THE SEVENTH DAY SERIES
Leslie Swartz

ISBN# 979-8-9859894-9-6

SERAPHIM

The devil can cite Scripture for his purpose.

William Shakespeare

Prologue

"Another one?" Lilith implored as Allydia emerged from the entrance of a chamber well hidden in the panels along the temple's far left wall, the stain of crimson still visible on her lips and chin.

"It was like being stabbed frantically with a stitching awl," Allydia complained.

Lilith giggled as she poured her step-daughter some wine. She admired the engravings on the gold cup as she handed it off and sat on her throne. The limestone was cool against her bronze skin which she had lovingly draped in a sheer, fringed shawl.

"Allydia, dearest," she condescended. "How many times must I explain that you have to *train* a man to please you? No man will ever seem worthy of you if you do not teach him to be."

"I refuse to put that kind of effort into a relationship I expect to last only until sunrise," Allydia retorted as she sat in her own throne, somewhat smaller and to the left of her step-mother's. "If a man can not satisfy me, he will be my dinner."

"You will never be satisfied. What you are disallows it," Lilith told her. "But, at least you'll be well-fed." They raised their cups to each other and drank.

"Mmmfff," the man sitting at Lilith's feet whined. She kicked him in the ribs before reprimanding him.

"I will give back your speech when I'm sure you've learned your lesson!" The naked man cowered and nodded, his lips still fused together. Several other servants stood around the throne room doing their best to remain still and silent, awaiting instruction, beratement, or torture. They only wished that the hoards of worshipers that gathered around the temple day and night would one day rise up against these creatures and save them from their servitude. They knew, however, that that was a hopeless fantasy, so they suffered, resigned to their fate.

"I'm bored," Lilith lamented. "I think it's time for us to move on. Spread out. Expand our empire."

"What did you have in mind?" Allydia wondered.

"I'm so glad you asked," Lilith said giddily. "I have great plans for us. Our army is set to invade all of the nearby cities, all at once! They only await my order. Nippur, Nineveh, Assur. Once I've taken control there, I can take what's rightfully ours."

"Babylon," Allydia concluded.

"Yes! *We* reign here, not them. We'll take the city and I will find a way to close the Gate, *permanently*. With that done, the entire world can be ours. It's so much bigger than you know. I can't wait to show you."

"My Queen," a man said from across the room. He had entered while the two were talking and didn't want to be punished for interrupting but this couldn't wait.

"Yes," Lilith said quizzically.

"I want to thank you for the honor of your presence and I've come today to ask that you please save my farm. My crops are dying," the man explained. "I have four children at home that won't survive if I can not feed them."

"If you were me," Lilith asked. "Would *you* care about that?"

"I've not come empty-handed, my Queen. I offer sacrifice." He unwrapped the bundle he'd been carrying to reveal a sleeping infant. Lilith's interest was piqued. She sniffed the air.

"Well, that baby is brand new," she said lustfully.

"Yes," he confirmed. "Born last night. I have no way to feed her. She is yours if you help me. I beseech you."

"Where is that child's mother?" Allydia asked.

"Dead," he told her. "The delivery proved to be too difficult."

"Dead?" Lilith queried. "It's not much of a sacrifice to offer a burden."

"Please, my Queen. I will give you anything. Take of me what you will."

"Fine," Lilith sighed. "I'm feeling generous. I accept your sacrifice."

"Thank you!" the man gushed, laying the baby at Lilith's feet, the mute servant staring in horror. "Thank you so much." He placed his hand over his heart and bowed as he left the temple, relief washing over him like rain.

"Why do they think I can solve their problems?" Lilith asked.

"They think you're God," Allydia reminded her.

"Oh, right," she chuckled.

Lilith bent down to retrieve the quiet bundle but before her hands could reach, the servant snatched the child up and ran.

"Is this a joke?" Lilith wondered. She flicked her wrist, snapping the man's neck from across the room. He fell to the floor, taking the child with him. She started to cry.

Just then, the Earth began to tremble. Wind blew in from the small entrance. They could hear the screams of people outside as the mud bricks of the building started to crumble. One of the servants, a woman whose own child was recently taken by her mistress, never to be seen again, took the opportunity to grab the wailing infant and flee. Suddenly, the shaking stopped and as the dust settled, they could see a figure standing before them.

"Sister," the man said slyly.

"It can't be," Lilith said, stunned. "I thought you were in, what did He call it?"

"Hell," he affirmed. "I was. I will be again. But I won't be going alone."

"You wish to imprison me, brother?" she guffawed. "On what grounds?"

"Well, there's a list, isn't there?" he jeered. "Crimes against humanity covers most of it. You know how He feels about His people. But, He's been willing to overlook that until now. Bigger problems to solve. But going after The Gate? Too far."

"I haven't done that yet," she challenged.

"But you would if left to your own devices. You forget He sees all. Nice to see you again," he said, turning his attention to Allydia.

"Don't know that I can say the same," she responded.

"Don't worry," he comforted. "I'm not here for you."

Lilith rolled her eyes. "I'm bored again," she huffed. "You, dear brother, have overstayed your welcome. Shoo." She waved her hand, sending him flying into the far wall, cracking it further.

"I was hoping to do this gently but you give me no choice." He opened his arms and waved his hands toward himself. The remaining servants all came forward, shock and horror covering their faces as they were forced to move closer and closer to their Queen. For the first time in her very long life, Allydia saw fear in her step-mother's eyes. The servants now rushed to Lilith, grabbing her and holding her steady. She fought them, tossing their bodies around like pillows. But they kept coming. Even the ones she killed reanimated and came for her. They forced her down into her throne and held her there as her brother neared.

"No!" she barked. "You can't!"

Allydia backed away, knowing what the man was capable of.

Lilith's anger turned to fear as her fate seemed sealed. "Please, brother," she begged. "We can all rule this world together. You don't always have to do what He says!"

"You know that simply isn't true," he said, kneeling before her and placing his hand on her head. He began the incantation while she screamed.

"Stop!" she pleaded. "Don't! Please! LUCIFER!"

Chapter 1

"How have I been since our last session?" Wyatt said impatiently, shifting a little in his seat. "Well, let's take stock. My wife left me because I'm not father material and I lost my job because, apparently, I'm too crazy to run into burning buildings. All in all, I'd say the last week hasn't been exactly stellar."

The therapist raised his eyebrows and took off his glasses. He sat them gently on the table next to him and picked up a pen. He scribbled something down and turned his gaze back to his patient.

"I'm very sorry to hear that, Mr. Sinclair. Truly," he told the man, who was visibly becoming more and more uncomfortable.

"Thanks," Wyatt said flatly.

"What would you like to discuss first?" the doctor asked, keeping his voice calm and soothing, almost monotone. His timbre seemed to annoy Wyatt more, but the doctor was steady, knowing that what this patient needed at that moment was a cool sounding board. That and a shit ton of antipsychotics.

"Work, I guess," Wyatt said halfheartedly. He was tired, not having slept in about thirty hours. Between that and days of weeping, his eyes were pained and bloodshot, barely able to stay open. Getting fired had pissed him off but losing his wife destroyed him. He would have to work his way up to talking about her.

"All right. Tell me what happened," the doctor instructed, readying his pen for what he was sure would be a lot of note-taking.

"It was the hallucinations," Wyatt confessed, brushing his dark hair away from his right eye. "They're not going away, no matter how many drugs you put me on."

"Are you not seeing any improvement?" the doctor asked.

"No," Wyatt answered, clearly upset. "I was *convinced* a woman was screaming for help inside an apartment next to one we'd just put out. I was so sure, I took an ax to the door. The eighty-seven-year-old man that lives there, who was the only person inside at the time, almost had a heart attack. He's suing the department."

Hallucinations continue. Need to up dosage of Risperidone, the doctor wrote. "And how does that make y--"

"I swear to God if you ask me how getting fired makes me *feel*, I'm leaving right now," Wyatt threatened. He slicked his hair back out of his face and took a deep breath. "I understand why they let me go. I don't blame them," he asserted. "I'm just sick and fucking tired of seeing and hearing things that aren't there." He again combed his hair back, trying and failing to keep it out of his eyes. He knew he was long overdue for a haircut, but he just couldn't muster the energy to care. He couldn't remember the last time he'd shaved. Probably four days ago, maybe five. Today was the first time he'd showered in that same amount of time. What was the point? Without Annie, life didn't seem worth living and the mundane routines of maintaining that life felt like a profound waste of time.

"I hadn't even told her," Wyatt admitted. "I was looking for another job, hoping I could just say I needed a change. Like it was *my decision* instead of having to tell my wife that I was put out on my ass for being a lunatic."

"Let's talk about Annie," the doctor insisted. "Clearly, that's what's bothering you the most." His voice was unconvincingly sympathetic and Wyatt struggled not to let his anger at the doctor's lack of sincerity ruin the session. Over the years, Wyatt had had many psychiatrists, none of which had been much help. While the hallucinations persisted, Dr. Stratford had been the only one to help him get through some of his more common issues like his mother's death, his father's distance and cruelty, and his general feeling of not belonging. The truth was, he was good at his job whether he actually cared about Wyatt's well-being or not.

"Sure," the patient started, taking a deep breath and letting it out slowly before he began. "I'd spent all day putting in applications at random places; gas stations, stores, restaurants. *Anything* to bring some money in while I figured out what my next move should be. Do I work at my father's firm like he'd always wanted? That sounded like being in Hell, but as long as going back to school and becoming a stripper were on the table, I couldn't rule anything out. But, on the way home I decided that I wanted to train to be an EMT, something where I'd still be helping people. Then, I remembered they don't allow people with severe mental illness to do that job so by the time I walked in the door, I was pretty messed up already." The aggravation on his face turned to sorrow as he thought about his wife and what he'd seen when he entered the apartment that day. Tears began to swell in his eyes. And here he was, thinking he had no tears left in him. He did his best to settle the anger that had again built up in his chest before continuing. "I got home and she was gone. Her clothes, her books, her computer. The art from the walls, most of the dishes. Her stupid cartoon character pillow that I made fun of her for keeping even though it was old and dusty and smelled bad. All gone. She left a note. Who does that? Sixteen years together and she writes a *note* after leaving the place looking like the scene of a robbery." He sighed heavily as his anger once again turned to sadness. "I must have read it ten times."

"Would you like to tell me what it said?" Dr. Stratford asked.

"No, not really but I will," Wyatt told him, pulling the letter from his back pocket. "I expected you might want to hear it," he said as he unfolded the paper. He cleared his throat and began to read.

"*Wyatt,*

I want to start by saying that I never thought I'd do this. You know I love you. Like, more than life. But your behavior gets more erratic every day. I watched you pull your hair out in a fit because 'the woman's voice' wouldn't be quiet. Your night terrors keep me awake because I'm afraid you'll hit me in your sleep. The final straw was when you broke the bathroom mirror in a rage fit because you didn't recognize your own reflection. You're on I don't know how many pills and none of them seem to be working and the worst part is how helpless I feel. I want to be able to make things better for you but I'm about as worthless as your prescriptions. The thing is, I want to have children. You know that. You must also know the reason why we've never tried to have any. Besides our kids potentially inheriting your disease, I just don't trust that you'd be a safe person for a child to be around. I know that you'd never hurt me or a kid on purpose but you have to admit, you're dangerous. It's not your fault and I'm not angry with you. You're a good person and you deserve to have a normal life, which is why I think a stay at a treatment center is something you should consider. I don't have the heart to commit you against your will, but I'm begging you to get the help you need. Sadly, I don't think you will so I have to think about my future. If I'm ever going to become a mother, I have to move on. I'm so sorry. -- Annie"

He wiped the tears from his face and put the letter back in his pocket. As he gathered himself, he noticed that the doctor, too, had gotten misty.

"You old softy," Wyatt teased.

The doctor gave a quiet laugh. "I'm sorry," he said, dabbing his eyes with a tissue before offering one to his patient. "That's inappropriate. I should be stoic and objective. But, I know how hard you've been working and what you've been through to make the progress you have. No matter how unflappable I should be here, that letter was a punch to the gut."

Wyatt was shocked. He'd never seen the doctor get emotional. He honestly didn't think he cared that much. He watched as the therapist wrote something on a prescription pad, set it aside, and put his glasses back on.

"I'm not sure what 'progress' you're talking about," Wyatt said.

"Well, you're here, aren't you?" the doctor pointed out. "The Wyatt Sinclair I met two years ago would still be in a heap on the floor if his wife left him. Or worse. But, instead of wallowing or hurting yourself, you came here to talk. That's progress."

"If you say so."

"I do," Dr. Stratford confirmed. "Now, how do you feel about your wife suggesting inpatient treatment? Had you discussed that with her before?"

"A couple of times," Wyatt told him. "My dad locked me up in one of those places when I was in college. Senior year for three months. I almost didn't graduate because of it. I think the only reason I got into law school was that he paid someone off."

"Yes," the doctor said. "I have the records from your time at Clear View. The doctors there marked your diagnosis as 'unchanged' when you left."

"Yeah, the place was useless," Wyatt stated. "That's why I told Annie I'd never go back."

"How do you feel now?" the therapist inquired. "Do *you* think you need hospitalization?"

He thought for a moment, admitting to himself that a stay in the loony bin probably wouldn't hurt. It at least couldn't make things any worse than they were now. But, he also had very little faith that one of those places could do him any real good.

"I honestly don't know," he conceded. "I know I need *something*, that's for goddamn sure."

"Let's put a pin in it for now," the therapist suggested. "The nightmares. Are you able to remember anything more about them?"

"Not really," Wyatt said. "It's just the same old thing. People getting hurt, needing help and me saving them, somehow."

"But, you don't know how."

"No."

"And you still can't understand what the people in the dreams are saying to you?"

"No. It sounds like they're speaking Latin or Greek or something."

"But, you know they need your help?"

"Yeah, they're bleeding and screaming and crying. It's chaos all around. Like a war zone," Wyatt remembered.

"But, you save them."

"Yes."

"Every time?"

"Yes."

"And it's important to you that you save people in your real life? Not just help them but save their lives?"

Wyatt hadn't made the distinction before but if he was being honest with himself, he supposed he *did* love the feeling he got when he saved someone from certain death. Seeing the joy, relief, and gratitude on the face of a person who, not a minute before, was sure they were about to die was maybe the only thing in Wyatt's life that gave him any real sense of happiness.

"I guess so," Wyatt confessed.

"Interesting," the doctor said, writing again in his notebook. "Tell me about the woman's voice. Is it still repeating the same question?"

"At least twice a day. But, lately, it's getting more, I don't know, annoyed. Like it's mad that I'm not talking back."

"So," the therapist asked, looking up from his paper and into Wyatt's eyes. "It wants to know, 'where are you?' Does it mean emotionally? Where you're at in your treatment? Is it asking if you think you're getting any better? Worse?"

"I have no idea."

"And you ignore it."

"Yes."

"And you think ignoring the voice is angering it?"

"I really couldn't tell you, doc. It's definitely pissed off about *something*. The last week, it's been so loud, I can't hear anything around me. It's like I'm on the truck with my ear pressed against the siren. It's getting to be unbearable."

The doctor sat quietly for a moment, tapping his pen on the rings of the notebook. After some thought, he leaned forward and looked Wyatt dead in the face.

"Next time it happens," he told the patient. "Answer it."

Wyatt's eyes grew wide. The doctor's advice was the opposite of everything he'd ever been told about how to deal with his hallucinations.

"Answer it?" he questioned. "That's not at all what any of you shrinks have ever told me to do. Wouldn't that make it *worse*?"

The doctor shrugged. "It could. Or not. The thing you have to remember about the voices in your head is that they're *you*. They're a manifestation of some part of your subconscious, as intrusive and bewildering to you as they may be. Maybe telling the voice what it wants to know, i. e., admitting to yourself where you believe you are emotionally and psychologically, is the first step to real improvement. I have to be honest with you, Wyatt, I'm increasing the dosage of your antipsychotics and mood stabilizers but I don't have high hopes of them being magic bullets. While you've learned how to cope with some of the deep-seated issues stemming from your childhood, you've made very little, if any progress in managing the symptoms of your schizophrenia. I want you to take these." He handed Wyatt the prescriptions. "Come back in three days and let me know if they're working any better. We'll go from there but if you're still having episodes that you can't control, like not recognizing yourself in the mirror, after a month of the new dosages, we may have to consider other options."

"Other options," Wyatt stated. "Like Clear View."

"I wouldn't recommend that particular facility but yes, somewhere like it."

"For the record, doc, I hope it doesn't come to that," Wyatt said, standing up to leave and reaching out to shake the doctor's hand.

"Neither do I, Mr. Sinclair." He took his patient's hand, jumping back a little at the static shock he felt.

"Sorry," Wyatt said.

The doctor smiled. "You'd think I'd be used to it by now. See you in a few days." He patted him on the shoulder and watched him leave. He could see him through the window of the small brick office as he got into his car and drove off. He genuinely felt bad for Wyatt Sinclair. Most of his patients were easily treated with antidepressants or antianxiety medication. But, Wyatt was the real deal. He needed real help that the doctor was worried he wasn't capable of providing. Recommending inpatient treatment was the last thing he wanted to do but he feared that, in this case, it might be the only viable option.

Wyatt was anxious to start his new prescriptions. Luckily for him, the pharmacy was just a few blocks away from the therapist's office. As he stood at the counter waiting impatiently for his scripts to be filled, he noticed how empty the store felt. There were a couple of employees milling around but otherwise, the building was quiet. He took his phone from his back pocket, hoping for a text or missed call from Annie but unsurprisingly, there was nothing. He sighed a little as he returned the phone and let his eyes wander, first to the pharmacist and then to the bottles and boxes on the shelves behind her.

Prepopik. Suprep. Moviprep. As he read, he was somewhat amused by just how bored he had to be that he was occupying himself by examining colonoscopy preparation kits from twelve feet away.

"It'll just be a few more minutes, sir," the pharmacist told him from behind the counter.

"Thank you," he replied.

Where are you? he suddenly heard. He looked around, hoping that it was the pharmacist speaking to him again. But, he knew better. It was 'her', the voice in his head. It sounded testy and Wyatt grew nervous. First of all, he wasn't stoked about the idea of losing it in public. Secondly, the doctor had told him that the next time the voice asked the question, he should answer it but was that smart? Would that give it more power over his mind? Make it more real?

Wyatt was startled by the sound of the door opening to three men arguing about how much beer they needed for the night's festivities. They were throwing a 'rager' and needed enough for everyone to get 'lit' and still have enough money to get tacos later. Wyatt rolled his eyes at how immature they seemed and how petty their problems, or even possibly their entire lives, must be. He remembered his own college days, getting wasted most nights, his friends thinking he was the life of the party. In reality, he had been trying, unsuccessfully, to drown out the noise of people that weren't there.

"Here you are, sir," the pharmacist said, handing him the bag containing his medication. "You have a good day."

"Thanks, you too," he said, unable to return her bright smile.

Where are you?! the voice insisted, louder and sounding more frustrated than before. Wyatt left the store quickly and fumbled with his keys as he crossed the parking lot. *Tell me where the fuck you are,* the voice demanded. *I'm sick of this shit.* It was angry now, the angriest he'd ever heard it. It was so loud, it completely drowned out the noise of the busy street in front of him. He made it to his car and tried to get the key in the door but his hands were shaking too violently. He looked around. The parking lot was empty aside from a few uninhabited cars and a truck he assumed belonged to the frat guys inside based on how badly it was parked. This was it, he decided. He would answer the voice as the doctor had suggested. He had to. Nothing could be as bad as how he felt right now.

"I'm a wreck!" he admitted. "I'm completely fucked up and I have no idea how to get better. As far as I can tell, there's not a way. You want to know where I am?! I'm at the corner of Miserable Avenue and Mad as a Hatter Boulevard!"

What the fuck? The voice asked. *Listen, we don't have time for you to have a meltdown right now. Tell me where you are, physically. I need a location so I can come get you. Freak.*

Wyatt dropped his keys. He was having a full conversation with a voice in his head and, not only that, it wanted to 'come get him'. Did he have multiple personalities on top of everything else? What was going on? He could barely breathe. He reached into the bag and retrieved one of the pill bottles but he was trembling so hard, he couldn't get it opened.

WHERE ARE YOU?! TELL ME WHERE YOU ARE! The volume of it was painful. It boomed in his head with such resonance, he thought he might have a stroke. He squeezed his eyes shut and put his hands to his head. His heart was racing and he couldn't think straight. What was happening?!

TELL ME!

"I'm at a pharmacy on Nine in Howell!" he yelled and as he did, a lightning bolt hit a lamppost, spewing sparks and filling the air with thunder and blinding white light. Wyatt fell to the ground, shaking, trying to catch his breath. His heart was pounding in his ears but that was all he heard. The voice was gone. The parking lot was silent.

He picked up the medicine and got in his car, finally able to unlock the door. He hurriedly opened the bottles, taking a pill from each one and dry swallowing them. He sat there, breathing heavily, trying to collect himself. Through his mirror he could see the frat guys leave the store, piling several cases of light beer in the bed of their truck before taking off. *At least no one saw me freak out,* he thought.

As he calmed down, he watched car after car speed by. The traffic reminded him of when he had moved there; of *why* he had moved there. Annie's mother lived in Howell and after graduation, she wanted to move back there to be close to her. So, they packed up their studio apartment and left the city. Manhattan had always been Wyatt's home but after law school, what did he have to stay for? He wasn't interested in becoming a lawyer as his father had always insisted. What he wanted was to save lives, so he bulked up and became a firefighter. His father was enraged. He remembered thinking that he'd never seen John so furious. After that, their relationship was strained, to say the least. They hadn't spoken since not long after the wedding; almost ten years. Wyatt wondered what his father would say when he found out that Annie had left him. He wondered how he was, if he was in good health. After all, he *was* getting older. Mostly, he wondered if he had forgiven him for leaving or come to terms with his son being 'different'. He sighed heavily. He was more relaxed but still a little shaken. He decided to go home, take some Xanax, and go to bed.

Three days had gone by and he hadn't heard the voice once. It was gone, just like that, and all he had to do was tell it what it wanted to know. It felt insane. He'd always thought he should never do what 'the voices' told him to. That that was how you end up becoming a mass shooter or a man that dresses like his dead mother and hoards cats. But, it worked. The voice was gone and Wyatt was starting to feel like he might be making some progress. For once, he was excited to see his therapist. He was feeling hopeful and as he sat down on the brown leather sofa in the doctor's office, Dr. Stratford could see the change in him. He looked healthier, stronger, and more relaxed than usual. He couldn't believe it. The new dosages must have done the job.

"Mr. Sinclair," the doctor began. "You look, dare I say, almost happy."

"Let's not get ahead of ourselves," he said. "But, I think I'm doing a little better."

"Tell me what's going on."

"A miracle, I think," Wyatt joked. "After I left here a few days ago, I heard the woman's voice again. I told it where I was, just like it wanted. I immediately started taking the new pills and I also took a Xanax that night." He sat back, feeling more comfortable there than he ever had. "I haven't heard the voice since."

The doctor looked at him with amazement. "Really?" he asked. "That's incredible. And what about your other symptoms? Hallucinations? Nightmares?"

"Still there," Wyatt told him. "But, if I can get rid of the voice, maybe I can eventually get rid of all of them."

"So, what your subconscious wanted was for you to address your own emotions after all," the doctor stated, proud that he had been able to finally help his patient have a breakthrough.

"No," Wyatt said. "It wanted me to tell it where I was. Like, the cross streets or something."

The doctor was baffled. "What?" he wondered. "It just wanted to know your physical location?"

"Yeah."

"And it gave you no more information? Why do you think that is?"

"Because," a woman explained as she burst through the office door. "I should really tell him what he needs to know in person." She sat next to Wyatt on the couch, a mischievous grin lighting up her face. She was beautiful with big brown eyes, high cheekbones, and dark hair.

"Excuse me, who are you?" the doctor asked sharply.

"Name's Taran Murphy but I don't really go by that. My parents were Irish but I feel like it's a little unfair to claim an ethnicity when I'm not really from here, you know?" She looked at Wyatt and smiled. "You can call me Gabriel."

He felt sick. Her voice. It was the woman's voice in his head. The incessant yelling, asking where he was nearly every day since he was eighteen. It was her, he was sure of it.

"You can see her?" he questioned the therapist.

"Of course," he answered matter-of-factly. "We are in session, Miss. You need to leave."

She leaned forward to more directly look at the doctor. "What are his issues, doc?" she taunted. "Let me guess. Sees things no one else can see. Hears things no one else can hear. Bad dreams. Maybe an issue with electricity, like, static shocks? Maybe," She looked back at Wyatt who had gone pale and felt like his heart would explode in his chest. "Lightning?"

"How do you know that?" Wyatt breathed. He had been convinced that the lightning in the parking lot was just another hallucination.

"I know everything," she replied nonchalantly. "For instance," She looked back at the doctor. "You were meant to be a concert pianist, but you never thought you were good enough, so you do this instead. All the joy you could have brought to people's lives, all that God-given talent, wasted. But, hey, a lot more stability in medicating the crazies, am I right?"

The doctor was stunned. "How could you possibly..."

"Did you not hear me when I *just* said I know everything?" She stood up, grabbing Wyatt's hand and pulling him up with the strength of a linebacker. "Come on, B, we gotta bounce."

She dragged him through the lobby and out to the parking lot like he weighed nothing. As the shock wore off, Wyatt, with much effort, yanked his hand away and stopped.

"Who are you?" he asked, not quite believing this person was made of flesh and blood and not just a figment of his imagination. "What do you want?"

"Short answer," she responded. "I'm your sister...kinda. We'll discuss it later. Right now, what I *want* is for you to call your dad *before* he calls you. It'll make him feel like you give a shit and he'll be less of a dick when you go see him. I'll meet up with you when you're done." She got into a tiny black sports car that Wyatt guessed cost more than what he made in two years at the department and looked up at him through the still opened door. "Listen, I get it," she told him. "You thought you were out of your mind so you ignored me. I'll get over it eventually but as of now, I haven't forgiven you for making me schlep out to Jersey so you owe me." She took the sunglasses from her dashboard and put them on. "Call your dad." With that, she slammed the car door shut and peeled out like a stunt driver.

Wyatt stood there, motionless, not sure what to do next. Behind him, he could hear the quick footsteps of someone approaching. He turned to see Dr. Stratford hurrying toward him.

"Are you all right?" the doctor asked.

"I'm fine," he lied.

"Who was that woman?"

"I don't have a clue," Wyatt told his doctor. "But, you could see her? She wasn't in my head?"

"I can assure you, she was very real. I have half a mind to call the police and report her as a stalker."

"You think she's a stalker?"

"It's the only thing that makes sense," the doctor surmised. "How else could she know about my past?"

How else indeed? A stalker. That was the only rational explanation. But, what about her voice? It was too curious of a coincidence for Wyatt to ignore.

"I'm going to have to reschedule our appointment if you don't mind," he told the doctor. "I need to handle some things."

"Of course. Just set it up with Marjorie."

The men nodded goodbye to one another as Wyatt headed toward his car. He sat in the driver's side seat and closed the door, looking at himself in the mirror.

"What the fuck?" he whispered to himself. "Okay, let's think about this logically. The receptionist saw her. Stratford saw *and* talked to her and confirmed she's a real person. Whoever that was is real, not a hallucination. So, she *can't* be the voice in my head." But, he was sure that the voices matched. He knew it in his bones. "But, how did she know about the lightning?" he asked himself. "How did she know about the dreams and the doctor? How--" he stopped, suddenly realizing what he was doing. "And I'm talking to myself. Awesome." He shook his head and turned the key in the ignition.

His head was swimming with thoughts as he drove home. Who was the woman, really? How was she connected to the voice in his head, if she was at all? Was he just projecting? And did she say she was his *sister*? Did his father have another kid he didn't know about? It was possible, he guessed. His mother had been dead for decades, and while he had never seen his father date, it was entirely in the realm of possibility that he just kept his girlfriends hidden from his son. As a child, Wyatt's father had all but worshiped his dead wife's memory. There were pictures of her everywhere, though he never spoke about her. To this day, Wyatt still had no idea how she died. All he was ever told was that she had died when he was a baby. He had always assumed it must have been during childbirth by the distance his father put between them his whole life. But, who knows? Could have been a car crash, suicide, rogue meteorite. Anything was possible.

At his apartment, Wyatt sat at his kitchen table, spinning his cell phone on the black lacquered wood as he procrastinated. He took note of the takeout bags that had piled up on the counters and the dishes that sat unwashed in the sink. Since his wife left, he'd really let the place go to shit. He could picture Annie at the sink, hands covered in suds, laughing while she scolded him about the mess. *We'll get ants,* she would have said. He'd just smile in agreement and throw the garbage in trash bags, tie them up, then kiss her cheek before taking them out to the community dumpster. Later, they'd have dinner and talk about their days, make weekend plans, and watch television before heading to bed where they'd have boring but satisfying sex, read a little, and go to sleep. *Get it together,* Wyatt thought, rubbing his eyes as he brought himself back to reality.

He took the phone in his hand and pulled up his father's number. He *had* been thinking about his dad recently and had wanted to reach out but it never seemed like the right time. Maybe the woman *was* a stalker, nothing more. Either way, it probably *was* a good idea to check in with his dad, if for no other reason than to rip off the band-aid of telling him about Annie.

"Let's get it over with," he said to himself as he hit the call button.

"Hello?" John answered, not recognizing the number. He rifled through some papers on his desk while he waited for a reply.

"Hey, Dad," Wyatt choked out, trying not to sound nervous. "How are you?"

John raised his eyebrows in surprise and sat slowly in his chair. "I'm all right," he responded coldly. "And you?"

He wasn't sure how to answer the question, so he settled on honestly. "Weird." He laughed a little as he said it.

"Well, that's not really news, is it?" John said. "How are things? How's Annie?"

"She left," Wyatt told him. "She wants kids and thinks I'm unfit. She's not wrong."

"I'm sorry to hear that," John said, almost dismissively. "Listen, I was just about to call you. There are some things we need to go over. When do you think you could make some time to come home?"

Home. The word sounded strange coming out of his father's mouth. The woman *did* say he would go see his dad and the truth was, he missed New York terribly. The pizza alone was enough to justify the trip.

"Whenever you want," Wyatt said. "I've got some time off."

"Great. Later today work for you? I've got some paperwork to finish up but I'll be done in a couple of hours."

"Sure. See you then."

"See you then," John hung up and continued going over his files.

Wyatt put the phone down and sighed heavily, relieved the call had ended but more confused than before he'd made it. The woman had been spot on about everything she'd said. His father *would* have called him if he hadn't called first and he *was* going to see him. If she was a stalker, she was incredibly thorough.

Chapter 2

Wyatt stood at the massive entry of his childhood home. The building that had been erected in eighteen eighty-four was as beautiful as ever. The history and grandeur of the place were still overwhelming. Looking up at the structure, the ornate iron gates and lanterns, and the gorgeous stonework, he was suddenly flooded with emotion. He had fond memories there, though few and far between. Playing in the courtyard with his friends, occasionally meeting celebrities. The first time he kissed Annie was right across the street at the entrance to the park. As far as places to grow up in the city went, this was one of the best, in his opinion. But, the loneliness of being left with nannies in an apartment, no matter how beautiful, while his father worked sixty-plus hours a week had left him feeling neglected and resentful. Combined with his dad's general disregard of him in their daily lives, that indifference had created a strange, almost professional relationship between them. In high school, Wyatt had acted out, smoking pot, drinking, staying out all night, all in an effort to get his father's attention. Once, when he was seventeen, John had caught him in his room with a girl. "As long as you're safe," he had said, leaving the teenagers to their business. It wasn't until the hallucinations started that Wyatt's father seemed to take notice. It was his buddy's eighteenth birthday and Wyatt had stumbled in at around four in the morning, drunk off his ass after a long night of partying. He must have passed out on the couch, though he had no memory of getting past the doorway, let alone making it all the way to the sofa. A few minutes later, he was awoken by the sound of a woman crying. It was loud and filled the room, like an announcement over a loudspeaker. He felt hot, so he took his flannel off and dropped it on the floor as he attempted to find the source of the sobbing. It was dark in the apartment, no lights from the television, so he thought it must be a person. He had been proud that his father had finally brought a woman home but why was she crying? Was his dad a date rapist? Was he going to have to kick his own father's ass to protect some chick? He checked every room and found no one. Every room but one. He approached his father's bedroom door and hesitated for a moment while reaching for the doorknob. He knocked quietly before entering, hoping to find his father listening to some weird radio show and not abusing some poor woman.

What he found was his father asleep in his king-size bed, oblivious to the woman crouched in the corner of the room under the window crying her eyes out. She was wearing a long dress and her long red hair had half fallen out of its bun to cover her face.

"Dad," he had whispered. "Dad, wake up."

John rolled over and stretched. "What is it, Wyatt? What time is it?"

"Dad, what the hell?" he had said, gesturing toward the very obviously upset woman in his room.

John looked to the window. "What?" he had demanded.

"What did you *do*, Dad?"

"What are you talking about? Are you just getting home? Boy, it's almost tomorrow. You should be in bed."

"The girl, Dad!" Wyatt had shouted.

"What girl?" John asked, turning his bedside table lamp on. They both looked to the corner and they both saw nothing. She was gone. Wyatt didn't hear the crying anymore.

"She was right there," he had told his father.

"Damn it, Wyatt. Go sleep it off. Tomorrow, we're going to have a serious conversation about your behavior."

The next day, Wyatt drank coffee while his father lectured him about responsibility and thinking about his future. "You're almost a man now," He had bellowed. "It's time to get your life together." As he droned on, Wyatt again heard the woman crying.

"Do you hear that?" he had asked.

"Hear what?"

"The crying."

"The what?" John had asked. "Are you still drunk?"

"No, I'm serious," Wyatt had insisted. "You really don't hear it? It's *so* loud." Just then, he saw the woman standing in the corner of the kitchen wearing the same long dress, her hair still disheveled.

Wyatt jumped up from his seat at the island. "There!" he exclaimed, pointing her out. "She's right there! I told you I wasn't making it up."

John looked at the empty corner of the room and back at his son. As a lawyer, John had ample practice at snuffing out liars. He looked Wyatt in the eyes and knew that he believed what he was saying. John's annoyance turned to fear and the next few years were spent visiting doctors and psychiatrists, trying this and that combination of drugs and therapies. Nothing worked. The hallucinations continued. Besides the crying woman, Wyatt soon started seeing other people that weren't there, and they were all over. The apartment, the subway, on the street. While accepting his diploma at his high school graduation, he heard the woman's voice for the first time. *Where are you?* It had caught him so off guard that he'd nearly tripped. The nightmares came later, in college. His roommate complained about him screaming in his sleep so much that Wyatt was given a private room.

Senior year, he had come home for Christmas and while there, he had a particularly violent night terror. John had found him, eyes still closed, trying to rip up the floorboards in the living room with his bare hands while screaming, "Hang on! I'm coming!" The next day was Wyatt's first day at Clear View.

Wyatt did his best to push the memories from his mind as he made his way to his father's apartment. He was more than a little surprised that his key still worked. He knocked loudly as he walked in.

"Dad?" he called.

"Study," John called back.

Wyatt opened the door to his father's office to find him on the phone with what sounded like a client. John motioned for him to sit in the chair across the desk and held a finger up as if to say 'one minute' before taking a sip of coffee. *Guarantee there's bourbon in that.* Wyatt thought, remembering his father's habits. He looked just as Wyatt remembered him; sleeves rolled up, tie loosened, cleanly shaven. His father, just like the apartment, hadn't changed a bit.

"All right, Charlie, let me know if anything changes," John said to the person on the other end of the call. "You, too. Tell Elizabeth I said 'hello'. Goodbye." He hung up and took a good look at his son. He was still more muscular than John thought was necessary and his face had grown mournful like life had beaten him down. He supposed his mental illness and wife abandoning him were the cause of that and decided not to bring it up. No need to upset him.

"So, how was the trip?" John inquired.

"Fine," Wyatt answered. "How's your life?"

"Oh, can't complain. Work keeps me busy, as you know."

"No girlfriend? Wife?" he asked, noticing John still wore his old wedding ring.

"I have a wife," John snapped. "She just happens to be dead at the moment." They sat in awkward silence for a few seconds before John pulled out a file from a drawer and slid it across to his son. "Speaking of which," he said. "Your uncle, Spencer died."

"My what?" Wyatt asked, having no memory of an uncle at all.

"Your mother's half-brother. You only met him once or twice as a kid. You were probably too young to remember. He lived in Indiana, barely kept in touch. Anyway, he didn't have any children and his wife passed a few years ago, so he left his estate to you. There's his house, of course, in a town called Southport. Bank accounts and stocks that have been transferred to you. There are also a few rental properties and a donut shop he owned that belong to you now to do with as you see fit. You *will* have to call the bank to get debit cards."

Wyatt was flabbergasted. The contents of this file solved his money problems. He no longer had to panic-search for a job. "I don't know what to say."

"Not much *to* say," John said. "People get old, they get sick, then they die."

"Is that what happened to Mom?" Wyatt asked. "Did she get sick?"

"Wyatt," John cautioned.

"Come on, Dad. It's been decades. Why haven't you told me what happened? This place is like a goddamn shrine. There's at least one picture of her in every room but you've never talked to me about her. Not once. Why have you *never* told me *anything* about my mother?"

"Because," John said, his face a combination of enraged and heartbroken. "Talking about her kills me." He took another sip of coffee, set it aside, and pulled a glass followed by a bottle of scotch from his desk drawer. He poured himself a little and drank it, ignoring his son's disapproving glance.

"I'd just like to know what happened to her," Wyatt said to his father as calmly as he could. "I'd just like to know something about her. *Anything*. Please, Dad."

John was nearly shaking, he was so angry. "You want to talk about this?" he threatened. "You *really* want to bring up all this old bullshit?"

"Um," Wyatt answered, taken aback by his father's demeanor. "Yes."

"Fine," he said, taking another swig and slamming the glass down on the desk. "Abigail was perfect," he began, tempering his tone. "She was brilliant, and funny, and so goddamn beautiful, she didn't look real. She liked The Beatles, Queen, and Elton John. She liked to read and watch movies and complain that the book was better. She loved history, especially English history. Henry VIII, Elizabeth I, stuff like that. She made me sit through the whole royal wedding, Charles and Diana, you know. I was bored to tears, but I would have done anything she asked of me. That woman was my whole life."

He poured another glass and took a sip before continuing. "She was a real estate agent and a damn good one at a time when women weren't taken seriously in that field. She was tough, put up with a lot of shit that nowadays they'd call 'harassment'. While I was striking out on my own, establishing my firm, *she* was the one paying the bills. *She* was the one that got us into this building and paid the mortgage. It wasn't easy, but she made it happen. This place was her dream. She worked hard, sometimes seven days a week, and she still had time to attend the events and dinners and bullshit elbow-rubbing functions I had to go to to get my name out there, form relationships with people that could potentially become clients. She was charming, graceful, poised. She was amazing on every level and it was because of her, because the fuddy-duddies and the DAR ladies all loved her so much, that my firm took off the way it did. In less than two years, I went from leasing an office to owning a building on the upper west side. She supported me and my dream and I always felt like I owed it to her to be successful, to put in the work to make it grow. Otherwise, what was the point of all her hard work and sacrifice?" He paused for a moment, bracing himself for what came next. "We had been so focused on our careers that we hadn't discussed when we'd have children. I knew she wanted them but it was always a 'someday' sort of thing. So, we were surprised when we found out she was pregnant but she was thrilled, and seeing her that happy made *me* happy. I was *so* fucking happy, I didn't recognize the signs."

"What signs?" Wyatt wondered.

John poured more scotch into his glass and took a drink. "Of her depression."

"Depression?" Wyatt asked. "You just said she was happy."

"She was. For a while. She put your nursery together, bought every toy in FAO Schwartz, I think. Spent hours in that room, just sitting in a rocking chair, rubbing her belly, singing to you. 'Hey Jude' on a loop. But, around the eighth month, she just stopped going in there. She stopped working altogether and started sleeping something like sixteen hours a day. I thought she was just tired from the pregnancy. She was edgy, easily irritated, but I thought that was normal hormonal crap. She complained that everything hurt. Again, it sounded normal to me. She was huge. Her back, her legs, her feet. It was all *supposed* to hurt. She stopped caring about how she looked, even when we went out. I wasn't about to comment on her appearance. I never bought into that whole 'pregnancy is beautiful' thing. It seems hard and miserable to me, so expecting her to be pretty during that time would have been ridiculous. Then, she stopped wanting to go anywhere. Ever. I wanted her to be comfortable in her last few weeks of pregnancy, so we stayed in. No big deal. But, then, she stopped reading. She stopped listening to music. That was *odd*, so I asked her about it and she said she 'just wasn't interested'. I called her doctor and he said it was 'baby blues' and it was fairly common and it would go away after you were born. It was maybe a week before her due date when she stopped eating. Said she wasn't hungry. At that point, I was worried. I did everything I could to get her to eat. I got her favorite take-out, bought all her favorite foods. Nothing worked. I got so frustrated, I tried to force a bite of pasta into her mouth. She threw the fork across the room and slapped me in the face. I was beside myself. I didn't know what to do." He paused. "You sure you want to hear this?" he asked his son. Wyatt nodded. John took another glass from the drawer, filled it with bourbon, and slid it across the desk. "All right," he began again. "So, one night, I get home from work, and the maid's freaking out, screaming something in Spanish. I don't know what she's saying, but she's banging on the bathroom door in hysterics. She runs up to me and the only words I can understand her saying are 'Mrs. Sinclair' and 'scissor'. So, I call to Abby to open the door but there's no response. So, I start kicking the door, trying to break it down. Finally, I throw all my weight against it and it opens." Tears started to pool in John's sorrowful brown eyes. Wyatt was getting nervous. He'd never seen his father show any real emotion *in his life*. John choked back the tears and did his best to still his voice. "She was on the floor, pale, not moving. There was blood and amniotic fluid everywhere. For a second, I thought she had gone into labor and passed out. But, then I saw the sewing scissors in her hand." He paused, clenching his jaw and taking a breath before continuing. "She had stabbed herself in the stomach, the doctor said eight times. She lost so much blood, by the time we got to the hospital, she was gone. They said it was a miracle you survived."

Wyatt stared at his father, stunned and speechless, and it was like he was seeing him for the first time. When he regained his motility, he picked up the glass in front of him and drank greedily until there was nothing left. He wiped away the tears that had fallen from his own eyes as he watched his father do the same.

"You remind me so much of her," John stated. "Smart, willful. Stubborn. You went off to New Jersey to be a fireman and I hated it. I mean, I *hated* it. But, I respected it. You did whatever the hell you wanted, just like your mother would have. Ballsy. It's strange. I look at her pictures every day and I'm fine. But it's always been hard for me to look at you."

"What?" Wyatt asked. "Why?"

"You never noticed?" John asked. "You look just like her. Your face is *her* face."

Wyatt looked at the picture of his mother that sat on his father's desk. He could definitely see the resemblance.

"There's a little bit of you in here, too, I think," Wyatt told him, pointing towards his eyes.

"You might be right," John agreed, taking another sip of scotch. The two men sat in silence for a while, both of them coming to terms with the conversation they'd just had. Wyatt understood now where his father had been coming from all these years. It didn't make him feel any better about their relationship but it did give him a certain kind of contentment. Knowing that there was nothing he could have done to change the way his father had treated him growing up, that John had his own issues that caused him to be distant and maybe blame Wyatt a little for his wife's death, was somehow comforting. His father was just a flawed, miserable, slightly alcoholic human being.

"Thank you for sharing that with me, Dad," Wyatt said. "I know that must have been really hard for you. I appreciate it."

"Yes, well," John said as if waking from a dream. He cleared his throat and composed himself. "*I* would appreciate it if we never spoke of this again."

"I concur," Wyatt teased.

"And there's the snark," John pointed out.

Wyatt laughed a little.

"I really am sorry about Annie."

"Thank you."

"All right, well, I have some work to do, so if you could lock up when you leave, that'd be great."

"Of course," Wyatt said, standing and making his way to the study door. "It was good seeing you, Dad. I'm glad you're well."

"Bye, Wyatt," John said, not looking up from the file he had just opened.

Wyatt took a quick glance around the room with its many bookshelves, filing cabinets, and paperweights. It all seemed smaller than it had when he first walked in. Less intimidating. He folded the file his father had given him and slid it in his jacket before pulling the door behind him.

"Bye, Dad."

"So, you're him, hmm?" Wyatt heard a voice from behind call to him as he exited the gates of his father's building.

"Excuse me?" he replied, turning to look at the slender Asian man addressing him. He wore a beautifully tailored suit, an oversized pair of sunglasses, and freshly polished shoes.

The man lowered his glasses to get a better look at Wyatt. "Yeah, it's you," he decided. "Come on." He began to walk, expecting to be followed. Wyatt stood in defiance.

The man turned back. "Did you not hear me?" he sassed. "Let's go before the princess loses her damn mind and starts screaming in ours."

"The girl," Wyatt said. "She sent you?"

"You know she did. For future reference, call her Gabriel. Anything else gets her panties in a twist. And, no, she's not a stalker. She told me that's what you're trying to tell yourself. I mean, homegirl can be overbearing as fuck, but a stalker she ain't. You coming?"

Wyatt followed the man across the street to the park.

"I'm Tae."

"Wyatt."

"Oh, that's cute," Tae complimented. "You're a tall motherfucker, aren't you? What are you, six-one?"

"Six-two," Wyatt corrected.

"Well, pardon me," Tae joked. "And those eyes. You must *slay*."

"You mind telling me where we're going?"

"It's just up here a little ways," Tae told him. "She thought you'd take the news better in a pretty environment. Before we get there, some things you should know. Bitch has a superiority complex because she knows every goddamn thing. She thinks she knows better than everybody and what's annoying about that is that she's right. You can't lie to her because she *knows*. Everything you've ever seen, heard, said, thought, or felt, she knows. Baby's telepathic, telekinetic, and pyrokinetic. She can heal the sick, raise the dead, and set up a duplex in your mind if she wants to. It's obnoxious."

I brought a picnic! Wyatt heard the woman say in his head.

"This bitch," Tae said. "Always gotta be extra. A *picnic*. I'ma have to tell her to reign it in."

Wyatt was dumbfounded. "You heard that?"

"Course I did. You're not the only one she pesters with that shit," Tae explained. "She's been chirping in my ear since Britney was still with Justin."

As they walked, they could see Gabriel sitting on some rocks in the distance. She looked up to meet their gaze and waved wildly as a huge smile stretched across her face.

"Now, listen," Tae warned. "She's about to tell you some shit you're gonna have a hard time believing. Trust me, when I first met her, I thought she was bat shit crazy. But, as fucked up as it is, it's all true."

Wyatt was more confused than ever as the two approached.

"Hey, girl," Tae said, taking a seat next to Gabriel and examining the contents of the picnic basket. "You really need to calm this shit."

"Raphael," she acknowledged.

"You brought a salad bowl of grapes and a jug of water," Tae griped. "What the actual fuck?"

Gabriel laughed and turned her attention to Wyatt. "Sit down, B," she said cheerfully.

"His name's 'Wyatt'," Tae told her as he munched on the grapes.

"I know," she said.

"You should probably call him that."

"Yeah, but I probably won't," she asserted before addressing Wyatt again. "Sorry your mom was animal crackers."

"Thanks," Wyatt said irritably as he sat across from the two in bewilderment. "Who are you people?" he asked.

"I'm Gabriel," she started. "This is Raphael. We're archangels, and, *surprise*, so are you."

"So you're deranged," Wyatt surmised.

"No, but I can understand why you'd think so," she told him. "You're not crazy, either, B T dubs. Just a freak show like the rest of us. Your real name's Barachiel."

Wyatt scoffed. "I'm an angel?"

"Archangel," she corrected. "Leader of four hundred and ninety-six thousand Guardians, Prince of Heaven, Angel of Blessings. You're kind of a big deal."

"Okay," he said, quickly standing up. "This is either some kind of scam, or you two are straight-up bats in the belfry. Either way, I'm out."

Gabriel tilted her head, staring at him blankly. Without altering her gaze, she raised her hand and flicked her wrist in the direction of some bushes that inexplicably exploded in flames, forcing a jogger to jump back and fall on her backside. Wyatt's eyes grew wide and his stomach dropped. He couldn't believe it.

"Come on," Gabriel laughed. "Burning bush?! That's *hilarious*."

"Was that necessary?" Tae snapped, grabbing the jug of water and rushing to put the fire out. "Pain in my ass."

Gabriel stood, giving Wyatt a knowing smile. "There's someone else you need to meet. She'll be able to clear things up for you a little bit."

Wyatt nodded, so overwhelmed by what just happened that he couldn't speak.

"You got this, Raph?" Gabriel called back as Tae struggled to put out the weakening flames.

"You best get the fuck out my face!" he called back.

She chuckled to herself as she led Wyatt out of the park. "Humorless, both of you."

Chapter 3

Walking along West 72nd Street, Wyatt took note of a sushi restaurant he'd never seen before.

"It wasn't here when you left," Gabriel told him, stopping several feet from the entrance. She smiled broadly. "There she is."

Next to the door was a pretty African American woman wearing jeans and a very large coat with several pockets. She looked somewhat perturbed as a man in a suit talking on a cell phone walked up, opened the door, and entered the restaurant. Behind him, an old man with a cane reached for the handle just as the door closed.

"Watch this," Gabriel said giddily.

The woman opened the door for the old man and followed him inside. After a few seconds, she reemerged, dragging the first man by his jacket. She snatched the phone from his hand and threw it in the street before opening the door of the restaurant once more, allowing a young couple to walk inside before letting go of the handle.

"How hard is that?!" she shouted to the suited man, who looked stunned and more than a little pissed off. He tried to retrieve his phone from traffic to no avail as he screamed obscenities in the woman's direction.

Gabriel was laughing so hard, she could barely breathe. "She's my favorite."

"Wyatt!" the woman exclaimed as she headed toward them. "It's so nice to meet you. You ready?"

"For what?" he asked.

"You didn't tell him?" the woman asked Gabriel. "I thought he'd be all caught up by the time you came to see me."

"You didn't tell me his dad was gonna take over an hour," Gabriel rebuffed.

"Bitch, I told you he was 'bout to catch him up on some family drama. That shit takes time," the woman said, turning her attention to Wyatt. She reached out for him to shake her hand, which he did. "I'm Valerie. Long story short, I'm gonna unclutter your brain a little. Help you distinguish what's normal and what's supernatural. What's a human voice and what's a ghost, stuff like that. I'm also gonna try to clean up those flashbacks you've been having so you can get some proper sleep."

"This is Uriel," Gabriel explained. "She's one of us. Divine visions, moral superiority, all-around badass. Today, though, she's gonna clean up what's going on in your head."

"I'm gonna try to," Valerie interjected. "But all those drugs you're on might make it difficult."

"You really need to stop taking that shit," Gabriel told him.

"For real," Valerie agreed. "Can we get going, 'cause I got a date in a couple of hours and I need to get home so I can get cute."

Gabriel chuckled as she attempted to hail a cab.

"So many things," Wyatt stated. "First, ghosts?!"

"Oh, yeah," Gabriel said. "Dead people are notoriously chatty."

"Yeah," Valerie chimed in. "You just have to ignore them. If they don't know you can hear them, they'll usually just go away on their own."

"Uh, huh," Wyatt said skeptically. "And, my nightmares?"

"Memories," Valerie corrected.

"Yeah, dude. That shit really happened," Gabriel informed him. "And before you ask, yes, we *really* want you to stop taking your meds because no, they're *not* helping you. They're just fogging up your brain, making it harder for you to see what's happening around you and making it impossible for me to find you. I've been looking for you since the turn of the century. Do you know how much easier things would have been if you had just answered me?"

Just then, a cab pulled up, but Gabriel shooed the driver away.

"No, sir, not you," she insisted. "You are already late for Izzy's recital and if you miss one more, Esperanza is going to stab you in your sleep. Go."

The cabby gasped, making the sign of the cross. "Bruja!" he shouted. "Eres del diablo!" He sped off, nearly taking out a pedestrian as he drove.

Valerie snickered. "Devil witch."

"He may be freaked out but I was serious," Gabriel told them. "His wife will literally murder him if he misses his kid's tap thing. That bitch is crazy."

"You know him?" Wyatt asked.

"No."

"That's gonna be your new nickname," Valerie laughed. "I'm gonna call you that from now on. Hey, Devil Witch!"

Gabriel rolled her eyes.

"What you been up to, Devil Witch?" Valerie continued. "DW Murphy, what's shakin'?"

"Okay, we're just walking," Gabriel conceded.

"Hey, Devil Witch, you got the time?" Valerie poked as she and Wyatt followed Gabriel.

A few blocks later, just past Broadway, they reached Gabriel's apartment. It was stunning. Entering through the double doors, the far wall directly in front of them was made entirely of windows. To their left was a kitchen with a large island and stools, marble countertops, and stainless steel appliances. To their right was a hallway with several doors next to a wall that housed a television that was at least seventy-five inches. Next to the kitchen was a set of french doors leading to a balcony where a table and two chairs sat. The cabinets, sectional sofa, and ottoman were all stark white which made the pink of the rosewood floors pop even more. Gabriel locked the door behind them and gestured to the couch. She got herself a bottle of water and leaned against the massive fridge.

"Go ahead, Uri," she commanded. "Fix him up so we can get the show on the road. We're already running late."

Valerie sighed. "It takes as long as it takes," she declared, annoyed with her sister's impatience. She sat on the sofa, patting the seat next to her. Wyatt joined her, not knowing what to expect, but feeling like nothing these women could do to him would be any worse than what he'd been living with lately.

"Just relax," Valerie instructed. "I'm gonna do all the work."

She put her fingers gently on his temples as Wyatt closed his eyes and took a deep breath. She took a few deep breaths of her own, not knowing what she'd see in there. Gabriel, as always, had been vague on the details.

She sorted through the haze of his still medicated mind for a few minutes before finding what she was looking for. She made quick work of mending his limbic system, allowing him to distinguish between normal and metaphysical beings as well as dreams and memories. One memory, though, she could see, was giving him particularly fitful nights. She decided to show him the memory in its entirety which would give him an understanding of it so he could move on.

Wyatt shuddered, suddenly feeling as if he'd been transported to another time and place. He was aware of everything going on in what he used to call his nightmare. Not only did he see and hear his surroundings, he could smell the air, feel the ground beneath his feet. And, he knew what was happening.

It was Verona, the year of The Consulship of Constantinus and Licinianus, and Constantine's forces had the city surrounded. There were men fighting everywhere Wyatt looked. Three different armies were battling it out in the city and the civilian population was getting slaughtered in the crossfire. As he watched in horror, an older woman quickly approached him, begging him to help her grandson. For the first time since he'd started having this dream, he could understand what she was saying. He followed the woman to an alley that was relatively quiet and they came upon a boy of about fourteen. He was lying there on the ground, the color drained from his face and bleeding heavily from the abdomen. His eyes had glossed over and were darting back and forth. He was almost gone.

The woman begged for his help, pulling on his clothes in desperation and despair. "If you can not save him, could you at least fetch some wine to alleviate the poor child's pain?" she pleaded.

Wyatt crouched down next to the boy and put his hand, which was much smaller and darker than his current one, carefully over the boy's wound. He looked up at the woman who stared, confused, and put his finger to his lips. She nodded and went silent, tears filling her forlorn eyes.

All at once, his hand and the wound underneath it began to glow. The boy's entire body began to glow as if it had been lit from the inside.

The woman fell to her knees in disbelief. She didn't know if this man was a good spirit or an evil one but if he saved her grandson, she didn't much care.

The wound slowly shrunk then disappeared completely and the boy gasped as if taking breath for the first time. He sat up, dazed, and stared up at Wyatt with stunned gratitude. Wyatt stood while the old woman hugged her grandson, kissing his cheeks repeatedly after inspecting the spot where his wound had been and seeing it was gone. She then began kissing Wyatt's feet and thanking him profusely. He lifted the woman to her feet and again put his finger to his lips. She understood. She would tell no one what had happened. Wyatt helped the two to safety before going back out into the war zone. There were more innocent people to be helped. Except, he wasn't Wyatt then and he knew it. Here, he was just Barachiel.

Wyatt's eyes flew open and he stared wildly at Valerie who had removed her hands from his head.

"Holy shit!" he exclaimed.

"Pretty much," Gabriel said.

"How did you do that?" he said, catching his breath.

"It's kind of my thing," Valerie bragged. "Now that you've seen it as a proper memory, it shouldn't keep you up at night. I also cleared up the confusion between your human side and the other. Now, when you see or hear a ghost, you'll know what it is." She stood to leave and headed toward the door while Wyatt just sat, still reeling.

"Shame you can't stay for dinner. I ordered pizza," Gabriel said, shifting her gaze to Wyatt. "You're welcome." Wyatt couldn't help but laugh a bit. He had been dying for a slice since he got to the city and he was starving.

"Shame nothin'," Valerie told her. "I've been waiting on this man for *weeks*. He finally asked me out and I'm not missing this date for *shit*. Besides, this one's got questions. Now he knows this is legit and he's all kinds of freaked out."

Gabriel laughed. "Remember when I first found *you* and you pulled a knife on me? That was hysterical."

"I do," Valerie teased. "And, just so you know, I still carry that knife with me, so watch yourself."

"You know you can't hurt me," Gabriel scoffed.

"I know. But, I can sure as hell show my disapproval," Valerie taunted as she opened the door to go. "Hey, new guy," she said as she walked out. "Ask Big Sis about her boyfriend."

"That was super cunty," Gabriel quipped.

"See you later, ho," Valerie joshed as the door closed behind her.

Gabriel threw Wyatt a beer and sat next to him on the sofa, putting her feet up on the ottoman.

"I'm gonna let you ask your questions since it'll upset your sensibilities if I just start talking," she said, taking a sip of water.

"I appreciate that," Wyatt sneered.

"Go ahead."

"First," Wyatt wondered. "Who am I?"

"Barachiel, leader of the Guardian Angels, all of which are currently in heaven, obviously, but most of the time, you tell them where, when, and how to save certain people from certain things. Can be anything from not letting an old lady slip in her tub to stopping a bomb from going off in a building. You also create and control lightning, which is why you're here now."

"So, saving people is,"

"What you were made to do," Gabriel finished. "Your whole life makes sense now, doesn't it?"

He nodded and took a sip of his beer.

"But," Gabriel wanted to make clear. "Your existence as *Wyatt* is just as real and valid as it ever was. Your life has meaning and purpose aside from the bigger picture."

"And, Valerie?"

"Uriel, Angel of Hope and Divine Visions. Besides reorganizing your brain, she gets random visions. Some things that will happen, some that have already happened. She also leads souls into Heaven, and by that I mean she tries to get people to do the right thing, hence the phone in the street." Gabriel giggled. "Raphael's supposed to be the funny one but she cracks me up. Raphael is our best healer, which is why he became a doctor even though he had started a travel agency in college. He ended up selling the agency to pay for medical school. He's also the Angel of Happy Meetings, which is why I had him meet you at your dad's. He makes the best introductions."

"So," Wyatt said. "Angels are real, so that makes..."

"God," Gabriel confirmed. "Yeah, He's real. Not like most people think, I mean, He's complicated."

"Complicated."

"Yeah, it's like, he's *everything,*" she explained. "The couch, the air, us. Every atom is part of God. So, He used to be this tiny little ball thing but he was bored and lonely, so he spewed himself all across the nothing and created Creation."

"Like the big bang?" Wyatt asked.

"Exactly the big bang," she told him. "So, think about everything in the universe like body parts. Cells in one unimaginably giant entity. And at the center of everything is God's consciousness, which I'll just refer to as 'God' from now on to make the conversation easier. Directly surrounding that is Heaven."

"His consciousness," Wyatt said. "So, he has like, a personality?"

"Totes."

"What's that like?"

"Oh, you know, self-righteous. Funny. He loves everyone and everything. He's basically a know-it-all father figure with a lot of dad jokes."

Wyatt laughed. "How do you remember this? Why don't I?"

"I don't actually remember it," she made clear. "It's more like I saw it in a movie or learned about it in school. I know this stuff like you know about Pearl Harbor. You don't *remember* it, but you can tell me what happened. And, while it seems like I do, I don't actually know *everything*. Just what God *wants* me to know. I'm His Messenger, so I know and relate pertinent information but there are a *few* things I don't know. For example, I have no idea if aliens exist. No clue. Could be none or there could be an alien city on the dark side of the moon. I'm oblivious. Fairies, unicorns, dragons, fucking Big Foot, I could not tell you."

"That's funny," Wyatt chuckled.

Abruptly, Gabriel jumped up and rushed toward the door. "Yay, pizza!" she sang just as there was a knock at the door. She opened it, smiling broadly. "Ethan, my precious," she said, pulling a twenty-dollar bill from her back pocket and handing it to the delivery guy.

"You don't have to pa--" the carrier stopped, seeing Wyatt who sat silently on the couch. "Who the hell's that?"

Gabriel tried not to laugh at Ethan's insecurity. "That's my brother, Wyatt." she snickered. "You don't see the resemblance?"

He looked Wyatt over suspiciously. "I guess you both have brown hair," he conceded. "So, I get off in a few hours. I was thinking, I could stop by and--"

"I know what you were thinking, sweetie, but it's not happening tonight," she rebuffed. "Family stuff."

"Okay, well call me when--"

"I'll call you sometime," she said, taking the pizza and closing the door. "Eventually, probably," she muttered as she placed the box on the island and opened it. She took a slice for herself and waved Wyatt over. They both sat and began eating.

"So, that's the boyfriend I'm supposed to ask about?" he baited.

"No, that's just Ethan," Gabriel said. "He helps me out sometimes. You know, sexually."

"Oh," Wyatt said, eyebrows raised.

"What?" she said, daring him to comment.

"I'm not saying anything."

"Mm-hmm."

"So, that's *not* the guy Valerie was talking about?" he asked, unable to stifle his curiosity.

"She wasn't talking about any one person in particular. She just has *opinions* about how I live my life, that's all."

"I see. So, is she worried about you or just nosy?"

"Thank you!" Gabriel exclaimed. "Bish all in my business and shit. I don't want a boyfriend. What's the point? Date some dude for so long he gets all attached and then one day I'm just like, 'Oh, by the way, I'm the fucking Messenger of God and I can't make it to dinner tonight because I have important saving the world shit to do. Sorry.' Or, I just hide who I am forever, and what kind of life is that? Keeping this secret would be like, effort, and I don't have room. Besides, when you know everything, pretty much *everyone* is too annoying to be around for more than a weekend."

"As long as you're safe, it's none of my business."

"Safe? What for?" she scoffed. "If I get sick, I heal myself. I can't get knocked up and I don't carry disease. Uriel just thinks I treat my partners badly by not ever committing to one. Says I might hurt their sensitive human feelings. But, I *know* what they're thinking and it has *never once* been 'Oh, I wish all this consequence-free sex came with more strings.'"

"All right, then," Wyatt said. "I'm sorry, though, about your fertility issue."

"Oh, I forgot to tell you," she realized, starting her second slice of pizza. "None of us can have kids. Like, ever. You boys are sterile and me and Uriel don't even get a monthly business. It doesn't suck."

"What do you mean, sterile?" he contested.

"Don't freak out, we're *angels.* We're *forbidden* from procreating, and when God forbids something, he doesn't trust people to do what he says. He just makes it impossible."

Wyatt could feel his life crashing down around him. Annie would never come back to him now.

"Hey," Gabriel said, rubbing his back. "In case you haven't noticed, I'm *loaded.* If you need money for adoption fees or a sperm donor or something, I'm here for you, bro."

"We just met."

"*You* just met," she corrected. "I've known you *forever.*"

"Thank you."

"Don't thank me yet," she warned. "I can give you a fuckton of money but that's not gonna bring your girl back. She's not gonna believe you magically got better overnight. And, I think you know you can't tell her any of this angel stuff."

"No, she'd think I'm crazier than she already does," he agreed. "Out of curiosity, why won't God let us have kids?"

"History lesson," Gabriel started. "Back in the old days, when humans were new and interesting, some angels got obsessed. They possessed the bodies of men to see how being human felt, and you know what it's like to be in here. You're hungry and thirsty, everything hurts and half the time, you're desperate for ass. Nothing ever satisfies for very long and it's just constant satiation of these stupid animal instincts. You and I were born into these bodies so we're used to it, but these motherfuckers just stepped right into the shit and couldn't control themselves. Some of them started seducing and even raping chicks, which resulted in offspring we called 'Nephilim'. Half angel, half human, those monstrosities were *unmanageable*. First, all the women that gave birth to them died. Their power was too great for a fragile human body to take. The fetuses grew something like three times as fast as normal pregnancies and then, instead of a normal delivery, the baby would force its way out, tearing at, we'll just say, *all the things*. Once born, they grew fast. By the time three years had passed, they looked, felt, and spoke like they were in their twenties. They were geniuses, master manipulators, and they were strong as fuck. They had the powers of their fathers but with human souls and brains, so they were *unbalanced*. Some forced people to worship them like Gods. Some went on murdering sprees. They were so hungry, they'd eat all the available food in a village and starve their neighbors to death. One asshole burned his whole town to the ground because the local winery couldn't make more wine because, after drinking it all, he ate all the grapes for miles. These abominations were fucking nuts. God eventually got sick of their shit, sent the angels that sired them to Hell and wiped the Nephilim from the Earth."

"How'd he do that?"

She took a sip of water before answering. "He made it rain."

"Oh."

"Yeah." She finished her pizza before speaking again. "After that, God took away our ability to breed, whether we be in a human host or otherwise."

"*Otherwise*. So, what are we *really*?"

"As angels, we're energy beings that don't really look like anything. We're invisible to humans unless we want to be seen, at which point, we can make ourselves look like pretty much whatever we want. Currently, the few of us that are here are occupying human bodies that would have died before birth. Had Wyatt Sinclair had a human soul, his mom's nutty-as-a-fruitcake moment would've killed him, and without you to be strong for, John would have spiraled into such hardcore alcoholism that he'd have lost his practice, his home, and he would have died penniless on the streets of cirrhosis in two thousand nine. Speaking of death, yes, we can die. We're basically human, our bodies just formed to be able to handle us. Because of our ability to self-heal, we probably have a longer than usual life expectancy, but we'll all ultimately die of old."

"I don't self-heal."

"Really?" she asked. "You ever get injured on the job? Smoke inhalation? When was the last time you were sick?"

Wyatt thought about it and couldn't remember. He recalled no instance of sickness in his life.

"Not even a cold," Gabriel stated. "Anyway, when we die, assuming we get cremated, we'll be pulled back to Heaven like we're on bungee cords. Our bodies act as a tether keeping us on Earth. They get destroyed, we go home. Otherwise, we're stuck here, roaming this dump until the Gates open. Yeah, yeah, the apartment's great but it's a third-world gutter in comparison, trust me."

"Gates?"

"And, to the reason we're here on Earth now," Gabriel began. "A few weeks ago, God started his rest. Every seventh celestial day, a 'day' being two hundred and forty-three Earth years, God shuts down his consciousness. Heaven's Gates and the Gates of Hell slam shut and any angel or demon still on this planet snaps back like a supermodel after a pregnancy. The only thing in or out are human souls. It's His way of ensuring humanity's control over their own evolution. The system has worked like gangbusters for infinity except now, a particularly fucked up so and so has thrown a wrench in the works and Dad needs us to clean up the mess while he's taking a nap."

"How do we do that?"

"We'll talk about it. Listen, I'm gonna put the rest of this pizza up for later. I know you want to, so go ahead and call your wife. When you're done, we need to get to work."

"Work?"

"Training," she insisted. "You need to learn to control your lightning and get yourself ready."

"Ready for what?"

"Anything. Your room's the first door on the left. That's where you'll be staying for a while, so get cozy."

"Yes, ma'am," Wyatt said jokingly. He made his way to the bedroom where he found a closet full of clothes in his size and an en suite with a sticky note on the mirror that read 'You still owe me for Jersey'. He laughed out loud as he went back to the bedroom, took his jacket off, and threw it on the chair in the corner, pulling his phone from his pocket. He dialed Annie. No answer. For once, he was excited to leave her a message because, this time, he wouldn't be crying and begging her to come back. This time, he felt like he had legitimate good news to share, even if it was under odd circumstances.

"Hey, baby," he began. "I just wanted to let you know where I am, in case you went by the apartment and I wasn't there. I didn't want you to worry. I'm in the city visiting family. Turns out I have some. Saw my dad which was," he paused for a second. "Interesting. I, um," Tears began to gather in his eyes as he tried to choke back the quiver in his voice. "I was hoping maybe you'd give me a call back, just to check in. I miss you. Okay, bye."

He hung up the phone and sat for a while trying to collect himself. He wiped the tears from his face, his mind wandering from thoughts of Annie to what Gabriel had said about his father. He had always known that he was a huge disappointment to his dad but knowing that had it not been for him, John would've died years ago turned the tables on their relationship in his mind somewhat. He felt a new appreciation and responsibility for his father and for the first time ever, he felt glad to have been born.

Looking around at the room, queen-sized bed and nightstand on one wall, television opposite, he decided he might as well stick around and help out with whatever big bad was coming. While he didn't know what exactly Gabriel had in mind, if this lightning thing was for real, he was actually kind of excited to see what he was capable of.

Chapter 4

The man's eyes bulged as life slowly left his body. Allydia's grip remained strong around his throat until she was satisfied that he had expired. Once sure, she left his body on the satin sheets of the four-poster bed and put her gown back on. She left the bedroom, entering her throne room. It was one of many in this city but it happened to be her favorite. Beautiful settees and chaise lounges lined the walls which were covered in gorgeous paintings and tapestries. The center of the room was adorned with a rug from the old country that Allydia had always loved and at the back of the room, opposite the door, was her throne. Beautifully ornate carvings filled the wood and it had extra thick padding under the purple upholstery to make it as comfortable as possible. She sat, watching the others indulge in all manner of drug and debauchery, as an assistant poured her a glass of Shiraz.

"Was he not to your liking, Majesty?" the girl asked, peering into the room and seeing the dead man.

"He disappointed me," Allydia sighed. "Be a dear and ask your Governor to have someone dispose of that."

"Of course, Majesty. Right away."

The girl scurried from the room while Allydia took a sip of wine but before she could swallow, her Governor of New York rushed in.

"Out!" he shouted. "Now! Everyone out!"

The room emptied and as the last person out closed the door behind them, the Governor knelt on the rug before his Queen.

"What is it, Tobin?" she asked dismissively.

"There are reports, Your Grace," he said shakily. "Of the creatures you described. Six eyewitnesses."

Allydia sat up straight and moved to the edge of her seat. "Are these witnesses trustworthy?"

"I believe so, Your Grace." He was nearly trembling with fear as he gathered the courage to look her in the eyes. "What are your orders, Your Majesty?"

Allydia sat back and thought for a few seconds. "Stay clear of them," she told him. "Ignore them unless approached and if they *do* engage, fight dirty, because they will."

"Yes, Your Grace," he agreed, standing to leave. "I'll put word out."

"Thank you, Tobin. You may go."

Once alone, Allydia's concern turned to excitement. She brushed her long dark hair off her shoulders and drank her cup dry. It had finally begun, what she had been waiting for all these years. She poured herself another cup, took a sip, and smiled mischievously. Revenge would finally be hers.

Chapter 5

"Okay, so the first thing you have to understand is that 'lightning' doesn't just come from the sky," Gabriel explained. "You can use the electricity from anything to create lightning bolts with varying degrees of electric shock. For instance," She took a D battery from her pocket and held it up. "You can take the charge from a battery and use it to make a small shock. It's enough to get someone's attention but not really enough to hurt them. You can pull the electricity from a wall socket, taking as little as a lightbulb's worth or as much as the entire power grid. You can take the energy from clouds, car batteries, cell phones, or even just the static in the air. There are two ways to do it. The first is focusing your intent and *feeling* what you're doing rather than thinking about it. That takes time and patience to get down, neither of which I have currently, so we're going option two, emotional upheaval. All the pain, depression, anxiety, and whatever bullshit just pisses you off is what you're gonna think about and focus on. Not what's going on in the room, not what you think you should be concerned with. Every strong negative emotion you've ever had, that's what needs to be in your brain. When you feel that shit bubbling up like you want to punch somebody, that's when you let it go. We'll start with this battery. Look at it, close your eyes, and think about something that upsets you."

"I'll give it a shot," he said, closing his eyes. He thought about the conversation he'd had with his father. He thought about his mother and what she had done to them and to herself. *How could she do that? How could she try to kill her own ba--*

"Shit!" Gabriel yelped.

"What?!" Wyatt shouted, his eyes flying open.

Gabriel smiled widely, opening her hand to show him the battery. It was completely destroyed, looking as if it had exploded in her palm, which was scorched and bleeding.

"Oh, God! I'm so sorry," Wyatt said.

"It's totally fine," she said, dropping the battery on the floor where the two sat facing each other. He watched in disbelief as her skin slowly healed itself. "Now, try the outlet."

He looked at the outlet on the wall and thought about the call he'd just made to his wife. He thought about how he didn't know where she was or if she was all right because she refused to call him back. He let himself feel how much he missed her as tears began to build in his eyes. Just as he remembered he was supposed to close his eyes in order to better concentrate, a bright flash erupted from the wall, setting the white faux fur rug ablaze.

"Holy crap balls!" Gabriel exclaimed. She jumped up and grabbed the small fire extinguisher she kept in a kitchen cabinet and put out the fire. "That was awesome!"

Wyatt was dumbstruck.

"Maybe you should practice on the roof from now on," Gabriel suggested.

"Probably wise," he agreed.

"Next, we'll work on aim," she told him. "Shouldn't be too difficult. You're getting the hang of your ability *with lightning speed*." She flashed an open smile as if to say 'Get it?' which made Wyatt chuckle.

Her phone vibrated on the counter and she picked it up, smirking when she saw the number.

"Hey," she said to the person on the other end of the call. "About half an hour. Just me and Barachiel." She turned to look at Wyatt who had moved to the bar and was drinking a beer. She grinned proudly and told the caller, "I think he'll be just fine. K, bye. Looks like training's done for the night." Gabriel said, placing her phone back on the counter. "We gotta go. Come on." She quickly walked down the hall to Wyatt's room. By the time he caught up to her, she was already rifling through the closet.

"What are you doing?" he inquired.

"Getting your outfit ready," she said, throwing a pair of black leather pants on the bed.

"I'm not wearing that," he said.

"Yeah, but you are," she insisted. "Where we're going, this tee shirt and jeans thing you've got going is not gonna fly. You will stick out like a pussy hat at an RNC convention." She tossed a dark burgundy shirt and a black vest down next to the pants, picked up a pair of boots, and handed them to him. "Wheels up in ten."

The two now stood in the alley next to a nightclub, Wyatt watching with condescension as people in clothing as preposterous as what he was wearing filed into the large brick building with blacked-out windows. He had begrudgingly worn what Gabriel had chosen for him and while he was wildly uncomfortable, he now understood her reasoning. She, herself, had gone full goth with black lipstick and eyeliner, navy velvet mini dress with extra long flowing sleeves, fishnets, and knee-high boots.

"I look ridiculous," Wyatt complained.

"Yeah, kind of," she agreed. "I look like nineteen ninety-six but what are you gonna do? This is their jam."

Wyatt noticed what looked like cat eyes at the other end of the dark alley. As they drew closer, he saw that they were too high to be a small animal. Out of instinct, he raised his arm in front of his new sister to protect her.

"Oh, that's precious," Gabriel chortled. "Completely unnecessary but still, super cute. Listen, when the delegation gets here, keep quiet. I'll do all the talking. Now, I have every confidence that we can handle ourselves but we need to lay low, so to keep these things at a distance, I need you to look tough. Like, full-on resting dick face."

He shot her an annoyed glance.

"Yeah, just like that," she approved.

He rolled his eyes a little. "What do you mean, 'delegation'?" he asked.

"She means us," a man said. Stepping out from the shadows of the alley were three men and a teenage girl. "Hattie, sweetie," he told the girl. "Stamp our friends."

"Yes, sir," she said, hurrying toward Wyatt and Gabriel and placing a red circle stamp on the backs of each of their left hands.

"I'm Tobin Abney, I'll be escorting you to Her Majesty this evening," the man informed them.

"Gabriel. This is Wyatt," Gabriel responded.

"Charmed," the man said kindly. "Follow me and do your best to stay close."

As they filed in, Tobin and the girl in the lead, Wyatt and Gabriel in the middle, and the two other men in the rear, Wyatt couldn't help but notice the unnerving amount of attention they were getting. People stopped what they were doing to stare as they walked past. Even the music, which Wyatt recognized but couldn't quite put his finger on, seemed to quiet slightly as they made their way to the back of the club and up a spiral staircase.

"Don't mind them," Tobin told them. "They're just curious."

Be careful, Gabriel warned as they approached the VIP section. *She'll have you feeding her peeled grapes by night's end if you don't watch yourself.*

The young girl pulled back a velvet rope and stood aside, allowing the others to walk through. Once on the other side, Tobin put his hand up, signaling for the others to stop before taking a knee.

"Your Majesty, I present Gabriel and Wyatt, as requested," he stated.

"Thank you, Tobin," a sultry voice said from the darkness. As Wyatt peered into the room, he saw the same kind of animal-like eyes as before looking back at him. As the woman came into the light, he could see that they belonged to her and that they now appeared normal. She was stunning in a black ball gown with dark hair, full lips, and vaguely Middle Eastern or Mediterranean features. Wyatt felt drawn to her somehow and as he couldn't help but stare, he wondered what her skin tasted like.

"Dude," Gabriel said pointedly.

"Sorry," Wyatt whispered as he gathered his senses.

"Leave us," the woman instructed the delegation. The others left and Wyatt and Gabriel sat in a booth next to the Queen.

"So," she said. "You call yourself 'Wyatt'."

"Yeah," he acknowledged.

"That's lovely," she breathed. "Allydia Cain," she said, holding her hand out for him to take, which he did, resisting the urge, just barely, to press his lips to it.

"All right, kids," Gabriel interjected. "Can you flirt later? We're here for a reason."

"Of course," Allydia said. "Later."

Wyatt let go of her hand and reminded himself that he was married.

"Pfft," Gabriel let slip.

"Hey," Wyatt griped.

"I'm sorry," she apologized. "But, I wouldn't call what you are *married*. Separated is more accurate. But, you're right. It's not my business."

"It's temporary," he insisted.

"Oh, sweetness," Allydia asserted. "Everything is temporary. *Life* is temporary. If a woman is feeble-minded enough to leave a man as beautiful as you, she lacks the sense God gave her and is undeserving of your patience."

"Anyway," Gabriel said. "I'm assuming you called because you have news."

"Yes," Allydia told her. "There are credible reports of demon activity in the city. Six eyewitnesses claim to have seen them, all on the Lower East Side."

"Demons?!" Wyatt blurted.

"Yeah, dude, chill," Gabriel directed. "Thanks, Dia. Call me if you hear anything else."

"I will," Allydia said as her guests began to leave. "And, Wyatt, just some food for thought, if your wife regains her faculties and comes crawling back, begging for another chance, perhaps you'll forgive her indiscretion. In the meantime, however, you would do well to remember that you're free to have some indiscretions of your own."

"Oh, gross," Gabriel winced. "Let's go." She led Wyatt through the crowd and toward the exit. Once outside, she smacked his arm in protest.

"What?" he laughed.

"Ew," she said. "Listen, I'm not your keeper. You do what you want but I'm telling you, that girl is bad news bears."

Wyatt scoffed. "I'm not interested," he claimed. "Despite what you think, Annie *will* come back to me. She just needs some time. Once she sees that I'm not crazy, everything will be back to normal."

"I hate to break the news," Gabriel told him. "But nothing is ever gonna be normal for you again. Just because you're not *crazy* doesn't mean things aren't severely fucked up."

Chapter 6

"So, demons?" Wyatt inquired, sitting at the island and taking a sip of his coffee. He had let it go the night before because he was exhausted after an unreasonably long day and just wanted to go to bed but it was a new day and he *had* to know what he had gotten himself into.

"Apparently," Gabriel replied. "The Gates of Hell aren't closed like they should be and that can only mean one thing."

"What's that?" he wondered.

"Girl!" Valerie called out as she let herself into the apartment. She closed the door behind her and quickly took a seat next to Wyatt at the island. Gabriel poured her sister a cup of coffee and patiently waited for her to tell her story, even though she knew everything she was going to say as soon as she saw her.

"I had a vision last night and I already texted Tae cause I knew you'd want to talk to him about it since it involved the hospital and he said he's on his way but first, let me tell you about my date," Valerie continued. "*This man*, first, as soon as he picked me up, announced we were going Dutch, and that's fine, like, I'm an independent woman, I got my own money. But, *damn*, why you gotta blast that shit in my face as soon as I open the door? Like he thinks I'm a gold digger or something, trying to extort him for some pasta. Then, we're at dinner and he sent his food back *twice* because the edges of the plates weren't clean enough. I was like, 'For real? You know what kind of awful stuff they're doing to your food right now?' and he told me they wouldn't *dare* because he's a health inspector. I don't care if you're the *mayor*, if you're that rude to your waiter, you're getting a spit sandwich. So, dinner's over and we're in a cab on the way back to my place, and I had *no* intention of letting him smash at that point. Like, if you treat your servers like shit, I just don't respect you, you know? So, we're in the cab and that's when the vision hits, so I probably look kooky as fuck, just staring off into the distance and shit for a good minute and a half. And, when I come out of it, this motherfucker is *kissing the side of my neck*, all uninvited, so I pushed his face away and I'm like, 'Uh, uh. You are *not* getting in tonight.' and this dude *took it out* and said *I* needed to take care of it."

"Oh, my God," Wyatt said. "That's awful."

"Wait for it," Gabriel smirked.

"So," Valerie told them. "We were less than a block away from my spot, so I yelled, 'Stop the cab!' and the driver pulled over, I opened the door, punched this dude in the face, and threw a travel size bottle of lotion I keep in my jacket at him and said 'Handle your own shit, baby dick'."

Wyatt and Gabriel couldn't help but laugh while Valerie nonchalantly sipped her coffee.

"I'm just salty because dude is *fine,*" Valerie confessed.

"Muffins!" Gabriel suddenly exclaimed, jumping up from her seat and rushing to the door. She reached for the handle as they heard the first knock. She flung the door open, snatched the box of muffins out of Tae's hands, and placed it on the counter. She opened it, picked one up, and took a bite before turning back to him, grabbing his face, and quickly kissing his cheek several times.

"I thought they'd please you," Tae condescended.

"Yeah, yeah," Gabriel dismissed. "All I eat is carbs. How am I so skinny? Do I know what vegetables look like? Anyway, now that everyone's here, we need to talk about what we're doing, like, on Earth, because the plan goes into motion *today.*"

"*Today?*" Wyatt asked.

"Relax," she told him. "You don't need to do anything just yet except practice. Today is just step one, getting the band back together."

"Girl, what are you on about?" Tae wondered.

"Uriel, please share with the class what your vision was about," she requested.

"All right, so," Valerie started. "It was a hospital room and there was a blond dude in the bed with like, tubes down his throat and shit and he was familiar to me but I didn't recognize him. Like, I *should* have known who he was and I felt like, nervous. Like I needed to get him out of that place. No offense, T."

"Mm-hmm," Tae sneered. "I mean, I *am* set to pull the plug on a John Doe in a couple of hours. He has blond hair."

"Yeah," Gabriel interjected. "I can't let you kill that guy."

"Bitch, I don't *kill* people," Tae rebuffed. "This motherfucker has been brain dead for a month. I am simply unplugging a machine."

"Okay," she agreed. "But, when you do, I need to be there to wake his ass up."

"What for?" he asked. "He one of your *companions*?"

"Oh, God! No! Ew!" Gabriel grimaced. "He's our brother."

"Another one?" Wyatt asked. "Jeez, how many angels does it take to screw in a--"

"Blond hair," Valerie blurted out. Her eyes became saucers and her mouth hung open as the realization hit her. "Are you serious?"

"Even when I'm joking," Gabriel declared.

"Which one?" Tae asked through a clenched jaw.

"Raphael."

"Which one?!" he shouted.

She looked at him knowingly.

"Bitch, are you out your goddamned mind?!" he snapped. "Are you trying to get us all *killed?!*"

"Calm down," Gabriel commanded. "He's on our side. Besides, between Barachiel's lightning and my all-around awesomeness, we'll be fine."

"Somebody gonna fill me in?" Wyatt asked. "Who are we talking about?"

"Motherfucking *Lucifer*," Tae griped. "This crazy bitch wants me to wake up fucking *Satan*. Mm mm. I am *not*. Not a chance in Hell."

"Lucifer?!" Wyatt gasped.

"He's not what you think," Gabriel said. "Exactly."

"No, not *exactly*," Valerie confirmed. "But, he *is* terrifying as shit."

"Sure, but he always does his job," Gabriel insisted.

"We are talking about the *Devil*, right?" Wyatt argued. "How are we considering this?"

"All right, kids, listen up," Gabriel began. "Back in the day, Lucifer was God's favorite. Not just His favorite angel, his favorite *everything*. He was the most beautiful, most powerful, and the most dedicated angel in Heaven. God loved and trusted him above all others. So, when the angels fell and God created Hell as a place to lock them up to protect humanity and the world He'd created, He knew there was no one else that could guard the Gates but his number one. Now, Hell's a big place, so every once in a great while, somebody will make a break for it and he has to come top-side to fetch them but for the most part, Lucy keeps those bitches in line. With him trapped in this John Doe, though, you know, the mice will play."

"The demons Allydia was talking about," Wyatt surmised.

"Yep."

"You make it sound like he's a good guy," Wyatt said, puzzled. "If he's just trying to keep demons from hurting people, what's the problem? These two are on the verge of panic attacks."

"Being the jailer means you have to spend your time in jail," she explained. "Hell is *separation from God*. Being in that place with those vermin, away from us, away from Grace, over time has had an e*ffect*. Which is why we need to find the monster we're after as soon as possible, he can take her back to where she belongs, close the Gates of Hell, sucking all the demons back in," she brushed her hands together. "Crisis averted."

Wyatt, Valerie, and Tae sat in mind-boggled silence for a few seconds.

"We good?" Gabriel asked, looking around at everyone stubbornly.

"We are definitely not *good*," Valerie answered. "Knowing the psychology of why someone's a barbaric, brutal psychopath doesn't make it *fine*."

"We need him," Gabriel said pointedly. "He's the only one of us capable of putting this monster back where she came from."

"She? You don't mean,"

"Lilith," Gabriel said plainly.

"Holy shit," Valerie all but whispered.

"Oh, fuck me," Tae said, sitting down. "I'm gonna need something stronger than coffee."

"You two have a vague idea of who this bitch is, but B's oblivious, so let me break it down," Gabriel related. "Lilith is Lucifer's twin sister. Take everything you've ever heard about Lucifer, most of which isn't actually true, by the way, and evil it up by about five thousand times. In our current states, we can't kill her but we can weaken her enough that Lucifer can drag her baby eating ass back to her cage."

Wyatt nearly choked on a bite of muffin.

"Yeah," Gabriel continued. "Bitch fucking *eats* babies, like, as snacks. And that's just the tip of her bat shit iceberg. She's *heavily* into dudes and once she picks one, things get real dark real fast. Lilith is twisted on a level that the human race hasn't seen since the Bronze Age. I can not stress this enough, guys. We *have* to take her down and we need our brother to do it."

"It's still morning and I'm already done with today," Tae muttered as he took a sip of coffee.

"The plan is pretty straightforward," Gabriel told them. "We get Lucifer functioning and on board, Barachiel, you'll keep practicing, getting stronger so you can play your part when we need you, Uriel will hopefully get some helpful visions along the way, and I'll do my best to keep Lucifer on a tight leash. Eventually, Lilith will contact Allydia. When she does, assuming we haven't found her ourselves beforehand, Dia will give us a location and that's when we'll go after her."

"And Allydia is?" Tae asked.

"Lilith's step-daughter. It's complicated," Gabriel said. "Point is, she doesn't know that Dia goddamn *hates* her. She's our way in."

"All right, girl," Valerie reconciled, standing up and drinking the last bit of her coffee. "Let's get to it, then."

"B, you stay here and practice," Gabriel commanded. "You never know when Lucifer's gonna get rowdy. Best to be prepared, just in case. You two with me."

The others left quickly while Wyatt sat, stunned, trying to digest all the objectively insane information he'd just heard. Feeling the likelihood of his impending demise, he decided to call Annie, maybe for the last time. The phone rang several times and then, a miracle. She answered.

"Hi, Wyatt," she said quietly. He was dumbstruck. For a second, he forgot how to speak. "Wyatt?"

"I'm here," he replied, clearing his throat. "I just wasn't expecting...how are you?"

"Fine," she told him, but she didn't sound like herself. Something was off.

"Are you? You sound strange."

"I'm okay, Wyatt. What do you want?"

"I wanted to tell you that I'm doing a lot better. No seeing things for a few days now. I had a procedure. Annie, *no voices*. I swear, I think I'm gonna be okay now."

"That's great for you," she said, not really believing him. "I hope that's true."

"It is," he assured her. "Listen, I'll be in the city for a little while, not exactly sure how long. Family stuff. But, when I get some time, I thought maybe--"

"Wyatt," she cut him off. "There's someone else."

His stomach dropped. "What?" he choked out. "What are you--"

"I'm sorry," she said, her voice beginning to quiver. "I'm so sorry, but--"

"No," he begged, tears streaming down his face. He began to pace around the apartment, his body starting to tremble. "Baby, I'm better, I promise. You don't have to do this. Please."

"It's done," she made clear, her voice shaking. "Please don't call again."

The line went dead as did any hopes Wyatt had for a reconciliation. He could forgive his wife for being afraid of him. It was completely understandable. He had been a train wreck the last couple of months before she left. He could forgive her for wanting to lock him up in an institution. He could forgive her for leaving, given the circumstances but he *could not* forgive her for sleeping with someone else. Even if she came back to him right then, he'd never be able to get past it. That was it. His marriage was really over.

He dropped the phone and fell to his knees. The pain growing in his chest was intense. He was gasping for air and he felt like he might throw up. The combination of rage and devastation was overwhelming as he gripped his chest and tried to control his breathing. Overcome with grief, he let out a booming scream and as he did, he lost all control. The room suddenly lit up with a dozen lightning bolts erupting from every socket. Appliances exploded in sparks, light bulbs blew out, and curtains burst into flames. He saw the fire through his tears and, for a second, wondered if he should let it burn. Let the smoke that was filling the room fill his lungs and put him out of his misery. His life was over now, anyway. After a few moments, he decided against it, knowing that he had a responsibility to literally help save the world, not to mention the fact that there were other people living in the building.

He tore the burning curtain from the wall and stomped out the flames. He coughed as he opened the doors to the balcony and threw the charred fabric onto the patio table.

"Girl trouble?" Allydia asked.

Wyatt was taken aback. "Where'd you come from?"

"Near the Red Sea, originally," she offered.

"How long have you been out here?"

"Just a minute. I heard a ruckus."

"What do you mean, 'a minute'? That doesn't--"

"Can I come in?" she requested. "It's getting kind of chilly."

He noticed her gathering the oversized hood of her long coat around her face. She did, in fact, look cold.

"Sure," he accommodated.

"Thank you, Wyatt," she purred, slinking closely past him into the apartment. She looked around at the mess and back at Wyatt, who had come inside and sat down on the sofa. She watched attentively as he wiped away some stray tears from his cheeks and smoothed his hair back from his face.

"Gabriel's not here," he told her.

"Oh, I know," she admitted. "What I need, she can't help me with."

"What do you want, Allydia?" he sighed.

"Say my name again," she said, sitting next to him.

"Are you hitting on me right now?" he asked.

She slid closer. "You can't be surprised," she presumed. "You're spectacular. You have mirrors, right?"

"I'm flattered," he said. "But, my wife just told me she has a new boyfriend, so I'm not exactly in--"

"Well, you know what they say," she cooed, swinging her leg over him and climbing swiftly onto his lap. "When one door closes."

"Allydia,"

"Mm," she breathed. "Yes, darling?"

As he tried to resist her advances, the pain he had been feeling so strongly was now slowly giving way to something else. All thoughts of Annie, Lucifer, and Lilith vanished. Even the room around him seemed to fade. All he could see was her.

She took her coat off and threw it to the floor. "Do you want me to go?" she asked quietly, leaning in, getting her lips as close to his as she could without touching. She gently stroked his face and looked into his eyes. He couldn't think. The world had disappeared. She was all there was.

"Wyatt, do you want me to go?" she asked more firmly. He didn't. That was the last thing he wanted. In that moment, all he wanted in the world was her.

He stared into her eyes and shook his head, allowing his hands to wander up her thighs as she straddled him. She smiled as she ran her mulberry-painted fingernails over the stubble on his cheek. She delicately brushed her lips to his and dragged her fingers through his hair. As he pulled her skirt up, he could feel she wore nothing underneath and began kissing her more deeply. With little effort, she quickly unzipped and removed his jeans along with his boxer briefs and set herself upon him again, this time placing him inside her. He tore open her blouse, sending buttons flying in all directions and exposing her full breasts, which he began kissing. His lips moved up her neck as he squeezed her backside. She writhed on top of him, her body quaking with pleasure. She grabbed the back of his head, gripping his lush dark hair and pressing his mouth harder against the side of her throat. They went on this way for a long time, both of them never having felt bliss like this before. He wrapped his arms around her, pressing her even closer and grunting with ecstasy as he came inside her. She gasped, her own climax exploding with sheer rapture. She could no longer hold back. Her eyes dilated completely and her fangs began to grow. Before she could stop herself, she clamped down on his neck, piercing his carotid, and allowed the sweet warmth of his blood to fill her mouth. She swallowed hungrily, unable to restrain herself.

The pain of the bite cleared Wyatt's head as if he were coming down from a high. "Stop," he said, trying and failing to push her off. "Allydia, stop!"

She didn't.

"Allydia!" he pleaded, his hands beginning to feel cold.

Again, she ignored him, grasping the other side of his neck.

The cold feeling was spreading to his arms and legs. He felt weak and a little numb.

"Allydia, get off!" he shouted, lightning spewing from his hands, throwing her across the room and into the wall. She fell to the ground and stood, smiling fiendishly as she looked up at him before wiping her bottom lip.

"I'm sorry," she claimed. "I couldn't help myself."

"What are you?!" he asked, pulling his pants up and putting his hand to his throat.

"I've been called a lot of things. 'Alukah', 'Estrie', 'Succubus'."

"You should go," he insisted.

"If that's what you want," she complied. She retrieved her coat, backed out of the apartment, and gave him a wink before closing the door behind her.

Wyatt finished getting his pants zipped and buttoned while looking around at the damage he'd caused. All of the appliances were destroyed. The television was hanging from the wall by its cords, which were fried. The can lights were all blown and there were scorch marks everywhere. He would do his best to clean up the mess but he knew Gabriel was going to be pissed.

He went to the bathroom to check out his neck. What looked like an animal bite slowly healed itself as he looked in the mirror in awe. He washed the blood from his skin and took off his blood-soaked shirt, looking, flabbergasted, at his reflection. "What is my life?"

Chapter 7

"So, how come he always takes up in a blond dude?" Valerie asked as she and Gabriel stood over the John Doe. The man looked fragile and weak, utterly helpless. But, Gabriel knew better. Once she undid whatever magic Lilith had done and Lucifer was awake and in control of the body he was in, he'd barely be manageable. She was banking on the fact that he hated Lilith more than he loved mischief, but she knew she'd have to keep a close eye because he wasn't exactly rational.

"He had a thing for Vikings back in the day," Gabriel explained.

"Did he like playing pirate or was he just down for killing lots of people?"

"Neither. He was up looking for an escapee and some Nordic villagers gave him beer and taught him how to play Nine Men's Morris."

"Booze and board games?" Valerie chuckled.

"I have cases of beer and a closet full of games and you know I didn't buy that shit for myself."

"I hope it keeps him occupied because I for damn sure don't want to find out what kind of trouble he'll get into if he's bored."

"No, you do not, ma'am," Gabriel agreed. "You should probably back up."

Valerie quickly shuffled away to stand next to Tae who was guarding the door to the room.

"You didn't give him an x-ray?" Gabriel accused.

"I did a CT scan of his brain, which is *procedure*," Tae rebuffed. "Are you a doctor now? You want to tell me how to do my job?"

Gabriel raised an eyebrow. "Course not," she told him. She held her hand up and suddenly, something burst out of John Doe's chest and flew into her waiting palm.

"Holy shit!" Valerie cried.

"What the fuck is that?" Tae stammered.

Gabriel looked at the blood-covered object in her hand.

"Amulet," she told them. "Old Aramaic binding spell. It's what's been keeping Lucifer trapped. Pull the plug."

"Oh, Lord, please do not let me regret this," Tae said.

"You know He can't hear you, right?" Gabriel bated.

"Bitch, can you *just*?" Tae yelled as he pulled the feeding tube from the man's throat. He flipped the switches on the machines, shutting everything down, and waited for the monitor to flatline. Once it did, he edged his way back to the door. "It's done."

"Get ready, kids," Gabriel said, tossing the amulet to the floor. "Shit's about to get real."

She stomped on the faience bobble, crushing it to dust, and waited. The three stood with bated breath for several seconds.

"Is that it?" Tae whispered. Valerie shrugged. All at once, the man leaped up in his bed, eyes open wide, gasping for air, the wound on his chest healing itself closed.

Gabriel rushed to his side. "It's all right," she said. "You're okay."

"Sister," he said, amazed. "How long has it been?"

"I have no idea," she laughed.

"Well, you look," he paused, looking her up and down. "Nearly human."

"Nearly," she agreed.

"Where is she?" Lucifer demanded. "Where is that jealous, miserable witch?"

"We don't know yet. Close, though, it looks like."

"What happened?" Valerie asked shakily.

"Uriel," he said. "It's good to see you. How did I become trapped in this wretched, albeit handsome, animalistic form? I was hunting a demon who'd escaped during, let's say, an *altercation*. I knew Father would be closing the Gates soon, so it was a nice excuse to pay one last visit to His Creation before being banned. I indulged in a drink and then, just as I almost had the creature in my grasp, there she was, hardly able to control her laughter as she did her vile magic, securing me in this body and cursing me to a never-ending slumber. Like a ridiculous fairy tale."

"You don't know how she got out," Gabriel stated, clearly disappointed.

"No," Lucifer admitted angrily.

"Lucifer," Tae said quietly.

"In the flesh, apparently. Nice to see you, too, brother."

"Why are you British?"

"I'm not *British*," Lucifer corrected, slightly annoyed. "I'm simply speaking the language of those around me, only properly. Now, be a lamb and get big brother some water. I'm quite parched."

Tae nodded and quickly left the room, relieved to get a break from the madness within. He got a cup from the nurses' station and poured some water into it.

"Hello, doctor," said the nurse behind the counter happily.

"Hi, Nurse Bowen. How are you today?"

"Oh, just fine," she responded. "Packing up my youngest for college. Time flies, doesn't it? Do you have children, Dr. Iha?"

"No."

"Good. Don't," the nurse warned him. "They're terrible. You'll spend all of your money on the best private schools only to find out they threw away their acceptance letter to Yale and decided to go to the University of Albany to follow their dumbass boyfriend who's majoring in Art History. What kind of job does a degree in Art History get you, doctor?"

"I don't know."

"No one does."

Just then, the phone rang. The two waved goodbye to each other as the nurse picked it up and Tae scurried off back to the room.

"Thank you, Raphael," Lucifer said as Tae handed him the water.

"No problem," Tae said with a hint of sarcasm. "Now, you all have to get out of here before someone notices you. I'll do the paperwork to make sure everything looks like it was done on the up and up because you know I'm not about to lose my job over this bullshit, but you've got to *go*."

Gabriel placed a duffel bag on the bed and closed the curtain around it so Lucifer could get dressed.

"You sure about this?" Valerie asked.

"Yeah," Gabriel confirmed.

"I'd be careful if I were you," Tae told her. "He *is* the motherfucking Devil."

"You know this drape isn't enchanted," Lucifer said from behind the curtain. "I can actually still hear you."

Gabriel giggled, the other two shooting her glances of derision.

"What?" she said through her laughter. "He's funny."

"What the actual fuck?" Gabriel griped as she walked through the door of her apartment, Valerie and Lucifer filing in behind her.

"I'm sorry," Wyatt told her.

"If this is what happens when he uses his powers, why aren't you having him practice somewhere else?" Valerie wondered. "Like an abandoned building or deserted island or some shit."

Gabriel looked at Wyatt, becoming aware of everything that had happened while she was gone.

"He just had a bad day," she decided. "It's fine."

"Barachiel," Lucifer said with a smile, walking toward him with his hand outstretched. "You're a fine mess. Human life not as worthy of saving when you're down in the muck, is it?"

"Probably not this one," Wyatt conceded, shaking his hand. "Lucifer, then?"

"Who else?" he quipped. "Well, you're not afraid of me at all. I'm impressed. Gabriel isn't, either, but she knows that she's my favorite sibling. Uriel, on the other hand, can barely keep her bladder in check. Seems she's caught a glimpse of some of my more rambunctious endeavors in a vision or two." He glanced back at Valerie. "Don't worry, love. I'm no danger to you. Scout's honor."

"So, I'm gonna go," Valerie announced. "If I have a vision, I'll call."

"Okay, but don't waste time with a phone," Gabriel told her, pointing at her temple.

"I got you," Valerie called back. She was already out the door.

Gabriel reached for her phone as it rang in her pocket and answered. "Hey," she said. "How reliable is this guy? Okay, keep me updated." She put the phone back in her pocket before addressing her brothers. "That was Allydia. She said one of her guys has tracked a few of the demons to an abandoned theater on Canal Street. She's sending a few guys tonight to check it out."

"Allydia Cain?" Lucifer asked. "How is she? Did you send her my love?"

Gabriel rolled her eyes. "All right," she said, ignoring his questions. "I'm gonna go get lunch because I know you're both starving. Lucy, I need you to stay here with B until I get back. Lilith knows what you look like, so if we're gonna maintain our element of surprise, you have to keep a low profile, cool?"

"Of course," he told her. He then stood very close to her and leaned in, speaking almost in a whisper. "But let us be clear, I take orders from *no one*. I will happily do as you ask as long as I see the benefit but I will not be controlled. And, my name is *Lucifer*. I understand it's your way of maintaining a certain distance, not using the names people choose to call themselves. Fear of intimacy and such. But, if you call me 'Lucy' one more time, I may be obliged to rip your throat out with my bare hands."

Wyatt grabbed him by the arm to pull him away but Gabriel had the situation well handled. She made a squeezing motion in the air with her left hand that sent Lucifer to his knees. He clutched his chest, blood beginning to dribble from his mouth as he gurgled, trying and failing to breathe.

"I don't like threats," she said. "We're all here, serving our purpose, playing our parts in God's production. We're on the same side, yeah?"

Lucifer nodded.

"And we're gonna have a nice, pleasant relationship while we're here, right?"

Again, he nodded.

"Awesome," she said chipperly, kneeling to look him in the eyes. "I realize that I tend to take things over and I come off as a little overbearing but I've been working on this plan since the fucking Fall, and if your ego gets in the way, I will figure out a way to deal with Lilith without you, do you understand what I'm saying?"

He nodded once more, his face turning a strange shade of purple.

"Great," she said, standing and relaxing her hand.

Lucifer coughed and took deep, labored breaths as he struggled to stand himself.

"Since it's so important to you, I'll call you 'Lucifer' from now on, okay?" Gabriel promised.

"It would be much appreciated," he told her, clearing his throat.

"Now, I'm going to get lunch and call some people to handle this mess. You boys play nice."

As she left, Wyatt couldn't help but snicker under his breath.

"What's funny?" Lucifer asked angrily as he took a seat at the island.

"Nothing," Wyatt lied, unable to control his laughter.

"Shut up," Lucifer demanded.

Wyatt settled himself. "So," he said, changing the subject. "You know Allydia?"

"I know her," Lucifer smirked. "Occasionally."

Wyatt felt a twinge of jealousy at Lucifer's innuendo but he ignored it.

"Have you met the others?" Lucifer wondered. "They worship her like a deity. It's obscene. Enlighten me, what's Earth like these days? It's been fifty years or so since I was last hereabouts."

"Uh," Wyatt answered. "Loud, stressful, overpopulated. What's Hell like?"

"Same."

They both chuckled a little.

"Beer?" Wyatt offered.

"Please," Lucifer replied.

Wyatt opened the refrigerator door and it fell to the ground, spilling leftovers and condiments all over the kitchen floor, while the light inside sparked and burned out.

Wyatt sighed. "It kind of got away from me earlier."

Chapter 8

Tae sat alone in his office, still shaking from the events of the day. *Lucifer*. He couldn't believe it. He wrung his hands anxiously as he considered all the ways things could go bad. What was the *literal Devil* capable of? Mass murder? Genocide? Triggering the Apocalypse?

"She knows what she's doing," he told himself, trying to trust that Gabriel's plan would work and that she could keep Lucifer well managed. "She *always* knows what she's doing."

Just as he let out a deep breath and felt like he was starting to calm down, the desk phone rang, startling him to jump in his seat. His hand flew up to his chest so fast, he physically hurt himself. He felt ridiculous as he reached for the handset.

"Dr. Iha," he answered. He put the call on speaker, his hands again trembling too hard to keep the receiver steady.

"Yes, hello, Dr. Iha," the woman's voice on the other end replied. "This is Headmaster Olivia de Barde at Emerson Academy. You're listed as your niece, Michelle Iha's emergency contact when her mother is unreachable."

"What's the emergency?" he asked, standing up as dread began to set in. The possibilities flooded his brain. School shooting, fire, kidnapping. His niece was the only human family he had left since his brother died in combat a few years before. At Reo's funeral, he had promised Michelle that he would do everything he could to make sure she had the life his brother had wanted for her. He sent her mother money every month for whatever they might need and he spent every other weekend with her so she'd still have a positive male role model in her life. And, he enrolled her in and paid for this stupidly expensive private school to give her the best education possible. She had become like a daughter to him. If the people he trusted to teach and protect her had let something happen to her, there would be hell to pay.

"Dr. Iha, I hate to be the one to inform you," the woman said. "But, Michelle's mother was killed today. Her car was involved in a crash. One of the officers let it slip that it was the fault of the other driver who failed a field sobriety test. I'm very sorry."

"Oh, my God," Tae uttered, falling back in his seat. Relief washed over him followed by sadness and worry. "Does Michelle know?"

"Yes, the school's counselor is with her now. She's taking it pretty hard, understandably. She's asking to go home early."

"Of course," Tae told her. "I'll be right there." He quickly ended the call, took off his lab coat, and looked at the clock. He left his office, throwing his jacket on as he walked.

"Nurse," he said as he passed the nurse's station.

"Yes, Doctor?" Nurse Bowen answered.

"I have to leave. Family emergency," he explained. "Can you please find someone to cover my rounds?"

"I'll do my best. Is everything all right?"

"Not even a little bit," he said as he hurried out the doors.

Tae rushed into the school and beelined it to the Headmaster's office where he was greeted by a man in his late twenties wearing a nicely tailored suit. The nameplate on his desk read 'Headmaster's Secretary, Harrison Marlowe'.

"Can I help you, sir?" the man inquired.

"Yes, hello," Tae replied. "I'm Tae Iha. I'm looking for--"

"OMG, of course," the man said jumping up from his desk. "Right this way." He ushered Tae into the Headmaster's office, looking him up and down as they walked.

"Have a seat." He gestured to a small leather chair facing a large desk. "She'll be right with you. Can I get you something? Water? Tea?"

"No," Tae declined. "I'm fine, thank you."

"Yes, you are," the man flirted, pulling a card from his pocket. "If you need *anything,* you just let me know."

Tae took the card. "I will do that," he said, watching the man walk out.

"Well, that was inappropriate," Tae whispered to himself. "Boy was sexy, though." He patted his knees as he impatiently waited, growing more nervous with every passing moment, knowing that he would have to somehow comfort his niece who had now lost both parents. He couldn't imagine how devastated she must be.

After what seemed like forever, Headmaster de Barde finally entered the room with Michelle following closely behind. The eighteen-year-old was very obviously heartbroken, her face sullen with remnants of smeared mascara still clinging to her cheeks as she dragged an overfilled book bag behind her.

Ms. de Barde shook Tae's hand. "Hello, Dr. Iha. Again, I'm so sorry for your family's loss." Michelle stood silently in the corner by the door, tucking her hair behind her ear and staring at the floor.

"Thank you," he said quietly.

"We were all just so sad to hear," she went on. "With her father gone and being one of only a handful of colo--" she stopped herself and cleared her throat before continuing. "*African American* students, things were hard enough on poor Michelle as it was."

"I'm sorry, but *what*?!" Tae asked heatedly. "Were you about to say '*colored*'?!"

The Headmaster shuffled quickly behind her desk and sat down.

"I'm sorry," she apologized. "As you can imagine, it's been quite a day."

"Uh, uh," he said. "You can not just gloss over the use of a racial slur. You are a grown woman. You know 'colored' is not acceptable."

"Yes, of course, you're right. I apologize."

"And she is not 'African American'. She is simply *American*. She was born in this country, as were her parents. Moreover, you didn't even get her ethnicity right! Her mother is Barbadian and her father, my brother, was Japanese, as evidenced by this beautiful Asian man sitting before you. If you're going to insist on categorizing people based on their race, you could at least use the term 'biracial' if for no other reason than accuracy."

"All right, Dr. Iha," she said, clearly getting annoyed. "Now, will Michelle be staying with you, or is there another family member that will be stepping in? We need to know who her legal guardian is now, for paperwork, you understand."

"Yes, she'll be staying with me," he replied coldly.

"Excellent. Now, our standard absence allowance for grieving is two weeks. Michelle has all of her assignments so she won't fall behind while she's out. Please make sure they're all completed before she returns."

"Damn, bitch!" Tae exclaimed. "You're not only *racist*, you're also *ice cold*."

"Excuse me?!" she gasped.

He stood, slamming his hands on the desk and looking the sixty-something-year-old woman in the eyes.

"This little girl's mother just died," he seethed. "Her daddy passed not too awful long ago and now all she's got in this world is me. Now, I may be goddamned amazing, but I am certainly not an adequate replacement for a teenage girl's momma. She is heartbroken and you have the indecency to sit there and demand she do *homework*?! Fuck that."

He turned and walked toward his niece, putting his arm around her. "Come on, baby," he told her. "You take as much time as you need." He glanced back at the Headmaster who sat in stunned silence. "There won't be any problems. I'm sure Olivia here wouldn't want the other parents finding out that she's an insufferably racist bigoted piece of shit, would she?"

Ms. de Barde opened her mouth to speak, but no words would come.

"Mm-hmm," Tae stormed out of the office, all but carrying Michelle with him. Harrison gave an approving slow clap as they passed, having heard the entire conversation.

"I'ma hit you up later," Tae said, looking back at the secretary as he and Michelle exited the building.

They had only made it a few steps when Michelle dropped her backpack, covered her mouth, and burst into uncontrollable tears. Her knees went weak and she nearly collapsed, save for her uncle taking her in his arms.

"I know, baby, I know," he said softly, holding her close and petting her hair. "You let all that shit out."

Bitch, you better not need shit from me for a while, he thought to Gabriel. *I've got other priorities.*

Chapter 9

Wyatt lay in bed, staring at the ceiling, unable to close his eyes, much less sleep. His wife, the love of his life and best friend was sleeping with another man. Yes, she had left him and maybe he should have seen it coming, but he hadn't. He was so sure that he could mend things between them at some point and now that that hope had been so cruelly extinguished, he was completely broken. The thought of Annie with someone else made his blood boil. How could she do this? And so *soon*. Was she having an affair before she left? How long did it go on? Was it someone he knew? Then there were the other events of the day that he couldn't stop thinking about. Between Allydia and Lucifer, he was feeling overrun by monsters. *I live in a freak show.* He thought.

Don't be so dramatic, he heard Gabriel's voice in his head. A few seconds later, she entered his room, sat in the chair, and covered her legs with the blanket she had wrapped herself in.

"Dramatic?" he retorted, sitting up in bed and switching on the lamp that sat on the nightstand. "Satan is sleeping in the room next door and I'm pretty sure I had sex with a vampire today."

Gabriel laughed. "You totally did. I tried to warn you."

"You didn't tell me she was a fucking *vampire*, or that vampires even *existed*."

"All right, my bad," she said sarcastically. "Next time, I'll be more specific about what *kind* of monster a bitch is."

"I'd appreciate it," he quipped. "Hey," he said, his tone more serious.

"No," Gabriel answered before he could ask. "I didn't know about your wife's new dude. I've never met her so I don't have access to her database, as it were."

"But, if you *did* meet her,"

"Yeah, I could tell you anything you want to know. I can track her down if you want."

Wyatt thought for a moment, then decided it was a bad idea. "Better not," he conceded. "It would probably just piss me off worse."

"Yeah," she agreed. "'What if' is generally better than confirmation of worse-case scenario."

"It doesn't matter. Before or after she left, she's still with someone else and she's still gone and without her, I'm--"

"What?" Gabriel prodded. "You're what? I will tell you. On one hand, you're Barachiel, leader of the Guardian Angels, Protector of Humanity, saving lives basically since people were *invented*. Arguably the most important angel in Heaven. On the other hand, you're Wyatt Sinclair, a little fucked up, but relatively normal dude that just found out he's got superpowers and is on a mission from *God* to save the fucking world. So, your ex has a boyfriend now. Fuck her. Shit gets a little dicey and she bolts? Fang bitch was right. She doesn't deserve you. *What are you* without a selfish, panicky, whiny, thirty-five-year-old toddler? Better off. You're an archangel, you're a goddamn superhero and you're my brother." She scooted to the edge of her seat and wrapped the blanket tighter around herself, looking Wyatt in the eyes. "I know we're not exactly a *normal* family," she admitted. "But, we *do* care about you." She stood and shuffled towards the door. "I know how you feel, like, literally, but you're not alone. Except for right now, because it's almost four in the morning and I'm sleepy as balls. Try to get some rest, okay? Your obsessive thoughts are keeping me up."

Wyatt chuckled. "I'll try."

"Night."

"Night."

As she closed the door behind her, Wyatt turned off the light and lay back down. He was touched by his new sister's words and he let them give him comfort as he closed his eyes and, after several minutes, fell asleep.

The next morning, Gabriel, Wyatt, and Lucifer sat around the kitchen island and had coffee and donuts from the shop around the corner.

"Some guys are going to be here in a few hours to fix all this," she informed them. "So, best behavior."

"Really?" Lucifer griped. "I quite like the place as it is. Reminds me of home."

"I'll pay for the damage," Wyatt offered.

"Don't," Gabriel refused. "I have a stupid amount of money. It's not an issue."

"How exactly did you acquire your wealth, sister?" Lucifer wondered, taking a sip from his disposable cup. Wyatt had been curious about that, too, but didn't think it would be polite to pry.

Gabriel swallowed a piece of donut before answering. "I inherited it."

"So, the humans that birthed you met an early demise, did they?" he sneered.

"Don't be a dick," Wyatt warned.

Gabriel sighed, visibly irritated to be talking about this. "Yeah," she said simply, shooting Lucifer an annoyed glance and taking another bite of her breakfast.

"Not going to elaborate, then?" Lucifer pushed.

"No," she flatly stated.

"What about you, brother?" Lucifer asked, shifting his attention to Wyatt. "Any interesting stories to share? Life happenings or goings-on? Anything you'd *bloody* well like to talk about?"

Lucifer and Gabriel quietly giggled as Wyatt irritably put his cup down.

"You told him?" he questioned his sister.

"No," she said defensively. "He figured it out on his own. You had some sort of micro-expression yesterday when you two were talking. Remember, he's *crazy*, not stupid."

"I prefer the term 'eccentric', thank you," Lucifer asserted. "So, are you and the vampire queen planning a spring or summer wedding? I assume it won't be too terribly soon, since we're all currently preoccupied with the plot to destroy her step-mother, not to mention winter in New York can be brutal. The traffic alone. The tourists, everyone scrambling to see trees and such."

Gabriel couldn't help but laugh.

"That's not funny," Wyatt said, struggling to keep a straight face himself.

"It's pretty funny," Gabriel said.

"Just mind the fangs," Lucifer jibed. "Certain acts can very easily become quite unpleasant."

"Oh, gross!" Gabriel exclaimed, covering her ears. "No, no, no. New subject."

"Did Allydia get back to you about the theater?" Wyatt asked.

"Yeah," she answered. "Her guy said he saw some people milling around, cleaning it up, but no Lilith."

"Okay, but how would he know? Couldn't she look like anyone she wanted?"

Gabriel and Lucifer looked at each other knowingly.

"You want to take this one?" she requested.

"Why not?" Lucifer accepted. "You see, my sister is unequivocally vain and she has particular tastes. She would be very hard to miss."

"Vain, so she'd be pretty," Wyatt surmised.

"Beautiful," Lucifer admitted. "But," he paused.

"But, what?"

"She likes to dress up like little girls," Gabriel blurted.

"When I saw her just before she attacked me, she was in the body of a fourteen-year-old-girl," Lucifer told them.

"Wait," Wyatt said. "She's *possessing* somebody?"

"Of course," Lucifer explained. "How else would demons gain access to the mortal coil?"

"And you're possessing someone right now," Wyatt remembered.

"Well, yes, but to be fair, Tyler here was only for this world a few more days."

"He always picks people who are about to kick it," Gabriel confirmed.

"Wouldn't want to piss Daddy off any more than we have to, would we?" Lucifer smirked. "See, a human body is weak, fragile. When an angel or demon takes up occupancy in one, the power is too great. The body breaks down, cell by cell. Eventually, it's completely destroyed."

"Like radiation poisoning," Gabriel explained.

"Yes, exactly," Lucifer verified. "Now, I have the decency to heal this body intermittently so I don't have to invade another. And, no doubt, my sister will do the same to maintain her attractiveness. The demons, however, are unencumbered by such matters. The longer they inhabit a body, the worse the damage. That's why I do my best to exorcise the intruder as quickly as possible, a job I should be getting back to while we wait for news on the whereabouts of that miserable, treacherous--"

"Okay," Gabriel interrupted. "Before this one gets all worked up and sucks the apartment up into a tornado or something, why don't we talk about something else?"

"What do you suggest, Gabriel?" Lucifer asked, incensed. "I've only been cognizant for a day. The only information I have access to is in this room, and since you're unwilling to discuss *yourself*, that leaves our dear brother. So, what shall it be? Barachiel's whore wife, his indiscriminate genitals, or the fact that he's currently bedding my, what's the term these days? Sloppy seconds."

Wyatt jumped up from his stool and punched Lucifer in the face, nearly knocking him from his seat. Lucifer licked the blood from his lip and grinned.

"That was a warning," Wyatt growled, standing over Lucifer, barely able to hold himself back. "Allydia was a mistake. Mock me all you want for it. I was stupid. But, when it comes to my wife, you *shut the fuck up*. If I even *think* you're about to mention her again, I will *end you*."

Lucifer looked at Gabriel in amazement. "He's really not afraid of me at all. I'm astonished."

"He's not afraid of *anything*," she declared.

"I'm going for a walk," Wyatt announced, grabbing his jacket from the hook and slamming the door behind him.

"You had that coming," she told Lucifer, who raised his eyebrows in agreement, rubbing his jaw. She handed him her cell phone.

"Let me introduce you to a little thing we like to call 'the internet'."

Wyatt walked briskly along the busy street, shoving his hands in his jacket pockets, the autumn air feeling colder as winter approached. As he wandered, from the corner of his eye, he thought he saw someone he recognized. He turned to look, but she was gone. *Strange,* he thought. He stopped at a magazine stand to check the recent headlines. Anything to get his mind off of his altercation with Lucifer. Not the act of punching him; that actually felt really good. But, what he had said, calling Annie a 'whore', did not sit well with Wyatt. No matter what she had done, he still loved her, even if he'd never be able to forgive her. Gabriel had also called his wife names the night before, but it hadn't bothered him, probably because, deep down, those were things he'd been thinking himself. 'Selfish' and 'panicky' just about summed up her actions. If he was being honest with himself, 'whore' didn't seem like that big of a stretch, either, especially since, as far as he knew, she hadn't even filed divorce papers yet.

As his eyes meandered around at the various magazine covers, he suddenly felt an odd sensation. He got chills, the hair on the back of his neck standing up, and it wasn't from the temperature. He turned to look around and saw, several feet away, a man hugging a trash can. He couldn't be sure, but it looked like he was eating the contents. What made it especially odd was that the man was wearing a nice suit and recently shined shoes. Definitely not homeless. As the man stood, Wyatt noticed that chunks of his hair were missing. Large bald spots covered the man's head. He turned around, as if able to feel Wyatt's stare. He looked ashen and sickly, eyes sunken with dark circles underneath. He opened his mouth to reveal holes where teeth used to be. *I'm seeing something weird,* he thought to Gabriel. Just then, the man vomited profusely on the sidewalk. The contents of his stomach were mixed with blood and people walking by scurried away as fast as they could to avoid whatever disease it was they assumed he had.

"Barachiel!" the man hissed in a voice that was not his own. Wyatt was shocked to hear the name. This was it. This had to be a demon. The man bolted down the street, bumping into pedestrians as he went, Wyatt chasing after him. He retreated down an ally as Wyatt followed. Now, he was trapped.

"How are you here?!" the demon screeched. "You're supposed to be in Heaven! I was told we'd have free reign! I was *promised!*"

"Somebody lied," Gabriel said, strolling up behind her brother. The demon made an animal-like shriek as she and Lucifer approached.

"No!" the demon cried. "It can not be!"

Lucifer rushed toward him, gripped him tightly, and threw him up against the fence.

"Where is my sister?" he demanded. "Tell me and I'll do what I can to make this painless."

"I will never tell you, Watch Keeper!" he squawked as Lucifer's hand wrapped around his neck. "She's going to save us from your torment! She's giving us our world back!"

"This world was never yours, you pestilent rubbish," Lucifer insisted. "Are you very sure you don't want to make things easier on yourself?"

The demon cackled. "Lilith will rid you from this place. She will have the humans worshiping at our feet, as it always should have been. And, when Father wakes, after we've exterminated the Earth of all those who oppose us, He'll have no choice but to let us keep this planet. Lilith will have Him bowing to *her*."

"Oh, my," Lucifer guffawed. "You are madder than a March hare, aren't you? You have *met* our Father, yes? What in all of history makes you think that what you're spewing could ever possibly occur? The Almighty would rather crush this world into nothing and start over than to ever bow before *anyone*. He would see us all burn before He would give up a monochrome of power. You forget of whom you speak. *God is all*."

"She is--"

"She is a scourge on this Earth and a pain in my ass," Lucifer proclaimed. "I will find her and when I do, I will not be gentle. As for you, since you've refused to be of any help to me, I'm going to do this slowly." He slammed his hand to the man's chest, a light glowing gradually around it. The demon shook, blood spurting from his mouth, his eyes rolling back in his head. He gasped for breath as what looked like a shadow seemed to peel off of him, slowly falling to the ground, shrinking, and finally disappearing. The man collapsed unconscious to the ground below him, color now returning to his face.

"Jesus," Wyatt said under his breath.

"Where?" Lucifer questioned.

Gabriel laughed. "All right boys, can we please get along better from now on?"

"Seems unlikely," Lucifer told her. "I'm a bit of an ass."

"At least you're self-aware," Wyatt poked.

"See?" Gabriel said. "We're all friends, right? A little bickering between siblings is to be expected. Come on, let's get out of the cold. Oh, yeah, just one sec." She knelt and placed a hand on the man's chest. His skin glowed, white light pouring out of his nose and mouth. His eyes opened wide and he shot up to a sitting position, scurrying away from them to sit up against the fence.

"You okay, buddy?" Gabriel asked.

"What the hell happened?" the man wondered, looking around wildly. "How'd I get here?"

"I don't know," she lied. "We were walking by and saw you lying here. We were about to call an ambulance. You all right?"

The man stood up, visibly shaken. "I think so," he said, patting himself down and feeling his wallet, phone, and keys still in his pockets. He looked at them suspiciously as he checked his wallet, finding the cash and credit cards all still there. He put it back in his jacket and nodded to them as he walked past. "Thank you," he told them as he staggered away.

"Is he gonna be okay?" Wyatt asked.

"He'll be fine," Lucifer assured him. "Our dear sister reversed any damage the possession may have caused. As for the demon, he won't be back."

The three walked back to the apartment in silence, all feeling a sense of accomplishment. No, this wasn't the monster they were after, but it was a start.

Chapter 10

Lilith stopped to admire her reflection in a store window as she made her way back to the theater she currently called home. It was temporary, of course, but she just loved being on a stage, her adoring fans looking on. *Soon*, she thought. *I'll live in the finest palace this world has ever seen.*

While the demons that followed her made attempts to provide her with the food she required, it wasn't enough to keep her satisfied. She had *other* desires.

As she brushed her long blond hair away from her roseate cheek, she noticed a man watching her. She smiled at him and he awkwardly smiled back. She approached him, fluttering her big blue eyes at him as she held his gaze.

"Hi," she said sweetly.

"Hi," he said nervously. "I'm sorry, I shouldn't stare."

"It's not a problem," she told him. "I like to be watched."

The man grew tenser as he sat on a park bench. "I'm just waiting for my bus," he explained.

"I'll wait with you," she cooed. "You know, you're a gorgeous man. Just lovely."

He smiled apprehensively. "How old are you?"

"Not much younger than you, I suspect."

"I doubt that. I'm twenty-two. If you're not at least eighteen--"

"Let's say I'm eighteen."

"Are you?"

She tilted her head and smiled broadly as she delicately touched his cheek. "I can be anything you want me to be," she said, her voice just above a whisper. She leaned in and kissed him, softly at first, and then with passion. *This* is what she had been missing. She quickly reached for his belt, taking him by surprise. He pushed her away.

"What are you doing?!" he asked. "This is a public street!"

"You don't want me?" she barked.

"Not in front of the whole city!"

"You're *ashamed* of me?!"

"What?!" he said, not sure of what the hell was happening. "There are *people*. We could get arres--"

Just then, a twenty-something-year-old-woman on her cell phone walked by and glared at them.

"Is it her?!" Lilith yelled. "Would you rather be with *her*?!"

"Oh, my God!" he shouted, standing up. "Am I being pranked? Is there a hidden camera somewhere?"

Lilith cracked her neck as she stood. "Why did you have to bring *Him* into this?" She grasped the young man's arm and pulled him to a nearby ally. He tried to get away, but couldn't. She was unnaturally strong.

"Stay here," she commanded, using her mind to lift him a few feet above the ground and paralyze him.

"Holy shit!" the man said shakily. "What the fuck?!"

She walked back to the sidewalk in search of the woman. After a few minutes, she found her. She grabbed her by the hair and dragged her on the ground to the ally.

"Is this what you like?" she asked the man, still suspended, forcing the woman up on her knees. She yanked the woman's head back and tore open her shirt, revealing her large breasts.

"Jesus Christ! Stop!" the man begged as the woman cried. Lilith watched angrily as his face grew more and more afraid. She slid her hand down the front of the woman's pants.

"Please," the woman sobbed.

"Don't worry," Lilith said as she fondled her. "It's almost over." She licked the side of the woman's neck and face while maintaining eye contact with the man.

"Leave her alone!" he shouted from above.

"Do you love her?" Lilith wondered.

"What?!" he howled. "I've never met her! You're psycho!"

"You know," Lilith told him. "In my day, youth was prized above all when it came to choosing a woman. These," she said, grasping one of the woman's breasts with her free hand, then gently caressing the nipple. "Were merely icing on the cake."

As her nether regions were being violated, the woman, though she fought the feeling, couldn't help but begin to orgasm. Tears streamed down her face as she came and she cried out in pleasure and torment.

"Why are you doing this?" she whimpered.

"Because, dearest," Lilith replied. "Everyone deserves one last orgasm. My Father's most wonderful creation, wouldn't you agree?" And with that, she whipped her hand out of the woman's pants and plunged it into her chest, tearing her heart from her body in one shocking, violent motion.

"What the fuck are you?!" the man screamed.

She opened his pants and pulled them down along with his underwear. She lightly licked him until he was fully aroused.

"Stop!" he demanded.

She laughed as she slammed him to the cold ground. She swiftly removed her panties and lifted her dress, sitting down on top of him and placing him inside of her. As she rode him, she forced his mouth open and shoved the woman's still warm heart into it. He let out a muffled scream as he looked at the dead woman's body lying in a heap next to him.

"Chew," Lilith told him. He began to cry.

"Chew!" she yelled, using her telekinesis to make his jaw move up and down.

"Yes," she gasped, a feeling of relief washing over her as she climaxed. "Yes! It's so good to be home!"

Chapter 11

"So audition," Valerie said, losing her patience.

"But, what about Corey?" the girl sitting across the desk asked.

"What about him?" Valerie asked, visibly annoyed. "Savannah, you are fifteen years old. Corey is not 'the one', I hate to break the news, and if by some one in a million chance he is, do you really think a couple months apart would be enough to break you up? More importantly, if he's the kind of boy that would hold you back from accomplishing your goals or chasing your dreams, is he worthy of you?"

"I guess not," Savannah admitted.

"Listen, the school can make accommodations if you get through, so you don't need to worry about that. If I were you, with all that talent, *I'd* be at that open call. In my professional opinion, girl, you should be singing."

"What do you know about music, Miss Moore?"

"I know I've been listening to it since before you were born. Now, get out of my office, you know what you want to do."

They both smiled as the girl stood and walked toward the door.

"Thanks, Miss Moore," she said. "I'm gonna go for it."

"Good," Valerie approved. "And have fun. Not everything's life and death."

"Miss Moore," another student said, entering the room, passing Savannah as she left.

"Hey, Javier," Valerie greeted the boy. "Have a seat. What can I help you with?"

The boy sat, face beaming, grinning from ear to ear. "I just wanted to tell you, I got in."

Valerie smiled broadly. "Oh my God, Javier! Congratulations!"

"It's my dream school," he told her. "I'm so excited. And I qualified for all the financial aid I need. I'm going to college and it's all thanks to you, Miss Moore. Thank you."

"Boy, all I did was help you with the paperwork. This is all you. I'm so proud of you."

"Thank you. I gotta get to class. Thanks again."

"Of course. You have a good day."

"You, too." He closed the door behind him and Valerie sighed happily. Javier had struggled to balance school and his job, which he had to keep to help feed his younger siblings. The university he chose was close enough that he could live at home and still work part-time. Valerie was thrilled for him. He deserved this opportunity and she was just grateful to have been of help.

Suddenly, she was startled by loud, incessant knocking on her door.

"Come in," she called.

The door flew open, a woman wearing a bright red sweatshirt with a white turtleneck underneath, faded jeans, and a necklace with wooden stars painted blue dangling from it burst in. She was clearly unhappy.

"Are you Miss Moore, the guidance counselor?" the enraged woman squawked.

Here we go, Valerie thought, doing her best to fake a polite smile.

"Yes," she replied. "How can I help you?"

"I'm Travis Dean's mom," the woman snipped. "You can *help me* by telling my son that you made a huge mistake when you told him to quit football."

"Have a seat, Ms. Dean."

"I will not," the woman said stubbornly. "Call him to your office and *fix this now.*"

"I'm not going to do that, Ms. Dean," Valerie told her as calmly as she could. "Travis has been cast in the lead role in the school's production of 'Hamlet', on top of which, he's now the captain of the debate team *and* the Mathletes. He simply does not have time to waste going to practices and sitting on a bench at games. He's just too busy."

"He's a *senior* this year!" Ms. Dean proclaimed. "He'll *finally* get a chance to play!"

"No, he won't," Valerie informed her. "I've spoken to the coach. Travis is terrible. He'll never see the field."

"How dare you?!" Ms. Dean exclaimed. "I'll have your job!"

Valerie stood as the woman turned to leave. "A little advice, Ms. Dean," she said. "Appreciate your son for who he *is*, not for who you *wish* he was."

The woman grunted, storming out in a huff and slamming the door behind her.

After a long day and what felt like an even longer walk home, Valerie finally made it back to her Hell's Kitchen studio. She took off her jacket, letting it fall with a thud to the floor. She kept her keys, wallet, phone, and pocket knife in the massive pockets so she didn't have to carry a purse, making her less of a target for muggers. The neighborhood was pretty safe, but she could never be too careful. The apartment was small, but it was close to school and rent was reasonable. Gabriel had offered to buy her a bigger place, but she had refused. The worst thing in the world for her was feeling like she owed somebody something. She worked hard for everything she had in life and she wouldn't let anyone, not even her sister, take that sense of pride from her.

She put the bag of fast food that would be her dinner on the coffee table, took a fry, and turned on the small television. She watched the evening news intently as she swallowed the french fry and took a sip of soda. Just then, she was startled, her eyes growing wide as she dropped her cup in her lap. She was being gripped by a vision, and it was a doozy.

It was dark, cold, and everything in sight was gray and bleak, seemingly covered in soot and ash. She could hear groans and wailing all around her and the feeling of despair was overwhelming. She could hear voices but wasn't sure where they were coming from. As she searched, noticing the strong stench of sulfur and the stone-like feel of the walls, she came upon two entities. She recognized one of them as Lucifer. She could tell the other was an angel, but she couldn't quite place him.

"The Gates close soon, brother," the angel said. "I'll no longer be able to come for these visits."

"Yes, well, what is a couple of centuries for creatures such as us?" Lucifer quipped.

"I look forward to our next meeting, then."

"See you when Father wakes."

The angel walked toward what looked like a black hole hovering in perfect stillness and turned to wave goodbye. Lucifer waved back and walked off, out of sight. When he was sure Lucifer was gone, the angel quickly turned away from the strange opening in space and instead headed down a darkened corridor. Valerie followed him through a maze of rooms, each containing black, shadowy figures that cried out in anguish as they passed. One contained a twisted, misshapen tree that looked as though it had been carved from lava rock. Another contained a tall, dull-gray obelisk that several of the shadows looked to be attempting to climb. Finally, at the end of the long hallway, the angel came to a locked cell. He looked around anxiously as he ventured to open it. As he struggled, the figure of a woman rushed to the bars. She looked like she was covered in tar, no real face could be made out.

"I'm here, sister," the angel told her. "You'll soon be free once more and while I'm trapped in Heaven, you'll create for us a world in which *we* may rule, as it should be."

After a few moments and a lot of effort, the shackles gave way and the cell door swung open. The woman timidly stepped out, as if in disbelief.

"It's all right," the angel said. "When back on Earth, you can make preparations to keep yourself there as well as Lucifer, should he follow. Come, now."

The two hurriedly sleuthed down the hall, gathering demons as they went, eventually getting back to the black hole, stepping into it, and disappearing, several demons going behind them.

Valerie gasped as she came out of the vision, slowly regaining her faculties. As she calmed her breathing and began to feel normal, she noticed her soda had spilled all over her clothes, the sofa, and the floor.

"Shit," she said.

Valerie pounded on the door, her rage growing as she waited. Wyatt answered, stepping aside to let her in and she passed by without acknowledging him. She stormed through the apartment, making a beeline for Lucifer who sat on the couch reading a newspaper.

"Oh, shit," Gabriel said as she took a chip out of the bag she was holding. She popped it in her mouth and stood next to Wyatt who closed the door and watched as Valerie all but attacked Lucifer. Within seconds, she was on top of him, grabbing the sides of his head with a little more force than was necessary. Lucifer took a shaky breath as he was shown his sister's latest vision. When he had seen it in its entirety, Valerie let him go and stood in front of him, so livid she was nearly shaking.

"You let him in, stupid!" she barked at him.

"That perfidious miscreant!" Lucifer shouted, jumping up, the paper falling to the floor. "I will kill him with my bare hands!"

"You want to fill me in?" Wyatt asked Gabriel.

"Turns out it was Samael that let Lilith out," she told him. "I'm not surprised."

"Who's Samael?"

"Angel of Death."

"Of course."

"Yo, Satan," Gabriel called from across the room. "Angels are taking sabbaticals in Hell now? You get a kickass DJ or something? Put out a spread?"

Lucifer was unamused. "As you may have guessed, Hell can be quite grim. Our brother will, on occasion, pay me a visit. It helps me stay sane."

"Ish," Gabriel joked.

"Yes," Lucifer agreed.

"The fuck were you thinking?!" Valerie demanded. "How could it not occur to you that letting someone like that into Hell might be a bad idea?"

"For context," Gabriel leaned in to tell Wyatt. "Samael can be a little unpredictable."

"Sure," Wyatt acknowledged.

"Do not lecture me, Uriel," Lucifer snapped, moving closer to Valerie and taking an offensive stance as if he were preparing for a fight. "You've seen the torment, felt the agony, the suffering. You've heard the screams of the damned. Imagine constantly existing in that for *millennia*, save the rare trips to Earth once or twice a century where you're tasked with dragging some poor soul right back to it. How would you maintain your identity? Stay vigilant? Remember who you are and whom you serve? You couldn't handle being me for a *day*, so don't you dare berate me for doing what I have to."

"All right, children," Gabriel said, pulling them away from each other with her mind. "Let's not get rowdy. Lucifer, why don't you come with me to get us all some dinner?"

He reluctantly stepped away from Valerie and followed Gabriel out the door.

"I'm really sorry," Gabriel told him as they walked toward the elevator. "I know how miserable it is for you there."

"I appreciate that sister," he said, regaining his composure.

"And Uriel's just--"

"Self-righteous and sanctimonious?" Lucifer interrupted.

"Kind of," Gabriel laughed.

"You okay?" Wyatt asked as he and Valerie sat at the island.

"Fine," she replied, struggling to calm herself.

"So, Hell is--"

"Bad," she confirmed. "Really, really bad."

"Right," Wyatt said. "Hey, you mind if I ask why you pulled a knife on Gabriel? Did she get in your head, too?"

"No," Valerie told him. "She broke into my house."

"Oh," Wyatt chuckled.

"See, when I was fifteen, I was staying with this family. Not the worst place I'd ever lived, but still, pretty rough. I was in foster care cuz my dad killed my mom when I was seven and then he went to jail, right? So, anyway, my foster mom was a junkie and she'd be passing out from too much heroin or whatever at like, nine o'clock every night and it was kind of a bad neighborhood, so I'd be afraid to go to bed, so I'd be up real late just being paranoid. Then, she got this real sketchy boyfriend but it was kind of comforting that there was a big dude in the house to scare off burglars and shit. So, one night, this little white girl comes banging on my bedroom window, telling me to let her in right now. I was like, 'Uh uh, I don't know you', so she broke the fucking window with her elbow and I was like, 'this bitch crazy', so I took my knife out my pocket and told her she needed to get the fuck out my house. About that same time, Russel, the boyfriend, drunk as shit, breaks my door down, yelling about how I should be in bed. So, this itty bitty teenage girl gets between us and tells this giant man to get away from me and says she knows what he's planning. He gets *pissed* and just starts punching her in the face. I run to the living room to get the phone, but Foster Bitch had left it off the charger all day, so it was dead. So, I run back to my room and he's still hitting her, except now he has her pinned up against the wall. I had my knife ready. I was about to stick this motherfucker, but Gabriel puts her hand up to stop me. Then, this crazy bitch starts laughing. Blood's gushing out of her face, her nose is broken, eyes swollen shut and she's *laughing*. So the dude loses it. He throws her down on the bed and tells me not to move. Said he was gonna do her, then me, and I better not tell *anybody*. Then he starts taking his belt off."

"Holy shit," Wyatt muttered, horrified by what he was hearing.

"Next thing I know," she continued. "This asshole goes flying across the room and hits the wall so hard he puts a hole through it. Gabriel looks back at me and tells me to run, but of course, I don't because I'm looking at some science fiction shit right here and I want to see what happens. So, the guy gets up and starts running at her but before he can do anything, she makes this little flip motion with her hand and the dude's head spins around *completely backward*. This bitch just broke this piece of shit's neck with a fucking parlor trick. So, then she goes to the bathroom and washes the blood off her face and she's like, *magically* healed. Eyes back to normal, nose fixed, like *nothing happened*. Then she tells me she found my grandma and she's there to take me to her. I didn't even know I had a living relative. So, at this point, I know this girl is some kind of supernatural *something*, and I'm a little freaked out, but she *did* save my ass, so I figured going with her was better than trying to explain to the cops what just happened. So, I pack my little bit of stuff in my backpack and we take off. I get the keys to foster bitch's car and Gabriel drives us from Camden to Harlem. She tells me who she is, who I am, the whole thing. Says I'll start getting visions when I turn eighteen and that we're gonna be best friends. I'm thinking she's nuts, but maybe she's not wrong. Now, I had never been outside of Jersey, so I wasn't fully believing that we were about to see my long-lost grandma, right? But, we get to this building and before I can stop her, Gabriel knocks on the door. It's past midnight. I was sure somebody was gonna call the cops. But, this old woman answers the door, just as calm as she can be. I tell her what my name is and that I was told she was my grandmother and she breaks down. Turns out, she was my mom's mom and when my mother was in high school, she dropped out to run away with my dad and never spoke to her again. She never even knew I existed. So, we get to talking and she invites me to stay with her, so I moved in. Gabriel stayed with us here and there, but for the most part, it was just me and my grandma until she died."

"I don't even know what to say," Wyatt admitted.

"Yeah, it's kind of fucked up, but it all worked out. Gabriel saved me and gave me my family. She *is* my family. I mean, listen, she's annoying as shit, but I love that bitch."

Chapter 12

While her demons remained nesting in the theater, Lilith had moved on to a suite at a luxury hotel on Fifth Avenue. The towering building with fifty-eight floors and gold embellishments was a much better fit for her current needs. Besides, the kinds of people she needed to aid in her efforts seemed to be quite comfortable there. Room service had prepared a lovely variety of pastries and fruits for her guests that would go untouched until their arrival. She had two meetings scheduled. One with Mitchell Spade, the CEO of Cardinal Rain, a well-known government securities company, and the other with Adam Smith, a cable news and talk radio host with a following greater than she'd had when she ruled Uruk. She had been feeding Adam talking points for weeks, skyrocketing his ratings and propelling him into seemingly overnight superstardom. This would be her first face-to-face with Mitchell, however, and she hoped it would go well. After all, he controlled the largest private military in the world and she'd need those numbers for her plan to run smoothly. Mitchell was the first to arrive.

"Is your mother here?" he asked as Lilith welcomed him inside.

"Well, that's condescending," she replied. "*I'm* Lilith. We spoke on the phone. Danish?"

"No, thank you," he declined, skepticism covering his chiseled, middle-aged face. "I'm sorry, is this some kind of school prank?"

"You continue to insult me as if I *won't* tear your entrails from your body and use them to hang you with."

"All right," he huffed. "That's enough. My time is very valuable."

"As is mine, Mr. Spade," she assured him, gesturing to a laptop on the coffee table next to her. He looked at the screen, dismissively at first, then more carefully.

"Is that," he started.

"One hundred million dollars," she told him. "Ready to be deposited into your private account in the Caymans. All I have to do is press 'enter'."

He studied the page, looking for signs of forgery. There were none. "What is it exactly that you want?"

"I need an army, Mr. Spade. As many men as you can gather. I'm specifically interested in your presence in Iraq."

"I have about eight thousand contractors in Iraq currently but they're--"

"I need ten times that amount," she explained. "To start. The best of the best, heavily armed and ruthless."

"What's the mission?"

"Let's not get ahead of ourselves. To begin with, I require full submission. Your men take orders from *you* and *you* will take orders from *me*."

He chortled. "That's not-"

"You're a mercenary, yes?"

"That's an oversimplification."

"That's *accurate*," she scoffed. "You provide soldiers and I provide money. There's a lot more where this came from."

"How did someone like you acquire that kind of money?"

"You'd be surprised, Mr. Spade, by what people are willing to do for me."

"I can get your men, but I can't agree to *anything* until I know what the mission is."

She slammed the computer closed in annoyance before taking a deep breath to calm herself. "Won't you sit?" she suggested, gesturing toward the sofa behind her. He nodded and they both sat. "There's something I need. Something I need to destroy, actually, in the ruins of the ancient city of Babylon. I can't get to it, however, because, as you know, Iraq has become infested with American military, Iraqi military, terrorist groups. It's one big dust-covered pain in my ass. To do what I need to do, I have to take out everyone in the way. That's a lot of dead warriors. The country's President, I imagine, will be displeased so, while I'm there, I may as well take it over."

"Take what over?" he asked suspiciously.

"Iraq, obviously," she told him. "First. Once we've recruited there, we can expand to nearby countries. Saudi Arabia, of course. Jordan, Syria," a sneaky smile stretched across her lips. "Israel."

"You want to *invade* Iraq, then seize power, for yourself, of the *entire Middle East*?" he guffawed. "You're a child!" he exclaimed, his laughter now uncontrolled.

Angered, Lilith closed her fist slowly in front of her and as she did, Mitchell's chortles turned to gasps as he lost the ability to breathe.

"I'm older than I look," she said through her teeth. The man's skin took on a purplish tint as he suffocated and Lilith debated whether or not she needed this arrogant blowhard. As his eyes bulged and glossed over, she decided he was too useful to kill just yet. She relaxed her hand and he began taking deep, labored breaths. "You're getting off light," she said. "I will not tolerate this insolence in the future."

As he got his bearings, the terror on his face was replaced by awe. "How did you do that?" he asked, his voice scratchy.

"I'm..." she searched for the right word as she stood. "Special."

"I can see."

"Are you in or not?" she pushed.

"What you're proposing is unheard of."

"Only in modern times," she said. "I've done this before. I can do it again."

"I don't understand."

"You don't have to. Can you get the men?"

"I would need some time."

"Not too much, I hope," she threatened.

"I, um-"

"I have a friend, he'll be by later today. I plan, eventually, to ask him for help in sending you recruits. They'll need training and discipline. They will be *in addition* to the one hundred thousand men you hire."

"A hundred thousand?!" he choked, standing in front of her. "I thought you said eighty?"

"Better safe than outnumbered."

"This is impossible, not to mention highly illegal," he told her. "This could trigger World War Three. It would *definitely* piss off the big guy upstairs."

"You let me worry about God."

"Who's talking about God? I meant the Pres-"

"Oh!" she chuckled. " 'Big Guy'. Oh, man. That's funny. But, yeah, fuck him, too." She opened the laptop and slowly typed. "You'll have to excuse me, I'm just learning how to use one of these things." She hit 'enter' and turned the computer to face her new General. "Show yourself out. I need to get ready for my next meeting."

As she sauntered off into the bathroom, Mitchell studied the screen, shocked at what he saw. The girl had deposited ten billion dollars into his account. He pulled his phone from his jacket pocket and called his bank, unable to believe any of what had just happened. After providing passwords and other assurances of his identity, the bank confirmed that ten billion dollars *had* just been deposited.

"Thank you," he said, nearly dropping the phone before he hung up. He let out a long sigh as he regained his composure and headed toward the door. "Time to get to work."

Chapter 13

It had been nearly two months since Michelle's mother had been killed and she still hadn't returned to school. She had somehow managed to keep up with her assignments, but she could barely get out of bed every day. She was sleeping until at least one in the afternoon and staying up at night until she physically couldn't keep her eyes open anymore. Her uncle was letting her get away with it, but she knew she needed to get it together soon. The school had called and emailed multiple times and she had received a letter in the mail stating that if she didn't come in for classes in two weeks' time, she'd be expelled. Her uncle hadn't mentioned it. He was allowing her to grieve as she needed to and she appreciated it. He had been so great, giving her space when she needed it and comfort when she didn't want to be alone. She owed him everything.

As she looked over the letter again, mentally preparing herself to go back, she heard a crash. She opened her bedroom door and slowly walked down the hall. Before she reached the living room, a book went flying past, coming very close to hitting her in the face. She stopped where she was and stayed quiet.

"I thought we could discuss this like civilized adults," she heard Tae say. "But, I guess this is what happens when you date an infant."

"You're calling me childish now?!" a second voice yelled. It was Mr. Marlowe. When he started seeing her uncle, he had told Michelle to call him Harrison outside of school. She couldn't bring herself to do it.

"What would *you* call someone that completely loses their shit if they don't get a text back within two fucking minutes?" Tae retorted.

"It's disrespectful and rude to make me wait!" Harrison griped.

"I was in surgery!" Tae explained for the fourth time.

"So, you were *in surgery* yesterday and three times last week and--"

"Yes, bitch! I'm a *surgeon*. That's my motherfucking job!"

"Now you're being condescending," Harrison said with attitude.

"And you're being needy as shit."

"Needy?!"

"I'm about to start calling you 'dough boy', you're so needy," Tae sassed.

"Well, excuse me for--"

"No, I can't hear it," Tae dismissed. "I don't have room for this kind of bullshit. I'm done. Just go."

"Are you breaking up with me right now?" Harrison whined.

"What was your first clue, genius?" Tae asked. "The 'I'm done' or the 'Just go'?" He impatiently waved him towards the door, but Harrison wasn't having it. He was furious. He picked up the closest thing to him, a lamp from an end table, and before he could stop himself, he raised it, intending to throw it across the room. Instead, he let his fury overtake him and he brought the lamp down onto his now ex-boyfriend's head.

"Uncle!" Michelle screamed from the hall. Harrison hadn't realized she was there. He looked stunned, staring at Tae lying unconscious on the floor. He slowly backed away, guilt and self-preservation setting in. He looked up at the girl's terrified expression. His heart raced and he couldn't think. After a few moments, he turned and darted out of the apartment.

"Uncle!" Michelle yelped again, tears starting to form in her eyes as she watched the pool of blood growing larger on the hardwood floor. She ran to him, kneeling as she cried. She shook him violently, but no response. She checked for a pulse but found none. This couldn't be happening. Not him, too! She sobbed as she rolled him over and slapped his face.

"Wake up!" she commanded. "Uncle, please!"

Tae groaned as he finally began to open his eyes. Michelle let out a sigh of shock and relief.

"Psychotic asshole," he complained, putting his hand to his head. He got up and stumbled to the kitchen sink where he used the sprayer to wash the blood from his head and face. As he dried himself with a dish towel, he noticed his niece staring at him in disbelief. She looked over his head and saw no evidence of what had just happened. There were no wounds.

"How the--"

"Don't worry about it," he ordered, putting the towel on the kitchen counter. "I'm fine. Get me some paper towels so we can clean this mess up."

She ran to the pantry and grabbed a roll of paper towels.

"What--" she started to ask.

"You know my name means 'to endure'," he said, picking up and placing the shards of ceramic and glass in a trash can. "I'm just resilient."

Michelle's hands trembled as she started to soak up the blood.

"Uncle," she insisted. "What *are you?*"

"Fine," he sighed, putting the dustpan and broom down and sitting on the floor in front of her. "But, this stays between us, you hear me?"

She nodded.

"I'm Tae Iha," he began. "Uncle, doctor, life of the party, all that shit. But, I'm also an angel named Raphael that took up occupancy in this body when it was a fetus. I heal myself, I'm really good with directions, but, otherwise, I'm a perfectly normal person. Please don't freak out."

Michelle sat there on the floor, her hands covered in her uncle's blood, shocked and confused by what she just heard. "And, you're not kidding?"

"Not at all."

"Angels are real?"

"Looks like."

"Are there others?"

"Yes, but I am not going to tell you about those people," he said. "They are seven ways to fucked up."

"Have you always known what you are?" she asked.

"No," he told her. "When I was a freshman in college, this girl showed up at my dorm, kicked my roommate out. He was so dense, he thought I was about to get lucky. She told me who I was, said she'd be checking in on me, making sure I was all right, not working too hard. Over the years, she's helped me in a lot of ways."

"She was an angel, too?"

"HBIC."

"So, if angels are real," she asked. "Why didn't one of them save my mom?"

Tae looked sadly at his niece, knowing there was no explanation he could give her that would be good enough.

"It's God's rest time, baby," he said. "It's complicated, I can't go into it. I know it's not fair and it feels like life is just one big heap of bullshit after another and I'm sorry I can't fix it for you. There are only a few angels here right now and they have a metric fuckton of their own shit to deal with. Saving the world type stuff."

"Why aren't you helping them?"

"I did my part," he said. "It's up to them to finish the job. My abilities are no longer needed. Besides, I have other things on my mind. You, work, filing a restraining order."

They both laughed and went back to cleaning. After a few seconds, Michelle's curiosity got the better of her.

"So," she started to ask. "Angels are allowed to be, um--"

"God doesn't give a fuck about our sex lives," he insisted. "Not mine, not yours, not anybody's. Assuming everything's consensual. I mean, from what I hear, there's a special place in Hell for predators."

"I was always told marriage is sacred and people shouldn't--"

"Marriage is *sacred* because two people make a promise to God to love, cherish, blah fucking blah," he explained. "When the preacher says, 'let no one tear asunder', he's talking to the couple. Those two people swore to God that they wouldn't be with anyone else. Breaking that promise is like lying to God, which is a surefire way to piss off the Almighty. But, if you're single, He couldn't care less about who you're sleeping with and he sure as shit doesn't give a fuck if you marry a man or a woman. We're all the same thing to Him."

"How do you know that?" she asked.

"When I was first told about who and what I was, I was scared," Tae admitted. "I thought I was gonna get punished or some shit for being gay. But, she explained it to me and I've been comfortable with myself ever since."

"The angel?"

"Not just any angel," he told her. "The highest authority on Earth. The Messenger of God."

Gabriel quickly put her shirt back on as she looked around for her sock. The woman rolled over in bed, felt that her playmate was no longer there, and opened her eyes. "Going already?" she asked, stretching and then covering her mouth as she yawned.

"Yeah," Gabriel said. "I have to meet my brothers for breakfast. Have you seen my--" she stopped, noticing the woman swinging her sock around in the air. They both smiled as Gabriel took the sock and put it on. The woman sat up and scooted herself behind Gabriel, moving her hair away from her neck then kissing it softly.

"I really have to go," Gabriel said.

"I know," she said, still kissing her.

"Beth,"

"It's Brie," she corrected her.

"Right, sorry," Gabriel apologized. She could hear the thoughts of a man in the apartment above. *Beth is so cool. I hope I get to see her today.* "Listen, I have your number. We'll do this again sometime, yeah?"

"Definitely," Brie agreed.

Gabriel got her shoes on and walked to the bedroom door. "I'll see you later," she promised as she left the room. Brie lay back down to get a little more much-needed sleep.

Gabriel found her coat on the living room floor of the boho-chic apartment and put it on. She checked her pockets for her phone, wallet, and keys and once she was sure they were all in their rightful spots, she exited the apartment, making sure to lock the door as she left. When she got outside, she had to look around to remind herself of where she was. She sighed. Long cab rides home were a drawback of picking up randoms at clubs. She caught a cab, told the driver the cross streets, and pulled her phone out to check her messages. Three texts. From Ethan, *U wanna cum over???* From Lucifer, *I find the programs on your DVR insipid. You should watch more documentaries. Expose yourself to some culture.* And from Allydia, *My man says he thinks Lilith's taken up with a new lover and has headed out of the city. Will keep you posted.*

"Fantastic," she muttered to herself. It had been months since they had exorcised that first demon. Gabriel was getting antsy. She thought Lilith would be back where she belonged by now and she was growing increasingly impatient as time went on. The plan was to lay low until they knew Lilith's exact location and then ambush her, but no one seemed to be able to track her down. Every night, Allydia's goons staked out the theater and, every night, it was filled with the same old demons but no Lilith. She thought about going after the nest because who knew what kind of trouble they were stirring up, but there was no way Lucifer could expel all of those demons at once. Some would get away and alert Lilith that not only was Lucifer awake and hunting her but that there were other angels after her as well. It would blow their cover and without the element of surprise, Lilith was sure to do an even better job of hiding and they might never get a chance to throw her ass back in a cell.

The cabbie pulled up in front of her building and she paid him, including a large tip that would pay for the prescription he'd been putting off getting because it was too expensive.

"Thank you so much!" he told her. "You don't know what a blessing this is for me."

"Yeah, I do," she said as she exited the cab. "Have a good one."

She walked into her apartment, doing her best to be quiet. The boys were still asleep and she didn't feel like having an awkward conversation with Lucifer about where she was all night. She took a quick shower, dried her hair, and put on fresh clothes. She went to the kitchen and opened the fridge to see what was available to make for breakfast. She was starving and it might be nice to make a proper meal for her family for a change. She grabbed a carton of eggs and some butter, then, after placing the items on the counter, got a pan from a lower cabinet and glanced around the room. She was still impressed with how quickly the contractors had gotten the apartment back in functioning condition after Barachiel's meltdown a few months before. The place was stunning. Hopefully, he'd be able to hold it together in the future.

She poured three glasses of orange juice and began to make scrambled eggs. After a few minutes, the pan started to smoke and the fire alarm sounded. She took a newspaper and fanned it until the noise stopped, but it woke the boys up, anyway.

"Everything all right?" Wyatt asked sleepily, taking a seat at the island.

"Fine," she answered. "Just making breakfast."

"What the bloody hell is the racket?" Lucifer called as he came down the hallway.

"She cooked," Wyatt told him.

"She *what*?" he griped. "Do you hate us that much, sister?"

"Shush your mouth," she said, setting plates in front of them.

The eggs were well overcooked and smelled awful. Wyatt took a bite out of politeness but Lucifer covered his nose. "I can't," he told her.

"They are not that bad," she said.

"Barachiel," Lucifer asked. "Thoughts?"

"I don't want to be rude," he said as he struggled to chew.

Gabriel took a bite of her eggs and immediately spit them back out onto her plate. "Okay, they're really gross," she admitted.

"So disgusting," Wyatt agreed, dropping his fork, relieved he didn't have to choke them down.

"This is why I don't cook real food," she lamented. "It's fickle. Toaster pastries never break your heart this way."

Wyatt chuckled as he stood. "If you'll both excuse me, I need to make a call."

"I already handled it," Gabriel told him, taking a sip of her juice.

"Handled what?" he asked suspiciously.

"Your landlord in New Jersey. I called him last week, pretended to be Annie, and paid off your lease. You have about four months before you'll have to renew. You're welcome."

"I don't need you to pay my bills."

"I know you don't," she said. "But, you're not working right now and most of what your uncle left you is tied up in property and you shouldn't be worried about selling houses seven hundred miles away when you're supposed to be focused on fine-tuning your lightning skills. It's unnecessary for you to be stressed out about money when I'm sitting on a stockpile of cash."

"She has a point," Lucifer chimed in.

"Pipe down," Wyatt told him.

"I don't know what your problem is," Gabriel said. "I mean, I do, but it's stupid. I'm just trying to be helpful. It's the sisterly thing to do."

"I don't need yo-"

"My charity, I understand," she sighed. "Ugh, you sound like Uriel."

"How is our lovely sister?" Lucifer asked. "It's been some time since I've seen her."

"That's because she hates you," Wyatt said.

"That's a bit of an overstatement," Lucifer rebuffed. "She just misunderstands me."

"No, she fucking hates you," Gabriel confirmed.

"Well, I'm insulted," Lucifer complained. "I have nothing but respect for our dear Uriel. She's helped me tremendously on dozens of occasions tracking down rogue demons. One incident I remember quite fondly. There was this king in Naples, I'm not sure of the year. It was five centuries ago or so, I believe. Anyhow, he was quite villainous on his own, but then--"

"Yeah," she interrupted. "She doesn't remember that."

"Of course not," Lucifer realized. "Perhaps I should remedy that."

"Don't get crazy," she warned.

"Me?" he said, feigning innocence. "I would never."

Chapter 14

Gabriel had agreed to take Lucifer to see Valerie in an effort to mend their strained relationship, leaving Wyatt alone to work on better controlling his abilities. He had come a long way and was now fairly skilled in keeping his emotions from getting the best of him. He stood on the balcony and watched carefully as he pulled a lightning bolt from the clouds and dragged it across the sky, making sure it didn't come down and hit anything. He felt a twinge of pride as it disappeared into the overcast. Just then, he heard something from the living room behind him. He entered the apartment and closed the glass door behind him, glancing around the room. He saw no one.

"You back?" he called. No answer. From the corner of his eye, he saw someone rush down the hall to where the bedrooms were. Concerned there might be an intruder, he readied a small ball of lightning in his hand as he made his way, finding his bedroom door to be open. He went inside and found a woman standing in the far corner. It was the same woman he'd seen on the street a few months before. She smiled at him and as he got closer and her face became clear, he realized who she was.

"Mom?" he choked out.

"Yes, Wyatt," she said. "It's me."

Wyatt nearly fell over, catching himself on the bed.

"You're," he started, but couldn't finish the sentence.

"Dead, yeah." She slowly approached and sat next to him. He scooted away from her a little as the shock began to wear off.

"And, I'm real, just to be clear," she told him.

He stared, unable to take his eyes off her face. His father had been right. He *did* look just like her. The faded photos from the eighties hadn't done her justice. "I don't know what to say to you," he admitted.

"You don't have to say anything. I just wanted to tell you how proud I am of you. Despite everything you've had to deal with, despite what I did, you've grown up to be such a good man. And I know you're an angel underneath, but to me, you're just my sweet baby boy that I never got a chance to meet. I can't tell you how sorry I am."

Tears filled Wyatt's eyes as all the long-buried pain of his childhood came flooding back. "It's not your fault. You were sick."

"I was. But, I'm okay now and I want to make sure you're okay, too."

"I'm fine," he said, wiping tears from his cheeks.

"Are you?" she prodded. "When was the last time you spoke to your father?"

"It's been a while. It's hard for him."

"Because you remind him of me," she said, tears welling her eyes now, too. "I'll never forgive myself for what I did to you both. John still hasn't recovered. Finding me like that destroyed him. It's my fault. Not his and most certainly not yours."

"He's a grown man," Wyatt said, resentment and anger building as he spoke. "I was a *kid*. A kid with no mother. I deserved better from him. He should have done better."

"You're right," she conceded, letting the tears fall. "He's been a lousy father. But, Wyatt, I *know him*. Before I died, he was a different person. He was so excited when I told him I was pregnant with you. He loved you so much, and he still does, just--"

"Not as much as he loves you," Wyatt told her. "No matter what I did, I was always just a reminder of what he lost. I will never be anything but an emotional burden for that man."

Abigail stared at her son's heartbroken face, crushed by what he'd just said. "I owe you more than I can ever give," she sobbed. "But, I swear, I will fix this for you." And with that, she was gone.

Valerie was enjoying a lazy Saturday. She had some high sugar cereal for breakfast, watched a bad movie on TV, and was still in her pajamas when there was a knock at the door. She ignored it as she scrolled through the guide trying to decide what to watch next. She heard the clicking sound of the door being unlocked, so she turned the television off, jumped up from her seat on the sofa, grabbed a knife from the kitchen, and prepared herself. The door opened and Gabriel and Lucifer came strolling in as if they'd been invited.

"Bitch, what the fuck?!" Valerie yelled.

"You gave me a key for emergencies," Gabriel reminded her.

"Is this an emergency?"

"Not really, but you know how pushy this one can get," she said, gesturing to Lucifer.

"All right, what do you want?" Valerie huffed, setting the knife on the coffee table and sitting back down.

"Is that how you greet guests?" Lucifer asked. "You don't say 'hello', don't offer a beverage? It's really rather rude."

"Lucifer," Gabriel warned.

"Fine, right to it, then," he said. "I just wanted to stop by and make an attempt, even if it proves fruitless, to mend what seems to be broken in our brother/sister relationship."

"Oh, my God," Valerie scoffed. "Are you serious?"

"Quite."

"Listen," Valerie explained. "There's nothing broken, nothing needing mending, okay? I'm not mad at you, I just don't feel comfortable hanging out with the Devil, you understand?"

"Well, that smarts," he admitted. "Might I remind you, sister, of some of our more cordial interactions? Times when we got along well. One might even go as far as to call us friends at certain times in our long history."

"I don't need a lesson in friendship, Lucifer. I'm just trying to have a peaceful--' But before she could finish, Lucifer grabbed her hand and placed it on his temple. She was immediately inundated with visions. Bits and pieces of Lucifer's memories of her. Most of them were of them hunting and exorcising demons. Others were of them fighting in wars together and of them in Hell, putting the Fallen in cells. When he was satisfied that she'd seen enough, Lucifer released her hand and backed away. She gasped and fell back into the couch, eyes wide, with a look of horror on her face. The feelings of despair from the Fallen combined with the fear and rage of the people and other angels in the wars was overwhelming. As the shock wore off, anger took its place and Valerie snapped. She leaped out of her seat, grasped the knife, and held it to her brother's throat. "I should kill you!" she screamed.

"Take it down a notch," Gabriel interjected, using her telekinesis to pull Lucifer back from Valerie's reach.

"What the fuck was that?!" Valerie yelled. "Why would you show me--" Suddenly, the knife in her hand exploded in flames. She dropped it on the table and it quickly went out without causing any damage. She stared at it in disbelief. "What the--"

Gabriel burst out in uncontrollable laughter. "It's, it's," she said. "It's your flaming sword!" She fell to the floor in hysterics, kicking her legs and pounding the floor with her fist. "Flaming sword!" she cackled again, wiping tears from her eyes. "I can't stand it!"

Lucifer snickered.

"I didn't think you'd ever get this power," Gabriel said, getting herself up off the floor and quieting her laughter.

"You knew about this?" Valerie asked. "Of course you did, look who I'm talking to. The fuck is it?"

"Uriel carries a sword engulfed in Holy Fire into battle," Lucifer explained.

"Apparently, you can access that shit if you get pissed off enough," Gabriel said. "Like B with the lightning."

"It's a good thing our brother wasn't here just then," Lucifer quipped. "His inner firefighter would have kicked into action."

Gabriel chuckled. "Imagine him hosing her down with the sprayer from the sink."

The two laughed while Valerie picked up the knife and returned it to the kitchen. "I need you two assholes to leave now."

"Come now sister," Lucifer said. "I don't like this rift between us."

"I just need a minute to get my shit together, okay?!" she snapped.

"We're going," Gabriel said, pulling Lucifer towards the door. "Relax, have a quiet day off. But, I do want you to make an effort to be less hostile toward our brother."

"Thank you, Gabriel," Lucifer said.

"Bitch," Valerie warned.

"Not today, calm down," Gabriel said. "In the future. Just think about it."

The two left, Valerie closing and locking the door behind them. She sat back down on the couch, propping an elbow up on the arm and resting her head in her hand. She looked around, confused. After a few minutes of quiet contemplation, she muttered to herself, "I need some weed."

"Son of a bitch," Gabriel said as she and Lucifer got back to her apartment.

"What now?" he asked.

"Goddamn ghosts, man," she complained as she headed to Wyatt's room. Lucifer sighed, not at all interested in what that was all about. He made himself comfortable on the couch and picked up the book he'd started reading the day before. It was a gripping tale of organized crime and family. One of the brothers was being ostracized for being different, not as well-liked as his siblings. He could relate.

Gabriel found Wyatt sitting on the edge of his bed weeping. She hurried to sit next to him and held him in her arms, cradling his head while he cried. "It's okay," she whispered, knowing that it wasn't, as she rubbed his back. "It's okay."

Chapter 15

John took one last sip of whisky before heading off to bed. He went around the apartment, turning the lights off and checking that the door was locked. Once in his bedroom, he took his cell phone from his pocket, turned it off, placed it on the charger, and turned to close the door. As he started to unbutton his shirt, he noticed that his phone was now on the floor, not on the bedside table where he'd left it.

"Strange," he muttered to himself as he put it back. As soon as he took his hand away, though, the phone flung itself from the table, back to the floor in the same position as before. *I've had too much to drink,* he thought, rubbing his eyes and shaking his dead. He took his shirt off, untucked his undershirt, and unbuckled his belt, leaving the phone where it was. As he began to unzip his slacks, the bedside lamp, too, suddenly fell over and rolled off the table. John looked around suspiciously.

"Who's there?" he yelled sharply, half expecting to be robbed at gunpoint. No response. "Who the hell's there?!" Still nothing. He went for his phone. "I'm calling the police!"

"And you'll tell them what, exactly?" a voice said quietly from the shadows.

"Who is that?" he shouted into the darkness, panic setting in as he reached for the fallen lamp, the only thing available to use as a weapon.

A form slowly began to manifest as if from thin air. John's heart raced and his breath quickened. He couldn't believe what he was seeing. After several moments, a face became clear and the woman appeared solid.

"Abby?" he marveled, falling to his knees, dropping the lamp and phone, and looking up at the vision of his dead wife.

"Hey, sweetie," she said as she knelt in front of him. John's eyes filled with tears. He tried to touch her face, but his hand went right through her.

"You're a," he uttered. "A ghost?"

"Apparently," she confirmed.

"How are you," he began to ask. "I mean, *why* are you--"

"I came to apologize," she told him. "What I did to you, Johnny is unforgivable. There aren't words for how sorry I am."

"Abigail," he assured her. "I understand. You weren't *you* at the end. *I* should have--"

"There's nothing you could have done," she explained. "I was determined. I would have found a way."

"Why, Abby?" he asked, tears streaming down his face. "Why did you leave me?"

"I was deranged. *Unbalanced.* I thought something terrible would happen if the baby was born and I didn't want to live without him, so in my insanity, I tried to kill us both. I was completely off my rocker. He did nothing wrong, and you certainly weren't at fault, either. It was *all* me."

"I miss you so much," John whimpered. "I miss you every minute of every day."

"I know that," she told him. "But, you have to let me go, John. It's not healthy for you to hold on to me like this. The pictures everywhere, not dating anyone else. The drinking. The drinking, Johnny, is catching up to you. You're not twenty-five anymore. And the way you've treated our son--"

"I know," he admitted. "I know. It's just so hard, Abby. Just looking at him kills me. He's so much like you."

"He's amazing," she said. "I've been watching, here and there. He's so special, John, you have no idea. But, he *needs* his father."

"He's an adult. I don't see a way of changing things between us."

"Find one," she demanded. "*I* know you love him, but *he doesn't.*"

John sprang up in bed, covered in sweat, his breathing heavy. The pale light of the sunrise filled the room allowing him to see his phone and the lamp in their proper places on the nightstand. *It must have been a dream,* he thought. He tried to steady his breathing, but after several moments, he realized he couldn't. He was suddenly overcome with a sense of vertigo, even though he was still sitting in bed. He felt nauseated and weak. Then, an abrupt, excruciating pain filled his chest and radiated down his left arm. Terror gripped him as he clumsily picked up his phone and dialed nine one one.

"Nine one one, what's your emergency?"

John fought to speak, struggling to get even one word out. "Heart," he managed to murmur before dropping the phone, falling back on his pillows, and losing consciousness.

Wyatt woke up still feeling drained from the events of the day before. He had been left reeling after his mother's visit. But, it was a new day and he intended on making the most of it by getting in as much lightning practice as he could. As he threw his blankets off and swung his legs over the side of the bed, he noticed on his nightstand sat a plate with a croissant, a cup of coffee, and a note that read,

It is my sincere hope that this will perk you up before joining the rest of us for the day. As you may have deduced, I'm cheerless enough without also having to endure your melancholy. L

Wyatt laughed a little, putting the note down and taking a bite of his breakfast. He checked his phone. Two missed calls from Tae. Odd. The two had a polite and friendly relationship, but they weren't what one would call close. Until now, the only time Tae had called him was an accidental butt dial. Assuming it must be important, Wyatt called his brother back.

"Wyatt?" Tae answered.

"Yeah, buddy. What's up?"

"Your last name is Sinclair, right?"

"Yeah."

"I thought so," Tae said, slightly embarrassed that he had to check. "You're listed as the emergency contact for a patient that came in a few hours ago. Jonathon Sinclair. From his age, I assume he's your father?"

Wyatt sat up straight. "He is. What happened?"

"He had an acute myocardial infarction. A heart attack. He's stable for now, but I'm keeping him at the hospital for a while. Just thought you should know."

"Jesus Christ, is he gonna be okay?"

"Hard to say," Tae confessed. "I'm keeping a close eye on him, but if you've got anything you want to say, I wouldn't dilly dally."

"All right, thanks, man."

"Mm-hmm."

Wyatt jumped out of bed and threw his clothes on as fast as he could. He took another bite of croissant and chugged the coffee before heading out. "Thanks for the breakfast, Satan," he said as he rushed by Lucifer and Gabriel who were sitting at the island playing chess on his way out the door.

"Is he unaware that I dislike that?" Lucifer asked.

"He knows," Gabriel giggled.

Wyatt hesitantly entered the hospital room where his father was recuperating. He looked fragile and smaller somehow as he lay there sleeping, IVs and monitors flanking the bed. *Nesiritide, Morphine, Saline,* the bags read.

"The good stuff, hey, old man?" Wyatt mumbled as he pulled a chair closer to the bed and took a seat. He wasn't sure what he should do in this situation. He hadn't prepared himself for a moment like this, though he realized he probably should have. His father was in his sixties and while he had appeared to be in good health until now, he drank heavily, worked constantly, and had no semblance of a social life. In hindsight, something like this happening seemed to have been inevitable. Wyatt glanced around the dimly lit room and took note of how cold it felt. The emptiness surrounded him like a breeze as he looked out the small window at the view of another building. Everything about this place felt hollow and impersonal and he wondered if it would aggravate his father to know this might be where he'd spend his final moments. He wondered if he'd care at all about the where and be more concerned with the how or why. And, he wondered if his father's ghost would someday visit him as his mother had or if he'd simply move on, unbothered, leaving this world with no regrets.

John's eyes slowly fluttered open and as he woke he was surprised to see his son sitting there. "Wyatt," he said, his voice scratchy. Wyatt poured a cup of water from the table next to him and carefully handed it to his father. John took a few sips and handed the cup back. "Thank you."

"You okay?" Wyatt asked. "How do you feel?"

"Let's just say, if I had a tail, I wouldn't be wagging it," John quipped.

"Do you need anything?"

"No, I'm fine," he said, trying to sit up and grunting with displeasure when he couldn't. "They shouldn't have bothered you. I'm all right."

"Dad, you had a heart attack."

"Just a little one."

"Dad,"

"Listen, while I've got you here, I'd like to apologize. I know I've been an asshole for the last, well, your whole life, and I want to make sure you know none of that was your fault. I mean, you know that, right? That was *my* bullshit."

"Oh, I know," Wyatt agreed coldly.

"You deserved more from me and I'd like to make it right. Is there anything you need? Money? Advice?"

"Well, if Annie ever gets around to filing divorce papers, I might ask you to go over them for me," Wyatt said, half-joking.

"Done," John chuckled. "She still hasn't filed?"

Wyatt shook his head.

"Huh. Maybe she's not sure."

"It doesn't matter," Wyatt told him. "She's seeing someone. I can't forgive it."

John raised his eyebrows in approval. "Good for you, son. Fidelity is the most important thing in a marriage. If you can't trust your partner,"

"You've got nothing left," Wyatt muttered, looking down at his hands in his lap for a moment, fiddling with the ring he still wore.

"Speaking of wives," John said in an attempt to change the subject. "I saw your mother last night."

"You *saw* her?" Wyatt asked, returning his gaze to his father.

"Well, not *her*, obviously," John corrected himself. "It was a dream or a heart attack-induced hallucination, but it *felt* real. She was as beautiful as I remember and she was wearing the dress I buried her in. She told me I needed to let her go. I don't know if I can. She was *everything*. The sun rose and set with her."

"I know what you mean," Wyatt said, again spinning the ring around his finger. "I can't imagine what it must have been like for you, seeing her, what she did. If I had been in your shoes,"

"You would have done right by your son," John presumed. "You're a better man than me, Wyatt. Stronger. Tougher."

"I don't know about that."

"I do. The things you've been through, having *me* as a father, and on top of that, your mental stuff. I'm amazed you can function at all, but here you are."

"Oh, um," Wyatt said. "I had a procedure. I don't have the hallucinations anymore."

"Really?" John said, sounding pleased. "A procedure? Like, electroshock?"

"Kind of."

"Well, that's great, kid. I'm happy for you. That's the best thing I've heard in a long time. Aside, of course, from 'No, you're not dead'."

As they laughed, a nurse came in carrying a large vase of flowers. "These came for you," she said as she placed it on the window sill and handed John the card.

"Best wishes on your current endeavor. The Rothstein Group," John read allowed then dropped the card on the table next to him. "I should maybe get some real friends."

Wyatt snickered.

"All right, Mr. Sinclair," the nurse said, releasing the brake on his bed. "Time for more tests."

"All right," John conceded. "Listen, Wyatt, go on home. I'm fine. I'll call you if anything changes."

Wyatt looked at the nurse who gave him a reassuring nod.

"Okay," he agreed. "I'll see you later."

"See you later," John said as he was rolled out of the room. "It was nice seeing you."

"You, too, Dad."

That night, after his shower, Wyatt took a good long look at himself in the bathroom mirror. It was time, he decided, that he come to terms with Annie being out of his life. His father wasn't the only one that needed to let a wife go. He looked sadly down at his wedding ring as he hesitantly slipped it off his finger and set it on the marble vanity, making sure it wasn't so close to the sink that it could easily fall in. He cleared the steam that had accumulated on the glass and again looked at his reflection as he applied a layer of shaving cream and picked up a razor. Until now, he had only used clippers to trim down his facial hair, not seeing the value in keeping properly groomed without Annie there to appreciate the effort. It was only about five millimeters of hair, but as he shaved, it felt like years falling away. There was a sense of relief he hadn't expected as he rinsed his face. It had been a long time since he had really *seen* himself and for the first time in months, he recognized the man looking back at him.

Chapter 16

"You've done excellent work, Adam," Lilith said, handing her guest a cup of coffee and sitting next to him on the sofa. "Since our last meeting, your ratings are up even more and you have over six million followers on social media, is that right?"

"Yeah, it's been awesome!" he said in his signature low, excited growl. "People are eating this shit up like ice cream! I'm talking to a guy about making my own line of-"

"That's great, Adam," she interrupted. "Really good news. You've succeeded in getting the people riled up. Enraged. Now it's time for phase two."

"What's phase two?"

She smiled sweetly and slid closer to him. "I need you to create posts on your social media accounts for Cardinal Rain. They're hiring."

"Oh, sure, no problem," he agreed emphatically. "Those guys kick ass! You know, I was in the National Guard back in the eighties."

"That's wonderful, Adam," she condescended. "I also need you to gently *nudge* your followers into taking up arms."

"Oh, my fans are well-armed, trust me. I did a poll a few weeks ago. Almost seventy percent are gun owners."

"Yes, but I need them to *use* those guns."

Adam set his cup down and turned to his benefactor. "What do you mean, use them?"

"Well, they know that big government is out of control," she explained. "They're aware, thanks to you, of the tyranny. The government can't be trusted. Law enforcement, politicians, the courts. It's all the same. Run by a criminal syndicate of elites that want them disarmed and weak so they can control them with indoctrination at public schools, mindless cogs in a--"

"Whoa, whoa, lady," he chuckled. "You know that's just bullshit, right? Stuff I say to provoke people."

"Of course, but your followers don't."

"It's just entertainment," he confessed. "I just say crazy shit people want to hear. It's just for ratings."

"But those ratings translate to real people with real weapons and those weapons now need to be turned on your government officials."

"Are you out of your fucking mind?!" he shouted, jumping up from the couch. "I'm not telling people to *kill* people!"

"It's the next logical step," she said, a little confused that he didn't know this was where things were headed.

"The fuck it is!" he barked. "What I do is *rhetoric*. It's soundbites and slogans short enough to put on a bumper sticker or baseball cap. I don't incite violence."

"Of course you do," she contradicted, standing to look him in the eye. "How many school shootings, pipe bombs, and ass-kickings are you directly responsible for? I've lost count!"

"I'm not responsible for crazy people doing awful things."

"Crazy people that listen to or watch one of your shows. Crazy people that think you're the only person being honest with them because that's what you've convinced them to be true. You are *covered* in the blood of innocent people that your followers deemed unworthy of life. All I'm asking you to do now is direct that energy to the people in charge. Declare the government the enemy of the people. Demand justice. Tell them-"

"Jesus fucking Christ, lady!" he yelled, backing away toward the door. "There is no way in Hell I'm doing that. I'm just an entertainer."

"This is the thing," she said, clearly irked. "If you won't do what I ask, I'll have to start over with someone else. I don't have time for that. People are looking for me. Now, I've done a cloaking spell, but it requires a tremendous amount of energy to maintain. I see no circumstance likely to weaken me occurring any time soon, but you never know. Cardinal Rain is deliciously close to beginning their mission and I need your government occupied here so they won't interfere with my plans. Now be a good boy and do what you're told." She dropped her hand down hard toward the floor, forcing Adam to his knees. She sat her computer in front of him on the floor and knelt beside him, stroking what little remained of his hair. "Log in to your account."

"No," he insisted.

"Fine," she sighed, rolling her eyes. She took her fist and crushed his hand into the hardwood. He screamed in agony. "Now, login with your left hand."

"I won't," he declared, tears welling in his eyes. "I'm not a monster."

"Pity," she said, standing up and taking a step back. "I am." She clapped her hands, crushing Adam's skull, causing it to cave in on either side. His eyes popped out of their sockets and dangled over his cheeks while blood and brain matter poured from his nose and ears. When his body fell, she kicked it under the bed and picked her phone up off the coffee table. She dialed Mitchell Spade's number as she opened the bedside table's drawer, pulling from it a small limestone box.

"Hello?" Mitchell answered.

"I'm sending you something to make your job easier," she told him. "You may not need it, and you should hope that you don't because using it comes with a price."

"What kind of price?" he asked.

"There are...side effects. It's only in case you come against a resistance you can't handle. Call it insurance. Hold out your hand."

"What?"

She quickly muttered the incantation, the box disappearing from her hand and reappearing in his.

"Holy shit!" he blurted.

"You're welcome," she said, hanging up the phone and dropping it to the blood-soaked floor. "I need a release," she said to herself as she went to the door and left the room, not bothering to close it behind her.

Chapter 17

Tae took off his surgical gown and gloves before washing his hands and heading to his office. He pulled a protein bar and bottle of water from his desk and sat down. He only had about ten minutes to eat while his next patient was being prepped. His late dinner tasted like a bad combination of sawdust and peanut butter, but at least he wouldn't be hungry while he cut into someone. As he guzzled his water, he heard a loud commotion coming from the hall. "What fresh hell?" he muttered as he went to the door and peered outside. At the other end of the long hall, just past the nurse's station, he could see a man flailing wildly as three orderlies tried to strap him to a gurney. He was screaming at them to let him go, blood pouring from his nose and mouth. As Tae got closer, he could see how pale and dull the man's skin was, his eyes sunken with only a few patches of thin hair left on his head.

"What's wrong with him?" one of the orderlies asked another.

"Radiation sickness, looks like," the second attendant answered.

"No way," said the third, struggling to hold the patient down. "By the time symptoms got this bad, he'd be so weak, he'd barely be conscious."

"Holy *shit*," Tae said under his breath.

The man stopped and craned his neck to look at Tae. "Raphael," he hissed.

"Mother f--"

"*Raphael!*" he screeched again, fighting even harder to break free of his restraints.

"Shit, shit, shit, shit," Tae whispered as he scrambled to think of what to do next. He hurried to a locked medicine cabinet, broke the glass, and retrieved a bottle of tranquilizer. He filled a syringe and raced to the gurney, jabbing the needle into the man's neck. The demon squealed and shook before finally passing out.

"Was that necessary?" the nurse asked, gawking at the broken glass on the floor.

"Woman, you have no idea," Tae insisted.

"What's he got?" one of the orderlies asked.

"I--" But, before he could answer, the demon sprang up from the gurney, pushing one orderly to the ground and punching another in the face.

"I'm calling security," the nurse announced as she pressed the alert button.

"Raphael," the demon seethed. "You shouldn't be here."

"Look who's talking," Tae said shakily.

"What are you?" the demon wondered, sniffing the air in Tae's direction. "*Human?*" he gleaned. He cackled, blood and bile spewing up out of his mouth.

Gabriel, I need you at the hospital. You and the Devil. There's a demon. Hurry, Tae thought as the monster ran at him, lifted him over his head, and threw him to the ground. As he tried to stand, he was gripped once more and, this time, dragged from the hall to the stairwell.

"Stop!" Tae could hear a security guard yell. "Stop right there!"

The demon continued, pulling Tae behind him down several flights of stairs. Two security guards followed, shouting and finally letting off a warning shot from one of their pistols. The demon laughed harder at their efforts as he threw Tae down the last few steps. He tried to fight back, but the demon was too strong.

Now in the basement, Tae was heaved up over the monster's shoulder. He kicked and punched to no avail. The demon walked briskly to the hospital's incinerator and opened the door, burning off a layer of skin as he grasped the white-hot handle. The security guards began to shoot, sending bullets into the demon's back and side. It didn't slow him down a bit.

"When you get home," he growled, standing Tae in front of him. "Tell those pharisaic prigs that this world belongs to *us.*" And with that, he bashed Tae's head into the hot metal before picking him up, shoving him inside, and slamming the door closed. The security guards were horrified, listening to the doctor's screams until the noise subsided. They continued to shoot, one bullet piercing the demon's heart and another landing between his eyes. He finally fell, laughing maniacally as he was forced out, slithering his way back to Hell, leaving the host body to die.

Gabriel, not willing to wait for Lucifer who was taking a shower, decided to go to the hospital alone. As she reached for the doorknob, she felt the strong sting of Raphael leaving the Earth. She clutched her chest and fell to her knees, unable to breathe, her eyes like saucers. The pain was intolerable. She stared into nothing, a single tear running down her cheek.

"Gabriel," Wyatt called, rushing to where she was, both her hands now on the floor. He knelt in front of her and put his hands on her shoulders. "Gabriel, what's wrong? Are you hurt?"

"I didn't see it coming," she said, her voice just above a whisper.

"Didn't see what coming? Are you all right?"

She looked at her brother's worried face, the concern in his eyes helping her to regain her faculties. He had enough problems. She didn't want to burden him with this until she had to. "I'm fine," she told him. "Something happened."

"What?" he fretted.

They both stood, Gabriel buttoning her coat. "I'll be back."

"Gabriel,"

"I'm okay," she insisted, opening the door and stepping out of the apartment. "Don't follow me."

Gabriel burst through the doors of the old, decrepit theater and strolled in, livid and determined. The building, mostly fallen apart, was crawling with dozens of demons. Some were on the floor and in old broken seats, having sex in seemingly uncomfortable, if not impossible positions. Some were hunched over large amounts of various foods, stuffing their mouths with as much as would fit. One was lying lifeless on the stage, the host's body having given out from being occupied too long. Two others stood over the corpse, splashing it with week-old soda. "Forty days and forty nights!" one of them cackled as the other laughed giddily. Their voices were loud and shrill, like nails on a chalkboard. It grated on Gabriel's nerves as she slammed the doors shut behind her with her mind, using her telekinesis to hold locked all the exits.

"Where's Lilith?" she called to the crowd. They all stopped what they were doing to glare at her in unsettled apprehension.

"Gabriel!" one of them shrieked in horror. Most of them darted for the exits, becoming hysterical when they realized there was no way out. A few brave demons came at her, but she immediately snapped their necks with nothing more than a thought.

"I would tell me if I were you," she warned the rest of them, frustrated that she couldn't decipher their thoughts. Demons' minds were tricky, clouded by the memories of those they inhabited. Nothing came through to her clearly.

"We will never!" someone shouted from the back of the room.

"It's in your best interest," she told them, throwing the two on the stage up into the rafters and bringing them crashing down onto the stage floor.

"No!" several of them shouted in unison.

"I won't ask again," she promised, bringing down a large chandelier, crushing a small group of demons underneath.

"We will not," one of them said, stepping forward, away from the rest as they cowered, blood and bile staining his white tee-shirt, nearly all of his teeth missing. "We have been liberated. Our redeemer *will* rule this place. You are no match. We will not betray she who set us free."

Gabriel sighed and addressed the crowd. "Does this one speak for the rest of you?"

"Yes!" some shouted while others just nodded.

"All right," she said, disappointed. "Don't say I didn't give you a chance." She opened her palms, raising her hands to her sides and as she did, every demon in the building erupted in immense plumes of flame and smoke. They howled as they burned and Gabriel watched, making sure every one of them had fled the body that held them and was sent screaming back to the cages they had come from. When she was satisfied they were all back where they belonged, she hurried out of the building, patting out a small spot at the end of her coat that had caught fire. Not wanting to further damage the historical building, she pulled her phone from her pocket and dialed nine one one.

"Nine one one, what's your emergency?" the operator answered.

"There's a fire," she told the dispatcher. "At the old theater on Canal Street between East Broadway and Grand."

"Is anyone in the building, ma'am?" the woman asked as Gabriel disconnected the call. She looked at the time. One twenty-seven AM. She pulled up another number and began to text.

U up?

There was an immediate response. *Fuck yeah.*

She sighed as she looked at the building, smoke coming from broken windows, the smell of scorched flesh filling the air. She walked the several blocks to Ethan's apartment, unnerved by the quiet stillness that always came after a big snowfall. She avoided stepping in slush or slipping on ice as she went, eventually making her way to her lover's door. He let her inside, gleeful and jittery, like a puppy whose owner just got home from work.

"Hey, sexy," he said as he closed and locked the door behind her. "What's u--"

"No talking," she demanded, quickly removing her clothes.

"You got it!" he complied, tearing his shirt off and pulling his pants down.

She stepped out of her panties and, once naked, walked to the futon which served as the entire living and bedroom in the tiny studio. "Go to town," she told him, lying down.

Ethan kicked his pants away and speedily climbed on top of her. He fervidly kissed her cheeks, neck, and chest, but when he got to her lips, she turned her head dismissively. Not allowing his bruised ego to get in the way of a good time, he again kissed her neck and earlobes, manually servicing her until she became wet. He entered her slowly, moaning with pleasure as he made love to her, knowing, after many past encounters, exactly what she liked. He pulled her legs back, giving her every inch of himself. Her breathing quickened as she became more and more aroused. The night's events melted away with her first orgasm, her mind clearing as her body trembled. *This is why I keep this dude around,* she thought, another wave of euphoria washing over her.

Gabriel returned home to find Lucifer sitting at the island, sipping a cup of tea and reading. She took off her coat, letting it fall to the floor. She opened the pantry and took out a bag of cookies, not bothering to close the door. She sat next to her brother, took a cookie from the bag, and slid the rest over. He took one, studied it, then put it back while Gabriel reached for another.

"Barachiel asleep, then?" she asked, already knowing the answer.

"Yes," he told her. "He tried his best to stay awake until you returned. The poor dear was worried sick. I assured him that you were fully capable of handling yourself and, eventually, he retired to his room."

"But you waited up."

"I wanted to finish my book."

"Right."

The two were silent for a few moments, Gabriel mindlessly eating several more cookies and staring off into space. Lucifer sighed and put down his book. "Do you want to talk about it?"

"Not especially," she replied, gobbling up another cookie and taking a swig of his tea. He raised an eyebrow.

"Come now, sister," he pried. "Tell me what's got you in such a fettle."

She groaned, resting her cheek to her hand. "A demon killed Tae, so Raphael went home and I lost it a little."

"Really?" he asked. "Raphael's back in Heaven?"

She nodded.

"Ah, well. He's in a better place, as they say," he commented, taking a sip of tea. "So," he wondered. "What did you do in your vexation?"

"I *may* have set fifty or so demons on fire, killing the innocent people they were inhabiting and destroying a perfectly good, albeit abandoned and run-down theater in the process and then banged some dude for three hours trying to forget about it," she confessed, taking another bite of cookie.

"Well," he said, both eyebrows raised now. "Seems like a perfectly reasonable response to me."

"Does it?" she asked, not convinced.

"Of course. I wouldn't beat myself up too hard if I were you. For the most part, as far as I can tell, you're taking your current predicament in stride."

"Which predicament?" she scoffed. "Not being any closer to finding Lilith, becoming a mass murderer, or making myself sick on sugar at four in the morning like a drunk teenager?"

"I was speaking of your humanity, Gabriel," he explained. "Uriel shudders with fear at the sight of me. Raphael was concerned with matters that were inconsequential at best, and Barachiel is a roller coaster of emotion and inner turmoil, but *you* remain steadfast in your duties, just like me. You haven't given up on finding Lilith, no matter how difficult it's been. So, you killed a few people letting off a little steam, who hasn't? Those humans were probably too far gone to be saved, anyway, and you needed to deal with your situation the best way you could. I, myself, indulge in the occasional fit of rage followed by long depressive episodes of solitude and reflection. At the end of the day, God's will is done, and that's what matters. If it makes you feel any better, had I developed a bond with the human version of our dearly departed brother, I would have slaughtered those people as well."

"It really doesn't," she smirked.

"What?" he mocked. "Knowing that you're just like *the Devil* isn't a comfort to you?"

She snickered as she got up, threw the empty cookie package in the trash, got a bottle of water from the fridge, and headed to bed. "Night," she called from the hall.

"Good night." Lucifer rinsed his cup in the sink and walked to the living room. He decided to catch up on world events by watching a few minutes of early morning news before going to bed himself.

"The grisly murders have law enforcement perplexed," the reporter read from her teleprompter. "All forty-one residents of the Delta Nu Phi sorority house at Burgoyne College in Schenectady were found late last night with their faces disfigured and their hearts removed. One witness said he heard screaming from the fraternity house across the street, prompting him to call for help, but did not enter the sorority himself for fear that someone may have a gun. The school had recently held active shooter drills where students were instructed *not* to engage an assailant under any circumstances. Classes have been canceled for the week and--"

Lucifer turned the television off, anger rising in his chest as he placed the remote gently on the ottoman. "This is *her* doing," he said to himself. He peered down the hall to make sure Gabriel hadn't heard. Once he was sure he wouldn't be followed, he carefully made his way to the door, being as quiet as he could as he opened it. He stepped out into the hall, locking up behind him. As he got in the elevator, a wicked smile crept across his face as he whispered to himself, "Field trip."

Chapter 18

Allydia looked on as Lucifer fled the building, no doubt going after Lilith himself after seeing the news of his twin's latest exploits. She doubted he'd find her, though. Lilith had proven impossible to track down, even for Allydia's most skilled hunters. She began to worry that her step-mother knew she was no longer the ally she once was. If so, she was no longer safe in the city and may need a change of scenery.

She flew up the side of the apartment building and snuck noiselessly in through Wyatt's bedroom window. She admired him fondly as he slept. Even when unconscious, he wore a pained expression. It wasn't surprising. She had been watching, taking note of his schedule, studying every move while she perched atop the building across the street. She had kept her distance, not trusting that she wouldn't hurt him again. But, this night, she could no longer control herself. She was enamored with him. Everything about him captivated her. From the way he wielded his power, moving lightning through the sky, to his general disposition; pensive and short-tempered. She found his indignation irresistible, his umbrage stimulating her sensibilities in a way no man before had ever been able to. He was *perfection* and after months of holding herself back, she *would* have him again.

She stood over him and brushed the hair away from his eyes. She delicately touched his face, beginning just above his eyebrow and sliding her fingers down, first to his temple and then down to his cheek. He woke with a start, grasping her wrist, a light electrical charge transferring from his hand to her. This only excited her more.

"Easy. I won't bite," she said seductively, pulling her arm away. "Well, I'll do my best."

"What are you doing here?" he asked, still half asleep.

"You know why I'm here," she said, removing her coat and dress with supernatural speed, throwing his blankets back, and climbing on top of him.

"Allydia," he admonished.

"Yes?" she cooed. As she moved her lips closer to his, the overwhelming sense of longing and serenity that had taken hold of him before returned, his will to refuse her fading.

"Last time we did this, we almost killed each other," he reminded her.

"I know, but was it not worth it?" she asked, gently nibbling on his lower lip and stroking his cheek. "I don't know if I like this," she told him, inspecting his skin, now visible after having been cleanly shaven.

"My face?" he asked, feigning offense.

"My father told me never to trust a man without a beard."

"My father told me never to trust *anyone*."

"That's not bad advice," she told him, taking his hand and placing it on the small of her back. "Touch me," she whispered, leaning in closer and kissing him softly. She slid her hand from his neck to his shoulder and as his arousal became apparent, she slipped him smoothly inside her, both of them letting out quiet sighs of pleasure. He took hold of her legs, pulling them apart even further and squeezing her thighs as she writhed, months of pent-up frustration finally being released. Within only a few minutes, she was already beginning to orgasm. In the dim light of the busy street several floors down that illuminated the room through the still open window, Wyatt could see Allydia's teeth starting to grow. He flipped her on her back and took her throat in his hand, holding her down on the bed while being sure not to squeeze too hard on her neck.

She gasped and smiled with delight as he took charge.

"No teeth," he grunted as he continued thrusting.

"As you wish," she breathed, watching intently at his changing face. The intensity of her orgasm triggered Wyatt's own frenzied climax, both of them struggling not to cry out in ecstasy for fear of being discovered. When they had finished, he removed his hand from her throat and looked into her eyes.

"Did I hurt you?" he asked.

"No," she assured him, touching his chin ever so gently with the tips of her fingers. "I honestly don't think you could." He lay down next to her, catching his breath. She looked again at the handsome man she now shared a bed with, and for the first time in millennia, she felt what she thought she remembered to be happiness. "I have to go," she told him, slithering out of bed and back into her dress. He sat up, noticing the time.

"The sun'll be up soon."

"Yes," she said, buttoning her long coat and throwing the hood up.

"So, is it like in the movies?" he wondered. "If sunlight hits you, would you burst into flames?"

She laughed a little. "No. I'm merely sensitive to the sun's radiation. It weakens and exhausts me. My children, however,"

"Your children?"

"Yes," she explained. "Every vampire in existence was either sired by me or by one that I sired. I'm the first of my kind, the strongest and most powerful. The sun, on its own, can't kill me. But, the others are more susceptible. Exposure to ultraviolet light for even a few seconds can," she paused. "Have you ever seen a hot dog being microwaved?"

"Ouch," he chuckled.

"Indeed."

"Hey, can I ask, why are you helping us? Gabriel said Lilith's your step-mother. Why do you hate her?"

"A long time ago, she took something that didn't belong to her," she explained. She went back to the window and sat on the sill. "Until next time."

She was gone, moving so quickly that it seemed as if she had disappeared into thin air. In her absence, Wyatt's mind cleared. He let out a long, disillusioned sigh and he rubbed his face in self-disapproval. "I'm an idiot."

The bodies had been cleared, but copious amounts of blood remained. It covered everything; the floors, the walls, the furniture. "Why would she do this?" Lucifer asked himself, peering suspiciously around the grim scene. The sorority house was dark, only a little light from the rising sun peeking through the curtained windows, which were also splattered with gore. "Her motivation for rampant violence is typically jealousy, but, why would she be--" And then it occurred to him. The quoted witness from the news had been lying.

He left the house and headed swiftly across the street. From the sidewalk, he could see through the windows that every light in the place was on. These boys had no doubt been shaken. He pounded on the door impatiently, a nervous-looking young man eventually answering.

"We already told the cops," he said, his voice trembling. "We didn't see nothin'."

"Well, hello to you, too," Lucifer greeted, glancing past the boy and taking note of several young men whose expressions ranged from terrified to ashamed. "I'm not with the police department."

"Like I said,"

"I know about the girl," he stated.

The man's face dropped and the house fell silent. "What," he stammered. "What girl?"

"Oh, I'm sure you know the one," Lucifer taunted. "Blond hair, wildly insecure. Underage."

The young man looked over his shoulder at his friends who pleaded with him with their eyes. "Look, man, I didn't know she was, I mean, she looked kinda young, but," he stopped and looked back again.

"It's all right, son," Lucifer told him. "You boys aren't in any trouble. The truth is, my colleagues and I have been looking for her for months. She's what you might call *special*."

"Like, some secret government experiment type of shit, right?" someone from inside shouted.

"Something like that," Lucifer said. "It would be very helpful if you could tell me what happened here tonight."

"Okay, listen," the first man said. "If I tell you, do you *swear* to keep it on the DL? We can't have this crazy shit getting out on the news. Our lives would be *trashed*."

"My word is my bond," Lucifer promised.

"All right," he said, stepping out onto the porch and closing the door behind him. "I don't wanna talk about it in front of them. A lot of 'em are really fucked up over it."

"Of course."

The man looked around to make sure no one was in earshot before he started. "Okay," he began. "So, my buddy, Mark, brought this girl back to the house and took her to his room. Now, I was *sure* she had to be a high school girl, but you can't tell Mark nothin', and she didn't look wasted or anything, so I figured she was into it. About twenty minutes go by and we hear Mark screamin'. Not like, *good* screamin', you know what I mean? Like, he was *hurt*. So, I get to the bottom of the stairs cuz I'm gonna go check it out. What if he accidentally choked the girl too hard or somethin', right? But, before I get up there, the girl comes out, completely naked, askin' if any of us know who Sydney is. Now, I know Sydney's Mark's ride or die, but I'm not gonna say shit cuz that's my boy. But, one of the new guys pipes in, sayin' she lives across the street like she's gonna hop on *his* dick for ratting Mark out or some shit. So, she comes down the stairs and asks me if Sydney's prettier than her. Now, I have *four* sisters and if there's one thing I know for sure, it's that if a girl with crazy eyes asks if some other chick is hotter, the answer is always 'hell no', so that's what I said. That must've made her happy, cuz she grabs me, drags my ass to the couch by my shirt, yanks down my pants like they're nothin', and starts ridin' me right there in front of everyone. It was a little weird, but you take it where you can get it, yeah? Next thing I know, me, Brayden, and my boy, J Dog are runnin' a train on this girl, and it's kinda fucked up, but I'm not havin' a bad time. After a while, though, I start hearing the guys on the other side of the room and they're yellin', freakin' out, straight up cryin' if I'm being honest with you. I look over and they're all buck-ass naked and doin' stuff, like, with *each other*. Dudes sayin' shit like, 'I'm sorry, I can't stop.' while they're giving it to some guy up the ass. Weird oral shit happening everywhere. And, no joke, the Freshman that ratted Mark out was pinned to the fuckin' ceiling, jerkin' it, jizzin' all over people. He was stuck up there by some kind of voodoo, bro, I'm not playin'. I see all this and I can't help but yell, 'What the fuck?' because I mean, what the fuck?! And the girl starts laughing like it's the funniest shit she's ever seen, gets up, puts on somebody's shirt she got off the floor, and leaves. Everybody stops fuckin' and the kid drops from the ceiling and lands flat on his fuckin' face, dick still in his hand. Nobody says shit. We just put our clothes back on and help the kid up, lookin' at each other like 'What the fuck just happened?' At this point, we hear Mark, still upstairs screamin' his fuckin' head off. So, me and Brayden go up there and he's tied to the bed, naked, and both his legs from the knee down are turned *completely backwards*. Bone's stickin' out and shit. So, we run over, get him untied, and asked him what the fuck happened. He points to his phone and there's a text from his girl asking if he's comin' over later. He says the girl saw it and asked who Sydney was. He tried to play it off, but the girl wasn't havin' it. She broke his legs with her bare hands. So, Brayden and J took him to the hospital and when I was helpin' get him in the car, I start hearing girls screamin' from across the way. No way I'm goin' over there after what just happened. No freakin' way. So I call the cops and tell 'em I hear girls screamin', but that's all I know. Cops show up and tell me all those girls are dead. *Dead.* I didn't tell 'em about the chick cuz it sounds crazy, right? Who's gonna believe that freaky shit? I'd end up in the loony bin and my boys would never forgive me for letting that shit out. They don't want people knowing about, *you know.*"

"Yes," Lucifer acknowledged, a little taken aback by his sister's latest shenanigans. "You boys have reputations to uphold, I'm sure. Do you happen to know where she went? See in which direction she headed?"

"No, man, sorry. You think she's gonna come back?"

"I wouldn't worry. She tends to leave carnage in her wake, but she rarely returns to the scene of her crimes. She gets bored quite easily."

"So, what is she?" the young man wondered. "Witch? Alien? Mutant freak?"

"She's much worse than that. The likelihood of her making another appearance is slim, but if you should see her again, I suggest you run."

"No doubt, no doubt."

As Lucifer walked away, the man opened the door to go back inside. "Stop cryin', Cody!" he could hear someone shout   from inside the house. Lucifer chuckled a bit as he headed back to the street where he found Gabriel waiting for him.

"I thought you were asleep, Gabriel."

"I find it amusing that you think I'd just ignore you sneaking out," she said.

"Yes, well, did you at least find anything useful while you were spying on me?"

"No," she admitted. "Security guard, groundskeeper, a couple of kids. None of them saw anything. I searched all over. She's long gone. Also, your sister's *fucked up*, bro."

"Does that surprise you?"

"No, but, I mean, she's *really* fucked up," she emphasized. "Like, she needs *massive* amounts of therapy. A team of specialists couldn't wrangle the army of cuckoo going on in her head. The girl has more issues than National Geographic. Crueler than a Congressman taking health care from kids."

"Are you quite finished?" Lucifer asked, annoyed that Lilith had slipped through his fingers yet again.

"Nuttier than squirrel--"

"Yes, she's unapologetically mad. Severely insane. I understand."

"Out of her tree," she joked. "Round the bend. Unzipped."

"Yes, yes."

"Flippity flop banana pants."

"What?"

"So unhinged, no one knows where the door went."

"All right!"

"Just one more," she promised. "Battier than the underside of a haunted bridge."

"All right, that one was pretty funny."

The two returned home a few hours later after stopping for pancakes and coffee. Wyatt emerged from his room just as Gabriel was setting out three plates and unpacking the carryout. "Oh, dude!" she said, exasperated. "*Again*? Now I'm gonna have nightmares."

"Can you turn that off?" Wyatt asked, irritated. "Do you *always* have to be in my head?"

"It's involuntary," she said.

"What has our little brother done this time?" Lucifer inquired.

"Dia," she told him.

"Really?" Wyatt griped.

"What? It's not like *he* can judge."

"Don't worry, Barachiel," Lucifer said. "I won't ridicule you for your lack of judgement. I know all too well the hypnotic seduction of Allydia Cain. It's preternatural. Not much you can do if she has you in her sights."

"Can we please not talk about this?" Wyatt pleaded, taking a cup of coffee from the drink carrier.

"Okay," Gabriel said. "You want to hear about Lilith's latest?"

"You know where she is?"

"No, but we sure as shit know where she was last night."

"What'd she do?"

Gabriel swallowed a bite of pancake before answering. "She killed a bunch of sorority girls and incited a forced orgy at a frat house." She gobbled up the rest of her breakfast while Wyatt stood in astonishment. "Oh, and she broke some dude's legs, but that's kind of low on the list as far as horrific shit goes, you know, comparatively." She stood, kicked off her shoes, leaving them on the kitchen floor, and headed to her room. "I'm taking a shower and a nap," she announced. "Can you fill him in?"

"Happy to," Lucifer agreed.

"What the hell, man?"

"You should sit down."

Chapter 19

Later that afternoon, Gabriel called Valerie over for a family meeting. She was reluctant to go, having stayed away as much as possible in an attempt to avoid Lucifer. But, her sister said it was important, so she went, telling herself it was only for a little while and that as soon as she heard whatever this big news was, she was out.

The four siblings gathered around the kitchen island, Wyatt and Valerie on one side, Gabriel and Lucifer on the other. The tension was high as Gabriel tried to find the right words, knowing that Wyatt would probably be fine, but no matter how she put it, she was about to break Valerie's heart. She and Tae had always been close and the news of his death was going to crush her. Gabriel cleared her throat and took a breath before starting. "Last night, Tae called to me, saying there was a demon at the hospital. He asked that we, Lucifer and I, come help. Lucifer was in the shower, so I decided to go on my own."

"Shit, girl, you okay?" Valerie asked.

"Yeah, I'm fine," she told her.

"Oh, God," Wyatt muttered, realizing what must have happened. "That's when you fell."

She nodded, keeping her eyes on her sister. "As I was leaving, I could feel him. He left."

"What do you mean, 'he left'?" Valerie snapped.

"He's not here anymore," she said. "He went home, to Heaven. So,"

"You're telling me Tae's *dead*?!" Valerie asked.

"Yeah."

"How is that possible?" she questioned. "We're fucking *self-healing*. The only way is if--" she stopped, horrified at the thought of how he must have died. "Fire?!"

"I'm gonna spare you the details," Gabriel said.

"You're gonna *spare* me?!" Valerie erupted in anger. "How the fuck did we not know this was gonna happen? Why didn't I get a vision ahead of time?"

"I don't know," Gabriel answered stoically, a phrase she didn't utter often.

"How do you not know?" Valerie shot back. "You know goddamn *everything*."

"Not everything," she corrected, starting to get irritated by Valerie's thoughts. She blamed her for Tae's death, angry that she didn't somehow prevent it from happening. Gabriel tried to keep a cool head, but after the events of the night before, her nerves were pretty much fried.

"Clearly," Lucifer chimed in.

"Dude," Wyatt warned him.

"What?" Lucifer asked as Valerie began to sob uncontrollably, Wyatt rubbing her back to try to comfort her. "I'm just pointing out the obvious. Our sister, in her current form, is not at full power. Had she been--"

"Had I been," Gabriel interrupted, her annoyance turning to anger. "You would still be in a coma until I handled this Lilith thing myself because I wouldn't need you."

"That may very well be true, sister, but as it stands, we're one angel down and no closer to finding my malfeasant twin. I can only hope we find and defeat her before the rest of you get picked off."

"I'm doing my best, okay?!" Gabriel barked. "Between Barachiel's meltdowns, your general douchebaggery, Tae ghosting for months, and Uriel's open disdain for you and your bullshit, I've been doing *everything* to keep this family together, civil, and on task. *None* of you make it easy. You think I'm not pissed off that Lilith's still out there? I'm *livid*."

"You're *seriously* thinking about the *mission* right now?" Valerie complained. "Our brother just died!"

"Our mission from *God* to save the human race from indentured servitude to a psychotic, baby-eating whore-monster? *That* mission?" Gabriel howled. "Hell yes, I'm thinking about that. I'm *always* thinking about that and if there's ever a minute in the fucking day when you're *not* thinking about it, then maybe I haven't made it clear to you just how fucking important it is. It is the *only reason* we're on this planet instead of in Paradise, which, by the way, is where our brother is right now, so you'll have to excuse me if I'm not blubbering like a toddler that got the wrong color sippy cup. There's work to do, and until it's done and that bitch is in a fucking cell, *nothing else matters*. Your job, your social life, your issues, and your motherfucking feelings are just gonna have to take a back seat!" Gabriel calmed herself as the others sat silently, not sure what to say. Her outburst had shocked them as none of them had ever seen her get agitated. "I'm sorry I yelled," she said, getting up from her seat and getting a bottle of water from the fridge.

"I gotta get out of here," Valerie said, wiping the tears from her cheeks and nearly knocking the stool over as she stood. She blew past Gabriel who let her go, not making eye contact. She slammed the door behind her, leaving Gabriel to lock it back.

"I could've handled that better," she recognized. She sat back down and took a sip of water.

"My 'meltdowns'?" Wyatt asked.

"You cry a *lot*, bro," Gabriel told him. He raised an eyebrow while Lucifer chuckled.

"Well," Lucifer said. "I, for one, am quite inspired by what you said, Gabriel. I'm proud of you for standing up for yourself and impressing on everyone the gravity of--"

She cut him off. "Just shut the fuck up."

Valerie was a little more than halfway home when she was suddenly struck with a vision that was so strong and clear that it knocked her to her knees right there on the sidewalk. She saw a building that she recognized as the women's clinic almost directly across the street from where she was. Inside, she could see a handful of people, some slumped in their seats or on the floor in the waiting room and others behind the counter, all dead, their necks broken. There was someone in the back, in a storage room far away from the offices and exam rooms. All she could see was a doctor lying in the hallway, blood pouring from his head, his eyes open and vacant. The door was cracked and there was light coming through, but she couldn't see who was inside. It didn't matter, though. Valerie could guess based on the level of evil she felt coming from that room.

"Miss, are you all right?" she heard a man ask as she came out of the vision. He was kneeling in front of her, one hand on her shoulder.

"I'm okay," she told him as they both stood.

"You sure?" the man asked.

"Yeah, I'm good. Low blood sugar, that's all."

"Okay, okay," he said, reaching in his pocket, pulling out a business card, and handing it to her. "Well, listen, I have to get to a job right now, but that last number is my personal cell. Maybe you could call me sometime and let me feed you."

The card read *Malik Perry, Private Chef and Culinary Instructor.*

She looked back up at him, just noticing how attractive he was. Tall and muscular with a shaved head, strong jawline, and wide smile.

"I'll do that," she flirted as he walked away and she put the card in her pocket. Once he disappeared into the crowd of pedestrians, she looked across the busy street to the clinic. "What are you thinkin', ho?" she whispered to herself as she began walking toward it, navigating through traffic, paying no attention to the crosswalk just a few feet away. She knew she wasn't thinking clearly, still reeling from the news of her brother's death. Even more than that, though, Gabriel losing her temper had thrown her for a loop. She'd never seen her like that. It had startled her, the look in her eyes downright frightening. Valerie knew she couldn't handle Lilith on her own, but she was *right there* and if she could save the people inside, convince them there was a bomb threat or gas leak so they'd evacuate *before* Lilith got there, she had to do it. Then, she'd call on Gabriel to gather the troops and wait for the bitch to show up. That was her plan. But, she was too late. As she entered the dimly lit building, she was sickened by what she saw. As it had been in her vision, everyone in the clinic was dead.

"Holy shit," she uttered under her breath.

"Uriel?" a voice called from the back. "What are you doing here?" A young girl came out from the shadows of the hallway and into the waiting room looking genuinely confused. Her hands, mouth, and chin were covered in blood as was the collar of the long white dress she was wearing.

"Lilith?" Valerie asked, her voice not much louder than a whisper as she was horrified by the realization of what she'd just walked in on.

"It's amazing," Lilith said, licking her fingers. "Entire facilities dedicated to the legalized murder of tiny humans before they've been born. Can you imagine? And people called *me* a monster just for finding them delicious."

Valerie edged toward the glass door that she'd come in, knowing she was no match for someone as strong as Lilith, not by a long shot. As her back touched the handle, she heard the door lock behind her. Her heart began to race and her mind swirled, unable to string a plan together, knowing there was nothing she could do.

"Was it you?" Lilith asked as she approached. "Did you kill my subordinates? Seems so unlike you, destroying all the so-called innocent people my followers were populating, but it *has* been a couple thousand years. People change."

"I didn't kill anybody," she replied, her fear turning to anger as she thought about the demon that killed her brother and how he was only there because of her, the psycho that now threatened to take her own life. She let the pain of her loss fuel her rage, believing it was her only chance of getting out of this alive.

"No," Lilith said. "I didn't think so."

"But, I'd have no problem putting your little girl wearing ass down."

"Well, that's hostile."

"I'm about to *show you* hostile, bitch!"

Lilith came closer, the look of bewilderment returning to her face.

"Even at full power, which you're obviously not, you don't stand a chance against me alone, and you *know that*. So, I ask you again, *what are you doing here*?"

Valerie shakily pulled her knife from her pocket and held it to her enemy's throat.

Lilith giggled. "You can't be serious."

"I'm dead fucking serious, bitch."

"Have it your way," Lilith sighed, waving her hand, throwing Valerie into a wall across the room. She slammed against it and crashed to the floor. She struggled to stand back up as Lilith moved toward her again. "If you didn't kill the demons in the theater," she gathered. "Then, someone else did. Who else is here? It can't be Michael, he'd never leave Father unguarded during his sleep. Is it Camael? I thought I felt his presence a few weeks ago, but it's been so long, I could have been mistaken." She grabbed Valerie by the throat and slammed her into some chairs. She climbed on top of her, squeezing with one hand her cheeks and chin while she decided what to do with her. "This is quite a beautiful body you've chosen, sister," she said, looking Valerie over. "Tell me, is incest still as taboo as it was in the beginning? So many things have changed."

Valerie panicked, adrenaline coursing through her veins. She started to hyperventilate, which only excited Lilith more. She slid her hand down from Valerie's jaw to her chest and began unzipping her jacket, a mischievous smile creeping across her face. As Lilith slipped her hand inside the jacket, running her hand along Valerie's left breast, the knife, which remained clenched in Valerie's hand, erupted in flame. Without hesitation, she plunged the fiery pocket knife into the monster's gut, again and again, lighting her dress on fire. Lilith flew back into the wall behind her, screaming in pain and surprise. She patted the fire out and fell to her knees, coughing up blood and trembling.

Lilith's psychic hold kept the door locked, so Valerie kicked the glass until it shattered, allowing her to squeeze through and make her escape. She ran and kept running all the way to her apartment where she collapsed on the floor, completely out of breath and terrified. She took her phone from her pocket and texted Wyatt, not wanting to get a lecture about not calling on Gabriel sooner.

Lilith's at the abortion clinic on Broadway. I'm pretty sure I hurt her real bad with my fire-knife.

After a few seconds, she got a reply. *Gabriel and Lucifer are literally cheering.*

Are you sure she's still there? she heard Gabriel ask.

Bitch, I don't know, she replied. *I took off. I'm not trying to die today.*

Chapter 20

The three siblings rushed to the clinic only to find it swarming with police and EMTs. Lilith was long gone, but they got a glimpse inside at the carnage she'd left behind. The scene was grim as body after body was loaded into the coroner's van.

"She knows we're here," Gabriel told her brothers. "If we don't find her before she heals, we're fucked."

"I'd like to say she can't have gotten far with her injuries," Lucifer said. "But, I don't feel her *anywhere.*"

"She's hiding out *somewhere,*" Gabriel said. "B, why don't you check out the theater. It's a long shot, but anything's possible. Lu--" she turned to look at Lucifer, but he was gone. "Fucking shit."

Wyatt entered the old theater, carefully making his way through every room and corridor, being as quiet as he could be. After about an hour of investigating, he was sure the place, smelling of char and decay, was empty. As an ex-firefighter, he recognized the lingering smell of burned flesh and knew something terrible had recently happened there. The main theater room was covered in soot, a lot of the wood having been burned away. Broken glass littered the floor, still wet from the fire department's efforts. Wyatt wondered what had gone on. Did Lilith kill her own minions? To hear Lucifer and Gabriel tell it, she was capable of anything. Did they set each other on fire? Was it an accident? Were demons even the ones that died here? No other clues remained, save a fast-food cup lying on the stage. He looked around one more time, his curiosity piqued, as he opened the door to leave.

"I'm sorry," Gabriel said, walking into her sister's apartment.

"Girl, for what?" Valerie asked. "I understand. After seeing that bitch in action, I get why you're all about the mission at hand."

"I shouldn't have yelled at you," Gabriel admitted. "Lucifer, sure, but you didn't deserve that. I should have been kinder, considering."

"Well, probably, but that's not really who you are, is it?"

"No, I guess not."

The two sat on the couch, Gabriel knowing what her sister was wondering about. "It was me."

Valerie stared at her, eyes wide. "What the--"

"I know," she said. "I know. If I had waited, brought Lucifer, maybe we could have saved those people. *Maybe*. But I was not in a good headspace."

"You crazy bitch," Valerie muttered. "You *killed* those people."

"Yeah," she said pensively. "But, when Tae died, Uri, I *never* felt like that before. I've never been upset like that."

"You've never been upset before?" Valerie condescended.

"I've never been *sad* before. Not really."

"Now I know you're lying. Your parents died when you were *fifteen*."

"I meant what I said," Gabriel insisted. The two sat quietly for a moment before Gabriel spoke again. "I didn't tell you everything about Tae's death."

"I know," she said, visibly miffed.

"When I said I felt him leave, that's not the whole story. I didn't just feel Raphael's absence. I felt *Tae die*. I *felt* him being burned alive. I *felt* his pain and his fear. I *felt* him suffocate. I heard him *begging me* to save him. And, I couldn't. I *couldn't*. So, I went looking for Lilith because I wanted to kill her with my bare hands. I wanted to wrap my fingers around her throat and watch the life drain from her eyes and I wanted to see her true form so I could burn it until there was nothing left. And, when those demons wouldn't tell me where she was, I lost it. I burned them all. I stayed in that room, choking on smoke until I was *sure* they were all back in cages and the worst part of it is that I don't feel bad about it *at all*. If I had to do it over, I'm not sure I wouldn't do the exact same thing because at least those things are off the streets and back where they belong." Tears filled Valerie's eyes, Gabriel putting a comforting hand on her knee. "I know that I don't usually let my emotions get the best of me," she said. "I don't typically *have* many emotions if I'm being honest. *Gabriel* is always reasonable. Always in control and level-headed. Doesn't get attached. But, *Taran Murphy* loves her family. You, Barachiel, Raphael, even Lucifer. The mission takes precedence because it *has to*, but you guys, you're *everything* to me."

Valerie wiped away her tears, considering everything she'd just heard. She thought for a while then sighed. "That's really deep and I feel like you need a hug," she told Gabriel. "But, *Taran Murphy* needs to get her shit together because *Valerie Moore* isn't gonna hang out if you're out there slaughtering people."

"I'll try to control myself."

"Try hard, bitch. I got enough stress without worrying about you, too." Valerie said, hugging her sister. She would forgive her for now, understanding her mindset at the time, she herself having gone a little homicidal on Lilith not an hour before. But, she'd be keeping a close eye.

Wyatt gathered the energy from the air around him to form balls of lightning, throwing them, one after another at the targets he'd set up on the roof a few months before. He hit one bullseye and then another, over and over, growing more confident in his ability to fight Lilith with every shot. He turned his eyes to the clouds, using his anger and grief to summon a thunderbolt and bring it down hard into the rubber mark. As it struck the target, Gabriel and Valerie were thrown back, having just walked onto the roof to find him.

"Oh, my God! Are you okay?!" Wyatt called. "I didn't see you."

"Show off," Gabriel joked as she helped her sister up.

"Are you all right?" he asked, hurrying to Valerie's side.

"Yeah, I'm good," she told him. "So, you and the vampire a thing now?"

"Come on! Why is everyone so concerned about who I'm sleeping with? I don't ask about *your* private life."

"If I had one, I'd share that shit voluntarily," Valerie scoffed. "I'd be so happy, I wouldn't be able to keep it to myself. Listen, I'm no expert, but according to every sitcom I've ever seen, talking about who we're fuckin' is just something family does."

Wyatt sighed. "No judgement?" he asked. Both women nodded. "It's like I can't control it," he admitted. "Like a fog comes over me and I *have* to--"

"That's vampire shit," Gabriel explained. "She, more than any of them, has like, a pheromone thing happening that makes her irresistible to men. The closer she gets to you, the stronger it is."

"Succubus," Wyatt said, remembering that Allydia had said she'd been called that in the past.

"Yeah," Gabriel confirmed.

"So, I'm getting roofied?"

"No, I mean, you don't lose free will," Gabriel said. "You're not getting knocked out, just a little impaired. It's kind of like she slips you ecstasy. You know what you're doing and you could stop if you wanted to, but you *really* won't want to."

"That's fucked up."

"Vampires, man," she shrugged.

"Did you find Lucifer?" he asked.

"No," Gabriel answered, obviously annoyed. "He went looking for Lilith. He hasn't found her, so now he's blowing off a little steam."

Chapter 21

"What can I get you?" the bartender asked sweetly as Lucifer sat down at the half-empty bar.

"A bottle of your strongest beer, and keep them coming."

"The one with the highest ABV that I've got is fifty dollars a bottle. You still want it?"

Lucifer pulled the credit card Gabriel had given him from his pocket and put it on the shiny marble counter. "Do your worst," he told her, smiling charmingly. She smiled back as she retrieved the bottle from under the bar and opened it for him, pouring him a glass.

"Thank you, love," he said, taking a sip.

"London accent?" she inquired.

"It would seem so."

"So, how long are you in town?"

"Hopefully not that much longer," he told her. "I have a little business to take care of before I return home, although I admit, I'm not exactly looking forward to the trip."

"Afraid of flying?"

"No, it's just that the place I call 'home' is," he thought for a moment. "Lonely. Dismal. *Ghastly*."

"Really? I've always wanted to visit the UK. So much history. Big Ben, the Tower of London, the Globe Theater. Seems romantic."

"It *can* be."

"How long have you been away?"

"From London?" Lucifer asked, trying to recall the year. "It was fifteen eighty-two, I believe."

"That long?" the girl chuckled.

"It's been quite some time."

She giggled, leaning forward, allowing him to see nearly halfway down her shirt. Lucifer noticed her attempts to flirt with him and he encouraged them. He continued to smile and held eye contact and she pushed her long, wavy, dark hair behind her ear. She put her elbow on the bar and rested her tawny cheek on her hand. Her big brown eyes and full coral lips had certainly gotten Lucifer's attention. He shouldn't let himself be distracted by this beauty. He needed to find his sister while she was still weakened, but this woman's cleavage seemed to be beckoning him and the truth was, one of the only good things about being trapped in a human body was the chance to indulge in the pleasures of the flesh.

"I'm Mariana," she told him.

"That's lovely. You can call me 'Lou'. Would you like to hear a story, Mariana?" he asked.

"Sure," she said emphatically.

"As I'm sure you're aware, this bar has stood since eighteen ninety-two and has changed very little over the years. However, in nineteen twenty, the federal government passed the Volstead Act, outlawing the sale or manufacture of alcoholic beverages, except for religious purposes. Of course, the law was never much enforced in New York, but when it was first enacted, bar owners were terrified of being put out of business, so they found creative ways of keeping their doors open. Instead of selling drinks, one might receive a free beer with the purchase of a bowl of peanuts that just happened to cost the same price as a beer had before Prohibition. Others ignored the law outright for fear of rioting. Most required a code word either for entry or to buy the forbidden products. As it became harder to acquire the alcohol needed to satiate the masses, bar owners resorted to bootleggers to meet demand, giving rise to organized crime. One night, one such bootlegger had become dissatisfied with the terms of the agreement he'd made with the owner of this particular establishment. He refused to deliver the goods that had already been paid for. Patrons lashed out, breaking glasses and screaming obscenities. Until a man, we'll call him 'Lewis', explained to the crowd that it was the seller, not the proprietor, that was to blame for the shortage. He then led the mob to the home of the bootlegger where they proceeded to *persuade him* to reconsider. By night's end, the bar was stocked once more and customers developed a loyalty to the place, feeling a sense of ownership for helping in keeping it afloat."

"What happened to the bootlegger?" she asked.

"He was fine after a short stint in the hospital. I'm sure he got what was coming to him, though."

"Miss!" an older man called from the end of the bar.

"Don't you move," she said as she walked off to attend to her customer.

"Wouldn't dream of it," Lucifer said, taking another sip of beer. He glanced around the room, impressed with how well it had been maintained. For a moment, he felt as if he were back in that time, rallying drunkards instead of on the hunt for his malevolent sister.

As his new conquest tended to other patrons, Lucifer thought about the last time he had visited Earth. Elvis was on the radio and there was a hydrogen bomb panic, giving rise to a bomb shelter industry whose underground bunkers would have been all but useless had an attack actually happened. It was in one such bunker that he had tracked the demon he'd been searching for. It had taken over the body of a little girl, about four years old, a crime Lucifer would not see go unpunished.

"Please!" the demon had squealed when he'd been found, cowering in the corner of the shelter. "Let me be!"

"You know that isn't possible," Lucifer had told him.

"I'll kill the girl!" he'd hissed, holding a fork to the child's throat. Lucifer rushed over, grasping the fork and flinging it to the floor. He placed his hand on the girl's chest, making quick work of the exorcism, enraged at the gall of the demon. To possess any human was forbidden, but to possess a child was superior in its repugnance. Once back in Hell, he'd be sure to reprimand the monster considerably.

The demon had taken its leave, Lucifer left holding the little girl as she struggled quietly to breathe. She was in bad shape, unable even to open her eyes, and wouldn't make it, even if he could get her to a hospital. He wasn't very practiced in healing and wasn't sure he could save her, but he knew his Father would be angered at the loss of this child to such circumstances as these, so he gave it a shot.

He placed his hands on the girl, one on her head and the other on her chest, and concentrated. Slowly, her skin began to glow and the damage the possession had done started to diminish. She opened her eyes with a start, jumping up and backing away.

"You're all right, now," he'd told her, feeling a little disoriented. Healing another while maintaining his own host body's integrity had taken a lot out of him. The girl looked at him, remembering everything that had happened to her over the last few days. She walked back to where Lucifer still knelt on the cement floor, threw her arms around his neck, and hugged him tightly.

"Thank you," she said quietly.

Lucifer gently hugged her back, surprised at how touched he felt by the girl's gesture. "You're very welcome," he'd told her.

She ran off, up the stairs, and out into the yard of the small Midwestern home. "Mommy, mommy, mommy!" she'd yelled. A woman stepped out onto the porch and fell to her knees at the sight of her daughter who, after days of looking progressively sicker with no diagnosis from the doctor, seemed to be her usual, healthy, happy self. The girl leaped into her mother's arms and the two held each other for several seconds. Tears of joy streamed down the woman's face as she looked up and saw Lucifer exiting the bomb shelter. He'd waved as he walked away, wanting to take the body he was in as far away from the family as possible before leaving it. No reason to traumatize them further.

As he sat at the bar, he wondered what had become of that little girl. Then, he remembered he had access to all the known knowledge of the world on the phone Gabriel had given him. He took it from his pocket and tapped on the button that brought up the internet. He typed in the girl's name and the state where he'd left her. Three people came up in the results, but only one was the right age. He clicked her profile and was pleased to find she was still living, a grandmother of four, and a retired social worker.

"Friend of yours?" Mariana asked, pouring him another beer as she'd noticed his glass looking dangerously close to being empty.

"You might say that," he said, putting the phone away.

"I'm jealous," she quipped. "So, what's your business? Must be important for you to come all this way."

"It is. I'm a headhunter of sorts. I've been tasked with finding a particular woman with a specific skill set. My boss insisted a long time ago that she be brought into the company, lest she take her abilities elsewhere."

"I see. And, from the look on your face when you talk about her, she's giving you a hard time?"

"You have no idea."

Just then, a group of men burst through the doors, laughing and talking very loudly. They sat at a nearby table and one of them called to Mariana, "Yo, can we get some whisky?"

She sighed softly as she placed four glasses on a tray, filled them, and walked them over. Lucifer watched as two of the men stared as she made her way back behind the bar while the others sucked their drinks down so fast, it was like they were trying to win a race. These were the exact kind of humans Lucifer tried to avoid. Brash, rude, and utterly uncivilized, seemingly missing the use of the higher functioning parts of their brains. The misogyny wafted like the scent of manure from the table, Lucifer able to hear the vulgar comments they whispered about the bartender. He was already feeling frustrated, doing his best to hold back from violence, and these sorry excuses for the masculine gender were testing his resolve by their mere existence.

"Well," Mariana said, continuing their conversation. "I'm sure you'll track her down. You don't strike me as the kind of guy to give up easily."

"Your instincts would be correct. I'm the epitome of conviction when it comes to my work." His eyes twinkled as the two flirted. He found her very attractive, with high cheekbones, rich olive skin, and just a hint of a Latin accent he couldn't quite place. Her beauty plus the beginnings of inebriation were a welcome distraction from his duties, which he knew he needed to get back to, just not quite yet.

"Baby!" one of the men shouted. "We need another round!"

"Be right back," she told Lucifer seductively as she got the order together and rushed it to the table. As she placed the glasses in front of the men, one of them brushed her leg. She pulled back quickly and gave him a look of warning.

"You got great tits," he said.

"This isn't that kind of place, guys," she told them.

"What kind of place?" one of the other men asked.

"Enjoy your drinks," she said, turning to walk away.

"Hey!" the first man shouted, grabbing her arm. "When a man pays you a compliment, you say 'thank you'." He pulled her closer, trying to sit her on his lap. She fought her way free only for him to grasp her arm again.

"Excuse me, love," Lucifer said, stepping between Mariana and the table. "Could you freshen my drink? I'm feeling a bit peckish."

She nodded and hurried back to the bar, relieved to put some distance between her and the men. Once she was safely behind the counter, Lucifer turned his attention to the table.

"Mind your fucking business, fa--" But, before the abuser could finish his sentence, he was met with a swift punch to the face. Lucifer hit him again, this time breaking his cheekbone and knocking him unconscious. The others appeared shocked as Lucifer went calmly back to his seat and took a sip of beer as if nothing had happened. They dragged their friend out of the building, shouting obscenities as they went, Lucifer smirking and trying not to laugh.

"Sorry for the ugliness, pet," he told Mariana. "Those cretins were being disrespectful and, to be honest, in my head, I'd already laid claim to you."

She looked at him hungrily, impressed and turned on by his defense of her. "Follow me," she commanded.

She led him to a storage room, pushing a pallet of boxes in front of the door to act as a makeshift lock. She kissed him hard, reaching under her skirt to slip off her panties. He held her face in his hands as they kissed and she unbuckled his belt and unzipped his pants. He lifted her onto a crate of pickled eggs and pulled his pants down, letting them fall to his ankles. She pulled him closer and ran her fingers over his manhood, subtly checking it for anything that felt like it could be an STD. When she found nothing out of the ordinary, she spread her legs wide, inviting him in. He accepted her proposal, sliding himself inside her and beginning the act he'd been denied the last sixty years.

"I only have a few minutes," she breathed, grabbing his posterior with both hands, urging him to go faster. "No one's watching the bar."

He touched her cheek again, looking into her eyes with determination and longing. "Your exquisite loveliness has captivated and beguiled me," he told her. "No offense to your work or this establishment, but they'll both have to wait. I plan on relishing you."

He kissed her neck as she moaned with pleasure, her eyes rolling back. She wrapped her legs around him and ran her fingers through his short, wavy hair. In her rapture, she decided getting fired would be well worth this highly satisfying experience.

Lucifer left the bar with Mariana's phone number written on a napkin securely in his pocket. He didn't know if he'd ever see her again, but it was nice to know that she would be available should he require her company in the near future. The sun had begun to set and it was quite dim in the alley, but he could very clearly make out the group of men from earlier there waiting for him.

"Isn't this a little cliche', boys?" he sighed as one of them started toward him. The man raised his fist, but Lucifer grasped it with his left hand, crushing several bones, causing him to cry out in pain. This angered his friends, all of them rushing to attack Lucifer at once. They tried and failed to lay hands on him. The four of them were no match for God's most powerful angel.

Lucifer beat them bloody, throwing one into the brick wall of the building next door, bashing the back of his skull in. As they fought, the anger and frustration of not being able to find Lilith bubbled over, the rage overwhelming him and, soon, he had lost all control. He noticed the man that had treated Mariana so inappropriately trying to flee. His fury was too strong and, before he knew it, Lucifer had taken the man by the hair and pulled his head savagely from his body.

As he looked around at the scene he had created, all four men dead, blood and gore everywhere, the madness slowly subsided. He didn't want Mariana finding this mess, becoming traumatized, and blaming him, so he stuffed all of the bodies, and their severed parts, into a nearby dumpster, took a lighter from his pocket, ignited the flame, and threw it in. The flames weren't as high as he would have liked, but with the small amounts of alcohol coating much of the garbage's contents acting as an accelerant, he was confident the fire would do the job. He hurried off, making sure there was no one around who would have seen what happened.

On to the next adventure, he thought.

Chapter 22

He walked for a long time, trying to calm the rage that had taken over, and he was almost feeling better until he heard it. The ravings of a zealot.

He followed the voice until he came upon a man handing out pamphlets and yelling at passersby. His words were the rantings of a fanatic, and most everyone on the busy street ignored him completely.

"Homosexuality is a *sin!*" the man shouted. "These politicians trying to *normalize* behavior that's *clearly* the work of the *Devil* are putting your children at risk of *eternal damnation!* This is the inevitable outcome of *decades* of going against *God*, ignoring the Scripture, and doing whatever feels good! First, it was interracial marriage, which is *clearly forbidden* in Genesis 28:1 and Leviticus 19:19. Then, it was allowing women to work instead of staying home with their babies as *God intended,* Titus 2:5. Then, gay marriage, Leviticus 18 and 20. Now, we have these freaks calling themselves *trans*. These abominations are--"

"Excuse me," Lucifer said, approaching the man, his anger growing. "You do realize that fanatics like you are the reason that people have turned their backs on God in higher numbers than ever before, yes?"

The man was visibly offended. "I'm trying to *save* people from the eternal Hellfire of the--"

"What you're doing," Lucifer interrupted again. "Is confusing your own bigotry with religion. Genesis 28:1 describes a conversation between Jacob and Isaac in which the latter warns the former not to marry a Canaanite because of the politics of the time. It had nothing to do with race and it's absurd to think that The Almighty would be at all interested, much less angered, by people with different skin tones marrying. That you honestly believe that God concerns himself with who you are or are not sleeping with is more tragic than your choice in trousers. Titus was an all right fellow, but a bit of a misogynist and *Leviticus*," he scoffed. "I'll just say that to call it nonsensical rubbish would be a kindness."

"*God said--*"

"You have no idea what God did or didn't say," Lucifer corrected. "I, however, was there for all of it. Let me enlighten you."

As the man opened his mouth to speak, Lucifer snapped his fingers, rendering the man paralyzed and silent. While his eyes frantically looked around for help, his captor continued.

"First," he began. "Race is just a set of genetic markers having to do with where your ancestors evolved. It has no bearing on your worthiness or ability or *anything*, really. Aside from looking ever so slightly different and a few health considerations, you are *all the same*. If you weren't, would you be able to breed? Can a dog and a cat make hybrid offspring? Of course not. But, an Asian and an African can produce beautiful children. More importantly, God doesn't give two shits about what you all look like. Your bodies are nothing but carts to carry your souls around in for a short period of time. Now, you may come from different countries and cultures, but those are human-made variations that, again, God doesn't care about.

As for homosexuality, it's nothing new. God decided when He created you that to prevent overpopulation, a certain percentage of you would be attracted to the same sex, just like most other creatures on Earth. We all thought it was quite genius at the time.

And, as for *allowing* women to work, or do anything else, for that matter, here's a newsflash for the misogynist in you: women are men's *equals*. Do I need to say that again? *Equal*. The reason men sought to oppress the females of your species was that my sister inflicted such unimaginable horrors on the earliest humans that they became paranoid beyond reason. Women decided to stay with their children while the men would go hunting because they feared, rightly so, for their safety. Over time, men's fear of Lilith became fear of women and that fear turned to anger, which led to a feeling of superiority. They turned their wives and daughters into servants and viewed them as a burden. They were considered the property of their closest male relative. In some cultures, they still are. The western world likes to think of itself as more inclusive and feminist than it once was, and for the most part, that's true. But, then, there are vile creatures like you. You, who wish to enslave your women and make second-class citizens out of entire groups of people. And based on what? Skin color? Sexuality? Gender? You're a buffoon. And you have the *gall* to assume you know what God wants? You're *oblivious* to His wishes. Do you know what infuriates my Father more than anything? Do you? Of course, you don't. I'll tell you. Misunderstanding. Specifically, misunderstanding that leads to disrespect, cruelty, or pain. Systemic racism, bigotry, sexism, with xenophobia being the most ridiculous since none of your religions have ever gotten it exactly right." He stepped closer, speaking directly into his ear. "From my perspective, it seems as though some of you just aren't happy unless you can look down on someone else. You're disgusting and barbaric, spewing rubbish and infecting the feeble-minded with your hateful disinformation. It's people like you, vile and contemptible, that keep your boot on the necks of those you call 'different' that are the real monsters of this world."

He glanced down at the man's hand and saw a wedding ring. "Well, that's horrifying," he determined. "I'm going to do the poor woman that chained herself to you a favor." He backed away from the man, far enough that people walking by wouldn't connect them. He held up his right hand and slowly made a fist. As he did so, the man began to quiver, then shake violently as he stood there on the sidewalk, still unable to move from that spot. Blood poured from his mouth, nose, and ears. Pedestrians screamed and several people called nine one one.

Lucifer smirked as he happily watched the man die, his internal organs crushed to the point of near liquefaction. When he was satisfied of the bigot's demise, he released his grip and allowed his body to fall to the cold concrete below.

The pamphlets the man had been holding were now scattered and blowing around on the pavement. Curious, Lucifer picked one up.

Wife talking back? Children sexually confused? Need help? Come learn how you can take back control of your family and put God back in their hearts.

Lucifer took note of the address and checked his phone for the time. "Better hurry," he said to himself. "Wouldn't want to be late."

Lucifer strolled casually into the church, irritated by what he saw there. Signs on the wall that read, *'Take back your God-given rights as the head of your household'* and *'Condemn the wickedness of the homosexual culture'*. The pews were full of middle-aged white men, all eager for the arrival of the dead man, hoping to be taught how to better control their families. Lucifer, instead, stood at the pulpit, being sure to leave the doors open to the street.

"Well, well, well," he addressed the crowd. "There's not a decent person among you, is there?"

The men muttered, confused and angry.

"Don't be so sensitive," Lucifer said. "I'm just acknowledging what you must already know. You're all trash. You've come here searching for a way to gain respect from your wives and children, but the truth is, and you know it to be true, that they don't respect you because you don't *deserve* respect. Let me ask you all a question. Have any of you ever tried just not being a dick? Just to see what it's like?"

"What the hell is this?!" a man yelled from the back. "I didn't come here for a lecture."

"Of course not. I'll get to the point shortly. But, first, I'd like to share a secret with you. Not a *secret*, really, more like a misconception. Hellhounds. Does anyone here know what those are?"

A man in the front row raised his hand.

"Yes," Lucifer called. "The man in the red hat."

"Giant monster dogs from Hell?" he guessed.

"So close, but no," Lucifer corrected. "That's the myth. See, over millennia, things get distorted, exaggerated. Men who shapeshift into wolves become giant wolf-men. Deer with a single horn become unicorns. And, an obedient worker with anger issues becomes the source of all evil. I'll be honest with you, that last one stings. Anyhow, the true story of the Hellhound is that the Devil, as you like to say, can control anything in nature. Plants, the weather, the sea. He can cause earthquakes, tidal waves, and volcanic eruptions. And, he can control and bend to his will all animals, including dogs. Dogs are his favorite because they can be the most precious, sweet-tempered, and loyal creatures on Earth, or the most vicious and deadly, depending on their mood. I can relate to that. So, when the Devil is particularly agitated, he likes to enlist dogs as his personal murder machines."

Another man raised his hand.

"Yes, a question." Lucifer nodded toward him.

"Look, man," he said. "I don't know what kind of preacher you are, but when are we gonna talk about how to get our women in line and turn our queer sons straight again?"

The crowd cheered. Lucifer was incensed and decided to move things along. "A question for the group," he began. "Who do you think God will be more upset with? You ignorant, abhorrent experiments in wickedness, or me, the dutiful, but admittedly quick to bouts of violence son who massacred the lot of you?"

They looked at him and each other, dumbfounded and enraged.

"I suppose we'll find out in a couple hundred years or so," he said, raising his fingers to his lips and whistling loudly. As he placed his hand back down on the lectern, dozens of dogs of various breeds rushed in through the open doors. Some stray, some with their collars and leashes still on, all wild-eyed and bearing their teeth. They growled and barked as the parishioners panicked, trying to run for the doors, but being held back by the ferocious canines.

Lucifer couldn't help but laugh as he watched the beasts attack, tearing flesh from bone, ripping out throats, and biting off noses and fingers. Two of them, attached by a double leash, worked together to pull out and feast on the intestines of a man who was not yet dead. Blood and gore covered every inch of the room, a mess of limbs and unrecognizable body parts littering the floor and seats   like garbage after a concert.

When his appetite for butchery was satiated, Lucifer walked calmly through the carnage, admiring the beauty and strength of the hounds, still chewing hungrily on what was left of the malicious fiends. He whistled again as he left the building, the dogs wandering out behind him, their usual dispositions returning.

The events of the evening, while enjoyable, did little to alleviate Lucifer's frustration. He knew that however he chose to distract himself, he would remain irate until he put his sister back in a cell. On the long walk home, he realized something else. Gabriel was going to be pissed.

Allydia watched from the roof of a building across the street as Wyatt walked from the kitchen to the living room sofa, giving his sisters bottles of water while they discussed strategy. She could hear them talking. They had scoured the city and were running out of ideas as to where Lilith could be hiding. She, herself, had men posted all over town with strict instruction to call her if they see any evidence of her whereabouts. So far, they'd come up empty.

She gazed fondly at Wyatt as he spoke to Gabriel and Uriel, occasionally brushing a rogue strand of hair away from his eye. She was completely captivated. So much so that she didn't bother turning her head when she felt Lucifer walk up behind her.

"It's a little unbecoming, don't you think?" he asked.

"Lucifer," she greeted him, still not facing him as he stood next to her.

"You must explain this to me. What is it about Barachiel that you find so interesting?"

"Nothing," she told him. "It's *Wyatt* that intrigues me. He's fascinating."

"Ah, the human persona my dear brother is currently chained to. Tell me, is it the personal baggage, the emotional instability, or the tendency to cry at the drop of a hat that gets your nether regions tingling?"

"It's his eyes, I think," she said, still watching through the windows. "And his intensity. He's all rage and despair. It's intoxicating."

"Well, that's unhinged."

"I would call it 'passionate'."

"And, I would call it stalking, but potato, potahto. Just don't let Gabriel see you. She's developed somewhat of a maternal instinct when it comes to our younger brother. If she knew you were camped out here, observing him like a zoo animal, she would be less than thrilled."

"I don't answer to your sister," she said firmly.

"Don't you?"

"Speaking of, how is Gabriel going to feel about all the people you killed tonight? I can smell their blood all over you. Lucky for you, I've already eaten."

"Yes," he said. "She'll be less than pleased, I'm sure. But, she can hardly lecture me about morality after what she's done."

"The demons in the theater?"

Lucifer nodded.

"One of my spies told me about that," she said. "I have to say, I was impressed."

"To be honest, so was I. I didn't think this version of my sister had it in her. Human emotions and the like. Well, I should go face the music, I suppose."

"Have fun getting your ass kicked," Allydia called as he scurried down the side of the building.

"I always do," he joked back.

"I remember."

Gabriel met Lucifer at the door. She waited for him to lock it back then grabbed him by the collar and dragged him down the hall to his bedroom.

"What was that about?" Wyatt asked.

"Looks like boss lady's about to whoop some ass," Valerie answered.

Gabriel closed the door behind them and telekinetically threw him across the room, slamming him hard against the wall above his bed.

"The fuck?!" she demanded.

"Come now," he said. "They had it coming."

"I'm not saying I don't understand the impulse, but that is *not* appropriate behavior," she spat. "You can't just go around killing every asshole that deserves a beatdown."

"Why ever not?"

"Because there'd be no people left," she explained. "You got pissed off at the awful things those pricks were saying. Imagine hearing the depraved shit everyone's thinking all the time. If I killed every dumpster-fire human that I deemed unfit to live, the population would plummet by like,--"

"Fifty?" he poked.

She sighed. "I was gonna say 'half', but I take your point. I'm not perfect, either. But--"

"They were brutish degenerates that were abusing their families," he interrupted. "The way I see it, I did the world a favor by removing their wretched chauvinism from the Earth, and in spectacular fashion, if I do say so myself."

"Are you just *too* fucked up?" she wondered. "Did I make a mistake? Should I have left you in a coma? Should I put you back in one?"

"Now, now, don't be cross," he urged. "We haven't much time before Lilith's healed. We should be searching."

"*We've been searching*. While you were off on a murder spree, we've been scouring the city. But, she's still out there, so fine. But, I swear to God, Lucifer, if you pull another stunt like that--"

"You'll what?" he asked, willing himself free and setting his feet on the bed. He stepped down to the floor and walked toward her. "Honestly. You know that I'm the only hope you have of caging our venomous sister and you're keenly aware that if you attempt to go up against her without me, you'll get yourself, not to mention our weaker siblings, killed or worse. She's stronger than you. Stronger than *all of you together*. You *need* me."

"Just because you're *right* doesn't mean you're not a *severe* pain in my ass."

He smirked. "I would apologize for my behavior if I were at all remorseful," he told her.

"As long as you understand why I'm pissed."

"I understand, but it's not as if you didn't know who I was. Now, why don't we move past tonight and focus on the job at hand? We have a monster to capture," he said, walking by her toward the door.

"Lucifer," she said, turning to look at him as he opened the door. He turned to face her again.

"Yes, Gabriel?"

She approached him and, without a word, punched him in the face, breaking his nose and knocking him to the floor. She stepped over him to leave the room as he healed himself.

"I deserved that," he muttered to himself.

"And I already know about crazy-eyes across the street," she called back to him as she walked down the hall.

Chapter 23

Allydia entered her penthouse and was stunned at what she found. Tobin, her Governor of New York, was lying dead in a pool of blood on her foyer floor, his intestines pulled out and strewn around him. She slowly crept down the hall, passing his heart mounted to the wall on a hook that had previously held a mirror, now broken, and his liver and kidneys on the floor among the shards of glass. As she walked into the living room, she saw his lungs lying haphazardly on the coffee table.

"He was one of my favorites," she said when she spotted Lilith clutching her stomach on her chaise. She looked pale and smelled of blood and burned flesh and Allydia wondered what weapon could have rendered her so weak and how she could get her hands on it.

"You shouldn't have had him spying on me, then, daughter," Lilith reprimanded.

"I had to be sure it was you," Allydia explained. "It's been a very long time."

"What is it they say now?" Lilith asked. "Bullshit? Yeah, I'm calling bullshit. And, since when do you lie?"

"Step-Mother, you don't understand,"

"I think I do. You're angry with me because you know what I did in Eridu. That's valid. Had you come to me with your grievances, we could have hashed it out. I may have even apologized. Probably not, but it might have been a possibility. But, you sought out the *angels* for help in getting your revenge, and I can't abide that."

She flicked her wrist, causing a large shard of broken mirror to fly up and plunge into Allydia's back. She gasped, then cried out in pain, reaching behind her to pull it out.

"Don't worry," Lilith told her. "I won't kill you. As disappointed as I am in you and your lack of decision-making skills, I'm hopeful that we can rebuild our relationship. We used to be such a good team, you and I. Do you remember? I miss those days. And the nights! The men and the blood. The *sex*. We can have it all again. Once I'm rid of the angel menace, you'll be by my side, aiding me in reshaping this hopeless planet into the kind of world we deserve. A place where we're worshiped and revered, as I once was before my Father so brutally thrust me into the darkness."

She waved her hand, bending Allydia's spine backward until it snapped. She screamed, falling on the floor in a heap. "Relax," she condescended. "You'll heal in a few minutes. I just want you to *really get* how angry you've made me."

As she lay there, Allydia got a glimpse at her step-mother's abdomen. She had a wound that looked charred at the center with dark lines spreading out from it and blood still slowly trickling out.

"What's wrong with you?" she asked, hoping that distracting her with a new conversation would end the torture.

Lilith looked down at herself and sighed. "This?" she asked, pointing to her stomach. "One of your new friends stuck me with Holy Fire." She waved her hand again, bringing a bookcase crashing down onto the vampire. "I should be fully healed in a few hours. If any of them still live by that time, I'll be able to handle them easily. But, I don't expect to have to."

"I won't kill them," Allydia asserted from under the mess.

"Of course not!" Lilith laughed. "You don't have that kind of power!"

Allydia crawled out from the rubble. "What did you do?"

"Well, they didn't kill *all* of my warriors," she explained. "I know you've been infatuated with one of the angels and I know where they are, thanks to your preoccupation with him."

"Lilith," Allydia warned. "You *can't.*"

"I *can't*? You are familiar with me, yes? I can do just about *anything* and I *do not* take orders from *you*. Besides, the demons should be there already, so learn to live with it."

Allydia tried to run for the door, but Lilith threw her to the ground and pulled her back into the living room, never getting up from her seat.

"Can you explain this to me?" she asked. "How is this man your type? Assuming he's roughly the same age as the human Uriel's in, he can't be more than what? Thirty-five? As I recall, older men suited you better. Or, is it that he's *really* several millennia old? Is that what does it for you? That he's ancient?"

The vampire's anger grew, the rage overpowering her common sense. She rushed toward Lilith who smacked her back with her mind like it was nothing.

"An *angel*," Lilith winced. "I thought you had better taste. No matter. He and the others will be gone soon enough and you'll realize that working *with* me instead of against is the right thing to do. We'll have these humans on their knees in a matter of weeks, especially now that you have an entire army of vampires at your command."

"I won't help you," Allydia declared, fighting to stand up again.

"Of course you will," Lilith scoffed. "What is the alternative?"

"I would rather *die* than be your bitch."

"Don't be ridiculous. We'll be partners. Well, seventy/thirty."

"I may not be able to kill you," Allydia said. "But, I will do my damnedest to *fuck you up*."

She lunged for Lilith again, who let out a loud sigh of derision. "Just take your punishment like an adult," she said, flicking her wrist to send Allydia flying through the room and out the window, smashing the glass with her head. She fell, hitting the pavement twelve stories below.

A woman screamed and Allydia could fuzzily see people around her as she struggled to get herself up. As she stood, she was met with a chorus of 'What the hell?'s and 'Holy shit!'s.

"Are you okay?!" someone yelled.

"I'm fine," she told the stranger, her sight restored.

She took her phone from her pocket, but it was crushed. She limped off, hobbling as quickly as she could, hoping she'd be able to warn Wyatt before it was too late.

"We're out of time. We need to get this bitch while she's weak or she'll take off to who knows where and we might never find her," Gabriel told her siblings. The four of them were gathered around the kitchen island, looking over a map of the city. Nervous energy filled the room as everyone was sure *this* would be the night.

"We know she was here," Gabriel said, pointing to the spot on the map where the clinic was located. "We've searched all over Manhattan. She's either left the island, or she's hiding somewhere we wouldn't think to look. At this point, thanks to someone's little adventure," she shot Lucifer an annoyed glance. He smirked. "She could be almost anywhere. I'm guessing she has about three hours before she's one hundred percent, so we need to figure this out and move our asses or we might lose our chance."

"Perhaps, Barachiel could entice his girlfriend to be more helpful in aiding in our efforts," Lucifer mused. "After all, she would most likely do anything he asked her to."

"Asshole," Wyatt muttered.

"That's not a bad idea," Gabriel said. "Dia was supposed to be our Trojan horse, but she's been completely useless so far. Maybe you could give her a call? See if she's been in contact?"

"Or, *you* could call her," Valerie chimed in. "You're the one that brought her into this, to begin with."

"Sure," Gabriel said. "But she's not in love with *me*."

"I don't think 'love' is the right word," Wyatt said.

"Okay," she clarified. "Psychotically obsessed with, then. Either way, you should call her. If she knows something, she's more likely to tell you than anyone. Have you ever read a book or seen a movie where the monster kills everyone and thinks people are garbage, but it has like, a pet? *You're* the pet."

Lucifer snickered.

"That's really condescending," Wyatt told her.

"I'm just being honest with you," Gabriel said. "You're like the bunny that got petted too much so now you have a bald spot. Or the cat that got hugged too hard and your ribs got broken."

Lucifer laughed harder, wiping a tear from his eye.

"Basically," Gabriel continued. "I'm saying the bitch be cray, but you can use that lunacy to maybe help us out."

"Fine," Wyatt agreed. "You'll have to give me her number."

"You don't have her number?" Valerie judged. "Aren't you fuckin' her?"

"Are you giving me shit, too?" he asked.

She threw her hands up and looked away.

He handed Gabriel his phone. She put the number in and handed it back. He put it to his ear, then ended the call and put it back in his pocket.

"Straight to voicemail," he told them.

"She doesn't recognize the number," Valerie assumed.

"That's not the problem," Gabriel said, her eyes darting to the door. "Get ready," she warned.

"Get ready for what?" Valerie asked.

Lucifer felt them now, too. "Demons," he answered, turning to face the door and bracing himself.

Just then, the door flew open, having been kicked in by one of the twelve men that came rushing through, all of them looking pale and sickly.

"Baneful scum," Lucifer vexed. The four stood as the demons rapidly advanced.

Valerie quickly grabbed a butcher's knife from the block on the counter and it instantly burst into flame. She stepped back, hoping to avoid the majority of the fighting while Gabriel began tossing the hellions around the apartment like rag dolls. Wyatt threw lightning at them as they approached, knocking them back hard as Lucifer started to exorcise them one by one.

"I just had this place redone!" Gabriel snapped, sending a demon flying into a wall.

As the others fought, Valerie was surrounded by three lumbering demons. They cackled madly as they closed in, taking twisted pleasure in the terror on her face. She made a futile attempt to stab one of them, but he knocked the blade from her hand, the fire extinguishing upon hitting the wood floor.

"Lilith is most angry with you," the demon hissed.

"Why isn't she here then?" Valerie lashed out. "Cuz she's a scared little bitch, that's why."

The demon growled as he threw his first punch, hitting her in the jaw and knocking her to the floor. The three cheered and laughed as they beat her savagely, punching her face and kicking her in the ribs, back, and head. Once she was motionless, the leader put his hand up for the others to stop and picked up the knife. He used it to brush the hair off her face so he could look into her now glazed-over eyes.

"You're lucky my orders are only to kill you," he wheezed, grasping her by the hair, pulling her head back, and slitting her throat. Blood poured and spurted from the gash as the life drained from Valerie's face. She fell limp to the floor while the three demons howled.

"Valerie!" Gabriel screamed, throwing demons out of her way as she raced to her sister's side. She dropped to her knees, immediately covering the wound on Valerie's neck with one hand and placing the other over her heart. Her hands glowed, white light seeping from the corners of the dead woman's mouth. "Wake up!" Gabriel cried. "I mean it, get your ass up!"

Gradually, the wound healed, and Valerie shot up, gasping for air. She tried to choke out a warning to Gabriel of the demon that was coming up behind her. Just as he raised the knife to stab Gabriel in the back, Wyatt launched a ball of lightning at him, striking him down and rendering him unconscious. Saving his sister, though, meant that Wyatt didn't notice the demon behind *him*, and now, suddenly, there was a cord wrapped around his neck and he was choking.

Before Gabriel could save her brother, another demon grabbed her by the hair and dragged her to the sofa where he began punching her in the face. Valerie hurried to her aid, picking up the knife as she went, leaving Wyatt to handle his attacker on his own. He grabbed the demon's wrists and used all the energy he could to electrocute him, but the supernatural brute was relentless.

Wyatt couldn't breathe, his face turning from red to deep purple as he struggled. The room grew dim and his vision became blurry. As he felt himself beginning to lose consciousness, he heard what sounded like footsteps speeding toward him. Suddenly, he was released, falling on his hands and knees, panting, his chest heaving as he labored to draw breath. He raised up and looked behind him, his vision clearing. He saw Allydia on the back of the demon, viciously tearing his neck apart with her sharp teeth, spewing blood, and flinging tissue everywhere.

Lucifer came to the aid of his sisters, sending the demon they were fighting back to his cage.

When Wyatt's assailant was dead, and the last demon was exorcised, the room went quiet. The human hosts that remained alive were catatonic, having been occupied for so long that their brains were all but destroyed. Gabriel assessed the damage done to her apartment while Valerie sat on a stool at the island, trembling, in near disbelief that she was still alive.

Lucifer paced angrily and Allydia threw up in the sink.

"You all right?" Wyatt asked her.

"Demon blood is highly acidic to things like me," she explained, turning on the faucet and rinsing her mouth out. "I'll be fine."

"You knew about this!" Lucifer accused, grasping Allydia's throat and lifting her off the ground. "I should kill you right now for your treachery."

"Hey!" Wyatt yelled, pushing his brother so hard, he stumbled and dropped the vampire.

"Are you seriously going to defend this creature after what she's done?!" Lucifer barked.

"She wasn't in on it, calm down," Gabriel told him.

"Really?" he asked, not convinced. "How, then, do you explain her sudden appearance only after the object of her affection was put in harm's way?"

Gabriel sighed. "Lilith kicked her ass after figuring out she was helping us, her phone got broken, so she ran over here as fast as she could to warn us," she made clear. "Well, warn *him*, but us by proximity."

"All right, fine," Lucifer conceded, looking Allydia in the eyes. "But, let me be clear. I don't trust you or your motives. Your kind are a plague on this world that, for the life of me, I can't understand why my Father hasn't yet wiped clean from it. If I discover that you assisted my sister in any way, I will rip your head from your body and put your heart in a jar like a trophy on my mantel."

Wyatt stepped between them, staring Lucifer down. "Settle the fuck down," he warned.

Allydia grinned slyly as she stepped away to speak directly to Gabriel. "It will interest you to know that Lilith is at my apartment recovering from whatever one of you did to her. She said it'd be a few hours before she'd be healed, so you can probably still catch her."

"I know," Gabriel told her, having gotten the information as soon as she came in. "I'm just giving these guys a second to get their shit together. Is everybody good?" she asked the others.

"Definitely not good," Valerie admitted.

"Let's go," Gabriel commanded.

As they stepped over bodies to leave, Allydia grabbed Wyatt's arm and he stopped. "Be careful," she warned him. "She's unlike anything you've ever seen. I'm not convinced the four of you can take her."

"I'll be all right," he said, moving her hand gently from his arm. He walked away and when he got to the door, he turned back to look at her for, for all he knew, the last time. "Allydia,"

"Yes," she said, a twinge of excitement flowing through her at the sound of him saying her name.

"Thanks for saving my ass."

"You're more than welcome," she said as he disappeared into the hall. "I'll just clean this up, then!" she called to no one. She looked around the room at the bodies littering the floor, some dead, some barely alive. "What to do with you?"

Chapter 24

The four siblings reached Allydia's apartment, Gabriel blowing the door open with her telekinesis. She and Lucifer began calmly searching through rooms, but Wyatt and Valerie stood motionless in the doorway, horrified by the carnage they saw. Valerie covered her mouth, swallowing a little bit of vomit that had come up in her throat. Wyatt recognized the corpse on the floor from the club and knew Allydia must be upset by the loss. He slowly stepped inside, avoiding slipping on recently removed organs. He made his way to the living room, joining the others. The signs of struggle were evident. The downed bookcase, broken window, and puddles of blood. It was clear to everyone that, had she been human, Allydia would have been killed. It was also clear that she would have been dead, regardless of her species, had Lilith wished it.

"I can feel her," Lucifer said. "She's not far."

"I hear her," Gabriel said, pointing to her temple. "She's on the roof."

They ran up the small flight of stairs that led to Allydia's private rooftop deck and garden. There, they finally found Lilith, sitting on the edge, taking in the view of the city.

"I was sure you'd all be dead by now," she told them, spinning around to face them. "I'd be impressed if I wasn't so irritated." She noticed Valerie, the last to get to the roof, still holding the butcher knife. "Fool me once," she said, shaking her head. She waved her hand in Valerie's direction, throwing her up against the door and wrapping it around her, trapping her in a coffin of metal. She screamed, banging on the door in a desperate attempt to free herself, to no avail.

"Brother," Lilith acknowledged Lucifer, her voice contemptuous.

"Pestiferous obstruction to my well-being," he greeted.

"That's not nice," she replied, holding her hand out. Instantly and with no warning, Lucifer's heart flew from his body and into her awaiting palm. He collapsed in a lifeless heap on the deck.

"Holy shit," Wyatt whispered.

Gabriel was unfazed. "That's a super cute body you've got there," she taunted. "Be a shame if something happened to it." She motioned toward her, engulfing her in flames. She screamed, using unnatural speed to quickly pat out the flames.

"Well, this dress is officially ruined," Lilith said, obviously annoyed. "*And*, you made me drop my new heart. *Gabriel.* You've been a pain in my ass since you were a kindle. Night night." She flicked her wrist, spinning Gabriel's head nearly all the way around, snapping her neck.

"So," she said, turning her attention to Wyatt. "You're the one my daughter's been so taken with." She looked him over, trying to make sense of the vampire's fascination. "I mean, you're *tall*." she conceded. "Are you interesting? Unusually smart or talented? I just don't see it. Not to be insulting, but what *is* it?"

"It's his eyes," Lucifer told her, springing up behind her, grabbing her by the hair and throwing her down onto a snowy patch of soil where, in warmer weather, gardenia's bloomed. "So I'm told." He kicked her hard in the stomach, directly in her mostly-healed wound, reinjuring it enough to put her off her guard for a split second, which was all he needed. He knelt, grabbed his twin's throat with one hand, and plunged the other into her chest. She screeched in agony as he ripped the amulet that kept her planted on the Earth from her body, crushing it to dust.

"How?" Wyatt wondered.

"I'm an archangel, brother," Lucifer explained. "You remove my heart, I'll just grow a new one."

"And I'm pretty quick to snap back myself," Gabriel said, standing up, her spine healed and head back in proper position. She made a fist and stared intently at Lilith, who seemed all but defeated as she coughed up the blood caused by Gabriel crushing her lungs.

Wyatt ran over to Valerie and tried to pry the door open to set her free. Just as he was making a little progress, Gabriel came flying into the wall next to them.

"What the," he started.

"I can't move," she told him.

He turned just as Lilith sent Lucifer flying over the side of the building. Above them, storm clouds gathered in the previously clear sky and the loud crash of thunder filled the air.

"Yo, B!" Gabriel called to him. He met her gaze and she glanced up at the stormy sky and back at him. "You're up." He nodded as Lilith began walking toward him.

"I don't believe we've ever actually met," she said. "You're what, the Protector of Humanity?"

"That's what they tell me."

"Sounds like a burden," she assumed. "No greater burden than what the rest of God's errand boys are tasked with, though, I imagine." She folded her arms and tapped her foot. "What to do, what to do?" she pondered. "Do I kill you so I don't have to look over my shoulder for the next sixty years, or do I spare you, thereby ensuring my daughter's loyalty? Decisions, decisions."

Wyatt quietly gathered all the energy around him, knowing he'd need all he could handle to take her down.

"Answer a question for me," she demanded. "Would it be possible for me to recruit you to my cause? Would you be willing to join me in conquering the human nuisance and ruling over them while waiting on my daughter and I, hand and foot?"

"No," Wyatt answered plainly.

"Pity. 'Protector of Humanity'," she scoffed. "I hate to be the bearer of bad news, but there's nothing you can do to save this world from me."

He gave her a knowing look and a condescending smirk as he raised his hand, rounded up all the energy in the clouds, and brought down a truly massive bolt of lightning. It ripped through the air, brighter than anything human eyes could tolerate and so hot, it melted the snow on the roof before striking Lilith directly on the top of her head, plunging through her, and knocking Wyatt back.

Lilith fell, dazed, her breathing shallow, her eyes glossy. Gabriel was released, her feet barely touching the ground before she used her telekinetic ability to free Valerie.

"Smite!" Gabriel exclaimed giddily.

Wyatt stood and approached Lilith. He raised his hand once more, preparing to strike her again, but before he had the chance, Lucifer appeared behind her, having floated up the side of the building. He knelt behind his twin, placing one hand on her heart and grasping her arm with the other.

"I realize it's been some time since we were last together on Earth," he said to her as the hand on her chest began to glow. "But, did you honestly forget that I can fly?"

Lilith's body shook as if she were having a violent seizure. Blood poured from her nose, mouth, and ears. Even her eyes spilled tears of blood. Lucifer's face remained determined, his eyes watching closely to make sure that after the darkness that was her essence slowly and painfully peeled away from the girl she had been inhabiting, it went back to where it belonged in the deepest and most secure part of Hell.

"See you at home, sister," he whispered as the last bit of her disappeared. "You're welcome," he said, looking up at Wyatt as the skies inexplicably cleared.

"That was you?" Wyatt asked.

"I thought you could use the assist. Now, if you'll excuse me, I need to get this girl to a hospital. Seems the poor dear has suffered a lightning strike." Lucifer grinned, gathered Lilith's ex-host, who remained unconscious, and jumped off the roof, floating down and running with inhuman speed to the nearest emergency room.

"Will she be okay?" Wyatt asked Gabriel.

"Not even close," she told him. "But, she's probably got family looking for her. At least they won't be left wondering if she's dead in a ditch somewhere."

"I guess," he muttered, feeling guilty about hurting the innocent child Lilith had taken hostage.

"Hey," Gabriel consoled. "You did what had to be done to save humankind. And, that poor kid's brain would've been mush no matter how or when Lilith left, just like the demons at home. Speaking of which, we should go figure out what to do with those bodies. I vote dumpster fire. Worked for Lucifer."

"What?" Wyatt asked.

"What?"

"So," Valerie asked. "She's gone? Like, all the way gone? We're done?"

"Totes," Gabriel responded.

"For real?"

"Yeah, bitch is gone."

"Well, shit," Valerie beamed. "I'm gonna go home, smoke a bowl, and relax for the first time in months!" She ran down the stairwell, got in the elevator, and was gone.

Gabriel laughed as she and Wyatt followed down the steps.

"You're not gonna follow Lucifer?" he asked. "You seemed pretty pissed when he went off on his own earlier."

"Nah," Gabriel replied. "I know what he was thinking about and it wasn't wreaking havoc. He met a girl."

"Ah."

"Yeah, a hot bartender chick."

"Nice."

"Like, really hot."

"Okay," Wyatt chuckled.

"I mean, like, *stupid* sexy."

"That's great."

"Slammin' body."

"Do you want to be alone?"

"No, but if I go out later, don't wait up," she instructed.

He laughed as they exited the building and began the walk back to Gabriel's apartment. "I guess I have to go home and pack up my place. I don't want to live there without Annie. It doesn't feel right."

"You know you can stay with me as long as you want," she invited. "Just because we don't have a villain to vanquish doesn't mean we're not still family."

"I appreciate that, but I need to figure my life out," he told her. "I have all this property to deal with, sell off, something. I should check on my dad before I go."

"This all sounds like future problems to me," she declared. "Tomorrow stress. Tonight, I say we watch bad reality TV and drink."

"What is with you and reality shows?" he wondered.

"When people are on TV," she explained. "I don't know what they're thinking. Makes me feel like a normal person. Or, what I think a normal person must feel like. Not knowing what someone's about to say or do. It's exciting. Like a roller coaster."

"Okay," he laughed. "But, can we eat? I'm starving."

"Pizza," she said knowingly.

"Obviously."

Chapter 25

The next day, Wyatt packed his car with the clothes Gabriel had bought him, at her insistence, along with the file of his uncle's properties, and began the sixty-eight-mile drive back to his New Jersey apartment. As he drove, he couldn't get the image of that poor girl out of his mind. Her dead-behind-the-eyes stare as Lucifer stripped Lilith from her haunted him. Who was she? What could she have grown up to be had she not been made Lilith's sacrificial lamb? What could her life have been like? Knowing that it wasn't his fault that she was comatose and that her family was surely devastated by her condition, which he knew to be permanent, didn't help him to feel any less guilty. She was just a kid. It wasn't right. It wasn't fair.

He was almost home, having gotten off I-95 on Garden State Parkway when his phone rang. He took it from his pocket and put it on speaker.

"Hello?"

"Hello," a strange man's voice replied. "May I speak to Wyatt Sinclair?"

"This is Wyatt."

"Mr. Sinclair, this is Dr. Laurence, your wi--"

"You're breaking up," Wyatt told the caller. "Did you say 'my wife'?"

"Yes," the doctor said, speaking louder as if that would somehow give Wyatt better reception. "Annie suf--,"

"She what?" Wyatt asked, his stomach dropping as he tried to focus on the road and make out what the doctor was saying.

Through the garbled, robot-sounding syllables and static, Wyatt could make out a few words: 'Central Medical Center', 'need you', and 'DNR'. His heart sank as the call dropped. 'DNR'. 'Do not resuscitate'. His hands shook and his heart raced. He thought he might hyperventilate as he altered course, speeding to the hospital, ignoring stop signs and traffic lights on the way, almost getting into several accidents, blind to the world around him. Once there, he raced into the building, barely getting the car door closed before he sprinted through the parking lot. He worked to stifle his anxiety as he quickly approached the front desk.

"I'm looking for Annie Sinclair," he told the receptionist.

She typed something in her computer before looking back up at him, concern in her eyes. "Second floor," she said quietly. "Room two-sixteen. But--"

"Thank you," he called as he ran to the elevator, frantically pressing the up button. It opened immediately and he stepped inside. As the doors closed, he took a few deep breaths and tried to calm himself.

When the doors opened again, he searched the room numbers along the hall. 208, 210, 212.

"Can I help you, sir?" a chipper nurse asked.

"I'm just looking for room 216," he told her.

Her face fell. "Are you Mr. Sinclair?" she questioned, her voice shaky.

"Yes."

"Wait right here," she instructed. "I'll get the doctor." She hurried back to the nurse's station and he watched as she made a call, the two other nurses there shooting him sympathetic glances. He knew it was bad. He again checked room numbers. 214 and, finally, 216. As he reached for the handle, a man in a white coat put his hand on his shoulder, gently turning Wyatt to face him.

"Mr. Sinclair, I'm Dr. Laurence," he said, removing his hand from Wyatt's shoulder. He reached out to shake Wyatt's hand, but Wyatt ignored it. "Mr. Sinclair," he continued, ignoring the snub. "I'm very sorry. We did everything we could, but--"

"But, what?" Wyatt asked, his voice raised.

The doctor was visibly uncomfortable but worked to maintain his composure. "I'm sorry," he said again. "I'll give you a few minutes to say goodbye before she's moved."

"Moved where?" Wyatt seethed.

"Mr. Sinclair, your wife made it very clear that in these circumstances, she wanted her viable organs harvested for donation. I know it sounds grim, but it's actually--"

"What circumstances?"

"Well, brain death, sir."

Wyatt was crushed. Tears filled his eyes as he felt the world come crashing down around him. He opened the door to the room and what he saw broke him. She was there, lying in the hospital bed, hooked up to tubes and wires, machines beeping all around her. He felt his legs go weak and he thought he might pass out.

"Take your time," the doctor said, closing the door, leaving Wyatt alone.

His heart pounded in his ears as he drew closer. How could this be happening? She was only thirty-five. He stood over her, touching her soft, blond hair, the sight of her chest rising and falling with such force breaking his heart even more.

He fell to his knees, sobbing, touching her face and burying his own in the pillow next to hers, the smell of her lavender shampoo filling his lungs. He screamed into the pillow, the sorrow overwhelming him. He had never felt such pain, the anguish taking him over completely. As he wailed, the lights in the room began to flicker. One of the bulbs in the overhead light blew out, shaking Wyatt free of his misery. *Of course.* His wife may have been technically dead, but she didn't necessarily have to stay that way.

Gabriel, he thought. *I need you. I need you right now.*

On my way, she responded.

"It's okay, baby," he said to the body, wiping the tears from his face. "We're gonna fix this. You'll be all right."

He sat in a chair next to the bed, holding the corpse's hand for over an hour as he impatiently waited, his leg shaking and his mind racing. Finally, Gabriel showed up, hurrying into the room, ignoring the nurses that tried to stop her.

"Jesus, B. I'm so sorry," she said, putting her hand on his shoulder. "What do you need?"

"I need you to wake her up."

"I don't think--"

"You did it for Lucifer," he reminded. "You did it for Valerie."

"Lucifer wasn't," she paused, trying to be tactful. "*This.* He was just stuck. And, Valerie would've been fine on her own, I just overreacted in the moment. I don't know if I can help here."

"Tae told me you could raise the dead. He *told me.* I've seen you. You can do *anything.* Please," he begged. "*Please.*"

"Okay, I'll try," she agreed, feeling his desperation. She went around to the other side of the bed and placed one hand on the dead woman's head and the other on her heart. Gabriel's hands glowed, but Annie's skin did not. After a few minutes, she gave up.

"I can't," she said softly, coming back around to stand in front of her brother. "Her soul's already gone."

"Then bring it back!" he commanded, jolting up from his seat.

"The Gates are closed. Only human souls can get in. I'm locked out."

"Do *something!*" he shouted, grabbing his sister's shoulders.

"Wyatt!" she said, her use of his human name jarring him into silence. He let her go and steadied his breath. "I'm really sorry, but your girl's gone."

He collapsed back in the chair, tears again streaming down his face. Gabriel knelt in front of him and took his hands in hers.

"Listen," she said. "I know, coming from a normal person, that saying, 'she's in a better place' would be cliche' and not comforting whatsoever. But, you can believe me when I tell you, Heaven is fan-fucking-tastic. I can guarantee you, she's happy as shit up there right now."

He wiped his tears away and tried to get it together. He looked over at his wife and stroked her hair one last time.

"It's not fair," he uttered. "We weren't together, but she was still--"

"No," Gabriel said, standing back up. "It's not fair. It's kind of bullshit. But, at least you don't have to think about her banging some other dude anymore."

"That's *really* not helpful."

A knock came from the door and it opened just enough for a nurse to poke her head in.

"He's all ready to go," she told them before quickly disappearing back into the hall.

Wyatt stood and started toward the door, giving his wife one final glance.

"What the," Gabriel whispered.

"She donated her organs," he told her. "The doctor's been waiting."

"That's not..." Her voice trailed off as they left the room, Wyatt stopping in the hall to look back inside, the space now filled with medical personnel blocking his view of Annie's face. He brushed away one last tear as he resigned himself to the fact that she was really gone.

"Here we are," the nurse said from behind him. He turned to see her standing beside a cart with bags on the bottom and a car seat on top. Strapped into the seat was a tiny baby covered by a striped blanket.

"I'm sorry, what?" he asked, profoundly confused.

"He's had all of his tests, his vitamin K and Hep B shots," she explained. "All the follow-up information is in the folder in the bag along with his diapers, wipes, and a few bottles of the formula he's been on. He's a very good eater, aren't you?" she said playfully, booping the infant's nose. "Oh! Almost forgot. Let me just get the scissors to take off his bracelet and you can be on your way." She walked off, disappearing into one of the rooms.

Wyatt walked closer to the cart, standing over the baby who looked up at him and cooed. He lifted the blanket and examined the bracelet around the child's ankle. It had Annie's name and the day before's date typed on it.

"Angel of Blessings," Gabriel muttered shakily.

"I don't understand," he said quietly. "She was having an affair for *months* before she left? That's--"

"Not what happened," Gabriel told him.

He looked at his sister who, for the first time since he'd met her, looked nervous. More than nervous. She looked downright scared.

"You're telling me he's *mine*?" Wyatt asked, disbelief coloring his voice. "I thought there was no way."

"He has your eyes," she said, her voice trembling.

He looked back down at the newborn and realized she was right. He looked *just* like Wyatt's baby pictures. "How?" he asked, a quiver now in his voice, as well.

Gabriel glanced around quickly to make sure no one was in earshot. "Lightning isn't your only thing," she explained. "Barachiel is also the

Angel of Blessings. Sometimes, when a woman prays for a baby, you make sure she gets one. I didn't think you could do that in this form. It requires a metric fuckton of power. But, she must have prayed to get knocked up while you two were boning and you unknowingly answered that prayer," she told him. "With your dick."

The nurse returned with the scissors and carefully cut the bracelet from the baby's ankle. "There you go, William," she said. "That's got to be more comfortable, huh?"

"Did you say, 'William'?" Wyatt asked.

"Yes," she said happily. "Oh, had you not settled on a name before?" she asked, realizing the situation. "I hope it's all right. She told the doctor his name should be William Ross Sinclair."

"It's fine," he said, his voice weak.

The nurse rubbed his arm in a pitiful attempt at comforting him while still remaining peppy. "Well, he's perfectly healthy," she said. "Congratulations." And with that, she was gone, scurrying into another room with another patient.

The siblings awkwardly made their way to the elevator, Wyatt carrying the baby in the car seat and Gabriel taking the bags.

"She named him William," Wyatt said, still in shock.

"Yeah."

"That's my middle name," he said as they boarded the elevator, the doors closing slowly behind them.

"I know."

"Ross was her dad's name. He died when we were in college. She always said if we ever had a kid, she'd want to name it after him. But, she put *my* name *first*."

"Mm-hmm."

"Don't you get it?" he asked, a small bit of happiness breaking through the waves of despair. "She never had a *boyfriend*. *He* was the other guy! She left me because she was worried I'd hurt him in a schizophrenic fit. She didn't stop loving me," he realized, looking down at his child in amazement. "She just loved him more."

The doors opened and they left the hospital, passing the concerned-looking receptionist as they went. Once at the car, Wyatt struggled with the car seat as Gabriel put the bags in the trunk on top of her brother's suitcases. She saw the file sticking out from underneath everything else and picked it up before closing the trunk and walking around to where Wyatt stood, finally having secured the baby in the back seat.

"I can't see him," she admitted.

"What do you mean?" Wyatt asked. "He's right there."

"I can *see* him, with my eyes. But, I can't *see* him, inside. I can't hear his thoughts or see his memories. I don't know what he's feeling. It's like he's not there."

"What are you talking about?" he questioned, suddenly feeling defensive and intensely protective of his new son. "What are you saying to me right now?"

"You know--"

"What?!"

"Barachiel," she said sternly. "He's Nephilim."

"No," he said firmly, closing the car door and standing between it and his sister. "Gabriel, don't even think it."

"I should kill him," she told him. "Now, before things get ugly."

Wyatt formed a ball of lightning and stared at her fiercely.

"If I was gonna do it, you wouldn't be able to stop me," she said. "But, I'm not going to, *against* my better judgement. But, Lucifer *will*. If he finds out there's a Nephilim on Earth, he *will* take him out."

Wyatt extinguished the lightning but didn't yet relax.

"I won't tell him," she promised. "Or Valerie. But, you have to go." She thrust the file with his uncle's property listings in it into his hand. "Take him somewhere *far*. Way away from people. He's gonna grow stupid fast and when he's done, he'll get his powers. He won't be able to handle them."

"I'll teach him."

"You'll try," she said. "You'll do everything you can to turn him into a decent person, but--"

"He'll be fine," Wyatt insisted.

"He'll be fucked the fuck up," she warned. "He'll get crazier and more violent and, eventually, he'll go completely off the rails."

"I can deal with it."

"If you can't," she urged. "If and when he gets too dangerous and you need help, *you call me*." She pointed to her temple.

He nodded.

She sighed, unsure of her decision. She threw her arms around Wyatt's neck and hugged him tightly, worried about what raising this monstrosity would do to him, but knowing that if she did what her instincts were telling her to, he'd never forgive her.

"I love you, you big, stupid crybaby," she told him.

He chuckled. "Love you, too."

"All right," she said, backing away. "I'll take care of your place, have your stuff shipped to wherever. Now, get out of here before I change my mind."

She didn't have to tell him twice. He hurried around the car to the driver's side door, opened it, and got in. "Thank you!" he called before slamming it shut.

"Don't make me regret it!" she called back as he sped away. "I already do," she said to herself. She sighed again, watching them drive off, her brother having no real idea of what he was getting himself into. She cracked her neck and groaned, "Fuck my life."

Wyatt made his way to I-276 and glanced up in the mirror at his new son who sat calmly in the backseat, the sweetest baby he'd ever seen. "Don't worry, Will," he said. "We're gonna be fine."

He checked the map on his phone to make sure he was going the right way. "Looks like we're moving to Indiana."

Chapter 26

Michelle tossed her diploma and cap on the sofa before collapsing onto it herself. She flopped her feet up on the ottoman and picked up the remote. While her classmates were off at their respective receptions and open houses, gathering gifts and 'congratulations', she was alone, watching TV and trying not to dwell on the fact that she had no family to celebrate her; no one to be proud of her.

The last four months since her uncle died had been tough. She barely made it through school and her social life was basically non-existent. She had isolated herself, for the most part, in the apartment Tae had left her, her only consolation being that, since he'd left her everything in his will, she didn't have to fret about college, work, or money. She was taken care of, and no matter what she decided to do with her life, she'd be okay, financially speaking. Emotionally, however, she was barely holding it together. Everyone she'd ever cared about or counted on was gone. She was sullen and resentful, jealous of the kids in her class that looked so happy after the commencement, posing for pictures and hugging their parents. It had taken everything she had to hold back the tears until she was safely in a cab and on her way home, away from the judgemental eyes of her classmates and the feigned sympathy of the parents and school staff. No one in that place had ever actually cared about her. She was friendly with a few of the kids, but there was no one there she'd really consider a true friend and no boys had ever taken any interest in her. The teachers were fine, but the administration was blatantly racist, whispering slurs when they thought she couldn't hear while parading her around during fundraisers and tours to show how 'diverse' the campus was. When her uncle died, Michelle almost dropped out, partly due to grief, but also out of spite. She knew they'd need her to be present at their mid-year open house and she so badly wanted to show up there with a bullhorn, give a brutal speech about how bigoted the Headmaster and her cronies were, and burn the whole place to the ground. She didn't, of course, because no matter how awful the people in that school were, a diploma from there was a guaranteed ticket to any college she wanted to attend, and more importantly, she knew how important it had been to Tae that she get a good education. So, she sucked it up, did what she had to, and graduated third in her class.

She glanced over at the dining table on the other side of the room, the pile of thick envelopes from all six universities she applied to sitting in the middle of it like a demanding centerpiece, mocking her indecision. She knew she had very little time to choose one, but the thought of going to college in the fall was overwhelming. Just the idea of opening the acceptance letters was stressful to the point of panic, and the longer she procrastinated, the worse her anxiety got. She looked back at the television and decided to put it off for another day. After all, she just graduated from high school. She'd earned a little relaxation time.

There was a knock at the door, which was odd since no one had been to visit in months. She turned off the TV, got up, and opened the door.

"Cute outfit," the woman in the hall said, referencing the gown Michelle had been too lazy to take off.

"Can I help you?" she asked.

"You can let me in," the woman told her. "Your uncle never gave my 'Sixteen Stone' CD back. I let him borrow it like, twenty years ago, thinking it'd open him up to different kinds of music than what he was used to. Classical and opera. I mean, I like a good Renaissance piece as much as the next girl, but come on. *All the time?* Snooze. I let him keep it because he kind of had a thing for the singer, but I mean, who didn't, right? Anyways, if I could get that back, that'd be awesome."

"I'm sorry," Michelle said suspiciously. "Who are you?"

The woman smiled. "Gabriel. Tae told you about me. He wasn't *supposed* to, but what are you gonna do?"

"You're," the girl breathed. "The Messenger of--"

"That's me. Now, can you let me in? We need to talk."

"Of course!" Michelle agreed, stepping out of the way to let the angel through. She stepped inside.

"I'm serious about that CD," Gabriel told her as the door closed behind her.

NEPHILIM

The pain of parting is nothing to the joy of meeting again.
Charles Dickens

Prologue

King Gevar paced the floor, the Mead Hall empty but for him. He grew impatient, his spies having told him of Chief Thryme's plan to invade nearly a month before. He downed a cup of ale, but it did little to calm his nerves.

Light poured into the room as the door swung open, making it difficult to see the man stepping inside. As the king's eyes adjusted, he was relieved to see the blacksmith edging closer, dragging a wagon overflowing with swords.

"You've done it!" he exclaimed. "I didn't believe it possible! How did you manage to create so many Ulfberhts in only a month's time?"

"I don't sleep," the man replied.

The king laughed and poured him a drink. "Come! I can think of no one more deserving of a pint than you."

He took the cup with no intention of imbibing its contents and nodded politely. "Thank you." The king offered him a leather purse heavy with coins, but he refused it. "I require no payment. Only the assurance that you will do everything in your power to keep your people safe."

"But I *must* pay you," Gevar insisted, inspecting the weapons. "These are impeccable. The work you put into them merits reward. If not coin, what would you have as compensation?"

"I need nothing," he claimed, his voice stern. It was then that the king noticed how piercing the man's azure eyes were through wisps of blond hair, striking as they seemed to look right through him. The blacksmith turned to go. "I should be getting home."

"Wait," Gevar commanded. "If you will not take silver, you must at least honor me by attending my daughter's wedding tomorrow. It will be here at sunset. You shall be my guest." The man thought for a moment, tightening the strap around the hammer that hung from his belt before nodding in agreement and taking his leave.

Hodr came upon a buck drinking peacefully from the stream, oblivious to the hunter and his intention. He pulled back on his bow, but before he could release the arrow, the snapping of branches startled him and the deer, which sprinted off, unharmed. Laughter wafted through the air from behind and as he turned, his annoyance turned to joy.

"Nanna," he greeted, a wide smile brightening his face.

"Beloved," she beamed, hurrying toward her betrothed. She flung her arms around his neck and kissed him sweetly.

"What are you doing here? Shouldn't you be preparing?"

"I will," she said. "I just *needed* to see you." She kissed him again, her skin warm with desire as she ran her hands over his chest before untying her cloak.

"What are you doing?" he asked, looking around for intruders.

"Just offering a taste of what's to come," she teased, opening her cloak to reveal the smooth, alabaster form underneath.

"Someone could see us."

"These are your family's private hunting grounds. No one will find us here," she reassured him, pawing at his belt.

"Your father would kill me."

"He wouldn't dare break his only daughter's heart the day before her wedding. Tomorrow, we'll be married, expected to start providing heirs to my father's throne. This is the only chance we have for it to just be about us." She took his hand and placed it on her backside, pressing her body to his. "Be with me."

He relented, grabbing her tightly and kissing her hard. As he struggled to get his trousers down, they were interrupted by an unnatural-sounding growl.

"Who's there?" Hodr called into the forest. Nanna covered herself quickly, her strawberry locks whipping in the cool autumn wind as they both scanned the woods for signs of life. They heard the odd snarling again, but couldn't place where it was coming from. Hodr readied his bow.

"It's only me," a voice called from beyond the trees. Slowly, a figure emerged from the shadows.

"Baldr?" Nanna asked. "I hardly recognize you. What happened to your face?"

He looked pale, gaunt, and sickly, not like the man that disappeared several months before.

"This man," Baldr said, slamming his hand to his chest as he stepped closer. "Has complicated feelings when it comes to you."

"You know this person?" Hodr asked.

"I used to," she admitted. "His uncle is the chief of the village across the lake. My father had arranged a marriage between us to keep the peace, but--"

"She found him to be brutish and lacking in proper hygiene," Baldr huffed, his voice sounding pained and raspy, not at all how Nanna remembered it.

"Why do you refer to yourself in the third person?" Hodr wondered.

"I refer to *this*," Baldr replied, again banging on his chest. "The one you call 'Baldr'."

"You should see a wound-healer," Nanna told him. "You're not making sense."

"Get behind me," Hodr instructed.

"What? Why?"

"Do it, Nanna," he commanded as he lifted his bow. "I do not think this creature is human."

"Guilty," the demon inside Baldr confirmed. "See, I only wanted to rape and pillage, but Baldr here has an intense desire to hurt the woman that broke his heart. He's just in here," he complained, pounding on the side of his head with his fist. "Screaming at me to do my worst. He wants death to come to you slow and bloody and he wants to feel these hands do the work of it. I will get no peace until it's done." He rushed toward the couple and as Nanna scurried behind her fiance, Hodr pulled back on his bow, releasing an arrow directly into the demon's heart. Baldr fell, a strange, black shadow peeling away from him as he hit the ground. The frightened lovers fled into the woods, afraid that whatever had left him would attach itself to one of them next.

That evening, Thryme, along with several of his most trusted soldiers, stormed into King Gevar's Mead Hall where preparations were underway for Nanna's wedding. He carried the body of his slain nephew on his shoulders until he reached the king's table where he slammed it down in grief and rage.

"Where is Hodr?!" he demanded. "Do not hide him from me. I will have vengeance!"

"Is that Baldr?" the king asked. "What's happened?"

"Hodr, the one you allow to defile your daughter, put an arrow through his heart. This will not go unpunished."

"Are you sure it was Ho--"

"Of course I'm sure!" Thryme shouted through his full, auburn beard. "I have spies everywhere. Now, give him to me!"

"I don't know where he is. He will be here tomorrow for the wedding. I'll question him then."

"There will be a wedding here tomorrow, but it will not be his," Thryme asserted. "If you wish to maintain peace between our lands, you have one choice. *I* will marry Nanna. She will give me sons, heirs to unite our people. Should she refuse, this time tomorrow, I will burn your village and every living thing in it to the ground."

King Gevar stood in stunned silence as Thryme lifted the corpse from the table and carried it back outside. His men followed, some glancing back at the king in derision, one even spitting on the floor. Gevar looked up toward his daughter's private room where he could see her peeking her head out, tears streaming down her lightly freckled cheeks.

The day of the wedding came. Guests filled the seats, ale flowed and the air smelled of roasting boar. The blacksmith peered into the hall, taking note of Thryme's men stationed on either end of the king's table. He turned to see Hodr walking confidently to the building.

"Are you suicidal?" the blacksmith asked, standing in the young man's way.

"I am not afraid of Chief Thryme or of his men," Hodr proclaimed. "I am to be married today."

"I see. You do not wish to die, you're simply an imbecile. Apologies." He slammed his large fist down on the top of Hodr's head, knocking him out cold. He then pulled the boy's tunic over his face and carried him over his shoulder into the building and up the stairs to Nanna's room. She was startled as the blacksmith dropped her fiance onto the bed and held his finger to his lips. "Stay here," he told her. "No matter what you hear, do not open this door. Do you understand?" The girl nodded, rushing to close the door behind the man as he left.

Thryme entered the hall, arrogance and body odor following him like sheep. The crowd stilled as they waited, all relieved, if not somewhat saddened to see Nanna descend from the stairs. She was as beautiful as she'd ever been, her soft hair flowing down her back, a silver bridal crown resting on her head. Her cheeks appeared flushed and her small but shapely frame was draped in the finest of fabrics. She approached her would-be husband, staring at him with such intensity that he began to feel uncomfortable.

"Nanna," he said. "You look lovely. I don't remember your eyes being so--" There was a thud between them. The two looked down to see a hammer lying on the floor, just beneath Nanna's dress. Thryme picked it up and handed it to her. "You dropped this," he said, confused. "From your... lap?"

"It was on my belt," she corrected.

"You're not wearing a--"

She brought the hammer back and swung it so hard into Thryme's face that it came out the back of his head. He fell to the floor, blood and brain spilling onto the large wooden planks. The berserkers rushed her and as they pulled their weapons, Nanna's appearance suddenly shifted from that of a young girl on her wedding day to that of the tall, muscular blacksmith. The man fought off three of the soldiers with his hammer, killing them with single blows to the head. As wedding guests fled, he seemed to create bolts of lightning from thin air and wield them as weapons, making light work of slaughtering the rest of Thryme's men.

As the smoke cleared, one man who had remained seated finished the last of his ale and began to clap. "Well done, brother," he said as he stood.

"Lucifer?"

"They call me 'Loki' here. It means 'lock'. I thought it somewhat fitting."

"Why are you here?" the blacksmith asked.

"Why am I ever anywhere? A demon got loose, so I came to fetch it. Turns out, it's been handled for me. Thryme, however, was a mess I should have cleaned up long ago. I appreciate your assistance, though I would have managed. Why are *you* here?"

"I came to protect this village from a maniac and his blind followers. I provided arms to the king in the hopes of avoiding spilling any blood myself, but after thinking on it, I decided it was too risky. Thryme was too dangerous. What did he have to do with you?"

"When his mother was pregnant with him, she became possessed," Lucifer explained. "I removed the demon, but the woman didn't survive. I should have left the child to die, as well. He'd been corrupted, his mind altered. But, I was weak and couldn't bear it. I thought, given time and a proper influence, the boy could overcome his less desirable instincts. So, I tore him from his mother's rotting womb and delivered him to his father. I've wondered for decades if I'd made the right decision. Clearly, I did not."

"I can hardly fault you for saving the life of an infant, Lucifer."

"Perhaps *you* can't, but no doubt our Father's been most disappointed in me."

"I doubt that," the blacksmith said, putting his arm around his brother. "Do you know how many times I've strayed from God's plan because I felt sorry for humans? Thousands. God still loves *me* and I'm not even His favorite. There is nothing you could do that He wouldn't forgive."

"I appreciate you saying that. Thank you, Barachiel."

The brothers left the Hall, closing the doors behind them. They didn't seem to notice King Gevar cowering under a table, not ten feet from where they'd been talking or Nanna and Hodr spying from above. Gevar rose and looked to his daughter, who now stood at the top of the stairs, quivering in fear and disbelief. The king clutched his chest, his hands and voice trembling as he said, his voice barely loud enough for the others to hear, "The man with the hammer...he controls the thunder."

Chapter 1

Lucifer's eyes slowly opened as he took back control of the body he'd abandoned nearly three years earlier. His amazement at the fact of its availability turned to anger when he realized how the feat had been accomplished.

He pulled the oxygen mask from his face and choked, his esophagus burning as he gingerly removed the feeding tube from his throat. The satin sheet beneath him was stained and smelled of old sweat as did his clothes, the same slacks and button-down he'd been wearing when he left. The garishly decorated room felt familiar, though he couldn't quite place it. He felt lightheaded as he sat himself up, noticing his arm connected by needle and tube to two bags, one filled with saline and the other brimming with his own blood. He extracted the needles, his skin repairing the small punctures left behind. He threw back the blanket to reveal another disturbing discovery; he'd been cathed. His lips pursed and a low growl escaped his larynx as he removed the device, the sharp pain enraging him further. His body felt weak as he stood and pulled his pants up, his eyes adjusting to the dim light that peeked through dark curtains. He saw four men lying on cots opposite the ornate poster bed he'd been in. They, too, were on breathing machines, unconscious and joined to IV bags similar to his. He recognized them as host bodies of some of the demons that had attacked him and his siblings in Gabriel's apartment. As he opened the door to the next room, a throne sitting at one end, bottles and paraphernalia littering tables and floor, he realized he knew exactly where he was. He seethed, "Allydia Cain."

"Lilith was a distraction," Lucifer growled, pushing past Valerie, stumbling into her apartment and dropping himself onto her sofa.

"You look like shit," she commented, closing the door. "And smell worse."

"Good to see you, too, sister."

"What are you doing here? Aren't you supposed to be in Hell, torturing people and shit?"

"I don't torture souls," he corrected. "That's a myth. Hell isn't what I think you think it is."

"Whatever. Why do you look like you just got done with six rounds of chemo?"

"It seems the vampire queen was keeping this body as an on-demand food source while I was away. Remind me to wring that foul creature's neck next time I see her."

"Jesus."

"I wish you people wouldn't use that name as a way of conveying astonishment. It's very confusing. As for why I'm here, tell me, have you had any visions lately?"

"Just personal stuff like when I was in high school. Nothing important since you chucked Lilith back in her hole."

"Well, that's disappointing," he complained. "Perhaps you need a jump start."

She backed away. "The fuck you mean?"

"Like a car battery. Just a little boost." He rushed her, grabbing her head and transferring memories to her, hoping they would trigger a related premonition. He knew she'd be cross with him, but he was desperate.

Her eyes grew wide as she was overwhelmed by information, the horrors of Hell flooding her mind, the despair of the damned like a weight on her chest.

"I hope that wasn't too unpleasant," he said, letting go and stepping aside as she staggered toward the couch. "You must understand the urgency." She nearly collapsed, but caught herself, unwilling to sit, instead turning back to her brother, rage twisting her features. She marched toward him, gaining strength with every step. He sighed, resigned to the coming punishment.

She punched him in the nose. "This is why I can't stand you!"

"Apologies," he said, realigning his broken nasal bones as they began to heal and wiping away the blood with the sleeve of his shirt. "But I need to know where to begin my search. That thing you saw is more dangerous than Lilith. He doesn't want to rule over humans; he wants to end them."

"Just close the Gate," she condescended. "Demons get sucked back in. Problem solved."

"Demons, yes. But what I'm hunting is something else entirely. He was an angel of the highest order, tasked with gathering the materials of the Earth that God would use to create the first humans. He was a devoted servant of the Almighty and watched over our Father's new creatures as a sort of guardian. This was, of course, before Barachiel was blinked into existence. He cared for God's people like pets, tending to their needs when they could not. Teaching them how to hunt, showing them which plants were safe for consumption, and providing comfort to them when they were hurt. He was kind to them. One might go as far as to say that he loved them. But, when the first son of man killed his brother, the angel was horrified. He never truly got over it."

"Are you talking about Cain and Abel?" Valerie asked. "That was *real*?"

"Indeed. As the humans multiplied and had their inevitable conflicts and the bodies of the murdered grew to be many, the angel became enraged. He was livid that he'd had a part in constructing such sadistic creatures. He used dark magic to bind himself, permanently, to the Earth and vowed not to rest until every human had been wiped from it. He used an army of locusts to destroy crops, starving a country's residents. When he became impatient, he cursed entire continents with plague. God was furious, so He fashioned Perdition, a literal bottomless pit made using Earth's magnetic field, and tossed the angel in. Later, Hell was created around that pit and I was tasked with ensuring it stay secure."

"So, while you were here, going after Lilith,"

"He got free," Lucifer lamented. "Before he left, however, he opened the cages, riled up the locals. There was a rebellion when my second in command launched a coup. I admit, it took longer to suppress than I'd like."

"Who's the angel?"

"We called him 'The Destroyer'. You may recognize his Hebrew name,"

"Abaddon," Gabriel chimed in, closing the door behind her as she entered.

"Sister," Lucifer greeted, unable to hide his relief. "How did you know I was here?"

"I put a tracker on you. Like the kind vets put in dogs in case they run away. I thought it was prudent after what happened last time you were in town."

"You knew what the vampire had done to me?"

"Duh," she scoffed. "I got the idea from Barachiel's wife. I thought it was pretty genius."

"*Your* idea?!"

"*You're welcome.* I knew when you came back you'd want to see that bartender chick and it would probably be helpful if she recognized you. Plus, I got used to you this way and a makeover would've just been obnoxious."

"This body was *tapped* like a *keg.*"

"You weren't using it," she rebuffed. "And neither was your host. His soul had already left for Heaven, I checked. Dia was just gonna feed on those guys that attacked us and burn their bodies, but after Barachiel took off, she didn't have it in her to hunt anymore, so I set this up. Two birds."

"Why are you helping the vampires?" Valerie wondered. "I mean, I know Allydia helped us out, but they're monsters, right?"

"I've been wondering the same thing," Lucifer said.

"A," Gabriel retorted. "I made a promise to Dia back in the day that I intend on keeping. Two, she's not anywhere close to done helping us and, also, no matter how he *wishes* he felt, Barachiel has a thing for her and he would never forgive me if I let her starve herself to death."

"Not everything is your responsibility, sister."

"The hell it's not."

"I thought we were done with this demon-fighting shit," Valerie huffed.

Gabriel rolled her eyes. "You've had a three-year break. Maybe don't complain so much. Come on, Satan. Let's get you a steak, you're low on iron. Shower first, though, because *fuck*."

"Barachiel's gone?" Lucifer asked, a twinge of disappointment in his voice. "Where's he off to?"

"She won't tell me," Valerie said, folding her arms.

"Oh, a mystery. Consider my interest piqued. What's he doing that's so secretive?"

Gabriel opened the door to leave as she answered, "What he's supposed to."

Chapter 2

Wyatt stared at the ax hanging on the wall of the old barn. It seemed to stare back as if the wood and metal knew its purpose, it too not looking forward to the task at hand. Melancholy set in as he lifted it from its hook and walked back outside. He knew what he had to do, but the closer he got to the house, the more he dreaded it. As he reached his destination, he took a deep breath, raised the ax, and brought it down hard, making sure he'd only have to strike once. The wood split perfectly and he reached for another log, chopping one after another until he had a suitable amount of firewood for the night. It wasn't the physicality of the chore that he minded; it was barely work for him at all. It was just another mundane activity that *had* to be done; something else to remind him of how boring he found living out here in the middle of nothing. The past three years had been an endless, mind-numbing routine of simple but necessary tasks. The monotony of his life had become a weight around his neck, dragging him further into the depths of his depression every day. There was only one thing keeping him going. One thing that made the quiet and the banality worth it. One thing that gave him joy.

"Will," Wyatt called as he entered the farmhouse. He placed a fresh log onto the fire before heading to the kitchen. "Indiana weather," he muttered to himself. The day before, it had been sixty-two degrees. That morning, though, it had dipped back into the thirties. It was early May; his wood chopping days should have been behind him weeks ago.

The oven's timer read two minutes, so he quickly threw the salad together and pulled two sodas from the fridge. "Will, dinner!"

"I'm coming!" the boy answered, bounding down the stairs and making a beeline for the living room window. "One second!" He pulled the curtains back just enough to peek through and watched, captivated, as the mail carrier pulled up next to the box at the end of the driveway, opened the little door, put some letters inside, and closed it back. Every evening at five on the dot, Will observed the fifty-something-year-old man deliver the mail, and every evening it brought him great happiness. He was the only person besides his father that he'd ever seen in real life, aside from his Aunt Gabriel who visited at birthdays and Christmas. Due to his condition, he wasn't allowed to leave the property or have visitors. All of his friendships were online. School, shopping, everything was done via the internet. He understood that his father was only being protective. After all, he was born three and a half years before but by every other measure was a typical sixteen-year-old. People wouldn't understand. They would bully him or worse...fear him. Will knew from watching the news that people become violent and cruel when they're afraid, even when their anxiety is unfounded. It seemed a sad truth of the human condition that people panic at the sight of something they don't fully recognize. His father was right to be worried.

"Lasagna again?" Will complained, brushing by his dad on his way to the table. Wyatt could feel a small static shock between them, but couldn't be sure of who it came from. Since Will had shown no other signs of getting his powers, he chose to ignore it.

"It's one of the few things I know how to make and can keep in the freezer for months, so yeah, lasagna again." They sat down and began to eat, Wyatt glancing at the newspaper. "Coyotes got two more dogs last night," he said after reading the front page. "You remember what to do if you see one and you're outside?"

"Keep eye contact, don't turn my back to it, and don't run."

"Good. Listen, next week I'll be doing some repairs at Pine's. I might be getting home late, so I got you some microwave dinners, just in case."

Will rolled his eyes.

"What?" Wyatt asked.

"Come on, Dad. You hate that place. I mean, I'll never complain about all the free donuts, but really. Why don't you sell it?"

"It's not that bad. I just find it tedious."

"Why do it, then? We don't need the money. We live off the money you got selling all those houses when I was a baby. There's money sitting in accounts we'll probably never need. Why do it to yourself?"

"It's not just about me, Will," Wyatt explained. "The people that work there depend on their jobs. If I sold the donut shop, a new owner would most likely cut hours, cut pay to minimum wage, get rid of their insurance. I couldn't do that to them. That's not how people should be treated. Also, it'll be a job you can do when I'm gone that won't make people too suspicious. No one does a background check on the son of the owner coming to take over the family business."

"You know what you just said, right?"

"What?"

"It's the same as always," Will said. "Everything you do is for someone else. Everything."

"Not *everything*," Wyatt assured him. "I bought that beer in the fridge just for me. Don't you even look at it sideways."

Will laughed. "Okay, Dad."

"How was school today?"

"I'm done," Will said, disappointment tingeing his voice.

"Done?"

"With high school."

"You just started."

"Like, eight months ago, Dad. I was twelve."

"My mistake," Wyatt chuckled. He didn't think he'd ever get used to how fast his son was growing. The school Will attended online was work-at-your-own-pace and his pace was rapid. Gabriel had been right about the speed of his progression and his intellect. Wyatt hoped that was all she was right about. "Well, congratulations. What do you want to do now?"

"I don't know."

"You haven't thought about it?"

"I have, it's just," He put his fork down, his face mournful. "There are some interesting degrees I could get online, but I'd have to take the SATs, so." The sadness in his voice cut Wyatt like a knife. Will was a good kid. In his entire short life, he'd never done anything worthy of punishment. He'd never once given Wyatt a reason to ground him, send him to time out, or even raise his voice. He was sweet and kind and the only thing he'd ever asked for was a faster internet connection. Wyatt couldn't bear breaking his son's heart, especially since he'd shown no signs of being dangerous. He would figure out a way.

"I'll talk to your Aunt Gabriel," Wyatt vowed. "I'm sure she knows someone who can get you some fake transcripts, social sec--"

"Really?!" Will erupted with excitement. He jumped up and hugged his father so tightly, he almost choked. "Thank you so much, Dad!" He sat back down to eat, his face beaming. He looked so much like his mother when he smiled. Wyatt now understood how his father must have felt over the years. It was heartbreaking but in the most beautiful way.

"You're thinking about Mom, aren't you?" Will asked, recognizing the pensive look on his dad's face.

"Yeah."

"Because I look like her?"

"A little, sometimes. When you're happy."

"What was she like?"

Wyatt sighed, readying himself before answering. He didn't want to be secretive about Annie the way his father had been about his own mother. He took a sip of soda and began. "She was sarcastic, like you. She was funny, sentimental, and smart. She was pretty and gentle, but strong. She was the strongest person I've ever met. She put up with a lot from me when I was sick. She saved me from myself when things were particularly bad. She was amazing."

"And she died," Will said, his tone somber. "Because of me."

"No."

"If I hadn't been bo--"

"No!" Wyatt insisted. Will had never seen his father look so stern. It was unnerving. "Your mother had a massive stroke that caused irreparable brain damage. It was *biology*. It was not your fault, do you hear me?"

Will nodded.

"I really want you to get this. You have zero blame in what happened to your mother. None."

"Okay," Will accepted. They went back to eating their dinner in silence for a while until Will spoke again, thinking it necessary to point something out. "Dad," he said, his voice quiet.

"Yeah?"

"It wasn't your fault either."

Wyatt looked up at his son, his features softening. He knew he needed to set a good example, to show Will that he didn't have to be burdened with guilt over things he had no control over, so he lied. "I know that."

A few days later, it was finally happening. His aunt had come through with the paperwork and gotten Will signed up to take the test. He was giddy, riding in the car for the first time, his father also smiling as they drove into town. Wyatt had never seen Will so happy, the spring wind blowing through the open window, gently tousling the boy's dark hair. They pulled into the high school's parking lot and found a spot.

"You have everything you need?" Wyatt asked.

"Yeah," Will answered, anxious to get inside.

"Okay, I'll be right here when you're done. Remember, it's not life and death, it's just a test. Have some fun."

"Thanks, Dad. I'll try." Will opened the car door and got out. He slammed it shut, not meaning to close it so hard, and waved goodbye, hurrying toward the entrance. Wyatt felt an immense sense of pride as he waved back, his anxiety about Will's first outing fading.

"He's a good kid," he reminded himself. "He'll be fine." As Will disappeared behind the double doors, Wyatt's phone rang. He glanced at the number. It was the shop. "This is Wyatt," he answered.

"Hey, it's Charlie," the woman on the other end said. "Can you come by? The girls aren't doing very well."

"What's wrong?"

She was quiet for a moment. "You haven't heard?"

"Apparently not."

"Can you just come by? I should really tell you in person."

"On my way." He ended the call and started the car. The SATs would take hours. He'd be back in plenty of time.

Inside, Will waited on pins and needles for the test to begin. The air was thick with the nervous energy of other kids, squirming in their seats, the cold cafeteria providing little comfort in its sterility. He tried to focus on the instructor at the head of the room, not wanting to miss anything important, but his attention was quickly diverted by a girl pulling up a chair next to him.

"Hi," she said brightly. She was gorgeous and smelled like birthday cake, one tawny shoulder peeking from the collar of her pink top. The fluorescent light bounced off her curls like starlight and the stare from her honey eyes made his stomach jump.

"Hi," he said shakily.

"I'm Michelle," she said. "First time?"

"How'd you know?"

"Most people only take the SATs once. This is my second time. I just wanted to see if I could get a better score."

"Oh," he said, relieved that she had been referring to the test and couldn't tell from his awkward behavior that this was the first time he'd ever spoken to a girl. "Do you go here? I mean, you look--"

"Old?" she giggled. "I'm twenty-one, so, no, I don't go here. I still haven't gone to college, though. I got into a bunch of schools, I just don't know if it's for me. What about you? College plans?"

"A few. I'm interested in Culinary Arts and History, but I'll probably get a Business degree first, just to be prepared."

"Sounds ambitious." She looked toward the front of the room where the instructor had begun passing out booklets. "Looks like we're starting." She got up and snuck back to her original seat and whispered, "Good luck."

"You, too." He readied his pencil, stunned that an impossibly beautiful girl had spoken to him out of the blue. If this was what being out in the world was like, he could very well become addicted. *Calm down*, he thought, the booklet sliding on the table in front of him. *Time to focus.*

Wyatt entered the donut shop to find the place nearly deserted, unusual for this early in the morning. Charlie, the shop's manager, rushed to greet him while Marley and Rose stood behind the counter, both barely keeping it together, the younger woman's cheeks stained with smeared mascara while Rose still wiped away tears of her own.

"What's going on?" Wyatt asked.

"It's Tim," Charlie explained. "He didn't show up to work this morning, so I called him, but no answer. The sheriff came in about an hour ago and told us," She paused for a moment to collect herself. "He said Tim's dead."

"Oh, my God," he said. Tim was the head baker at Pine's and everyone in town loved him. He was a veteran of the Iraq War and had received a Purple Heart after saving a convoy, taking an IED blast that eventually got him fitted with a titanium leg. Despite the severe spinal nerve pain he lived with every day, he always seemed to be in a good mood, putting a smile on the faces of everyone he came across. He was the closest thing Wyatt had to a friend in this town. He would be missed. "How?"

"They found him in the creek by the park. The sheriff said it looked like a coyote attack. He's asking the mayor to let people hunt them. He thinks there's at least one that's gone rabid."

"Okay," he said, placing a comforting hand on the older woman's shoulder. "You should all go home. I'll close up."

"Are you sure?" Rose called from the counter, finally getting her emotions under control.

"Yeah, go ahead. I'll pay you for eight hours. Take the day, get some rest. Customers will understand. Marley, I'm promoting you to head baker. Can you start tomorrow? Take over Tim's hours?"

She was flattered. "Really?"

"You know the job, you've filled in before. I can find another cashier, but teaching someone new to make the donuts like Tim did?" He shook his head. "You're the only one."

"But, Rose has seniority."

Rose laughed. "Dear, I'm retiring in a month. No way I'm taking on more responsibility."

"You can do this, Marley," Charlie assured her.

The twenty-year-old couldn't believe it. This was her dream job, having grown up eating there every Saturday since she was a baby. She felt guilty for being happy in that moment, but couldn't help but smile. "Thank you, Mr. Sinclair."

"Wyatt," he insisted. "You guys get out of here. Take some donuts with you. I'll see you tomorrow."

The ladies collected their belongings, each taking a dozen donuts as they headed out. Wyatt cashed out the drawers and put a help-wanted sign in the window before filling several boxes with the remaining donuts and leaving himself, locking the door behind him. He got in his car and sat, the gravity of Tim's death hitting him like a ton of bricks. While he felt the loss wholly, he knew there was someone else taking it much harder. He leaned back in his seat and closed his eyes for a moment before whispering to himself, "Shit."

Wyatt knocked on the door of Tim's house to no answer. His wife, Sydney, was either not home or couldn't bring herself to come to the door. As he was about to leave, he noticed the letter carrier stopping at the mailbox.

"Hey, Arthur," he called as he approached.

"Wyatt," the man said gloomily. "Sorry to hear."

"Yeah, listen, I know it's not technically allowed, but Sydney's not home and I'd like to leave her something. Could I maybe sneak it in the mailbox?"

"Well, that's against Federal law," Arthur reminded him. "But, I can't report what I don't see."

"Understood."

"Such a shame about that boy. At least he didn't leave any kids behind. His poor wife, though."

Wyatt nodded in agreement.

"Well, I better get back to it. Not rain, nor sleet nor dead war heroes."

"I'll see you later, Arthur."

"See you later."

Wyatt waited for the mail truck to turn the corner before placing the envelope in the letterbox. The thirty-five thousand dollar check inside would do little to alleviate the despair he knew Tim's widow must be feeling, but a year's wages was all he could think to offer. She shouldn't have to worry about paying her bills on top of everything else. He knew what it was like to lose someone and Tim was such an important part of Pine's and the community, it was the least he could do.

"How was it?" Wyatt asked as Will got in the car.

"Awesome!" Will gushed, smiling from ear to ear. "I was nervous being around all those people, but it was *so* worth it. When can I go out again?"

"We'll see."

"You don't understand. It was amazing. Dad, a *girl* talked to me."

"A girl?" Wyatt chuckled as he drove from the parking lot to the street. "I've given you 'the talk', right?"

"Yeah, Dad," Will sighed, rolling his eyes. "A bunch of times."

Wyatt laughed again. "Okay, as long as you remember the three golden rules."

"Respect, consent, and condoms."

"Good boy," Wyatt snickered. "Seriously, though, I'm really proud of you. Finishing school, being around people. You're doing well. You're a great kid."

"Um, thanks."

"You know you're the best part of my life, right?"

"I know."

"I love you like crazy. And your mom loved you, too. More than anything."

"Why are you being weird?"

Wyatt sighed. "Something happened today that reminded me how important it is to let the people you love know how much they mean to you. I don't want you to ever not know how loved you are."

"Okay, Dad. I love you, too," Will said, patting his father on the arm. "Now, let me tell you about this girl."

Chapter 3

The eerie glow of the computer screen lit up Lucifer's face as he searched the internet for news of outbreaks and for a moment, Gabriel got a glimpse of how the Fallen must see him in Hell; cold, focused, and creepy as shit. She got a bottle of water from the fridge and set it next to him on the bar.

"Thank you, Gabriel," he said, unscrewing the cap. "I was getting quite parched."

"I know," she said, shoving her phone in her back pocket and rifling through kitchen drawers. "Have you seen my checkbook?"

"You still use one of those? I thought they went extinct, like black and white televisions or common courtesy."

"Believe it or not, if you look hard enough, you can still find those things."

"I'll take your word for it. I may have seen it in the pantry this morning when I was attempting to locate something edible. I failed miserably, by the way."

"You didn't eat?" she asked, finding what she was looking for and setting it on the counter. *Five million dollars*, she scribbled in the amount section.

"Everything calling itself 'food' in this apartment is either full of chemicals or dripping with sugar, mostly both. I ordered in. Someone will be delivering it shortly. I took the liberty of purchasing you something, as well."

"Thank you, Lucifer, that's very kind. Save it for me, will you? I have to run an errand. I shouldn't be more than an hour." She finished filling out the check and tore it from the book. As she headed toward the door, she called back to her brother, "Try not to kill anyone while I'm gone."

He waved, not looking up from the screen in front of him. "Demons running amok," he muttered to himself, unhappy with how long this was taking. Nearly a week had passed since he'd been back and he still had nothing to show for it. His impatience grew like weeds, fertilized by guilt. "I will set things right, Father. I swear it."

Gabriel walked into the small Chinatown shop, her boots clicking on the tile as she passed towering displays of colorful, unrelated items. Handbags on a rack with bathing suits hung next to a table of cleaning supplies and baby-proofing devices. As she approached the counter, the old woman behind it barked, "Ni xiang yao shenme?!"

"She says, 'How can we help you?'" her grandson told Gabriel, who knew that wasn't *exactly* what she'd said.

"There's an amulet in a silver-lined black box on the top shelf of your storage room, closest to the office. I need it," Gabriel answered plainly, taking the check from her pocket.

The older woman recoiled, having gone from suspicious to horrified. She yelled at the teenager in Mandarin, ordering him to make the stranger leave. Gabriel's exasperation was evident to the boy, the shop owner's panic-induced word vomit bordering on insulting.

"Oh, Christ, I'm not a witch," she rebuffed. The woman silenced herself, surprised that the stranger understood. The two watched as she unfolded the check and slid it across to them. "I know you've been getting a lot of shit from your asshole landlord," Gabriel explained. "He's raising the rent and being an all-around dick because he wants to sell the building. This is enough to buy it yourself and tell him to fuck off."

They examined the check, their jaws dropping.

"I need that item," she demanded. The boy rushed to the back to retrieve it while his grandmother wrung her hands.

"It's okay," he whispered to the old woman as he handed the box to Gabriel. "She doesn't know how to use it."

As she left, Gabriel turned back. "I know exactly what I'll have to do with it."

Gabriel closed the door behind her after entering the apartment to find a note on top of a takeout container next to the still-open laptop.

Measles outbreak in the Philippines. Will check in if any news.

"This motherfucker," she murmured. She hid the box in the back of the pantry and sat at the bar, opening the container to find an egg white omelet. She took a bite and gagged as she swallowed. "Spinach," she choked, covering her mouth. "At least it's not cold." She took another bite, wincing as she chewed. She logged onto a crowdfunding site and searched for medical fundraisers. She lazily clicked, fully funding several of them as she ate.

I'm bored. Come over, she thought.

I'm at work, Valerie responded.

Quit your job. I'll give you ten million dollars right now.

You know I'm not doing that.

You're dumb.

Bitch, bye.

Fine. She took a sip from Lucifer's half-empty water bottle before contacting another sibling. *Hey, B.*

Hi, Gabriel, Wyatt replied.

How's Will? Murdery yet?

He's fine, he thought with derision.

Good, that's good. How are you? You need anything? Money? A babysitter? Five minutes back in civilization just to remember what it feels like?

I'm all right. What about you? You sound--

Bored?

Lonely.

Gabriel raised her eyebrows in silent agreement before noticing the time. *I have an appointment. Talk to you later. Keep an eye on that kid.*

I always do.

"We need to talk about your spending," he said, his voice stern. Gabriel sat across from the accountant who stared at her, clearly displeased. The office was stark and flooded with light coming in from the windows behind the middle-aged, balding man who sat straight up in his chair, not an ounce of calm in his demeanor. She tried to focus on the view, but couldn't get the image of him and his cleaning lady out of her head. The two had had a tryst the night before on this very desk and since he was still thinking about it, she too was stuck with the mental impression.

"Okay," she dismissed.

"It's reckless."

"Reckless," she scoffed.

"Ms. Murphy,"

"You're getting bent out of shape over charitable donations."

"You're giving away *sixty percent* of your money."

"Sixty percent of three billion dollars still leaves me with stupid amounts of money to blow on takeout and candy."

"You're being glib."

"I'm being honest. Listen, I know you want me to invest in stocks, buy rental property, create my own foundation as a tax haven; all that normal rich person bullshit. But, I'm not going to. To be honest, I plan on giving *more* money away. There are a lot of people that need it way more than I do."

The accountant sighed and rubbed his brow, looking fondly at his client who he'd been working with for the past two decades. "I'll be straight with you," he said, folding his hands and leaning across the desk. "I admire that you want to help people, I do, but I wouldn't be doing my job if I didn't warn you against what you're doing. If you keep spending at this rate while leaving your automatic monthly donations in place, you'll run out of money in less than a hundred years."

"I'm relatively certain I'll be dead by then, bro."

"Don't you want to leave something for your children?"

Gabriel laughed. "I'm *definitely* not having those."

"Oh."

"I understand your concern. You're just doing your job, and you're good at it, really. But, using my parents' money to help people that need it is like my silver lining. I *have* to do it."

"I see. It makes their deaths seem like they weren't in vain."

"No, it makes their lives seem like they were worth something. Those people were trash."

"Oh, uh, um,"

"We done?" Gabriel asked, standing to leave.

"I suppose."

"Awesome. See you next month."

Gabriel stood in the mausoleum, not really sure what she was doing there. She almost never thought about her parents anymore, since doing so only made her angry and she had enough to worry about without being distracted by emotions that no longer mattered. She folded her arms and looked over the plaques.

James R. Murphy 1948-1997

Esther M. Murphy 1953-1997

Beloved parents

"Bullshit," she whispered to herself. She glared at the stone wall for a few more seconds, the rage bubbling over. She didn't like how she felt and she hated more that she was wasting her time and energy on criminals that should have been long forgotten. Before she turned to leave, she took a step closer to the tombs. She knew they couldn't hear her, their souls firmly in Purgatory, but she had to say it anyway. "Fuck you."

Chapter 4

"Last one," Wyatt said to himself, twisting the light bulb into place. "Fixed," he sighed, proud of the job he'd done repairing the sign. He'd been told that it was a lost cause, that the decades-old sign should be replaced, but he knew what the shop meant to the people of Southport. It was a landmark to them, part of the town's history. He was still a relative newcomer and if he started making big changes, it may not sit too well with some of the residents. The last thing he wanted to do was bring negative attention to himself.

As he made his way down the rickety ladder, he heard the sound of glass breaking. It was late, well after most people on the quiet street were typically out and about. He walked around the building, following the noise to the dumpster in the back. At first, he thought it was the rabid coyote that had been terrorizing the town, but the dumpster shook, scooting a little on the concrete underneath. Something was inside and it was way bigger than a coyote. *Teenagers*, he thought.

"Hey!" Wyatt called. No answer. It occurred to him that the person inside might be homeless, hungry, and looking for food. "Hey, if you're hungry, I have a few donuts left from this morning! You're welcome to them!" The shaking stopped. "I'll go put those in a bag for you! Meet you out front!" He turned to enter the building through the service door, but before he could get the key from his pocket, he heard a low, guttural growl.

"Oh, shit," he whispered. Wyatt had been warned about the woods behind the donut shop, that on a rare occasion, a black bear might wander through. He'd never seen one there, but he now gathered the electricity from the air and formed a ball of lightning, ready to face the beast. He spun around, ready to fire, but he was so taken aback by what he saw that the electricity gathered in his hand dissipated, curiosity and confusion clouding his judgement. What stood on the lid of the dumpster in front of him was a man, only not. He was naked, covered from head to toe in long, dark hair with flecks of gray about the face. His arms seemed stretched and spider-like with black claws erupting from four gnarled fingers on each oversized hand. His legs were bent backward, the way a dog's would be. Large, pointed ears sprung up from his malformed head above eyes that shone in the dark like a cat's.

Gabriel, Wyatt thought.

Yeah, B? she replied.

Quick question. Are werewolves real?

Eh, kind of. There used to be a few Native American tribes that could shapeshift into wolves for hunting purposes, but the Colonists killed most of them off in the seventeenth century. There have been a handful of times when a half-person/half-wolf monster movie type of thing would pop up, but there hasn't been one of those for like, two hundred years or so. Why?

Because I'm either hallucinating or I'm looking at one right now. He told his sister, watching the creature slowly climb down.

For real?! Light that thing's ass up! It will rip your throat out before you can say 'lycanthropy'. You're not on drugs, right? No brown acid?

Stone-cold sober.

Well, damn, dude, get to smiting. Pew pew!

The beast growled again, bearing his long, pointed teeth. He moved carefully, examining his prey. In an instant, he pounced, leaping forward with unnatural speed. Wyatt threw a bolt of lightning into the monster's chest, sending it falling back and yelping in pain. He darted on all fours into the woods just as the sign in front sparked and went out.

"Fuck me," Wyatt muttered.

You okay? Gabriel asked.

Yeah, but it got away. I'm going after it.

Not what I would recommend, but you do you, fam.

Wyatt entered the woods, the lush greenery blocking out all light from the street. He searched for several minutes, the moon his only guide. There were no signs of the creature. Wyatt was about to give up when he heard a branch snap. He went in the direction of the noise but was stopped in his tracks by a middle-aged woman with gray hair and almond-shaped eyes.

"You need to leave," she commanded.

"You shouldn't be out here right now, ma'am," he told her.

"I'm aware of the creature. My people have ways of dealing with things like this, but you are not safe. Go, before it returns. Here," She handed him a business card. "If you see it again, call my brother. *We* will handle it."

She walked off into the dark, leaving Wyatt feeling frustrated and useless. He hated the idea of that thing still out there, hurting people. It had killed his friend. Who would be next? He looked down at the card. *Mills Auto Sales.* He let out a defeated sigh and put the card in his pocket, trekking back to the shop. After taking the electricity from the sign to fight off the werewolf, it was, again, in need of repairs.

Michelle sat at the small table in the donut shop, going over her application for the second time, making sure she'd filled everything out properly. She was pleasantly surprised to see no box for race, assuming it meant that the management wasn't overly concerned with a potential employee's ethnicity. She took a bite of the free donut the manager had given her while she waited, glancing around the room, taking note of where the exits were and what everyday items could be used as weapons in an emergency. The building was old, but clean and had a hominess about it that reminded her of her grandparents' house. They had died when she was small, but she could still remember making dorayaki with her baa-baa every Saturday in her small, upstate kitchen. The donuts here were good, but they couldn't compare.

"You all done?" Charlie asked. Michelle nodded and the older woman sat across from her, taking the application and giving it a quick once-over. "So, you used to be a personal assistant?"

"Yes, ma'am."

"You can just call me Charlie. We're not sticklers for formality around here," the manager said, a friendly smile crossing her unpainted lips. "What were your job duties?"

"Answering the phone, making appointments, running errands. Anything my boss didn't want to deal with herself. Most of the time, it was just a lot of store runs for chocolate."

Charlie laughed before moving on. "In 'special skills' you wrote, 'Krav Maga' and 'Brazilian Jiu Jitsu'."

"I also type fifty-five words a minute."

Charlie laughed again. "I like you. Can you start tomorrow? Five-thirty AM on the dot. Starting pay is twelve dollars an hour. That goes up to fifteen after thirty days which is also when your insurance kicks in."

"I get insurance? But, I'd only be part-time."

"The owner's a nice guy. Not like the last one, who was a real hard-ass. Don't tell Mr. Sinclair I said that, though. He was his uncle. When Wyatt took over about three years ago, he raised everyone's pay, got us better insurance, upgraded our equipment. He's the best boss I've ever had. You'll like him."

"He sounds like an angel," Michelle said, struggling not to laugh.

"He's been one for us."

"I will definitely see you tomorrow," Michelle told her, standing to leave, taking what remained of her donut with her.

"See you then!"

The two shook hands and Michelle left the building, popping the donut in her mouth before taking her phone from her pocket and texting, *Job secured.*

Chapter 5

Valerie woke up shivering, her blanket having been stolen by the handsome man sleeping next to her. Sunlight filled the room, causing her to squint while she sleepily looked at the time. "Oh, fuck!" she blurted, jumping out of bed and racing around the room, picking up pieces of clothing as she went.

"What's up?" Malik asked, rubbing his eyes as he sat up.

"What's up is I'm three hours late," Valerie griped. "My alarm didn't go off. Help me find my bra."

Malik grinned as he pulled the garment from under his pillow and twirled it in the air. "You're not late. Come back to bed."

"Boy, you see what time it is? Quit playin'."

"Your alarm went off. I called the school and told them you were sick so we could spend the day together."

She tilted her head and looked him over. "I don't know if that's cute or intrusive, but you lookin' sexy as hell, so I guess I'm okay with it." She giggled as she hopped back in bed, taking the bra from him and throwing it to the floor. She climbed on top of him and started to kiss him, but he protested.

"Hold up," he said, opening and reaching into the nightstand's drawer. He took out a small box and opened it to reveal a white gold and diamond engagement ring. "Valerie Moore,"

"Yes!" she squealed.

"You gonna let me ask?"

"Nuh, uh!" she said, taking the ring and putting it on her own finger. "I don't wanna give you a chance to change your mind."

He laughed. "I would never."

"You better not."

Lucifer sat pensively, the computer screen mocking him with its aggressively bright light and lack of useful information. Every lead so far had turned out to be an utter waste of time. The world had become a cesspool of disease, famine, war, and poverty. It was impossible to distinguish demonic activity, Abaddon's handiwork, and humanity's own self-destruction. He was beyond frustrated and needed to kill something.

"Cheer up, Satan," Gabriel poked. "At least you got a little color while you were out chasing the big bad."

"I do wish you'd stop calling me that," he sighed. "Satan is a myth, a figment of mankind's imagination, used to scapegoat their own less socially acceptable behaviors. I, as you can see, very much exist."

"Yes, you do. Speaking of things that exist, a little birdie told me there's a demon nest in the Atlantic Avenue Tunnel. I was thinking we could check it out, exorcise some bitches then hit the speakeasy." She did a little dance while Lucifer moaned in annoyance.

"These demons," he complained. "Every time I send five back to their cages, ten more appear in their place. Like gray hairs or Hydra."

"Shh," she instructed, waving for him to be quiet. She looked to the front door, then back to him. "Be nice." She opened the door before Valerie could knock, which Valerie usually found irritating. Today, though, she was too happy to notice, excited to share her news with her sister. She held her hand up to show off her new ring, her smile infectious.

"Congrats, lady," Gabriel said, taking Valerie's hand to look at the ring more closely.

"You're getting married, Uriel?" Lucifer questioned. "Is that wise?"

"What did I tell you?" Gabriel scolded.

"I'm only curious as to how our dear sister will keep her true identity from her beloved. Tell me, is he a religious man?"

"Uh-uh," she dismissed. "Not today, Satan. You are not getting to me *today*. I came here to celebrate with my girl."

"Yas, bitch," Gabriel agreed. The women broke out into an impromptu dance-off, further worsening Lucifer's vexation.

"I will handle the nest alone," he decided, standing from the barstool and leaving the apartment.

"Don't let the door hit ya!" Valerie called, still dancing.

"I have to do it," Gabriel said, pulling up a video on her phone.

"Don't you do it," Valerie joked. "Don't do it!"

"I'm doing it!"

As the song began to play, their dancing became more coordinated.

"Girl," Valerie said. "You know I have to shake it to a song named for me."

"You wouldn't happen to know where Abaddon is, would you?" Lucifer asked the demon he'd beaten nearly to death. He'd made quick work of exorcising the rest of the nest and he was sure this one would have no answers for him, but he had to make the attempt.

"Abaddon?" the demon laughed, blood pouring from his nose and mouth. "You should be focusing your efforts on more pressing matters, Watch Keeper. Abaddon is but one, while we are Legion. There are thousands of us on Father's precious planet. How angry do you think He'll be with you when He finds out you let us roam free in order to chase one rogue angel?"

Lucifer seethed, fully aware of the consequences of his prolonged search. He punched the demon several more times, even after the vermin had lost consciousness, trying to release the discontent he felt. He then placed his hand on the man's chest, watching with delight as the shadowy figure left the body and went screaming back to its cage. Lucifer brushed his hands together, glaring at the bodies around him before opining, "This is taking too long."

"Next weekend, Atlantic City, family and close friends only," Valerie said.

"You know I'll be there," Gabriel told her.

"And invite Wyatt. I haven't seen that boy in forever. There's no excuse good enough for missing your sister's wedding."

"I don't know if that's a good idea. He's pretty busy."

"Bitch, I couldn't give less of a fuck if I was born without reproductive organs. You make sure he gets his ass there."

"Okay," Gabriel chuckled. "It's your day. I will make it happen."

"Good."

"What about Lucifer?"

"Ugh, do I have to?"

"Uriel,"

"Fine, but he better be on his best behavior. I can't have him embarrassing me in front of Malik's parents. Those people barely tolerate me as it is."

"I promise to throw him out a window if he acts up."

"That's all I ask. I'm gonna go. Mrs. Perry wants to take me dress shopping. Wish me luck. I'm gonna need it." As Valerie closed the door behind her, Gabriel's phone rang.

"Hey, Hattie," she answered. The girl on the other end was distraught, barely able to form words. Too impatient to tell her to calm herself and slow down, Gabriel instead simply said, "On my way."

Gabriel peeked into Allydia's room, what she saw there giving her a better understanding of Hattie's panic. The vampire was ghostly pale, her hair dull and unwashed, eyes distant, lying on top of the sheets, her face gaunt.

"It's worse than before," Hattie said quietly, coming to stand next to Gabriel in the hall. "She's not only refusing to hunt or feed, she won't even take blood from a glass. At least before, she was drinking *something*. Now, she desiccates. She will die if she continues this way. I'm at a loss. I've never seen her like this."

"I have," Gabriel said. "A long time ago." She stood there for a few seconds, watching Allydia's stillness, a twinge of guilt gnawing at the back of her mind. She had done the right thing in sending Wyatt away. Still, Allydia's reaction was more dramatic than she'd anticipated. She genuinely felt sorry for her and hoped she'd be able to pull herself out of this depression faster than she had the last time. "If she's still not eating in two days, call me back. I'll hold her down so you can feeding tube the drama queen. Even in her weakened state, she's stronger than any of you." She walked to the door and looked back at Hattie who was feeling relieved and grateful for Gabriel's assistance. "She just needs time."

Chapter 6

Wyatt placed his hand over the coals of the grill. *Not hot enough*, he thought. He took a deep breath, the fresh, "green" scent of a just-mowed lawn hanging in the finally-warm air. One of the few things he enjoyed about living out here was how picturesque it was when spring hit. Everything was flowering and full of life. The landscape was so beautiful, he forgot for a moment about the creature that had attacked him two nights before. But, as his eyes lifted to the woods beyond the barn, he couldn't help but remember, hoping that the strange woman he'd met that night had taken care of it.

"You finally gonna let me wield the spatula?" Will teased, bringing the steaks out from the kitchen.

"You know what? I think I will," Wyatt agreed.

"Seriously?"

"Sure, you're in college now. I think you can handle it."

"Thanks, Dad!"

"Grill's not ready yet, though. Give it a few minutes."

Will nodded and put the plate down on the picnic table a few feet away, his eyes glued to the low flames stirring under the coals. "Oh, crap!" he shouted. "What time is it?"

Wyatt checked his phone. "Five o two."

"CRAP!" Will darted back into the house and headed for the front window. He was sure he'd missed Arthur delivering the day's mail, but to his delight, the carrier was still there, setting letters in the box. "Whew," Will breathed. He watched the man walk back to his truck, but instead of getting inside as Will expected, he gathered a package from behind the seat and began the long walk to the front porch. "Oh, jeez," Will mumbled, leaping from the couch and running through the house to the backyard. "Dad!" he called.

"What's going on?" Wyatt asked.

"The mailman's coming to the door."

"Okay, I'll get it. You know what to do."

He did. It had only happened a few times over the years, but there was a routine in place for when someone unexpectedly dropped by. Will would stay in the kitchen while his father got rid of whoever was at the door. There would be no way to explain who he was to people without coming up with an elaborate story that wouldn't hold water a few months later when he'd have grown another two years. It was safer for him to avoid being seen as much as possible until he was an adult and the aging process normalized.

The carrier knocked just as Will stood behind the wall that separated the kitchen from the living room. He gave his father a thumbs up from the entrance and Wyatt opened the door.

"Hey, Arthur," he said cheerfully. "You need me to sign for that?"

"Yeah," the man stated, handing Wyatt a pen. "It's marked 'signature required'. Must be important." Wyatt glanced at the return address on the box. It was from his father. He scribbled his name and returned the pen.

"Hey, is that one of those 4K TVs?" Arthur asked, pointing to the entertainment center.

"Yeah," Wyatt confirmed. "A gift from my sister."

"I've been thinkin' about gettin' me one of those. I've had the same old plasma screen since 'Monk' ended." He stepped forward to have a better look, poking his head in the doorway and bumping into Wyatt. "Ope."

"You're fine," Wyatt told him, but as the man stepped back, his face changed. He looked distant, then aggravated. "You okay, Arthur?" Wyatt asked, worried the older man was having a stroke. Arthur put his hand on his chest and moved closer, placing a hand on Wyatt's shoulder. "I'm calling an ambulance," Wyatt said, taking his phone from his pocket, but before he could dial the number, he noticed the man's skin slowly covering itself in a thin layer of hair. Arthur sniffed the air, then Wyatt. His eyes grew wider and began to change shape, becoming rounder with longer lashes as he stared angrily into the eyes of the man he now knew had hurt him two nights before. His teeth lengthened, cutting his bottom lip, and as he gripped Wyatt's shoulder, he let out a low, quiet growl.

"Holy shit," Wyatt whispered. Without hesitation, he shoved the man off the porch, slamming the door shut and locking the deadbolt and chain. He ran to the kitchen and took the business card from the junk drawer, handing it along with his phone to his son. "Call this number," he instructed. "Tell them 'it's here' and give them our address." Loud banging came from the door, violently shaking it and startling Will. "Go to the basement. Lock the door. Don't come out until I tell you. Now!" He pushed Will in the direction of the basement door just a few feet away. The boy complied, moving as quickly as he could. He dialed the number on the card and waited impatiently for someone to pick up.

"Mills Auto Sales," the man on the other end said. "We've got what you're looking for. How can I help you?"

"Hi, um, I'm supposed to tell you, 'it's here'."

The man was quiet for a second before responding, his tone changed. "Where are you?"

Will gave him the address and the man ended the call without another word. Will pressed his ear to the door, hearing a crash and the sound of glass breaking. "Arthur!" he could hear his father yell. "Snap out of it! Remember who you are!"

But he couldn't. The wolf had taken over. He lunged for Wyatt, who held him off with small, low energy lightning blasts. "I don't want to hurt you!" Wyatt shouted. The wolfman kept coming, all but ignoring the shocks, seeming to develop an immunity.

Will felt afraid, wanting to help his father, but not knowing how. He did the only thing he could think of. He called his Aunt Gabriel.

"Hello?" she answered.

"Aunt Gabriel, it's me, Will."

"Hey, sweetie. What's up?"

"I don't even know. Dad's fighting with the mailman or something. It's really loud. I'm in the basement, but--"

"But nothing," she said sternly. "You stay your ass there until your dad comes to get you, do you hear me? He can handle himself, trust me."

"That's what he told me to do, but what if--"

"Stay. There."

"But--"

"Boy,"

"Okay, okay." He heard another crash, this one so violent, it shook the lightbulb that hung overhead. "I have to go."

"Will--" Gabriel protested as he hit the 'end call' button. He again pressed his ear to the door to try to hear what was happening on the other side.

"Arthur, stop!" Wyatt shouted, throwing a low voltage bolt into the creature's chest. He was as he had been behind Pine's, tall, animal-like and crazed. He swung his elongated arm, knocking Wyatt to the floor. He grasped him by the throat with one giant, clawed hand and slammed him down through the coffee table. Wyatt grabbed the beast's arm and shocked him again, this time with more force. The wolfman winced but did not relent. He held Wyatt there, choking the life from him.

Will could hear his father's gasps for air and the odd growling of an animal he didn't recognize. His heart pounded in his chest as he put his hand to the doorknob. His dad was dying. He was *dying*. He had to do something, so he opened the basement door and raced to the living room where he was stunned by what stood before him. It was like something out of a comic; a monster, enormous and looming, hovering over his father, one gigantic hand around his neck, the other in the air, ready to strike. Wyatt's face was purple, his eyes bulging. Spurts of blue light erupted from his hands every few seconds, which seemed to hurt the animal, but not enough to stop it. Adrenaline surged through Will's veins as panic set in. His heart was beating so loudly in his ears that he could no longer hear the creature's growls. Wyatt's head tilted back and for a second, he and Will locked eyes.

"Run," he gurgled, but Will shook his head. Instead, he rushed forward, throwing himself, full speed into the monster. When he made contact, a hot, white light poured from his hands like water through a busted dam. The power of it was so strong that it knocked the boy back and to the ground. The light flew into the wolf, causing it to convulse and foam at the mouth. It fell back, its eyes bursting in its head and smoke rising from its singed fur.

Wyatt coughed, putting his hand to his throat and taking slow, labored breaths, rolling over and eventually standing himself up. Will, too, stood, looking at the dead creature and down at his hands. "What did I do?" he whispered.

"It's okay," Wyatt said.

"It's not okay! What did I do, Dad?!"

Wyatt hugged his son tightly, grabbing the back of his neck and kissing his head. "It's okay," he repeated.

"What did I do?" the boy said again, tears streaming down his face.

"You saved me," Wyatt told him, tears now in his eyes, as well. "You saved us both."

"I didn't mean to hurt him," Will sobbed into his father's shoulder. "I didn't mean to, to--"

"I know."

"I just wanted to get him off you," the boy wept. "I didn't want to--"

"I know. Listen," Wyatt said, releasing his embrace and taking Will's face in his hands. "Arthur was a good guy, but that thing wasn't Arthur. It was a monster that took him over. It killed Tim and it would have killed us and who knows how many more people if you hadn't stopped it. I know it hurts, believe me. I've felt the guilt you're feeling, but you saved lives putting that thing down. I wish you didn't have to. I wish there was something I could've done to save Arthur, but there wasn't. Arthur was gone. Do you understand?"

Will nodded, wiping the tears from his cheeks.

"Hello," a man said, walking into the house through the opening where the front door used to be. He stood over the corpse, a puzzled look coming over his face. "How did you do this?"

"We electrocuted it," Wyatt said.

"With what, the power grid?"

"How did this happen? I was told werewolves haven't existed for centuries."

"He was out hunting a few weeks back," the man explained. "He came across one of us and her cub. He thought they were normal gray wolves, got nervous, raised his gun. The baby got scared and bit him, just trying to protect his mother. He's only four years old. He didn't know what he was doing."

"Would he have ever gone back to normal?" Will wondered.

"No," the forty-something-year-old man answered, sweeping his long hair off his shoulder. "Once the wolf has you, there is no going back. The man would have slipped away over time, losing all memory of his former self. His humanity would be lost. All there would be for him was the kill."

"That's enough, Joseph," the woman from the woods said as she entered with another man. "You two, take the body to the truck. I'll finish up here."

The men wrapped the creature in a blue tarp and lifted him up, struggling under the weight as they carried the wolfman out of the house.

"I assume I don't have to tell you that this can't get out," she said.

"No shit."

"Will," Wyatt scolded, never having heard him use that language before.

"Sorry."

"Good," the woman said, glaring at Will and back at Wyatt. "I need to speak to you. Alone."

Wyatt motioned for Will to go upstairs and he did, no questions asked.

"What happened here?" she asked. Wyatt gave her a look of refusal and shook his head. "Fine," she said, looking up the stairs. "We're all entitled to our secrets, but I have a bad feeling about him. I don't know what that boy is, but you keep him on a tight leash." She stormed out, again leaving Wyatt with more questions than answers.

Yo, B, you okay? he heard in his head.

I'm fine, he responded. *Werewolf's dead. Locals came and picked it up.*

Cool. How's Will? He was pretty shaken up when he called.

He's okay. I have some cleaning to do. I'll talk to you later.

K.

Wyatt looked up to see his son creeping down the stairs. "I saw their truck leave from my window," he said.

"Are you all right?"

"Not really."

"I'm sorry. Listen, Will, we need to have a talk. There are things you don't know. Who we are, what we can do."

"At the risk of getting snapped at again, no shit."

"Will,"

"You've been lying to me. I don't just have some super rare aging disorder, do I?"

"No. I didn't tell you because I was hoping you wouldn't inherit my--"

"Can we talk about it after dinner, Dad? The grill's gotta be hot by now and I'm starving."

"So, what are we, Dad?" Will asked, dropping his fork and folding his arms. "Aliens? We're aliens, right? Is there a ship buried under the barn? Are we waiting for someone to beam us up and fly us to our home planet? Is Gabriel really your sister, or is she a government spook assigned to make sure we don't blow up the planet with our advanced technology?"

"I don't appreciate your attitude," Wyatt said, finishing his last bite of steak.

"I don't appreciate being lied to."

"Fair enough." He took a sip of beer while he tried to put the words together. He'd dreaded this conversation, hoping they'd never have to have it. He put the bottle down and reluctantly began, deciding that the only way to explain it was to just spit it out. "My body is human. I was born like everyone else. I have parents, I grew up on West 72nd Street in Manhattan, went to school, had friends. All the things I told you about my life are true. But, a few years ago, Gabriel came to me and told me who I was inside. Basically, instead of a soul, I have...I'm an angel."

Will chuckled, thinking his father was pulling his leg in an attempt to lighten the mood. But Wyatt's face remained still. He wasn't kidding.

"Really?" Will asked. "An angel?"

"Guardian angel, specifically. Barachiel, Angel of Blessings, leader of--"

"An *angel*?"

Wyatt nodded. "I didn't believe it at first, either. I thought Gabriel was full of--"

"Is she Gabriel from the *Bible*?"

"Yeah."

"Holy crap."

"That's what *I* said."

"She's a big deal."

"She knows it, too, believe me."

"So, am I an angel, too?"

"Half," Wyatt told him. "Your mother was human. It shouldn't have been possible for you to be born. You're a miracle."

"So, I have your light-from-the-hands power, but--"

"Electricity. We can use the energy around us to create lightning. Now that you have the ability, I'll have to train you on how to control it."

"But, inside, I'm human?"

"Yeah, you have a proper human soul. You're a person like you've always been. The thing is, though, that the angel part of you might be a little hard to manage."

"What do you mean?"

"It might feel overwhelming. Gabriel said you could get headaches, have nightmares; even feel like you can't control yourself. These powers can make us dangerous to other people. If you ever feel like you can't handle it, if you feel yourself slipping, you have to tell me."

Will looked behind him into the living room, the broken furniture and boarded up doorway filling him with shame. "I didn't mean to--"

"Hey," Wyatt said, reaching his hand out and patting his son's arm. "I know that. Tonight, we'll clean up this mess. Tomorrow, we start training. A big part of controlling your lightning is knowing how to suppress it. That'll be lesson number one."

"Okay, Dad," Will said, picking up his soda can and taking a sip. He put it down and looked at his father. "*Angels*?"

Chapter 7

A strange man left Gabriel's apartment, passing Lucifer on his way to the elevator. As Lucifer went to open the door, it flew open in front of him, a beautiful woman also leaving, winking at him as she passed.

"Holy fuck buckets, that really watered my crops," Gabriel said, taking a water from the fridge, wearing only a thin, silk robe.

"I've only been gone a few hours. How did you manage to--" Lucifer stopped himself, realizing he had no interest in his sister's extracurricular activities. "Never mind."

"Don't go all 'Uriel' on me."

"Wouldn't dream of it. I just never understood the attraction to men." He sat at the bar, picking up the book he'd left there.

"Except you always choose a man to occupy when you're here."

"Yes, because I wish to indulge in the female body. This," he said, gesturing to himself. "Is purely for function."

"The functionality of the male body is precisely why I like it. And, FYI, most of the time, a woman better satisfies another woman than a man because she knows what feels good. Something to think about before your next trip topside."

"I'll take it under advisement."

Gabriel slammed her water bottle down and lifted Lucifer from his seat. "You have heroin?!" she accused, reaching into his pants pocket and pulling out the tiny bag of powder.

"Is that what it is? I took it off a demon after I sent him packing. He was so calm while I removed him. Piqued my curiosity."

Gabriel stormed through the hall and into the bathroom, tossing the bag into the toilet and flushing it.

"Well, that was rather rude," Lucifer complained.

"Don't bring that shit into my house."

"Why so vexed, sister? It was only for fun. Why should my experimentation irk you so?"

"You don't know everything about me." She charged past him, following the sound of her ringing phone. She took and quickly ended the call. "I'm gonna take a shower, then I have an errand to run."

"Does your errand have something to do with that phone call?"

"Yes."

"Might I join?"

"No."

"This is the thing," Gabriel said, plopping herself down to sit next to Allydia on her bed, the faint smell of death floating up from the decaying vampire as she remained unmoved. "When I get a call from a twenty-year-old ginger vampire, hysterically sobbing into the phone, making it impossible to understand what she's saying through her already barely coherent Scottish accent, I feel compelled to come see exactly what the fuck. Now, I've already been down here twice in the last week; this is getting ridiculous. They told me you took your feeding tube out as soon as I left. You know this behavior is--"

"Go away, Gabriel," Allydia said, her voice weak.

"Can't do it. If I let you die, my brother would be hella salty."

"Your brother doesn't care for me," the vampire bemoaned, tears forming in her eyes. "He disappeared. No explanation, no goodbye."

"About that, he left because I told him to go. It had nothing to do with you."

"You what?" Allydia hissed, struggling to set herself up.

"Can you keep a secret?"

Allydia nodded, her despair replaced with anger.

"He had a kid. Shouldn't have happened. I still don't know how it did. *I* don't know. Craziness. Turns out his wife left him because she was pregnant and thought he'd mess the kid up somehow."

Horror spread across Allydia's face. "A Nephilim?"

"Totes magotes. Which is why I made him leave the city, take that thing to the middle of nowhere, and hope nothing bad happens, but you remember what they're like. No way he grows up functional. He's been a good kid, though, so far. Sweet as can be. I love that little monstrosity."

"You allow the child to live?"

"Against my better judgement. I was kind of hoping Barachiel was right about him. That he might not ever get powers. But he did. He killed a *werewolf*."

"A werewolf? That takes me back."

"Right? The kid's emotional, undisciplined. B's trying to teach him to control it, but you know as well as I do--"

"There is no controlling a Nephilim."

"Nope."

"You should have killed him when he was an infant."

"You think so? How do you think my brother would've reacted? You think he would've forgiven me? Because I don't."

"He would understand, eventually."

"The way you understand what Lilith did?"

"You know that's different."

"He wouldn't see it that way," Gabriel said, opening Allydia's nightstand drawer and pulling out a pen and a sheet of paper. "*Barachiel* would understand. *Barachiel* would probably thank me.

But *Wyatt*? That motherfucker would set my bony ass on fire." She scribbled down an address and handed it to the vampire. "I'm trusting you'll keep your mouth shut. Lucifer's back and you know what he'll do if he finds out there's a Nephilim running around."

"I remember."

"All right, I'm gonna go, but for real, get it together. You're a goddamn queen. Take a shower, put on something fabulous, maybe a little blush for color. I don't want to be a dick, but you look like shit. And for fuck's sake, bitch, eat something."

Gabriel brushed by Hattie on her way out the door.

"Hattie, dear," Allydia called. The young vampire rushed to the queen's room.

"Yes, Your Majesty?"

"Be a lamb and run me a hot bath. While I wait, bring me a blood bag...or ten."

Chapter 8

Abaddon stared from the edge of the bed in the rundown motel room at the blurry television screen, the local news informing him of just how evil mankind still was. Arson, theft, and murder; so many murders. Every day there was something new for him to be incensed by. War, corruption, greed. It turned his stomach, now that he had one. The body he'd chosen had taken a bit of getting used to. It required food, water, and sleep, not things he'd taken into consideration before having made the journey to Earth. It felt confining and rigid. He'd been watching people on television, studying their movements and vernacular, waiting until he felt well enough acclimated to venture out without being noticed. Lucifer would have undoubtedly followed him, after pushing back the resistance among the damned, and Abaddon had research to do before forming a plan, let alone enacting one. Blending in was the priority for now.

The news was horrifying, but he still wasn't sure if humanity as a whole needed to be wiped clean from the Earth or if there were some people worth saving. He needed more data before making a final decision and he knew just where to go first to get it. Several commercials aired on cable news, each more obnoxious than the last, but one seemed to run more frequently than the rest. It was for a department store that sold everything from groceries to power tools. The ads always showed the inside of the store crawling with people, filling their carts with all manner of items, from the sensible to the absurd. He would go there now to observe more closely what had become of humanity since last he was corporeal.

"Well, aren't you fancy?" the older woman asked as he walked into the store. "Coming from work?"

"Always working," Abaddon answered, perplexed by the strangers greeting. She smiled as if to prove herself friendly, yet her comment on his appearance felt insulting somehow. He adjusted his suit jacket and glanced around, noticing immediately that he did seem overdressed for the setting. Most people wore shorts or jeans and tee-shirts. A few of the women wore sundresses. He realized his mistake. He'd dressed like the anchors on the news, not like the people in the commercials. He felt an odd sense of insecurity as he walked through the aisles, the puzzled looks on people's faces as he passed making him self-conscious. He straightened his tie and smoothed his lapels, the urge to do something with his hands overwhelming.

"Can I help you, sir?" a young man in a vest asked. He wore a name tag, indicating that he worked there, giving Abaddon a false sense of familiarity with the boy.

"Yes," he told the clerk. "How many people would you say the average person kills in their lifetime?"

"What? None."

"None?" Abaddon asked in disbelief. "Your news programs tell a different story."

"Look, man, I know you're not from around here, but--"

"What do you mean? How do you know that?"

"Uh, your accent, dude."

"What accent?"

"The British one."

"What is 'British'?"

"Listen, buddy, not all Americans are murderers. We don't all have guns and we don't all hate this race or that religion. The ones that do are just real loud."

"I see," Abaddon said. "And you yourself have never killed anyone?"

"Of course not, man!"

"Huh. Interesting."

"Do you need help finding something, or what?"

"Do you sell history books here?"

"Not really. There are a few on the website, but if you want to save some money, just check out Wikipedia or go to a library."

"And what is a Wikipedia and where is this place you call 'library'?"

The clerk glared at him. "Bro."

Abaddon scoured the history section of the library, nearly overwhelmed by the number of books on the subject. To make it more manageable, he started with American history, since he happened to be in the United States. He'd follow that with English history, since he, apparently, was speaking with an English accent, and go from there. He'd read every history book in the library. He wanted to get as much information on the evolution of the human species as he could. Perhaps if he understood *why* they behaved the way they did, he wouldn't have to slaughter them en masse. After all, the boy at the department store wasn't altogether awful, though maybe a tad condescending. Also, the woman that helped him find the history section of the library was quite pleasant and everyone in the building was polite and quiet. He gathered the books and sat at a table, noticing the sense of calm in the room as people minded their own business, only whispering when speaking at all. He liked it here.

He began reading a book detailing the American Revolution. It was brutal. It started with people being treated unfairly by their government and ended with approximately fifty-thousand people dead from battle wounds and disease. Men were taken prisoner, never to be heard from again. Cities devastated by fire. Children orphaned.

He continued reading, books chronicling The War of 1812 and The American Civil War. He was disgusted and outraged. He read about children working in factories, men dying in mines, and women burning alive in a garment factory, having been locked in their workrooms for no other reason than the greed of the men that owned the building. More wars followed, as did criminal leaders and assassinations. Terrorism, bombings...it was too much to take.

He decided to move on to English history, the country the Americans found too cruel to remain subject to. He thought there was no way they could have been as bloodthirsty and devious as the Americans. He soon discovered that the English were, in fact, even worse. The Crusades, Colonization, the many, many wars...the slave trade. He'd had enough. People throughout history had proven themselves evil beyond measure. He sat back in his seat, arms crossed, reflecting on what he'd learned. His stomach was in knots, rage mingled with something else. What was it? He couldn't remember the feeling. He then felt a warm tear slip down his cheek and he realized, it was sorrow. Sadness filled his chest as he covered his mouth, not wanting to bother anyone with the sound of his weeping. This is what humanity had come from; violence, injustice, malice. No wonder they still displayed such savagery. He wiped the tears from his face, put the books back where he'd found them, and headed toward the door. He'd come back tomorrow and learn the histories of African and Middle Eastern countries. Those were places he remembered as thriving and peaceful, for the most part. Surely, their stories would be easier to take than the ones he read today.

Chapter 9

"Dad!" Wyatt was jolted out of bed by the volume of the word. "Dad!" It was coming from the bathroom across the hall. The overhead light exploded. "DAD!" He opened the door and was taken aback by what he saw. It was Will, but it wasn't. Though his growth had always been accelerated, it had also been steady; subtle enough that Wyatt felt he was watching his son mature into every age. This was like nothing he'd seen before. Last night, Will went to bed a sixteen or so-year-old-boy. Today, he'd woken up a man in his mid-twenties. Wyatt was speechless.

"What happened to me, Dad?!" Will shouted, the lights above the mirror flickering.

Wyatt got his bearings and took his son's face in his hands, studying the changes that had occurred. It was like looking in a mirror to the past. He looked exactly like Wyatt's younger self, the resemblance to Annie all but gone. "It looks like you grew up."

"Overnight?!"

"Apparently. You okay? How do you feel?"

"Old."

Wyatt laughed and hugged him, Will trembling in his father's arms. "You're okay," Wyatt told him before calling to Gabriel. *Will looks twenty-five. Is that what's supposed to happen?*

Using his powers probably triggered a growth spurt, she answered. *He's done growing and I know you know what that means. Keep a real close eye on him. If he gets out of control--*

I know.

He pat Will's shoulder and looked him in the eyes. "We'll have to work hard to make sure you can control your powers and *yourself.* Lightning training every day. Maybe some meditation or something to keep you calm when you start to feel stressed or angry."

Will nodded in agreement.

"The good news," Wyatt said. "Is that you'll age like everyone else from now on. If someone comes to the door--"

"No more hiding?" Will asked, his anxiety giving way to hope.

"No more panicking at the sight of people," Wyatt corrected. "As far as going out, I don't know--"

"Come on, Dad. What's the worst that could happen?"

"Power outages, electrical fires, death and destruction."

"Dad,"

"All right, listen, I have some paperwork at the shop I need to deal with. I'll only be there for an hour or so. The truth is, I don't want to leave you alone right now, so you can come with me, but if you start feeling--"

"If I get overwhelmed, we'll come home. I get it."

"Do you? Because it's the most important thing in the world as far as you're concerned. With our powers, things can go from zero to Apocalypse in seconds."

"I understand, Dad. I promise I won't put anyone in danger."

"All right," Wyatt said, still unsure if bringing him along was the right thing to do.

"Thanks, Dad. What's for breakfast? I feel like I haven't eaten in a week."

Wyatt laughed as they headed down the stairs. "Oh, and Will, if anyone asks, I had you when I was a teenager."

"Your office is smaller than I thought," Will said, looking with interest around the room. "Offices on TV are big, have windows and plants. This is a dungeon with a desk."

"Hey," Wyatt chuckled. "I also have a safe and a file cabinet, so, you know, I'm living the dream." He went back to filling out purchase orders, not noticing his son peeking out into the shop.

So many people, Will thought. He watched them like a movie as they ate, stood in line, and spoke to one another. Being out in the world again was exhilarating. He could feel the energy coming from the room just beyond the door. It was magnetic. He wanted desperately to be part of it, to be among the people. Then, he saw her.

"Dad!" he whispered. "That's her! That's the girl from the SATs. I didn't know she worked here."

Wyatt got up from his seat and peered through the crack in the door. "I haven't seen her before. She must be the new cashier Charlie hired."

Will abruptly closed the door. "Am I attractive?" he asked.

"I'm sorry, what?"

"Am I good-looking? I mean, you see her, she's gorgeous. Do I have a chance?"

"I don't know how to answer this question."

"Should I ask for her number?" Will wondered. "Am I allowed to date? What do people even *do* on dates?"

"Slow down," Wyatt instructed. "Breathe. Don't worry about dating just yet. You haven't even introduced yourself. As far as she knows, you're a complete stranger."

"Right," Will realized. "The guy she met at the high school was ten years younger."

"Exactly, so don't freak her out by asking for a date first thing. Girls don't like to feel ambushed. You can't just walk up to her and ask for her number. You have to be casual. Have a normal conversation."

"Okay," Will said. "Yeah, just talk to her like a normal person. Except *I don't talk to people, Dad.* What do I say?"

"Hi."

"Dad,"

"You say, 'hi'. Let her take your order. If she's interested, she'll give you an indication. Prolonged eye contact, smiling, touching her hair. Now, some of that is just being friendly or even just polite because she's working in customer service, so don't get your hopes up. Ask a question. Nothing personal, just small talk. See how the conversation goes. Tell a joke. If she laughs, you have a shot. If she touches your arm, she's most likely into you. Don't ask for her number. It's not like you'll never see her again, she works here. Give her space so she feels comfortable."

"Okay," Will said. "Solid advice. Insightful."

"Thank you."

"How'd you get so good at this?"

"Practice."

"You had a lot of girlfriends?"

"In my younger days."

"What happened?"

"Don't worry about it."

"Come to think of it, have you been on a date since Mom--"

"Are you gonna talk to the girl, or not?"

"Yeah," Will nodded. He took a deep breath and let it out slowly. "Okay. I'm going for it." The two stood, neither of them moving an inch.

"Soon?" Wyatt teased.

"I just need a second." Will cracked the door and looked out into the room. The line had dwindled and Michelle had no customers. "Okay, I'm going."

He nervously approached the counter, glancing back at his father who gave him a reassuring nod. Wyatt closed the door, wondering if he'd made a mistake letting Will go. On one hand, he was a grown man now, and keeping him locked up at home seemed barbaric and slightly abusive. On the other hand, he knew what his son was capable of and while he'd shown no signs of being unnecessarily angry or otherwise insane, his personality could turn on a dime, according to Gabriel, who had been right about everything else, so far. He leaned against the door, uncertainty taking hold, and said to himself, "Parenting is hard."

Michelle struggled to get the coin wrapper open, the roll of quarters slippery in her hands. As she finally made some progress at ripping the paper, the whole thing fell apart, spewing coins in all directions.

"Come on," she whispered, crouching on the floor to pick up the rogue change. She looked up, seeing a man also crouching on the other side of the glass donut case in front of her. As the two stood, Michelle quickly noticed how cute he was. Dark eyes and hair, kind of tall, wearing a tee-shirt that seemed a touch too big for him. He moved awkwardly, as if nervous, which endeared him to her even more.

"You dropped these," the young man said, placing the three quarters he'd picked up on the counter.

She took them and put them in her drawer, hoping she'd found them all. "Thanks."

"Don't worry," he said. "I didn't take any."

"Oh, I know," she said, not actually knowing that at all, but feeling compelled to put him at ease. "What can I get you?"

"Um, two glazed, please."

As she reached for the donuts, she could see him fidgeting with the empty coin wrapper, signaling to her that he was anxious to speak to her. It was precious.

"You don't have to be nervous," she told him, placing the donuts in a bag.

"What? I'm not, I mean, it's just,"

"Just what?"

"I'm sorry, I'm trying to think of something funny to say, but you're so, you're..."

"I'm what?"

"You're just so pretty. Sorry, I'm probably staring like a creep. I'll leave you alone." He paid for the donuts and took the bag, sure he'd blown it. He started to walk off, but she called him back.

"Hey," she said, writing her cell number on the coin wrapper. "I'm Michelle. We should hang out sometime." He took the paper, a tingling sensation building in his stomach.

"Cool," he said, the delight in his voice evident. "I'll call you. Tomorrow. I'll call you tomorrow."

"Hey," she called after him as he headed to the back of the shop. "What's your name?"

"It's Will. Will Sinclair," he called back, disappearing into the owner's office.

Her heart sank. "Oh, fuck me," she said under her breath.

"She gave me her number!" Will said, showing Wyatt the torn wrapper.

"That's great," Wyatt said, trying to cover his apprehension and sound supportive. "What are you gonna do now?"

"Eat these donuts and have a mild panic attack."

Chapter 10

Will looked down at the skates, now securely tied. He'd never worn skates before, let alone been to a roller rink, but it's what Michelle had suggested they do and he couldn't refuse her. Something about her smile made him weak and when she took his hand to help him to his feet, he thought he might faint.

"You okay?" she asked, now holding onto both of his hands to keep him steady, her soft skin giving him chills.

"Yeah, I'm fine," he said, shaking, trying hard not to fall.

Michelle laughed. "Maybe we should stay in the arcade area for a while. It has carpet."

"Let's do that," Will said, unable to hide the relief in his voice. "I'll get some quarters." He awkwardly scooted himself to the change machine and put in a five-dollar bill. He gave twelve quarters to Michelle and pocketed the rest.

"Thank you, Will. That's nice of you," she told him.

"If three dollars in change impresses you, wait til I buy you nachos later."

"I will never not be impressed by nachos."

"And cotton candy."

"Now you're just showing off."

The two played for about an hour, beating each other in several racing games. The building was relatively quiet for a Friday night, only a couple dozen people on the rink itself and less than a handful in the arcade. The restaurant area was nearly empty when they sat down to eat.

"As promised," Will said, setting the plate of nachos in front of his date as she took a sip of soda.

"And you're officially the coolest person I know in this town," she complimented. He gave a shy laugh and sat, his own nachos beckoning him like sirens. He shoveled them into his mouth a few at a time, paying no mind to the cheese dripping to his chin.

"Hungry?" Michelle asked.

"Always." He drank his soda and sat quietly while Michelle ate. *Ask questions*, his father had told him. *Be interested. Listen.* "So, what did you do before you started working at Pine's?"

"I was a personal assistant."

"What was that like?" he asked, wiping the cheese from his face with a napkin.

"It was a lot of work," she told him, remembering the long hours of martial arts training. "But, I learned a ton. My old boss knows all kinds of interesting stuff. And she's not a bad time to be around. She's real funny."

"Why'd you leave?"

She knew she couldn't tell him the truth, but she felt strangely guilty about lying to him, so she compromised. "It was just time for me to get out of New York."

"New York? That's where my dad's from. What's it like?"

"Busy."

"A lot of people, right?"

"Yeah."

"I've always wanted to go, but it's probably not in the cards," Will said, the disappointment in his voice apparent. "At least, not for a while."

"Why not?" Michelle reflexively asked, already knowing the answer.

"Being around a lot of people is, um...worrisome."

"Oh."

"I mean, I like people. I don't have social anxiety or anything, it's just," he paused for a moment, trying to think of how best to explain it to her without revealing too much. "Growing up, I had to stay away from people because my dad was worried they wouldn't understand me. I had a condition. Now, I just really hope I am who I think I am."

"Well, not that my opinion means anything, but you seem okay to me."

"Your opinion means *everything*."

She stopped eating, a twinge of emotion bubbling up in her stomach. She was crushing hard, a direct violation of the rules. She wasn't even supposed to have a conversation with Will that went beyond small talk, let alone be on a date with him. She watched him as he smiled at her, taking her trash to the garbage before heading back to the concession stand to buy dessert. She knew Gabriel would be pissed, so she decided not to get too attached. *Keep it casual*, she thought, deciding there was no harm in befriending him, as long as that's as far as it went. *No kissing*, she vowed, but as he walked back to the table, cotton candy in hand, she knew she was kidding herself. Besides being the first guy to show any real interest in her, he was cute as could be, smart and charming. No one had ever looked at her the way he did, like she could do no wrong, and as he handed her the cotton candy, a tiny static shock passing between them, butterflies in her stomach, she thought, *I'm fucked*.

Wyatt drained the hamburger he'd browned and returned it to the pan. Will would be back any second and he wanted to surprise him with a special meal to either celebrate his first date or comfort him if it had gone badly. He'd put the pan back on the stove when he felt an eerie sensation, compelled to look out the window above the sink. It was dark and he could barely make out the shadowy form of the barn at the back of the yard and the treeline just past it. Nothing seemed out of the ordinary, but he was sure something was off. As he reached for the back door's knob, he heard the front door close. He went to the living room to find Will back home.

"How was it?" Wyatt asked.

"Amazing," Will said, locking the door behind him. "She's amazing. She's funny and interesting and, jeez, Dad, she's so pretty. I probably freaked her out staring so much."

Wyatt laughed. "I'm glad you had a good time."

"I had a *great* time. One thing, though. Can you teach me how to drive? It's kind of embarrassing being twenty-five with no license. I don't want her to think I'm weird."

"Sure," Wyatt agreed. "We'll have to start lessons next weekend, though. I have to go to the city for a couple of days. There's food in the kitchen and I'll leave you some money for pizza. You think you can handle being here alone until Monday?"

"Sure."

"While I'm gone, no powers, okay? We can get back to practicing when I get home, but I don't want there to be any mistakes, you understand?"

"I get it, Dad. I'll be fine."

"All right."

"I get why I can't go with you," Will said. "But will I be able to someday? Go to New York? See where you're from, where you met Mom?"

"Of course," Wyatt said, putting his hand on his son's shoulder. "You're doing well controlling your abilities and being out in public. No incidents, so far. I think with a few more months of training and meditation, you'll be ready to live a normal life like everyone else."

"I hope so. I'd like to see what all the fuss is about. New York, I mean. Not a normal life. Although, that too, to be honest."

Wyatt laughed again, heading to the kitchen. "You hungry? I'm making tacos."

"You're *what*?"

"I can make tacos."

"Since when?"

"Since college. I just don't do it very often."

"I have no recollection of you ever--"

"Do you want tacos, or not?"

Will nodded.

Wyatt got a box of shells from the pantry and read the instructions. Will could see the concentration on his father's face and decided it would most likely be a while before dinner would be ready, so he went up to his room, sat on the end of his bed, and called Michelle.

"I just wanted to make sure you got home safe," he told her.

"I'm still driving," she said.

"Oh, right. I didn't-- hey, would it be weird if I asked you out again? Is it too soon? You had a good time, right?"

"I had a really good time."

"My dad's going out of town, so I should probably stay in, but maybe you could come over? We could watch TV or something."

"I'll bring some DVDs," Michelle agreed. "There's an awesome show that's like, mandatory viewing. See you Sunday?"

"Sunday's perfect! Listen, I'm sorry if I made you uncomfortable tonight. I didn't mean to stare."

"You didn't."

"Oh, good. You're just...I really like you."

There was a long pause.

"Michelle? Are you there?"

"I'm here," she said.

"Sorry. Did I freak you out? Am I coming on too strong? I shouldn't have said any--"

"I like you, too, Will."

"Oh," he said, relief washing over him. "Thank you. I mean, good. I mean--"

"Can I call you back when I get home? It's starting to rain and I should concentrate on the road."

"Oh, yeah, of course. I'll talk to you later."

"Okay, bye."

"Bye." He put the phone down and fell back onto his bed. He couldn't stop smiling, Michelle's voice lingering in his mind. *I like you, too.* It was the most beautiful thing he'd ever heard.

"Will! Dinner!" Wyatt called.

Will jumped up, the smell of taco seasoning filling his nose. As he raced down the stairs, he couldn't help but say, out loud, "Best day ever."

Later that night, Michelle called back and they talked for hours about everything from the crazy Indiana weather to their mother's deaths. They had so much in common including their tastes in music, food and never feeling like they belonged anywhere besides home. Will was thoroughly smitten and after their conversation, he was sure she was super into him, too.

Will sat in the silence, the empty house feeling bigger with his father gone. He had been reading, but his mind wandered to thoughts of Michelle. They had plans for the next day to binge episodes of a show he'd never heard of that she swore was incredible. It would be only them, together, in the house, alone. He was nervous, so he put the book down and opened the laptop. *What to do when you're alone with a girl*, he searched. "Nope," he said, closing the window that had become covered in pornographic imagery. He knew from several awkward conversations with his dad that porn and real-life rarely had anything in common. Besides, he wasn't expecting things to move that quickly with Michelle. He was just hoping for some helpful tips on how to behave that were more specific than the 'just be yourself' speech his dad had given him. He closed the computer, dissatisfied with what he found on the subject, and took a sip of water before placing the bottle back on the kitchen table. He glanced up at the window, noticing the storm raging outside. Hail the size of golf balls was raining down so hard, it put a dent in the grill. The sky was dark and swirling, the angry clouds looking lower to the ground than usual. Then, he heard it... the siren. As he started to head to the basement, a knock came on the front door. He wasn't sure if he should answer it. Normally, he would hide until the person left, but a person shouldn't be out in this weather, so he hesitantly opened the door.

"Michelle," he greeted. "I thought you were coming over tomorrow."

"I am," she said, grateful to be under the porch and out of the hail. "But, my apartment doesn't have a basement and I'm not used to this weather. Would it be okay if--"

"Of course!" he blurted, stepping aside to let her in. "Come in. I was just about to head downstairs." They hurried to the basement, Will turning on the dim overhead light before joining Michelle on the old, dusty sofa. They watched the hail pile up outside the small windows near the ceiling, both of them feeling anxious, but for different reasons.

"So, this happens a lot here?" she asked.

"No, just like, twenty or so times a year."

"Oh, is that all?" she giggled.

"It's not that bad. I've lived here my whole life and have never had anything particularly bad happen because of a storm."

"Okay," she said, her shoulders relaxing. "That makes me feel a little better."

"The good thing about tornadoes is that even if they're right on top of you, they're gone in like, two minutes."

"Yeah. You're right. We should maybe try not to think about it. So, what have you been up to today?"

"Reading some Dickens. What about you?"

"Ignoring friend requests and blocking people on social media."

"Why?"

"People in high school weren't exactly nice to me. There was a lot of racism and at the time, I ignored it, but these people all of a sudden out of nowhere deciding they want to be friends or whatever is...like, I want to ask them if they're lost."

"I'm so sorry. I can't imagine what that must have been like for you."

"Yeah, you're pretty white." They both laughed before she spoke again. "It's just hard when you already don't feel Black enough or Asian enough and then you have all these white kids calling you 'ugly' and on top of it, the Dean is--"

"Ugly?!" Will interrupted.

"Yeah. I mean, I know I shouldn't listen to tha--"

"You are the furthest thing from ugly. You're so far from ugly, ugly couldn't see you with a telescope. *You*, you're the most beautiful girl I've ever seen. *Ever*. And that includes lingerie models I saw on a TV special once."

"That's nice of you to say," she told him, pushing her hair behind her ear.

"I mean it. You're *gorgeous*. Anyone that would say otherwise is either lying or needs glasses."

"Thanks," she said, her insecurities giving way to something else. The somewhat manageable crush she had before was growing stronger and as she looked into his eyes, she felt the will to hold herself back leave her. Before she knew what she was doing, she leaned in and kissed him. He was surprised, then delighted. He'd never kissed anyone before and it was everything he'd thought it would be and more. Not wanting it to end, he took her face in his hands, letting them wander into her hair and back. He felt warm all over like he'd been wrapped in a heated blanket. As the world fell away, the light above flickered, then went out completely. They didn't notice.

Chapter 11

"Look at you, you gorgeous bitch," Gabriel beamed.

"I know, right?" Valerie said, checking herself out in the mirror. "Get back here and zip me up. It's almost time." Gabriel complied then hugged her sister from behind.

"I'm really happy for you," she told her. "Malik's a good dude, not to mention sexy as fuck. Honestly, nice haul."

"Girl, I will hurt you."

"May I come in?" Lucifer called from the other side of the dressing room door.

"Yeah!" Gabriel called back, ignoring Valerie's annoyed glare.

"Well, you look lovely, Uriel," Lucifer said as he entered the room. "I just wanted to give you my gift now as I'll be leaving after the ceremony to attend to more pressing matters. Congratulations." He handed her an envelope. "I've booked you a honeymoon in Venice. I haven't been there myself in a few hundred years, but the travel agent assured me that its retained it's romantic ambiance. Do mind the ghosts."

"Thank you, Lucifer. That's actually very sweet," Valerie said, surprised by his kindness.

"Thank Gabriel. It was her money I spent."

"You know I give zero fucks about money," Gabriel interjected. "If I did, I'd give you a lecture on the benefits of *free* internet porn. My credit card statement looks like I live with a teenage boy on Rumspringa."

"All right, let's not make me throw up while I'm in my dress, okay? Thank you," Valerie cringed.

"For real," Gabriel continued. "You should hit that bartender chick up. Get it out of your system."

"I will consider it," Lucifer told her. "And, I'll abstain from viewing certain websites, on the condition that you eat something green that grew from the ground every day."

"That's...you know what? Look at whatever porn you want. It's none of my business."

Lucifer smirked. "I will go take my seat now," he said, leaving the room.

"Hey, can I talk to you for a second?" Valerie asked.

"About the kid thing?" Gabriel asked.

"Yeah. Can you get in Malik's head and see if he-- I mean, he knows I can't have kids, but I think he wants them."

"He does."

"Fuck."

"It's cool. I put a hundred thousand dollars in your checking account this morning."

"Bitch, you did what?"

"Happy wedding!"

"Girl,"

"Adoption's expensive, plus you'll have to buy a crib and diapers and shit."

"It's too much."

"A, no it's not, and two, what we are shouldn't prohibit you from living your life. Don't forget, I know what you want. I know you better than you know yourself. You deserve everything good in the world and it would make me happy to make you happy. So, quit being stubborn and take the fucking money. And, thank your lucky stars I didn't give you more, because I wanted to, but I knew what kind of fit you'd throw."

"I don't kno--"

"Just accept my love!"

"Fine, Jesus," Valerie chuckled. "But I hope you don't think I'll be asking you to babysit."

Gabriel scoffed. "You better not. I am not equipped."

"And, now that I'm all in my dress, *of course,* I have to pee." Valerie shooed Gabriel from the room for privacy.

"It's not like I haven't seen it!" Gabriel called through the door.

"Bitch, stay out of my head!"

Gabriel waited impatiently, looking onto the crowd of people, trying to block out the thoughts of Valerie's coworkers and college friends. Each one saw her slightly differently. To some, she was the reliable friend that got them home safely after happy hour. To others, she was someone they could trust to give them the best advice. To her college roommate, she was the straight girl she still had feelings for but never had the guts to tell. Gabriel wouldn't spill the woman's secret; it would only make things awkward and she knew how much her friendship meant to her sister.

"Barachiel," Gabriel whispered to herself, feeling him enter the building. She rushed to find him placing a package on the gift table. "B!" she nearly shouted, throwing her arms around his neck and hugging him tightly.

"Gabriel," he said, a broad smile covering his face. "How are you?"

"Awesome," she said, pulling away to look at his face. "First, I want you to know that I've missed you terribly, but also," She smacked his arm hard.

"Ow!" he laughed.

"You let him kill the werewolf?" she whispered.

"I didn't *let* him. The thing was killing me. He got scared. And why could he kill it, but I couldn't? I gave that thing everything I had and it didn't make a dent."

"Because he's stronger than you, stupid. You have to pull energy from somewhere else. Static in the air, light sockets, the atmosphere. Meanwhile, Will has a battery inside him with more power than the goddamn sun. A human soul is condensed creation. Nothing in the universe is stronger than that but God, and He's on vacation. That's what makes Will so dangerous."

"He's not dangerous," Wyatt insisted.

"Are you sure? Because if he goes dark side, you won't be able to control him."

"He's fine."

"Wyatt!" Valerie squealed, hurrying to give her brother a quick hug. "I'm digging the suit. You clean up nice."

"Congratulations," he told her.

"Thank you, thank you."

"Gabriel tells me Malik's a decent guy."

"He's perfection personified. Listen, I was wondering since I don't have a daddy or anything if you'd walk me down the aisle? I know we haven't seen each other in a minute, but--"

"I'd be honored."

"That's good because it's time to start. Go ahead, girl. Kick this shit off." They headed to the ceremony room and paused outside the entrance, Valerie jumping in her skin as she took her brother's arm. Gabriel walked to the rose petal-covered aisle runner and waited for the music to start. When it did, she took one slow step after another toward the arch at the other end where the minister, Malik, and his best man stood. She took her place and listened to Valerie's fiance's thoughts.

Who is this white boy walking her down the aisle? Must be one of her foster brothers. Damn, she looks good. I can't wait to get my hands on her tonight.

Ew. Gabriel thought.

What is this music? Lucifer asked.

The Wedding March of Osterdalen, Gabriel answered. *I thought you'd appreciate it.*

Wyatt left Valerie at the altar and took his seat next to Lucifer.

"Nice to see you, brother," Lucifer greeted.

"Lucifer."

"Does this song remind you of anything?"

"It's vaguely familiar," he admitted. "I can't place it."

"We heard something like it once at a wedding in Norway. Let's hope this one ends differently."

"Oh. I'm sorry, I don't remember that."

"It's probably for the best. This version of you probably wouldn't have the stomach for what came after the music ended."

"We've gathered here today," the minister began. "To celebrate the joining of this man and this woman in Holy Matrimony. If anyone here objects to this union, please speak now, or forever hold your peace."

Lucifer jokingly whispered, "Should I--"

"You better not," Wyatt warned.

"If there are no objections, we'll begin," the minister continued. "The couple have written their own vows." He gestured to Valerie to start. She nodded and looked into Malik's eyes. He could see how nervous she was, so he took her hands in his and offered a reassuring smile. She smiled back and cleared her throat before speaking.

"Love is patient. Love is kind. I'm neither of those things." The crowd quietly laughed as she continued. "But, I promise that I'll try, every day, to be whatever it is you need me to be. If you're upset, I'll comfort you. If you're sick, I'll heal you. If you're hungry, let's be honest, you'll probably have to feed yourself, but I can set a table like nobody's business." Malik and the crowd laughed again. "Seriously, though, you're the best man I've ever known and I'll do everything I can to always make you happy. I love you."

"Thank you, Valerie," the minister said as Malik kissed her hands. "Now, Malik."

"Valerie Moore," Malik said. "You are crazy and wild. You're argumentative and stubborn and you always have to have things your way." Again, the crowd chuckled. "And I have loved every second of being with you. You make me laugh. You make me whole. The light you bring into my life has made me a better man. You, Ms. Moore, are the absolute best thing that God has been gracious enough to bless me with and I will spend the rest of my life working to be the man you deserve. I love you more and more every minute of every day. Thank you for the honor of allowing me in your life."

Smooth, Gabriel thought.

Isn't he, though? Valerie responded.

"And now," the minister said. "The rings." Malik's best man gave him the white gold band. "Repeat after me. With this ring, I thee wed."

"With this ring," Malik repeated, slipping the ring on Valerie's finger. "I thee wed."

Gabriel handed Valerie Malik's ring. Again, the minister said, "Repeat after me. With this ring, I thee wed."

"With this ring," Valerie said, placing the ring on Malik's finger. "I thee wed."

"By the power vested in me by the Sikes Memorial Methodist Church and the state of New Jersey, I hereby pronounce you husband and wife. You may kiss your bride."

Malik kissed his new wife with a little more tongue than was appropriate as the attendants cheered. They turned to face the crowd, held hands, and gleefully jumped over the broom Malik's mother had placed on the floor, the guests again erupting in applause. They walked back down the aisle and into the ballroom as "That's How Strong My Love Is" by Otis Redding played overhead.

"Give our sisters my best, won't you?" Lucifer said quietly as he stood.

"You're not staying for the reception?" Wyatt asked.

"No time. While Gabriel, to my dismay, seems less than fully invested in the mission at hand, I intend on bringing Abaddon to justice in a much more timely fashion than we did Lilith. It really was good to see you, Barachiel. Perhaps, when the world as we know it is no longer in danger, we can catch up properly." He pat Wyatt on the back before moving past him to leave.

"Hey, you like Foo Fighters, right?" Gabriel asked on her way past Wyatt.

"Sure," he said, gently taking her arm to stop her.

"Good, because I have a surprise for Uriel. She has no idea--"

"Abaddon?" Wyatt interrupted. "Were you ever intending on filling me in?"

"No. It's not for you to worry about," she told him, pulling her arm away. "Unlike Lucifer's rowdy twin, Abaddon has no way of hiding where he is from me. Don't tell you-know-who. The wild goose chase is keeping him out of trouble, for now. I can't have him going on another murder spree."

"Gabriel,"

"Relax. I know what Abaddon's after and where he plans on getting it and he's not there yet. I'm keeping an eye on him, don't worry. I'm honestly trying to give him a chance to change his mind, redeem himself. It's probably not in the cards, though."

"Do you need any help?"

"Nah. You just have a good time at the reception, come back to my place for pizza and beer, and in a couple of days, go back to the sticks and make sure your spawn hasn't gone full psycho."

"Will is--"

"Nope," Gabriel stopped him, putting her hand up and turning her head. "I can't think about that right now. I have a party to get to."

"I'm fine, Dad," Will said.

"Are you sure?" Wyatt asked, his phone pressed to one ear and his hand to the other in a feeble attempt to block out the music blaring in the ballroom just beyond the doors where he stood, barely able to hear his son's responses to his questions.

"Yes, Dad. Nothing is gonna happen in two days."

"You remember what we talked about? If you ever feel like you're losing control--"

"Deep breaths, count to ten and call you right away. I know."

"And?"

"And no powers. I know all this, Dad. You don't have to worry about me. Go have some fun. You deserve a break. Spend some time with your sisters. I know you miss them."

"All right, call me if--"

"Bye, Dad."

"Bye." Wyatt ended the call and put his phone back in his jacket pocket. He knew he was being paranoid. Gabriel had gotten in his head, but Will was right. He *had* missed his sisters, more than he'd realized until he saw them again. "All Of Me" was over, which meant so was Valerie and Malik's first dance. Wyatt made his way to the ballroom where he saw Valerie and Gabriel dancing to a version of "In Da Club" he hadn't heard before and as he watched them, he felt calm, their happiness giving him a sense of well-being. If they could celebrate this unencumbered while Abaddon, whoever that was, was on the loose, he could relax a bit, too, for a change.

When the song ended, Gabriel ran to the DJ booth and took the microphone. "Can I get everyone's attention, please?" she piped. The room went quiet. "As some of you know, I'm Gabriel, Valerie's sister. For those of you that look confused, yes, we have different parents. Don't think about it too hard. So, when we were teenagers, we had pretty different tastes in music. Try as I might, I could never get her to like certain bands I was in to. One day, though, we were listening to a radio show that shall remain nameless and the guest played an acoustic version of my favorite song. By some miracle, Valerie loved it. About a decade later, they released that version on an album that I bought several copies of, and over the years, we've spent many nights eating junk and listening to that song on repeat. Just like that song, marriage is new to my girl, but I'm sure she'll love it just as much. Congratulations." She handed the mic back to the DJ as "Everlong" began to play. Suddenly, a curtain opened revealing a wall of windows showcasing a beautiful ocean view and something else.

"You didn't!" Valerie squealed among the gasps and cheers from the wedding guests.

"Bitch, you know that I did," Gabriel said, smiling wide as she gave her sister a hug. They listened intently until the song was over and applause broke out.

"Hey, Wyatt," Valerie said as he came to stand with his sisters. "Can't talk now. I'm gonna go meet Dave Grohl!" She rushed off toward the stage, leaving Wyatt and Gabriel alone.

"Impressive," he said.

"So, the kid says he's fine."

"Yeah."

"All right. If you trust him, I trust him." *Trust, but verify*, she thought as she checked her phone for messages from Michelle. Nothing new.

"Where'd your phone come from?" he wondered, noticing she wasn't carrying a bag.

"This dress has *pockets*!"

"If I eat any more, I'm gonna die of cheese," Gabriel complained.

Wyatt laughed, taking a final sip of beer before standing and putting the empty pizza box in the kitchen.

"Hey," Gabriel said, getting up from the sofa and following her brother, sitting at the bar and drinking the last of her soda. "I'm sorry I called Will psycho. Or said he *would be* psycho. Or whatever I said. You know I love that kid, right?"

"I know," Wyatt acknowledged, sitting across from her.

"I just worry."

"Yeah, well, so do I," he admitted. "He hasn't done anything to make me think he'll go dark side, as you put it, but when he killed the werewolf, I felt sick. I felt guilty. I should have been able to protect him from that. He's distracted right now since he's discovered girls, but I know it bothers him. It's a burden, the regret of what he did. He understands that he had to, but deep down--"

"He's not over it."

"No. And if he gets...if he loses control--"

"You're a good dad, B. Better than yours and light years better than mine. Who knows? Maybe he'll be fine. The Nephilim back in the day had no mothers and their fathers all left them before they were born. They had no one to teach them how to be what they were. You being around could be the thing Will needs to stay Will and keep him from flipping his shit."

"Do you believe that?"

"Fifty/fifty."

"That's encouraging."

"I'm going to bed. Your room's where you left it." She got up and headed down the hall. "Love you!" she called.

"Love you, too!" he called back, checking his phone before heading to bed himself. A text from Will sent a little over an hour before read *Going to bed. Night.* Wyatt let out a sigh of relief as he put the phone down on the bar. Will was okay. Everything was okay.

Chapter 12

"Seven seasons," Michelle said excitedly. "A hundred and forty-four episodes."

"That's a lot," Will pointed out.

"That's just the beginning. There's a spin-off series almost as awesome. I brought those DVDs, too."

Will laughed. "There's no way we're getting through those today."

"No, but we can *start*. I'll leave everything here for you to watch when you feel like and we can talk about the episodes later. You ready?"

He nodded and handed her the remote. His arm felt like home to her as she wrapped it around her shoulders and snuggled in next to him. She couldn't help but dance a little in her seat as the show's theme played. They stayed there all day, watching hour after hour, eating candy, and cuddling on the couch. They'd gotten through the seventh episode when Will hit pause.

"So," he said. "She kills--"

"Yeah."

"But, she's in love with--"

"Yeah."

"That's gonna be awkward later."

"You don't even know."

"Does she kill him?"

"No spoilers!"

"Seems like a waste," he bemoaned. "Why have this whole love story if she just ends up killing him?"

"It's romantic."

"It's depressing."

"That's what romance is," she told him. "Romance can't exist without tragedy. How do you know if something was worth having if you've never felt the pain of losing it?"

"That's dark."

"That's life."

"What about happily ever after?"

"Like fairy tales?"

"No, like," he thought for a second. "Take Charlie, for example. She's been married to the same guy since she was eighteen. Their oldest kid is about to have a kid of her own. It's nice."

"Okay, but, best-case scenario, they're together until one of them dies, leaving the other one alone and miserable."

"Sure, everyone dies, but isn't it love that makes life worth living? Spending however long you have with someone that understands you and makes you feel--"

"Happy?"

"Worthy. Useful. Seen. Building a life and maybe a family with someone, feeling like you belong somewhere. 'Romeo and Juliet' isn't aspirational, it's *sad*. A little old lady and a little old man holding hands on their front porch while their grandkids play in the yard, *that's* something to strive for."

"God, you are just," She touched his cheek, letting herself fall into the whirlpool of his eyes. "So fucking awesome." She pressed her lips to his and climbed onto his lap, the heat between them rising like the tide. As they kissed, Will was overtaken by lust. He wrapped his arms around her and laid her down, the feeling of her beneath him the rightest thing he'd ever known. He moved from her lips to her neck, breathing her in like life. He then felt himself, now hard as stone, rub against her. Embarrassed, he backed away.

"I'm so sorry," he said, covering himself with a throw pillow. "I got carried away."

She slipped her jeans off, keeping her eyes locked on his. His heart pounded as she opened her legs in front of him.

"Are," he said, hardly able to speak. "Are you sure?"

She nodded.

He threw the pillow to the floor and tore his own pants off, never having moved that fast in his life. He climbed on top of her and asked again, "Are you sure?" Again, she nodded. He looked at her, honored and amazed that someone so incredible would be with him. He kissed her, all thoughts of restraint fleeing his mind like passengers on a sinking ship. He heard her take a sharp breath as he entered her. "Am I hurting you?" he asked.

"No," she assured him. "No, keep going." He obeyed, doing his best to be gentle. The sensations were overwhelming. The world went away. The room, the television, even the couch all disappeared. All he could feel was her engulfing him like a slow-moving hurricane. She was his entire universe. Her heavy breathing synced with his as he felt her pulse around him. He tried to stop himself from coming inside her, realizing he'd forgotten to use a condom, but he couldn't. He let out a breathy moan as he finished before again apologizing.

"I'm sorry. I forgot a condom."

"It's okay," she said, steadying her breathing. "I'll take care of it."

He brushed a few stray hairs away from her face and looked at her adoringly. "You're stunning."

"Am I romanticizing you or are you just like, the perfect man?"

"I don't know about perfect," he told her. "Happy, though. You make me feel...I can't explain it. You just, you make me *feel*. I'm so grateful for you, Michelle." A flood of emotion and hormones washed over them as they kissed, Will reentering her with more ease than before.

"Again?" she breathed.

"And again," he said, kissing her neck. "And again, and again."

Wyatt dropped his bag and closed the door behind him. "Will!" he called. As he entered the living room, he saw several cleaning products on the coffee table. He then saw what they were for. On the sofa was a large stain that could only have been made by one thing... blood. Wyatt's heart sank. "Will!" he called again.

"Hey, Dad," Will said, bounding down the stairs. "Don't worry, I'm cleaning it up right now. Nothing was working, so I looked it up. Supposedly, peroxide gets it out like magic." He opened the small bottle and dumped its contents onto the couch. The stain began to lighten. "Well, I'll be damned."

"What did you do, Will?" Wyatt asked, seeing that the boy wasn't hurt himself.

"Please don't freak out."

"What did you do?"

"I had sex. Are you mad? Oh, and I forgot to use a condom, but she took the morning after pill, so everything's fine. She didn't tell me until after that she was a virgin, too. I would've put a towel down or something."

"Oh, God," Wyatt said, relief replacing dread. He pulled his son in for a hug. "I thought something bad happened."

"You're not mad?"

"No, I'm just glad you're okay," Wyatt replied, patting him on the shoulder and stepping back.

"Good, because I have questions."

"I'm sure you do," Wyatt chuckled.

"What does love feel like?"

"Love? Don't you think it's a little early?"

"I have no idea, that's why I'm asking you. I haven't seen what a relationship is supposed to look like. You haven't dated anyone, as far as I know, my whole life, and you're my only role model, so--"

"All right," Wyatt said defensively. "I've had a little bit of a dry spell."

"Dry? Dad, there's more rain in the Sahara."

"Okay, just sit your ass down. I'm gonna give you an education." He took a DVD from the cabinet and put it in the player. "My wedding to your mother." He skipped ahead a few scenes. "Watch me when she's saying her vows. See that look on my face? See my eyes? That's what love looks like."

"And you haven't had any relationships since Mom?"

"Not any healthy ones," he said, pausing the video on a close-up of Annie's face. "She was the love of my life."

"But, there *was* someone, after?"

"It doesn't matter."

"Why not?"

"It's complicated."

"I know you're lonely."

Wyatt sighed.

"It looks to me like you miss her, this mystery woman."

"Will,"

"You should call her."

"I shouldn't," Wyatt told him. "The truth is, I do miss her. More than I'd like to admit. But she's not--"

"Interested?"

"Human."

"Oh."

"When you were born, I left the city to keep you safe. I didn't tell her where I was going or even that I was leaving. I ghosted because I knew she'd follow me and you wouldn't have been safe from somebody like her."

"Why no one else, then? A regular person. Why haven't you been on a date in the last three years?"

"I've been kind of busy raising a smart-mouthed son that ages at Mach ten."

"Fair point, but I'm not a baby anymore, Dad. I don't want you to be alone because of me. Call your girlfriend, the whatever-she-is."

"She's a vampire."

"Those are real?! What are they like?"

"Obsessive."

"Is she hot?"

"Shit, yes."

Chapter 13

Wyatt turned off the TV, the remote feeling like failure in his hand. Sleep eluded him, his mind occupied with thoughts of Allydia. Will had been right about him being lonely and as much as it disturbed him to admit, he'd thought about the vampire a lot since leaving the city. She was complicated and a little psychotic, but she wasn't boring, and that alone made the idea of reaching out to her tempting. The last three years hadn't been exactly exciting. Aside from a couple of bouts with a werewolf, life had become unbearably dull. He was used to putting out fires, saving lives...hunting demons. Lately, though, all he seemed to be in life was 'Dad'.

He got up from his chair and headed to the kitchen, deciding he needed a nightcap before trying to get some rest. But, as he took a bottle of beer from the fridge, that eerie feeling once more came over him. He peered out the window, seeing nothing unusual, but the feeling remained. He went out into the backyard, careful to close the door quietly behind him. Will had gone to bed hours ago and he didn't want to wake him. As he walked across the grass, the feeling grew stronger. He knew *something* was out there and had been for a while. The night wrapped around him, the warm, still air of spring like a hug from an old friend. Fireflies danced under the clear sky and the sound of cicadas was the only thing he heard. Maybe he was being paranoid. He was about to turn back when he saw a glimmer among the trees, distinct from anything else in nature. He slowly moved toward it, gathering static electricity from the air in case he needed it. As he drew closer, the shimmering eyes became clearer and as she stepped out from the edge of the forest, he could see that they in fact belonged to Allydia.

"Oh, thank God," he muttered to himself, breaking into a full sprint to meet her. She leaped into his arms, wrapping her legs around him and kissing him fervently. She smelled like gardenias and felt like contentment, her pheromones doing their work to calm and entice him, not that he needed any persuading. He took her to the barn and pressed her to the wall, wasting no time getting his pants down and her skirt up. Her body was like a glove around him, her husky moans like a song. She shuddered against him, the intensity of the moment overwhelming her. He laid her down on the dusty wood floor and continued making love to her, so caught up that he didn't notice the hardness of the ground beneath them. She, too, was oblivious. The only thing she felt was him.

When it was over, he held her face in his hand, watching her eyes as she examined his expression. "Why are you here?" he wondered.

"You know why," she said.

"I missed you."

"Did you?"

"I did."

She ran her fingers down from his forehead to his cheek. "That's nice."

"I'm sorry about taking off like that."

"I understand," she said, turning her head to look toward the house. "And I hope *you* understand why I can't let that boy hurt you." She darted up and out of the barn, running too fast for Wyatt to stop her. He struggled to get his pants on and chase after her at the same time.

"Allydia!" he called. "Wait!" He got to the house to find her standing outside Will's room. He slept soundly, unaware of the threat at his door. "Allydia, stop!" Wyatt whispered.

"What have you done?" she asked.

"It's okay."

"This is a lot of things, Wyatt, but 'okay' is not one of them."

"Come downstairs," he said, taking her hand. She reluctantly followed.

"Do you have any idea what he is?"

"He's fine. He's a good kid."

"He's 'fine'? The last time things like that roamed the planet, your sister had to move me to Spain because your Father destroyed an entire continent to get rid of them."

"Gabriel saved you from the Flood? I didn't know that."

"How else would I still be here? Listen to me, you have no idea what he's capable of. You're not safe here. Come home with me and tell your brother. Let Lucifer handle this before it's too late."

"*Do not* tell Lucifer about Will."

"Wyatt,"

"I mean it."

"I don't appreciate your tone."

"Allydia, he's *my son*. I will *kill* Lucifer before I let him anywhere near--"

"Fine," she said, memories long buried creeping into her mind. Realizing that he'd never forgive her if she was the reason he lost his son, she agreed to back off. "But, if he hurts you, I will take him by the throat and drown him in your bathtub myself."

For the next few nights, Wyatt snuck Allydia up to his room after Will had gone to bed. It was like being in high school again, which somehow made the trysts even more exciting. When she went back to the city, Wyatt couldn't help but miss her. He'd grown fond of having her around; knowing she was keeping an eye on him from the woods was oddly comforting. Twisted and completely unhealthy, but comforting all the same.

Chapter 14

"Close your eyes," Will said, leading Michelle through the woods.

"You know this is how horror movies start, right?" she joked.

"Relax," he chuckled. "Just a few more steps." They finally reached their destination and stopped. "Open your eyes."

She gasped, the beauty of what he'd created surprising her. Twinkling lights wrapped around the trees. A dozen paper lanterns hung overhead, dangling from the branches. Solar-powered lights stuck up out of the ground, encircling an air mattress covered in a blanket. A picnic basket rested on one side of the mattress, the babbling creek on the other. They sat down, Michelle still looking up at the lights.

"Jesus, you're beautiful," he told her, noticing the way the soft light of the lanterns and the early evening sun made her skin glow and her eyes sparkle. She smiled widely and touched his hand and that's when he saw it; the same look that was in his father's eyes in the wedding video was in hers now. She loved him, too. His nerves disappeared as he held her hand, her touch soothing. "I brought you here and I put this together because I want to tell you something. Something important, and I wanted it to be perfect."

"Will," she grinned. "You didn't have to go to all this trouble."

"I did because you deserve it. You deserve more than I could probably ever give you. You're unbelievable and wonderful and I don't know if it's normal to feel like this this soon, and if you can't say it back, I'll understand, but it won't change how I feel about you. Michelle, I am completely, utterly, hopelessly, out of my mind in love with you. It's okay if--"

"I love you, too, Will," she said, squeezing his hand.

"Oh, good. That could've really sucked."

She laughed before kissing him, climbing on top of him, and pushing him to the bed.

"Are we--" he asked. "I mean, do you want to--"

"Do you not want to?" she asked, pulling her top off over her head.

"Oh, I *always* want to, I just didn't want to presume."

"I mean, you *did* bring a picnic. We could eat first if you want."

"No, no, we can eat after. It's not a problem."

"Good," she smirked, unhooking her bra.

As she bent down to kiss him again, he wondered out loud, "Good God, how did I get this lucky?"

He held her as she slept, her head resting comfortably on his chest. He kissed the top of her head through piles of soft curls, the sweet smell of her hair enveloping his senses. He looked up at the starry sky and took a deep breath, happiness blowing through him like wind. It had been a perfect night, one that he knew he'd remember for the rest of his life.

Somewhere in the distance, he heard the rustling of leaves. He lifted his head and looked around, but didn't see anything. Then, on the other side of the creek, as if from thin air, it appeared. Will's eyes became slits as he stared at the wolf, all but daring it to come closer. He held Michelle tighter, continuing to stare down the animal on the other side of the water. The wolf turned away and moved on, vanishing into the dark woods.

"Wake up," Will whispered.

"What?" Michelle asked groggily. "Did I fall asleep?"

"Yeah. It's late. We should go."

She nodded and started putting her clothes back on. They finished dressing and Michelle began deflating the mattress.

"I'll come back in the morning and pack this all up," Will told her. "The lanterns have all gone out. It's pretty dark and there could be wild animals. Let's just go."

"Okay," she agreed, still half asleep. She picked up the picnic basket. "I'm taking this, though. You need to eat."

Michelle woke up the next day to a string of lecture texts from Gabriel.

I didn't think I had to tell you not to date my nephew. You know what he is.

Also, you're almost related. Not really, but still.

Do you have a hormone imbalance that makes you want to hop on the first dick you see or are you just dumb as shit?

That might have been out of line, but I stand by it. I sent you strictly to monitor and report back if he got out of control. THAT'S IT. Fuck!

Try not to die.

Michelle rolled her eyes and set the phone back on the nightstand, pulling her comforter up to her chin, her mind swirling with memories of the night before. The lights, the soft sound of the creek, the warm night air, and Will. Thoughtful, gentle, loving Will. He was sweet and charming and handsome and he loved her. *He loved her.* When he looked at her, she could feel it all through her body, making it that much easier for her to let herself love him, too. She hadn't planned on falling for him so hard, but here she was, aching to see him again.

She picked up the phone to call him, but quickly remembered that he was driving with his father today. She remembered when her uncle had taught her to drive, his hysterical stomping on the nonexistent brake as he sat in the passenger seat of his sports car, clinging to the door handle with one hand and covering his eyes half the time with the other. He eventually sent her to driver's ed classes, telling her he didn't have the disposition to put his life in someone else's hands. She missed Tae every day, but meeting Gabriel had helped her deal with the loss immensely. She'd told her stories about his college days and explained what Heaven was like. Michelle knew her uncle was all right where he was and she'd see him again, someday, along with her parents and grandparents. She was grateful for Gabriel, even if she was wrong about Will. He'd shown no signs of psychopathy, sociopathy, or rage. She'd never seen him use his abilities, much less lose control of them. Gabriel trained her to be able to defend herself in case he ever went crazy, but she was sure Will was no threat to her. He was a good person and he was in love with her. *I'll be fine*, she texted Gabriel back. *Will is okay.*

Chapter 15

Researching humanity's evolution had left Abaddon profoundly disappointed. History was littered with genocide, torture, and war. Every time they seemed to be making progress, people would revert even further into cruelty and narcissism. God had sworn never to rid the Earth of them again, but he'd made no such promise. If his Father would not do what needed to be done, he would simply have to do it himself.

He sat on a park bench, watching the children play. These were the human race's only hope; innocent and gracious. The bit of God in them still shown and as he looked on, he considered the possibility that maybe humanity could be saved after all. Maybe all that was required was a reeducation. When he thought about it, nearly everything a human was was learned behavior. If he could isolate the children, teach them kindness, compassion and selflessness, perhaps the next generation would grow into the people God had always told him they could be. He'd need at least a hundred children to begin the experiment; enough to repopulate if he indeed needed to rid the world of the rest of humanity. He'd need a place to shelter them, as well. There was a cave in Vietnam that could work. It had fresh water and plenty of plant life. He was sure he could grow food there and--

A boy, no more than seven years old, pushed another off a swing, causing Abaddon to lose his train of thought. The second boy cried while the first took his spot on the swing, smiling.

"Or, never mind," Abaddon said to himself, realizing that even the children were tainted. There was no saving these people. He would simply have to remove them like a cancer, forcing his Father to start over, better guiding a new crop of sentient beings, instead of allowing their more animalistic impulses to influence so much of their decision-making.

The second boy ran to his mother, who offered him no comfort as she was preoccupied with the electronic device in her hands. Abaddon wasn't sure if she even knew he was standing there until he saw her reach in her bag and pull out a juice box, handing it to the child without ever taking her eyes off of the screen.

"Shameful," Abaddon groused. He looked back to the first boy who swung gleefully, giving no regard for how he'd made the other boy feel. The disgraced angel became enraged. He reached into his suit jacket pocket and took out a hantavirus carrying rat. He whispered something into its tiny ear and released it on the ground in front of him. The rodent scurried toward the swinging boy, but before it could reach his shoe, its neck inexplicably snapped, its head spinning around one hundred and eighty degrees. The boy screamed and ran off, allowing the crying boy to retake his rightful place on the contraption. Abaddon scanned the area but saw no one who could perform such a trick. Lucifer was nowhere in sight and while he was aware of the demons that escaped Hell along with him, none of them had telekinetic powers. Someone else must be on Earth. Someone powerful. He stood and left the park, not wanting to risk a run-in with whoever was following him.

Gabriel got home from the park and read Michelle's reply, *Will is okay.* "You better be right, bitch," she said under her breath.

"I'd better what?" Lucifer asked.

"Not you."

"Right, well, the polio outbreak in Myanmar proved to be caused   by a lack of vaccine, not Abaddon."

"Back to square one, then?"

"Unfortunately," Lucifer said. "Would you mind ordering lunch? I'm feeling rather peckish and the only food you keep here is artificially flavored."

Gabriel ignored his comment and opened the laptop to order food. Lucifer hovered behind her, groaning in disapproval when she chose two servings of mashed potatoes for herself. She let out a sigh of derision before slamming the computer closed and asking him, "Why are you like this?"

Chapter 16

"So," Malik said. "You ready to move in with your husband?"

"Mm, 'husband'," Valerie said, her lips curling into a smile. "I like the way that sounds." She kissed him hard as the cab drove on, the Manhattan traffic moving slower than the Venetian gondola rides she'd gotten used to. The past week had been a feast of food and sex, occasionally at the same time. She was still surprised that she had Lucifer to thank for setting it all up. Maybe he wasn't so terrible, after all.

The cab stopped, jolting the couple from their newly-wedded bliss. They had been so distracted, they hadn't noticed that the driver had pulled into an alley and was now quietly laughing.

"Why'd you stop?" Malik snapped.

"Ask your friend," the cabbie hissed, still giggling.

"Oh, shit," Valerie gulped, realizing what he was. She could see through the mirror his ashen skin and sunken cheeks; his bloodshot eyes and teeth half-missing.

"Hey, man," Malik started, but Valerie cut him off.

"Get out," she told him.

"What?"

"Get out the cab! Get the fuck out!" she ordered, pushing him to the door, but it was too late. The demon threw itself into the back seat and began clawing at them like a rabid animal. Marks appeared on Malik's face, blood dripping from them to his shirt which the demon clutched in his veiny hand. Valerie opened her door and squeezed out, the alley barely wide enough for the cab to fit. She reached through the driver's side window and took the keys from the ignition. She opened the trunk and rifled through her husband's bag. "Kick its ass, baby!" she called, hoping Malik could hold his own until she got back. Finally, she found what she was looking for. She took the biggest knife from her husband's chef knife set and watched as it burst into flames. She ran to Malik's door and yanked the demon out of the cab by his hair. She stabbed it repeatedly until fire spread over its entire body, its screams deafening as it fell to the ground. She dropped the blade and helped Malik from the car, looking him over for wounds.

"Are you okay?" she fretted, seeing the many scratches and bite marks that covered his face and arms.

"What the hell was that, Val?!" he asked, more like an accusation than a question.

"Don't yell at me."

"Valerie, what the fu--"

"It was a demon."

"A *what*?"

"I should probably tell you something."

Lucifer prowled the streets for hours, but no demons could be found. It was odd because he knew there were thousands of them on the loose and he'd assumed at least some of them would have stayed in the city. The high concentration of people made it hard to resist. Since demons didn't bother tending to their hosts, body-hopping was necessary if they wanted to stay on Earth for more than a month or so. Manhattan should have been crawling with the fiends. They were up to something.

As he passed an alleyway, he felt a familiar sensation. The hair on the back of his neck stood up and he felt slightly nauseated. He walked toward a cab parked precariously in the alley, a satisfied smirk crossing his lips as he bent down to inspect the body that lay next to it, the corpse burned nearly to ash.

Seeing the puncture marks on what was left of the torso, he laughed, "Welcome home, Uriel."

He was bored; with no demons to exorcise and no idea where Abaddon was, he grew increasingly impatient, restless, and angry. He knew it wouldn't be long before he did something he'd no doubt get a lecture from Gabriel for. Perhaps his sister was right. Yes, Mariana was a distraction, and yes, he would be shirking his duties by taking time to meet with her. But, he needed to blow off some steam, and spending time with a beautiful woman was less regrettable than mass murder. Usually.

He called the number she'd given him years earlier, hoping it still worked. It did.

"Hello?" she answered.

"Mariana, hello. I don't know if you remember me, but-"

"Lou?"

"Yes. You recognized my voice?"

"Of course. I think about that day *a lot*."

"Well, that's lovely to hear. I'm recently back in town and I was wondering--"

"I'll text you my address."

Lucifer opened the door to the five-story walk-up, checking the mailboxes to make sure he was in the right place. Behind the first set of stairs, a teenaged boy threw lit firecrackers at a stray cat. The feline hissed and backed away, but the boy had it trapped in a milk crate fortress. *Obnoxious little prick*, Lucifer thought. He made a gesture toward them, giving the cat the courage to defend itself. It leaped at the boy, clawing at his face and eyes. The boy screamed and tried to run, tripping over himself and falling on his behind. The cat kept coming, mauling his face into a bloody mess. Lucifer snickered as he made his way up to the third floor. He got to apartment 3C and lifted his hand to knock, but before his knuckles met the door, it flew open, Mariana having been watching through the peephole for the past few minutes in anticipation of his arrival.

"Hey," she purred.

"Mariana," he said. "You're looking ravishing as ever. Might I--"

"Get in here," she ordered, grabbing him by the shirt and pulling him in, kissing him with three years of unrequited passion. Lucifer was delightfully surprised, wrapping his arms around her waist and kicking the door closed behind him thinking, *Wouldn't want the moment to be ruined by the screams of a psychotic juvenile.*

Chapter 17

Valerie walked into Gabriel's apartment without knocking and sat silently on a stool at the bar. She looked tired and had obviously been crying.

"You want me to hurt him a little?" Gabriel asked, getting her sister a soda from the fridge.

"No, girl. I just didn't want to go back to my apartment. It's too quiet."

"What's happened, sister?" Lucifer asked, joining the women in the kitchen. "Married life not all it's cracked up to be?"

"Not now, Satan."

"I am not-"

"Yo, Daddy's favorite," Gabriel warned. "She said not now."

"Are you jealous?" Lucifer poked.

"Nah, I got cooler powers."

"Did you? Tell me then, when was the last time *you* flew?"

"When was the last time *you* set something on fire with your brain?"

"I know I said my place was too quiet," Valerie told them. "But do you two ever shut the fuck up?"

"Look at me," Gabriel said, sitting across from her at the island. "Are you looking?"

"You see I am," Valerie sighed.

"Malik will come back when the shock wears off. He will. It's just gonna take a minute for his tiny human brain to wrap itself around all this new information. It's not every day you find out your wife's an angel, like, literally. His face when you told him about Lucifer," she giggled, having seen how the conversation had played out as soon as Valerie walked in. "I'll be laughing about that for *days*." Valerie shot her an annoyed squint. "Sorry."

"Was he scared?" Lucifer asked.

"Shitless," Gabriel confirmed.

"Really?"

"Figuratively."

"Well, that's mildly disappointing."

"I just," Valerie croaked. "I just wanted this so bad. Something normal. Husband, kids, maybe a fuckin' dog. A regular, safe, stable life. After all the bullshit growing up, I thought I deserved something better. He was my chance."

"He'll come back," Gabriel said. "And, if he doesn't--"

"If he doesn't, I'll kill him," Lucifer promised.

"No," Gabriel said.

"I can make it painless if you prefer, though that takes all the fun out of it."

"*No.*"

"Why ever not? He's hurt our sister. That alone demands retribution. Not to mention the fact that *he knows what we are.* Humans can't handle that kind of knowledge, as well you know. Wars have been fought over it. People go mad. We can't allow this to get out. Not while Father slumbers. If he tells anyone--"

"He won't," Valerie assured him.

"But, if he does--"

Valerie gasped, her eyes opening wide.

"Are you all right?" Lucifer asked.

"She's having a vision," Gabriel explained. "I haven't been here for one of these in years." She grabbed a bag of chips and eagerly watched what was happening in Valerie's mind while Lucifer placed a hand on her temple so he, too, could enjoy the show.

The silent street was littered with bodies, the air heavy with the stench of death. Broadway had never been this quiet. Valerie stepped over the corpses, mutilated and disfigured, some looking as though they'd rotted from the inside out. She realized those must have been the hosts for long-gone demons while the rest were innocent people, caught in the crosshairs of evil. She came upon a newspaper box and took note of the date, only three days away. She then heard the unmistakable sound of a demon screeching in the distance. As it got louder, she could tell that it wasn't just one voice, but several. The closer it became, the more voices she could make out. There were dozens, then hundreds, then thousands. It was so loud, it vibrated the glass on the surrounding buildings. Electric billboards shook and exploded. Car alarms sounded as the ground beneath her trembled. This wasn't the sound of a few escaped Fallen. This was Hell itself. Every damned soul, every once imprisoned monster now laid claim to the Earth, extinguishing humanity from it like a twisted exterminator. Nowhere was safe. The world was theirs.

Valerie shivered as she came reeling out of the vision, terror replacing the sadness she'd felt just moments before. Gabriel went to the pantry and pulled the small box from behind the cereal, tossing it to Lucifer and giving him a knowing stare. He opened it, looking pensively at the amulet inside and back at his sister.

"You don't have a choice," she told him.

"I don't know that our Father would see it that way."

"When I get up there, I'll explain it to Him. Right now, though,"

"Yes," he agreed. "You're right, as always." He lifted his shirt and took a deep breath, plucking the amulet from the box and plunging it into his chest, grunting as the stone sank beneath the muscle and rested just over his heart.

"What the fuck?!" Valerie yelped, jumping up from her seat.

"I'll be back," he told them, turning toward the balcony and wiping the blood on his pants.

"Where you goin'?"

Lucifer opened the French doors, grateful night had fallen, the chances of someone seeing him fly overhead lessened. "Yonkers."

Locals called this abandoned power station "The Gate to Hell". They didn't know how right they were. Underneath the graffiti, broken bricks, and barred windows lie something darker than the water outside under the moonless sky. The vortex, not visible to the human eye, stood open and unguarded, leaving anything to get out that had the courage to try. Few demons on the streets meant that they were gathering somewhere, plotting. Lilith was under lock and key, he'd made sure of it, but others, no doubt, had taken up her mantle. Hell on Earth had been the pipe dream of every demon since their imprisonment. With Lucifer gone and the Gate wide open, this was their chance to make that fantasy a reality.

Though it pained him, he waved his hand over the mass of dark, watching as it drew in on itself. The shrieks of the damned were so loud and high pitched, it made his ears bleed. Thousands of screaming shadows poured into the building, fighting futilely against the pull of the murky whirlwind. The vortex closed, every demon back where it belonged, the Gate locked tight. Lucifer dropped to his knees, the guilt of what he'd done, what he had to do, like a weight on his spirit. There was no way of going back for him until his Father woke and there would be no exorcising Abaddon now. Death was the only option.

He again lifted his shirt and tore the amulet from his chest, howling in pain as blood seeped from the wound. While he healed, he looked over the stone, Chinese engravings and beautiful embellishments covering its face. Gabriel had known this would happen; that it would *have* to happen. She was prepared. "What else are you hiding from me, sister?" he muttered. He shoved the rock in his pocket and walked out to the edge of the river. He cleaned himself up and looked back at the building. He couldn't shake the guilt, knowing it was against God's Law for him to remain on Earth as long as he'd now have to. The feeling was unpleasant, so he decided to replace it with another. He took his phone from his back pocket and called Mariana.

"Hello, love," he said when she answered. "I realize it's late and we've just seen each other, but, would you perhaps be up for another round?"

Chapter 18

"Just aim for the pins," Michelle said.

"I know the rules of bowling," Will told her. "I've just never actually played before."

"Okay, but you've been standing there for three and a half minutes staring at the lane like you don't know how to roll a ball, so."

"I'm going," he said, stepping forward and releasing the ball down the smooth wood floor. The pins sounded like thunder as they flew and fell to their sides.

"Strike!" Michelle yelped, standing from her seat in the booth to give her boyfriend a quick peck on the cheek. "Good job, sweetie."

"See? I just had to take my time."

"Oh, okay," she teased, taking her ball and waiting for the pins to reset. As she stood there, she noticed a middle-aged man in a torn tee-shirt and faded jeans two lanes over watching her. His unkempt dirty-blond hair fell over one eye, sticking out from his backward blue baseball cap. *Well, he's creepy,* she thought. She rolled her ball down the lane; a seven-ten split.

"You got this, M!" Will called from the booth. When the bar raised, she took her shot. She threw the ball hard toward the pin on the left, sending it careening across to the other side. The pins collided, both of them falling. "Holy crap!" Will exclaimed. He picked her up and swung her around, kissing her before setting her back on her feet. "Where did you learn to bowl like that?"

"My uncle used to take me. Once a month, we'd go blacklight bowling. He said it was the only sport he was good at, but I think he just went to pick up dudes."

Will laughed. "Well, I'm glad he took you because you are an amazing teacher." He kissed her again before taking his ball and stepping forward. She tried to ignore it, but she could feel the man in the other lane still staring. She could see him from the corner of her eye, facing her, not even attempting to be subtle. She made the mistake of letting her eyes wander in his direction and regretted it immediately. The man held up two fingers, pointed at his own eyes, and then to her. It felt like a threat of some kind and she grew increasingly uncomfortable; so much so that she didn't see Will's second strike of the night.

"Are you all right?" Will asked, seeing the distress on her face.

"Can we go?" she asked quietly.

"What do you mean? We just started."

"I don't want to be here. I want to go. Can we go?"

She looked nervous, downright afraid. "Yeah," he said, putting his ball down. "Yeah, let's go." They changed their shoes and headed for the door as the man continued to watch. Michelle put Will's arm around her as they reached the parking lot and walked toward her car.

Just a few more steps, she thought.

"For future reference," Will said. "If you ever want to leave a place, you don't need to ask. Just tell me we're leaving. I'll go wherever you want me to."

"Thanks, sweetie."

"Isn't that precious?" the man from inside scoffed, running in front of them, blocking their path. "Where do you think you're going?" he asked the couple, the smell of stale beer and cheap cigarettes wafting off of him.

"Excuse us," Michelle said politely, hoping to avoid an altercation.

"Maybe you didn't hear me," he said, his voice raised. "I asked where the hell you think you're going."

"What's your problem, man?" Will demanded.

"I wasn't talking to you, bitch," the man dismissed, pushing Will to the ground. He grabbed Michelle's arm and pulled her close to him. "You're not going anywhere."

She struggled to free herself and before she could whip out her best Krav Maga moves, Will was on top of him. He threw the man to the ground, sitting on his chest and hitting him repeatedly, breaking his nose and jaw. He could feel himself losing control, but he didn't care. No one hurt Michelle. *No one*. He hit the man again, breaking his left eye socket, and again, knocking out a few teeth. With his final punch, his fist sparked with electricity. On impact, the man began to shake as if he were having a seizure. It was then that he realized what he'd done and could finally hear Michelle's screams.

"I'm sorry," he said, standing, his hands trembling. The man's face was unrecognizable. Will feared the worst, but as the bully lay there twitching, he could hear him groan in pain. He was alive.

"We have to go," Michelle said, grabbing Will by the shirt. "Come on!" She looked around to make sure no one saw what had happened and got in the car. Once Will was in, she sped off, concern growing in her like fungus. "What the hell was that, Will?"

"He was hurting you. I just...snapped."

"You can't lose control like that. I know he was a dick, but--"

"He was *hurting you*. I don't know if he's racist or if that was like a 'me too' thing, but I had to protect you. I *had* to."

"Why, because you're the guy?" she condescended.

"No, because you're important," he told her. "I love you. If someone grabbed *me* like that, what would *you* have done?"

"Fine, but you're lucky that guy's not dead," she lectured, turning onto Will's street. "It could've been really bad. You know that, right? You understand what could've happened, right?"

"I know."

"You hit him really hard."

"Yeah," he said, thankful she hadn't seen the electrocution. "*Really* hard."

"I'm not fragile. I can take care of myself."

"I know you can. I wasn't trying to--"

"And I don't want you thinking you have to swoop in and rescue me all the time. If you'd given me a few seconds, I would've handed that guy his ass myself." She parked in the driveway and turned off the engine. "I appreciate that you care about me. I do. But, I don't need you to be my knight in shining armor. I don't need a bodyguard. What I *need* is for you to stay as sweet and kind as you've always been. I don't want anything bad to happen to you."

"Okay," he told her. "I promise, from now on, no more saving the day."

"Thank you. Now, go ice that hand before it swells." She kissed him softly and watched as he made his way to the door and inside the house. She looked down at her phone, debating whether or not to tell Gabriel of the night's events. She knew he just did what any boyfriend would have in that situation, but his strength was far greater than that of a regular guy's. The raw power with which he beat that man bloody, while sexy, was dangerous, and the burst of electricity from his hand troubled her. Gabriel had told her what he was capable of, but she hadn't quite believed it. She'd never seen anything like it.

"This is why she said not to get too close," she said to herself, remembering the speeches about keeping a safe distance, staying an acquaintance, nothing more, and watching from afar. She wasn't sure if her feelings for him were clouding her judgement or if the incident really wasn't that big of a deal. She put her phone down and started the car, deciding not to involve Gabriel. One outburst of violence in defense of the person he loves didn't constitute a flag red enough that he deserved to die. She would keep watching, waiting, and hoping that everything would be all right.

Will went straight through the house, closing the front door behind him and heading out the back. He hadn't wanted to scare Michelle, so he had feigned calm in the car, but he was *not* calm. He was angry to the point of rage, still seeing the man's hand on his girlfriend's arm, manhandling her with such entitlement, as if she were his property. He needed to vent, to rid himself of this negative energy. Though the man in the parking lot may have deserved an ass-kicking,

Will had scared himself with the electrical discharge. He hadn't meant to do it and a loss of control like that *couldn't* happen again. He decided to go into the woods where his father had set up a few rubber targets. They'd been practicing aim, restraint, and authority over his ability, and if the night's events proved one thing, it was that he was *not* in full control. He needed *a lot* more training.

He threw one ball of lightning after another, telling himself to constrain them to no more powerful than a car battery. But, as he continued, his rage only grew stronger, and so did his blasts. He launched another and another, their size and power increasing with every throw. He pulled his arm back like a pitcher in a baseball game and released a surge of lightning so forceful that the tree the target was strapped to snapped and fell backward, crashing loudly to the ground. He was stunned, never having wielded that much power before. He was sure the noise had woken his father, so he turned to exit the forest. In the distance, he could hear a wolf howl. His anger not yet dissipated, he changed his mind and headed back.

"Will?" Wyatt called from upstairs.

"Yeah, Dad, I'm just getting a snack!" Will called back, having finished two sandwiches already. He took some pain reliever and started on sandwich number three.

"You ready for your next driving lesson tomorrow?" Wyatt asked as he came down the stairs.

"Yeah, it'll be nice being able to pick Michelle up for a date instead of the other way around all the time. Hey, Dad,"

"Yeah?"

Will paused. He knew he should tell his father what had happened. It was rule number one. If he ever lost control or scared himself, he was supposed to tell. But, he was afraid. He didn't want his dad to think of him differently or lock him up somewhere. "I, um, I smashed my hand in the car door," he lied, showing Wyatt his banged-up knuckles.

"Oh, man!" Wyatt said, inspecting Will's fist. "Let's get some ice on that. What happened?"

"I just got distracted. Michelle was--"

"Say no more," Wyatt chuckled, wrapping a bag of frozen peas in a paper towel and handing it to his son. "You able to drive? Hold the steering wheel properly?"

"I'm pretty sure, yeah," Will told him, amazed he hadn't mentioned the tree falling. He hadn't heard. Since Valerie cleaned up his subconscious, he slept fairly heavily. His alarm barely woke him. He had to have it set to ring continuously until it was manually turned off, just in case. After years of torment, his mind now rested soundly, making up for lost time.

"I was planning on waiting until you got your license, but,"

"But what?" Will asked, unable to hide his excitement.

"Look in the garage."

"You didn't," Will said, running to the door and swinging it open into the three-car garage. There, next to his father's car, was another. Its gunmetal paint shined under the dim overhead light, its smooth curves reminding him of a toy he played with as a child. "You did! That's for me, right? Dad, I love it!"

"I thought you might," Wyatt grinned, accepting the hug his son gave him.

"And I can take it out tomorrow?"

"Sure, just be careful. I don't want to have to pay to fix a car I just bought."

"I'll take care of it, I promise. Michelle's gonna love it."

"Kid, if she was the kind of girl that got impressed by the kind of car a guy has, she wouldn't be dating someone that can't drive."

"Yeah, she's awesome."

"So, things are going well?"

"Yeah, she's the best," Will gushed.

"Good, that's nice for you. And, who knows? Maybe your old man's not out of the game, after all."

"The vampire?!"

Wyatt shrugged coyly and went back inside.

"Dad," Will pried, following him. "Come on, Dad! I need details!"

Chapter 19

Lucifer slept comfortably in Mariana's bed for the second night in a row. He would never tell her, but Gabriel had been right about him needing to take a break. He felt recharged, ready to take on Abaddon, wherever he may be. He'd get back to the search in the morning, after one more go-round with the beauty sleeping beside him. As he fell deeper into his slumber, he began to dream, first of Mariana and then of home. Not Hell; his *real* home. He dreamed of his brother, Michael, telling him that he was doing exactly what he was meant to and that their Father was pleased with him. He could feel the warmth of Heaven, the complete, unconditional love of every soul there. He could hear the distant hum of God's voice and as he turned to look, thrilled by the promise of seeing his Father's face after so many millennia, the scene changed. Now, he stood in a cheap motel room, a burnt orange blanket on the bed, pea soup green shag carpet covering the floor.

"What is this?" he griped, lucid and resentful.

"It's no Perdition," Abaddon quipped. "But it's been home."

"You repugnant, loathsome--"

"Now, now, don't be cross. I come in peace, as they say."

"I will pull your lungs from your body and watch with glee as you suffocate."

"I will ignore that, seeing as how I interrupted your homecoming fantasy. Your vexation is understandable. I, too, have wished, in vain, to go back to Heaven. But we will never be welcomed back through the Gates, as you well know."

"*You* won't. But, I--"

"You were condemned to Hell in service to our Father for infinity. You will never go home. When the scourge of humanity is scrubbed clean from this world, God will only create another race of pets he can fawn over that will no doubt need protecting. You will forever be charged with keeping the demons at bay, unless you give up your mantle, and join me."

"*Join you?*" Lucifer scoffed. "I mean to *kill you.*"

"Come now, brother. Try to remember Earth as it was before the human curse. Tranquil and serene. Clean. It could be again."

"And when God wakes? I don't think you've thought this through. Besides, what's the point of being on Earth if you can't enjoy humanity? There are benefits to these bodies that you've clearly failed to explore."

"You're more brutish than I remember," Abaddon complained.

"And you're more deluded."

"Have it your way, but I won't spare you when I end this ridiculous experiment."

"And how do you plan on doing that? People aren't as helpless as they once were. They've developed medicines. You'll have a difficult time plaguing them all."

"I've discovered something called 'internet'," Abaddon explained. "Have you heard of it? I have access to all the world's knowledge on a device called 'computer'."

"Yes, I'm familiar."

"The one thing humanity seems to be unrelentingly skilled at is the development of weapons of war. I will use their own wickedness against them and wipe them clean from the Earth, once and for all."

"You will regret--"

"My only regret will be that they'll die too swiftly to recognize the evil in their own hearts."

Lucifer woke abruptly, springing to a sitting position and startling Mariana.

"Are you okay?" she asked, half-asleep.

"Fine, love," he told her, catching his breath. "Go back to sleep. I'm off. I'll call you later. I have work to do."

Lucifer stood outside the motel, contemplating exactly how he'd make his presence known. He'd recognized the interior of the building from the last time he'd been on Earth, having tracked a demon nest there when he went searching for Lilith. Abaddon had been so smug, thinking he could hide from him forever. He would soon find out how wrong he was.

Lucifer made a turning motion with his left hand, raising it to the sky, his eyes fixed on the building in front of him. The clouds above began to swirl, the gentle spring breeze growing in speed. The skies darkened as a funnel cloud formed, the wind pushing cars around the parking lot like toys. The roof of the building peeled away, leaving screaming residents to scramble to lower ground. All but one. Abaddon looked through the now broken window of his room, shocked that he'd been found. Lucifer sneered back, bringing his arm, and the tornado, down, ripping through the building and sending Abaddon flying into a car just a few feet from where Lucifer stood, a smirk on his face and delight in his eyes.

"You should have stayed hidden," he said, allowing the skies to calm and the weather to return to normal.

"You will not stop me," Abaddon told him, getting to his feet, blood trickling from his mouth. He lifted the car and hurled it at Lucifer, who stepped slightly to his right, avoiding an impact and rolling his eyes.

"You'll have to do better than that. Remember who I am."

"Yes," Abaddon mocked. "God's favorite son. The most beautiful angel in all of Heaven."

"Yes, that, but more importantly," he picked up a truck and hit him, swinging it like a baseball bat, sending him hurling into what was left of the building. "The strongest."

Abaddon struggled to stand, blood pouring from his mouth and nose. He held his ribs, the broken bones taking more time than he'd like to heal. He coughed, unable to get his balance. "Was it you, then?" he accused. "In the park? Like a sick game of cat and mouse, biding your time, letting me think I was safe?"

"I haven't been to a park in ages," Lucifer said. "Must have been Gabriel. What'd she do? Move you against your will? Set you on fire? She does have an affinity for pyrotechnics."

"Gabriel? How is *she* here?"

"You know our Father, all-knowing and such. He saw you and Lilith coming and sent some of our more agile siblings as a means of defense." Lucifer retrieved a downed lamppost, hoisting it over his shoulder. "We put Lilith back in a cage, which was the fate I'd intended for you. But, sadly, the demon hordes got antsy waiting for my return, so they came forth, overrunning this planet and planning an Apocalypse. I had to send them back from whence they came by locking the Gate."

"You didn't. You would never disobey so blatantly. Too afraid of God's wrath."

"I did what I had to. So, no way back in for us, and since I can't allow you to destroy the human race, well, you see where that leaves me."

"You can't kill me," Abaddon dismissed. "I'm immortal."

"Did I not mention the presence of our dear sister? Her Holy Fire can eradicate even your true form. You won't die, per se. You'll simply cease to exist."

"Where is she?" Abaddon shouted, Lucifer relishing the hint of anxiety in his voice.

"Oh, who knows. Her schedule of errands and meetings with this or that lover is impossible to predict. However, I can summon her here with a thought, and I will, once I've had my fun." He swung the post back and brought it forward, but before it could make contact, Abaddon was gone, teleporting off to who knows where. Rage replaced glee as Lucifer dropped the post, a scowl covering his once contented expression. He growled under his breath, his fists and jaw clenched. He knew now what Abaddon was planning, it was simply a matter of location. He flew off, knowing he didn't have much time to narrow it down.

Chapter 20

Abaddon materialized in the Sonoran desert, not far from Mobile, Arizona. He walked for miles, having no idea what direction led to where, deciding that a place this desolate was perfect for hiding from Lucifer for a time. He was tired and hungry, the body he'd chosen never relenting in its petty weaknesses. His ribs were still not fully healed and the pain was getting to be more and more of a nuisance as he wandered, the heat making him reconsider the jacket he wore. He went to unbutton it, but his fingers didn't cooperate. The sun beat down on him with such unyielding warmth that he, in his current condition, could not withstand it. His knees buckled and as he fell to the scorched earth below, his blurred vision went dark. By the time his head hit the ground, he could feel nothing, all of his senses having left him, floating away into the arid afternoon air.

Abaddon woke with a start, the vibrations underneath him foreign and unpleasant. He was seated inside of a truck, not unlike the one Lucifer had struck him with. He was unamused by the irony.

"You okay, buddy?" the man in the driver's seat asked, reaching for a bottle of water from the cup holder and handing it to him. He was older, probably in his sixties or so, with eyes as blue as the pattern on his flannel shirt. "You need a doctor? Want me to call someone for you?"

"No, thank you," Abaddon replied. "I'm fine." He sipped the water, annoyed by how delicious it tasted, maddened by his need for a human host, to begin with. Everything about a physical body was aggravating and tedious. He took no pleasure in occupying one and was sickened by his unwilling relief as the water soothed his throat and cooled his internal temperature.

"I found you face-planted a few miles back. You are not 'fine'. Blood on your face, no wallet or phone. Looks like you got robbed."

"I wasn't, I assure you. Thank you for the water. You can let me out anywhere."

"Buddy, I don't know how they do things where you're from, but around here, if someone needs help, which you *clearly* do, you help them. Now, I can understand not wanting to go to the hospital. Can't stand the places myself. But, I'd be a grade-A piece of shit if I didn't at least give you somewhere to clean up. You hungry? I'm grilling burgers for dinner. You're more than welcome."

"That's very compassionate of you," Abaddon said, surprised by the stranger's generosity.

"No problem. And you don't have to tell me what happened to you out there. None of my business."

"You wouldn't believe me."

"Don't go piquing my interest," the old man snickered, reaching over to shake his passenger's hand. "Name's Ed, Ed Stone."

Abaddon shook the man's hand, having seen the custom dozens of times on television. "Abaddon."

The man laughed. "You are foreign, ain't ya? What kind of name is that? Greek?"

"Hebrew."

"Huh. Well, it's definitely interesting. You Jewish, then? Lot's of Jews out this way. I'm Baptist, myself, but, to each their own."

"I don't participate in the mass delusion of organized religion, no offense."

"None taken. Everyone's entitled to their own beliefs. The love of my life was Muslim. I don't judge." They pulled into the driveway of a small suburban home, Abaddon taking note of how similar all of the houses on the street looked. They exited the red pickup and headed to the door, Ed unlocking it and inviting his guest inside. "Bathroom's the second door on the left," he offered, pointing down the hall. "You can get cleaned up while I get the burgers on. You want something to drink? I have soda and juice. I don't drink alcohol, so no beer, sorry."

"Water's fine, thank you," Abaddon told him before entering the bathroom. He wet a hand towel and wiped the dried blood from his nose, mouth, and chin. Lucifer had done a number on him, but he couldn't do any permanent damage. He and Gabriel together, however, could very well be a different story. He'd have to avoid them until he regained his strength. Perhaps he should speak to Gabriel, one-on-one. The only way she could be outside Heaven's Gates was if she, too, was tethered to one of these miserable corporeal forms. Maybe he could convince her that ridding the planet of these wretched bodies was in her best interest. She'd be free of the constant torture of putrid bodily fluids and functions, the biological urges and requirements that her true form didn't need. She could shed herself of it and go home, back to Heaven, where she belonged.

He dropped the towel in the hamper behind him and looked back in the mirror, studying the face of the man he inhabited. He wasn't sure what would happen to him once his work was done. If he allowed this body to perish with the rest of humanity, where would he go? Not back to Hell, thanks to Lucifer. Not to Heaven; he was banned, not to mention the spell he'd cast all those millennia ago. He was fixed to the Earth, but without an anchor in the form of a human host, his atoms would scatter. He'd lose his sense of self and become little more than dust in the wind. No. As much as he hated the confinement of this body, he'd have to protect it.

He left the bathroom and gave himself a tour of the house, peeking into rooms, examining the art on the walls, and inspecting the books on the shelf in the living room. Two Bibles, one King James, and one New International version. Books on architecture, bird watching, and entomology. As he looked around, he was confused by the lack of pictures in the home. He'd never actually been inside someone's home before, so it probably wasn't that unusual, but homes on television always had photos in frames sitting on end tables or hanging on walls. Tables here held only golf magazines and coasters and the art on the walls consisted of watercolor paintings of fish, bears, and deer. It was obvious to him that the man must live alone, but what of the 'love of his life' he'd mentioned?

"Burgers are done!" Ed called, opening the sliding glass door that led to the back patio and poking his head in. "Perfect medium-rare." He took the plate of meat to the kitchen and began building burgers, placing lettuce and pickles on the bottom buns and squirting ketchup and mustard on the tops before adding the patties and closing them up. He put a heap of chips on both plates and brought them to the dining table where Abaddon had politely sat. "Bon appetit!"

"Thank you," Abaddon said, eating a chip, angered by how amazing the burgers smelled.

"So, Abaddon, what do you do for a living?"

"Do you mean for money?"

"Well, yeah."

"Money is a man-made construct I don't quite understand. It only has value because someone says it does. I suppose that's true of most things here, but I find it perplexing. What people are willing to do for it and the desperate longing they feel for it. It's obscene."

"You're right about that. 'The love of money is the root of all evil'. Inflation being what it is, young people can't afford to live the way my generation did. Living with their parents until they're thirty, can't afford a house, student loans taking what little income they have. It's not right." The man took a bite of his dinner, nearly choking on it when Abaddon spoke again.

"So, where's your wife?"

"My wife?" Ed sputtered, taking a sip of his soda.

"You mentioned her on the way here."

"Ah, 'the love of my life'." A forlorn stare into the distance replaced the chipper smile on the man's face, heartbreak apparent in his voice. "She left, a little over a year ago."

"I'm sorry. I shouldn't have asked."

"No, it's fine. It's good to talk about her. Remembering the good times makes it less painful."

"What was she like?"

"She was beautiful. Big brown eyes, skin the color of coffee. She wore henna on her hands and a hijab on her head. Her name was Sabita and she was wonderful. I miss her every day."

"It sounds like you loved her very much."

"I still do. I would do anything to bring her back if I could." The men finished eating in silence, melancholy hanging like fog in the air. Evening turned to night, Ed sharing stories of Sabita, his work at the church, and his latest fishing trip to Saguaro Lake. His life was lonely but full and Abaddon felt a strange sense of guilt thinking about how he'd die in a blanket of fire and ash later.

"It's getting late," Ed sighed, his joints cracking as he stood from the sofa. "You look a lot better than you did, but not a hundred percent. There's a guest room down the hall if you'd like to stay the night."

"That would be very helpful, thank you," Abaddon accepted.

"All right, I'm going to bed. This old man can't burn the midnight oil like he used to."

"Goodnight, Ed."

"Goodnight." Ed shuffled off to his room and closed the door, Abaddon following behind to the guest room. He sat on the bed, pondering the generosity and kindness of the man, a stranger to him until today. He'd found him, unconscious and bleeding, and instead of leaving him to die or merely calling the authorities, he'd taken it upon himself to feed and shelter him for the evening for no other reason than it's what he considered to be the right thing to do. Ed was a genuinely decent human being. Had he judged humanity too harshly? How many more people were as honorable as Ed? Was the human race worth sparing? Perhaps instead of a mass execution of the entire species, he could spend some time extracting the good ones from the general population and protecting them from what was to come. It would take time and much more effort, but men like Ed were a beacon of goodness in an otherwise festering cesspool of immorality. More like him could teach future generations what it means to be human, the way God had originally intended. His Father would undoubtedly be miffed that he exterminated most of his favorite pets, but once He saw the utopia Abaddon created, He'd have no choice but to let it stand. Who knows? He might even forgive him.

He stood, unbuttoning and removing his suit jacket. He opened the closet door and hung it on a hanger. As he placed the hanger back on its rack, he took notice of a jewelry box on the floor in the back left corner of the closet. Curiosity got the better of him and he picked it up. It was a pale shade of pink and played a quiet melody when opened. What he found inside horrified and enraged him.

At the bottom was a neatly folded pair of girl's panties. Atop that was a lock of hair and pictures of what he recognized from the internet as 'kiddie porn'. Polaroid after Polaroid of children in compromising poses, some in just underwear, some in nothing at all. A stack of photos that had been separated from the others, tied together with a red ribbon, infuriated him more than anything else he'd seen. They were all of the same girl who looked to be ten or eleven years old with dark skin, large, frightened eyes, wearing a hijab. "Love of his life," Abaddon seethed.

"Hey, buddy," Ed said, opening the door to the guest room, carrying a bottle of water. "Thought you might need--" He stopped, seeing what Abaddon had discovered. "You don't understand."

"You're right," Abaddon agreed, setting the jewelry box and its contents on a shelf in the closet and loosening his tie. "I don't understand. I don't understand how a race that was handed Paradise can destroy it without a second thought. I don't understand how you all abide unjust and corrupt laws designed to make a very few of you even more wealthy. I don't understand murder, genocide, slavery, greed, lying, or hatred. I don't understand the cruelty in which you all seem to relish. And, mostly, at this moment, I don't understand how a creature as vile as *you* could have fooled me into thinking you were worth saving."

"I didn't hurt them," Ed insisted. "I just took pictures."

"And what became of those children after you'd taken your sick pleasure? What became of Sabita?"

"Well," he hesitated. "She told her parents, so,"

"So what, Ed?" Abaddon barked, his rage growing.

"I had to."

"You had to what?!"

"I, I called ICE."

Abaddon's blood boiled. "You're telling me you had a family deported to spare yourself justice?"

"I know, it's bad, but it's not what you think. It's a *disease*."

"A disease," Abaddon rasped. "Funny you should mention." He waved his hand in Ed's direction, a calmness returning to his demeanor. "I don't pretend to know what living with the mind of a pervert is like, but I do know that God gave you all highly functioning brains, capable of self-control and rational thought. You *decide* how you treat others and if you can not, you seek the help of professionals that can teach you, or, if no other recourse can be taken, can lock you away from civilized society."

Ed began to feel a burning sensation in his genitals. It got worse quickly, forcing him to drop his pants and examine himself right there in front of his guest. Red bumps had appeared all over his penis and testicles. "What's happening?!" he howled.

"I've given you a particularly nasty STD. They call it 'donovanosis'. It starts as deep-red bumps. Gradually, the skin wears away. Eventually, all genital tissue rots. I've accelerated the process, of course."

Ed screamed in agony as the infection did its work.

"You disappoint me, Ed," Abaddon said, taking his jacket from the closet and putting it back on. "More than the rest of them. You had me fooled. For a *split second,* I was considering sparing some of you. How naive I was." He watched as the man's sexual organs disintegrated into nothing. When he was satisfied he'd been tortured enough, he walked past him to vacate the room. "I will leave you to tend to your disfigurement, content in the knowledge that you'll soon burn with the lot of them." He stopped and turned back. "On second thought," He grasped the man by the hair and bashed his skull into the wall, blood and brain matter splattering onto his face. He dropped the body and used his sleeve to wipe his cheek clean. "You don't deserve even one more moment of life."

He left the house, walking peacefully into the night air which was significantly cooler than the day's. He still wasn't at full power and he couldn't risk Lucifer catching up to him before he was. So, he would stay in the confines of this desert town for a little while longer before enacting his plan. That didn't mean, however, that he couldn't have a few laughs while he waited.

"Order up!" a woman yelled from behind the counter. The diner was loud, the voices of dozens of patrons chattering in his ears, the volume like thunder in his head. Abaddon stood near the entrance, watching the people eating happily, discussing this and that as they shoveled in vast quantities of artery-clogging food, blissfully unaware of what would soon befall them. Their gluttony was embarrassing. None showed any consideration for the millions of people that starved right now in their own country, let alone the rest of the world. Worse, still, were the plates of half-eaten food left by consumers whose eyes were bigger than their stomachs. The greed and entitlement of these people knew no bounds. They hoarded resources, growing fat and happy while their fellow man lived in hunger. It was repugnant.

Abaddon gestured with both hands toward the crowd, his mouth curling into a sly smirk. One by one, diner-goers began to hold their stomachs and cover their mouths. Some ran for the bathroom, but most didn't make it. They threw up, vomiting violently onto the floor, into trash cans, and on their plates. A waitress in a yellow, fifties-style uniform attempted to run to the back, but slipped, falling into a puddle of someone's regurgitated dinner. She stood and as she reached for the towel usually used for cleaning the counter, thin, liquid excrement spilled from under her skirt, down her leg, into her shoe, and to the linoleum floor. A look of shocked horror came over her face, but her humiliation lasted only a few seconds as one person after another shared her predicament.

"And their bowels boiled, and would not rest," Abaddon muttered to himself, pleased with the performance of the norovirus.

Chipper conversation had been replaced with screams and retching. None were left clean, most being covered in not only their own filth and sick, but that of their neighbors. Abaddon laughed quietly, exiting the building, the smell repulsive. He put his hands in his pockets and whistled the tune of the commercial for the big box store he'd seen well over a hundred times. It lingered in his brain like lost love and as obnoxious as it was, he couldn't remove it from his thoughts. It didn't matter. Soon, he'd never have to hear it or any of the other insipid melodies created by the human botheration. He looked forward to the only sounds being the waves of the ocean, the wind in the trees, and the rain falling to the ground. "Not long now," he told himself, feeling his strength returning. "Not long at all."

Chapter 21

Will swallowed two acetaminophen tablets along with the last of his soda, setting the empty can on the coffee table, his eyes never leaving the screen. He sat, transfixed, as the fictional town collapsed into the massive crater. Michelle had been right; this *was* a great show.

"Whatever the hell she wants!" he cheered, answering the final question asked by the main character's sister. He got up, went to the entertainment center, and retrieved the DVD from the player. As he placed it back in its case, he felt a white-hot pain shooting from his temple to the back of his head. It was so sharp, it knocked him to his knees. He'd had the same headache for more than a week, but it had been manageable with pain medication. This was different. He'd never felt anything like it before. He winced in pain, putting his hands to his temples as his vision became fuzzy.

Suddenly, he was bombarded with images he couldn't quite make out. There was a bright light, a man in a lab coat coming at him with something metal. Scissors? "Is he okay?" he heard a woman ask. "He's perfect," the man in the coat said. Will was now looking at the face of the woman. He recognized her from pictures and videos his father had shown him. She was his mother. "William," she said. "My angel. I love you so much." She smiled, kissing him on the forehead. She smelled like lavender, her skin soft and warm. She studied his face while he wrapped his tiny fingers around her thumb. "You look just like your fa--" She stopped, her face falling and the light in her eyes fading. She fell back into the hospital bed, the doctor preventing Will from falling as she went limp. The piercing sound of beeps and alarms startled him, causing him to scream and cry as a nurse took him away. He reached his arm out, grasping at the air for his mother, but he could see from the doorway that she wasn't moving, and as the door closed, his delicate, newborn heart was shattered.

Will's vision cleared, the stinging pain in his head replaced by a familiar, dull ache. Tears streamed down his face as the shock of what he'd seen wore off, the realization of what it was gripping him tight. This was a memory; the memory of the day he was born. He was overcome with emotion, covering his mouth with both hands and bawling, never having experienced anything so tragic. It was physically painful, his diaphragm feeling constricted like someone was sitting on it. He wanted to call his father, but he was in an important meeting with suppliers at Pine's, so he sat on the carpet, using his tee shirt to wipe the tears from his face. He knew he couldn't tell Michelle what just happened; she'd think he was either lying or crazy, but he didn't want to be alone. He pulled himself together, gathered up the discs, and headed to the garage. He'd go to her apartment under the guise of bringing her DVDs back and he'd stay there until he felt better, no matter how long it took.

"Will!" Michelle said excitedly, stepping aside to let him in. She closed the door behind him then threw her arms around his neck. "I wasn't expecting to see you today!"

"I just wanted to drop off your DVDs," he said, handing them to her. "It's a really good show. I'll probably start the spin-off tomorrow. You want to come over?"

"Sure!" she bubbled, putting the discs in a cabinet. "Are you okay? Your face looks kind of puffy."

"I'm all right, just a headache."

"Are you sure?"

"Yeah, I'm fine. What have you been up to today?"

"Well, after work, I went to the grocery store, put gas in the car--"

"What was your mom like?" he interrupted. "Sorry, I was just... I was thinking about mine today and how I never got to know her and thought-- never mind. I shouldn't have asked. I don't want to upset you."

"It's fine," she told him, sitting on the couch and waiting for him to sit next to her. When he did, she continued. "Let's see, she was strong-willed and a little impulsive. She married my dad after knowing him for less than three months, which is insane. I mean, who does that, right?"

"I would marry you *tomorrow*," Will confessed. The shock on her face made him immediately regret saying it. "I mean, I'm not proposing. Don't be nervous."

She giggled. "I'm not nervous. I was *going* to say, it sounds crazy to tie yourself to one person forever that soon and I never understood how they could've made that decision. I didn't think love was that strong of an emotion, until I met you."

He looked at her fondly, touching her cheek, tears filling his eyes again as he kissed her. "You know how much I love you, right?" She nodded. "I want you to always know that, okay? No matter what. People die; my mom, your parents, your uncle, but I will *always* be here for you. I will *always* love you."

"You can't make that promise. There are things you don't know. Things that would--"

"I don't care," he professed. "There is nothing you could do, ever, that would make me stop loving you. You have my whole heart."

She kissed him, holding his face in her hands, the tears in his eyes falling to her fingers. She wiped them away and looked inquisitively at the face of this man she just could not get enough of. "Are you sure you're all right? You can tell me anything."

It was nice of her to say, but he knew it wasn't true. If she knew what he was, she would run from him, screaming. "I'm okay," he assured her. She nodded and kissed him again, leaning her body into his. She sat up, preparing to straddle him. Just then, he got another stabbing pain in his left temple. It burned through his skull like fire, a cloud of images once again flooding his mind.

He gently pushed her away and put his hand to his head. "I have a headache," he said.

"Are you kidding?"

"No," he declared, getting up and walking quickly to the door. "I need to go take some pain medicine."

"I have some here," she offered.

"That's okay, I need to go home, anyway. Dinner with my dad. I'll see you tomorrow? Around seven?"

"Sure," she agreed.

He left the apartment, not one hundred percent sure if he'd closed the door all the way. He stumbled down the stairs and out the lobby doors to the parking lot. He hadn't made it to his car when the memories overtook him. He dropped to the sidewalk, clutching his head in anguish, flashes of memory after memory filling his brain, the real world disappearing from view. He trembled, his mind unable to process this much information so quickly. Blood trickled from his nose as he toppled over, his head hitting the pavement with a ghastly thud. He laid there, shaking, as the sun set on the horizon. Michelle, oblivious, searched her closet for an outfit to wear to her date tomorrow, excited to spend more time with her beloved.

Chapter 22

Death rose like steam from the streets as Lucifer walked through the Old City. Blister-covered bodies lay everywhere, some still clutching phones or grocery bags. "Leprosy," he uttered, covering his nose, the stench of decay making him gag. He hadn't seen a plague like this in thirty-five hundred years. Disease that struck down this many people this swiftly could only be Abaddon's doing. He searched high and low but turned up nothing. He knew what he was planning. "A weapon to wipe out all of humanity." He leaped into the sky, flying out of Israel and back to Gabriel's apartment. He was going to need her help.

"Ada!" fifteen-year-old Gabriel screamed from the road, watching in horror as the building burned. Security guards threw her in the back of a town car and sped off as she sobbed, the cries of her friends still ringing in her ears.

"That must have been unbearable," a guard said, a menacing smile creeping across his face.

"What?" she asked.

"Tell me, did you know it was them, or did you go years thinking it was an electrical malfunction as the investigation implied?"

"This is a dream," she realized, her current visage replacing her teenage self.

"Yes, and you'll be waking soon, undoubtedly full of self-righteous indignation and contempt, but, I want to be clear, you can not defeat me and you shouldn't want to."

"Uh-huh," she dismissed.

"Think about it, Gabriel. These people are little more than vessels of malfeasance, destroying without a thought what our Father so graciously gave them. They kill each other and this planet with no remorse. I've spent weeks trying to find *anyone* worth redemption. *One person* worthy of sparing. I could find no one. They are flawed, resentful, and angry. They hate for sport. They do not deserve life."

"Yeah, people are generally trash cans."

"So, you agree?"

"No one's *perfect*," she told him. "I mean, *shit*, I've known *my whole life* the secrets of the universe; God and Heaven, Purgatory, all of human history, and I'm *severely fucked up*. Imagine having none of that knowledge, just guessing and hoping, clawing around in the dark for something that felt like right. People are wild animals with souls pulling them in a direction they don't understand. They're just trying their best."

"They are failing."

"They are orphans of the Throne, just waiting to get back home."

"As are you?" he asked. "Wouldn't you like to go back to where you belong?"

"You think I'd be welcome if I stood by and let you blow the planet to shit?"

"God would forgive you. He always does."

"You know He loves them, right? Like, *a lot*."

"He will start over when He wakes," he sighed. "This time, giving them proper instructions."

"Last time He told them what to do, it didn't work out so well."

"Their stupidity is egregious. How difficult is it to love one another? How confusing is kindness?"

"I'm picking up what you're putting down, but I still can't let you kill them."

"You've been among them too long," he griped. "You're weak. Your subconscious is riddled with childhood traumas. Your mind is tormented by guilt over things you can not change and you, like Lucifer, are obedient to a Father that puts you second, preferring these primates to His first-born."

"Can we wrap this up? I'm losing interest."

"You will not stop me."

"You think?"

"Your human body lessens your abilities, I'm sure. In your current state, you have no chance against me."

"In my current state, bitch, I'm *Irish*. I will cut you like soap."

Gabriel woke to find Lucifer standing over her bed, impatience covering his face. "Let me guess," he said. "Abaddon infiltrating your dreams?"

"Yeah, he tried to give me the whole 'they deserve it' speech," she sneered, getting up and heading to the kitchen. She put two frozen waffles in the toaster and opened a can of soda.

"Somehow, your eating habits never fail to disturb me," he snorted, peeling himself a banana.

"Dude, it is four in the morning. I need caffeine."

"Most people drink coffee."

"Most people hate themselves." She dumped an unnecessary amount of syrup on her now plated breakfast and began to eat.

"That's disgusting."

"It's delicious."

"Why do you eat so much sugar, sister? You must know it's unhealthy."

"Dopamine."

"Yes, well, do hurry. Abaddon's already released a plague on Jerusalem and I think you can guess where his next stop is."

"I know. I've been keeping an eye. I gave him a chance to change his mind, but--"

"You what?!"

"He hadn't hurt anyone until now. Waited til I was asleep. Pretty smart. Or maybe just lucky."

"Either way, this fight could get rather messy. Are you sure you're up for it?"

She finished her waffles and downed the rest of her beverage before responding, "Oh, if this motherfucker wants to *go*, we'll *go*."

Chapter 23

Valerie paced the living room floor, her siblings having woken her when they left, off to who knows where to do who knows what. She was staying in Wyatt's old room, unnerved by the fact that she was sharing a bedroom wall with the Devil. Gabriel had assured her that he was behaving himself since coming back, and he had given her a nice honeymoon, showing a more thoughtful side of himself that she didn't know existed before. Maybe he wasn't *so* bad. *Maybe.*

The sun wouldn't be up for half an hour and she wasn't due back at work until next week. "Fuck this," she muttered, picking up her bong from the bar and grabbing a lighter. She would smoke herself sleepy and go back to bed, saving the stress of her probable divorce for a later time. As she put her mouth to the glass, there was a soft knock at the door. "Who's there?" she called, expecting to have to shoo away one of her sister's many companions.

"It's Malik!" said the voice from the other side. She put her things down and ran to let him in.

"Baby!" she cheered. "How'd you know where I was?"

"When you weren't home, I figured you came here. I hoped, anyway."

She embraced him, kissing him for several seconds before he pulled away.

"Stop, stop," he told her, holding her at arm's length. "We've got to talk about this. Now, I've calmed down, but you've got to explain this to me."

"Okay," she agreed, closing the door behind him and following him to the sofa. "Ask me anything."

"Demons. How big of a problem are they? Are they everywhere? Are we gonna get jumped again?"

"No, Lucifer put them all back in Hell. There won't be another one on Earth for at least two hundred and forty years."

"And Lucifer's *Lucifer*, Lucifer?"

"I mean, yeah."

"And he's what, their king?"

"Shit, no. He's more like a prison guard."

"But he's the Devil, like, the fucking Devil."

"He's harmless to you."

"*Harmless*? We were *attacked by a demon* and you're telling me *Satan* is *harmless*?"

"Oh, he's scary as shit, but he won't hurt you, I swear. I mean, I can't say he *never* kills people, but--"

"What the fuck, Val?!"

"Racists, homophobes, misogynists, all kinds of bigots; that's who needs to be worried about pissing him off. I'm not saying it's cool, but I can understand where he's coming from. He hasn't killed anybody in years, though, so--"

"You're defending *Lucifer* to me now?"

"I'm as surprised as you are, but he *is* my brother."

"Your *what*?"

"I told you I'm an angel. Were you not listening?"

"It must not have registered while I was bandaging up the bite wounds I got fending off a fucking *demon*."

"You remember the blond dude at the wedding? The one that left before the reception? That was him."

"Satan was at our wedding?"

"Yeah, and see? Everything was fine."

"This is a lot for me, baby," he sighed.

"I understand, but you're focusing on the negative shit. Hell's real, but so is Heaven. I'm a fucking angel. I've got superpowers and shit. You have got *nothing* to worry about."

"What does that mean, though? Is 'Valerie' just an act for you?"

"No, 'Valerie' is who I am. I was born and I grew up like everybody else. My experiences and genetics formed my personality. Uriel is me *inside*. It's like, normal people have souls that act as their conscience. Uriel is that for me. The instinct to do the right thing, the moral compass, that sort of thing. And, when my body dies, Uriel will go back to Heaven, remembering everything about this life, just like a human soul would."

"I'm gonna have to think on this," he told her. "The Lucifer thing freaks me out, I'm not gonna lie, but that's just a small part of it. I'm sayin', I'm *nothing* compared to you. I don't have special abilities, I don't have thousands of years of stories to tell. I'm just a man. How could I ever be enough for you?"

"Baby," she chortled, touching his cheek. "I'm an angel, but I'm human, too. I love you more than I've ever loved anyone. You might be a regular-ass man, but you're fine as hell, you lay down that d like none other *and* you can cook. I could comb the universe and never find anything better than that."

He laughed. "I just don't want to disappoint you."

"You could never disappoint me," she said, kissing him gently.

"Wait, wait, wait. So, your sister is Gabriel from the *Bible*?"

"I guess we're not done talking."

Chapter 24

Wyatt awoke much groggier than usual. He felt heavy, his limbs like stone. He turned off his alarm and slowly crept down the stairs, eager to get some coffee in his system. When he got to the kitchen, he found Will already awake and making breakfast.

"Hey, Dad," he said, flipping something in a pan on the stove. "I think I've got this pancake thing down. I put a touch of vanilla in the batter. You sleep okay? You look terrible."

"I just need some coffee," Wyatt slurred, pouring himself a cup, grateful for his son's skills in the kitchen. "And send two of those pancakes my way."

"No problem," Will said, placing them on a plate and setting it on the table. "There's also bacon in the oven. It'll be a couple of minutes."

"Thanks, buddy." He chugged his first cup and poured another, ignoring the heat that scorched the roof of his mouth. He took the syrup from the pantry and as he sat to eat, his phone rang.

"Hello?" he answered.

"Is this Wyatt?" the voice on the other end asked.

"Yes."

"Hello, Wyatt. This is Bob Wilkins. You may not remember me. I'm your father's lawyer. We met twenty years ago or so when you--"

"I remember," Wyatt said, recalling the incident in college when he'd destroyed his dorm room in what he thought had been a psychotic episode. A window, bed frame, and desk had been broken. Bob convinced the university to settle, ensuring that Wyatt would be able to finish school there.

"Of course," The lawyer cleared his throat before continuing. "I'm sorry to be the one to tell you this, but, last night, your father passed away."

"What?" Wyatt stood and walked to the living room, not wanting Will to hear. "What happened?"

"The doctor called it 'ventricular fibrillation', but that's just a fancy way of saying 'heart attack'. I'm sorry, son."

"Do you know if," Wyatt choked, unable to hide the quiver in his voice. "Was it painful?"

"It was very quick. He most likely felt a sharp jolt for a couple of seconds before losing consciousness. A neighbor found him and called an ambulance right away, but--"

"Okay."

"Everything's been taken care of. After the first heart attack a few years ago, he put a plan together. All I have to do is execute it.

He wanted it over with as fast as possible, so your grief wouldn't be dragged out."

"He was nothing if not efficient."

"The funeral's today at one. Most of his belongings will be boxed up and donated next week, but there are a few sentimental things he wanted you to have, along with the rest of the estate."

"Sentimental? We are talking about *my* father?"

Bob chuckled. "I'll leave them for you in his-- *your* apartment. I'll text you the funeral details."

"All right, thank you, Bob."

"Of course, son. I know you've moved out of state. Will I see you this afternoon?"

"Yeah, it's only a two and a half hour flight. I'll be there."

"Okay, see you then."

Wyatt ended the call and looked back into the kitchen where Will sat, speedily eating what must have been his sixth pancake. He didn't know how to tell him. He didn't *want* to tell him. News like this could trigger him, potentially causing him to lose control. He couldn't risk it. He'd go to the funeral alone and tell Will what happened when he got back.

"Dad?" Will said, noticing the tears building in Wyatt's eyes. He got up from the table and went to his father. "Dad, are you okay?"

Wyatt pulled his son in for a hug, letting one tear fall to his cheek and wiping it away, suppressing the emotion he was feeling. "I'm fine," he said, pulling away. "I have to go to the city. I'll try to make it back by tonight. Stay here, okay? Promise me you'll stay here."

"Michelle's coming over later to watch TV, but if we get hungry--"

"I'll leave pizza money. Just don't leave the house. I mean it. If something happened to you, I don't know how I'd--"

"Okay," Will promised. "Okay, I'll stay here while you're gone. Are you sure you're all right? You do not look 'fine'."

"We'll talk about it when I get home. I'll be okay, I swear. As long as you stay safe."

"I'll do my best."

Wyatt stood over his father's fresh grave, the loneliness of being the last mourner to leave like rocks in his gut. He had been fine throughout the service, cold and stoic, showing no emotion whatsoever. Now, though, the sinking in his stomach was too much. He could no longer stifle the tears that fell hot on his cheeks in the afternoon sun that shone too bright to be tolerated by a man missing his father.

"I should have called more," he bleated. "I should have made more of an effort." He stared at the headstone, his tears blurring his vision so much that he could no longer make out the inscription. "There were things I couldn't tell you, that I really wanted to. What I am, what I can do. That what I was seeing weren't hallucinations. That I talked to Mom. And you were right, she was really beautiful. I didn't tell you that you have a grandson or that he's a genius, taking classes for three degrees at the same time. Now, he'll never get to know his grandfather. I took that from him because I didn't want to scare you. I finally felt like I was more than a burden to you and I didn't want that to end, so, I'm sorry. I'm sorry I didn't trust you with who I am." He walked around the mound of earth, placed a hand on the cool, smooth granite of the headstone, and knelt next to it as if telling it a secret. "I wish you were here."

Wyatt sat on the sofa in his father's living room, the silence of the apartment suffocating. He loosened his tie and rolled his sleeves up before examining the contents of the boxes Bob had left on the coffee table for him. Pictures of his mother, his parents' wedding album, and his father's music collection were what had meant the most to the old man and Wyatt was thankful to have them now. He put a CD in the stereo and quietly played "Here There and Everywhere" as he flipped through the photo album, taking note of how happy his father looked. He'd never in his life seen his dad smile like that. It was jarring and comforting at the same time. "At least you're together now," he muttered. He set the book aside and found another small, leather album at the bottom of the box. He was astonished upon opening it to see pictures of himself as a child; baby pictures, school pictures, and a few from his wedding to Annie. He didn't know his father had kept any of them. Tears again began to build. He stood and paced the hardwood floor, the sound of his steps echoing as he thought about the first time he'd left Will home alone. He'd spent so much time worrying if his son would be all right that he hadn't really enjoyed the visit. John talked mostly about work and they discussed the possibility of franchising Pine's, which Wyatt had no intention of doing, though the idea was intriguing. They'd joked about Indiana weather and the use of the word 'ope'. John didn't have one drink that day and Wyatt had been glad to see his father taking better care of himself. Not better enough, though, apparently.

A knock on the door broke Wyatt from his memory and he answered it, forgetting to turn the stereo off.

"Do you want to be alone?" Allydia asked. He shook his head and let her in. She removed her cloak, a necessity she wore, even in the June heat, as it was still day. He closed the door and went back to turn off the music. "Leave it," she requested. "I love this song." He did and returned to his seat on the couch. "I heard about your father."

"How?"

"I have people."

"Right."

"I'm very sorry."

"Thank you."

"Are you all right?"

"I'm okay, just," he sighed, the heaviness of the day making him feel weak. "I don't know how to deal with this. How did you?"

"How did I what?" she asked, sitting next to him.

"Deal with losing your parents."

"You mean my mother? She died when I was two, so I don't remember what that was like. I'm sorry I can't give you any advice on the matter."

"What about your father?"

"Cain? He's cursed to eternally wander the Earth, never able to stay in one place for more than--"

"Your dad's *Cain*? Like, Cain and Abel, Cain?"

"I thought you knew."

"How would I have known?"

"If your siblings didn't tell you, I would have thought my surname made it clear."

"I honestly thought you'd made that up."

"What?"

"Because it sounds...never mind."

"I did drop the 'ibnat'. Being called 'daughter' seemed disingenuous, after."

"Cain. Well, that is just...something."

"Can I get you anything? Water? Food?"

"No, I'm fine, thank you, though. It's nice of you to come by."

"I have ulterior motives," she admitted.

"Don't you always?"

"I know this isn't the appropriate time, but, I'd like to speak to you about our," She thought for a moment. "Whatever we are."

"You want to have the 'where is this going' talk *now*?"

"Not especially, but I feel I must say this before I get...frisky."

He chuckled. "Go ahead."

She moved to sit on the table in front of him to better look into his face as she spoke. "I don't know what this feeling is. I was married in my previous life, before I was what I am. I loved my husband and I was bereaved when he died. I was grief-stricken when my children were taken from me. I lamented for months. But, I've never been as devastated as I was when you left. I spent more than three years confined to my private room, unable to hunt or feed. Some days I couldn't drink at all. I made myself sick missing you. What I feel for you is stronger than I know how to handle. According to your sister, you feel as though no one has ever put you and your needs first, but *I do*. I will *always* put you ahead of *anyone*, including myself. That's why I want to give you the choice. I know what it's like for men to be near me. I don't want you to feel tricked into being with me. If we're together, it has to be because you wish it so and if you want me to go, I'll go. You'll never have to see me again if that's what you prefer. But, if you want me, I will never leave your side."

He stared at her, awestruck and mute, his mind swirling with the emotions of the day. His silence lasted too long, a clear indication to Allydia that she should leave with what remained of her dignity. "I understand," she told him, getting up and walking toward the door. She opened it slightly, but it slammed in front of her.

She turned to find Wyatt standing over her, his eyes like fire burning through her. He brushed the hair away from her eyes, watching them as they watched him, sparkling in the dimly lit room and beginning to dilate. Unabashed happiness filled her as the hushed command left his lips, "Don't go."

Chapter 25

Will swallowed the acetaminophen, his third dose of the day. His headache was getting worse and with it, flashes of memories he had no business remembering. He pushed them away and ordered pizza in preparation for his date with Michelle. He tied the bag of trash that filled the kitchen garbage can and took it outside where he stopped to admire the early evening sky, painted in varying shades of red and orange. He'd just turned to go back inside when he heard it...the low, quiet growl of a wolf.

Two gray wolves stepped out of the woods, then six more. They crept toward him, snarling and baring their teeth. He moved to run back into the house but was blocked by another wolf, this one larger than the others with a darker coat. It howled in his face, a signal to the rest of the pack, before leaping at him, knocking him to the ground. It stood upon his chest, howling once more. They all came at him at once, biting his back and legs as he went fetal, instinctively protecting his neck, chest, and stomach. The pain was blinding. He knew if he didn't do something soon, he'd die, so he managed to get up on his knees and begin to fight back.

He grasped the mouth of one of the beasts and pried its jaws apart, snapping the bone. It yelped, backing off a bit, but not surrendering. He threw another one off of him, sending it flying all the way to the roof of the barn. He stood, waiting, hoping he had scared them enough that they'd now run away. They didn't. Following the big one's lead, they came for him again, clamping down on his arms and legs, rendering him immobile. He glanced around wildly, the amount of blood that covered the animals and himself, all of it his, was alarming. He'd lost too much and was beginning to feel dizzy. Terror set in as the pack's leader approached him, its eyes fixed on his now exposed throat. Adrenaline rushed through his veins, his heart pounding in his ears like a drum. His mind went blank. No plan could be made to get himself out of this. They had him. He was sure he was going to die.

As the wolf lunged, Will could feel something hot inside him, rising like steam from his solar plexus to just under his skin. It burned like acid as it spewed from him out of every pore, a wave of white lightning, bursting out in all directions, killing all eight of the wolves instantaneously. Their bodies dropped, singed and smoking.

Will fell to his knees, hurt and trembling, horrified by what he'd done. "You had no choice," he told himself, catching his breath. "They would've killed you. You *had* to."

He got to his feet, hunger replacing fear, and hurried inside where he took several slices of bread from the package and gorged himself, devouring one after another until there was none left in the bag. Blood dripped from his arms to the floor, leaving small puddles everywhere he went. Suddenly, his headache went from bad to intolerable, shooting through the nerves like a bullet on fire. He dropped to the floor, more memories flooding his mind. He remembered Gabriel telling his father that she should kill him and seeing the fear in her eyes as she looked down at him through the car window. He remembered his mother's voice when she'd spoken to him while he was in the womb, her guilt about hiding him from his father, and explaining her reasons for doing it. He remembered being born. Tears fell like water from a faucet from his bloodshot eyes, the memories more painful than his wounds. He went to take his phone from his pocket, desperate to call his dad, but it wasn't there. It must have fallen out during the fight. He slapped himself in the face, trying to free himself of the visions that ran rampant in his brain, but he couldn't shake them. They kept coming, clouding his judgement and whittling at his sanity. He was so lost in his head that he didn't hear the front door open or the knocking that had come before.

"Will?" Michelle called. "Will!" She crouched next to him on the tile floor, taking his face in her hands. "What happened? Will, what happened? Talk to me."

"They attacked me," he told her, his shaky voice barely above a whisper.

"Who did?"

"Wolves."

"What? Okay," she said, calming herself and examining the gashes, bite marks, and places where entire chunks of flesh had been torn out. "Okay, come on. We have to get you to a hospital. Can you stand?"

"I'm not going anywhere."

"Will," she pleaded.

"I promised my dad I'd stay here until he got back. It shouldn't be long."

"Will, we can call your dad from the car. Please!"

"You should go."

"Are you crazy?! I'm not leaving you like this. You could die!"

"There's only one thing that kills something like me."

She backed off, noticing a change in his tone. "Will, you're scaring me."

"I don't want to," he said, tears again forming in his eyes. "I don't want to hurt anyone. I don't want to hurt *you*, Michelle. You're--" He paused. "You know what you are to me. I'm not okay. So, go, please. Please, just go."

She nodded, wiping tears from her cheeks and kissing him gently before getting up and leaving the house, calling Gabriel from the porch. No answer. As she hurried to her car, she passed the pizza delivery man on the long sidewalk. "Run," she warned him, not breaking her stride. He gave her a puzzled look and continued to the front door as she drove off. He knocked a few times before growing impatient and letting himself in.

"Hello?" the twenty-something-year-old man called. "Pizza! Anyone here?"

Will staggered to the living room. "You have to go," he commanded. "Leave the pizza."

"Dude! Are you okay?! You need an ambulance?" He took his phone from his pocket and started to call nine-one-one.

"No ambulance," Will said.

"You need a hospital, bro," the man insisted, putting the phone to his ear.

"I said 'no'," Will grunted, shoving him to the ground, the pizza box falling open, spilling its contents onto the carpet. *"I can't leave."*

"What the fuck?! Man, you need help. You're lucky you're already fucked up because if you weren't hurt, I'd kick your scrawny ass myself. Now, I'm calling an ambulance, like it or not."

"I can't let you do that," Will insisted, kicking the man in the face, sending blood and teeth flying. "They'd take me to the hospital, which means I wouldn't be here when my dad gets home and I promised him *I'd stay here."* He knocked the man unconscious with one blow to the top of the head. Worried he'd gone too far, he checked that he was still breathing. When he could feel the warm air coming from the man's gaping mouth, he relaxed, sitting next to him on the floor. He moved the pizza box to the coffee table, out of the way of the food that lay in a mangled pile on the carpet, and started eating directly from the floor, the pangs of hunger now completely overwhelming.

Chapter 26

"Okay, I'm chartering a jet for the trip back. That was *unpleasant*," Gabriel griped after Lucifer set her on her feet.

"Agreed," he said. "Flying with a passenger isn't my cup of tea, either, especially when they're squirming."

"Dude, it was *really* high."

"Yes, well, it cut our travel time by half, and as you can see, time is of the essence."

The fly-covered bodies that lined the streets had taken on a foul stench so putrid, even stray animals stayed away.

"I'm gonna throw up," Gabriel complained, covering her mouth. "No, no, I'm good. Let's just find this asshole so we can get home. I think I left my phone on the counter. *Or* I dropped it somewhere over Ireland."

"You're worried about social media *now*?"

"There could be an emergency."

"A bigger emergency than *this*?" he gestured to the decomposing Israelis that littered the pavement like confetti after a parade.

"Apples and oranges."

"What on Earth could be more pressing than preventing humanity's complete annihilation by way of nuclear missile?"

"Probably nothing, but--" Just then, a far-off buzzing filled the air. "The fuck is that?"

"He knows we're here," Lucifer surmised. The sound grew louder, the high-pitched screech roaring above them. They could see now that the noise came from what must have been millions of locusts, the wall of them so dense, it blotted out the sun. The sound was deafening as they descended, swarming, covering the siblings in suits of living hum.

"Can you do something about this, please?!" Gabriel yelled. Lucifer forced the insects off of them, sending them high into the air. He drew them to each other, the buzzing of their wings replaced by the crunch of their bodies as they were compelled together. Lucifer enforced his will on them, driving them to commit suicide by flight until no sound remained. The ball of macerated bug parts fell to the ground in front of them with a sickening, wet thud. "That's fucking gross," Gabriel observed. "But I appreciate you."

They'd started walking, heading to the not-so-secret site of Israel's nuclear weapons stash when they heard a rustling behind them followed by a deep moan. They turned to see the dead rising, their vacant, unsettling stares more unnerving than the haphazard way with which they shuffled toward them.

"Are you serious right now?" Gabriel whined. "I forgot he can make zombies. Pain in my ass."

"Would you mind, sister?" Lucifer asked, motioning toward the dozens of ghouls approaching them from all sides. "I'd like to save my strength for the main event."

"Yeah, I'm just waiting for them to get a good distance from the buildings." She crossed her arms as they drew nearer.

"We have little time to waste," he scolded.

"I am not about to destroy a city block over a few creepers."

"I see over a hundred, which I would venture to say counts as a horde. And, might I remind you, that while they may not be able to kill you permanently, if they liberate a limb from your body, it will not grow back."

"Fine," she sighed, rolling her eyes. She waved her hands up to her shoulders, engulfing the mob in flames. Some fell instantly while others continued, mindlessly staggering onward until they, too, dropped a few feet away from where the two stood.

"Well done," Lucifer praised. "And you managed to avoid any structures. Now, on to Dimona."

The site appeared desolate. It was Chernobyl in its silence. They entered the facility, the cold sterility of the military installation cutting through them like shards of glass. The lights were all on and computers remained opened on the oversized, oval table that sat in front of a wall of screens. To their right was a control panel, its lights flashing and a timer counting down the seconds until the launch. 29, 28, 27. To their left, a man sat, listless on the floor, propped against a wall of clocks. He had a rash, a nosebleed, and had very clearly recently vomited on himself. 26, 25, 24.

"What disease is *that*?" Lucifer cringed.

"Dengue fever," Gabriel told him, bending down to heal the dying man, whose temperature had run up to a hundred and ten degrees.

23, 22, 21, 20.

"Is now the best time for that?" Lucifer prodded.

"Hey, I may be a garbage human, but I'm not heartless."

19, 18, 17

"I never implied tha--"

The man jumped up, terror on his face and gratitude in his eyes. He ran off, being of no help in their current predicament. 16, 15, 14.

"Wonderful," Lucifer exasperated, the counter ticking down. 13, 12, 11, 10, 9. "How do we stop it?"

"I got it," Gabriel assured, flipping the correct switches and ending the sequence. "You didn't think I knew how to shut down a nuclear launch?"

"Honestly, sister, I didn't believe it would be that easy."

"Well, we're not done yet, are we?"

"No, we're not. Remember, when we find Abaddon--"

"Yeah, yeah. Hold him in his body so you can beat his ass. Seems like a time suck, but whatever you want."

"Now to find the miscreant."

"I can hear him," Gabriel said, pointing to her temple. "Underground bunker. Guess he didn't want to ruin his man-suit killing off the rest of the planet. Honestly, he thinks nothing through. Like, how did he *not know* that blowing up the planet with fucking nuclear hell-fire would devastate *everything*? Plants, animals. This dumb motherfucker thought he'd just get rid of people and the rest of nature would be *fine*. He'd have all the food and clean water he could handle, living in a new Garden of fucking Eden, all alone until God woke up. Stupid as *shit*."

"Yes, he's always been emotional, reason never playing much of a role in his decision making."

They got in the elevator and headed down to the underground bomb shelter where they found Abaddon, genuinely surprised that they'd found him.

"You're too late," he told them. "Any second, the bombs will fall. I have one pointed at every major city on Earth. Soon, this world will be free of the human scourge and you wi--"

"Yeah, I shut that shit *right* the fuck down," Gabriel declared. "No explosions today. Sorry, bro."

"You did *what*?!"

"A few switches here, a couple button pushes there. It wasn't hard."

"I will tear your foul tongue from your mouth and use it to strangle the life from you, once and for all."

"Give it a shot," she goaded. He rushed toward her, but she held her arm out, throwing him back with the power of her mind. "You know, I understand the child molester thing. That piece of shit got what he deserved. But the diner people? That was just rude." She flicked a finger in his direction causing a gash to appear on his left cheek. He winced, staring angrily at her while she smiled. "I told you," she giggled. "*Like soap.*"

"Gabriel," Lucifer scolded. "Remember what we talked about."

"Lucifer, from God's favorite son to His biggest disappointment," Abaddon poked. "Imagine how angry He'll be."

"He'll get over it," Gabriel interjected.

"Now, Gabriel, you know how He can get."

"Bitch, I don't know what you're talking for. You must have forgotten how *I* can get." She started to raise her hand, but Lucifer held it down.

"This fight is mine, sister."

"Are you sure? I can just--"

"Yes, but I've waited a long time for this."

"All right," she grumbled, again lifting her hand and making a fist.

"What are you doing?" Abaddon accused.

"Call it a cage match," she smirked.

He needed to get back to the control room and restart the launch sequence. He would then handle these two. He tried to teleport but realized he could not. She had bound him, rendering him trapped, unable to leave this body or to transmit it to another location. Now a fair fight, Lucifer pounced, landing a hard right hook into his brother's eye. He went down, touching his face and laughing.

"You want to fight this way?" he jeered. "Like these creatures our Father takes so much pride in? Like *animals*?"

"I find it cathartic," Lucifer commented. "The Gates are closed. There's no redemption for you to be had. This ends now."

"So be it," Abaddon growled, getting to his feet. "But, how can you be sure that it will be *my* end and not the two of yours?"

Gabriel snickered.

"*You* against God's most powerful angel and a firestarter?" Lucifer scoffed. "You wouldn't stand less of a chance if you were human." He punched him again, breaking his nose, and again, cracking his cheekbone, and again, breaking his jaw. Abaddon fought back, throwing punishing blows to Lucifer's stomach and face. They went back and forth, exchanging jabs, both of them bloody and broken.

"Are you done yet?" Gabriel whined. "My arm's getting tired."

They continued to brawl, pushing each other into walls, smashing screens, and putting holes in the concrete. Lucifer, growing tired, lifted Abaddon over his head and slammed him through a table, sending bits of metal flying in all directions and shattering most of his enemy's vertebra. He was unconscious, his ability to heal slowed by the amount of punishment Lucifer had inflicted.

Lucifer left him, looked to his sister, and walked from the room, telling her breathlessly as he passed, "Go ahead." She turned to follow him and flicked her wrist behind her, igniting the angel in flames so hot, he was completely incinerated within seconds, his body and the true form within it gone before the sprinklers turned on.

"That wasn't so difficult," Lucifer remarked, peering out the window of the small jet as it took off.

"I told you we wouldn't need the others," Gabriel reminded.

"Speaking of the others, why have you been so secretive about our dear brother's whereabouts? Uriel doesn't even know his location and the two of you are thick as thieves. I admit, though I've been preoccupied, I have been curious."

"I can't tell you."

"Come, now. I just helped you save the world...*again*. You can trust me. I won't tell a soul."

"No."

"Fine, then answer something else for me, because I don't quite understand. Wyatt, emotional powder keg though he may be, is a grown man. Why are you so protective of him? *He* was the one of us created for protecting others. Why do you baby him so?"

"I owe him."

"For what?"

"It's my fault," she confessed. "Everything wrong with him, psychologically, is because of me. You feel guilty about closing the Gate and staying here. You feel like you failed God. Well, I failed Wyatt. I failed him *hard*."

"You can't blame yourself for his afflictions. You didn't know where he was for *decades*."

"I did. I did know, once. When I was fifteen, I saw him at a party. I could feel him. I *knew* it was him, but I didn't say anything. I don't even think he saw me. I just let him walk by. I didn't tell him who he was because I was *too high to care*. He spent twenty years thinking he was insane, being locked up in institutions and drugged, his friends abandoning him. His wife left him, his dad treated him like trash. You don't know *half* of the fucked up shit he's been through and all of it was because I let my personal bullshit matter more than the mission. I know that he's not the Barachiel you remember and I know you miss him, but he's in there. Under all that pain and anger and depression, the brother you know is *in there*. You know as well as I do that he's the best of us, and I fucked him up, so, yeah, I baby him a little. I worry about him. I let him get away with things I know I shouldn't. I let him make mistakes because I don't want to be the one to hurt him again, but, *shit*. What would *you* do, if you were me?"

"Me?" Lucifer considered. "I'd probably drown my sorrows in gluttonous amounts of alcohol and women, followed by years of regret and self-loathing."

"Bro, you just described my twenties."

Chapter 27

Will tossed the last wolf's body onto the pile, covered the heap in lighter fluid he'd gotten from under the grill, backed away, and chucked a ball of lightning at it. The mound of corpses erupted in a plume of smoke and flame, the fire growing hotter the more it consumed. He went back inside for a snack, his hunger raging once more. He opened a new package of bread and made a sandwich, then another. He was so hungry that eventually, he stopped assembling and ate the ingredients separately, shoving lunch meat, cheese, and bread in his mouth as fast as his hands would allow. More memories flooded his brain, these not even his own. They were his mother's memories and they were brutal. He knew what she had been thinking and feeling when he was developing inside of her. He could see his father through her eyes, throwing furniture and breaking mirrors, screaming nonsense. She was afraid of him.

Will made his way up the stairs, deciding he should get cleaned up before his dad got home, but as he reached the landing, a wave of pain hit him so hard, he collapsed. Blood poured from his nose as more memories cascaded in. They seared his brain like a hot poker, causing him to convulse. Visions of his childhood, his mother's voice, and the fear in his aunt's eyes flashed like cameras. He cried out, his hands gripping the sides of his head. He hyperventilated as he seized, his nervous system overloaded with information. He opened his mouth to scream again, but just as the sound was about to escape his throat, everything went dark. He was limp, his breathing shallow, his heart barely beating.

Wyatt drove up to the house, stopping before reaching the driveway. He and Allydia watched as the pizza delivery man ran out the front door and got into his car, speeding off, nearly taking out the mailbox as he went. The two got out of the car, immediately getting soaked by the rain that fell hard from the night sky. Wyatt could smell fire and went around the house to find a smoldering pile of ash in the backyard. He couldn't tell what had been destroyed there, but whatever it was, it had been big.

Allydia entered the house first, a feeling of unease washing over her. "Wyatt," she all but whispered as he came in behind her, her eyes dilating and hunger pulling her toward the stairs. "Wyatt, I smell blood."

He moved past her and darted up the stairs to find his son, bleeding and unresponsive. "Will," he croaked. "Will!" He shook him, but nothing. He listened for a heartbeat. It was there, but it was slow. There was no time to get him to the hospital. He'd have to heal him himself. He placed his hands on the boy, one on his head and one on his heart, and concentrated.

"What are you doing?" Allydia asked.

"I'm trying to heal him."

"Do you know how to do that?"

"Not a clue," he admitted. "But I've seen Gabriel do it. I've seen Barachiel do it. I just have to focus." He thought about the memory Valerie had shown him years before, where he'd healed the boy in the alley. He thought about how that had felt and tried to recreate it. "Come on," he cried. "Come on!" Finally, white light glowed from his hands. Will's skin, too, began to illuminate, the marks on his arms shrinking and disappearing. Will sprung up, clutching his chest and coughing, the sudden rush of air in his lungs painful.

Wyatt leaned against the wall, exhausted and weak, the healing taking all of his strength.

"Dad?" Will panted, looking down at his arms. "Did you fix me? I didn't know you could do that."

"Neither did I," Wyatt wheezed, finding it difficult to catch his breath, as well. "What the hell happened?" He sat on the stairs, leaning against the railing. He glanced down to the living room where he saw Allydia, hovering near the front door, looking afraid.

"I'm a monster is what happened," Will answered, tears welling in his eyes. "I'm not okay, Dad. You should've let Gabriel kill me when she had the chance."

"How do you know about that? Did she talk to you? She had no right--"

"I remember it," Will bellowed, jumping up and heading down the stairs, ignoring the vampire's cautious stare. "I remember everything. I remember my mom talking to me before I was born. I remember how she felt when you'd go off the rails, how afraid she was. I remember how, despite that, she almost didn't have me so she could stay with you. She made an appointment and everything, but I grew too fast."

Wyatt teetered down the stairs to join the others, lightheaded, his balance unsteady. "I'm sure that's not true," he challenged. "I knew your mother. She wouldn't--"

"She would have," Will asserted. "She would have for *you*. And I wish she had because knowing I killed her is--"

"You *didn't* kill her."

"I did. I did, Dad. I *remember* it. *I tore that woman apart.* She didn't give birth to me, I *fled* her. I could hear her heart above me getting weaker. I could feel her pulse getting fainter. If I didn't get out, I would have been dead, so I left. And after everything I put her through, she asked the doctor if *I* was okay. She was worried about *me*. She loved me, and I watched her die. I'm a monster that never should have been born."

"You're not a monster," Wyatt choked. "You're a good kid. You're smart and caring and--"

"I'm not a kid anymore, Dad, and I'm *not* good. You have no idea what I've done." He opened the door to the garage and slammed it behind him. Wyatt tried to follow, the muffled sound of Will's car starting giving him a sense of urgency, but Allydia stood in his way.

"Move," he demanded.

"What are you doing?"

"I'm going after him, what do you think?"

"You're spent. You're in no condition. You should call your sister."

"Get out of my way, Allydia."

"You can't move me unless I allow it. I'm stronger than you, especially in your current condition, so unless you're planning on electrocuting me--"

"He's my son."

"He's dangerous. He's killed someone. He wears the stench of death like cologne."

"Did you see him?! He was obviously attacked."

"Wyatt,"

"And how many people have you killed? Hundreds? Thousands?"

"None since you left!" she defended. "I wanted to be good enough for you. *Honorable*. That boy has had the benefit of your goodness his entire life and he *still* became the thing your sister feared. I've seen first hand what the Nephilim are capable of and once they turn, I'm telling you, there is *no* saving them. *Call your sister*."

"You told me your children were taken from you. Did you mean vampires, or did you have real kids, before?"

"Why would you hurt me with that question?"

"What would you do, if he was yours? What *wouldn't you do* to help your kid?"

She thought about her daughters and the resentment she still felt for not being able to watch them grow up. Wyatt would never forgive her if she didn't let him try, so, she stepped aside, allowing him to open the door. As he walked out, she followed closely behind, unwilling to let him face this danger alone.

"I need you," Will quavered, tears spilling over his cheeks.

Michelle pulled him into the apartment and hugged him tightly. "What happened?" she asked, closing the door and looking him over. "How are your wounds gone?"

"My dad, he...I don't know where to start."

"Okay. Why don't tell me how you got hurt?"

"A pack of wolves attacked me in my backyard. I had it coming."

"Why did they--"

"Because I killed one of their--" he struggled to get the rest out. "One of their kids."

"You what?"

"A four-year-old kid. He bit someone I cared about and turned him into-- it doesn't matter. I should've gone home. I should've let it go, but that night, after the bowling alley, I was so angry. I couldn't calm down. I tried to stop, but I couldn't control it. I couldn't--"

"Oh, God, Will."

"That's just the beginning. I killed the whole pack when they came for me. I almost killed the pizza guy. Michelle, I killed," he stopped himself, afraid to say it out loud, the realness of the words in his head like a knife to his heart.

"Who?"

"I didn't mean to," he sobbed. "I swear, I didn't."

"Will, who was it?"

He wiped the tears from his face and with a trembling voice told her, "Michelle, I killed my grandfather."

"Jesus, Will."

He broke down, taking her in his arms and pulling her down with him as he fell to his knees. He cried into her shoulder, holding her so tightly that it hurt. She was a lifeboat in a sea of chaos, the only thing that made sense to him anymore. She pet his hair and rubbed his back, tears forming in her own eyes as her greatest fear was being realized. "Okay," she settled, knowing what she had to do. "Okay, why don't you get yourself cleaned up and I'll make us something to eat and we can figure out what to do next, all right?"

He nodded, getting up and walking towards the bathroom, the blood on his clothes leaving Michelle's shirt and carpet stained. Once she was sure he was in the bathroom, she took out her phone and texted Gabriel everything she'd just heard. It destroyed her to do it, the pit in her stomach urging her not to. But, it was the right thing. Will was out of control and had to be stopped. She rubbed the tears from her eyes and as she hit send, she could feel him behind her.

"Gabriel?!" he shouted. "You told my aunt?! Do you know what she'll do to me?!"

"I'm worried about you," she cried, spinning around to face him. "What you've done, it's--"

"Did she send you?" he accused. "Did you come here to spy on me? Was any of this...were we real for you?"

"Of course we're real, Will. I love you. I love you so much. Nothing that happened between us was fake, not since--"

"Since?"

"I wasn't supposed to like you. I was supposed to work at the donut shop, watch from a distance, pop up where you happened to be once in a while, like at the SATs."

"You knew who I was?"

"Yeah, but I didn't recognize you at the shop. I didn't know you'd grown like that. I just thought you were a hot guy trying to ask me out. But, when you told me your name--"

"You went out with me, anyway? Knowing what I was? You do know, right? That I'm a freak? A monster?"

"You're not," she whimpered. "You're not a monster to *me*. When that tornado came through and you let me in, you were so kind to me. No one had ever treated me like that before. No one ever saw me the way you did. I fell for you that day."

"You fell for me, and now you're sentencing me to death. You love me, but you'd let me *die*?"

"I don't really think she'd kill you. She loves you."

"She *will* kill me. She will. She knows what I'm turning into. And, the thing is, I don't blame her. She's not wrong."

"You're a good person, Will. She knows that. I'll tell her--"

"So, you did see, didn't you? The night at the bowling alley. You saw what I did to that guy."

"Yeah."

"Why didn't you call her *then*?" he barked. "I was slipping. You could've prevented *all* of this."

"Because I'm in love with you. I didn't want to lose you. If there was a chance--"

"Does it look to you like there's a chance?" he yelled, grabbing a knife from the kitchen drawer. "Do I look like someone that can be saved?" He held the blade to his throat. "Is this what I deserve? Because this is what she'll do."

"Put the knife down."

"Don't worry, this can't kill me. It'll just put me down long enough that I won't be able to hurt anyone else until my aunt gets here. Or maybe you can do it yourself? You have a tub, right?"

"Stop," she sobbed.

"You can drag me in, hold my head under. Take the knife with you, in case I struggle. Stab me in the heart. That should knock me out long enough for you to get the job done."

"Stop it, Will," she begged, taking the knife from his hand and throwing it to the floor.

"How could you do this to me?" he sniffled. "You're the only girl I've ever loved and you broke my heart."

"I won't let her kill you," she promised. "I'll tell her--"

"You can't stop *her*. Do you know what she is? My dad told me about her powers. She can do *anything*. She's a force of nature."

"She's your aunt. She won't--"

"She's an angel first, above everything else, and she's coming to kill me, thanks to you."

"No, Will," She took his hands, but he pushed her away, a bolt of lightning exploding from his hands to hers. She fell, her body shaking violently on the floor, her eyes glazed over, her mouth foaming. She went still, her vacant eyes staring into nothing.

"Michelle," Will whimpered, kneeling beside her. "Michelle, please," He checked for a pulse, but there was none. He listened for her breath and heartbeat. Nothing. He fell back, new tears pouring down his cheeks. He buried his face in his hands. There was nothing for him left in the world. Without her, he was lost. Loneliness filled him like hot chocolate on a cold night, it's comfort strange, but right somehow. He stood, listening to the thunder clap outside, the flashes of lightning brightening the dimly lit apartment. *This is it*, he thought. *This is who I'm meant to be.*

Chapter 28

"Bitch, what the fuck?!" Valerie snapped as Gabriel and Lucifer entered the apartment. "You left your phone. I saw *all* that shit. Why didn't you tell me there was a fucking Ne--"

"Lucifer, go to your room," Gabriel ordered.

He guffawed.

"Please, go."

"All right," he acquiesced, intrigued. As Gabriel led Valerie to the sofa, Lucifer quietly stole the phone from the counter and took it to the hall where he stayed, out of sight, but well within earshot. He scrolled through the texts as he listened, growing more and more agitated as he read.

"Tae's niece?!" Valerie screeched. "You sent that poor girl to do *your* dirty work?"

"Tae told her who I was, *what* I was. She was the only person I could trust that Barachiel wouldn't recognize. She was just supposed to watch and report back. If he started showing signs, I--"

"You what?"

"I would have handled it."

"You would've killed him? Wyatt's son? Fuck, bitch, hasn't that boy been through enough?"

"Obviously. That's why I didn't kill him when he was a baby. I almost did. After B took him away, I went to his house when he was asleep. I snuck in, stood over Will's crib. I was gonna drown him in the sink, dry him off, try to make it look like SIDS. But B would've been devastated." Tears fell from Gabriel's eyes, something Valerie had never seen before. "He'd just lost his wife and, God, Uri, the look on his face when I couldn't bring her back. It broke me. He was *gutted*. This kid gave him hope, something to live for. If I took that from him, I don't know that he would've recovered. So, I checked in, visited a few times a year, talked to B every couple of days to make sure everything was all right. And, when Will started going out into the world, I sent Michelle. I had her in martial arts classes so she could defend herself, just in case, and I made it very clear that it was too dangerous to get friendly. Casual acquaintances tops. Nothing else."

"Well, she must not have listened, since he was at her place. That poor girl's probably dead, along with a kid and Wyatt's dad. His *dad*."

"Will's fucked up," Gabriel worried. She glanced up toward the hallway, knowing her brother had been listening the entire time. "That whole town's in danger. Southport, Indiana better lock its doors and close its windows because if he's half as nutty as I think he is, there's gonna be hell to pay."

Lucifer slunk to his bedroom and opened the window, rage coloring his face like rouge. He climbed out and took off, determined to make this right.

Wyatt drove down the dark road, the too-few street lights little help in seeing through the downpour. "Wyatt, look out!" Allydia yelped, able to see the figure lurking in the middle of the street. He slammed on the breaks, the car sliding and drifting sideways before coming to a stop. The man approached and soon, in the brightness of the headlights, they could make out who it was.

"Lucifer," Wyatt commanded, exiting the car, not bothering to close the door. "Go home!"

"You know I can't do that, brother. Not after what you've set upon us."

"Did Gabriel send you?"

"No, our sister is feeble when it comes to you. She believes the loss of someone else you love may drive you mad. I suspect she's right, but in your heart, you know what must be done."

Wyatt stepped closer, getting directly in Lucifer's face. "You leave my son alone."

"Have you any idea what he's done?" Lucifer barked back. "He killed a family of shifters, a four-year-old child, and your father."

Wyatt backed off, his stomach falling. "You're lying."

"I'm not. Gabriel's spy told her. I read the messages myself. A girl named Michelle."

"Gabriel *planted* her?"

"Of course. She may put your delicate feelings above her common sense, but she's not *stupid*. Now, it seems your progeny has killed the girl, as well. I overheard Gabriel telling Uriel all about your offspring's misadventures. She'll be a tad cross with me when I return, but I trust she'll understand. She learned long ago to put what's right ahead of her emotions."

Suddenly, the boom of an explosion rang out in the distance. They could see plumes of smoke rising from the center of town and the orange glow of flames tinting the sky above. Overhead, several lightning bolts stretched across the overcast, heading in the same direction and, eventually, all coming down on buildings on the same block.

"I see he shares your flare for the dramatic as well as your powers," Lucifer quipped.

"Jesus Christ," Wyatt breathed.

"How many times must I ask that you not say--" Another explosion erupted, this one louder than the last. "I'm sorry, brother, but you know what I must do." Wyatt grabbed one of his arms to stop him, but Lucifer wrapped the other around him as if in an embrace. "Have it your way," he sighed. "You won't be the first person I've had along for a ride today." He carried Wyatt as he flew over the town, coming down hard on the sidewalk across from Pine's, now engulfed in flames. The auto repair shop next door and several homes, too, were on fire, the rain of no help in putting out the blaze that lit up the street so well, it was as if there were a spotlight on the block.

"Dad?" Will called, emerging from around the corner, his shirt singed and his demeanor off.

"Hello, nephew," Lucifer greeted.

"Who's this?" Will wondered, crossing the street to meet them.

"What did you do?" Wyatt asked through the tears that mingled with rain on his cheeks.

"I saw it on a show," Will explained. "If I destroy the town, everyone will leave. They'll be safe and I can stay, alone. I'm too dangerous to be around people. It's the right thing to do."

"You're killing people."

"That's what I'm telling you. I'm unsafe. I killed that kid that turned Arthur into that thing, the pack that came for revenge,"

"And my father?" Wyatt asked, his voice breaking.

"That was an accident," Will insisted. "I just wanted to meet him, see if we looked alike. But, he thought I was a burglar, called the cops. I told him who I was, but he didn't believe me. He just kept yelling at me to leave. When I wouldn't, he grabbed me, pushed me, and I...it just came out of me, like instinct. The electricity in his heart, I sped it up. I didn't mean to, I swear. When he let me go and my mind cleared and I realized what I was doing, I stopped, but...he fell down."

Wyatt covered his mouth as he sobbed, the awfulness of what he was hearing too much to take.

"I tried to save him," Will continued. "I tried to restart his heart, but nothing happened. I called nine-one-one. I didn't know what else to do."

"How did you get into the city?"

"It's only a two and a half hour flight. I slipped some antihistamine in your drink with dinner and snuck out. You're already a heavy sleeper. It was easy."

"You drugged me?"

"You wouldn't have let me go. To be honest, I'm surprised you're so upset."

"Surprised?!"

"You think I don't know how miserable that man made you? I do. I remember everything Mom thought about while I was in her. At college, the booze, the drugs, the suicide attempts. *Three times* you tried to *end it* because of him. He was a dick that made your life such hell that you didn't want it anymore. But no amount of pills can kill things like us, right? Only one thing can kill me." He held his hands out and let the rain fall through his fingers. "And only one thing can kill you. Is that why you bailed on the Bar exam and started Leroy Jenkins-ing into burning buildings? Were you trying to *die*?"

"That's enough," Lucifer growled.

"Seriously, who *are* you?" Will inquired.

"I'm your dear uncle, come to end this madness once and for all." He rushed toward him, reaching for his collar, but Will threw a bolt of lightning, sending Lucifer flying through the window of a house behind him.

"Wyatt!" Allydia called, running toward them. Will knocked her back with a ball of electricity, rendering her unconscious on the pavement.

"You have to stop this," Wyatt pleaded. "I don't want to hurt you."

"It's okay, Dad," Will said, hugging his father. The two cried there for several seconds in the rain before Will spoke into Wyatt's ear. "I know it would devastate you to hurt me. Don't worry. You won't have to." He squeezed him tight and let the full power of his soul loose, white lightning pouring from him like a river through a broken levy into Wyatt's torso. He shook, his heart exploding, blood oozing from his mouth, nose, and ears. The heat was so intense, it melted his skin before his body caught flame. Will let him go, watching sadly as he fell, a heap of little more than charred bone.

"WYATT!" Allydia screamed, scrambling to her feet and racing toward them. Lucifer staggered from the house, livid, his eyes set on his monstrous nephew. Allydia collapsed to her knees in the road, the flames too high for her to get near. She wailed, the sorrow unlike anything she'd felt before.

"Who are you?" Will shouted at Lucifer from afar.

"Your ignorance is insulting," Lucifer huffed. "No matter. Soon, you'll be in Purgatory, left alone in the cold and dark to think about the terrible things you've done. When your time is served, I hope your next life sees you more stable. If not, I'll meet you there, as well."

"Lucifer," Will realized. He backed away and started to run. Lucifer stood over Wyatt's burning corpse, the knowledge that there was nothing he could do to save him inciting in him a feeling of despondency, an emotion he hadn't felt in centuries. He took a deep breath and crossed the street, walking past the smoldering donut shop, following Will into the woods. It was darker there, harder to see, but he navigated his way through the trees and brush, more determined than ever to end the destruction caused by the abomination he called 'nephew'. He could hear the boy in the distance, snapping twigs and rustling leaves as he made his escape, but just as Lucifer was sure of which way to go, he was halted in his tracks by the feeling of something familiar. He turned, and there, standing among the trees, was his brother. Not Wyatt, but the Barachiel he remembered, looking just as he had in Norway all those years ago.

"Barachiel? How is this possible? You should be home."

"The vampire," the angel explained. "She fed on me once, taking so much blood, it became part of her DNA. Had I been human, I would have perished that day. I'm trapped here, until the Gates open, as long as she lives."

"Would you like me to kill her? Set you free?"

"Thank you, but, no. There's more work to do. Gabriel will fill you in. I'll heal my body and return to it, once I've ended this. It was nice getting a chance to speak with you without my human filter. Being Wyatt has been difficult. There's a disconnect between us, the human brain being so fragile. I appreciate you coming to protect me. How does it feel, doing my job?"

"Burdensome."

Barachiel laughed.

"Why did you do it?" Lucifer queried. "Why did you bring a *Nephilim* into the world?"

"As Wyatt, I was so in love with Annie that not much else mattered. I could feel her pulling away. She was frightened of me. She had prayed for a baby before things got bad, and I thought if I gave her one, she'd stay with me. Turns out, though, the baby was the thing that took her away. You have to understand how muddled the human mind is. Reason is often ignored. I'm not myself when I'm him. I wish we had more time, but when Wyatt has a natural death, we will be together again, I'm guessing for a hundred and forty years before we go above and below. It'll be good to catch up. As for now, though, I have a mess that needs tending to. If you'll excuse me."

"Let me do this for you, brother. Please. You shouldn't have to--"

"He's my Thryme," Barachiel maintained, disappearing into the night, his true form pure energy, unencumbered by the constraints of matter. Lucifer sighed and headed in the direction Will had been running in.

Will sat on the soggy ground, the storm having passed and the fireflies floating by, reminding him of the night he and Michelle had spent there. He was alone now, as it always should have been. He could finally breathe, knowing there was no one left for him to hurt.

"I'm sorry I let this happen," Barachiel apologized, appearing before him, his blond hair and cobalt eyes striking, even in the moonlight. "I shouldn't have been so careless."

"Who are you?" Will asked, getting to his feet.

"You really are so much like me. Well, not *me*, but, the *other* me."

Will studied the man's face and looked into his eyes. Then, it occurred to him. "Bara--"

Barachiel grasped the boy's throat and lifted him off the ground. Will tried electrocuting him, but his bolts went right through him.

"I really am sorry," Barachiel lamented as he carried Will closer to the creek and slammed him down into it. The boy thrashed, struggling to get free, unable to get hold of any part of the angel. "You're fundamentally good. Wyatt's influence, no doubt. It's your physiology that's the problem. You will get another chance and when you do, I will help guide you to be the best version of yourself. Remember, child, that you are loved."

As Will's body went limp, Barachiel waved goodbye to the soul that drifted off to its next destination. He placed the body on the ground and smoothed the hair away from the boy's closed eyes.

"Are you all right, brother?" Lucifer asked as he approached. "That must have been--"

"Once I'm Wyatt, I won't remember," Barachiel told him. "You should tell me. I might need to be watched to make sure I don't do something rash, but I'd much rather know the truth than think he did this to himself. Promise me."

"I will do what's right, Barachiel. I swear it."

Allydia continued to weep, her face pressed to Wyatt's exposed ribs. His top half was nothing more than bones and ash, still warm from the fire that had gone out just moments before. She put her hand to his forehead, but the skull crumbled at the touch. She wailed again, her heartbreak all-encompassing. As she cried, the smell of blood drifted up from the corpse. A warm wetness on her cheek forced her eyes open and she couldn't believe what she was seeing. Muscle and organs formed, a heart appeared and began to beat, the skull reformed, skin covering it. Soon, he was again whole, the lover she thought she'd lost. His eyes flew open as he took what felt like his first breath.

"Wyatt," she whispered, astonished and grateful. "Wyatt!" She held him in her arms as he sat upright, inhaling the sweet smell of his skin and bathing herself in his body heat, the most perfect warmth in existence.

"Where is he?" he asked, shakily standing.

"He went into the woods, but, Wyatt, your brother went after him."

Wyatt barreled through the forest, his instincts telling him in which direction to run. Allydia followed, dodging tree branches and tripping hazards as she went. As the sound of the rushing creek grew louder, so did Wyatt's dread. His chest tightened and his heart pounded as he felt something entirely foreign to him...fear.

They came to a clearing and there, on the edge of the creek, was Will's body, wet and still, sinking into the mud beneath him.

"No, no, no, no," Wyatt repeated, hurrying to his son's side. He began CPR, giving thirty chest compressions followed by a breath. "Wake up," he sobbed, starting more chest compressions. "Please. Please, wake up." But there was no life left to save. Allydia placed a sympathetic hand on Wyatt's back as he scooped the boy up in his arms and wept, his lungs feeling as if they could not take in air. The vampire wrapped her arms around his shoulders and kissed the back of his head as he grieved.

"You should run," she warned, feeling Lucifer approach them from behind the trees. Wyatt looked up and saw him there, a pained expression on his face.

"I'm sorry, brother," Lucifer said quietly.

"I don't know how," Wyatt swore through tears and strained breaths. "But I *will* kill you for this."

"I expect you'll try. I can't blame you, I understand. If *you'd* murdered someone I--"

"*I said run*," Allydia ordered.

"Very well," Lucifer complied, flying off, leaving Wyatt to mourn, unwilling to break his brother's heart further with the truth.

Chapter 29

Gabriel was a wreck. Feeling Wyatt die and come back had been an emotional roller coaster of devastation, physical pain, and relief. She was confused as to how he'd returned but was so grateful that he had that she almost thanked God before remembering that He couldn't hear her. She anxiously paced around the living room while Valerie took a late-night nap on the couch.

"Oh, shit," Gabriel muttered, rushing toward the door.

"What?" Valerie asked, popping up from her slumber.

"Be nice," she instructed, opening the door. Lucifer came in, his face ashen, despair in his eyes. Gabriel threw her arms around him, cradling the back of his neck with her right hand. He hugged her back, allowing her to comfort him as a single tear made its way down his cheek.

"We must let him believe it," he said into his sister's hair. She nodded, tears in her eyes now, too.

Michelle rolled over, wiping the drool from her mouth as she stood, her skin tingling and her head feeling heavy. She stumbled through the kitchen where she opened the freezer door and took out a frozen pizza box. She reached her hand inside and pulled out the bag of human blood she'd been hiding there and tossed it in the microwave. "Won't need *you* anymore," she sighed, taking the vial of Hattie's blood from the fridge and dropping it in the trash. The timer beeped and she emptied the contents of the plastic medical bag into a glass and drank greedily. She licked the blood from her lips and picked up her phone, dialing Hattie's number and holding the cell to her ear.

"Plan V in full effect," she told her friend when she answered. "Thanks for saving me."

"Are you sure this is what you want?" Hattie asked. "It's not an easy life, being what we are."

"It's better than being dead."

"What other secrets have you been keeping?" Lucifer asked, standing at the bar, taking a sip of Earl Grey as the sun rose, neither of them having yet been to bed. "Barachiel told me there's more for us to do."

"A ton more," Gabriel confirmed. "We're not even *kind of* done. You think Lilith was just a distraction. She wasn't. She started something when she was here, something I've been prepping for *for years.*"

"Do tell."

"You're gonna want to sit down."

ELOHIM

The boundaries which divide Life from Death are at best shadowy and vague. Who shall say where the one ends, and the other begins?

Edgar Allen Poe

Prologue

Six-year-old Gabriel slid a piece of paper to her father. He sat next to her at the long table in the conference room, the sleazy smile of a used car salesman plastered on his face. The two men on the other side were visibly uncomfortable, squirming in the leather seats and fiddling with papers and pens as they nervously awaited Mr. Murphy's offer. They knew him by reputation, the stories of his shrewd genius having made their way around town for years. Every CEO in Manhattan dreaded the day they had to come to Murphy Equity Group. James Murphy's style was well known. He'd exchange pleasantries, sit quietly for a few moments, then make his offer: the lowest possible amount the seller was willing to take. He somehow always knew and his chipper demeanor made his low-balling all the more insulting.

Mr. Murphy glanced at the note, folded it, and slipped it into his jacket pocket. "Well, Gentlemen, I won't waste your time. My team has crunched the numbers and the best I can do is seven million. I'm sure it's lower than you were hoping, so if you can't accept, no hard feelings." He stood, pulling his daughter's chair out and helping her down. "If you'll excuse me, I have to get this one to school. I'll give you until the end of the day to think it over."

"Wait," one of the men sighed. He stopped, a knowing grin creeping across his face.

"Go wait for me with Mrs. Lee," James whispered to Gabriel, who nodded and left the room. "Yes?"

"We'll take it," the other man said, disappointment and defeat clear in his tone.

"Excellent!" James said, shaking the man's hand. "Let's get those papers signed, shall we?"

In the lobby, Gabriel hovered near the secretary's desk. Mrs. Lee chewed on the end of a pen, the waiting driving her crazy. The doctor should have called by now. What was taking so long?

"Don't worry," Gabriel assured her. "He's fine."

"What?" Mrs. Lee said, just noticing the girl. "Oh, hi, Taran. How are you today?"

"A little sleepy. Daddy got me up early again for his meeting."

"Well, that's no fun. Would you like a pen and some paper to draw with while you wait?"

"No, thanks. I'm not particularly artistic. But he is," she said, pointing to the woman's stomach.

"Who is, sweetie?"

"Daniel. That's what you'll name him, after your husband's dad. He's gonna be a famous painter when he grows up."

The secretary's mouth hung open as she ignored the phone ringing next to her. "How...what?"

"Let's go, Taran," James said, exiting the board room, carrying the signed sales agreement. He placed the papers on the desk and took Gabriel's hand. "Time for school. Kim, take care of these while I'm gone, would you?" The secretary nodded, dazed by the girl's words. Gabriel waved as father and daughter stepped into the elevator, Mrs. Lee slowly raising her hand to wave back. As the elevator doors closed, the phone rang again.

"Murphy Equity Group, how can I direct your call?"

"Is this Mrs. Lee?" the woman on the other end asked.

"Yes."

"Hello, Mrs. Lee, and congratulations! Your suspicions were correct. You're pregnant! We'll need to set up an appointment to determine how far along you are."

She almost dropped the phone. How could the child have known? She hadn't told anyone she thought she might be expecting, not even her husband. And how did she know her father-in-law's name?

"Mrs. Lee?"

"Yes, yes, I'm here." *How did she know?*

"How does it feel, being a *teenager* now?" Gabriel's mother asked, lighting the thirteen candles on the cake that sat in front of her, cloying pink icing spelling out her human name in awkward cursive.

"The same," Gabriel responded, blowing out the candles before her mother was finished.

"You didn't make a wish," Cam said. He was her only friend and the solitary party guest.

"You know there's no point."

"Taran, dear," her mother condescended, her words slurred and her breath reeking of gin. "Don't be so dramatic. A wish is a dream your heart makes. Or is it the other way around?"

"Mother, you're wasted and you're embarrassing me. Can you leave us alone? Please?"

"How dare you speak to me that way?!" Esther shouted. She raised her hand and slapped her daughter hard, causing her mouth to bleed ever so slightly. Cam jumped up from his seat, grasping the cake cutter. Gabriel covered his hand with hers and shook her head. He sat back down. "When your father gets home and he finds out what you said to me--"

"You mean when he gets back from Amber's?" Gabriel shot back. "Oh, I know all about Dad's girlfriend. Well, the chick he pays to bang on weekends. I would have said something, but you already knew. Just didn't want to admit it to yourself. You *should* tell him what I said. You should *also* tell him it's real shitty to miss his only kid's birthday for a cheap fuck."

Esther slapped her again, wishing at that moment that the fall she'd purposefully taken down the stairs when she found out she was pregnant with her had done its job. Gabriel's skin burned hot and her cheeks turned red as she rose from her seat. Without thinking, she used her telekinesis to lift the cake from the table and throw it across the room, sending it smashing into the wall behind her drunk mother. Esther backed away, horror and confusion covering her overly painted face. "What are you?" she all but whispered as she hurried from the room.

That night, James came home to find his wife distraught and more inebriated than usual. She looked terrified and what she'd told him didn't make any sense. He chalked it up to the booze but went up to Taran's room to get her side of the story, anyway. He let himself in, angered at the sight of her smoking a joint, the music from her stereo blaring so loud, he couldn't hear himself yelling at her to turn it down.

"What do you think you're doing?!" he shouted, taking the joint and putting it out with his fingers.

"I'm just trying to calm down," she told him. "Mom was, well, *Mom*, and I--"

"You told her about Amber? How did you know about that?"

"How do I know anything? How do I know *everything*? Don't act surprised. You've been using me for my 'insights' since I was four."

"Taran Ann, there is a difference between work and family. You do not invade people's minds for personal reasons. It's an intrusion."

"It's involuntary."

"Young lady, you will not--"

"Can you go? I need to be alone."

"*Taran Ann Murphy,*"

"Dude, all I can see in my head is a naked blonde from behind and, thanks to you, I know what she feels like on the inside. Please, *get out.*" She opened the door behind him without ever leaving her seat on the bed on the other side of the room. James felt his heart jump in his chest. He left the room, his hands trembling, sweat beading on his brow. For the first time, he was afraid of his own daughter.

Fifteen-year-old Gabriel kissed her girlfriend goodnight before falling asleep next to her. Ada's parents had no idea what went on at their sleepovers and Gabriel wasn't sure how long they'd remain oblivious, so she enjoyed it while it lasted, knowing that the strict Catholics would put an end to the relationship if they ever put two and two together. As the girls slept, a man crept into the room. He covered Gabriel's nose and mouth with a rag doused in chloroform, ensuring she'd remain unconscious as he took her from the bed and carried her out of the house.

She woke with a start just as one of her father's security guards was loading her into the back of a town car. She looked behind her, groggy, her head pounding like a drum. Her vision was blurry, but it wasn't hard to make out the house, fully engulfed in flames. "Ada!" she screamed. "ADA!"

A few days later, Gabriel snuck into the city, her best friend by her side, to attend the party of a girl she'd never met, but was said to have the best drugs in Manhattan. While Cam headed to the bathroom to do a bump, Gabriel floated on a heroin cloud, blissful nothing replacing the constant barrage of other people's thoughts in her mind. She fell back into the couch, allowing the fog to carry her away. It was the closest thing to Heaven she'd felt since before she was born.

As she lay there, she suddenly felt something familiar; a knowing. A longing. A pull in a particular direction. It was one of them. She glanced around, her eyes eventually falling to a boy about her age, beer in one hand, a girl's waist in the other. He was tall with dark hair and a no-fucks-given attitude. She recognized him immediately. "Barachiel," she whispered. She giggled, unable to muster the energy or gumption to get up and speak to him. He walked off, taking his girlfriend into a bedroom and closing the door.

"Heroin, really?" Cam lectured. "You know how addictive that shit is?"

"It makes the voices disappear," Gabriel explained. "Shh."

"I know you're messed up about Ada, but this is too much."

"I said, 'shh'."

"You can't ignore what happened forever. You're gonna have to deal with it, preferably before you OD."

"It just hurts too much right now. I'll talk about it when I can go five sober minutes without wanting to hurt someone."

"All right, let's get you home before someone calls the cops on this party." He picked her up and threw her over his shoulder, carrying her from the apartment and to the elevator.

"My pal, Cam. Always taking care of me."

"Somebody's got to."

The two arrived back at Gabriel's house just after three in the morning, the drive from Manhattan to Fairfield taking about an hour and a half. They were greeted by a gun in their faces, James thinking he'd heard an intruder.

"Taran, what were you doing out so late?" he barked, putting the gun down.

"Since when do you have a gun of your own?" Gabriel wondered. "Where are your security bros?"

"They're off for the night. Where were you?"

"Probably fornicating with that boy," her mother slurred from the top of the stairs.

Gabriel laughed. "Dude, gross," she snickered as Cam helped her up the steps.

"That's not something you have to worry about, ma'am," Cam assured Esther, taking note of the gin and tonic in her hand.

"You keep acting this way, you'll end up pregnant," Esther warned.

"Guess again," Gabriel chuckled.

"Why not? Because you're an abomination?"

"What?"

"We know about that girl," Esther spat.

"Esther!" James cautioned from the foyer.

"Oh, I already know," Gabriel told them. "I know you killed her, and her parents, and her fucking dog, you pieces of shit. Dad had his goons burn her fucking house down and made it look like an electrical fire because you couldn't stand the thought of your country club buddies finding out you had a gay daughter. How *embarrassing* that would have been for you. Did you honestly think I didn't know? Why do you think I've been stoned out of my gourd all week? Or were you too busy banging hookers and hiding in a bottle to notice?"

Esther dropped her glass and threw her hands into her daughter's chest, sending her flailing backward and down the marble staircase, her anger getting the better of her.

Cam watched in horror as Gabriel's neck snapped, her limp body hitting the floor, blood gushing from her head at her father's feet.

"Oh, my God!" James gasped.

Cam's rage overtook him, the world around him going black. He grabbed Esther by the hair and slammed her head into the banister, over and over, until there was nothing left but a mangled lump of unrecognizable flesh where her face used to be. James shot up at the boy, but he barreled down the steps, unfazed, the bullets hitting his chest seeming to have no effect. When he reached the last step, Gabriel stood, rubbing her neck as it put itself back in proper alignment.

"That was rude," she muttered.

James clutched his chest. "What the hell are you?"

"You wouldn't believe me."

"You're possessed!" he blurted. "You're a demon!"

"Wow."

"It's the only thing that makes sense. You're a monster!"

"I'm not a monster," she snapped.

"Demon!" he shouted, shooting Gabriel in the heart. She fell, dying at the hands of her parents for a second time. Cam's eyes became slits and his blood pressure rose. He punched James, breaking his nose before gripping the sides of his head and spinning it around, snapping his neck. As the man's body fell, Cam's mind cleared. He got his breathing under control and wiped the blood from his hands onto his jeans.

"Gabriel," he said, trying to gently shake her awake. "Gabriel, you okay?"

"I'm fine," she grunted, getting to her feet. "It'll take a lot more than a couple of fucked up parents to kill this bitch."

"I'm sorry. I lost it," he admitted as she looked over her dead parents' bodies.

"Yeah, you did. It'll be fine. I'll clean up, change clothes, tell them I was asleep and heard gunshots, woke up, and found this. You have to go, though."

"I don't want to leave you alone."

"I'm all right, I swear."

"But, your parents--"

"It doesn't matter."

"G, are you sure?"

"You'd be a suspect."

"But--"

"Camael, please. Go home."

"All right," he said, giving her a quick hug before opening the door to leave. "Love you, sis."

"Love you, too." She closed the door behind him and leaned against it, looking down at her shirt and around the room. "What a mess."

Chapter 1

Wyatt stood over his son's fresh grave, his face sullen and his body numb. He hadn't eaten or slept in the last two days, the pain in his gut replacing all other sensations. He felt no fatigue or hunger. He was oblivious to all manner of discomfort, including the heat of the summer sun beating down on him as he stood, alone, tears blurring the words on the headstones. His wife and his son, buried not far from his parents, all dead because of him, in one way or another. Guilt, grief, and rage mingled in his chest as he tried to maintain an upright position, a feat that proved more difficult by the second.

"You should go over there," Valerie told Gabriel as the two watched their brother from behind a tree a few yards away.

"He doesn't want to see me," Gabriel said. "The whole 'sending-Michelle-to-spy' thing. I'm gonna give him some space. You should talk to him, though. Keep an eye. He shouldn't be alone."

"He's gotta be devastated."

"He is." She wiped away a tear as she observed him, his misery overwhelming, even at a distance, and her own feelings of loss proving difficult to manage.

"Girl, are you *crying*?" Valerie asked.

"I'm not made of stone."

"All right, but this is the second time I've ever seen you cry *in my life.*"

"Just because he was fucked up, doesn't mean I didn't care about him. He *was* our nephew. I loved that kid."

"Well, damn, if you're over here shedding tears, Wyatt's gotta be--"

"Broken," Gabriel said, her voice shaky. "He's completely destroyed. I have a plane to catch, but you should talk to him."

"You have a *what? Now?*"

"Girl, I've got so many balls in the air, I could join the circus. Don't leave him alone." Gabriel walked back to her car, texting Allydia once she was inside. *As soon as the sun goes down, you get your fangy ass to Wyatt's dad's place. Do not let him be alone. Not for a second.*

"How are you holding up?" Valerie asked, rubbing Wyatt's arm as she stood next to him.

"Not well," he grumbled.

"I'm so sorry. Is there anything I can do?"

"Unlikely."

"You know I'm here if you feel like talking."

"I know." He looked up from the headstone. "Gabriel didn't show?"

"She was here. Said you didn't want to see her."

"She's not wrong."

"Hey, you wanna come over for dinner tonight? Malik can make anything you want."

"No, thanks."

"Maybe I'll just bring you something, then."

"Don't," he ordered. "I want to be alone."

"I feel like that's a bad idea. Gabriel said--"

"I couldn't care less what Gabriel said. *She's not here*. She's probably with Lucifer at her place, celebrating."

"Man, that girl was crying. Her. *Crying*. She might not have many emotions, but she loved Will, too. Maybe don't be so hard on her."

Wyatt sighed. "Fine. Where is she? Home?"

"No, she said she had a plane to catch. You should call her, though. No sense pushing her away when you need your family most."

"A plane?" he asked. "To where?"

"Beats me."

"Huh." His expression turned from that of despair to angry determination. "Interesting."

"Boy, what are you thinking?"

He glared down at her, the look on his face making the hairs on the back of her neck stand up. "Don't get in my way."

The door to Gabriel's apartment flew open, Wyatt having kicked it in. He had a key, but not the patience for using it. Lucifer stood from his spot on the couch, setting his book on the end table.

"Brother," he greeted. "Apologies for missing the funeral. I assumed my presence there would have been in bad taste."

Without a word, Wyatt hurled a bolt of lightning into the devil's chest, sending him flying back into the sofa, smoke rising from the seared flesh now exposed by the hole burned in his button-down.

"That smarts," Lucifer complained, setting himself up.

"Wyatt, stop!" Valerie yelped, running in behind him as he marched toward Lucifer, unable or unwilling to hear her. "Wyatt!"

He threw a ball of electricity into his brother's chest, then another. Lucifer winced but didn't fight back. "It's all right, sister," he said, raising a hand to keep her back. "We all know I deserve it."

Wyatt leaped over the ottoman and wrapped his hands around his brother's neck, squeezing so hard, his nails drew blood. He then unleashed all the power he could muster, taking it from every source in the apartment, causing lights to shatter and appliances to explode. Lucifer's eyes bulged and his nose spewed blood as his body shook violently, his mouth foaming.

"Wyatt, stop!" Valerie pleaded. "You're killing him!"

"That's the goal," Wyatt grunted, the look in his eyes that of a rabid dog.

Her heart racing, Valerie grabbed the sides of Wyatt's head and showed him his own memory, revealing to him what had actually happened the night his son died. He saw it all; his conversation with Lucifer in the woods, holding Will under the rushing water of the creek. He could feel the boy thrashing in the water, then going limp. He watched as his soul drifted away. He remembered instructing his brother to tell him what he'd done and returning to his body, recreating its organs and structure. He even remembered the affection he, as Barachiel, had for Lucifer, his older but damaged and somewhat needy brother, that he'd missed terribly since the last time they'd been together.

Valerie let go and backed away as Wyatt stumbled, collapsing onto the ottoman, short of breath and eyes wide.

Lucifer healed and jolted up. "Why did you do that?!" he barked at his sister. "Those memories were meant to stay buried!"

"Uh, *you're welcome*," she snapped.

"The blame should have been mine to bear."

"Are you stupid? He was *killing you*."

"I would have been fine. Besides, look at him now. He can't handle the burden of what he's done! He's much too fragile. *We went over this*."

"I couldn't just stand here and let him--" She stopped as Wyatt got up and staggered toward the door. "Where you goin'?"

He walked to the hall, not looking back. "Leave me alone."

Wyatt rifled through his father's desk, falling into the chair when he found what he'd been looking for. He opened the bottle of scotch and guzzled the contents, ignoring the empty glass that sat in front of him. The study was dim and dust had begun to collect on the globe in the corner next to the shaded window. The room itself felt lost, serving no purpose since the passing of its former occupant, another loss Wyatt still hadn't fully dealt with. When the bottle was empty, he searched for another, tossing papers and books from the desk drawers before throwing the lamp, shattering it against the wall, and heaving the desk from its place to the other side of the room, blocking the doorway. He fell to the floor and sobbed, his chest tight and heavy as he trembled, his wailing piquing the interest of the ghost that resided there. She lurked in the far corner, kneeling and folding her hands as she watched him, curious. She hoped that he would stay. She'd missed him.

Chapter 2

In life, Margaret had been an immigrant to this city. Having left Ireland in the hopes of a better life, she quickly learned that New York was no place for a young woman on her own. Luckily, she'd been taken in by The Whyos who gave her food and proper clothes. They'd even found a job for her working as a maid for a prominent businessman. He'd recently rented an apartment in a newly constructed building in a remote part of town and wanted to keep it in pristine condition, even though he had no intention of actually living there. She stayed in the servant's quarters: a tiny room with one window, a mattress on the floor, and not much else. It was small, but so was she, standing five feet exactly and weighing about ninety pounds. Other people may have seen her room as cramped or inadequate, but it was warm and dry with a beautiful view. As a poor, illiterate farmer's daughter who'd grown up fighting for scraps, never having owned a pair of shoes until she'd been given refuge in The Bowery, servant's quarters seemed like a luxury.

She'd been washing the windows when the man made his first appearance. Until then, she'd never actually met her employer. Once a week for two months, he'd leave her payment on the desk in the study. She'd never seen his face. She didn't even know his name.

He'd ignored her at first, busy with some sort of paperwork. She had curtsied when he entered the room, but she was sure he hadn't noticed. She continued with her work, leaving the man to his, assuming it must be important. He'd spent all day in the study, looking over papers, occasionally scribbling something on one of them. She'd made sure to stay quiet, not wanting to break his concentration. She'd heard horror stories of abusive employers, beating their servants with belts or even whips for minor infractions. One girl that worked as a nanny in the building had several marks on her arms; burns from her master's cigars. She had been lucky, the girl had told her, that her boss was never around. Now that he was, she couldn't help but be nervous. Still, the sun was setting and it was time for her to retire for the evening. She couldn't just do that, though. She knew the protocol. She had to ask permission. So, she made her way to the study, her heart racing and her throat going dry.

The door had been left ajar. She gently tapped on it before entering, keeping her eyes on the floor. "Excuse me, sir." She curtsied again.

He looked up from his mound of paperwork. "Yes?"

"I've finished for the day, sir. Is there anything else you need?"

"Stand up straight, girl. Let me get a look at you."

She did as she was told.

"You're a pretty little thing, aren't you?"

"If you say so, sir."

"I absolutely do. How old are you?"

"I turned eighteen last month, sir."

"Very good. Tell me, can you read?"

She was embarrassed to answer but choked back her pride. "No, sir."

"Ah. Well, then, I suppose I'll have to teach you. Come, sit."

"Yes, sir." She sat in the chair across from the desk, but he shook his head.

"No, girl. *Here*." He patted his knee. She swallowed hard and did her best not to show how uncomfortable it made her as she went around the desk and sat on his leg. "First, you'll have to learn what the letters are. See this right here?" he pointed to a mark on a page from the pile.

She nodded.

"That's 'A'. This one here, that's 'B'. Do you know the sounds they make?"

She shook her head.

"That's fine. You'll get there. Now, this letter is 'C'. This here is 'D'."

She looked at the marks as he pointed them out, trying to memorize them. She didn't know why he wanted her to become literate. Most employers didn't care, so she'd been told. Some even preferred their staff to be unable to read. Less chance of them moving on to better jobs and leaving them in the lurch. Plus, reading a book could make a person lose track of time, time that would be better spent working. But, if he needed her to read, she would learn. Anything to keep her position.

As he spoke, the low, soothing sound of his voice distracted her. She snuck a look at him, noticing the way his eyes sparkled, green as the grass back home. He was older, at least forty, but handsome with wisps of gray running through his otherwise deep chestnut hair. He smelled of cedar and tobacco and his leg felt warm underneath her. His left hand was firmly placed on the small of her back, presumably to keep her steady. But, as he went through the alphabet, that hand began to lower, brushing over and then settling on her backside.

She knew that was inappropriate but as anxious as it made her, there was part of her that didn't mind. It felt nice to be getting attention from a man, even if it was her boss. No man had looked at her twice since she'd arrived in this country, and this was a fine man, indeed. She wondered if she could ingratiate herself to him. Seduce him, even. If she could find a way to make him fall in love with her, maybe he would marry her. She could live a life of luxury and opulence instead that of a poor maid. *Fairytales*, she thought as she pushed the daydream aside and tried to focus. She concentrated on the marks on the page, following his words as best she could. But, as he spoke, his voice became fainter. She could feel his breath on her cheek, warm against her skin. He went quiet, his right hand moving from the papers to her leg.

He pulled up her skirt and petticoat, slowly as to gauge her response. She allowed it. He slid his hand up, gliding over and between her legs as he nuzzled her neck. She fluttered with anticipation, wanting to behave demurely, but aching for his touch. He gently pushed her legs apart, just enough that he could slip his fingers inside. Her breathing quickened as he massaged her. She could feel her body responding to him, unable to control the movements of her hips. She threw her arm around his shoulders to balance herself. He took that as an invitation to take things to the next level.

He hoisted her onto the desk, carefully pushing his papers to the side. He pushed up her clothes, revealing her pale, freckled skin. He hastily removed his trousers and pulled her to the edge of the desk, opening her legs and thrusting himself into her. She gasped, the combination of pain and pleasure flooding through her. He grasped her rear, squeezing as he continued. She lay back, grinding against him, her hands over her head holding on to the desk for stability. She bit her lip, stifling the cries that begged to escape her lips. She'd never felt anything like this. Was this what an orgasm felt like? She'd never had one but had been informed by the other servant girls in the building that they *were* possible. The boys she'd been with back in Ireland had been so quick to finish, it was hardly pleasurable for her at all. Now, though, her skin felt hot, like bathwater washing over her. Wave after wave of euphoria gripped her as she held on to the desk, her knuckles going white. He continued to buck, pushing hard and fast into her. She was sure she'd have bruises where his fingers dug into her behind, but she didn't care. She exploded with pleasure, every part of her tingling. Finally, the man grunted, his face twisting as sweat ran down his temples. His face had gone red and he trembled as he filled her.

When he was done, he put his pants back on and wiped the sweat from his brow. He didn't look at her. He gathered his papers and walked toward the door. "That's all for today." He left the apartment, leaving Margaret in a state of shame. She slid off of the desk, standing and adjusting her dress, her legs weak. It had been a ruse. The man had had no interest in teaching her to read. It was an excuse to get her close.

"I'm so stupid," she whimpered, holding back the tears that threatened to fall. She refused to let them. "It's all right," she told herself. "I'm fine."

But she wasn't, and she could feel in her gut that she would never be fine again.

Months had passed. By the time the man returned, Margaret had begun to show. She had tried to hide her condition with an oversized uniform, but there was no disguising her bump given her small frame.

She'd curtsied as he entered the apartment, keeping her eyes averted. He paused to look her over before heading to the study, this time closing the door. She let out a sigh of relief. She knew she'd have to tell him. She'd have to do it today. It could be *another* six months or more before she'd see him again. Her heart thumped in her chest as she awaited the conversation, unsure of what exactly she'd say. She didn't want to sound bitter, though she was still angry with him for using her the way he had. She wanted to appear strong, capable of handling this on her own if that's what he wanted. He would *not* get the best of her. He would *not* see her cry.

As the sun set, he finally exited the study, a stern look sharpening his features. She turned to face him and curtsied again. Before she could say a word, he took her hand and thrust fifty dollars into it.

"Sir?"

"There's a man in Syracuse, a doctor," he told her. "His method is less painful, I've heard. Safer."

"I don't understand, sir."

"I believe that you do." He glanced down at her belly.

She was horrified. "You want me to--"

"I'm a married man, girl. My wife has given me six children and while I may indulge in the occasional indiscretion, I will not shame her by fathering a bastard with *the help*. You *will* see the doctor. I trust you'll be discreet." And with that, he took his leave.

She stood there, mouth agape and head spinning. What he was asking was impossible. She was too far along. She'd felt the quickening. To end the pregnancy now would be a sin. She couldn't do what he'd demanded. She simply couldn't.

Two months later, the man returned. She shuddered at the fire in his eyes, his face red with rage.

"You defied my orders!" he bellowed.

"I'm sorry, sir. It was too late. I couldn't--"

"I don't want to hear your excuses! You have no idea what you've done!" He paced the floor as she cowered in the corner, hands folded, bracing herself for the beating she was sure she was about to receive.

"I haven't spent the money. I left it in your desk. I don't want anything from you."

"It's not about the money, you stupid girl!" He bounded toward her, his face twisted in anger. She could see that he wanted to hit her. She recognized the look. Her father used to look at her mother like that just before he'd start in. He didn't do it, though. Instead, he disappeared into another room. When he came back, he was carrying a toolbox. Sweat beaded on his forehead and his face had gone pale, the look of a man who knew he was about to do something truly horrific.

He left, slamming the door behind him. She was stunned. She'd been sure he'd reprimand her in some way. When no punishment was allocated, she breathed a sigh of relief. He was angry, yes, and she'd have to raise her baby alone. She would have to concoct a story of a fake husband. Maybe a

Marine, killed in the Rebellion in Hawaii. It would be difficult, but it was doable. She would find a way. She would have her baby and she would show him the love she'd never known herself.

She'd been so lost in her own thoughts, she hadn't heard the pounding. It was coming from the door. She thought the man had come back. Perhaps he'd left his key in his rush to get out of there. She went to answer, but the door wouldn't open. The knob turned, but it wouldn't pull to. She pulled harder. Nothing. She kept pulling, but it wouldn't budge.

"Sir?" she called. "Sir, the door's stuck!"

No answer. Just more pounding.

"Sir? Sir?!"

Again, no answer. The pounding stopped.

"Sir, I can't open the door!" She smacked her hand against it a few times, hoping he'd be able to hear her now that he'd stopped knocking himself. "Sir!" She hit the door a few more times, confusion giving way to panic. She stepped back, catching her breath.

Her hands shook and her eyes became saucers as she realized what had happened. He hadn't been knocking. He'd been nailing the door shut. He'd trapped her inside.

She threw herself at the door, screaming and banging her fists against the wood. "HELP! HELP ME, PLEASE!" But no one came.

There was no food in the apartment. She was sure she would starve. But, it was worse than that. The next day when she awoke, she discovered the water had been shut off. She would be dead inside of a week with no water. He had done it purposefully. He was trying to kill her.

She should have been afraid. She wasn't. She was enraged. She drank the water from toilet tanks and convinced herself she'd survive on spite alone. He'd have to come back eventually. The smell of a rotting corpse would surely draw suspicion. He'd have to dispose of her body. So, when he came back, she'd have her revenge. She slept with a kitchen knife under her pillow and waited.

Another week had gone by. She'd run out of water and she hadn't felt her baby move in two days. She'd noticed the blood before she'd felt any pain.

On her mattress in the servant's quarters, she gave birth to her son. His skin was gray and his body limp. He never cried, but she did. For three days, she held her bundle and sobbed. She was hot with fever and would soon join her boy in death. It was her only consolation. She would forever hold her baby in her arms.

On the fourth night, the man returned. Dropping his toolbox at the sight of the dead child. He covered his mouth and sank to his knees.

"You did this to us," she spat, her voice barely audible. "I will tell everyone what you've done. I will--"

"You'll tell no one." He growled, pinning her to the blood-soaked bed. He sat on her chest, holding her arms down with his legs. The knife peeked out from under the pillow. He took it and grasped her jaw, holding her mouth open. She tried to bite him, but he persisted in overpowering her, not a difficult feat, considering. He couldn't get a proper grip on her tongue, so instead of a clean cut, he hacked at it, mutilating it, sending bits of tissue flying in all directions. "You won't tell a soul. If only you could write."

She screamed in pain, blood gurgling in her throat and pouring out her mouth. Even when he stood, she couldn't move. Between infection and blood loss, she was too weak. Her vision became blurry, but as she faded, she saw the man take a tool from his box and begin to pry up a floorboard.

When she woke, the man was hammering a nail into the floor. She looked around wildly, digging through the sheets. Where was he? Where was her son? She pleaded with her eyes, but the man just gathered his tools. He grabbed her by the arm and started to drag her from the room. She yanked on his coat and pointed to the bed as they left.

"The child?" he mocked.

She nodded.

"He's where no one will ever find him."

Her eyes darted back to the room, then up at him. *Holy God*, she thought. *He's put him in the floor.*

It was late, just after two in the morning. The entire building was asleep. She tried to scream as he carried her from the apartment to the elevator, but her voice was faint. She tried to claw at him, but her hands were numb. She didn't make a scratch. Once outside, he raced to the park across the way, nearly dropping her as he hurried. He found a wooded area and set her on her feet. She couldn't stand on her own and tried to balance herself by holding on to his shoulder, but he pushed her away. She fell to the cold ground, the light snow stinging her exposed skin like a thousand tiny needles. He walked off, never looking back.

She tried to crawl to the street, but she was so far gone, it may as well have been a million miles away. She collapsed, the exhaustion overwhelming her. She drifted off and as she pictured her son's tiny face one more time, a single tear fell to her cheek. *At least he never saw me cry.*

Suddenly, she was back in the apartment. It had changed, having been remodeled. Everything was different. She'd tried to go back to the servant's quarters, to find her baby, but the room was gone. It was now part of a parlor decorated in strange furniture and inhabited by people she didn't recognize. There was a man, a lawyer from what she gathered, having listened in on his conversations, and his very pregnant wife. They were happy. It was nice. But, it was immediately clear to her that they couldn't see her, which could only mean that she had died in the park that night and was now haunting this place as a ghoul. She grew depressed, spending all of her time crying over her baby's wooden grave and stalking the mother-to-be, who she could tell was beginning to be impacted emotionally by her presence, but what could she do? She couldn't leave. Not without her son.

As her depression grew, so did the woman's. She began behaving erratically. Margaret knew she was adversely affecting her, so she maintained a distance, keeping to the corners and staying quiet. Not that she could speak if she'd wanted to. Not without her tongue.

Soon, the day came when the lawyer brought his new son home. He was perfect with dark hair and eyes and a sweet disposition. She fell in love with the boy, watching as nannies and maids cared for him. The mother hadn't returned from the hospital and the father became more and more absent as the boy grew. She decided he'd be hers, a replacement for the child so cruelly taken from her. She spent years watching over him, taking pride in his accomplishments and joy in his sweet smile.

The years passed, though, and the boy grew into a man. It wasn't long before the ache of losing her own son returned and she again cried for him. She thought she would suffer alone for eternity, until one night, the boy called Wyatt heard her.

She tried to get his attention, to tell him what had happened. If she could just see her baby, hold him one more time, maybe she could move on. But, the boy went away, shipped off to college by his father who meant well but was very clearly not equipped to handle the job of 'parent'. But, then, a Christmas miracle. The boy had returned. When she was sure the father was asleep, she snuck into Wyatt's room and grunted at him until he woke. Still half unconscious, he'd sprung up from his bed and rushed to follow her to the spot. She'd pointed to it and he'd begun working, trying his damnedest to pull up the boards. The lawyer caught him, though, and that was the end of that.

She couldn't say that she'd been sorry to see the lawyer die. He'd reminded her of the man that murdered her and stole her baby in that he was a workaholic, cold, and seemed to lack empathy. But, as she watched Wyatt, the boy she'd adopted in her heart, now a man with a broken spirit mourn what she assumed to be the loss of his father, she couldn't help but mourn with him. Maybe she'd misjudged the lawyer. Either way, she still had a soft spot for the man before her. The boy she'd thought of as her own.

Chapter 3

Gabriel stared through the window of Mitchell Spade's suburban Virginia McMansion. The man sat in a high-backed chair in his home office, his messy desk littered with files. He was talking on the phone, too quietly for Gabriel to hear through the glass. She flicked her wrist, attempting to snap his neck. Nothing happened. She waved at the desk, trying to set it on fire. Nothing. It was as she'd suspected; he was invulnerable. Lilith had placed a protection spell on him, rendering her powers useless. "Well, that frosts my cookies," she muttered, turning to leave. It had been a long shot, but she'd hoped Lilith had neglected to insulate her general from supernatural threats. It would have been so much easier, just a quick motion of her hand and the whole thing would have been over. The lives that could have been saved, not to mention the time she could have spent keeping an eye on her grieving brother, making sure he didn't do anything crazy. Now, she'd have to rely on the others to watch over him and *none of them* were equipped.

I know it's daytime, but I have a bad feeling, Gabriel texted. *Get your ass up and get to Wyatt's NOW.* She sat, shifting in her aisle seat as the plane made its way to the city. It was only a little more than an hour flight, so she'd decided to fly commercial. Judging by the turbulence, that had been a mistake. The flight attendant, a pretty blonde with a chipper smile, made the usual 'everything's fine' announcement and instructed the passengers to fasten their seat belts. Gabriel took note of how attractive she was and was thinking about striking up a conversation once the plane landed when she was jolted forward. The plane shook violently. A bird had flown into one of the engines and the pilot was unable to compensate. Oxygen masks dropped and she could feel the other passengers panic as they scrambled to put them on, screaming and texting goodbyes to their loved ones. They were falling fast, a crash inevitable. Just as Gabriel was about to use her telekinesis to hold the plane up, she saw the flight attendant raising her hands to her shoulders. She was whispering something Gabriel couldn't make out from that distance; a chant? The plane slowly corrected itself as the woman muttered under her breath. "What fresh hell?" Gabriel said to herself.

"Attention passengers," the pilot's voice murmured over the intercom. "We're experiencing some technical difficulties and will be making an emergency landing in Harrisburg for repairs." Gabriel couldn't hear the rest of his announcement over the moans of derision from the other passengers. *So ungrateful,* she thought.

She waited until the other passengers had all deplaned before approaching the flight attendant. She was surprised when she got close that she couldn't hear her thoughts. She tried to look inside her mind, but all she saw was the face of another woman, yelling at her to 'get out'.

"Was that Violet?" she wondered allowed.

The flight attendant's face went pale. "Excuse me?"

"In your head. That was Violet, right? Tituba's daughter? Wow. I thought her line died out *years* ago."

"I don't know what you're--"

"It's okay," Gabriel assured her. "I won't tell anyone. I was just coming to see how you saved the plane, but that question's been answered, hasn't it? You're a witch. A *powerful* witch. Descendant of Tituba Indian. I'm not often impressed, but--"

The flight attendant looked around nervously. "How did you know that?"

"I'm not exactly 'normal'. What are you doing right now? You wanna get some dinner? Looks like we're stuck here for a while. I've never actually been to Pennsylvania. What's there to eat around here? I'm starving."

"Um,"

"I'm Gabriel."

"Wendy."

"It's nice to meet you, Wendy. Anyone tell you lately how gorgeous you are? Like, *stunning*."

"Thanks," she tucked her hair behind her ear as they left the plane. "How did you--"

"We'll talk about it later, maybe someplace less people-y. You hungry?"

"Usually." Wendy blushed, a rush of excitement running through her as Gabriel brushed the hair off her shoulder, her touch electric.

"Let's go, then."

"You're hitting on me, right? I have a hard time distinguishing flirting from people just being nice."

Gabriel smiled. "Oh, I'm *definitely* hitting on you."

Chapter 4

As the tub filled, Wyatt took a swig from a freshly opened bottle of whisky he'd found in his father's pantry. He slipped off his shoes and his jacket before climbing in, not bothering to turn the faucet off. The water was cold and sent chills all through his body as he lay himself down, the icy pool covering his face. He looked up at the ceiling, then closed his eyes, opening his mouth and inhaling the frosty liquid. It felt like needles in his lungs, stinging and sharp as he seized. The pain was intense but soon was over, replaced by quiet nothing.

"Wyatt?" Allydia called from the front door. She let herself in and took off her cloak. The sun wasn't quite down, but Gabriel's incessant texting had woken her. Any other time, her phone would have been off while she slept, but with her lover being in such a fragile state, she couldn't risk it. She had to make herself available to him any time of the night *or day*. "Wyatt?" She followed the sound of water running and entered the bathroom, horrified at the sight of his lifeless body in the tub. "WYATT!" She pulled him from water that overflowed to the tile floor. She pounded on his chest until he sprung up, hacking up fluid and gasping for air. "Why would you do this?" she cried, turning off the faucet.

"Leave me alone, Allydia," he commanded, taking the whisky from the vanity and gulping it down as he sat in the inch of water that now covered the floor.

"I won't. Your sister was right, you are not to be left to your own devices."

"My sister," he scoffed. "*Of course* she sent you. I don't need a babysitter."

"I beg to differ."

"I'm fine."

"You just tried to kill yourself! You aren't in the same *hemisphere* as '*fine*'."

"It's not like I'll *stay* dead," he asserted, drinking the last of the whisky.

"You need help. Let me be of assistance."

"There's nothing you can do. My father's dead and I killed my son. I don't deserve saving. You should have left me where I was."

"What are you saying? *Lucifer*--"

"Took the fall," he interrupted, trembling with rage and guilt as he spoke. "*I* killed Will. I remember it. I can still feel my hands on his neck, holding him under until he stopped moving. *I'm* the monster. Lucifer tried to *protect* me. He didn't want me to know what I'd done when I was *him*, this *thing* inside. This *angel*."

"Barachiel," she realized.

"Just go."

"Wyatt,"

He smashed the bottle on the side of the tub and held the jagged edge to his wrist, slicing it open.

"Wyatt!" She jumped back, the scent of his blood causing her eyes to dilate and her heart to race.

"Get out!"

She backed out of the room, running from the apartment, afraid of what she'd do, the intoxicating aroma of his blood calling her to drink him dry. She phoned Gabriel, but no answer. She knew Lucifer would be of no help in this situation, so she called the only person left.

"Hello," Valerie answered.

"Valerie, hello. Gabriel gave me your number in case of an emergency and I'd say your brother repeatedly committing suicide in his bathroom counts as such, yes?"

"Holy shit! I'm on my way."

Valerie entered the dark apartment, fumbling around for a light switch. She'd never actually been to Wyatt's place before and at first glance, it seemed typical of a stuffy old white guy, which his father had been. She passed the bookshelves, stereo, and television, noticing how archaic they seemed. Who had a stereo anymore? She found Wyatt in the kitchen, sitting on the island, drinking scotch straight from the bottle, his clothes wet and his sleeve covered in blood.

"I'm finding them everywhere," he slurred, holding up the bottle. "In cabinets and dresser drawers. I found a flask in the *couch cushions*. I didn't know he had that big of a problem."

"Your girlfriend called," Valerie said, hopping up to sit next to him. "You have any idea how un-fucking-nerving it is to have a *vampire* call you saying your brother's *killing himself*?"

"She shouldn't have bothered you."

"I'm not bothered. I'm *angry*. What the fuck do you think you're doin'?"

"Don't lecture me."

"I'm not saying don't be fucked up," she made clear. "It's a fucked up situation and I can't even imagine what you're going through, but repetitive suicide? You know that is not okay."

"Leave me alone."

"That is *not* happening."

"Go!"

"Boy, don't yell at *me*. Your girlfriend might put up with that shit, but *I* won't."

"Sorry."

"You're exhausted. Go put on some dry clothes and go to bed. I'll be here when you get up."

"You don't have to--"

"I've lost one brother. I won't lose another one, you hear me?"

Wyatt sighed and put the whisky on the counter before heading off to his childhood bedroom.

"Love you!" she called after him. "I'll be checking in on you periodically to make sure you're still breathing, so don't lock that fucking door!"

Chapter 5

"So, what are you, psychic?" Wendy asked as she and Gabriel sat down in the back booth of the restaurant, out of earshot of the other patrons.

"Sort of. I'm telepathic, empathic, telekinetic, and pyrokinetic."

"*Pyro*kinetic? I didn't know that was a real thing."

Gabriel took a bite of bread. "It's pretty rare."

"So, you can *literally* set stuff on fire?"

"Yeah. It's not that interesting. Tell me about *you*. Why did I think the Tituban line was extinct?"

"It mostly is." She took a piece of bread from the basket and smoothed on a pat of butter. "After World War Two, a lot of guys came back still in a combative headspace. With no more Nazis to fight, a group of dudes targeted witches. My grandmother's coven was wiped out. She and her sister were the only ones that got away. They left Tarrytown, moved to New York. They figured a city that big would be a good place to hide, get lost in a sea of people. My grandmother eventually moved back and that's where I grew up."

"And Violet in your head?"

"Before she died, my grandmother used one of Violet's protection spells to keep other witches from reading my thoughts. She was afraid of them getting hold of our spells, stealing our magic. It's too powerful for most witches. They can't handle it. It corrupts them, makes them violent and power-hungry."

"Wow. So, it's just you left?"

"Me and my great-aunt, but I've never met her. She and my grandma had a fight in the fifties about what they should do with their magic. Grandma wanted to keep it in the bloodline. Grace couldn't have kids, so she wanted to start a new coven and share her power so it wouldn't die with her. Standard family feud."

Gabriel laughed. "Yeah, totally normal."

Wendy smiled. "What's *your* family like?"

"Big, complicated. Kinda dark."

She laughed. "So, brothers and sisters?"

"Tons."

"Parents?"

"Died when I was in high school."

"Oh, sorry."

"Don't be. I'm not."

"I feel like that should freak me out, but it doesn't."

They both laughed. They chatted for several minutes, unable to take their eyes off each other even to order. They barely noticed when the food came as their flirtation continued. Gabriel sipped her soda while Wendy finally cut into her steak, her face falling in disappointment.

"What's wrong?"

"It's fine," Wendy accepted. "I ordered medium. It's rare. It's not a big deal."

Gabriel looked around to make sure no one could see them and slid Wendy's plate to her side of the table. She covered the steak with her hand, a flame appearing between them, cooking the meat to temperature like a broiler. The fire dissipated and she slid the plate back.

Wendy was clearly impressed. "That was damn sexy."

Gabriel gleaned. "I'm a sexy bitch."

She giggled. "You really are. You wanna get a hotel room after this?"

She showed her the confirmation screen on her phone. "Girl, I already booked one."

When dinner was over, they took a cab to the hotel. As they traveled, they let their hands wander up one another's thighs. Feeling frisky, Gabriel glided her hand underneath the skirt of Wendy's flight attendant's uniform and slid her fingers between her soft cotton panties and her skin.

She touched her arm and whispered, "What if he sees?"

Gabriel glanced at the driver and back at her. "I'm making sure he keeps his eyes on the road. Telekinetic, remember?"

"Oh, we're gonna have *all kinds* of fun together." She kissed her softly and opened her legs, pulling her closer. Gabriel continued to touch her until they reached their destination. Once in their room, the kissing became more intense. They kicked off their shoes and stumbled to the bed. Gabriel slipped off Wendy's panties and pushed up her skirt, beginning the marathon lovemaking session that ran into the early morning hours.

"I've never done this before," Wendy admitted, feeling shy as she brought the sheet up to her chin.

"A chick?" Gabriel asked.

Wendy laughed. "No, taken someone back to my place after just meeting them."

"Oh, well, to be fair, this isn't *your* place so...record still intact."

They both giggled.

"Do you do this a lot?"

"Not *a lot*."

"You're lying," Wendy smirked.

"I'm clean if that's what you're worried about."

"It's not. I've just never been someone's one-night stand before. Not sure what the etiquette is. Do I offer you a beverage? Make you a snack? Pretend to sleep so you can sneak out to avoid an awkward conversation?"

"Like this one?" Gabriel snickered, touching the woman's cheek.

Wendy grinned.

"For the record, this isn't a one-night stand for me. I like you."

"I like you, too."

"Good. So, you ready for round three? Or is it four?"

"Already?"

"I'm insatiable," Gabriel teased.

"Well, I already know *that*," Wendy beamed, scooting closer to kiss her new playmate, running her hand down her body and slipping her fingers once more inside of her. Gabriel pulled her on top of her, holding her face in her hands as she kissed her hard. Wendy's hair fell around her face, enveloping her in a mane of blond, the dim light of the bedside lamp filtering through, lighting up her face in a glowing halo. She was amazing. For the first time in decades, Gabriel was excited to get to know someone. She knew she'd have to leave as soon as she could get a flight, but she didn't want to go. She was happy, an emotion mostly foreign to her. She lost herself in Wendy's warm touch, her soft hair like silk against her skin. Her responsibilities were urgent and many, but for now, they'd just have to wait.

Chapter 6

Lucifer quietly entered Wyatt's apartment, finding Valerie asleep on the living room sofa. "Not very diligent, are we?" he muttered to himself. "Uriel," he whispered, nudging her awake.

"Finally," she complained. "Gabriel won't answer her phone and the vampire's staying away until she's sure he's stopped cutting himself, which he *hasn't*. Every time that boy goes to the bathroom, I end up giving him a lecture about self-harm. I got all the knives and razors out of the house, so this motherfucker broke the mirror and used the shards to slit his wrists again. I can't take it anymore. Can you talk some sense into him?"

"I doubt it. I'm not his favorite person at the moment."

"Then tie his ass to his bed or some shit until he snaps out of it."

"Is that why you called me here? Brute force?"

"You *are* God's strongest or whatever. I'm exhausted and I've missed too much work already. Can you stay with him until Gabriel gets back from wherever the hell she is?"

"I suppose," he agreed, setting his duffel bag on the coffee table. "Where is the poor lamb?"

"Locked in his room," she said, pointing down the hall as she headed for the front door. "Don't kill each other."

Lucifer waited until she'd gone to open his bag and remove a large bottle of whisky. He knocked on the bedroom door and when no answer came, he opened it, breaking the lock with minimal effort. He held the bottle inside, keeping his eyes averted. Wyatt took the offering and slammed the door back. The brothers sat on the floor on either side, Lucifer calm with his hands folded and Wyatt, drinking until his throat hurt.

"I *am* sorry about your son, Barachiel."

Wyatt scoffed. "You would have killed him if I hadn't."

"That's true, and if you weren't so stubborn, I could have spared you from the guilt you're feeling now."

"Go away, Lucifer."

"Afraid I can't. You've given our sister quite the fright and as angry with her as I am for revealing to you the events of that evening, she still deserves peace of mind."

"And what do I deserve?" Wyatt growled. "I'm pretty sure filicide gets you the death penalty in Indiana, except I *can't die*."

Lucifer sighed, wishing there was something he could do to alleviate his brother's suffering. "You only did what had to be done. You always do. It's the burden of what you are. You deserve all the best things this world has to offer, as well as the next. It would serve you well to remember that."

"I deserve to burn."

"You gave that boy a chance, which is more than I would have done.

Had he been *my* son, I would have slaughtered him in his crib the moment I learned of his existence."

"That's fucked up."

"Yes, well, God's will and all that."

The two were silent for a while before Wyatt leaned against the door and spoke again, his words slurred. "The only time I don't want to die is when I'm dead."

His pain cut Lucifer like a knife. "It's late. Get some rest, brother. I'll be here."

Chapter 7

"Phindi will have an update for you tomorrow," the young vampire said. "Still no word on Hattie, but I'm happy to serve as your assistant for as long as you need me."

"Thank you, Hart," Allydia replied, slumping in her seat in the throne room, her thoughts with Wyatt. "Tell me, have you ever taken a human lover? Since you became one of us, I mean."

"Not for more than a few days, Your Majesty. They're frail and need constant tending to."

"So you ended things with your human consorts because they were weak?"

"I didn't *break up* with them so much as I *ate* them," he confessed. "In my defense, men these days are *delicious*. Have you ever fed on a fruitarian? *Like candy*."

She smiled. "I have, actually. It's been a while, though."

"Would you like me to send for one?"

"Thank you, Hart. That would be delightful. I could use a little dessert."

"Right away, Your Majesty." He snapped his fingers at the guard standing at the entrance to the room. The man nodded and hurried off. Hart went over his notes before again addressing his Queen. "I've chartered the planes, so that's been handled. All the monthly expenses have been paid. There's just one more order of business."

"What is it?"

He took a deep breath and shifted his weight from one foot to another.

"Hart," she said, her patience wearing thin.

"It's Mason, Your Majesty. He's stirring up trouble. Blaspheming. He's saying...he's telling people..."

"Spit it out, Hart."

"He's saying you're not fit to lead. That you haven't killed in years. That you're soft."

She tilted her head and raised her eyebrows, throwing her hair over her shoulder and clearing her throat.

"Forgive me, my Queen." He looked down at his platform boots and did his best to steady his breathing.

"That's all right." She crossed her legs and sighed dismissively. "More often than not, *someone* has something negative to say. It's not usually worth my time, but, 'not fit to lead'? That's treason."

"Yes, Your Majesty."

"Do you know what my punishment is for treason, Hart?"

"Yes, my Queen."

She twirled her hair and tapped her foot. "I really don't have time for this."

"Would you like me to take care of it, Your Majesty?"

"Only if you can handle it personally. I wouldn't want anyone else thinking I'm too 'soft' to handle my own business."

"Of course."

"Very well. But make sure he understands why he's being punished. Make sure he knows I sent you."

"Yes, Your Majesty."

"All right, you may go. I'd like to be alone with my thoughts."

He bowed and left the room, closing the door behind him.

Allydia's mind wandered again to Wyatt, the blood spilling from his wrist like a siren song. Had he been anyone else, she wouldn't have bothered stifling her baser instincts. As it was, she knew she had to stay away or risk devouring him whole, the image of which she played in her mind like pornography. She would keep a distance, for now, trusting his siblings to keep him safe.

"Hart!" Mason greeted as the Queen's assistant entered the apartment. "I wasn't expecting you. Did we have a date tonight?"

As the door closed, Hart pulled a gun out from under his leather duster and shot the other man in the gut.

"What the hell?!"

"Queen's business."

Mason fell back into a recliner, covering his wound with one shaky hand. "UV bullets?"

Hart nodded.

"You told her? You betrayed me?" His lip quivered under his jet black goatee, blood starting to ooze out from his mouth.

"You know I had to."

"But we are lovers."

He smacked his lips and rolled his eyes. "Getting together a few times a month to bang it out and never speaking otherwise hardly makes us 'lovers'. Besides, my loyalty is to the Queen. You know that."

"Some Queen you serve! Forcing you to do her dirty work, knowing that we were sleeping together. The cruelty!"

"She didn't force anything. I volunteered."

"You...ah. You think you can endear yourself to her."

He clicked his tongue. "She *already* loves me."

Mason wheezed, a knowing smile turning up his lips. "She will never give you what you want."

"You don't know that."

"Foolish boy," he coughed. "She will *never*--"

"Don't call me 'boy'!" His heart beat fast as he shouted.

"You should go home and shave. Your five o'clock shadow is showing."

He pulled his dagger and plunged it into the other vampire's chest. "You shouldn't have blasphemed. You should have kept your trap *shut*."

Mason shook violently as Hart carved, tearing at muscle and breaking through bone. Blood splattered across his face as he reached his hand inside the condemned man's chest.

"Please," Mason gurgled.

He ignored him, got his fingers around the slippery organ, and yanked it from his body. Mason looked at his own heart beating in the man's perfectly manicured hand, the shiny, black nail polish now caked with gore. Hart held it there, showing it to him until the light faded from his eyes.

Death came to all traitors of the Queen, but that wasn't the real punishment. The *real* punishment was watching their hearts beat outside of their body, then stopping. It wasn't enough to kill them. They had to watch, not just feel their lives leave them. They had to be terrified.

It's done, Hart texted. *Is there anything else you need?*

No, the Queen replied. *Thank you. I will see you tomorrow.*

He put his phone on the coffee table and sank into the couch. "Hey, Marilyn," he cooed as his cat climbed up into his lap. He pet her gently as she purred and curled up for a nap. "I missed you, too. Did you have enough to eat while I was gone?" He glanced over to the food dish and saw that there were still a few bits of cat food uneaten. "That's good. Did you have a nice night? Mine kind of sucked. Killed a dude, and not because I was hungry, so that was no fun. Now I have to find a new fuck buddy and you know how I hate shopping for dick. Maybe I'll just be celibate for a while, shut it all down. Put up a sign, 'this booty's closed for repairs'. Not that I'm broken, mind you. Just a little...bent." He tilted his head as he gazed down at his pet as she slept. "You ignoring my existential crisis? That's cool. *I've* been doing it for *years*. The Queen will grant me this, right? She's not *unreasonable*. Just because Mason's like, two hundred or whatever, doesn't mean he knows what he's talking about. Right?"

The cat continued to sleep.

"Fine. You rest. I should probably get some sleep, too. It's been a *night*. Let's go to bed." He carried her to the bedroom and sat her on her princess kitty bed before taking off his boots and letting himself fall into bed, crashing down onto the black comforter and groaning as his face hit the hot pink pillowcase. "So tired."

The cat scratched at the sparkly crown emblem on her bed, licked her paw, and curled up on the plush fabric.

Hart looked over at her one more time and closed his eyes. "Thanks for being a good listener, M."

Chapter 8

Gabriel returned home to Valerie who'd been waiting there, her impatience evident.

"Bitch, where the fuck you been?" she griped. "Me and Lucifer have been taking turns keeping Wyatt from offing himself for *days*. I can't handle this shit."

"I'll go over there after I eat something," Gabriel said, taking a bag of cheese puffs from the pantry.

"Speaking of food, that boy eats *a lot* of pizza. You'd think he was raised by a giant rat in the sewer."

Gabriel laughed. "It's a psychological thing. A 'fuck you' to his dad. He was a very knife-and-fork kind of dude, thought pizza was 'uncivilized', like, peasant food. He was real boujee. Don't tell B that, though. He just thinks he likes it because it's delicious."

"I still can't believe he got back with the vampire. They're a full-blown couple now."

"Right?" Gabriel said, taking a bite and avoiding eye contact.

"Girl."

"Hmm?"

"Girl! You set them up?"

"Only kind of. I didn't *have* to take him to the vampire club to find out where Lilith's demons were. She *could* have told me over the phone."

"The fuck, bitch?"

"I knew she'd get obsessed and start following him around. I knew she'd look out for him, and us in turn, with that whole Lilith thing. I knew she'd protect him. I wasn't counting on him getting so involved, though. I warned him not to get too close. I made it very clear she was--"

"She's a *vampire*," Valerie yelled. "She called *me* because she couldn't handle seeing his blood. What if she--"

"If she ever lays a finger on him, I'll fucking kill her."

Gabriel entered Wyatt's apartment, the stench of booze punching her in the face. Empty pizza boxes lay haphazardly on the coffee table and island while sorrow hung in the air like smog. She looked Wyatt over, his unconscious body on the floor, leaning against the sofa, a nearly empty bottle of scotch in his hand. She took it from him and went to the kitchen where she drained the contents into the sink.

"Gabriel," Lucifer said, looking up from his book. He put it down on the counter and sat up straight on his bar stool. "So good of you to grace us with your presence. Was your trip a success?"

"Not really," she replied, taking the last three bottles of whiskey from the pantry and dumping them, as well. "It's like I thought. He's warded. I did meet a girl, though, so not a total waste of time. What's with the ghost?" She gestured toward the far corner where the phantom that haunted the building stood creepily still, watching in silence.

"The poor dear's been fixated on our bereaved brother. I think she's lonely. Seems harmless enough."

"Ugh, I can't deal with dead people on top of everything else. Yo! Hey, honey! It's time to go home."

"That's rather rude, don't you think?" Lucifer lectured.

"Fine," Gabriel huffed, walking over to speak to the spirit face-to-face. "Hello. I'm Gabriel, Messenger of God. It's time for you to go to Heaven."

The ghost looked at her with hope in her milky eyes before turning her gaze to Wyatt. Worry covered her face as she looked back at Gabriel.

"He'll be fine," Gabriel promised. "I'll stay with him."

The specter didn't look convinced.

"I'm an angel of the highest order. I won't let anything happen to him, I swear. You need to go now. Your baby's waiting for you."

The ghost smiled, looked up, and breathed a sigh of relief as she faded, then disappeared.

"Well, I'm off," Lucifer announced, slipping his book into the duffel bag and zipping it closed. "I could use a decent night's rest. I trust you'll watch over Barachiel, now that you're back."

"As long as he needs me. Listen, you know what's coming. This is gonna be an all-hands-on-deck situation. Uriel can't be fighting with a fucking pocket knife, do you understand what I'm saying?"

"I do, indeed. Have no fear, sister. I know just where to find what she needs."

"Good. And, Lucifer," she said, looking over to Wyatt and back at him. "Thanks."

They exchanged knowing glances as Lucifer picked up his bag. "It was my pleasure." He left the apartment, leaving Gabriel to pick up Wyatt's broken pieces. She took a trash can from the bathroom, set it in her brother's lap, and smacked him in the face. His eyes flew open and she flicked two fingers toward herself, causing the contents of his stomach to come flooding up and out of his mouth. When he was done vomiting, Gabriel took the now full can back to the bathroom before returning and sitting herself down next to Wyatt and patting his knee.

He looked at her, tears filling his eyes as he began to tremble. "I'm not okay," he croaked.

"I know," she told him.

"You were right. About everything."

"See, if you people would just keep that in the back of your minds--"

"How could I do it? What kind of monster am I inside? *I killed my son.*"

"To be fair, he killed you first. I know because I felt that shit. It was brutal. I'm still having nightmares."

"I don't know how to live with this. It's too much."

"I know. Come here." She wrapped her arms around him as he lay his head down in her lap, weeping and grabbing onto his sister's hand, afraid to let go. Tears welled in her eyes, too, as she bent down to kiss the top of his head. She brushed the hair away from his face as she whispered, "I'm sorry. I wish there was something I could've done. God, B, I'm so, so sorry."

"I want to die. I don't want to *exist* without him here."

"Shh." She squeezed him tighter. "I know. The thing is, I need you alive. Valerie's off with her dude most of the time. You're my only friend. Plus, who's gonna put Lucifer in his place if you're gone?"

"I feel like you can handle him on your own."

"Yeah, but Jesus, that's exhausting. He's a handful."

He wiped away another tear.

"I know it sucks. I know how you feel, literally. I'm having a hard time not falling apart, myself. Would it make you feel better if I told you he'll be back someday?"

He sat up. "What do you mean? Isn't he in Heaven?"

"Fuck, no. He killed people. He's in Purgatory. It's like jail for souls. He'll be there for a while, thinking about what he's done, and eventually, he'll be born again. I mean, as someone else, but--"

"When?"

"I don't know."

"How can you *not* know?"

"He's there until he thinks he deserves another chance. He has to forgive himself. Could be a few years, could be a few centuries. It's up to him."

Wyatt stared at his sister, his bloodshot eyes wide and frantic. "Will I see him again?"

"Yeah. I mean, of course. Human souls are never *gone*, just moved. It probably won't be for a long time, though. After Wyatt's dead and you're just Barachiel again."

"Great." He slumped back against the couch and hung his head.

"Sorry. Didn't mean to get your hopes up."

"It's fine."

"He *will* get to Heaven. They all do, eventually. No matter how many times it takes. God doesn't give up on people."

"That's comforting."

"I know you're being sarcastic, but I also know that it *does* make you feel a little better."

He sighed. "Of course you do."

She took out her phone. "I'm ordering food. Not just pizza this time. I'm also getting you some cake."

"Why?"

"You know, sugar, chocolate. It'll make you feel better."

"I don't deserve to feel better."

"Well, I do and I want some cake. Also, that's bullshit. You deserve a medal for what you did for Israel in 1967 alone."

"I have no idea what you're talking about."

"Maybe just trust me then."

He grunted.

"Hey," she tapped his nose with her finger. "Love you."

"Love you, too."

"You'll be all right. Over time."

He nodded but wasn't convinced. They sat in silence, each letting the other grieve in their own way.

Chapter 9

Wendy beamed as she walked to her Chambers Street apartment, lunch from her favorite chicken spot in hand. She couldn't help but smile. It had been a long time since she'd had so much fun with someone. Gabriel was funny, interesting, and to call her 'sexy' would have been a gross understatement. The few days they'd spent together in a Harrisburg hotel room were maybe the best in her life. They'd gotten so lost in all the sex and talking, they'd forgotten to eat. They slept only for a couple of hours at a time; naps between marathon sessions of mind-blowing lovemaking. She'd had more orgasms in the last three days than she'd had probably in her entire life. Just thinking about it got her excitable. The lightness of her touch. The smoothness of her skin. The way she looked up at her with those big brown eyes as she went down--

A chill went through her, her thoughts interrupted by the feeling that someone was following her. She glanced around, seeing no one and quickening her pace. Someone was there. She could feel them closing in, just a few steps behind. She rushed into her building, making a beeline for the empty elevator. As the doors closed behind her, she thought she could finally relax. She was wrong.

"I didn't mean to scare you," the girl claimed as she appeared. "I had to use a cloaking spell so no one would see."

"You're a witch?" Wendy asked, catching her breath.

"They call me 'Poe'. The leather and black lipstick." She gestured to herself and hit the emergency stop button. "You get it. The others don't know I'm here."

"What others?"

"I'm from Grace's coven. She wanted you to have something." The girl, no more than sixteen, held out an envelope. Wendy hesitated before taking it. "Don't open it until you're alone. If the others find out I gave that to you, they'll kill me. Or worse."

"What is it?"

"I can't say." Her eyes darted around the lift. "Not out loud, just in case. You shouldn't, either. They have eyes and ears everywhere." She pulled a newspaper from her jacket and handed it to her. "I marked the page. If you decide to come, use a cloaking spell. If they see you," She shook her head. "Stay hidden."

"How did you find me? I'm shielded."

"Not from your own magic." Poe restarted the elevator. "I was never here, okay?"

Wendy nodded.

The girl was again invisible and as the doors opened to the lobby, Wendy could feel her brush by, leaving her alone. She hit the button for her floor and watched with furrowed brow as the doors again closed. *Her own magic.* That could only mean one thing; Grace must be dead.

She set the bag of chicken on her table and opened the paper to the page with the dog-eared corner. Obituaries. Halfway down the page, she found her great-aunt's name. She'd died of a stroke a few days before. She was ninety-one. Her funeral was set for four o'clock that day.

She opened the take-out container and took a bite of chicken before opening the envelope. Inside was a necklace and note that read, *It's your responsibility now.* She reached inside again and pulled out the cat's eye amulet, a mournful sigh escaping her lips. It burned hot in her hand, radiating power, like the glow from a nuclear reactor. She knew instantly what Grace had done. She'd bound her magic by blood to the amulet, assuring that only a witch that shared her genes would have access to it. It was drawn to her like a magnet, undoubtedly leading Poe right to her.

"Well, I can't deal with *this* right now," she muttered, walking to the desk in the corner of the room and opening the drawer, tossing the necklace inside, and waving a hand over it. "Abscondo." It was now hidden from everyone but her.

She finished eating while contemplating what this all meant. Grace had stayed away, never having made contact with her. Wendy wasn't even sure if her aunt had known she existed. Why would she leave her magic to her? It didn't make sense. Usually, when a witch dies, their power is absorbed by her coven. To bestow her power to anyone outside of the coven would have been seen as a betrayal of the highest order. No wonder Poe had been so afraid. The others must be furious.

Chapter 10

"I'm moving them from Siberia as we speak," Spade told the man on the other end of the call. "I'll join them once I've made arrangements here."

"Will they be ready?" the caller asked.

"Of course. They've been training for years. My soldiers are the best of the best."

"I admire your confidence, Mr. Spade, but you have no idea what you'll be up against."

"We can handle *anything*."

"I hope that's true because your opposition will be unlike any you've ever faced."

"Yes, Lilith told me," he sighed, rolling his eyes. "They have superpowers or something. We have AK-47's. I'm not concerned."

"You weren't privy to all of Lilith's secrets, but trust me when I tell you, she was one of the most powerful creatures to ever walk the Earth and these people took her out in a matter of minutes. Underestimate them at your peril."

"If you say so. I know you don't like me questioning you, sir, but can I ask one thing?"

"If you must."

"The site," Spade wondered. "Why go to all this trouble? Why not just drone-bomb it? Seems so much more efficient."

"It's not enough to destroy the Gate physically, you imbecile. You must also destroy the keepers of it. As long as even one of them remains on Earth, so does the tether."

"You know this sounds like bullshit, right?"

"I would caution you to remember to whom you're speaking."

"I can't remember what I've never been told."

"I'm the man who signs your checks, Mr. Spade. The money Lilith paid plus everything I've been gracious enough to pay you since can all be taken away."

"Yes, sir. I understand."

"Good. Call me with any updates."

As the line went dead and Spade put the phone down, his daughter wandered in, still in her pajamas. "Aubrey!" he called to his wife, who was already rushing to the office.

"I tried to stop her, but she wanted to see you before you left on your business trip," she explained.

"It's all right," he said, his voice calm. "Can you find my passport while I say goodbye to Jenny?"

"Sure," she smiled, leaving father and daughter alone.

"What have you been up to today, Jenny-Bean?" he asked playfully. The girl sat on his knee and giggled. She was eleven with the intellect of a toddler and the communication skills of an infant. She was born with a myriad of mental and physical disabilities, symptoms of her extreme DWS, some of which had been corrected with experimental and impossibly expensive surgeries and treatments. After the influx of money Spade had received by taking the job Lilith had originally offered, he'd been able to pay for all of it, in cash. At nine, Jenny finally took her first steps. Two years later, she was walking almost normally. She still hadn't spoken, but doctors were confident that she could understand when others did. He'd hired a private tutor to teach her to read and write, but she didn't seem to be catching on. It had been a challenge, but Spade was determined to give his daughter the best life he could, no matter the circumstances. "I'll only be gone for a little while," he promised. "A week, I think. Give your mother lots of hugs while I'm away, okay?"

The girl smiled.

"That's my girl," he said, hugging her and kissing her forehead. "That's my good girl."

Chapter 11

Lucifer stood in the center of Saint Michael's Tower on Glastonbury Tor, admiring the craftsmanship of the stonework. It had been centuries since he'd watched it being built, and while it was all that was left of the original building, it was as beautiful as he remembered. All, that is, above ground. As much as he enjoyed a good tourist attraction, he had work to do and he couldn't get to it with all of these people milling around. He looked to the sky through the open roof and allowed a smirk to cross his lips as clouds gathered, thunder sounded and rain poured down. The visitors scattered, covering their heads with picnic blankets and papers, running hastily down the hill. When he was sure everyone was out of harm's way, he walked out onto the grass, hoping his memory was correct about the exact spot. He knelt and placed a hand on the wet ground, causing it to tremble beneath him. As the quake grew in power, the earth opened before him, a wide chasm splitting the clay and shale. He peered down, relieved to see what he'd been after. He stood and jumped in, falling nearly two hundred feet before landing on the stone sarcophagus below. He stepped off and looked it over, noticing how lovely the engravings still were. He tossed the lid off, revealing the ancient skeleton inside, well preserved in the hill's cool conditions. "Hello, Arthur," he said, moving a dragon-embossed banner aside to uncover the corpse's hands, still clutching the Celtic long sword. "Sorry about desecrating your grave, but that's what happens when you're buried with things that don't belong to you." He tore the sword by the horn hilt from the body's grip, almost taking the hand with it. "Do say 'hello' to your sister for me." He winked, leaping up out of the rift. He waved a hand to close the schism as the skies cleared before taking off, flying back to Gabriel's apartment for some much-needed rest, Uriel's sword in hand.

Chapter 12

"It has been a *day*," Valerie griped, plopping herself down on the sofa after a particularly stressful day at work.

"What happened?" Malik asked from the kitchen several feet away.

"Parents whining, mostly. 'Why can't Austin get into Columbia?' 'Why does Xander want to go to film school instead of med school?' It's a lot of 'Why isn't my kid a totally different person than he is' bullshit. *And* I got a visit from the PTA lady, bitching about the safe-sex brochures in my office. Like, sorry, Brenda, but this is high school in Hell's Kitchen, not a fifties sitcom."

Malik chuckled. "Did you say that?"

"No, I put on my fake-polite voice and told her the statistics and how it's the school's policy to prepare kids, blah, blah blah. I still think she left madder than when she came in."

"That place doesn't deserve you."

"Probably not, but the kids need me."

"Speaking of kids, the adoption agency called today."

She sat up straight, her chest tightening. "What'd they say?"

He came out from behind the bar and sat next to her, taking her hand in his. "We got approved."

She covered her mouth as she gasped. "So fast? I thought it'd be--"

"*Approved*, but the waitlist is long. She said it could be up to seven years before we get a baby."

"*Seven years?*"

"I know you're disappointed, but we've been approved. A lot of people don't even make it *that* far."

She nodded and he kissed her hand before heading back to the kitchen, the dinner he was preparing almost ready. He was right. She *was* disappointed, but part of her was relieved. While she desperately longed for a family, a life she could call 'normal', she had always suspected 'normal' wasn't really in the cards for her. Angel business aside, the way she'd grown up had her questioning her abilities as a parent. She had no example of what a good mother looked like. Her grandmother was the closest thing, but by the time she'd met her, she was almost grown and left pretty much to her own devices. If she was being honest with herself, Gabriel had been the most motherly influence in her life. She was always there for her, taking care of her when she needed it, protecting her. She knew her sister worried and cared about her. She loved her. But if *Gabriel* was what Valerie thought a mother was, she was definitely not ready for the responsibility.

"Hey, are you sure--" But before she could finish her sentence, a knock came on the door. "I'll get it," she offered, standing up. "You just keep cooking. Something smells delicious and I'm starving."

"Hello, sister," Lucifer greeted as she opened the door. "How are you this evening? You look tired."

"What do you want? Is Wyatt all right?"

"As far as I know. Gabriel's with him presently. I came to return something to you." He held the sword out to her by its hilt.

"What the fuck?" she muttered, pulling him inside and closing the door, hoping her neighbors didn't see this white boy strolling through the hall with the weapon.

"It's your sword," he explained. "Well, one of them. The only other left on Earth is in an abbey in Tuscany, so in the name of discretion--"

"Why are you bringing me this?"

"There's a battle coming. The world needs Uriel at full power. Pocket knives and kitchen utensils are quaint but relatively useless against an army of paid mercenaries. Speaking of kitchen tools, how are you, Malik?"

Malik grunted from the kitchen as he worked.

Valerie took the sword, the weight of it surprising her. "I don't know how to use this."

"Of course you do, you've just forgotten. Simply do for yourself what you've done for Barachiel. Search your mind for the memories, and do make it snappy. There's not much time."

"Take this to your brother," Malik said, shoving a plastic container into Lucifer's hands. "Chicken, risotto and broccoli rabe. Val told me he's been living on pizza and whiskey. No doubt he could use a home-cooked meal."

"Well, thank you, Malik. That's very thoughtful. I'm sure he'll appreciate the gesture."

"Why is it that even when you're being nice, you sound condescending?"

"It's a mystery."

"Bye, Lucifer," Valerie said, opening the door and pushing him out. She looked over the sword in her hands, a strange sense of nostalgia washing over her.

"Battle?" Malik asked.

"Looks like I need to have a talk with my sister."

Chapter 13

"A gift from Uriel's husband," Lucifer said, setting the container on the counter. "*Uriel's husband*. I don't believe I'll ever get used to that."

Gabriel inspected the contents of the lidded bowl before pushing it away in disgust.

"It's not for you," he reassured her.

"I know, but still."

"How is he?"

"A little better. He's in there taking a shower without breaking anything, so, you know...progress."

"Something's different," Lucifer noticed, glancing around. "Did you clean?"

"Did I *what*? No, I hired a maid service. Did I clean?" she scoffed. "Like I have time for that."

"A sword?" Valerie called as she entered Wyatt's apartment. "Really, bitch?"

"I got you a back-scabbard, too," Gabriel replied. "Lugging that thing around by hand would be--"

"The fuck's goin' on?"

"Keep your voice down," Gabriel ordered. "I don't want to bother B with this until I have to."

"Is he okay?"

"Meh."

"What's happening?"

"Lilith's army is still going after the Gate. I have one more Hail Mary, but if that doesn't work, things are gonna get real bloody. You have to be prepared."

"To fight an *army*? Girl, are you crazy? I'm not a soldier."

"*Valerie's* not, but *Uriel's* one of God's finest. Ask this one," she said, gesturing toward Lucifer. "He can tell you stories."

Lucifer nodded in agreement.

"Fine, but how are the four of *us* supposed to go up against *an army*?"

A sneaky smile crept across Gabriel's face as she took a sip of water before answering, "We'll have backup."

Phindi watched from a distance as her soldiers trained under the night sky. Finding a Krav Maga instructor who was also a vampire had proven impossible, so she'd created one, with her Queen's permission, of course. He was still fairly nervous being around so many of them, but she'd assured him that as long as he did his job, no harm would come to him. Still, training nearly three thousand vampires at once in a field upstate would have been difficult for anyone, let alone a fledgling vampire who hadn't quite gotten the hang of things. He was always hungry and had a hard time controlling his urges, but Phindi kept him and the others in line. As the general in her Queen's army, she had a responsibility to train and protect her subordinates. It was a duty she'd been born for, her father having been a great warrior in the Ndwandwe-Zulu War. She was honored to serve her Queen in such an important role, even if she didn't fully understand who, or what, her soldiers would be fighting against.

Chapter 14

Wendy silently made her way through the natural burial ground, having cloaked herself before entering the cemetery. It had been years since she was last here, or in the quiet town that surrounded it. Not since her grandmother had died. It was as peaceful as ever, the soothing sound of the Pocantico River the only thing she could hear. She loved the city, but the longer she walked, the more she realized how much she'd missed the town, the quiet...the nature.

She trekked through the soft grass, admiring the greenery all around her. The trees whispered in the breeze as she strolled, so at ease in this idyllic location, she'd almost forgotten why she was there. A deer moseyed past, unable to see her thanks to her spell. *Good*, she thought, sure now that the coven, too, would be unaware of her presence.

She made her way through the trees and finally came to the clearing where the funeral was being held. Mourners gathered in a crescent shape a good distance from the altar as one after another shuffled to it, kneeling and whispering their final goodbyes to the body lying there. The shroud wrapped around her great-aunt's corpse was sheer enough that she could just make out the woman's face as she stood over her. Her skin was almost as gray as her hair, her cheeks sunken. But, she looked to be at peace. Wendy smiled, tears forming in her eyes. Grace looked so much like her grandmother and seeing her like this brought back all the pain she'd felt when she'd lost her. She'd hated that she hadn't reconciled with her sister before she died, but she'd understood.

"Why did you do it?" a young woman whispered into the dead witch's ear. Wendy had been so lost in thought, she hadn't noticed her approach. She stepped back but listened intently. "Your magic should have passed to us. Why did you hide it? Without it, we--"

"Julia," another woman warned.

"I'm sorry, but we're all thinking it."

"This *is not* the place."

"I know." She stepped toward the group and stared them down, daring them with her eyes to try to silence her. "But we are flailing. Leaderless. This was Grace's coven and it never occurred to anyone to demand she name a successor."

A few of the witches laughed. "*Demand*? Who would dare demand anything of Grace?" one of them scoffed.

"She would have you shunned for even suggesting someone question her," another said.

"Yes, probably," Julia huffed, throwing her long, red hair over her shoulder. "But she's no longer with us and we are desperate. Without the Tituban magic, we're weak."

"We're *witches*," one of them sneered. "We're anything but weak."

"Compared to what?" she griped. "The other covens? Once they hear of Grace's death, the Dyer's will be coming to pilfer our members and the Gowdies will move to eradicate us completely."

"The other covens fear us," Poe chimed in. Wendy hadn't spotted her until now. She looked small; timid compared to the rest.

"*They feared Grace*," Julia corrected. "Without her power, we are sitting ducks."

"You're paranoid," the first woman told her. "It's been three generations since our coven has been attacked."

"Yes, three generations. Since just after Grace put us together. Others tried to dismantle and destroy us and it was *Grace* that shielded us. It was *Grace* that protected and defended us. It was *Grace* that all other covens feared and respected. Without her and her power, we are nothing."

"Enough," an older witch commanded. "You will not disrespect our founder with your dramatics. We will stand in reverence as she moves on to the Summerlands. We will return her body to the ground and *you will show some respect*."

Julia huffed. "Very well. But we *will* have this discussion."

The group quieted themselves, bowing their heads as another witch knelt before their fallen leader. When everyone had had a turn, a few of them told stories, reminiscing about the many ways Grace had impacted their lives. Healing sick children, delivering justice to men that had wronged them, aiding them financially when they were in need. Wendy was fascinated. She'd never known any of this. Her heart warmed at the knowledge that her great-aunt had lived such a full and happy life, even if without her sister.

Poe stepped forward, addressing the crowd as it was her turn to speak. "As you all know, I was in pretty bad shape when Grace found me. My parents kicked me out. I had nowhere to go. I was living on the streets, sleeping in shelters. One day, I was panhandling, starving, and she told me she knew what I was. I didn't know what she meant at first. She said I could stay with her and she'd teach me. She saved me that day." She wiped away a stray tear, her eye makeup smearing across her cheek. "She showed me how to access and control my magic, do spells. She fed me and bought me clothes. She even left me her house here in town." She choked back her sobs before finishing. "Nothing I could do would ever be enough to repay her for her kindness. I owe her my life."

Another woman wrapped her arm around the girl's shoulders and rubbed her arm. "She'll be greatly missed."

Poe nodded. "I just need a minute." She walked off alone into the woods, unable to stifle the tears that streamed down her face, grief mixed with eyeliner staining her flushed cheeks. Wendy couldn't help but feel sorry for her, the urge to hug her too strong to fight. Poe jumped at her touch. "Who's there?"

"It's me, Wendy," she whispered. "Are you okay?"

Poe looked around wildly. "Shh. If anyone catches you here--"

"I'm leaving. I just wanted to say I'm sorry and I'm glad my aunt had someone that cared about her as much as you. Thanks for being there for her."

Tears again formed in Poe's eyes. She rested her head on Wendy's invisible shoulder, grateful for the comfort. "She was like a mother to me. Way more than my real mom was." She wiped her face with her sleeve and gave Wendy a final squeeze. "All right." She backed away, clearing her throat and pulling herself together. "You have to go."

"I'd tell you to call if you ever need to talk, but--"

"I know. Too dangerous."

"Take care of yourself."

"I always do."

"Bye, Poe."

"Bye."

Before leaving Tarrytown, Wendy stopped at a Thai place for dinner and admired a statue off Old Broadway that had been deemed a landmark. She had missed this place, its history, and lore. It felt old, like stepping back in time. There was a gentleness in the air that swept through her, drawing her in and making her wish she could stay. She promised herself she'd return sometime soon. Maybe, if things worked out with Gabriel, she'd bring her along, show her where she grew up. *Please work out*, she thought as she began the fifty-minute drive back to the city, her thoughts drifting again to the amazing time they'd spent together.

Hours later, she lay awake in bed, her thoughts bouncing between Gabriel and the witches at the funeral. The coven had relied so heavily on Grace's magic. She almost felt guilty for keeping it from them. She knew, though, that it was given to her for a reason. Grace clearly didn't trust her fellow witches with it once she was gone. They didn't seem particularly menacing to Wendy; typical witches, as far as she could tell. Maybe it was as simple as Grace having a change of heart. Maybe she knew, like her grandmother had, that the average witch couldn't handle Tituban magic, and instead of allowing her power to turn her coven into monsters, she chose to bind it, protected by cat's eye, accessible only by shared blood. But had Grace even known there were descendants left? That Wendy existed? She had to. Unless she was so worried about her magic getting into her coven's hands that she'd rather see it locked away forever than risk them using it. Poe had certainly seemed rattled when she had brought the necklace to her. Perhaps they were more dangerous than she knew. "My responsibility."

She pushed the worry away as memories of Gabriel crept into her mind. She smiled in the dark as she remembered her lips on her skin and her hands on her body. She smelled like chamomile and tasted like strawberries and Wendy couldn't wait to see her again. She ached to feel her on top of her, in her, and around her. She didn't know where things were going with her. If it was just for fun or something that could turn serious. A fling or the beginning of a relationship. They'd exchanged information when they'd gotten back from Pennsylvania. Maybe she'd surprise her for a late-night booty call later. Right now, though, she was too aroused to get out of bed, the visions of Gabriel's body floating in her mind. She slipped her hand underneath the covers and into her pajama bottoms, closing her eyes and taking in a sharp breath. Yes, she'd *definitely* have to stop by Gabriel's place later.

Chapter 15

"So, what's on the agenda?" Lucifer asked as he and Gabriel took their seats on the plane. "Please say unrelenting torture."

"I'm putting a tracker on his phone so I know where he is and I'm hacking his computer to find out exactly how many troops he has and the details of his plan. I know he's still going after the Gate, I just don't know when or how. You're coming with because my powers don't work on him. I need you to keep watch so I can book it if need be."

"Well, this should be painfully boring."

"I hope so, bro. I am not trying to get shot tonight."

"Shot?"

"Yeah, dude. Spade's office is on his pseudo-military base. Base of operations? You know what I mean. We'll be going in when most of the contractors are sleeping, but that place will still be crawling with people, all armed."

Lucifer smiled. "This may be more fun than I thought."

"Don't get excited. This is a recon mission. We can't touch Spade, which means we can't kill him. But, if I know where he's gonna be, I can call in some favors. Get him tied up in so much red tape, he'll maybe decide it's not worth it. Better yet, get him arrested the minute he steps foot in Iraq. So, best behavior. This trip is strictly to get intel. You hear me?"

He groaned.

"Lucifer."

"Fine." He sighed and leaned back in his chair, struggling to get comfortable. "You know, we'd be there by now if you'd let me fly us."

"Stop complaining. It's a private jet. Have some champagne. Take a nap. Enjoy your life."

"Speaking of enjoying life, do you think Barachiel will ever get better, or is his current state of melancholy a permanent affliction?"

"I don't know, man," she confessed. "Dia's with him now, so at least he's not alone. She doesn't really know how to handle stuff like this, though."

"What do you mean?"

"As I was leaving, she saw him sitting on the couch all depressive and shit and I heard her think to herself, 'I just want to fuck him until he's not sad anymore'."

Lucifer chuckled. "You don't know. A distraction might be just the thing he needs. If memory serves, she's quite skilled in that department."

"Oh, shit," Gabriel giggled. "Don't let him hear you say that unless you want him to strangle you again."

"You're still here?" Wyatt grunted as he emerged from his bedroom after a long nap.

Allydia's leather-clad legs hung over the arm of the chair she'd draped herself across. She watched him shuffle to the couch and drop into it, his eyes still barely open. "I will always be here."

"I'm all right. You can go."

"I think we both know neither of those things is true. I would offer you a drink, but your sister warned me against it. Something about a familial predisposition."

"She's probably right, *as always*."

"She cares for you," she told him, detecting the disdain in his tone.

"I know."

"Then why do you sound angry with her?"

"It's not her I'm mad at." He sat up to look her in the eye. "I *hate* this *thing* in me. *I hate him. 'Protector of Humanity'*," he sneered, trembling with rage. "I say, 'him', but he's me. The real me, inside. Lucifer was right. I'll always do what's in the best interest of everyone else, no matter what it costs me. The greater good will *always* come first. That's who I am." Tears welled in his eyes as his voice broke. "What does that mean for me? Should I give up hope of ever being happy? Am I just not built for it? Will I ever have *anything* that's just mine?"

She left the chair and knelt on the floor in front of him, cupping his face in her hands. "*You will have me.*"

His features softened as tears spilled onto his cheeks. "I thought I'd pushed you away."

She smiled. "It would take a lot more than an *attitude* to get rid of *me*."

A quiet laugh escaped his lips as he took her hands in his.

"Do you need to talk?"

He shook his head, breathing in her pheromones and letting them work their magic.

"Would you like me to comfort you?" she asked, tugging at his pajama pants.

He nodded, his mind too hazy now to form words.

She smiled again. "Good thing I'm already on my knees."

"Are you nearly finished?" Lucifer complained as Gabriel downloaded the relevant files to a flash drive.

"Just stay there," she ordered.

"This is absurd. We've snuck into the enemy's lair. We should take offensive action *now* to prevent--"

"The people here haven't done anything, yet. We can't just preemptively slaughter thousands of people."

"Of course we can."

"Okay, I'll rephrase. We *shouldn't* slaughter thousands of people. There's a chance they might reconsider. Disobey orders. Bail on the mission."

"They're *soldiers*. It goes against who they are to be defiant."

"I didn't say it was a *good* chance." She started hiding cameras while Lucifer waited outside the door, keeping watch like a burglar too incompetent to be part of the actual crime. He peeked his head in, saw that his sister was thoroughly distracted, and left his post.

He headed to the mess hall, conveniently located at the center of the compound. Directly surrounding that were the barracks where more than one hundred thousand military contractors slept. "It's almost too easy," he smirked. He punched through the walls behind the ovens in the kitchen, tearing out and snapping apart the down gas lines that fed them as he quietly sang 'Devil in Disguise'. He picked up a few forks and threw them in a microwave, setting the timer for five minutes. He smiled to himself as he hurried back to the office, knowing that he'd get a stern talking-to from his sister, but delighting in the forthcoming carnage all the same.

As Lucifer approached the office door, shots rang out and an alarm sounded. He raced inside to find Gabriel on the floor, unconscious and bleeding out, three bullet holes gaping in her chest.

"Spade, I presume," Lucifer seethed, his gaze shifting to the man with the gun.

"Who are you people?" he barked, pointing the revolver at the intruder.

"Did Lilith not tell you? Of course, she didn't. Always with the secrecy, that one. No matter. I'm her brother and this is our sister. Don't worry, she'll be fine in a few minutes."

"What...what have you done with Lilith? I was told she was 'taken out', but--"

"Oh, she's back where she belongs, in a cage, locked away as to prevent her corrupting any more unsuspecting souls. You'll soon be in your own prison of sorts. Tell me, Mitchell, are you a religious man?"

"That's enough," Spade said, shooting Lucifer in the chest.

"Well, that's inconsiderate. Do you treat all of your guests so brutally?"

"How--"

"I'm much stronger than my sister," he explained. "Her body is a part of her, whereas I'm only visiting mine."

Spade fell back, barely catching himself on his desk. Lucifer moved toward him, holding his hand out in front of him. It was repelled by an invisible force; the warding his twin had put in place.

"Pity," he grumbled, gathering Gabriel in his arms. "Ah, well. We'll meet again, very soon, I imagine. I'd tell you to pray for your safety, but, unfortunately for you, God's not on your side in this war." The room shook, a loud explosion booming in the not so far off distance. Lucifer grinned.

"What have you done?" Spade spat.

"Until next time." He took off, flying straight through the ceiling, Gabriel limp as he carried her. He hovered over the base, giddy at the sight of the smoldering buildings. "Sorry, sister," he whispered. "But, you were wrong on this one."

Chapter 16

Eighteen-year-old Gabriel sauntered through the door of her Fairfield home to find Camael there waiting. They'd lived there together for the last few years, both now free from their abusive parents since Cam's had kicked him out, his violent outbursts having frightened them. He ran a hand through his dark, wavy hair as he prepared himself. His bright blue eyes followed his sister as she sat next to him on the sofa. He was *not* looking forward to this conversation. "How is he?"

"He's good," she said. "Calls himself 'Tae'. He's pre-med, runs a travel agency. Smart."

"And he's on board?"

"Took a little convincing. I had to rearrange his furniture with my brain, but," She shrugged.

He chuckled. "At least you didn't have to kill anyone this time."

"That dude had it coming. Uriel was in danger. I was just--"

"I know, I know." He put his hands up in retreat, the smile fading from his unshaven face. "Any luck with Barachiel?"

"No," she said. "It's like he's hidden from me. Every once in a while, I'll get a glimpse. I'll hear a thought or feel him for just a second. I try to break through, asking where he is, but, nothing. It'd be so much easier if I knew his human name. Why didn't God think that was prudent information?"

"Maybe you're not supposed to find him, yet."

"Bro, I *need* to find him *fast*. From the little bit I've seen in his head, he is *fucked up*."

"More than we are?"

She laughed. "Is anyone?"

He smiled and looked down, his demeanor changing. As his thoughts became clear, Gabriel's eyes widened, horror spreading across her face. "*No,*" she commanded.

"G,"

"I said, '*no*'." She bolted from her seat and ran to the window. "Come on. We have to go before they get here. We can stay with Uriel and her grandmother until we--"

"Uriel doesn't know I exist."

"Well, she *will*. You're not a secret."

"Maybe I should be."

"Stop being dramatic. Get your ass up before I come over there and drag you to the car myself."

"Gabriel, sit down."

"Camael, let's go. *Now.*"

"I waited until you found the others. I didn't want you to be alone."

"Cam, please."

"I'm dangerous. I scare my parents. I *killed* yours."

"That was--"

"G, I'm *Wrath*. I serve one purpose. I shouldn't be here."

"But, you *are* here. You know as well as I do, God doesn't make mistakes. You're here for a reason."

"Do you know what that is?"

"Not yet," she admitted, tears forming in her eyes. "I don't know everything all at once. Some things come to me later, when He wants me to know them."

"Well, when the old man fills you in, you know where to find me." He stood, seeing the police car's lights as it pulled into the driveway.

"Cam, no. Please. Please don't leave me."

He held her face in his hands as he tried to make her understand. "It's getting harder to control. I don't want to hurt you." He kissed her forehead before opening the door. "Visit me?"

She nodded as she choked back sobs, covering her mouth as she watched him put his hands up and drop to his knees. She fell to hers as well as he was handcuffed and read his rights. He nodded to her as he was shut inside the car.

You'll be fine, he thought.

'Fine' is a relative term. She nodded back as the car pulled out of the drive. As she cried, she could suddenly no longer feel the porch beneath her. The colors of the sky and grass muted. *This is a dream*, she realized. She'd had it before, thousands of times over the years. The memory of that day still stung in her mind as one of the worst of her life. She hung there in her past as her body healed, her anger at Cam's confession still haunting her two decades later. Yes, he'd killed her parents, but it wasn't like they hadn't deserved it.

Chapter   17

Lucifer lay Gabriel on the sofa and stood over her, waiting impatiently for her to come to. He folded his arms and began tapping his foot, trying to decide if he should linger or finish the book he'd been reading. He chose the latter, but before he could pick it up from its spot on the ottoman, he was thrown into the television hanging on the wall, shattering the screen. "Murus!" he heard a woman say. He was pinned there, unable to fight his way free.

"That's just impolite," he quipped, seeing the blonde woman emerge from the kitchen.

"What did you do?!" she barked.

"Nothing to *her*, I assure you."

"Obcillo!" His arm snapped at the word, the bones cracking loudly in his ears. He winced but didn't cry out, his pride stronger than any pain. She took her phone from her pocket and began to call nine-one-one, but before she got to the second 'one', Gabriel gasped, her eyes flying open.

"Wendy?" she asked, slowly sitting herself up and placing a hand on her fully healed chest. "Oh, man, that was unpleasant."

"Holy crap," Wendy breathed. "I thought you were dead."

"I was, but just for a few minutes."

She rushed to sit next to Gabriel and examined her shirt, poking a finger through one of the holes. "Are those bullet holes?"

"I'm fine," Gabriel promised.

"Sister," Lucifer called. "You didn't tell me your new friend was a witch."

"Sursum," Wendy spat, dragging him up the wall and pressing him to the ceiling.

Gabriel laughed. "That's hilarious." She kissed her companion and took her hand. "You can let him go. He's my brother."

"He didn't hurt you?"

"He wouldn't dare. He loves me." She looked up at him squirming and giggled. "Don't you, you dumb fuck?"

"Gabriel," he sneered.

"He's all right, I swear."

"If you say so. Occumbo."

And with that, he fell, grunting as he hit the floor. He righted himself and rubbed his arm as it healed.

"What are you doing here?" Gabriel asked.

"The maid let me in," Wendy explained. "I thought we could get breakfast or--" She stopped and looked over at Lucifer whose arm had fully recovered. "Honestly, what the fudge?"

"Well, it seems you have plans," Lucifer chimed. "I'll just be off--"

"You stay where you are," Gabriel commanded through her teeth, holding out her fist, rendering him immobile. He grunted and folded his arms. She turned her attention back to Wendy. "Can we make it lunch? I need to have a chat with my brother."

"Sure," she agreed. "But we need to have a serious talk about what you--"

"I know."

"All right. I'll see you later." She gave her a quick peck before leaving the apartment.

"What the fuck is wrong with you?" she scolded, standing up and dropping her hand, allowing Lucifer to move freely. "Do you have any idea how many people you just murdered?"

"A hundred thousand, give or take."

"It's not funny."

"Perhaps not, but it *was* necessary. Your humanity is clouding your judgment, Gabriel. This is war. We're defending the Gate to Heaven from those that seek to destroy it. As you once said, it's the only reason you and our siblings are here on Earth. *You should remember who you are.*"

"It's maybe *you* that should remember who I am. It's like you forgot that I know things you don't. Those soldiers were regular people. They would have been easy as shit to take down *if* it came to that."

"Yes, but now we don't have to. It's over. Spade's finished."

"He's *what*? Goddamn, you're usually the smart one. Spade will *never* be finished. He's going after the Gate in four days. You took away his army, so now he has to raise a new one."

He scoffed. "He doesn't have time for that."

"He does if he uses what your psychotic twin gave him and, thanks to you, he has no choice. You fucked us."

"I come bearing pasta," Gabriel said, holding the bag of takeout in front of her like a gift.

"I *guess* you can come in," Wendy teased. They sat, opening the containers of cavatappi and bruschetta.

"So, what are you?" Wendy blurted. "Your aura's brighter than anything I've ever seen and it's the color of the freakin' rainbow. That means you have a really strong link to the other side or a powerful spirit guide or--"

"Heaven."

Wendy froze. "Like, Heaven, Heaven? You're kidding, right?"

"I'm a funny bitch, but no."

"So, you're what? A ghost?"

"What? No, girl. I'm Gabriel."

"I know your name."

"*No*, I'm *Gabriel*."

"You're...like, from the Bible? The angel? Now I know you're messing with me."

"I'm not."

"Like, told Mary she was gonna have *Jesus*, Gabriel?"

'That's not *exactly* how it went down, but--"

"Are you fucking kidding me?!"

"You're freaking out."

"I am *definitely* freaking out."

"To be fair, you're a witch, so..."

"Witches are human beings."

"I'm *human*. Sort of."

"And your brother? Is he an angel, too?"

"Technically, but he's, um,"

"What?"

"Don't panic."

"Don't panic? You mean *more*?"

"The brother you met was...Lucifer."

"Holy shit!" Wendy gasped, bolting up from her chair.

"It's okay. He won't hurt you."

"He won't? He's *Lucifer*."

"He's not what-- I mean, he *is*, but he's--"

"So, Heaven's real? And Hell? And *God*?"

"Yeah, it's a little different than-- never mind. Listen--"

"God is real?! Am I going to Hell? Should I stop practicing the craft? I try to only use it for good, but--"

"No, He doesn't-- listen, I'll answer all your questions, but two things first. You can't tell anyone about this. Ever."

"Who'd believe me?"

"And, are we okay? I mean, we spent a few awesome days together and I like you, a lot, but this is real new and if you can't handle it, I mean, I'd understand if--"

"I don't know," Wendy admitted. "This is a *lot* of information. I really like you, too, but I'll have to digest this for a while."

"Okay."

They sat in awkward silence for a few moments, eating and taking sips of soda. Wendy put her cup down, folded her arms, and looked Gabriel over. "So, you can have sex?"

She looked up from her lunch. "You know I can." She winked.

She blushed. "I do. I just thought angels, if they even existed, were like perfect, sacred, virginal beings."

Gabriel burst out laughing. "You thought we were *what*? Maybe go back and reread Genesis 6."

"So, the Bible's...accurate?"

"Bits and pieces."

"What other myths are true? Vampires? Demons? Werewolves?"

"Yes, yes, but they're locked up in Hell, so no worries, and yes, it turns out, sometimes."

"Wow."

"Yeah. To be fair, most people think witches are myths, too."

"Yeah, but that took hundreds of years of hiding and propaganda. We *convinced* people not to believe we existed. Religion has--"

"Religion and truth aren't exactly best friends. Most of the time, they're not even casual acquaintances. Perpetuating one generally has nothing to do with the other."

Wendy raised her eyebrows. "I don't know what to do with all this."

"Sit with it. See how you feel after thinking about it for a while, then call me."

Chapter 18

Gabriel let herself into Valerie's apartment and groaned as she plopped herself down on the couch.

"I guess I'll leave you two alone," Malik chuckled, retreating to the bedroom.

"What now?" Valerie sighed, sitting next to her sister.

"Lucifer screwed us with his latest massacre, which I saw coming, but it still pisses me off."

"Massacre?"

"Yeah, but that's not what's bothering me."

"Why the fuck not?"

"I'm worried about Wendy."

"Who the hell's Wendy?"

"My girlfriend, kind of. Maybe. I don't know, man. We just met, but she's goddamn amazing. She's a Tituban witch, super powerful. You remember Violet, Tituba's daughter?"

"No."

"Right. Well, anyway, Wendy's grandma did one of her spells on her. I can't see in her head. I have no idea what she's thinking or feeling, what her life's been like. Being with her is like being on vacation. If she's not talking, it's just *quiet*."

"Well, good. It's about time you find somebody you can deal with for more than a night."

"I may have fucked it up already."

"Course you did."

"She found me a little...dead."

"Girl, what?"

"Long story. Point is, she knows everything. Who I am, what we are. I don't know if she can hang."

"Jesus fuck, bitch. What were you thinkin'?"

"You told Malik," she defended.

"He's my *husband*. We've been together for *years*. And what was I supposed to say when a demon kicked his ass and I set it on fire?"

"The girl found me not breathing with holes in my chest. There was no glossing over that."

"Fine. So, she's not taking it well?"

"Not super well, no. Better than I expected, but,"

"And you like her? For real? Not just for a weekend?"

"I feel like I'm falling for the girl."

"Damn, bitch. I've never heard you talk about somebody like *that*."

"I've only felt like this one other time."

"Really? What happened?"

"My parents killed her."

Valerie's eyes widened. "You wanna unpack that?"

"Nope."

"I guess we're blowing right by it, then. Listen, just give her a little time. A wise woman once told me that it takes a human brain a little time to catch up."

"I know. Anyway, have you made any progress with your sword?"

"You know I haven't."

"Yeah, but I was trying to be nice, you know, nudging you to get your shit together instead of giving you a lecture."

"Appreciated."

"We only have four days, though, so maybe get on it."

"You sure this is something I can do?"

"I'm always sure."

That night, after Gabriel left and Malik had gone to bed, Valerie sat on her living room floor staring at the sword in front of her. "Come on, bitch," she whispered to herself, mustering the courage to relive her memories as Uriel. "We got no time for you to be scared." She took a deep breath and placed one hand on the sword and one on her temple. "Here we go." She closed her eyes and after a few seconds of searching, a flood of images poured into her mind. She saw the sword in her hands, engulfed in flames, mowing down demons after The Fall. She watched as men whose bodies had been all but destroyed by possession fell under her blade, the thick stickiness of their captors peeling away and being sent screaming to cages. She saw herself somewhere in the Middle-East, driving the blade through soldiers of an enemy army. She watched Barachiel follow an old woman to an alley as she fought to protect civilians in Verona. The sound of people wailing as she struck them down, the begging in their eyes, was more than heartbreaking. Her hands, stained with blood, were all she could see. The image stayed with her for several seconds until another finally replaced it. She saw water below her as she hovered above it. Soon, she felt the sweet relief of the sword leaving her hand as she heaved it into Colliford Lake, painfully aware of the wizard watching nearby.

Tears filled her eyes as she opened them, her hands now covering her mouth as she wept. *All those people,* she thought. *I'm a monster.* She got up, leaving the sword where it was, and headed to her room.

"You all right?" Malik wondered, hearing his wife sniffles.

"No," she whimpered, crawling into bed and his arms, resting her head on his chest as she cried. "I'm really not."

Chapter 19

Camael sat alone at a table in the yard, the books from the prison's library the only company he needed most days. As he read, he could feel the stares from the other inmates. They usually kept a safe distance, having seen too many times what happened to men that challenged him. Every once in a while, though, a newbie would decide to pick a fight, thinking if he kicked the ass of the scariest guy here, he'd avoid trouble with anyone else in the future. It never ended well for them.

He shifted his gaze from the pages to the group. They immediately looked away and began nervously talking among themselves. He returned to his book, having no interest in whatever shenanigans they were planning. From the corner of his eye, he could see one of the men standing. He took a shaky step toward him, fists at his sides. "Are you sure that's wise?" Cam asked in his thick Brooklyn accent, not bothering to look up.

The man looked back at the group. They all shook their heads. "It's not worth it," one of them whispered.

"He's right," Cam said, putting his book down and standing up. The other men rushed away, scurrying like rats on a sinking ship, leaving the first man to face him on his own. He mustered his courage and sprang forward. Cam sighed as the man charged. "This is exhausting." With one punch, he knocked his would-be assailant out cold, breaking his cheekbone.

"Oh!" the other men cringed. A guard approached him, contempt flashing in his eyes.

"You saw that, right?" Cam asked. "I tried to warn him. You know I'm trying not to fight no more."

"Yeah, I saw," he said, bending down to revive the prisoner.

"Yo, Lee!" another guard called from the entrance. Cam looked over to meet his gaze. "Visitor."

He followed the guard to the visiting area and was happy to see Gabriel sitting on the other side of the glass, phone already in hand. He sat down and picked up the receiver, smiling from ear to ear. "Every week, like clockwork."

"How are you?" she asked, already knowing the answer.

"I'm all right. How's Barachiel doin'?"

"Still fucked up."

"To be expected, I guess."

She nodded.

"What's with *you*? You look pensive."

"A couple of things. First, Lucifer royally fucked us and now we're gonna have a full-blown war to deal with. I swear to Christ, this motherfucker *never listens*."

He laughed. "Did you expect him to?"

"*No*, but it would be super awesome if he surprised me *just once* by doing what I goddamn tell him to."

"He's a loose cannon, but when the chips are down, you know you can count on him to have your back."

"I'm worried it won't be enough." She pushed her hair behind her ear and let her hand fall, hitting the table with a thud. "I can't get to Spade, Uriel's taking her sweet ass time getting *her* shit together, Barachiel's useless right now, Lucifer's a giant pain in my ass, as usual. This whole thing could go sideways. I could really use your help."

He gestured to his surroundings. "I'm a little tied up."

"It would take nothing to break you out of here."

"We've had this conversation a million times."

She rolled her eyes.

"Remember last time?" he reminded her. "When Lilith was a problem, you begged me to let you get me out of here, and what did I say then?"

She glared daggers at him.

"I said you didn't need me and I was right."

"You never should have confessed."

"I confessed because I'm guilty." They stared at each other for a few moments before he spoke again. "So, what's the other thing you're upset about?"

"It doesn't matter."

"Come on, G. Tell me what's going on."

She let out an annoyed breath. "There's a girl."

"Oh, juicy. Give me the details."

She whispered, "She's a Tituban witch."

He raised his eyebrows.

"*I know*. She tossed Lucifer around like a rag doll. Broke his arm with a *word*. The best thing, though, is I can't hear her thoughts. Her mind is spelled. I can't see in. I can *breathe* around her."

"So, what's the problem?"

"She *kind of* saw me a *little bit* dead. I had to tell her who I was. She freaked out a smidge."

"She'll get over it."

She tilted her head and raised an eyebrow.

"*She's a witch.* If she was normal, maybe you'd have to worry. But someone like *her,* from *that* bloodline...if *anyone* can handle it, it's probably her."

"I hope you're right." Just then, Gabriel's phone buzzed. Her eyes lit up. "It's her."

"Go." He waved her away. "Get outta here."

"Love you."

"Love you, too, sis. Go get your girl."

Chapter 20

Wyatt opened his eyes, the early morning light seeping in through the space between the blackout curtains. He kissed the top of Allydia's head as he carefully moved out from under her to close the drapes, not wanting the sun's rays to hurt her. He knelt next to the bed, studying her sleeping face. He brushed a few stray hairs away from her eyes as he took her in, grateful for her existence in his life. She, more than his siblings, had pulled him back from the brink. He realized as he watched her how much he needed her and how hard it would be to leave her now.

He stood and got dressed before checking the plane ticket on his phone. He sat on the bed and rubbed Allydia's back until she woke. "Hey," he said quietly as she sat up. "I have to go, but I didn't want to leave without--"

"Where?" she asked.

"Back to the house in Southport. I need to pack it up and get it on the market."

"You don't have to do that now. You're grieving."

"I need to get it over with. Putting it off won't make it any easier and thinking about all of his things sitting in an empty house is--"

"Very well," she said, touching his cheek. "I will come with you."

"I appreciate the offer, but I need to do this alone."

"Are you certain?"

He nodded. "I'll be back tomorrow."

"Promise me," she demanded, the worry on her face breaking his heart. "Promise you will return to me."

He took her hand and kissed it. "I promise. I'm not *good*, but I'm done hurting myself."

"I'm worried that you'll abandon me again," she confessed.

"I won't," he swore, tucking her hair behind her ear. "You're what I'm living for, what's keeping me going. You're my survival."

She took his face in her hands and kissed him, the sharpness of his stubble a welcome discomfort. "I'll be here when you get back." He nodded and kissed her cheek before leaving the room, then the apartment. She sat there in the dimness, the sheet pulled up around her, debating whether or not to follow him. She decided against it, not wanting him to feel suffocated by her constant presence. Still, she was concerned, so she picked up her cell and called his sister.

"Hey, Dia," Gabriel answered, sounding half asleep. "Is he okay?"

"Yes, but he's leaving for Southport. He feels it necessary to pack his son's belongings *now*. He wants to be alone, but,"

"On it," Gabriel huffed, ending the call.

Allydia set the phone back on the nightstand and let out a sigh of derision. "That was abrupt."

"Hey," Wendy said, the sound of Gabriel's voice waking her. "What time is it?"

"Early," she whined, throwing her arm around her and closing her eyes. "Go back to sleep."

"Can't. The smell of your chamomile shampoo is getting me hot."

Gabriel laughed. "I'm glad you called."

"Me, too. So, who's calling at," She checked her phone for the time. "Five-thirty in the morning?"

"My brother's girlfriend. He's been in a bad place lately, so she's worried about him. I'll check on him later. He probably needs a little space."

"Lucifer has a girlfriend?"

"Sort of, but I meant my other brother."

"Other? How many of you are there?"

"Millions."

"On Earth?"

"Oh, five."

"I have to admit, I'm still not sure how I feel about this whole thing. Angels, demons, vampires...it's a lot."

"I know. When my sister's husband found out, he *freaked*. It didn't help that a demon attacked him and he had to watch her kill it with a knife she set on fire, but--"

"Um, what?"

"Never mind. Listen, I like you, a lot, but I don't want to push, so if you need some time--"

"I like you, too. It's weird, for sure. If you asked me a week ago if I believed in angels, let alone would have one for a girlfriend, I would have called you crazy, but--"

"Girlfriend?"

"Oh," Wendy said. "Now I'm being the pushy one. Sorry, forget I said anything."

"What if I don't want to forget?"

"Really? You want to jump into something this soon?"

"I mean, I'll give it a shot."

"Awesome." She kissed her softly, breathing her in like oxygen.

"Okay," Gabriel gleaned, sitting up and throwing back the covers. "If I'm up, I should probably--"

"Where do you think you're going?" Wendy, asked, replacing the covers and pulling on Gabriel's arm. "I wasn't kidding about that shampoo. Get your sexy ass back here."

Chapter 21

"What do you mean, ninety percent?!" the man roared.

"I apologize, sir," Spade said. "We were ambushed. I can't explain it. The one calling himself Lilith's brother...I shot him point-blank in the chest and he *didn't flinch.*"

"I told you these creatures would be difficult to kill. How many men do you have left?"

"Not quite ten thousand, sir."

"That won't be enough. You know what you have to do."

"Sir, I can recruit more--"

"There's no time! You have *three days*. Do the spell."

"Sir, with all due respect--"

"Did I stutter?!" the man barked.

"No, sir. I'll do it today."

"*Now*. Our entire way of life is at stake."

"Yes, si--" The call ended, cutting him off and leaving him feeling defeated and annoyed. He stood among the rubble of what used to be the mess hall, cadaver dogs still finding bodies. "You!" he called to the first person he saw, a young contractor who had been the only person in his building to survive the blast.

"Yes, sir," he said, adjusting the sling on his arm as he approached.

"I need a tattoo artist. Make that a hundred. Hell, call every tattoo shop in the state. Get 'em down here now. Tell 'em I'll pay triple. Every soldier left is getting ink."

He paced around the hotel room, his disappointment in Spade clawing at his peace of mind like a jackal. Perhaps he should have chosen another to lead the siege on the Gate. Lilith had been so sure he would be up to the task, but she had been wrong before. He should have known not to trust her judgment. It was too late now, though. They had three days at most to destroy it and while Lilith had wanted it gone to rule over humanity, *his* reasons were more personal.

"Can you please pipe down?" he snapped. "I can't think straight with all of your blubberings."

The young man sniffled, the duct tape over his mouth muffling his cries. He quieted himself as he attempted to break free from his restraints. The chains dug into his wrists as he struggled, pulling ever so slightly away from the radiator and back again. It was useless. The man had him.

"I'm sorry," he said, kneeling in front of him and stroking his cheek. "I shouldn't have raised my voice. Do you forgive me?"

The young man nodded, confusion and fear filling his bloodshot eyes.

"Aaron is your name, isn't it?"

He nodded again.

"You'll have to excuse my curious nature. I couldn't help but check your identification. Your wallet's lovely. Quality craftsmanship. I just love the feeling of real leather, don't you?"

Aaron didn't respond, staring blankly into his captor's inquisitive face.

"I must be going soon. Have you considered my offer?"

Again, he simply stared.

"Will you not answer me, then?" he roared, tearing away the tape from Aaron's lips. He winced and squeezed his eyes shut. "Answer me!"

"I...I don't know what to say."

"Say that you'll join me," the man all but begged. "We can travel the world, dine in the finest restaurants, visit museums, and take in the theater. We can sleep in palaces and watch the sunrise from the Eiffel Tower. You'll want for *nothing*. All you have to do is *stay with me*."

Tears again fell to Aaron's cheeks as he shook his head. "You're crazy."

The man's eyes darkened. He grasped the younger man's face in his hand, unable to stifle the desperation building in his chest. He stood and stormed across the room, flying into a rage. He tore the linens from the bed and threw the pillows. He lifted the television from its spot and smashed it on the floor. "I tried so hard with you! I gave you everything!" He pulled his instrument from its lined steel case and marched back. "*Why won't you love me?!*" He plunged the point deep into Aaron's chest, his eyes bulging as he watched the blood pour from the young man's mouth. The gurgling of his last breath soothed him. He pulled the iron from his body as he calmed himself. He used the comforter to wipe it clean and replaced it in its rightful spot, closing the case and taking a deep breath. "Why don't they ever love me?"

Spade stared at the security feed, watching as the last few soldiers got their marks. He fiddled with the mortar and pestle he'd used to create the special ink for the tattoos; a mixture of graveyard dirt, silver shavings, and his own blood. He felt a twinge of guilt as he sat in his office, knowing that the men and women that served him would never be the same. It had to be done, though. His benefactor had grown impatient and if he had any hope of paying for his daughter's treatments, his mission *had* to succeed. Luckily for him, unlike Lilith, the man had no desire to conquer Iraq or the surrounding countries. He just wanted some ruins blown to shit. But, after seeing what the people that protected it were capable of, he couldn't afford to take risks. He *had* to use Lilith's spell, but before he could trust it in battle, he'd have to test it in the field.

Chapter 22

"Where is she?" Valerie quizzed Lucifer as she entered Gabriel's apartment, sword in hand.

"Nice to see you, too," he said. "She's run off after our bereaved brother who's decided *now* would be an appropriate time to rifle through his dead child's belongings. A bit soon, I think, but I'm no expert on grief, never having felt it myself."

"When she gets back, tell her I'm *out*," she stated, placing the sword on the island. "I got a glimpse of the horrific shit I did back in the day and I want *no part* of whatever it is you two got goin' on. *I'm done.*"

"Horrific? Don't be so melodramatic, Uriel."

"My name is 'Valerie'. Uriel is a sociopath with a habit of slaughtering folks."

"Come now, sister," he guffawed, rolling his eyes. "The people you killed in the past all had it coming, I can assure you."

"It doesn't matter. I'm not a murderer. I won't--" Just then, a thud came on the door. As Lucifer began to walk toward it, the door crashed down into the apartment. A man wearing a sling stepped inside. His face was still and emotionless, his eyes appearing dead.

"And who might you be?" Lucifer asked. The man didn't speak. Instead, he rushed toward them, using his good arm to knock Lucifer back before turning his attention to Valerie. As he came for her, she acted on pure instinct, grasping the hilt of her sword, swinging it back, and cleanly lopping off the head of the intruder.

"I'm a fuckin' monster," She dropped her blade, hands trembling as the weapon hit the floor and the man's body fell.

"You're not," Lucifer told her, kneeling and looking inside the decapitated head's mouth. "You're an agent of the Almighty, doing what He set you upon the Earth to do. This, on the other hand," He pulled down the bottom lip and showed her the word printed on the inside. "*This* is a monster."

Chapter 23

You were right, Lucifer thought to Gabriel. *One of Spade's creatures attacked. Uriel handled it nicely. I'm confident she'll be ready when the time comes to go to battle.*

For real, I need you to stop questioning me, she warned as she walked up the steps to the porch. *I do actually know what I'm doing.*

Fine, fine. Have you convinced Barachiel to join our efforts, or is he still too wretched to be of use?

Working on it. She stood at the door for a while, listening to Wyatt inside. He'd packed up most of the house and was sitting on the couch, holding one of Will's tee shirts and weeping. She noticed the pile of boxes on the porch and the open moving van in the drive. To kill some time while she gave her brother a moment, she began loading boxes. Halfway to the truck, she set the first box on the sidewalk. "Seems inefficient." She looked around at the empty street and vacant fields surrounding the property. When she was sure no one was there to see, she waved her hand at one box after another, loading them onto the truck telekinetically.

"What are you doing here?" Wyatt asked from the doorway.

"Helping you move? That's what family's for, right?"

"I don't need a babysitter," he told her. "Anymore."

She walked towards him to get a better sense of what he was feeling. He wasn't lying. The suicidal thoughts were gone and while he was still crushed, he was relatively functional. "Yeah, well, maybe I needed to say 'goodbye', too."

He nodded and stepped aside, letting her walk into the house. She glanced around the living room, nostalgia sweeping through her. The air was different here. Still. She'd only been there a dozen or so times, but it was strangely comforting, somehow feeling like home. Or, maybe it was her brother's presence. His mental state had settled a bit and she was no longer brought to tears just by being near him. She could feel the tears coming, though, her own grief threatening to bubble to the surface any minute.

"Remember when he made me give him a horsey ride right there?" she reminisced, pointing to the floor near the entrance to the kitchen. "*Twenty minutes.* My back hurts just thinking about it."

Wyatt laughed.

"The first time he told me he loved me, he must have been around three, he grabbed my face and kissed my cheek and said, 'I love you, Aunt Gabriel'." She wiped a tear away as she spoke. "It was the first time someone had ever said that to me where I didn't feel like they felt obligated to. I'm not an emotional person, usually, but goddamn it, I loved that kid."

Wyatt pulled his sister in for a hug and kissed the top of her head as she cried, tears welling in his eyes, as well. She sobbed into his chest, allowing herself, finally, to feel the loss wholly. She'd been avoiding it, keeping herself distracted. She had to be strong for the others, to make sure they stayed focused, but Wyatt was different. She knew he would do as she asked simply because it was the right thing to do. He didn't need to be scolded or threatened or harped at. She could relax when it was just the two of them and at that moment, she could not have been more grateful to have found him.

"All right," she said, pulling herself together. "What is there to eat around here?"

"There's still a lasagna in the freezer," he shrugged.

"Well, heat that bitch up. I'm starving."

They sat quietly, eating straight from the pan, the plates already packed and on the truck. "It's nice out here," she observed. "Peaceful."

"Yeah," Wyatt agreed. "And boring, and lonely."

"Still, it's good to have a place far away from people. The only thoughts I can hear are yours. No neighbors stressed out about the news or health issues. No one worried about relatives overseas or wondering if their high school crush likes them back. It's soothing."

"I suppose."

"Let me buy it."

"The house?"

"Yeah. You're selling it, anyway. I could use a place to get away from everything, especially once this whole golem thing is over."

"The what?"

"The other reason I came by," she said, putting her fork down and taking a sip of soda. "Long story short, Lilith's army is still going after the Gate. We have a few days to get our shit together and haul ass to old Babylon to protect it. It was already a nightmare, then Lucifer decided to go rogue and kill off most of the soldiers, so Lilith's general, a guy named Mitchell Spade, you know, the Cardinal Rain guy? He used a spell Lilith left for him, like a break-glass-in-case-of-emergency sort of thing, and turned what's left of his army into golem. Basically, puppets that'll do anything he wants. They can't be hurt by anything living. Luckily for us, your girl is providing *her* army of undeads to kill them all while I hold them back from the Gate and Lucifer takes out tanks and drones. Still not sure how to stop Spade, himself, though. Lilith warded him. Anyway, your lightning skills would come in real handy, but I'd totally understand if you're not up to it."

He glared at her. "You just said a lot of things."

She shrugged and nodded in agreement.

He leaned back in his chair and folded his arms. "When do you need an answer?"

She looked at her phone, reading the text from the pilot saying the jet was gassed up and ready for departure. "I have to go," she said, getting up from the table. "You have an eleven-hour drive to think about it."

Chapter 24

"I just don't know what to do now," Ms. Landry sniffed, sitting down across from Valerie, the desk between them more cluttered than usual. "The after-school drama program is *working*. Giving these kids an outlet, keeping them out of trouble. They'll be devastated."

"Man, these budget cuts are out of control," Valerie bemoaned. "Did you know they're getting rid of SAT prep? They say their goal is to get every kid 'college-ready'. How do they expect--"

"Ms. Moore," the principal's secretary said, poking her head into the office.

"Hey, Karen."

"Principal Simpson would like to see you."

"Oh, lord," she said, getting up and heading to the door.

"Good luck," Ms. Landry said, patting her arm as she walked by.

"Thanks, girl. I'm probably gonna need it." As she walked across the hall to the principal's office, she was almost run over by the boys' gym teacher. His face was red and he muttered obscenities under his breath as he passed. "That's not encouraging," she uttered to herself as she went in.

"Ms. Moore, have a seat," the weary principal offered.

"What's going on? Andrea's in my office on the verge of tears and Bill just came out of here lookin' like you smacked his momma."

"It's the damn budget cuts," he grumbled. "I'm having to make some tough and, admittedly, unfortunate decisions."

"It's really that bad?"

"It's worse. I hate to do this, but I have no choice. I have to knock you down to part-time. Two days a week, a third of your current salary."

"The fu--" She stopped herself. "Sorry, I mean, what?!"

"I know," He rubbed his temples. "I know. But my hands are tied. Even with all the cuts, we'll barely have enough money to keep the lights on. Mentoring programs, after-school programs, all gone. Any teacher without tenure will be replaced by a newbie at half the salary. The union's gonna have a field day with that one. I really am sorry. I wish there was something I could do."

"All right, you know what? There is no way I'm trying to do this shit *part-time*. I'm a guidance counselor, not a cashier. If I wanted to work for less money than it takes to live, I wouldn't have worked my ass off putting myself through college. I tried to be professional, but *fuck this*. I quit."

"Ms. Moore, please don't--"

"It's Mrs. Perry and I've got more important things to do, anyway."

Chapter 25

"Fair warning, Uriel's in a mood," Lucifer said as Gabriel entered the apartment. "She's on the roof, honing her swashbuckling skills. I offered to assist, but she said if I dare follow her, she'd lop my head off the way she did the golem this morning."

"Fucking Lilith," she complained. "Ten thousand golem we have to deal with now. Next time I tell you not to kill people, can you just listen? For fuck's sake. No, you know what? After we secure the Gate, maybe just don't kill anyone ever. How 'bout that?"

"You really know how to take all the fun out of being alive, don't you?"

She rolled her eyes.

"Perhaps if you'd be willing to share more vital information, we wouldn't be in this predicament."

"You know I can't."

"Yes, yes. God's 'need-to-know' policy. You know all and the rest of us are left scrambling."

"I don't know *all*," she asserted. "Just more than *you*, so it would be super helpful if you could just trust me."

"It's not that I don't trust you, it's that I'm impatient and impulsive."

"Maybe something to work on."

"Speaking of things that would be helpful," he cajoled. "Now that our enemies are no longer human, your witch friend could prove useful."

"No."

"Think about it, sister. A Tituban witch *happens* to fall in your lap just as we're in need of--"

"I said 'no'."

"You're being unreasonable."

"Probably."

"Gabriel,"

"I'm not putting her in danger."

"She's a *Tituban witch*. She's hardly defenseless."

"She's still human."

"What do you remember of Salem?"

"It doesn't--"

"Children attempting to summon me, demons torturing them instead. Tituba was the only real witch among them. *She* drove out the demons on her own. I didn't have to lift a finger. No other witch in history had that kind of power. None human, anyway."

"Wendy isn't Tituba. She's a white girl from Tribeca. The genes are so watered down--"

"Perhaps, but if she possesses a tenth of her ancestor's power, she's still the strongest enchantress on Earth. Do you honestly think meeting her now was a coincidence?"

"No," she conceded.

"Then find out what she's capable of. You're derelict in your duty to our Father if you don't use every weapon available to contain this threat."

"Trying to give me dad-guilt?"

"Never. Just trying to win this war."

Valerie was getting used to the weight of the sword as she grew more comfortable with every swing. The setting sun's light glinted off the steel as she sliced through the air, again and again, her anger fueling her effort. Furious and resentful, she threw the blade, embedding it in the building, barely missing her sister's face as she stepped onto the roof.

"I should have brought you some fries to go with all that salt," Gabriel teased.

"Unfunny," she huffed as she pulled the sword from the stone.

"Sorry about your job. I know it meant a lot to you."

"Gives me more time to kill monsters, right?"

"I know it's not what you want to be doing, but--"

"I know, I know. God's will or whatever. Is this it, though? This fight with the monster army? Is our angel-work done after this?"

"Well,"

"Man, what the fuck?! How long is this gonna go on?"

"Just like, three or so years, give or take."

"So you're telling me I have to tell my husband we can't have a baby for at least three years? If the adoption agency calls, I have to tell them 'not right now'?"

"I didn't say that."

"Well, bitch, I'm not trying to raise a kid in the middle of this bullshit! Everywhere I go, something's trying to kill me."

"I mean, I see what you're saying, but--"

"So, what's up with your girl? Lucifer thinks--"

"I know what Lucifer thinks."

"Well? If she's as powerful as he says she is, maybe--"

"She could get hurt."

"Girl, so could we. Besides, you're the one that keeps telling me our mission is the most important thing in the world. That still true?"

She folded her arms. "Yes, and Lucifer's *probably* right. Don't tell him I said that. If his head gets any bigger, his neck won't be able to support it."

Valerie laughed. "What about Wyatt? Is he coming, or is he still too fucked up?"

"He's thinking about it."

Wyatt ate in the cab of the moving van, not feeling up to being around strangers. He'd driven in silence, mulling over everything Gabriel had told him. He needed more information. He sat his sandwich on its wrapper and called Allydia. The sun had been down for hours; she should be awake.

"Yes, darling?" she answered.

"Hey, what can you tell me about golem?"

"You spoke to your sister. I hope you're not angry with me for keeping you in the dark. I didn't want to burden you."

"No, I understand."

"Thank you. So, golem are living dolls, bound to their creator by blood magic. They're fiercely loyal and will carry out his wishes even without him having to say a word. They feel nothing. They're creatures of blind obedience."

"Do you need me?"

"I always need you."

He smiled for a moment. "For the fight."

"Oh, I don't know. My soldiers are quite capable. Still, the last time I talked to your sister, her heart was beating more rapidly than usual. I'd dare say she was nervous."

"If *she's* nervous, it must be pretty bad."

"Yes, I suppose it is."

"All right. I'll be home in a few hours."

"I'll see you soon, then."

He ended the call and went back to his sandwich, thinking as he chewed. He was tired, not physically or mentally fit for battle, but what choice did he have? It was the *Gate to Heaven*. He knew how important protecting it was, that it was the reason he and his siblings were born. It was why Lucifer was on Earth. It was why he'd had to put that poor girl that Lilith had been possessing in a coma. While an army of golem was the *last* thing he wanted to deal with, his family needed him; the only family he had left.

He bagged up his trash and took it to the bin next to the entrance. He noticed, through the glass door, the many people sitting down together, enjoying their meals. Couples and families, laughing and talking, oblivious to the dangers Gabriel wanted him to help her fight against. He knew it was big. Even Allydia was offering up her army to aid in the battle. As he watched a young boy dip a french fry into a shake, a tear came to his eye. He couldn't let anything bad happen to anyone else's son. He got back in the truck and began the last two hours of his trip home. As he pulled onto the highway, he thought to his sister, *Looks like we're saving the world.*

Chapter 26

A guard Camael had never seen before opened the cell door, waking him from a dreamless sleep. "Move it, Lee." He shot the guard a confused glare but followed him to the visiting area. He was surprised to see Gabriel there, impatiently waving him over.

He sat in front of her and picked up the phone. "It's the middle of the night. How'd you arrange this?"

"I'm rich."

"Oh, right," he laughed. "So, twice in one week. What's the occasion?"

"I need your counsel."

He raised an eyebrow in interest.

"Lucifer and Uriel think I should ask Wendy to help with the Gate."

"You probably should."

"Damn it, Cam. You, too?"

"You came for my opinion, right?"

She grunted, then nodded.

"She's a witch. She could help."

"Something could happen to her."

"Again, *she's a witch*. You probably don't need to worry about her so much."

"I worry about *everyone* I care about."

He tilted his head and smiled, his eyes wide.

"I think I'm falling for her. I mean, hard to say, but it's like...it's kind of like--"

"Ada?"

Gabriel's face fell. "Not exactly. Wendy and I don't have to *hide*."

His features softened. "You never had to hide from *me*."

"I know, and I appreciate you, more than you know. This girl, though. Dude, I'm *concerned*."

"I think she'll be fine. What's the worst that can happen? If she gets hurt, you can just heal her."

"It's not only that. What if she sees it, what it's actually like to be with me? The monsters and the killing. What if she decides it's too much?"

"Some unsolicited advice?"

"Why not?"

"It sounds to me like you love her. As far as I know, that's only happened for you one other time, so if there's a chick out there giving you the warm and fuzzies, I say enjoy it. You deserve to be happy, despite what you think about yourself most of the time."

"What if she bolts?"

"Then you'll be sad for a while. Who cares? Wouldn't you rather have something amazing for a little while than sentence yourself to a life in solitary?"

"I see what you did there."

"Don't worry so much about it ending that you push her away."

"That's some strong wisdom, bro."

"I'm in prison. All I have to do all day is work out and read."

They both laughed.

"Listen, get through the next couple days, defend our way home, defeat the bad guys, and then have some fun. Take your girl on a trip. Somewhere tropical. A beach. Chicks love beaches."

She bit her bottom lip and chuckled.

"I mean it. Get out of town for a while. Go on vacation."

"I can't leave. Barachiel--"

"Is a grown man, with the Queen of all vampires lookin' out for him. What are you worried about? It's not like he can die. I know you feel guilty about what happened when we were kids, but you can't beat yourself up over that forever. At some point, you have to forgive yourself and live your life."

"I'll consider it. All right, I'm gonna go talk to Wendy. Maybe she can give me a charm or something to break Lilith's warding. I'll see you next week. Love you."

"Love you, too." He waited until she disappeared behind the door before standing to go back to his cell.

"*Goddamn*, your sister is *hot as shit*," the guard blurted.

"What did you just say to me?"

"She slipped me a grand to sneak her in tonight, but with tits like that, I would have done it for a lot less, if you know what I'm sayin'. Tell her next time she can visit whenever she wants, *if* she spends some time with *me*, that is."

Camael gripped the guard by the throat and threw him into the wall. "The fuck did you say?!" He grabbed the back of his head and slammed it onto the table. "That wasn't very polite." He gritted his teeth, his whole body shaking with rage. He took the phone from its cradle and smashed it into the man's temple, again and again, sending blood and bits of flesh flying. His skull shattered, the impact of Cam's blows growing in strength as he relented to his impulses. When the guard's head was little more than a puddle, he dropped the phone and backed away, his chest heaving as he struggled to calm himself. He looked at his reflection in the glass, the blood splattered on his face and clothes filling him with shame. His shoulders slumped and he looked down at the floor. "I'm sorry." He took the keys from the guard's belt and turned to take the long walk back to his cell. Once there, he locked himself back in and hid the keys in a hole he'd dug into the wall, carefully placing the poster back over it. He washed away the blood as best he could, assuming the guard had turned off the security cameras before retrieving him. The block was quiet. If anyone had been awake to see him, they weren't saying a word. And they wouldn't. They wouldn't dare risk that he'd come after them next. This wasn't the first time Cam had lost his temper, and every prisoner there knew what he was capable of. Unfortunately for the rookie guard, no one had given him the memo.

Chapter 27

Gabriel took Wendy's face in her hands and kissed her hard.

"Well, hello," Wendy giggled, closing the door as Gabriel entered the apartment. "It's late. Everything all right?"

"I have to ask you something," Gabriel hesitated. "I don't want to. I wanted to keep you as far away from this as possible, but you might be our only hope."

"Your only hope for what?"

She cringed a little before saying it. "Saving the world."

She laughed.

"I'm not kidding."

"What are you talking about?"

"There's a place in what used to be Babylon. We, my siblings and I, have to protect it, like, at *all costs* and there's an army of golem headed there *right now* on a mission to destroy it. You're a witch, so--"

"Hold on. You and your siblings, the *angels*, are in a war with *golem*? The clay to life puppet monsters from Jewish folklore?"

"Sort of. Religion never really gets the details right. Doesn't matter. Point is, if they blow this place up, me and my family don't get to go home when we die. *No one* gets to go to Heaven when they die. My Father's plans get flushed down the toilet and we're all pretty much fucked for the next two hundred and forty years."

"Your Father...you mean *God.*"

"Yeah."

Wendy's eyes were wide, eyebrows raised. She didn't hesitate. "Tell me what you need. It's yours."

"A protection spell. Something to guard the place while we take out the baddies. Maybe something to remove warding? Give me whatever ingredients and words to say and I'll--"

"That's not how it works. Something that powerful I'd have to do myself. No offense to you, but you're no witch. Even if you were, my spells are too strong for most to handle."

"Okay. Never mind, then. I'll figure something else out. I always do."

"Don't be crazy. I'm coming with you."

"No."

"Gabriel,"

"I won't put you in danger. If something happened to you--"

"I can take care of myself. Not to toot my own horn, but I'm pretty badass. Besides, it's for *God.* Who am I to say no?"

Tears formed in Gabriel's eyes as she feebly tried to wave them away.

"Why are you crying?" Wendy asked, touching her girlfriend's hair and cheek.

"I don't want you to get hurt."

She kissed her and wiped away her tears. "It's sweet of you to worry about me, but you don't have to."

"You'll see things...see me do things. I'm afraid you'll think less of me. Be afraid of me."

Wendy laughed. "I'm not exactly a stranger to spooky shit."

"Aren't you scared?"

"Of course, it's an army of monsters with guns. I'm badass, not stupid."

"I didn't mean about the war."

Wendy looked at her fondly. "A little. But, you're pretty cute, so I think I'll risk it." They both laughed before kissing again. "So, when do we leave?"

Chapter 28

"Three years?" Malik asked.

"That's what she tells me," Valerie huffed.

"And she swore it'd all be over then? No more fights with this demon or that mythical creature? You'd be free?"

"Supposedly."

"Well, okay. That's not that long. Hell, we'll probably still be on the waitlist. Plus, it gives us time to find the perfect house, settle in, get a minivan."

"A minivan? Who are you right now?"

He laughed. "I'm just excited to start our family. Maybe not a minivan. An SUV?"

"We'll talk about it." Her face fell, her expression solemn.

"What's wrong?"

"What if I'm not cut out for it? Parenting, I mean."

"What are you talking about?"

"You know, growing up in foster care, bouncing around, all the abusive shit. I don't know how to be a mother."

"Val, up until this morning, you were a *guidance counselor. Your job* was helping kids."

"High school kids, picking colleges, classes, and careers. Their parents did all the actual work. I just helped them get to where they wanted to be."

"Well, Val," he chortled. "What do you think parenting is?"

"That's the problem. I couldn't tell you."

"Baby, all it is is giving them what they need to become the people they want to be...and keeping them alive." He winked.

"Oh, shit. I didn't think about it before now, but how's it gonna be for them, having *Lucifer* for an uncle?"

They both laughed.

"Well, I don't know. Maybe he only visits when your sister's around. She seems to keep him on a pretty tight leash most of the time."

"She *tries*." She covered her mouth as she giggled.

He took her hand. "You have nothing to worry about. I'm a thousand percent sure you're gonna be an excellent mother."

"How?"

"Because I know you, better than anyone."

"Do you?"

"Well, maybe not as well as your sister. She has the advantage of being able to read your mind." He smiled. "Speaking of, wouldn't she try to talk you out of it if she thought you weren't mother material?"

"Yeah, she's not shy about telling me what she thinks I should or shouldn't do."

"No. So can you stop second-guessing yourself now? Unless there's something else goin' on."

"What do you mean?"

"I mean, if you don't *want* kids--"

"Oh, no, I do. I definitely do. I'm just afraid I'm gonna mess them up."

He kissed her hand. "Every parent worries about that. *Especially* the good ones."

"I guess."

"So, tell me about this thing you're getting ready to do. How dangerous is it?"

"Extremely. I'll basically be beheading dudes in the desert for as long as it takes Lucifer to disable bombs. An army of vamps will be doing most of the fighting, I think, but it'll be a miracle if I don't get shot."

"And I'm supposed to be okay with this?"

She shrugged. "Not really. Shit, *I'm* not okay with it, but if Wyatt can drag his ass out there after everything he's been through lately, I have got no excuse to sit mine at home."

Chapter 29

Wyatt walked into his apartment after leaving the contents of the moving truck in a storage unit on West 55th. It was late and he felt drained. He kicked off his shoes and collapsed onto the sofa, barely able to keep his eyes open.

"Mr. Sinclair," a voice called from behind.

He sat up, turning his head to see a man he didn't recognize sipping from a blood bag.

"I'm Hart, the Queen's assistant. She wants me to tell you she's attending to her army, but she'll be back in a flash." He came around to the front of the couch and looked Wyatt up and down, taking another sip and nodding in approval. "Okay, I get it now."

"She could have left a note."

"She wanted me to make sure you were all right. You need anything? I can order you some take-out, give you a massage, run you a bath. *Anything* you want."

"I'm fine."

"I can see that."

"I thought that girl, Hattie, was her assistant."

"Mmm," Hart acknowledged, sitting next to him and rolling his eyes. "She *was*, but she disappeared without a trace a couple of weeks ago. Rumor has it, she sired a new vampire without the Queen's approval. I don't know if that's true, but if it is, best she stays away *for good*."

"Why's that?"

Hart put his hand to his chest. "Are you kidding? Have you ever seen Her Majesty angry? I wouldn't wish her wrath on my worst enemy."

"Really? She seems so,"

"Fair? Generous? Kind? Loving, even?"

Wyatt nodded.

"She is. But, get on her bad side," he shook his head. "I don't recommend it."

"Good to know," he chuckled. "I appreciate that she cares enough to send you, but I'm all right. I'm just gonna go to bed. You can leave."

"I can't. As rude as it is for me to stay when you want me to go, if I leave before the Queen gets back, she'll skin me alive."

"You mean that metaphorically, right?"

Hart took another sip from his blood bag, his eyes fixed on Wyatt's, and shook his head.

Chapter 30

Allydia looked over her soldiers, arms folded and a scowl on her face. Red war paint had been smeared in stripes on their cheeks to symbolize the blood-bond they all shared. Some carried swords, others machetes. Some held no weapons, instead relying on their hands to do the work of removing head from body. Those were the ones that gave her the most pride...and the most concern.

"Are they ready?"

"Yes, my Queen," Phindi said confidently. "They have been trained in the ways of the Israeli's, as you commanded. I would trust any one of them with my life, in battle or otherwise."

"Thank you, Commander. You've proven yourself invaluable. Should we prevail, I will give to you anything you desire. Money, title. Simply name it and it's yours."

"You are very kind, Your Majesty. But, you have already been so generous. I require nothing but to keep serving you as long as I am needed."

"It's not about what you *require*. It's about what you *deserve*. Come out of this with your head and heart intact and I will give you the world on a platter."

Phindi stood straight, honored, and proud. "Whatever you wish, my Queen."

"It's nearly morning. Get some rest. When the sun sets again, make sure everyone's well fed. They'll need their strength."

She nodded. "The plane's windows have been blacked out. We will sleep there so there will be no delay in our departure." She turned to face the soldiers and gave the order. "Planes, now!" The soldiers spun on their heels and began to file into the five double-deck aircraft Hart had chartered.

"I will meet you there. Remember, keep everyone on the planes until I arrive. I don't have to tell you how unforgiving the desert sun is to things like us."

"Yes, my Queen." She bowed and made her way to the lead plane, leaving Allydia alone on the tarmac. She sighed heavily. She hated putting her people in harm's way. But the fight was just and besides, this was the last favor she owed. After this battle, it would be Gabriel's turn to deliver on her part of their arrangement.

"He's all right, I trust," Allydia said as she entered the apartment, closing the door behind her and taking a seat at the kitchen island.

"Yes, Your Majesty," Hart assured her, hurrying to fetch her a blood bag from the fridge and tossing it in the microwave. "He's been asleep for just over two hours."

"Good. Thank you, Hart. The sun will be up soon. You may go."

"Actually, there's something I'd like to discuss with you, if I may." He removed the blood from the appliance and poured it into a glass before handing it to her and kneeling, his eyes fixed firmly on the floor.

"Of course. What is it?"

"I've been struggling with how to bring this up, and I know it's maybe not the ideal time, a war on and everything, but--"

"You have a request?"

"I do," he told her, his voice shaky.

"All you need to do is ask."

"Okay," he gulped. "Your Majesty, I want to...I *need* to..."

"Yes?"

"I'd like to...transition."

She burst into laughter, setting her glass on the counter. "Hart, remind me of the night you turned."

He shifted a little as he remembered. "It was the summer of 1969. I was outside a club in Greenwich. Some guys had beaten me up. I was bleeding from the head. I tried calling out for help, but it was so crazy, I didn't think anyone heard me. But then, you came. You asked if I wanted to live a life free of hate and fear."

"And have I provided you with that life?"

"Yes, Your Majesty."

Her voice softened. "Then why would you think you had to ask my permission to be who you are?"

Tears started to form in his eyes.

"Look at me," she ordered. He raised his eyes to meet hers, the tears now spilling out. "I don't care what you look like or what you identify as. Change your clothes, change your name, change your gender. It's all just window dressing to me." She touched his cheek and smiled. "You're perfect. You've always been perfect. And, whoever you become, however you wish to present yourself to the world, you will always be perfect to me."

Hart covered his mouth, muffling the sobs he didn't want her to hear. He did his best to gather himself before standing. "Thank you, Your Majesty." He hurried to the door, locking it behind him as he left.

Allydia went to Wyatt's bedroom where she found him standing in the doorway, having listened in on her conversation. He took her face in his hands and kissed her sweetly. "You don't seem scary to me."

"I don't? Maybe you don't know me as well as you think you do."

He laughed. "You're probably right about that."

Chapter 31

Hart woke early the next night, having set an alarm for just after sunset. He was too excited to start his new life to sleep in. He tied back his shoulder-length hair and slipped on a satin robe before heading to the bathroom. In a rush, he applied the shaving cream and lifted the blade from its place on the vanity. He shaved quickly, one smooth swipe of the razor after another, rinsing the blade periodically. When he was sure all the stubble had been removed, he splashed his face with cold water and patted it dry with the hand towel that hung just above the light switch. He took a deep breath and blew it out slowly, his hands trembling in anticipation.

After a few contemplative moments, he opened the drawer and beamed at the sight of its contents. Pallets upon pallets of eyeshadow and blush. Tubes of lipstick, bottles of foundation, compacts of powder, bronzer, and contour, all unopened. His face lit up as he took a tube of BB cream in his hands and broke the seal. He squeezed a small amount onto his finger, rubbed it on the back of his hand to warm it up, then dotted it all over his face. He blended it in with a stippling brush until his skin looked flawless. Next, he applied the contour, doing his best to remember the techniques he'd seen on internet how-tos. "Blend, blend, blend." he reminded himself. He then turned his face up in an exaggerated smile, brushing on the soft-pink blush to the apples of his cheeks and eye-lids. He used transparent powder to set before he turned his attention to his eyes. He lined them in deep black before applying mascara and false lashes. Finally, he carefully spread the blood-red lipstick to his full lips then went over them with a clear gloss.

"Almost," he breathed, closing the makeup drawer and opening the medicine cabinet. He'd taken out the shelves and added hooks, allowing him to easily store his many hair extensions. He separated his hair, tying most of it up before clipping in the first extension. He repeated the process until he was happy with the length and fullness. He then added waves with setting spray and a curling iron. He tousled his hair until he was satisfied that he had a natural, "beachy" look.

He stared at himself in the mirror, puckering his lips and tilting his head in different poses. This was it. *This* was who he'd always been meant to be. Hart was over. Dead. He had ceased to be. From now on, there was only Hartley.

"There you are, you beautiful bitch."

Chapter 32

Wendy left Gabriel in bed while she went to pick up a fast-food breakfast; sausage biscuits, hash browns, and apple pie. She had food at her apartment, but she needed an excuse to get some fresh air, the short walk guaranteed to clear her head. She had agreed to help Gabriel without giving it much thought at all. How could she refuse her? She was talking about guarding the *Gate to Heaven*. That wasn't something she could just ignore. Still, it was risky and she could be putting herself in more danger than she realized. She went over the checklist of things she'd need for the spell: Amethyst, Goofer Dust mixed with dirt from her grandmother's grave and a few other things, black, blue, and red candles. She felt like she was forgetting something, but what? Hopefully, it'd come to her once she got some food in her stomach.

Gabriel was still sleeping when she got home. She watched her for a second before deciding that was probably creepy and went to the desk where the cat's eye necklace remained. She debated with herself whether or not to use it, activating her great-aunt's magic and taking it into herself. On one hand, the more power the better. On the other hand, there was no telling what Grace's magic would do to her. It was strong. She could feel it from across the room. It would take time for her to learn to control it...time they didn't have. No. It was too much of a gamble. She'd leave the amulet where it was. At least, for now. She was confident she could do the spell on her own, no assistance required. As she took the food from its bag and set cans of soda on the table, she hoped she wouldn't regret her decision.

"Hey," Gabriel greeted, sauntering into the kitchen wearing nothing but a tee-shirt. "Yay, food!" She kissed Wendy's cheek and sat down, curling her legs underneath her and shoving a bite of biscuit into her mouth. "You have everything you need?"

"Yeah, my duffel's already packed." She pointed to her bag by the door.

"So prepared."

"Like a boy scout."

"Are you sure you want to do this? It's gonna be hella dangerous."

"I'm sure. I thought about it on the way to get breakfast. What kind of person would I be if I said 'no' to protecting *Heaven*? I mean, really."

"With the threat of getting shot or blown up looming, I'd say 'normal'."

"I'm not normal, though," she smirked.

"Join the club, sister."

They clinked soda cans and drank, their smiles fading as Gabriel held Wendy's hand, kissing the back of it and sighing heavily. "I won't let anything happen to you."

She shook her head. "I don't think you can promise that."

"*Okay*, I promise that if something *does* happen to you, I'll do everything I can to fix it and then take revenge on the dumb son of a bitch that dare lay a hand on you."

She giggled. "I don't doubt that for a second."

They finished eating and moved to the couch, not having to leave for the airport for several hours.

"So, who else is coming? What other angels can I expect to meet today?"

"Lucifer will be there. He's instrumental. He can fly, so we need him to--"

Her jaw dropped. "He can *fly*?"

"Oh, yeah. He'll no doubt whine all the way there about how slow planes are in comparison. Now, he gets a little murdery sometimes, but as long as you don't say anything overtly racist, he won't--"

She chuckled. "Murdery?"

Gabriel shrugged. "Uriel will be there. She likes to be called 'Valerie'. She gets psychic visions sometimes. Kind of judgemental, but funny."

"Not to be a dick, but, how is that helpful in a war?"

"Fiery sword."

She raised her eyebrows. "Oh."

"Then, there's Barachiel, human name Wyatt. His son just died, so be nice."

"Oh, God, that's awful. Wait, angels can have kids?"

"No, not usually."

"Uh, huh. And what's his deal?"

"Protector of Humanity, lightning powers. Then there's his girlfriend."

"I thought you said the angels were like siblings. Oh, gross."

Gabriel erupted in laughter. "No, no. His girlfriend's not one of us. She's a vampire. *Queen* vampire. She's letting us borrow her army to fight off the golem."

"Queen?"

"First of her kind."

They were quiet for a while, the upcoming battle feeling more real as it grew closer. Wendy tapped her bottom lip with her finger. "Is it weird that I'm starting to get excited? Like, giddy, even?"

"Yeah, kind of."

They laughed as Wendy climbed into Gabriel's lap, pinning her to the back of the couch and kissing her playfully. "Do you think we have time to..." She let her voice trail off.

"Oh, we will *make* time."

Valerie decided to get one more practice in before leaving for Iraq, flourishing her sword and moving about the roof of Gabriel's building as if in a choreographed dance. The more she worked with the sword, the more it felt like a part of her, an extension of her arm. It seemed lighter and less cumbersome, easier to control. Once she'd accepted it as hers, once she'd finally fully accepted who she was, the movements came to her like second nature. She was Uriel, Regent of the Sun, Flame of God, Archangel of Salvation. She *would* defend the Gate and cut down any ghoul or goblin that got in her way. Not that she wanted to do it. She couldn't wait for this day to be over. She hadn't gotten much sleep the night before. She'd been too anxious. This wasn't one little-girl-wearing psycho terrorizing frat houses. That had been bad enough. This was an army of freaks, all with two things on their minds: blowing the Gate to shit and slaughtering anyone trying to protect it. She was *not* looking forward to it.

"I see your training has come along nicely." Lucifer leaned against the stone wall next to the door. "Not as well as if you'd let me assist you, but all in all, not too shabby. Pity you have no practical experience."

"I remember enough."

"Do you?" He pulled a sword of his own out from behind him and rushed toward her, raising it above his head and bringing it down hard on her awaiting blade. "Good instincts, sister. Now, let us see how skilled you are when your opponent isn't thin air." He swung again, meeting her sword with a sharp clank. Over and over again he swung at her and over and over again, she deflected. "You seem to have nearly mastered the art of defense. I'm almost impressed." He kept pushing her, switching up his attacks, keeping her on her toes. "Good," he sneered. "Very good, indeed. Now, take an offensive stance."

"What?"

He struck her blade once more. "Come for me."

"I don't--"

He swung again, the force of the blow nearly knocking her down. She righted herself and stared him down, cracking her neck and lifting her blade. "Boy, you have done it now." She flew forward, crashing her sword into his, one furious swing after another sending him reeling back, laughing as he held her off.

"Excellent! Look how far you've come, Uriel. Dare I say, I'm quite proud of you."

She threw her sword down again, this time allowing it to burst into white-hot flame as it met Lucifer's. His eyes grew wide and he scurried backward, putting some distance between himself and the blaze.

"Are you mad?" he admonished, throwing down his sword and folding his arms like a disappointed father.

The flame went out and she sheathed her weapon. "What?"

"Are you trying to kill me just as we're about to go into battle? You do realize the rest of you will *not* be victorious without my help."

"I'm not trying to-- hold up. I thought *nothing* could kill you. God's strongest and whatnot."

"You wield *Holy Fire*. That can kill *anything*. Well, *nearly* anything."

"Really?" she smirked. "That is very interesting information. Good to know. *Good to know.*"

"Don't go getting all high and mighty, sister. You're still incredibly undisciplined and lack the proper footwork to--"

"Why do you continue to hassle me?"

"*I'm helping you.* You may have bested a single golem, but you've never come up against *ten thousand* of them, not even in your true form. You have no idea the danger you're in. While I have every confidence that we will prevail, I am *not* certain that you and the others will make it out of the desert with your heads still attached. Barachiel is the only one of you that can survive such a fate as beheading and *that's* assuming his vampire doesn't get herself killed. You must be prepared."

"Aww, Lucifer. Are you saying you care about me? You gettin' soft?"

He rolled his eyes and let out a sigh of derision.

"Fine. You were helping. But I'm good. Don't you worry your pretty little head."

He growled under his breath.

She giggled. "All right, come on. Let's get something to eat before we go."

"As long as it's real food."

"So, nothing from downstairs."

"Definitely not."

"You should get some sleep," Wyatt said, adjusting his pillow as Allydia rolled back to her side of the bed.

"I'll sleep on the plane. Until we leave, I will cherish you."

His dark eyes lingered on her face as she smiled at him. He tucked her hair behind her ear, sending shivers down her spine, the gentleness of his touch like catnip. "I could stare at you all day."

"And I you," she purred.

"We will have to get out of bed, eventually."

"Yes, *eventually.*"

As he looked at her, his thoughts turned to the upcoming battle. "How dangerous will this be for you?"

"Mild to moderate."

"I'm serious. Are you worried?"

"No."

"No?"

"I've come up against worse and won."

"Worse than an army of unkillable monsters?"

"They're not unkillable to things like me. All one need do is remove the head. My soldiers and I can do that with one hand tied behind our backs. In fact, on one occasion, I had to do just that. I had been vacationing in Santorini, I think it was around the end of the nineteenth century. Beginning of the twentieth? I had gotten a tad reckless, exposed myself. The locals discovered what I was and before I knew it, they had me strapped to a stake. They were cocky, so sure of their vampire hunting abilities. The smug looks on their faces made my blood boil even before the fire was set. The man with the torch made the mistake of getting just a little too close--"

"I feel like I don't want to hear the rest of that story."

"Oh. Then, perhaps you'd like me to tell you about the time I aided the Ottoman Empire in taking down one of my own? It was December 1476. He'd been drawing attention to himself for *years* and the number of dead he left as trophies, just out in the open, was a *clear* violation of my laws. I could not abide it. So, I found him in Bucharest--"

Wyatt shook his head, indicating that he didn't want to hear *that* story, either.

"The Crusades?"

"No."

"Pompeii?"

"Uh, uh."

"Battling the Neph--" She stopped herself.

He gave her a stern look of warning.

"Of course," she said, touching his cheek. "My point is, you don't have to worry about me. I've been taking care of myself for a very long time."

"I know that, but it doesn't change the way I feel."

"And, how do you feel?"

He brought her hand to his lips and closed his eyes, taking in the sweet scent of the perfume she had made from the gardenias that grew in her rooftop garden. It rose from her wrist and enveloped his senses with nearly the same intoxicating quality as her pheromones. His hunger for her again began to build as she moved closer. His mind went foggy as she brushed his chin with her fingertips.

"Wyatt, how do you feel?"

He struggled to speak, her pheromones taking hold. He ran his hand over her body, starting at her neck and gliding his fingers down. "Are you tired?"

"Almost," she breathed, her cheeks flushed and her skin tingling. Her eyes bore into his, the intensity between them growing. "I want you to exhaust me."

Unable to hold back, he threw himself on top of her, spreading her legs wide and entering with more force than usual. She drew in a sharp breath as he buried his face in her hair and kissed her neck, her hands sliding down his back. She writhed against him, hushed moans escaping her lips as her body quaked. All thoughts of the upcoming conflict and inevitable bloodshed fled their minds. At that moment, there was only this room, this bed, and each other. Nothing else mattered.

Chapter 33

Spade and his men had just made camp in the Iraqi desert, taking time to rest before the impending battle. The soldiers moved like robots, never speaking and doing as they were told with efficiency. If things continued to run this smoothly, they'd have their target destroyed and be on their way home by lunch. He didn't want to get too arrogant, though. The scout he'd sent to the apartment of the woman whose clothes he'd put a tracker on had never returned, most likely meaning that he'd been killed. In war, things can go sideways at the drop of a hat. Best not to get too comfortable.

In the distance, he spotted a convoy of pickup trucks heading toward the camp. As they drew closer, he could see the machine guns mounted on them with men in the beds at the ready. Typical Islamic extremist fighters. He'd dealt with these groups dozens of times over the years and prepared himself to talk them down, hoping to avoid a conflict.

The trucks stopped and one man walked toward him, apparently the speaker for the group. He held a rifle but didn't point it at him. Instead, he looked him over, distrust and contempt evident in his eyes. "What are you doing here?" he asked, more of an accusation than a question.

"We've gotten word that a neo-Nazi outfit is here looking to destroy Muslim cultural sites," Spade lied, feeding him the same story he'd told authorities when he'd arrived. "We're here to apprehend them and take them back to the States for prosecution."

The man was clearly skeptical.

"Have you seen this man?" Spade pulled a picture from his pocket and showed it to him. It was of the wounded soldier that hadn't returned from the scouting mission. "We believe he's the ringleader of the operation. Goes by 'Charlie'."

The man shook his head after examining the photo.

"All right, well, we'll be here for a few hours to grab some shut-eye then we'll be out of your hair."

"No," the man insisted. "You will leave now." He raised his hand, signaling the others. They began knocking things over and using knives to tear at the tents the soldiers were sleeping in.

Spade frowned. "We don't want any trouble."

"But, you have found it. We will take your weapons and tanks and leave you to die. That will teach your government to interfere in matters that don't concern them. If there *are* people trying to destroy our history, *we* will handle them, our way."

The commotion woke the soldiers who stumbled out of the tents, their eyes distant. They stood quietly, waiting for orders, unable to make a move without instruction. Thousands of them gathered, silent as the extremists readied their weapons.

"Are you sure you want to die?" Spade asked the leader.

The man scoffed. "It is *you* who wi--"

Spade pulled his side-arm and shot the man in the forehead. "Kill them!"

The soldiers leaped into action, shooting, stabbing, and strangling everyone in the opposition. As they, too, were injured, they kept attacking, ignoring their own bullet wounds. Spade ducked behind an LUV and watched enthusiastically as his men took out the enemy without hesitation. They had no fear, no survival instinct, and seemed incapable of feeling pain. They were murdering machines devoid of emotion or thought. They had a singular goal: to carry out their Commander's orders. Perfect soldiers. "Thank you, Lilith," Spade whispered.

When the dust settled and the last of the extremists was dead, he called to his men, "At ease!" They stopped in their tracks. After assessing the damage, he gave the next order. "Put the bodies in the trucks and confiscate the weapons." The men did as they were told, carrying two corpses at a time to the pickups and throwing them in the beds. They gathered the guns and laid them in a pile at Spade's feet. "Pack up. Once we get moving, we'll IED those sons of bitches." The soldiers got to work with no complaints, some bleeding from the chest, a few spilling blood and brain matter from gaping head wounds. He watched in awe as they labored, the guilt of stripping them of their humanity replaced by excitement. He was confident now that they would have no problem completing their mission and fulfilling his duty to his employer. From there, the sky was the limit. With an army of unkillable soldiers, his business would become even more profitable. Since they were basically robots, they would never need to go home. He may even get away with not paying them. He felt invigorated and was actually looking forward to the next battle.

The men filled the LUV's and DPV's after setting the bombs and as they drove away, the timer ticked down. The last vehicle was less than half a mile away when the timer reached zero, setting off a chain of explosions so loud, Spade worried that more hostiles would show up, causing another conflict. As he looked over the three soldiers in the vehicle with him, stone-faced and diligent, he smiled and said to himself, "Let them come."

Chapter 34

"Who's she talking to?" Wyatt asked, watching Gabriel pace around the back of the plane as he absentmindedly stroked Allydia's hair, her head in his lap as she slept.

"The president of Iraq," Lucifer answered, sitting across from him and next to Wendy. "The area needs to be evacuated."

"How does she plan on getting him to do that?"

"Bribery, I imagine."

"Is she all right?" Wendy wondered, looking at Allydia's motionless face.

"She's fine," Wyatt insisted.

"It doesn't look like she's breathing."

"That's because she's a vampire," Lucifer informed her.

"Well, sure." She looked her over, head tilted and eyebrows furrowed.

"What?" Wyatt scowled.

"Nothing, I just didn't think they'd be so *hot*. I had this whole pale, sunken in cheeks, Nosferatu picture in my head. Also, I'm a little surprised they don't sleep in coffins."

Lucifer chuckled. "I like this one."

"We should *all* be getting some sleep," Valerie interjected from across the aisle. "Thousands of what-the-fucks aren't gonna kill *themselves* and I don't know about you, but I want to be alert when I get to head-chopping."

Wendy smiled. "You're amazing."

"All right, kids," Gabriel said, sitting across from Valerie and putting her phone in her bag. "He's evacuating a fifty-mile radius. Should be plenty to prevent any civilian casualties."

"How much did that cost you?" Lucifer inquired.

"Two million."

"Holy crap!" Wendy gasped.

"It's all right, love," Lucifer told her. "My sister has nearly limitless funds. Inherited wealth, you understand. She didn't tell you?"

She shook her head.

Gabriel shot him a look. "It's not important."

"Of course not," he smirked. "But, seeing as how you've yet to tell any of us how exactly you came to acquire your family fortune, one can't help but wonder."

"I didn't kill my parents, dick."

"No, I wouldn't think so. But, *something* happened to them and your refusal to discuss it must mean that their deaths weren't purely natural."

Wyatt stared him down. "Do I have to get up?"

Lucifer raised his eyebrow.

"Can we focus?" Valerie snapped. "You all know we're heading into a war zone, right? We're about to be knee-deep in zombie-soldiers shooting at us, armed with nothing but a sword, some crystals, fireworks, and a bunch of blood-suckers who, for the life of me, I can't figure out why they'd be helping us. Exactly why in the ever-loving fuck are you bickering right now?"

The group was silent for a moment before Lucifer snorted. "They're not 'zombies'. They're *alive*, just--"

"Are you *fucking* kidding me?"

"Okay, there's obviously some tension here, so," Wendy waved her hand at them. "Somnus."

Wyatt, Valerie, and Lucifer fell unconscious as Gabriel beamed. "You're the best thing ever."

"Really?" she flirted, gliding across the aisle and into the seat next to her. "You wanna maybe," she slid her hand up Gabriel's thigh. "Spend some quality time?"

"They could wake up."

"Not for eight solid hours. The plane could burst into flames, crash into the ocean. We could all get eaten by sharks. They'd sleep right through it. There are about ten hours left on this flight. That gives them all kinds of time to wake up, eat and prepare themselves."

"Eat?"

She pointed to her duffel in the overhead compartment. "I brought snacks."

Gabriel grabbed her face and grinned. "Damn it, you *are* the best." She kissed her and began fiddling with her belt buckle. "What's this pants crap?"

They woke up to the sound of individual chip bags being placed in front of them on treys. Bottles of water and sandwiches accompanied them. "It's crunchy peanut butter with strawberry jam because that's my favorite," Wendy informed them. "I also have chocolates for dessert."

"Well, aren't you two perfect for each other?" Lucifer quipped. "Shared unhealthy eating habits as well as a penchant for using your powers against the rest of us."

"I'm sorry," she claimed. "But you were all too rowdy. Snapping at each other, being rude. Valerie was right, you needed a nap."

"Who are you?" Allydia asked, having fallen asleep before Wendy had boarded the plane.

"Gabriel's new playmate," Lucifer told her.

"Girlfriend," Gabriel corrected.

"Really?" Allydia asked. "I didn't think you were capable of monogamy, Messenger. Are you finding it difficult?"

"No."

"It's okay if you are," Wendy assured her. "Allydia, I made a sandwich for you, too, but Gabriel just told me you can't eat regular food."

"That's all right, I brought my own." She pulled a blood bag from the cooler next to her and began to drink.

Wyatt averted his eyes. "Still not used to that."

"Thanks for the food," Valerie said through a mouthful of chips. "But, don't fuck with me like that again."

"Cross my heart," Wendy giggled.

They ate in silence for the next several minutes, all of them anxious about the upcoming battle. All except Wyatt, who no longer *wanted* to die, but wasn't one hundred percent against it, either.

The jet landed in the middle of the desert, as per Gabriel's instructions. The planes carrying the army of vampires were already there and as Allydia headed toward the door to leave, she turned to address Lucifer. "Would you mind?"

"Not at all." He exited first and looked up to the midday sky. He took a deep breath and as he exhaled, the sky became overcast with thick, dark clouds. Now safe from the sun's radiation, Allydia went to join her general and assemble her soldiers.

"Neat," Wendy approved as she and Gabriel stepped onto the sand.

"You're not the only one with tricks up their sleeves."

"You ready for this?" Valerie asked as she and Wyatt walked to meet the others.

"Not at all," he admitted.

"Yeah, me, neither."

They made the short hike to the ruins of ancient Babylon. As they drew closer, the ground became greener. There were palm trees and shrubbery all fed by the Euphrates River.

"You can set up right here," Gabriel told Wendy, who nodded and began placing large amethysts in a circle.

"So, this is Babylon," she said. "Pretty."

"It's buried a few miles down. Is that an issue?"

"Not as long as I'm right on top of it." She poured the Goofer Dust around the stones and set candles in between. "Crap in a hat!"

"What?"

"I didn't bring a lighter. I knew I was forgetting something."

Gabriel chuckled. "Girl, I got you." She waved her hand, lighting all the candles at once.

"Goddamn, you are *handy*."

"And here come the vampires," Valerie groaned, leaning on her sword. The others turned to see thousands of the creatures, somehow their allies, headed toward them, Allydia and another woman in the lead.

"They really *will* do anything she asks," Wyatt said.

"You just figuring that out now?" Gabriel asked.

"I told you," Lucifer groused. "They worship her. They revere her as a mother, savior, judge, jury, and executioner. She's a god to them. It's disgusting."

"Don't start," Gabriel warned.

In the distance, they could see them coming; the military vehicles approached like a herd of wild horses, loud and fast. Valerie lifted her sword, igniting it in a burst of flames. Wyatt began gathering energy from the blackened sky and Lucifer clenched his fists.

Wendy got on her knees in the center of the circle and began to chant, "Praesidio in loco isto."

"Get ready, kids," Gabriel said, stepping forward. "Shit's about to get dicey."

Chapter 35

Allydia stopped and faced her soldiers, an army of the undead, ready to kill or be killed for their Queen. They halted and knelt before her as she began to address them, none of them looking her in the eyes.

"My finest warriors, you humble me with your willingness to fight. You honor me with your sacrifice. I am proud beyond words to call you my children. Some of you may die here today, far from home and for a cause you may not see as your own. Take solace in the fact that what you do here is just and I am grateful for your contribution. Take pride in knowing that until your dying day, you served your Queen well and you will not be forgotten."

The crowd cheered, standing as she turned away. "Assume your positions!" Phindi called.

Lucifer stepped away from his siblings to speak into Allydia's ear as she approached. "If anything happens to my brother, I will hold you personally responsible."

"If anything happens to your brother, I will rip out my own heart with my bare hands."

As a swarm of drones flew overhead, Lucifer rocketed up to meet them, swatting them into each other, exploding them in the sky above. When the last craft was disabled, he moved on to the vehicles, pouncing on them and lifting them up before dropping them on the enemy soldiers below. He was a one-man army, plowing through LUV's, tanks, and DPV's. All that was left were the golem themselves, which he was useless against in his host body. He rejoined the others as Wyatt pulled bolts of white-hot lightning from the clouds and threw them into the crowd. The army of monsters was stunned, but got up and kept coming.

"Well, that's unsettling," he complained.

"Stay behind me," Allydia instructed.

"I can take care of myself."

"Nothing living can harm them. If they get close, I'm the only one here that can protect you."

"Ready!" they heard Phindi shout. The vampires were in formation, stationed between the Gate and the golem. As the enemy got closer, the vampire general raised her hand. Her soldiers nearly vibrated with excitement, hungry for the fight that was to come. "Remember, if you can't get their heads off, just the bottom lip will do!" The general dropped her arm. "Attack!"

The vampires raced to the opposition, hacking off heads with swords as bullets began to fly. Vampires carrying no weapons flung themselves on enemy combatants like spider monkeys, tearing the bottom lips from their vacant faces and watching in amazement when they fell.

"How is that killing them?" Wyatt wondered.

Lucifer folded his arms. "They've been marked with the Word of God, enslaving them to the one whose blood was used in the ritual. One of Lilith's spells. Always with the blood magic, that one. She was obsessed with trading one life for another. Or many. Isn't that right, Your Majesty?"

Allydia shot him a look.

"The Word of God?" Wyatt asked.

Lucifer nodded. "One of His names. Considered sacred by humans of certain religions, though it matters little to Him what people choose to call Him. Imagine if the bacteria in your gut had a name for you. Would you mind?"

Suddenly, an explosion boomed above them, the grenade crashing into the invisible wall Wendy's protection spell had put in place. It was hit with another and another and Wendy's arms began to shake as she chanted louder, the shield weakening with every blow.

The fighting between the two armies continued. Vampires were slaughtered en masse with bullets through the heart. Golem were torn to shreds by vengeful vampires. The battle drew closer to the Gate and as the wall began to thin, a stray bullet got through, hitting Wendy in her liver. She bled out and as the light from her stormy eyes faded, the wall dissolved, leaving the Gate and the siblings vulnerable.

"Wendy!" Gabriel cried, rushing to her girlfriend's side. She pulled the bullet from her body with her mind and placed her hands on the wound. Her skin glowed and the wound slowly healed, but her eyes remained closed. "Wake up. Please, wake up." Gabriel's heart pounded in her ears and her mind raced. She thought she might hyperventilate. "Lucifer,"

"Yes, sister?" he answered, crouching next to her.

She looked at him, the fear in her eyes unsettling him. He'd never seen her afraid. She choked back tears, her voice shaky as she spoke. "I think I'm in love with her."

"Oh, fuck this shit," Valerie blurted, stepping outside the circle and swinging her flame-engulfed sword, lopping the heads off every golem she came across. Wyatt, too, stepped away from the group, throwing balls of lightning at the soldiers as they swarmed.

"Remember what I said," Lucifer warned, jumping up and grabbing Allydia by the arm.

She shot back, "Wyatt is the most important thing to me in this world. I will not fail him." She went after her beloved, planting herself between him and the monsters.

Horror covered the face of one of the vampires, seeing his Queen put a human before her own kind, before her own life, filling him with anger and disgust. He ran off, deserting her and her cause, unwilling to risk himself for a Queen whose heart was not fully with him and his people.

"Please be okay," Gabriel whispered as she put her ear to Wendy's heart. She couldn't hear over the sounds of the battlefield. She pressed harder but nothing. She put her fingers to her wrist to feel for a pulse. It was there. Faint, but there. After a few seconds, it got stronger and she opened her eyes.

"You were right, dying is *really* unpleasant."

"Are you okay?" Gabriel fretted.

"I think so," she said, struggling to stand.

"Stay here. Get the spell back up if you can."

"Where are you going?"

"To fight," she said, marching toward the action. "I'm in a mood." She raised her hands, determination and rage coloring her face. As she concentrated, the remaining golem burst into flames. It didn't kill them. They carried on, shooting and fending off vampires. Eventually, the flames went out, Gabriel being alive rendering her powers all but useless against them.

"It was you," Wyatt realized. "In the theater with Lilith's demons. *You* killed those people."

"Lecture me about it later." Just then, Spade came barreling through the crowd, pistol drawn, a smug grin plastered on his five o'clock shadow-covered face.

"We meet again," he smirked, pulling the trigger and shooting her twice in the stomach.

Allydia held Wyatt back as he tried to rush him. "She will heal."

"And you," Spade scoffed, approaching Lucifer. "Flying. Impressive. Let's see if you can survive a straight shot to the temple."

As he pointed the gun at Lucifer's face, the shot ringing out and the bullet being released, they heard Wendy cry out, "Subsisto!" The bullet stopped in mid-air and fell to the ground between the two men. Lucifer sneered.

"How is that possible?!" Spade spat.

"He's the one that can't be hurt by supernatural creatures?" Wendy asked.

Lucifer nodded.

"Interesting spell. My grandmother told me about a witch who could work it, back in the day. Not easy."

Spade shot again, and again, while Wendy easily stopped the bullets. "What are you people?!"

"There's no way to straight remove it," Wendy continued. "All you can do is," She held her hand out, palm facing him, and flicked her wrist, pointing her fingers toward herself. "Transuerso."

"What did you do?" Spade demanded.

Lucifer stepped toward him, his face twisted in an evil grin. He slapped him and laughed. "She shifted the warding to herself. I knew a Tituban witch would come in handy. A lesson for you, Wendy. My Father will occasionally put people in our lives for a purpose. As for you, Mr. Spade, sadly, your time here has passed."

The general tried to run, but Lucifer snatched him by the hair. "A coward on top of everything else? Shameful." He threw him to the ground.

"Lucifer," Gabriel called, clutching her bleeding gut, unable to move from where she'd fallen as she healed.

He gave her a sideways glance in acknowledgment.

Through heavy breaths, she all but ordered him, "Make it hurt."

He smiled again and returned his gaze to the fallen general. "As you wish, sister." He tore off Spade's right arm first, assuring he wouldn't be firing his gun again. He plucked off the other, then his legs, reveling in the savagery of it. He was nearly laughing as blood sprayed in all directions.

Spade howled, the pain so intense it brought tears to his eyes. "My employer won't stop!" he swore. "He'll find another way! He *will* destroy this place!"

Gabriel walked up, inspecting the holes in her shirt. She sighed and stood over him, looking him in the eye. "You let *me* worry about Cain."

Lucifer plunged his hand into Spade's gut, pulling out intestines like a magician pulling scarves from his sleeve. The man convulsed, blood sputtering from his mouth. He went ghostly white, his eyes glazing over. Finally, he stopped moving, the life leaving him. When he was dead, the last of the golem fell, their lives having been intertwined with his. The battle was over.

Chapter 36

Only nine hundred vampires remained. They lined up their fallen and paid their respects, Allydia and Phindi watching as they said goodbye.

"Africa," the Queen told her general. "The entire continent. And the Middle East. They're yours now."

"Your Majesty?"

"Duchess Phindi, Ruler of The Old World's, yours *and* mine. Second only to me, you answer to none of my Governors anywhere in the world."

"That is too great of an honor, my Queen."

"You deserve it. You've proven yourself loyal and worthy. You're strong. A leader."

"I am humbled. It is a privilege."

"It's what you've earned." She held back the urge to shed tears as she watched her people mourn. "Do you know how old I am?"

"You are the first of our kind. I assume you must be thousands of years old."

"Yes. Almost as old as humanity itself. I've seen wars, famine, and plague. I've seen the rise and fall of nations and empires. Through it all, I've maintained our way of life. *Us*, the vampiric race. I've kept us out of human affairs, for the most part, separating us from their petty skirmishes. But, *this*...I couldn't ignore this."

"May I ask why, my Queen?"

"The people I traveled with, you saw what they can do?"

"The man that wields lightning as a weapon? The woman that heals herself from death?"

Allydia nodded. "They're not *strictly* human. They're something else, something older. It devastates me to see my people die and more to see the ones that did not suffer the loss. But, these people speak for something higher. I could not refuse them."

"Higher? What could be higher than *you*, my Queen?"

"Only one thing."

She was taken aback. "You speak of a Creator?"

"We called Him 'Elohim'. I thought my father had invented Him. An easy explanation for the things in life he couldn't account for. I only believed him after my stepmother made me this."

"You talk of *God*."

She nodded.

"I don't know what to say."

"You'll say nothing. I trust only *you* with this."

"Why not tell the others? Forgive me, my Queen, but this is--"

"The ability to believe what one wishes without actually *knowing* keeps people sane," she told her. "I'm old enough to remember a time when God spoke directly to humans. They took His words out of context, bastardized His commands, killed each other for the right to call themselves His. The only true difference between us and the humans is that we feel more deeply. Imagine the zealotry that could emerge, the harm they could do to each other. Better God remain a vague idea than something tangible to be acquired like love or fear. You will keep this to yourself, yes? My faith in you has not been misplaced?"

"Of course, Your Majesty. I serve at your pleasure. And...do you serve God?"

She laughed. "I serve no one. But I do respect Him."

The vampires boarded the planes, leaving their comrades where they lay. Allydia joined them and they took off, heading quickly back to the States.

Once she was sure the vampires were out of sight range, Gabriel waved her hand at the makeshift memorial, then at the pile of golem, setting ablaze the thousands of bodies, Spade's mangled corpse thrown in with his soldiers, his dead eyes seeming to stare her down as they burned.

Back on the jet, Valerie curled up in a window seat and closed her eyes. "Hey, witch, any chance of getting another one of those power naps?"

Wendy giggled. "I thought you said--"

"Girl, I know what I said, but I'm tired as hell."

"All right, then. Somnus."

Valerie passed out, a light snore the only sound she made for the rest of the trip.

"So, problem solved?" Lucifer asked.

"For now," Gabriel told him.

"Wonderful," he rejoiced. "I should like to visit a certain bartender. It's been some time since--"

"I am begging you not to finish that sentence."

Wendy took her arm and led her to the back of the plane, out of her brother's view.

The two men sat quietly for a time until Wyatt's curiosity got the better of him. "You were willing to take the fall for what I did to Will. Why?"

Lucifer raised his eyebrows and sat back in his seat. "Your personality is quite volatile. You aren't always rational. I thought the knowledge of what you'd done would torment you, push you over the edge. I was right."

"I could have killed you."

He laughed. "You could have *what*? At *full power,* you couldn't kill me, much less in this meat puppet you're wearing."

"Still,"

"You already weren't very fond of me. Hating me would have been easy and I would have allowed it to spare your precious human emotions."

"Why?"

"Because that's what brothers do."

After a long silence, Wyatt spoke again. "You're God's favorite."

"So they say."

"So you know Him, what He's like?"

"If memory serves."

Wyatt let out a breath and looked into his brother's eyes. "Does He hate me?"

"What? Of course not. He doesn't hate anyone, especially His Protector of Humanity. You're special to Him, as am I and Gabriel and--"

"Did I do something to make Him angry? Did I offend Him somehow?"

He snickered. "Contrary to social media's comments sections, our Father isn't offended by much of anything."

"Then, why would He allow this? I know He's asleep or whatever, but Gabriel told me He made it *impossible*, so how did it happen? *Why* did it happen? Why would He give me a son only to turn around and take him away from me?"

Lucifer didn't know how to answer that, but he'd brought up a good point. "I don't know, brother."

Wyatt wiped away a stray tear. "It's not right."

"No," he agreed. "No, I don't believe it is."

Chapter 37

Gabriel watched the girl playing in the front yard. Her mother was inside, grief-stricken, leaving the child alone as not to burden her with her tears.

"Jenny," Gabriel said as she approached. The girl looked up and Gabriel studied her; she seemed unafraid, naively trusting. She took her hand and urged her to sit on the ground next to her, which she did. "I'm sorry about your dad. He loved you very much. He prayed every day that you'd get better. That's why I'm here. To make you better."

The girl didn't seem to understand. She continued playing with the blocks, all but ignoring the stranger's presence.

"I'm gonna touch your head now," Gabriel warned. "It'll feel weird for a second while I repair some connections in your brain, but when it's over, you'll be good as new, okay? Here I go." She placed her hands on the girl's temples, lighting up the skin on her face. Her eyes grew wide and she dropped the toys, the light stinging sensations surprising her. Her eyes rolled back and her bottom lip quivered as every vein in her face became visible. After a few moments of concentration, Gabriel took her hands away, satisfied with the healing. "How do you feel?"

The girl looked at her, directly this time, shock and gratitude in her eyes. "Ah," she croaked. "I feel like I'm here. Really *here*. What are you?"

"Angel. Don't tell anyone, though. They'll think you're crazy. Just tell your mom you hit your head. She won't question it. They'll call it 'a miracle'."

She nodded.

"I'm gonna go before someone sees me. Remember," she covered her lips with her finger as if to say, 'shh'. The girl nodded again.

As Gabriel stood and walked away, she could hear the girl yell, "Mom! Mom!" Once across the street, she turned to look as the woman rushed outside and fell to her knees, tears spilling down her already puffy cheeks. The two embraced and Gabriel left, her guilt over Spade fading. He may have been an evil piece of shit, but he *was* human. Healing his daughter seemed like a good enough way to right things. Hopefully, when she saw her Father again, He wouldn't be too terribly upset with her.

Chapter 38

Hattie placed a log on the fire. The Highlands could feel chilly, even in the summer, especially in old stone buildings like this one.

The man struggled to free himself, but she'd tied the ropes tight around him and the chair he sat on. He wasn't going anywhere. Screams from the next room drowned out his muffled pleas as she released the valve on his IV, allowing his blood to flow into the awaiting glass. Tears fell from his eyes as she replaced the valve.

"Stop complaining," she dismissed. "I already told you I'm not going to kill you. When you've lost so much blood, you'll pass out, I'll drop you at the pub and the barmaid will call a doctor. You'll be fine."

He cried through the gag in his mouth.

"Come now, I can't just let her die, can I? It's not as though she's in a condition to feed herself." She patted him on the back and left him there, scurrying to get the fresh blood to her friend before it went cold. "Here we are." She held the glass to Michelle's mouth and she drank, unquenchable thirst driving her nearly to the point of madness. She was drenched in sweat, exhausted, and in pain. The blood helped, but it wasn't enough.

"I need more," Michelle breathed.

"I told you, only so much at a time. If we drain him too quickly--"

"More!" she bellowed.

"All right, all right. Here," she held her wrist out. "Take some of mine. It's not the same, but it'll hold you over until we can tap Callum again."

Michelle's pupils dilated and her fangs grew. She bit down hard into her friend's wrist, greedily taking as much as would come. After a few moments, Hattie yanked her arm away. "That's enough, now." She got the towel from the bowl of water on the nightstand and wiped it over Michelle's forehead. The girl fell back into the pillows, letting the sense of relief wash over, knowing it was only temporary.

"Why?" Michelle whimpered.

"I don't know, dear. We've had this conversation already. I'm not the person to ask. Almost over now."

Another wave of excruciating pain gripped her, this time accompanied by a puddle of blood seeping from her nightgown to the bedsheets. She cried out in anguish as Hattie went to the end of the bed and lifted the gown. "It's time, girl."

"No. I can't. This isn't right."

"Right or not, it's happening. Now, pull yourself together and push!"

CAIN

He who has a why to live can bear almost any how.
Friedrich Nietzche

Prologue

"I will call her Thaddea because she is my heart," Allydia said, her voice barely above a whisper as the light in her eyes began to fade. She looked down at her newest daughter and smiled.

"You are pale," Lilith fussed. "There is too much blood. Your father will not forgive me if I let you die."

"But I *am* dying. There is nothing you can do. He will understand."

"He will leave me."

"Perhaps he can ask his God, this Elohim he claims to worship, to save me," she smirked.

"I wouldn't mock such things if I were you, girl."

"Tell Farhan I am sorry. I failed to give him a son...again. You will help him, won't you? Help care for my daughters?"

"I will not have to," Lilith insisted.

"I can feel death's grip tight around my throat. The dark fog of him shrouds the room. I am leaving this world."

"You are not." But as she said the words, her step-daughter's eyes rolled back and closed. Her chest, once heaving as she labored to breathe, fell and went still. She was gone.

Lilith gathered the baby in her arms, left the birthing tent, and presented her husband with his grandchild.

"A girl," she told him. "To be called Thaddea."

Cain took the infant, gave her an approving nod, and handed her back.

"Forgive me, husband, but your daughter..."

"My daughter what?" he snapped.

She took a step back. "She is gone."

Cain's eyes flashed and his jaw tightened. He turned toward his son-in-law sleeping next to the fire and pounced. He pulled him up by the hair and began punching him. The startled man backed away and put his hand to his jaw, the look of confusion on his face driving Cain further into madness.

"You knew this would happen!" he spat. "You knew a woman in her thirty-first year can not withstand childbirth, yet you insisted. You forced her to endure this *again* because *you wanted a son.* Now, you still have no son and I have no daughter. *You took her from me* and I will make you suffer for it." He grasped Farhan's throat and squeezed until his hand cramped. His heart pounded in his ears as he allowed the rage to overtake him. The man tried to fight back, but as he struggled, he caught a glimpse inside the tent where his wife's body lay. As his heart broke, he accepted his punishment, the thought of living without her too much to bear.

Cain pulled a knife from his belt. "I will ensure you never get what you want." With three quick strokes, he cut through the man's genitals, mutilating them beyond use and causing him to bleed out. "I only wish your death to be slower and more painful than hers." He dropped Farhan to the sandy ground and kicked him in the ribs before entering the tent. There, he saw his daughter, ashen and lifeless, and fell to his knees.

"My sons have all left me," he sobbed as Lilith followed him inside. "She followed me here to Eridu so I wouldn't be alone. She gave me grandchildren. She befriended you the moment I announced our marriage. She was kind, even when I showed her no mercy. She is the only one of my children that doesn't despise me. She deserves better than this." He looked up at his wife, tears streaming down his face. "Is this another one of His punishments? Banishing me from my home, compelling me to wander, never able to settle...is that not enough? Does He hate me this much?"

"It's unlikely my Father has thought of you in years." She placed the baby again in his arms. "He tends to put a plan in motion and move on, having His minions do His work for Him." She knelt next to him and put a comforting hand on his shoulder. "I could bring her back if you like."

"With your magic?" he sneered, rocking the quiet baby as she slept.

"Yes. Powerful blood magic. It would have to be done quickly, before her soul reaches Heaven."

"Are you serious?"

"Deadly. But," she pushed the blanket away from Thaddea's face. "It would require a sacrifice."

Cain's expression turned dark as he realized what she was getting at. "Farhan is near death already. *He* will--"

"It must be a blood relative."

"Then take my life. It's not as though I won't return."

"That is precisely why it can not be you. It is no sacrifice if a life is not extinguished...permanently."

Tears again filled his eyes as his pain clouded his judgement. "She will hate me."

"She never has to know. We'll tell her the child died. It happens all the time. Two of her own children were stillborn. One died in her crib. It won't be a terrible shock." She stood and looked the body over, seeing the soul start to slip away. "It is up to you, my love, but it is the only way and if I am to save her, I must do it now."

He stood, looking from the baby to his daughter. "If you do this, how long will she live? Twenty years? Thirty? Or will she succumb to sickness in a few months and this was all for nothing?"

"Forever," she promised. "I'll take not just the life force of the child, but of all future generations that would have been. An infinite number of souls will fuel her existence. She will never have to leave us."

"Forever? Are you sure?"

"Only an act of God will be able to snuff her out."

He looked down one more time at the child in his arms before handing her over. "All right," he agreed, wiping the tears from his face. "Do what you must. Just bring my daughter back to me."

He left the tent, unable to watch what came next. He looked in on his three granddaughters sleeping soundly in their own tent a few yards away. Allydia would survive the loss of the child for the sake of the others. Most importantly, *she would survive*. He walked back, warming himself by the fire, glaring at his son-in-law who was still somehow not quite dead. He paced, hands on his hips as he waited. Finally, Lilith stepped out of the tent.

"It worked. Just, not exactly how I intended."

"What does that mean?"

"As I was doing the spell, I discovered that the child would only have three generations after her. Our Allydia would die in seventy years. That was not what I promised you, so I improvised." She held a cup next to Farhan's neck and slit his throat, blood filling the chalice, the man already so close to death that he could not object. "This," she explained. "Will be what sustains her. The blood of others will replace food and drink. *Life* in liquid form. There will be side effects, but--"

"What kind of side effects?"

"Aversion to sunlight, firstly. It will tire her, make her weak. But, she'll be strong in the night. Almost as strong as me, and fast. Men will fall at her feet, catering to her every desire, of which there will be many. The hardest thing will be controlling her blood-lust. She will crave it like air and will do anything to get it."

He felt nauseous.

"Don't worry," she tried to reassure him. "I will guide her, show her how to use her new abilities and how to stifle herself when needed. She is back with us and that is all that matters, yes?"

He stared as she reentered the tent, watching in horror as his wife held the cup to his daughter's lips. She drank hungrily, her pupils dilating until the entirety of the irises had gone black.

He gasped and backed away. "Dear God, what have I done?" he whispered, crumpling to the ground and gazing into the fire. "Forgive me, Grandfather. My grief has made me a fool and a contributor to evil. I have made her a killer, just as I am, but worse. I am unforgiving and brutal but she will be a rabid animal, unable to be contained. She'll be something dark, born of the witch's black magic. I should have known better, Grandfather. I should have--" He stopped, the rustling from the children's tent snapping him to attention. He jumped up and ran to them, his still innocent granddaughters. They slept, unaware of what had befallen their family that night. "They won't be safe," he muttered to himself. His heart raced and his breathing quickened as he took them from their beds, gently as not to wake them. He piled them in the cart and made sure it was fixed tight to the donkey's harness. He led them away, fleeing the city, never to return.

Allydia pulled her sword from the fallen Nephilim and turned to face another as he barreled toward her. Stone-faced and with an exasperated sigh, she lifted her weapon and swung, slicing off her would-be attacker's head with minimal effort. She trekked up the hill to get a better vantage point and assessed the situation. The battle raged on, her vampires making quick work of taking down the Nephilim menace. As the torrent of rain poured, ankle-deep water mixed with blood caused a sea of red to rise over her enemies' bodies. She smirked as she began her descent. She'd won. But as she reveled in her presumptive victory, the dead began to wake. She looked on in horror as they stood, again reaching for their weapons and attempting their assault. She cracked her neck, raised her sword, and raced to the field. Just as she skidded to a stop in front of a seven-foot-tall Nephilim holding the severed head of her general, the rain stopped. The monster was gone. Her army had disappeared. The muddied battlefield was replaced by a rocky landscape with grass so green, she could see its brilliant color even in the moonlight. Before her was a lake mirroring the starry sky and in the distance, she could see a snow-capped mountain.

"What trickery is this?" she wondered aloud, taking in her new surroundings.

"Not trickery," a voice from behind her spoke. "I simply moved you, for your own safety."

She spun around to look her kidnapper in the eye. "Who are you?"

"My name is Gabriel. I'm an angel of the Lord your God. I apologize if I frightened you. That was not my intention."

"An angel? Like Lilith?"

"*Not* like Lilith."

"Why have you brought me to this place? Where are we?"

Gabriel appeared to take a deep breath as she looked around, though Allydia heard no sounds of life come from her. No heartbeat, no air moving through her lungs. It was as if the woman before her was made of pure light. The angel smiled. "They call it, 'Tarshish'. Beautiful, isn't it?"

"I demand you take me back. The Nephilim--"

"Are being handled."

"Handled?"

"It is not your fight," Gabriel insisted.

"It most certainly *is* my fight. Do you know what they have done? They consume everything they come across. They starve the humans, that is when they're not slaughtering them en masse. Those people are my people's food. Without them, we will die. That is why I declared war on the Nephilim scourge. I *must* defeat them."

"Worry not. My Father is purging them from the Earth as we speak." She cast her a quizzical glare. "The rain?"

"The rain."

"But, everyone else. My people. The humans."

"A temporary loss. The souls will all be reborn, over time."

"Why spare me, then?"

"My Father commanded it. Your assistance will be required in a future altercation. Your stepmother will escape from her prison and He'll need you and an army of your kind to fight against her and those that follow her."

Allydia scoffed. "Why would I help Elohim in a fight against Lilith? He didn't save me from death, *she* did. He cursed my father. He let four of my children die."

"Three," the angel corrected. "He allowed *three* of your children to die. The fourth was not His doing."

"Thaddea--"

"Would have lived a long and healthy life. She would have had children and grandchildren. She didn't *die*. Lilith killed her."

She took a step back. "You're lying."

"I'm not. She would have done anything to prevent Cain from leaving her. She has a fear of being alone. Men give her a sense of stability. So, she brought you back as a gift to him, knowing that he wouldn't forgive her for allowing you to perish. She sacrificed the child in the spell that forced your soul back into your body."

"How could you know this?"

"I know anything God wants me to know. I'm His Messenger."

"So, does He want me to know this? So I'll help Him?"

"He wants you to know the truth. What you do with it is up to you, but there *is* an incentive."

Allydia folded her arms and raised an eyebrow.

"Your father took your daughters. He married them off and they were lost to you. Generations have passed and you have no way of tracking their descendants. But, God does. He knows where they are and if you help Him--"

"He will tell me." Her features softened and tears began to form in her eyes.

"In a few thousand years, I will come to you again. I'll look different and my speech will be riddled with expletives as I'll be born as a human, but my knowledge will remain. I'll tell you then that the time has come for you to do your part. When Lilith and her soldiers have all been defeated, I will give you the location of your remaining descendants. I won't know until the war is over, but as soon as I do, I *will* tell you."

She wiped away a stray tear and looked the angel over, her oddly pale skin seeming to glow and her fiery hair somehow still in the cool breeze. "I accept Elohim's terms. I will help Him."

"In that case, I look forward to our next meeting."

"Dia," a voice whispered in the dark. "Dia, wake up." The light came on, jolting the vampire from her sleep. She knew without opening the curtains that it was still day.

"Who dare--"

"It's me, Gabriel," the woman said, sitting next to her in her bed. "It's time to get this party started."

"Messenger?" Allydia asked, looking the woman over. "You *do* look different."

"I know, right? I was going for a whole ethereal, otherworldly thing back in the day. Thought it would drive home the point, you know? Me angel, you Jane. Sorry to wake you up and everything, but if I tried to sneak in here at night, somebody would *definitely* try to eat me, and not in the fun way." She handed her a piece of paper. "This is my number. Lilith hasn't Shawshanked it just yet, but when she does, she'll be bringing a bunch of demons with her, so keep an eye out and call me if you see any. Nice club. Reminds me of high school, all goth and shit. I was more of a hippy myself, you know, hemp necklaces, flannel. Now, though, I alternate between classy and sophisticated and tight jeans and band T-shirts. Depends on my mood. Anyway, it's a nice little empire you've built for yourself. I'm gonna skedaddle. The sun'll be down in about five minutes and I don't want to be here when the creepy-crawlies wake up. Have some fun tonight. Relax. Pretty soon, things are gonna get bloody and not in the way you like."

She watched Gabriel leave the room, scowling as she set the paper on the nightstand. She'd had almost five thousand years to rethink the decision to aid God in his battle against her stepmother. She'd gone over it again and again and the more she'd thought about it, the angrier she became. Lilith murdered her youngest daughter and her father had stolen the rest. They should both be in the ground as far as she was concerned. Now, finally, her chance at revenge on her stepmother was soon at hand. She leaned back into her pillows, a wicked grin creeping across her face. She took the brush from the drawer and ran it through her hair as she said to herself, "Not long now."

Chapter 1

The bullets whizzing by as she crouched behind a display of snack cakes didn't faze Yara, a decade on the force having given her nerves of steel. Her partner had the lookout cuffed and was using him as a shield as he barked orders at the two gunmen, one shooting at the officers from the center of the store and the other with a gun to the clerk's head, demanding to be let go.

"Drop your weapons!"

"Suck my dick, pig!" the first gunman shouted, again shooting in his general direction.

"Drop your weapons, now!"

"We just wanna get out of here," the second man said. "We don't wanna hurt nobody."

"Could've fooled me," Officer Jackson said, his eyes plastered to the first shooter.

"That's just Popcorn," the lookout told him. "He ain't been right since cops killed his daddy."

"Why you sayin' my name, bro?"

"Why you shootin' at *cops*?"

"You on their side?"

"Yo, I didn't sign up for this. Y'all told me this was 'bout to be easy money. You said there wasn't even bullets in your guns."

"You bought that?" the officer chortled.

"Hey! No one's talking to you!" Shots rang out again, bullets bursting bottles of wiper fluid and bags of chips as the clerk squeezed his eyes shut in fear. The gunman had had enough. He only had a few bullets left and he wanted to make them count. He strode out of his hiding spot and raised his weapon, shooting Officer Jackson in the shoulder and busting out the glass of the door behind him. The officer dropped his gun and fell back, losing his grip on the lookout.

"Fuck this," he said, running from the building, hands still cuffed behind him.

"Not so talkative now, are you pig?" Popcorn stood over the policeman, gun cocked, but before he could pull the trigger, a shot rang out from behind. He went to turn around but realized he couldn't. He'd been hit. He fell, blood soaking through the back of his white tee-shirt, the gun clanking on the floor.

"Jackson, you all right?" Yara asked as she edged toward the counter, her eyes fixed on the remaining gunman.

"Yeah, Rocha, I'm fine." The officer sat up, covering his wound and catching his breath.

"You look pale."

"I'm Black."

"You need an ambulance. Call it in, I got this."

"Stay back, lady," the gunman warned. "I'll shoot him, I swear to God."

"I believe you. Put down your weapon." She inched closer.

"I said stay back!"

"So, your friend's name was Popcorn. I have *got* to hear the story behind that."

"Lady,"

"Was he corny with a tendency of popping people or did he just really like movies?"

"Bitch, I said get back!" He turned his gun on her, releasing the clerk who dropped to the ground and covered his ears. Without hesitation, she mowed him down, emptying her clip into his chest. He fell in a heap next to the clerk who screamed and scurried away.

"A little excessive, don't you think?" Jackson commented.

"What?" She holstered her weapon, feigning innocence. "You saw him aiming at me. I was in fear for my life."

"You goaded him into it."

"Hey, if you commit a crime in *my* neighborhood, expect to pay."

He raised an eyebrow.

"You know what they say. Don't start nothin', it won't be nothin'."

"You're fucked up."

"I'm a cop. I do what needs to be done. You don't see him complaining, do you?" She pointed to the clerk, still shaking on the floor. "He was a criminal. As far as I'm concerned, he had it coming."

"Yeah, Chief?" Yara said, entering the police chief's office.

"Close the door, Rocha," he instructed, taking a sip of coffee. "Sit down, we need to chat."

She did as instructed, folding her hands in her lap as she waited for what was sure to be another lecture on excessive force.

"I read your report and I have some questions."

"Which report, sir?"

He took the file from a drawer and slid it across the desk. She opened it, pretending to skim it over when she knew full well which report he was talking about. "Ah, the convenience store robbery."

"Yes, the robbery that somehow ended with one of my officers in a sling, two suspects dead, and another in the wind. You want to explain to me what happened?"

"It's all in the report, sir."

He squinted at her and snatched up the file, putting on his reading glasses and clearing his throat before reading aloud. *"I told the suspect to put down his weapon. He did not comply. Instead, he turned it on me. I could see the safety was off and I felt that I was in immediate danger, so I reacted."*

"Yes, sir."

"And that's all there is to the story?"

"Sir?"

"Your partner issued a report of his own. Said you provoked the suspect. Said you fanned the flames and that it could have gone down differently. Said it seemed to *him* like you *wanted* to kill that boy."

"That's ridiculous."

"Is it? Because this isn't the first time something like this has happened. This isn't even the first partner of yours that's come to me with concerns."

She rolled her eyes. "Sir,"

"That boy was seventeen, did you know that?"

"No."

"He was a *kid*. I've gotten a dozen calls today from people demanding I investigate. They want the surveillance and bodycam footage released to the public. His parents will probably sue. Do you have any idea the position you've put this department in?"

"I understand."

"Do you? Because I'm looking at you and you're cold as ice. You have no remorse. You don't give a--"

"My partner was down. He was about to get killed, so I had his back. When he was safe, I focused on the last perp. The kid had a gun to an old man's head and told me he'd kill him. What should I have done? I had three choices: let the suspect go, let the old man get killed, or take the shot. I took the damn shot. Yes, it's sad that he wasn't *quite* an adult, but come on. He was a criminal and if I'd let him off the hook--"

"I don't want to hear any more. You're suspended pending an investigation, but if I were you, I'd hire a lawyer and start thinking about career options."

"Are you serious?"

"You see a brick wall behind my head? Yeah, I'm serious. Gun and badge."

She scoffed as she stood, shaking her head and placing the items on the desk. "I can't believe this. After everything I've done for this community."

"I'm not discounting the work you've put in, Rocha. I'm telling you you've gone too far, *again*. Maybe you should get some help."

"Help? Like a shrink? You think I'm crazy?"

"I think if a medical professional could testify that you weren't in your right mind when the incident occurred, you might avoid jail time altogether."

"Jail time? I'm sorry sir, but are you on crack?"

"Get out of my precinct, Rocha."

She stormed out of the office, slamming the door behind her and ignoring everyone in the building as she made her way out, their self-righteous stares like daggers in her back. Ten years she'd dedicated her life to this place, to these people, to this city. *Ten years.* Her mind raced as she walked home. Should she try to fight this? Try to get her job back? Or should she track Jackson down and give him a talking to about ratting out your partner? Maybe she should say, 'fuck it', buy some fertilizer, and blow the whole precinct to shit. She took a deep breath, cracking her neck as she tried to calm her mind. "The point is to stay *out* of prison," she whispered to herself. But thoughts of revenge lingered. She imagined shooting the chief between the eyes, setting pipe bombs, and watching as people she once called friends get blown apart in a fiery shower of blood and broken badges. She thought about breaking into Jackson's apartment and wrapping her hands around his rat-fink throat until his eyes popped out of their sockets and he passed out. Mostly, she thought about the kid and how good it had felt to put all those bullets in him. Seventeen or not, she was glad he was dead. "One more criminal off the streets."

"You talkin' to me?" a man asked as she passed. She shook her head and kept moving, a sly smile creeping across her lips. Yes, she was glad the boy was dead. Her only regret was that his friend, the lookout, had gotten away. She was sure she'd see him around the neighborhood, eventually. She was looking forward to it.

Yara jumped at the sight of a man sitting on her couch as she opened the door. On instinct, she reached for her sidearm before remembering that it wasn't there. "What do you want?"

"To talk," the man said, putting his hands up as if he was about to be arrested. "I would have waited outside, but this isn't exactly a safe neighborhood."

"Who are you?" She stayed in the doorway, ready to bolt if things got out of control.

"Come sit."

She scoffed.

He sighed and stood up, buttoning his suit jacket. "I really do just want to talk." She tried to back out of the room, but he was too fast. He grabbed her arm and pulled her inside, closing the door and standing between it and her. He put two fingers to his temple, gently massaging it for a few seconds as he looked her over. "I don't wish to harm you, Yara, honestly."

"How do you know my name?"

"I know all of my descendants' names. I've kept track."

"Your what? Man, who the hell are you?"

"My name is Cain. I'm your one hundred and eighty-first great grandfather. I was hoping we might--"

"So, you're not a burglar, you're a lunatic. All right, bro. Get out of my house."

He rubbed his temple again, this time closing his eyes and wincing.

"Hey, man, you all right? Listen, I'm sorry. Mental illness isn't a joke. But you can't just--"

"I'm not mentally ill," he insisted. "Why are you people always so quick to assume a person is out of their mind? Just because you don't understand something, doesn't make it insane. Let me explain. As I said, I am Cain, son of Adam, father of Enoch, Allydia--"

"Cain? Like, from the Bible? That's who you think you are?"

"*No*, that's who I *am*. Anyhow, my son, Olad, had children who had children and so on through the millennia until we come to you. I really didn't mean to frighten you. I would just like to get to know--" He reached up with both hands and held his head, gritting his teeth.

"Do you need an ambulance? I'm calling--"

"Don't!" he snapped. "This is just what happens when I stay in one place too long. Part of God's curse."

"God's curse? Bro, you're whacked. You need help. I'm calling someone."

She went for the phone in her pocket, but he grabbed her arm again. "I said, '*no*'." He flung her to the ground. "Please, believe me, granddaughter. *Please*. I want us to be friends. I want to know you. We're family, after all."

She glared at him, her anger from the day's events bubbling over. It would be irresponsible of her to go after the boys in blue, but this guy? He was an intruder. He'd attacked her. She had every excuse in the world.

She looked past him, just long enough for him to turn to see what she was looking at. When he did, she swept her leg across the back of his, knocking him to the ground. She leaped on top of him, punching him in the jaw before pressing down on his throat, using as much of her body weight as she could to crush his windpipe. He gripped her wrists tight, prying her hands off of his neck. Sure that he would overpower her, she switched strategies, kneeing him in the groin and jumping up, making a beeline for the door. Just as she was about to turn the knob, she felt the pain of her skull being cracked. He'd hurled something at the back of her head, causing her to drop to her knees. She touched her head and looked at her hand. It was covered in blood. The room seemed dimmer as she tried to stand, her legs not wanting to cooperate. Suddenly, she felt a sharp pain flood through her, starting between her shoulder blades and coming out her chest. She looked down and could see what looked like metal poking out from between her breasts. Blood flooded from her mouth onto the carpet as the weapon was yanked from her body. She fell forward, her head crashing into the door with an audible thump. Her vision had gone blurry, but she could just make out the silhouette of the man as he wiped her blood from something before placing it in what looked like a briefcase.

"I really didn't want to do this, Yara," he told her. "I was hoping things would be different with you. I'm starting to believe you're all the same. I can't tell you how disappointed I am in you." He left the apartment, scooting her across the floor as he opened the door, her vision now completely black. She couldn't feel anything anymore; not the pain, not the floor, not even her anger. There was just...nothing.

Outside, Cain set his case on the sidewalk and took a pen and a small, leather-bound notebook from his jacket pocket, opening it to the last page with writing on it. He crossed off the name *Yara Rocha*. There was only one name remaining. He put his things back in his pocket, picked up the briefcase, and took a breath. "Well," he murmured. "I guess I have a plane to catch."

Chapter 2

"I hate this," Wendy complained as she twirled Gabriel's hair between her fingers. "I wish I didn't have to go back to work already."

"You don't *have* to," she told her, gently pulling her toward the entrance of her building.

"I'm not taking your money."

"Come on, just a little. Ten million. You could quit your job and we could be on vacation all the time."

"As tempting as that sounds, I do actually like my job. Plus, I don't want you to think I'm taking advantage of you."

"Please, I know you're just in it for the sex," Gabriel teased.

"And the jokes."

"Well, sure. I'm pretty hilarious."

"I really have to go. I'll call you as soon as I get back."

"Fine, but I'm agreeing under duress."

"Noted." She kissed her and touched her cheek. "I'll see you later."

They parted ways, Wendy heading back toward the subway and Gabriel walking into her building alone. As she entered the elevator, she was struck with a familiar but overwhelming feeling. She was knocked to the ground by a flood of new information filling her brain, dropping her suitcase, and swallowing the bile that rose in her throat. She clutched her chest with one hand and searched for the railing with the other as she tried to catch her breath. The world around her seemed to spin and go dim. She managed to crawl to the front of the lift and hit the emergency stop button, ensuring none of her neighbors would stumble upon her in this state. She closed her eyes and took deep breaths, blowing them out her mouth as her organs vibrated, the power of what waited for her upstairs shocking her system. She sang 'Sherry Fraser' to herself as her body adjusted, having always found the melody soothing. She finally got her bearings and was able to stand, putting her hand to her forehead as her mind cleared. She hit the button for her floor and readied herself. "Get it together, bitch."

The doors opened and she found Michelle sitting in front of her apartment. She stood up and threw her arms around her neck. She was trembling as Gabriel hugged her back. "I didn't know what else to do," the girl said. "I don't trust anyone but you."

She pulled away and picked up a blanket that had been covering the car seat. Gabriel held back tears as she looked down at the baby resting peacefully, knowing that maintaining her composure was vital under the circumstances.

"Come in," she said, unlocking the door. Michelle picked up the carrier and followed her inside, locking the door back behind her. "I thought you were dead."

"I'm not *not* dead," the vampire joked, setting the carrier on the island and stepping back. "Will?"

Gabriel shook her head.

She swallowed the lump in her throat. "I figured. Is his dad okay?"

"Okay's maybe a stretch. He's alive, taking care of himself. He'll be all right."

"You know why I'm here."

She nodded, looking down at the infant.

"And you know what the Queen will do if she finds out a damphyr has been born, much less one with Nephilim powers."

"I do know."

"Hattie said nothing on Earth is stronger than a human/vampire hybrid. Is that true?"

"Usually."

"I took the morning-after pill."

"I know."

"I don't want you to think I was irresponsible."

"Girl, I see you."

"Yeah. So, you'll take her?"

Gabriel sighed.

"Do you know what the punishment for a vampire siring without permission is? I'll be thrown in a cage until Allydia can track Hattie down. Once she does, she'll make her kill me before yanking her fangs out with pliers and chaining her on the roof just before sunrise. If she finds me with Sinclair, she'll drown her in front of me. That's what I named her, Sinclair, for her father. I thought about Willa or Willow, but when I saw her face, Sinclair just felt right."

"It suits her," she said, letting the baby grab onto her finger.

"Hattie won't leave Scotland and without her, I'm having a really hard time controlling myself." She glanced at the baby and back to Gabriel. "She smells like food."

"Jesus, yes, I'll take her. Here," She took a key from the junk drawer and handed it to her. "Go to the house in Southport. B's all moved out, so it'll be empty, except for the furniture." She rifled through her purse, found her wallet, and pulled out a credit card. She gave it to her and touched her arm. "I'll send a steady stream of blood bags so you can ride out the new-vampire urges without killing anyone. Call me if it gets too bad and I'll rush right down."

She nodded. "Thanks. And you'll protect her, right?"

"Her whole life." She picked up her phone and texted the pilot to have the jet gassed up. "The plane will be ready to go by the time you get to the airport."

Michelle wiped away a tear as she took one last look at her baby. "Will she be okay?"

"She'll be perfect. And, yes, I'll tell her you love her and you gave her to me for her own safety. I promise she'll understand."

"How do you know?"

She gave her a condescending glare. "Who am I?"

She laughed. "Right."

"I'll have a box of blood waiting for you when you get to the house."

"Okay." She turned to leave.

"Michelle,"

"Yeah," she said, grasping the doorknob.

"I'm glad you didn't stay dead."

She smiled and nodded, opened the door, and left.

As the door closed, Sinclair let out a quiet cry, again reaching for Gabriel's finger. She picked the baby up and held her close to her chest, rocking back and forth, letting the tears she'd been stifling fall down her cheeks. She sang 'Golden Slumbers' as they cried, the child's broken heart more painful to Gabriel than the loss she'd felt when Raphael had gone back to Heaven. The child wanted her mother and the only thing Gabriel could think to do to ease her suffering was to give her a new one.

Wyatt ran his hand over Allydia's forehead and down her cheek as he kissed her, indulging in her body for the third time that night. It had been two weeks since the battle for the Gate and in that time, the two had barely left the bedroom, worshiping each other and blocking out the world around them.

Yo! he heard in his head.

He stopped what he was doing and grimaced. *Not now, Gabriel.*

When your girlfriend leaves, book it to my place. It's urgent.

"What's wrong?" Allydia asked.

"Nothing," he said. *Bye, Gabriel.*

Say 'okay'.

Fine, I'll see you in the morning.

K, bye.

"Well, that's over," he huffed, rolling back to his side of the bed.

"Your sister?"

"Yeah. Apparently, there's some big emergency."

"Isn't there always?" she quipped, pushing the hair away from his eyes.

He chuckled.

"Speaking of your sister, there's something I need to talk with you about."

He raised an eyebrow.

"There are things I haven't told you, not because I wanted to deceive you, but because it's hard for me to think about. You asked me once why I hated Lilith so much."

"I remember."

"I told you it was because she took something that didn't belong to her."

He nodded.

"What she took, what she snuffed out, was the life of my youngest child. She murdered her as an infant in order to make me what I am."

"Jesus."

"I did not ask for this life. I was fine with dying when I did. But my father could not endure it. Lilith manipulated him into allowing her to bring me back this way because she was afraid of being without him. When he saw what I'd become, he was worried that I would harm my daughters, so he stole them away. As much as it pained me, in retrospect, he was probably right."

"God, I'm so sorry. That must have been awful."

"It was. But, years later, Gabriel came to me, saved me from your Father's flood. She told me that one day, she would come again and call on me to aid in a battle against Lilith. In return for my assistance, she would give me the location of my daughters' descendants. Earlier this evening, she sent me two addresses."

"She found them?"

"Not so much found as was gifted with the knowledge. I would like to see them."

"Of course. You should."

"I don't want the others to know where I've gone. There's talk of rebellion among my people. If my enemies discover I have human family, they could use them. They could hurt them. They wouldn't dare attempt to harm *you*. Word of your abilities has spread. They fear you. But humans...I can't risk it. I need to go on my own as not to raise suspicion."

"Sure, go ahead. Take as much time as you need."

She touched his face and stared into his eyes. "Will you be all right?"

"I'll be fine," he assured her, taking her hand in his and kissing it. "This is your family. You *have* to go. I'll be okay, I swear."

"Thank you." She got up and put her clothes back on, slipping the wispy sundress over her head and pulling it down around her. "Hartley will be at your disposal, should you need anything. I've already told her to treat your calls as if they were mine."

"That's not necessary."

"Perhaps not, but it brings me comfort knowing she's watching over you when I can not."

"You don't have to treat me like I'm made of glass."

"So you say, but my heart still breaks remembering you floating in the tub."

"I'm sorry about that," he said, sitting up and pulling her to his lap.

"I know you are." She wrapped her arm around his shoulders and touched his chin. "And I *will* learn to give you your space, in time. But, for now, while I'm away, I'd like to enjoy myself instead of worrying about your safety. Can you understand my perspective?"

"Yes," he sighed. "I suppose I can. As long as *you* can promise to start trusting me."

"I will." She got up, slipped on her shoes, and headed for the door. "As soon as I get back."

Chapter 3

"All right, I'm here," Wyatt called as he entered Gabriel's apartment. "What's the big problem *now*?" He closed the door behind him and walked to the living room where he nearly tripped over the baby lying on a blanket in the middle of the floor. "Oh, sorry, sweetie," he cooed, kneeling down and tickling the child's stomach. "I didn't see you there." She giggled and grabbed his hand.

"Hey," Gabriel said as she appeared from the hall.

"Hey," he said, standing up. "Cute baby. I'm a little surprised somebody's letting *you* babysit."

"Haha."

"Who is she?"

"You should sit."

"Why?"

"I recommend sitting."

"Gabriel," he prodded.

"Barachiel," she mocked.

"Who is she?"

She furrowed her brow and folded her arms.

He tilted his head and raised his eyebrows.

She rolled her eyes and sighed. "She's your granddaughter."

He laughed. "She's what?"

"Michelle brought her to me. Turns out, Hattie snuck some of her blood to her before Will zapped her. She was pregnant when she turned."

His face went ghost-white and his mouth fell open. He turned to look down at the infant playing happily with a rattle. He knelt back down and covered his mouth as tears began to form in his eyes. "That's not possible. She would have only been pregnant for, what, two months?"

"She's not exactly human, B. The rules on what consists of a normal gestation period don't really apply." She sat next to him and patted him on the back. "Michelle can't keep her. She's not in control of her vampire shit, yet. She thinks she might hurt her. I'm gonna give her to Uriel."

He flashed her a look. "The hell you are. She belongs with *me*."

"Listen, B,"

"No," he said, getting to his feet and pulling her up by the arm. "I know Valerie wants a kid, but you can't just--"

"*Allydia will kill her.*"

He dropped her arm and took a step back.

"This kid isn't normal, B. She's what the vampires call a 'damphyr'. Stronger than vampires, able to walk in the sun, can survive on blood *or* normal food. Your girlfriend has rules about stuff like this. *Laws.*"

"She wouldn't."

"I know her a lot better than you do. Trust me on this. Dia will drown her, tear her to pieces, and burn the parts to ash. *I've seen her do it*, and that was with regular damphyrs. One with lightning-controlling Nephilim powers? She might put her through a meat grinder just to be safe."

He stared at her, horrified, his mind racing.

"If you leave, she won't spiral into a depression again. This time, *she will hunt you*. Besides, I know how you feel about her."

"What," he choked. "What do you mean, 'Nephilim powers'?"

The baby giggled and grabbed his ankle, sending a small jolt of electricity through his jeans, causing the hair on his leg to stand up.

His eyes widened as he looked down at her and back to his sister. "Already?"

Gabriel bit her bottom lip and nodded.

His throat went dry and his voice quivered. "Will she be okay, or is she like...is she--"

"She'll be fine." She picked her up and handed her to him. "She'll age fast. Faster than Will. She'll have some growing pains, but eventually, she'll be good as new."

He held her in his arms and couldn't help but smile through his tears. "She's perfect."

"I know, right? Oh, Michelle named her Sinclair."

His face brightened.

"I thought you'd like that."

"Wait," he worried. "Where's Lucifer? If he even *thinks* about--"

"Settle down. He's been shacked up at the bartender's place for days."

Wyatt's shoulders relaxed, but his jaw was still tight as he looked down at his granddaughter's smiling face.

"You can visit any time," Gabriel comforted. "Just make sure it's during the day."

"So," he said, tears again threatening to fall from his worried eyes. "Sinclair Perry?"

"Maybe Sinclair *Ann* Perry, for her grandmother."

Tears streamed as he nodded and took a shaky breath.

"Ann happens to also be *my* middle name, but that's just a happy coincidence."

He laughed and the baby giggled and kicked her legs. "I think she likes it."

"She doesn't care about her name. She just likes seeing you happy."

Wyatt turned his glance back to his sister. "You know that?"

"Obvs."

"I thought you couldn't see--"

"She's not the same as Will. Not exactly. Just like you and Lucifer and Uriel, I can hear her thoughts, feel her emotions. I'll always know what she needs and she can call on me whenever. Trust me, you don't have to worry about her. She's gonna be awesome."

"And you're sure Valerie can handle this?"

She scoffed. "That bitch can handle *anything*."

"Spider, spider!" Valerie yelped, pointing to the ceiling and backing away.

Malik chuckled as he took the stick vac from the hall closet, plugged it in, and proceeded to suck the tiny creature into it. "Demons, monsters, and Lucifer you can handle, but one little bug, and you're heading for the hills."

"Not *all* bugs. Just *those* things, *especially* when they're up high. They can fall and get in your hair and get stuck." She shuddered. "I don't even want to think about it."

He laughed, put the vacuum away, and kissed her cheek. "I'll be gone for a couple days for that class, but when I get home, I'll have a dozen new recipes in my repertoire. Think about what you want for my first dinner back *now*. I don't wanna have the 'I don't know, what do you want' conversation for half an hour *again*."

"I mean, *okay*, but just so you know, we probably will."

He laughed again, picking up his suitcase as he left, waving goodbye and closing the door behind him. She sat down on the couch, crossed her legs, and looked around the apartment. She tapped her fingers on her knee and began to chew on her bottom lip. It had been like this since she'd gotten back from Iraq. With no job and no monsters to deal with, she didn't know what to do with her time. There was no urgency. Nothing needed done.

She flopped her head back and let out a frustrated sigh. "*I'm so bored.*" She picked up the laptop from the coffee table and searched job listings with no luck for the third day in a row before putting the computer back in annoyance. Just as she was about to get up to mindlessly snack on something to pass the time, the door flew open. From the hall, she could hear Gabriel singing 'Circle of Life' as an empty car seat floated into the room.

"The fuck?" Valerie muttered.

Soon, her sister appeared holding a baby up in front of her, still singing, a goofy smile on her glossy lips. She closed the door with her mind and handed the child over, unable to stop herself from giggling.

"Aren't you the cutest little light-skinned baby ever?" Valerie said, looking down at the gleaming infant. She instinctively began rocking back and forth as she turned her attention to her sister. "What kind of moron let you watch their kid?"

She folded her arms. "Okay, this is getting insulting. Just because I'm not *parent material*, doesn't mean I'm irresponsible. I can take care of a baby for a *day*."

"Uh, huh. For real, whose kid is this?"

She looked her in the eyes and did the floss before answering, "Yours."

She raised her eyebrows. "Girl, did you kidnap this baby?"

"No, jeez. Let's sit." They moved to the sofa, Valerie bouncing the girl on her knee. "So, her name's Sinclair Ann. She's Barachiel's granddaughter."

Valerie tilted her head and widened her eyes.

"I know, right? So, you know how Will was boning Michelle, but then he accidentally killed her with his emotional-break-down-lightning?"

"Yeah."

"Well, while Hattie had been helping train her to protect herself before she went to Southport, they became real good friends."

"Hattie's the vampire's assistant, right?"

"Was. So, apparently, when Will started showing signs of going dark side, Michelle had her overnight her some of her blood. She put a little in her orange juice every morning. Grody, I know. So, instead of staying dead, she turned. Unbeknownst to her, she was knocked up at the time, and that's how our great-niece came to be."

"That's a different level of fucked up."

She shrugged.

"All right, but I can't keep her. She should be with Wyatt. He's--"

"Banging a vampire."

"Yeah, but--"

"Sinclair isn't human, Uri. She's half vampire, half Nephilim. Dia will *slaughter her* if she finds out she exists. I went over this with B. He gets it. He doesn't *like* it, but he gets it. He knows the only place she'll be safe is with you."

"What about me? What about Malik? Are *we* safe with *her*?" She looked down into the baby's seemingly innocent face. "No offense, cutie, but my man's just a dude and you're--"

"Family," Gabriel insisted. "She's our family, Uri. She's got no one else."

She went quiet, thinking about the years in foster care, the loneliness, and the trauma. She remembered the abuse. She looked her sister in the eyes, warmth washing over her as she remembered how grateful she'd been when she'd brought her to her grandmother. She knew she was just trying to do the same thing for Sinclair now. "You're right," she said, smiling down at her new daughter. "She can stay here."

"Good. There's formula in the bag. If you run out, she can drink blood in a pinch, but she'd really rather not. Also, the diapers I have are size one, but she'll outgrow those in a couple days. I'll just send over some supplies."

"A couple days?"

"She's gonna grow fast. Like, 'take-a-ton-of-pictures-because-you'll-forget-what-she-looked-like-from-one-day-to-the-next' fast."

"Wait, did you say, '*blood*'?"

She got up and headed for the door, twirling her hair as she went. "Yeah, it's not important."

Wyatt sat on the grass of his wife's grave, his back against the headstone, eating the candy bar his sister had given him on his way out the door. He hadn't realized how hungry he was until now, having skipped breakfast in his rush to get to Gabriel's. She did, though. She always knew.

"It's been a while since we've talked. I know you can't hear me, I'm not *crazy*...turns out. I just need some perspective. I thought if I came here, got some things out, I might feel better about this whole absentee-grandfather thing. *Grandfather*. That's so weird." He took another bite and leaned his head back, watching the clouds as he chewed. He stretched his legs out, crossing one ankle over the other as he finished the candy, crumpled the wrapper, and shoved it in the pocket of his jeans. "I should trust Gabriel here, right? She always knows what she's doing, except maybe for that whole theater incident. I'm still not sure how much slack I should cut her there. On one hand, those people were possessed and probably wouldn't make it, anyway. I saw her when Tae died. She wasn't okay. Doesn't seem like much of an excuse, though, does it? I mean, she hasn't shown *any* remorse about it and that's just weird, right? I don't know. Maybe it's different for her, being God's taskmaster, knowing what He wants from her and the rest of us, what He *expects*. It's probably a huge burden, knowing all the big picture stuff. Fifty lives is a drop in the bucket to someone like that. Plus, constantly having other people's thoughts in her head can't be exactly peaceful. Feeling everyone else's emotions. I'm surprised she hasn't cracked up more often. Still." He tore up a bit of grass and let out a breath. "Valerie will be a good mom. She's worked with kids for years, she'll be fine...I hope." He ran his tongue over his back teeth and folded his arms. "There's something else I wanted to talk to you about. There's this girl. I don't know *what's* going on. It's completely unhealthy, codependent, potentially dangerous. There's something about her, though. She makes me feel needed and wanted. She looks at me like I matter. Like I'm the only person in the world. She makes me a priority. I don't know if anyone else has ever cared about me like that. I feel like I need her. It's insane. I don't know, maybe I *am* crazy. I wish you were here. I could really use my best friend right now." As he stood to go, a gentle breeze rustled his hair, the scent of lavender wafting by, ever so briefly, the air like a kiss on his cheek. He looked around, trying to figure out where the smell was coming from. The cemetery was deserted but for him and the landscaper, and of all the flowers on graves he could see, none of them were Annie's favorite. He kissed his fingertips and touched the headstone. "I should really get back into therapy."

Chapter 4

Cain sipped his brandy, admiring the view from the small window of the plane. He looked down at the Atlantic through the wisps of clouds, noticing how peaceful the world seemed from this altitude, nothing but an ocean of blue below him. He imagined that's what Heaven must be like, not that he'd ever get a chance to know that now. His plan had failed. His curse remained.

He straightened his tie and cleared his throat, pushing away the anger and closing his eyes as he composed himself. He needed to be pragmatic. He took a deep breath and cleared his mind, letting the magazine that he'd been reading fall to the floor.

"Here you are, sir," the flight attendant said, hurrying to pick it up and set it on his tray. "Can I get you anything?"

"No, thank you," he replied, meeting her gaze and feigning a smile.

"All right. Enjoy the rest of the flight."

"Actually," he said. "What's your name?"

"Wendy."

"Hi, Wendy. Could I get another brandy? I've almost finished this one."

"Of course. Give me one second." She smiled sweetly and scurried off to fetch his drink. He watched her go, his lips turning up into a devilish smirk. The angels had destroyed his only chance at breaking God's curse, and while he had no way of doing them any physical harm, he *would* make them suffer for it.

Poe set her basket down on the soft grass, the heat of the afternoon sun making her rethink her decision to wear patent leather pants and a black tee-shirt to do the day's gardening. "Ah, well," she shrugged. "Already writing the ticket." She reached up and bent the stalk of the first mullein flower down, being careful not to break it, and plucked off its buds and flower spikes one by one, dropping them into her basket. She moved on to the next one, the six-foot stalks nearly a foot taller than her, reminding her, as Grace always had when they were harvesting, that she was one small part in a much bigger universe.

As she went for her third flower, she heard a rustling in the grass just past the garden. She brushed her short, dark hair away from her eyes with the back of her hand and squinted in the harsh daylight as she went to investigate. She covered her mouth and gasped when she came upon it, the small, brown and white rabbit, convulsing on the ground.

"What happened, baby?" she wondered. "What did you--" And then she saw it: purple flowers, some half-eaten, strewn across the grass a few feet away. "Foxglove. Oh, shit." She scooped the bunny up and hurried back to the house. "Sorry about the sticky fingers, cuteness. Don't worry. We'll get you fixed right up. I promise." She kicked open the screen door and rushed in. Once in the kitchen, she dumped the apples from the bowl on the table and set the bunny inside. She then got to work, pulverizing as many bayberries as she could using a mortar and pestle. Once she was satisfied with the consistency, she used a needleless syringe to administer the medicine to the rabbit. Within seconds, it began vomiting. "Good job, buddy," she cooed as she pet its fluffy back. When she was sure there was nothing left in the animal's stomach, she went to the pantry and found the jar marked *activated charcoal powder*. She dumped some in a bowl with a little water to make a paste and used a clean syringe to feed it to the bunny. She then fed it some water through the syringe and gave it a bath in the sink, the animal too weak to put up a fight.

For the next few days, Poe nursed the rabbit back to health, feeding it water with the syringe and holding out pieces of kale for it to munch on until it could lift its head and feed itself. She held the bunny close on her chest when it slept to make sure it was breathing and when it seemed to be on the mend, she bought a bale of hay and a collar with a bell on it so she'd always know where her new friend was. She let it roam the garden, thinking that, eventually, it would wander off, never to be seen again. But it never did. It stayed with her, sleeping in her bed, hopping along wherever she went. It was the best friend she'd ever had.

"I'm gonna call you 'Raven'," she told the bunny, petting it as it ate from its bowl on the kitchen table. "You can stay with me as long as you want, but if you ever want to go, I'll respect your choice." As she watched the bunny eat, she realized that she was smiling for the first time since Grace died. It had been strange, living in her house without her; lonely and sad. But, having a pet had given her purpose and she was finally on her way to feeling like herself again.

Poe was in the garden gathering herbs when she heard a noise coming from inside the house. She thought Raven had knocked something over, so she went in, expecting to have a mess to sweep up, but what she found would take a lot more than a broom to clean. Julia and two other witches from her coven were standing in her kitchen, rifling through drawers, and emptying jars of herbs. There were piles of powders and dried leaves all over the counters and Grace's recipe cards were scattered across the table. Julia stood over them, flipping through the pages of a spellbook she'd found in a cabinet.

"What the hell are you doing?" Poe shouted, frantically looking around the room.

"It's none of your concern," Julia told her, not looking up from the book.

"The hell it's not. I live here!"

She sighed, closing the book and folding her arms, finally meeting Poe's gaze. "We're looking for Grace's magic. She hid it from the coven. It's not right. It has to be here somewhere."

"It's not."

"It *has* to be."

"I'm telling you, I live here and I don't feel it anywhere."

"What part of, 'she hid it' is confusing to you? Grace was the most powerful witch I've ever known. If she didn't want something found, there is no way someone like *you* would be able to find it."

"Someone like me?"

Julia rolled her eyes. "Don't get offended, you know what I mean. You're young, barely trained."

"Personally trained by Grace herself. I'm not as weak as you seem to think I am."

"You're a child, but, fine. Let's say you're as strong as the rest of us. It means nothing. Without the Tituban magic, we're all as good as dead."

"You still think the other covens are coming after us?"

"Not yet, but they will be. I don't know about you, but I don't want to be a sitting duck. Look, I'm sorry about the mess, but this is important." She looked the girl over. "You and Grace were close. Like, mother and daughter, close."

"So?"

"So, are you *sure* you don't know where she put her magic?"

"She didn't tell me. I was as surprised as you when it didn't pass to us."

"When it didn't pass to *us*," She put her hands on her hips. "You mean the coven?"

She nodded.

"You know, we've been working under the assumption that Grace didn't bother choosing someone to take her place, but what if she did? What if she cared so much about you, that she wanted *you* to take over when she died?"

Poe scoffed. "*Me*?"

"Not the obvious choice, of course," Julia said, tapping her fingers on the spell book's cover. "You're the youngest member of the coven, the least experienced. But, she did love you. We could all see it. She fawned over you like a pet. She would have known that the rest of the coven would hate it if she left you in charge, especially the elders. Can you imagine Libby's face if Grace had told her that her eighty-year-old ass would be taking orders from *you* from now on?"

The other women laughed.

"But, if she left all of her magic to you, *just you,* we would have no choice."

Poe swallowed hard. "I don't have it."

"You don't?"

"No."

"How can you tell?"

"What do you mean?"

"Grace could have hidden it in you, dormant, until you needed it. You wouldn't even know it was there."

"That's crazy."

"Is it? Let's find out. Quassatura."

Searing pain ripped through Poe's arm as a deep scratch opened up across her skin. "Ow! What the fuck, Julia?"

"Well, damn it. I thought I was on to something."

"I told you, I don't have it. It's not here. You're wasting your time."

"Maybe you're right," she huffed. "But, if it's not with you, the only other place it could be is--"

"The elders," another woman said.

Julia nodded. "But, why would they keep it from the rest of us? Why wouldn't they use it? Doesn't make sense."

"Did you ever think that maybe Grace hid it to protect us? You know how powerful she was. What if it's too much for us?"

"Too much? We're *witches.*"

"Yeah, but--"

"But nothing. That power belongs to the coven and I'm *going* to find it."

She stomped out, the other two following closely behind. As the door slammed shut, Raven popped out from under the sink, hopping over and sitting at Poe's feet. The young witch picked up the rabbit and sat in a chair, hoping to be comforted by its affection. But, she couldn't shake the feeling of dread twisting in her stomach like a knife. Julia was out of control and something bad was going to happen. She could feel it.

Chapter 5

Allydia perched herself on the roof of the building across from the first address Gabriel had given her, a one-bedroom flat in the heart of Camden Town. It had been some time since she'd visited London and as she waited, she wondered if Queen Mary's Rose Gardens were as beautiful as she remembered. She first saw them in 1934, the day they opened to the public. She remembered thinking how worth it it was, being out in the daylight, to see such vibrant colors. She'd only stayed a short time, of course, but she could picture it in her mind even now. She'd be sure to stop by for a stroll before she left.

Her ears pricked up at the sound of a doorknob turning. She watched as the door to her descendant's building opened and a man walked out. He was in his late-twenties to early-thirties with dark hair and a skin tone that resembled her own. He was slender and tall, wearing khaki cargo pants and a plain, black tee-shirt. As she focused her vision, his face became clear, even at this distance. He was clean-shaven with full lips, and even though she was sure it was impossible, she would have sworn on her life that he had Farhan's eyes.

He walked for a few blocks, Allydia hopping from one rooftop to another as she followed. He stopped in front of a shop, but before he could open the door, it burst open, an older man bounding out to meet him.

"Navid!" He slapped him on both shoulders, a wide grin peeking out from his full, gray beard. "So good of you to come. Are you well?"

"I am," he replied. "And you?"

"We're wonderful, thanks to you. Business has *tripled* since you got those hoodlums off the street. Come, come. Shadi has a gift for you; her famous bamieh, to say 'thank you'."

"Bamieh?" the younger man asked, placing a hand on his stomach. "Well, let's get inside before I start drooling all over the pavement."

The men laughed and went in, the door closing slowly behind them. Allydia crouched down, trying to get a glimpse inside, but there were too many people. It was a party of some sort, inside what looked like a bakery. There was a counter and a glass case full of pastries, a few tables, and a sign on the door that read, 'closed'. It was loud inside, at least two dozen voices talking all at once. She'd lost track of him for now, so she'd wait, the early evening sky quickly turning dark giving her the cover she needed. She stared at the door, anxious to get another look at him, to compare his features with her own. "Navid," she whispered to herself, the sound of his name like a warm blanket around her shoulders. She wondered what his life was like. He was obviously beloved by the people in his community and from the conversation he'd just had, she assumed he worked in law enforcement. Was he happy? Content? She couldn't leave until she knew.

After more than two hours, Navid emerged, waving to the other party guests and carrying a tin. He began the short walk home, taking a pastry from the container, and eating as he went. Allydia again followed, shimmying down the side of a building and sticking to the shadows on the sidewalk across the street. The scent of rose water and saffron wafted from his hands as he closed the tin back, reminding her of something she'd eaten as a child. She thought those memories had been all but lost to her, her human life having ended so long ago. A lump formed in her throat. It was all she could do to stop herself from tearing up.

As Navid approached the door to his building, he stopped, looking around as if he knew he was being followed. Allydia slunk back into an alley, out of sight, or so she thought. In her excitement, she'd forgotten the way her eyes shone in the dark, reflecting what little light was available. For a short time, the presence of a blood relative had made her forget what she was; not only inhuman, but a predator.

He looked across to where she stood, unable to see anything through the dark but her eyes, yellow and glowing. She could hear his heart skip a beat as he swallowed hard. He rushed to get inside and bounded up the stairs to his apartment, nearly dropping his pastries as he hastily got the door unlocked. Once safe, she could hear his breathing steady. She felt a twinge of guilt for frightening him, but couldn't resist the urge to keep following. She *had* to know he was all right.

She crept across the street and climbed up the side of the building, looking in windows until she found him. She could hear him on the phone reporting a strange animal sighting. He thought he'd seen a lion or cougar stalking him on the quiet city street. The man on the other end of the call laughed but said he'd send someone to check it out. As she listened, she took note of his surroundings. A small sofa served as the only seating in the living room. Two bar stools stood in front of an island with one cushion far more worn than the other. In the bedroom, there was a nightstand on one side of a twin-sized bed. He clearly lived alone.

Her eyes again fell to him. He wore no ring, so he had no wife. The only pictures she could see were of an older couple who she assumed must be his parents, though neither bore any resemblance to him. No other photographs could only mean that he had no children that he knew of. It seemed that he led a solitary life, with work and friends taking up most of his time. He was relatively young, so she didn't jump to any conclusions about how that affected his happiness. She, though, was ecstatic to see him, offspring of her offspring, alive, healthy, and thriving.

He set the phone on the counter and turned toward the window, Allydia able to hear his heart beginning to race. She skidded down to the sidewalk and darted across the street, clawing her way up a building and again crouching down to watch him from afar.

Navid hid in the tall shrubs, watching with intense concentration as the woman walked through the gardens, stopping for a time to admire the Boy and Frog statue. It was early in the morning, but the temperature had already risen to nearly seventy degrees Fahrenheit, and yet, the woman was almost completely shrouded in a heavy cloak. Who was she? He had to know.

Chapter 6

Once in Tripoli, Cain headed straight for an apartment building near Saint Vasilios Square where he knew the last of his descendants took residence. She was a sixty-year-old retired nurse and while she wasn't his first choice, she was all that was left.

"Yes?" She said in Greek as she opened the door.

"Hello," Cain replied. "Are you Dimitra?"

"I am. And who might you be?"

"My name is Cain. This may sound crazy, but I think we're related."

"Oh! You've done one of those DNA tests, haven't you?"

"Something like that."

"Well, come in! I'll make tea." She showed him in and headed to the small kitchen. "Have a seat. We can tell each other stories. I've been alone for so long, it's wonderful to know I have family out in the world. Where are you from? I can't place your accent."

He sat on the couch, set his briefcase next to him on the floor, and placed his hands on his knees. "I was born in what they call Iraq, but I've traveled all over since then. I've lived on every continent except Antarctica, though if things don't change for me soon, I may end up there, as well."

"That sounds exciting," she said, setting two cups on the coffee table and joining him on the sofa. "I must tell you, your Greek is perfect. So, you travel for work?"

"Sometimes. Mostly, I just feel compelled to move on from one place to another...frequently. You might say I'm forced."

She raised her eyebrows and sipped her tea. "So what is it that you do?"

"For work?"

She nodded.

"I sell antiques, some antiquities, mostly at auction. When you're as old as I am, you tend to accumulate a lot of unnecessary trinkets. It's quite lucrative."

She snickered. "You think you're old? What are you, late-thirties? You're a baby." She patted his cheek before putting her cup back on the table.

"I'm older than you think."

She gave him a condescending glance.

"By thousands of years."

Her face fell as she saw the seriousness in his eyes. "How did you say we're related again?"

"Dimitra, there's no reason for you to be nervous."

"All right," she said, putting some distance between them on the couch.

"I am Cain, son of Adam, banished by God from my home, never able to create another for myself. *You* are my last living descendant."

She stared, her heart pounding.

"Good," he smiled. "The others laughed, at first. They didn't believe me. But you do, don't you?"

"I don't know what to believe." She took another sip of tea, the cup clinking against the glass of the table as she put it down, her hands trembling. "It sounds insane, but,"

"But?"

"There is something familiar about your face. In the cheeks and around the eyes. So much like my father's. When you said we were related, that's why I believed you. You must be a cousin."

"I'm not."

"I am a religious woman, but,"

"Look in my eyes, Dimitra. *Look at me.* Do you think I'm lying to you?"

A shaky hand covered her mouth as she looked him over.

Relief washed over him. "Good, that's good. Thank you, granddaughter. You're the first to see the truth. I've spent *millennia* searching for *one* to understand. You've made me very happy today."

"What do you want from me?"

"What I've always wanted. *Family.* One that wouldn't hate me for abandoning them when God's curse compelled me to leave. One that would remember me."

She could feel how tense her muscles had become. She took a deep breath and tried to relax, but her body wouldn't cooperate. "How can this be true? If you are who you say you are, how can you still be alive?"

His expression went dark as he remembered. "God punished me with eternal life when I killed my brother. He cursed me with the inability to stay in one place. I *need* to leave, sometimes after two weeks, sometimes twenty years. I get an urge, like a drowning man longing to breathe. I've tried forcing myself to stay put, but that ends in..."

"In what?"

"Bloodshed. I lose control. I lose my sanity. I slaughter those I love."

She stood and backed away.

"I won't hurt you, Dimitra. I swear it."

"You just admitted to *killing people. Your family.*"

He stood and walked toward her. "Yes, but it won't happen with you."

"How can I know that?"

He thought for a moment. She was older, not exactly someone he could take along on his travels. He couldn't stay with her, of course. Besides his curse, he had revenge to take. "You're right. You have no reason to trust me. I'll go." He picked up his case and went to the door. As he turned the knob, he suddenly got excited. "We can exchange letters! You can keep me apprised of your life's happenings. I can tell you all about my adventures, send you pictures of the places I go, things I see. We'll be pen-pals. I'm off to America next. New York. I'll send you something Statue of Liberty related." He smiled from ear to ear, the joy he felt in his heart like nothing he'd experienced before, at least, not that he could remember.

"All right," she agreed, her hand on her chest.

"Thank you, granddaughter. You have no idea what a blessing you are to me." He closed the door behind him as he left, the smile still plastered on his face. *Finally*, he thought. *A real family.* But she would only live another thirty years, at most. She would have no children. Soon he would be alone again, this time with no hope of ever being anything but. As he stepped out onto the pavement his anger returned. He'd spend as much time as he could visiting and corresponding with his new-found granddaughter, indulging in the love of family for what little time she had left. For now, though, he would have his vengeance.

Chapter 7

Michelle sat cross-legged at the top of the staircase, running her hand over a spot on the carpet still slightly tinted pink. The floors had been cleaned, but she could still smell the blood through the chemicals; Will's blood.

She had held herself together in front of Gabriel, but now, as she stayed alone in his house, the memories of her lost love had her reeling. Hattie had explained that her emotions would be amplified, but this was overwhelming. Her chest was tight, her stomach hurt, her head pounded. Her entire body ached for him. She couldn't sleep because every time she closed her eyes, she saw him, covered in blood, holding the knife to his throat, his bottom lip quivering. It must have broken his heart, living with what he'd done to her, even if for only a short time. She knew it had been an accident. He wasn't in control. She would have given anything to tell him she was okay and that she understood. The truth was, she would have forgiven him anything. She loved him with her whole heart and nothing, not psychosis, murder, or death could change how she felt.

Tears spilled down her cheeks as she lay down on the stained carpet, breathing in what she could of his scent. She sobbed, digging her nails into the soft floor and allowing the quiet cries to escape her throat. She didn't know how she'd go on, but she would. Somehow, she would get herself through this because she knew in her soul that Will would have wanted her to.

"I'm back!" Malik called, entering the apartment and dropping his suitcase at the door. "Val? Val, you home?" He looked quizzically at the baby-gym on the living room floor and the high-chair in the dining room. "You went shopping?"

"In here!" she called back.

"A little soon to be--" he stopped in the doorway to what used to be the guestroom, now decorated as a full-blown nursery, a crib against one wall, a changing table on another, and in the corner by the window sat his wife in a rocking chair, holding what looked to be a six-month-old baby in a pink onesie. "What's this?"

"We need to talk."

"I see that." He knelt next to her and took the infant's small hand. "Who's this?"

"Sinclair," Valerie told him, smiling down at her and back at him. "Sinclair Ann Perry."

He looked up at her, his eyes wide in surprise and confusion.

"Gabriel brought her to us. *For* us...to raise."

"Your sister, what?"

"She's my great-niece, Will's daughter."

"Will? The half-angel psycho that lost his mind and killed a bunch of people?" He felt a small jolt of electricity zap his hand. He pulled it away from Sinclair's grip and stood up. "What the..."

Valerie giggled. "I guess she doesn't like you talkin' shit about her daddy."

"What the hell is she?"

"*Be nice*. She's part-angel, part-vampire, part-human. One hundred percent family."

"Val, we can't...I mean, this is..." His voice trailed off as he folded his arms, furrowing his brow as his mind raced.

"The fuck we can't."

"Shouldn't Wyatt take care of her? She's *his*--"

"If the vampire he's fuckin' finds out she exists, she'll put her in a wood chipper. If Lucifer finds out, same thing. Gabriel's not exactly down for diaper duty, so we're it. This child has got no one else. Yes, she's a little complicated, but--"

"Val, she just *electrocuted me*. And, did you say, '*vampire*'?"

"Gabriel promised she's harmless. This isn't up for debate. She's *our* baby now. Only question is, what kind of father are you gonna be?"

The statement took him off guard. His jaw clenched and his heart leaped to his throat. He could tell she was dead serious. He would lose her if he didn't act right *quick*. So, he pushed his concerns aside, relaxed his arms, and softened his features. "I'm gonna be the best dad I can be." He knelt back down and pinched the infant's cheek. "But no more shocking me, okay?"

She giggled.

He laughed, too. "Awe, you're a good baby, huh? You eating real food, yet?"

"Still on baby food," Valerie said.

"Well, I make a mean sweet potato/banana puree. Maybe carrot applesauce? Just wait for those teeth to come in. You'll be eatin' real good."

The baby giggled again.

"You sure you're okay with this?" Valerie asked.

"Do I have a choice?" he chuckled.

"No."

"I'm cool with it. You're right. She's family. Besides, she's a baby. What's the worst that can happen?"

Michelle slurped the last few drops of blood from the final bag that Gabriel had sent. It should have been enough to last a week, but she was insatiable, emptying the stash in three nights. She was restless and tired of mourning. All she did was sit in the silence of her dead lover's house, missing him and thinking about their daughter. She knew giving her to Gabriel had been the right thing to do. There was no doubt in her mind about that. Still, she couldn't get the image of her face as she left her out of her mind. She looked so heartbroken. Like she knew. Michelle obsessed over that night, and the twisting guilt in her stomach mixed with her grief over Will had her mind swirling. She needed to get out of this house for a while. She needed to get away from herself.

She texted Gabriel, *Need more blood.* She immediately got a text back that read, *On its way.* It would be the next night before it arrived and while she knew logically that she should wait it out, her instincts were telling her something different. She was crawling out of her skin and she was hungry.

She decided to take a walk. The warm, late-summer breeze felt soft against her skin as she tied her long curls up in a scrunchie, her short sundress blowing lazily around her legs. She'd walk along the road for a while before turning back and going into the woods to hunt. Maybe she'd get lucky and find a deer or two. If nothing else, a rabbit or a squirrel might be enough of a snack to hold her over until her next shipment of human blood got there. Just a short walk, then a quick hunt. That was the plan. However, after only just losing sight of the house, a truck pulled up next to her.

"Get in," the driver demanded.

She sighed as she saw the man's face. It was the creep that had harassed her at the bowling alley the night Will first started slipping. It was his fault. If he hadn't provoked him, threatened her, Will never would have snapped. *He would have been fine,* she thought. *Everything would have been fine.*

"Bitch, I said get in." He slammed on the breaks and got out of the truck without turning off the engine. He stomped toward her, his jaw and fists clenched.

"You really should be running," she warned.

"You should be screaming," he retorted, reaching out to grab her by her ponytail, but before he could make contact, she grasped his wrist, twisted his arm behind him, and swept his leg out from under him, knocking him to the ground. He yelped in pain and surprise.

"I told you to run." She snapped his arm, the satisfying cracking sound sending a chill up her spine. He cried out, another sound she relished. She could hear his heartbeat quicken and feel his pulse speeding up under her thumb. He was afraid and she loved it.

"Let go of me you crazy bitch!"

"Let go? Is this not what you wanted?" She flipped him onto his back and swiped her nails across his cheek, leaving four perfect lines of blood dripping onto the pavement. The smell of it sent her into a frenzy. She was losing control. Her eyes flashed in the light of his high-beams and he gasped.

"What the fuck are you?"

"I'm a wild animal dressed like a princess. You wanted me in your truck. Let's get in the truck." She lifted him up by his collar and threw him, one-handed, into the driver seat. She was a blur to him as she sped around to the passenger side and slid in. "What's your plan, cornbread? What did you think would happen once I was trapped in your car?"

He held his arm, holding back tears as rage, pain, and terror mingled on his face. "I was gonna play with you a little first, but now I'm just gonna kill you."

She laughed, holding her stomach as she bellowed. "You're gonna *what*? Oh, man, that's amazing. Oh, Jesus, I can't tell you how much I needed that. Thanks for the laugh, buddy, really. Much appreciated." She continued to cackle as his face went red.

He moved closer in a sad attempt to overpower her, but she grabbed him by the throat and shoved him down into his seat. "You know," she remarked. "I've had a real shitty past few months. Like, *the worst*. I blame you. Maybe that's ridiculous. Maybe things would have gone sideways no matter what. But I'm putting it on you. Your fault. You fucked it all up. And, yet, I was willing to walk away, be the bigger person. I tried to tell you. I said, 'run'. Did you listen? Of course not. You're a sociopath. Serial killer? Racist? It doesn't matter. You're bleeding now and I'm starving, so." Her eyes dilated and her fangs grew. He screamed, using his good hand to try to push her away. She slammed it into the door before pressing his head to the side, exposing his neck. Her skin felt hot as she caved to her instincts and bit down, gulping mouthfuls of the warm, salty fluid that escaped his veins. He fought against her, kicking and pushing, but she was too strong. His squirming became weaker as she drank and when he'd lost too much blood, he passed out. She kept drinking, unable to stop herself. Eventually, she felt his pulse on her lips stop. His heart went quiet.

She pulled back and looked him over, her belly full and her eyes and teeth returning to normal. She felt no guilt for what she'd done. She knew she should, that it was horrible not to. Monstrous. But in that moment, all she felt was justified.

A flash of light drew her attention to the windshield. Another car was approaching. She hurried out of the truck and rushed to the field beyond the road, hiding in the tall stalks of corn. She watched as the car stopped and a man got out to investigate while a woman in the passenger seat waited.

"Call nine-one-one!" the man yelled. The woman complied as the man felt the corpse's wrist for a pulse. Michelle scurried away, unnoticed by the pair. She ran straight back to the house, locking herself inside. She washed the blood from her lips, nose, and chin, threw on a pair of pajamas, and went up to Will's old bedroom. If the police came, she'd say she'd been sleeping and didn't know anything about what happened to the stranger just down the road.

Chapter 8

Wendy dropped her bag and kicked off her shoes. The last few days at work had been exhausting and she was glad to finally be home.

"Hello, Wendy," a voice said from the dimly lit kitchen. "Don't be startled. I'm a friend of your girlfriend."

"Are you?" she asked, unconvinced, recognizing him from her flight to Greece a few days before. She walked toward the man, showing no fear, which seemed to surprise him.

He took a knife from a drawer and spun it on the counter. "Oh, yes. We go way back. Several times over the years I asked God to lift the curse He placed on me. Begged Him. And every time, Gabriel would come to me and say that He would not. No explanation, just refusal."

"God cursed you? Doesn't sound like Him."

He smirked. "You should reread Genesis."

"And you and Gabriel are friends?" she condescended.

"Well, maybe not 'friends'. But I *do* know her. She's not the only person we have in common. I believe you've also met my daughter, Allydia."

She tilted her head as she put together who he must be. "Cain?"

"In the flesh."

"Huh. I thought you died like, five thousand years ago."

"Would that I could."

"Uh, huh."

"You see, I had a plan. Destroy the Gate to Heaven and kill the angels, thereby severing the link between God's consciousness and Earth and in turn, breaking my curse. I would be free to settle, marry, and have a family. I would grow old and by the time God woke and repaired the Gate, I would have been long dead, my soul in Purgatory, on its way to being reborn. I could have been a normal man, Wendy. I could have had *a life*. But the angels robbed me of it."

"Okay, but didn't you like, brutally murder your brother over some bullshit? Seems like you had the whole curse thing coming."

He slammed his fist down on the counter. His jaw tightened and a low growl escaped his throat. He dabbed the sweat from his brow and collected himself before addressing her again. "My brother and I had come to an amicable distribution of the world's resources. He would rule over the creatures of the Earth and the land would be mine to cultivate. I grew olives, figs, and pomegranates. I had fields of barley and wheat. I grew melons bigger than your head, and when I offered my finest crops to Elohim as a tribute, he rejected them. But my brother slew a few lambs and *that* was considered a proper sacrifice. I was jealous of my brother and couldn't control my resentment." He paused, picking up the knife and gazing into it like a mirror. "When He asked what I'd done, I lied. *That's what He hated.* He didn't care that Abel was dead. He was angry that I attempted to deceive Him."

"Cool story, bro. So, why are you here, exactly?"

He set the knife down and closed the distance between them. "The angels stole my chance at happiness. Snatched it from my hands just as I was reaching for it. So, I will take from them what gives them joy, starting with you." He reached for her throat, his face twisted in a maniacal grin. But before his fingers could touch her skin, he was thrown back, slamming into the dining table and falling to the floor.

"Yeah, I should have told you," she said. "When I helped save the Gate from your lackey, I also took the warding your ex had given him. Technically, being immortal and all, you're a supernatural creature. You can't hurt me. Although, if I'm being honest, if you were just a dude, I would have kicked your ass pretty hard, anyway, because spells."

He picked up the knife and hurled it at her face, but it bounced off an invisible shield that seemed to surround her. He took the spike from its case and stomped toward her, but when he got close, he was again sent flailing, crashing hard into the upper cabinets and dropping down to the gray, slate tiled floor.

He stood, brushing off the sleeves of his suit jacket and letting out an angry sigh. He huffed past her and left the apartment, muttering under his breath, "*Witches.*"

Allydia stood in the empty apartment, her brows furrowed as she placed her hands on her hips. It felt suspicious. She'd called Gabriel to confirm the address and she'd told her that, indeed, one of her descendants did live there. But there was no one. The only things left were a few scattered papers on the floor and two teacups sitting on a glass coffee table, still mostly full of what smelled to her like Sideritis and honey.

She walked through the rooms, wondering what had happened, why someone would have left in such a hurry. She hoped whoever had resided there was all right and that she'd be able to track them down one day.

"You're back!" Gabriel gleaned as she ushered Wendy into the apartment. She hugged her tightly and kissed her, her excitement clear on her face.

"I'm back," Wendy smiled, taking her girlfriend's hands in hers. "I have to tell you something. That Cain dude showed up at my place today."

She bit her lip and cupped Wendy's face in her hands, "Are you okay? You don't look hurt."

"No, I'm fine. Lilith's warding. He can't touch me."

She let out a sigh of relief. "Right. Good. Okay. Maybe you should stay with me for a few days, though, just in case."

"I can take care of myself. He's pretty pissed we ruined his master plan, though."

"Yeah, but you know what they say. While we make plans, God laughs and says, 'Not so fast, dumbass'."

"Oh, is that how the saying goes?" she snickered.

"That is *totally* the unredacted version," Gabriel giggled.

They kissed again, allowing their hands to run over one another's bodies. "Lucifer here?"

Gabriel shook her head. "Still with the bartender."

"Well," she slipped her fingers into the waist of her lover's jeans and pulled her closer, fiddling with the top button. "Maybe I could stay *one* night."

Chapter 9

Lucifer brushed his lips along the side of Mariana's neck as she buried her face in her pillow, reaching back and taking a fistful of his soft, blond hair in her trembling hand. She moaned in aching pleasure as she submitted, the pressure of his body on her back, dominating her like a hungry beast sending chills up and down her spine. She couldn't get enough of him. He was a drug and she was addicted.

"Am I hurting you, love?" he asked, his voice quiet and husky in her ear.

She opened her mouth to answer, but her mind was too clouded by bliss to form words, so she shook her head and steadied herself on the mattress as she began to climax. As they finished, light from the rising sun filtered through the rose-colored blinds of Mariana's window, illuminating the small bedroom in a pinkish hue. Lucifer stood, finding his slacks and swiftly pulling them on.

"What are you doing?" She clicked the lamp on and pulled the blanket up around her.

"I need to stop by my sister's for some fresh clothes and a shower."

"You can shower here."

"Yes, but I've been wearing the same trousers for three days. It's obscene."

"On the rare occasion that you're actually wearing pants," she teased.

He flashed a flirty smirk, kissed her cheek, and finished dressing. "Would it be too forward of me to pay you another visit tomorrow?"

She smiled, getting up on her knees and letting the blanket fall. She sucked on her bottom lip and ran her hand over his chest. "I'd be offended if you didn't."

"Very well." He gave her a once over, held her face in his hands, and kissed her hard. "I will see you soon." He left the room and the apartment, making sure to lock up before closing the door, and heading down the stairs.

The early morning air was still as he began the long walk to Gabriel's apartment. The quiet of the usually busy street allowed his mind to wander. He thought about the time he'd spent with Mariana and how relaxing it had been. He'd never been on Earth long enough to develop an attachment to a human before. He wasn't sure what he was feeling, but he *did* know that he'd grown fond of her company and was looking forward to seeing her again. Perhaps he'd follow in his sister's footsteps and open up to Mariana more. Not about who he really was, of course, but maybe a conversation where both parties were fully clothed wouldn't be the *worst* thing.

"Coming!" Wyatt called as he hurried to pull up his jeans and throw on a tee-shirt, the sound of persistent banging on his door waking him from a too-short sleep. He rushed to answer it, not recognizing the man standing before him. "Yes?"

"You call yourself 'Wyatt', yes?" the man asked.

"That's my name."

"Is it? My ex-wife told me something different. Unless you're *not* the angel that wields lightning?"

He glanced around the hall to make sure none of his neighbors had heard. It was empty. "Who are you?"

"My apologies. I should have introduced myself sooner, considering you're sleeping with my daughter."

Wyatt raised an eyebrow and stepped aside, allowing the man to enter. "Allydia's not here. I expect her back tonight, though. I can tell her you stopped by."

"That won't be necessary. I know not to attempt a visit with her during daylight hours. I came to see you."

"If you want to know what my intentions are, I honestly couldn't tell you. Coffee?" He poured two cups, relieved to have a coffee maker with a timer. He wasn't twenty anymore and staying up into the wee hours was beginning to take a toll.

"I'd love some, thank you."

"How do you take it?"

"Black as my soul."

Wyatt snickered as he handed him the cup and gestured toward the barstool across from him.

Cain sat, taking a sip and setting the drink down on the smooth countertop. "It's very good."

"Filtered water," he said, gulping it down and pouring another cup. "A trick my son taught me."

He tilted his head. "You have a son?"

"Not anymore."

He sat up straight. "Well, my condolences. I know what it's like to lose children."

"I'd imagine."

"Yes. Speaking of children, I came to warn you of one of mine."

"Warn me?" He wiped the sleep from his eyes and did his best to focus on what Cain was telling him through the fog of exhaustion.

"I've watched my daughter over the years, hoping that as she learned to control her urges, she'd return to her once sweet-natured ways. You should have seen her, helping me in the fields, tending to her children.

She was a light in the dark for me. But the years have made her hard. She's grown sadistic. My fault, if I'm being honest, either by my actions or sheer genetics. Either way, it would be in your best interest to flee from her before she turns her anger to you...and kills you."

He chortled. "As long as she's alive, I can't die."

"'Alive' being a relative term."

He sighed and folded his hands. "What are you doing here?"

"As I said--"

"You're trying to get me to leave my girlfriend, your own daughter. You hate her that much?"

"I don't hate her," he insisted, his jaw tightening. "*I miss her.* It killed me to abandon her."

"And kidnap her kids?"

"I did what I had to!" He slammed his hand down on the counter, his face turning a deep shade of red. "You didn't see what I saw. *She was gone.* The witch brought her back with the darkest of magic and made her a creature I didn't recognize. She would have butchered those girls had I not saved them from her clutches."

"So, you're not just immortal. You're also psychic."

"Be glib all you like, but I was right. It broke my heart to do it, but *I was right.*" He calmed down and took another sip of coffee as Wyatt stared daggers.

"You should go."

He looked him in the eye and sat back, breathing a sigh of defeat as he looked the angel over. "She's dangerous."

"I know that."

"But you won't heed my advice. She's gotten her hooks in." He squinted as he studied his face. "You love her." He stood, drank the last of his coffee, and walked back to the door. Taking the knob in his hand, he turned to address Wyatt one more time. "You're a damn fool."

Cain's attempt at killing two birds with one stone had failed spectacularly. The angel, Barachiel, had very few people in his life that he cared about and they were all other angels, aside from Allydia, who was also too powerful for him to take down. Breaking up their romantic relationship was all he could think to do to punish them for what they'd done. They'd have to go unscathed, for now.

Enraged by his second failure, he turned his attention to an easier target. He bounded up the steps to the apartment Lucifer had been spending so much time in lately. He was certain there was a woman inside; a *human* woman, weak compared to the others and perfect for taking out his frustrations on.

He made his way to her door and kicked it in, breaking the frame and sending bits of wood flying. She screamed, jumping back and running to the bedroom where she tried to lock him out. But he was too strong and pushed his way in with ease.

"You're quite pretty," he panted, already tired from physical exertion. "I'm not surprised. Lucifer always did have excellent taste."

Mariana grabbed the lamp from the nightstand and raised it, but as she brought it down, Cain caught it, avoiding a head injury and becoming more irritated. He threw it against the wall and shook his head, setting his briefcase on the bed, opening it, and pulling out the iron spike. She tried to run, but he grabbed her by the hair, yanking her back and tossing her to the floor. He stood over her, his heart beating out of his chest. He felt exhilarated, the panic on the girl's face like a jolt of caffeine. Finding her body would surely anger God's favorite son. It might even make him a touch sad. Cain laughed as he gripped the spike, lifted it up, and plunged it into the girl's heart.

She gasped, blood bubbling up and spilling from her quivering lips. He pulled his weapon out and stuck her again, this time in the abdomen. He smiled gleefully as blood splattered across his face. He stood upright, wiping his instrument on her bed-sheets and placing it back in its case. After a few seconds of convulsing, the girl's body went limp, her hands dropping to her sides, and the light in her eyes going dark.

He turned to the makeup table, using a tissue to clean his face. As he looked in the mirror, he wondered how he'd make sure Lucifer would know it was he who'd laid out this fantastically brutal scene for him to find. He tapped his fingers on the whitewashed wood and looked down. That's when he saw the makeup brushes and smiled.

Chapter 10

"I'll be back in a few days," Wendy giggled as Gabriel pet her hair and stuck out her lip.

"Fine, but next time someone calls in sick to a flight to goddamn *New Zealand*, fake a cold, maybe."

"I'll try." She kissed her goodbye and left the apartment.

"Well, it was nice seeing your significant other again, even if only for a few minutes," Lucifer said from the sofa. "Seems things are going swimmingly."

"Yeah, it's going great. Makes me feel like something bad's gonna happen any minute."

"Don't be so pessimistic, sister. She adores you, I can see it in her eyes. What could possibly go wrong?"

She gave him a knowing look. "All the things."

"All right, what's bothering you? Something's on your mind, I can tell. What is it? Barachiel in another depression? Did Uriel's husband leave her? Did one of your favorite reality stars get the clap?"

She laughed. "That would be hilarious, but no. I've recently been made aware of something and I'm struggling with it."

"Do tell." He sat across from her at the island, his interest piqued.

"I have to do something. It's not optional, it's God mandated. Gabriel knows it's the right thing to do. *Gabriel* understands."

"Ah, but *Taran Murphy*--"

"Can't bring herself to do it."

He folded his hands and leaned forward. "My advice, should you be willing to hear it,"

She nodded.

"Take your time. You know as well as I do that you will do as He commands. You will always aid our Father in his endeavors. It's how you were made. But, if it's hard, procrastinate." He gave her a wink and sat back.

"I don't think I should. I'd like to, I really would, but he's already attacked Wendy. He could come after any--"

"Who did?"

She sat down, folded her arms, and crossed her legs, a look of aggravation on her face. "Cain. He's in town and on the warpath. I guess he's salty we fucked up his big plan."

He rolled his eyes. "*Cain*. He's been a thorn in my side for years. Recent events aside, he used to follow me when I'd be here on the hunt for demons. Seems he thought we should be allies of some sort. He was a pest, always trying to endear himself to me, bringing me gifts, as if my friendship was somehow useful to him. That all changed when he found me with his daughter in Akrotiri. I'm not sure if he was offended that I'd bedded her or if he was simply so afraid of her that he decided not to risk another encounter. Either way, I was free of him after that."

She shot him a look. "Why would you put that image in my head? I already have to see that shit every time B's around. At this point, I feel like *I've* been fucking her."

"I'm surprised you haven't been."

"She only likes dudes."

"Oh, that's right."

"You hungry? I'm making dinner."

"You're *what*?"

She picked up her phone and showed him the restaurant's website.

"In that case, yes, I'm famished."

Chapter 11

Allydia sat on her throne, relieved to be back in the city she called home. She rifled through the papers on the small, marble table next to her, deciding none of it was worth her time. She was excited to get back to the apartment...to Wyatt.

"Your Majesty," her assistant said, bowing as she entered the room.

"Yes, Hartley, what is it?"

"How was your trip, my Queen?"

"It was fine."

"Your dress is beautiful. I especially like the corset. The black really brings out your--"

"Why are you stalling?"

"I apologize, Your Majesty. I hate giving you bad news."

"What is it?"

"While you were away, I personally kept watch of your lover at night, as you instructed."

"Yes?"

"And during the day, I had my most trusted human stake out his place. I told him that if anyone suspicious came around, to take a closer look and make sure nothing happened."

She sat up straight, her cold stare giving Hartley chills.

"He's fine," she assured her. "I went as soon as the sun went down myself to look in on him. I made sure he didn't see me. He was eating something from a box, looked like pizza. I have someone there now, just in case, but I thought I should show you this myself." She approached her, keeping her eyes averted as she pulled up the photos on her rhinestone-encrusted phone. "My man got pictures of a guy going into his apartment. Now, it's been a few decades since you showed me the portrait in the basement, so call me crazy, but is that the same man? Is this," She pointed to the face on the screen. "Is he the man you told us to avoid at all costs? That he was too dangerous? Is *this* the only man you fear?"

She studied the picture, squinting to get a good look. When she was certain, she stood up, the quickness of her motion startling her assistant, nearly causing her to drop the phone. "Fear has been replaced with indignation. Yes, that's him. And you're sure Wyatt's all right?"

"Yes, Your Majesty." She swiped the screen a few times and showed it to her Queen. It was a live feed of Wyatt, still sitting at the kitchen island, finishing a soda. It was clear that the video was being taken through a window with a zoom lens as the quality was somewhat grainy but clear enough to ease her mind.

"Good. Did your man follow the man in the picture?"

"No, he stayed watch, but he did send someone else. From what he told me, dude's kind of a psychopath."

"And you know where he is now?"

"Yes, my Queen."

She stomped to the door, her leather boots clicking on the wood sounding like urgency mixed with rage. "Text me the address."

She moved through the crowd like wind, fast, squeezing past vampires without them noticing. The music was loud and so were they, laughing and singing along as they drank. The lights were dim, but she could still make out the familiar shape of the man she'd only recently been stalking. She halted, tilting her head in confusion as he rushed up to her, vampires licking their lips as he passed.

"Why were you following me?" he accused. The eyes of the crowd turned to them.

"You shouldn't be here," she warned. "It isn't safe for you."

"I can handle myself. Who are you?"

She grabbed his arm and sped him out of the club, not stopping until they were several blocks away. She pulled him into an alley and folded her arms like an exasperated parent. "Why are you here, Navid?"

"What the hell? How did we get here?"

"Navid."

"How do you know my name? Why were you following me?"

She shifted her weight from one foot to another and sighed. "I'm impressed that you found me. I'm normally much better at covering my tracks."

"I'm a detective. Hunting people down is in my blood."

"Yes, I suppose it is."

"So, who is it, mm? O-Tray-One? ABM? Who sent you and what for? To kill me? Take your shot, but I warn you, I have no problem defending myself, even against a woman."

She chuckled. "You're feisty."

"I mean it. If one of them white boy gangster wannabe's has a beef and are too chicken-shit to come at me proper, deciding to send a girl to do their dirty work--"

"I would never hurt you, Navid. No one sent me."

He stepped back, the anger in his expression turning to confusion. "What, then? Woman as beautiful as you wouldn't be interested in a nobody bloke like me, definitely not to the point of criminal following. You a debt collector? I owe nothing, but you never know with identity theft being what it is."

"Nothing like that. I just wanted to get a look at you."

"What for?"

She peeked her head around the corner to make sure they hadn't been followed before looking him squarely in the eye. "We're related. Very,

very distantly. I wanted to make sure you were all right. That's it. I promise, from now on, I will leave you alone."

"Related? How? That doesn't make sense."

"I have to take care of something and as I told you, you're not safe here. I need you to leave." She left the alley and didn't turn back, not wanting anyone who may be watching to see them together.

"But I have questions!" he called.

She quickened her steps. "Go home!"

Allydia opened the door to the first-floor hotel room, easily breaking the lock and startling the man inside. "Hello, Father."

He jumped up from his spot on the edge of the bed and backed away, catching his breath as he tried and failed to hide his terror. "Daughter."

"When was the last time our paths crossed? Do you remember?"

"It was 1583, The Battle of Torches, I believe."

"That's right. You came upon me feasting on a half-dead soldier and proceeded to vomit all over your boots."

"I remember."

"You scolded me. You called me a monster, said I was no daughter of yours. You told me that if you ever saw me again, you'd kill me. I believed you."

"Allydia, you must understand--"

"So, I kept my distance. I hid from you. I created a network of spies to inform me of your whereabouts to avoid you at all costs, and now you're here, in my city. Why? What have you been up to, Father? Besides harassing the man I love."

"Love?" he chortled. "Honestly, daughter. *Love?* He's not fit for *you.* One day, he will see you for what you are and he will run from you, if you don't destroy him first."

"You lost the right to an opinion on my love life when you murdered my husband."

"I faulted Farhan for your death, you can hardly blame me."

"Why are you here, Father?" she barked.

He jumped. "To bring justice to those that wronged me."

She tilted her head and folded her arms.

"*The angels*, girl. I had a chance at a normal life. If the Gate had been destroyed, if the angels were back in Heaven, the link between God and Earth would be severed. His power would no longer reach me. I would be able to have more children, age, and die. By the time He woke from his slumber, I would have been reborn, or at least, on my way to it. I'd be able to settle on a farm somewhere, live a life. It's all I've ever wanted. *A family.*"

She scowled, fighting the tears that threatened to come as she clenched her teeth. "You lost your chance at a family when you left me."

"I didn't leave *you*," he said, his voice shaky. He took the spike from the case. "My daughter was already dead." His words were stern, but his heart was racing, and beads of sweat formed on his temples. He was afraid of her, a realization that both saddened and amused her.

"The plow you used to slaughter your brother? It's a little melodramatic, don't you think?"

"I'll give you one chance to leave. You know you can't hurt me."

"And you know that's not true."

"Allydia,"

"I absolutely can. I shouldn't. There's a slight difference."

He backed away again, his back almost to the wall.

"I wouldn't kill you, of course. But there are other ways of making you suffer. Apply pressure here, remove an organ there."

"Allydia ibnat Cain."

"No ibnat!" she shouted, rushing toward him. "Calling me 'daughter' is another right you lost long ago."

He swallowed hard, tightening his grip on the iron spike. "Fine. But I did not lose all hope of family when you died. There's another. I met with her. We are to be friends. So, your angels didn't take *everything* from me. I will have a few decades with--"

"The woman in Tripoli?" she asked, stepping back.

"How did you know that?"

"I stopped by her apartment. By any chance, did she serve tea when you visited?"

His face fell. "What did you do?"

"I did nothing. She was gone by the time I arrived. The only things left were two teacups, still half full. She must have left in a hurry. I believe you frightened her."

"You're lying."

"You know I don't lie."

He fumed, nearly shaking in his anger.

"Seems you are alone, Father. As God intended." She opened the door. "Stay away from Wyatt. If you come near him again, I won't hesitate." She left the room, hurrying out of the building and making her way to a nearby bus stop where she sat down, the cool metal of the bench a sharp contrast to the heat in the air.

She covered her mouth and cried, allowing herself one brief moment of weakness, her father's words cutting her deeper than his weapon ever could. She heard footsteps approaching from behind her, so she wiped her tears away, sat up straight, and turned to see Navid, his face sorrowful and bewildered.

"Are you all right?" he asked, sitting next to her.

"I'm fine. I told you to go."

"There's no way I'm leaving now. Not after what I've just seen."

"What did you see?"

"I was watching through the window. I heard everything."

She looked around, checking for passersby. The street was quiet.

"You called that man 'Father', but he looks no older than you and he hasn't aged a day since I saw him murder my mother."

She looked at him, her features softening. "What?"

"He didn't know I was there. I was hiding, stuffed in a hamper. I was four years old, but I'll remember his face for the rest of my life. *It was him.* Wasn't it?"

"Probably, yes."

"And he wants to kill you, too? He called you a monster? Why?"

"Because I *am* a monster. Queen of monsters. I'm very sorry about what happened to your mother. I don't know why he would kill her. Just his nature, I suppose. You should go home. Forget you ever met me. Forget what you heard. *Forget* about my father." She stood to go, but he grabbed her wrist.

"You said we were related."

"It doesn't matter."

"You said distantly, but how distant can it be if you have my mother's eyes?"

She stopped, her heart leaping to her throat.

"My mother was my only living relative. I was adopted by strangers from another city. Who are you? Please, I need to know who you are so I can understand who *I* am."

"All right," she relented. "Where are you staying?"

Chapter 12

Wendy arrived at the lodge, exhausted after an eighteen-and-a-half-hour flight. There was a lovely patio with an umbrellaed table, a cozy living room, kitchenette, bathroom, and spacious bedroom where she dropped her bags, then herself, onto the queen-sized bed. Just as she was about to kick her shoes off and settle in for a nap, a knock came on the glass patio door. She groaned and got up to answer it, bumping into the dresser as she went, grunting, more agitated than hurt.

She recognized the older woman waving excitedly as she slid the door open to let her in as the witch that had called her here, begging for help.

"Wendy!" she chirped, giving her a quick hug. "So glad you're here. How was your flight?"

"Long," she said, flashing her a smile.

"Right," she laughed, her accent so endearing that Wendy's annoyance drifted away. "Well, I'm Charlotte. Sorry to bug you already, but this is pretty time-sensitive."

"I understand. Let's sit." They took a seat on the blue, leather sofa. "So, what exactly are we dealing with?"

"You know the legend of Maui?"

"Just the cartoon version."

She held back a snicker. "Well, the myths deviate quite substantially from his actual history."

"Why doesn't that surprise me?"

"Maui was a warlock, born into a family who controlled very strong magic. As a child, his grandmother told him stories about an island that sank to the bottom of the ocean many generations before. She told him about the beautiful beaches and interesting wildlife. She spoke of waterfalls and mountains and sunsets so spectacular, they were like something from a dream. His brothers told him it was a fairy tale, but he so loved it that he was determined to make it real. When his grandmother died, he used her jawbone, his blood, and a karakia to work a spell. Now, no one knows for sure if he created the island or just pulled it up from the depths, but either way, it's now called 'Te Ika-a-Maui', or 'The North Island'."

"Where we are now."

"Yes, exactly. Seems well enough, right? But, as Maui got older, he became obsessed with ruling over his island. He loved it so much, he never wanted to leave it. Like, *never*. So, he sought out a powerful witch who was said to know the secrets of immortality named Hine-nui-te-po. She lived deep in a cave, in hiding from her handsy father. He wooed her with gifts of exotic birds whose songs were the most beautiful she'd ever heard. He bottled the rays of the sun, giving her light where she'd never had any. He made her happy for maybe the first time in her life. He tricked her into falling in love with him, thinking that she would share her secret spells. One night, when they were...*together*, she noticed one of the birds, a fantail. Unbeknownst to Maui, one of her powers was animal communication. The bird was nervous, so she went into its mind and saw its memories, memories of Maui making plans to deceive her. She was livid, so she took a dagger made of obsidian and jammed it into his back."

"While he was still," She made an awkward thrusting motion.

Charlotte nodded, eyebrows raised. "She stuck him a few times, actually, until he stopped moving. When she was sure he was dead, she vowed that one day, she'd be reborn and she'd take her revenge again, this time by plunging his precious island back into the sea. Then, she worked a spell using his blood, the blood of the bird, and her own. For the spell to work and bring her back, she had to sacrifice her life, so she slit her throat."

"Holy crap balls. So, you need me because you think she's back?"

"We're fairly sure. There have been a lot of earthquakes lately, geysers are more active. Almost four million people live here now. It's the perfect time for her to return if her goal is to inflict as much damage as possible. My coven and I are little more than holistic medicine peddlers. We're no match for someone like her. But a Tituban witch might stand a fighting chance."

Wendy chewed the inside of her cheek as she pondered, her mind so fatigued, it was hard to string a coherent thought together. "Okay, I'm having some serious brain fog right now, so let me get a few hours of sleep and meet me back here with the coven in the morning."

"Oh, of course. Get some sleep. The girls and I will see you bright and early."

Wendy had just pulled on her sweater when she heard chattering coming from the living room. When she got there, she found twelve women, talking and seeming to be in good spirits, sitting around the coffee table.

"Wendy!" Charlotte greeted, breaking away from the group. "Come, sit. We've brought meat pies and L&P. Alice makes *the best* pies."

A woman, presumably Alice, waved from the sofa. Wendy smiled and took a seat next to her, picking up a pie from the table and taking a bite. Her eyes widened and she nodded. "She *does* make the best pies."

"Why, thank you, dear," the woman, who had to be in her late seventies, said. "I'll be sure to get you the recipe."

"Thank you." She tried to sense the magic in the room, but only a tiny bit sparked from Charlotte. Everyone else here was almost void of it entirely. *This isn't a coven,* she thought. *It's a goddamn book club.* "So, do you ladies know where we might find the resurrected witch we're after?"

The room went quiet, all of the women turning their eyes to Charlotte, whose expression went from chipper to defeated. She took a deep breath and folded her hands in her lap, appearing to be afraid of how Wendy would respond to what she had to say. She looked her in the eye, took another breath, and answered, "We have no idea."

"All right. I'll walk around the island, see if I can sense her."

"Just like that?" Charlotte exchanged dumbfounded glances with some of the other women. "You can just...*feel* her?"

"I can feel *magic* and if she's as strong as you say she is, it won't be hard to point her out in a crowd." She took another bite of pie. "*God,* these really are *good.*"

"It's the garlic," Alice said proudly. "I add a little extra."

"Hmm."

"You can *feel magic*?" Charlotte asked, visibly stunned.

"Yeah, I'm a witch. So, I'm gonna walk around, see what I can see. Who knows? Maybe what's going on with the island is completely natural."

The women exchanged knowing glances which made Wendy think of the phrases, 'Oh, girl' and 'Bless her heart'. She ignored it and took a sip of soda as she stood to go. "Stay here, make yourselves comfortable. I'll be back when I know something. Hey, can I take another one of these pies with me?"

Alice grinned from ear to ear. "Of course, dear."

"Thanks." She took a pie, her soda, and a napkin and headed out, half expecting to find nothing at all.

Chapter 13

Michelle tossed an empty blood bag on the pile on the coffee table. Her leg was nearly vibrating, she was tapping her foot so fast. No one had come by asking about the man in the truck and she wasn't sure if she should be relieved or if it had just not occurred to the police to interrogate her...yet. She gathered up her trash and shoved it down into the can in the kitchen before washing her hands. She paced the room, memories of finding Will on the floor, bleeding and covered in wolf bites clawing at her mind. Tears filled her eyes as her hands began to shake. It was all she could do to keep herself from going up to his room, throwing herself on his bed, and never getting up again. She wanted to exist there, desiccating in her own misery until even the hunger left her. She could go up there right now, lay down, and let herself die.

She shook her head, pushing the thought from her mind and sitting at the dining table. She held her hands together and tapped them on her forehead as she tried to get herself together. In the distance, she could hear a wolf howl and her despair turned to rage. "Don't do it," she told herself. "Stay your ass here. Do not leave this house." She put her head down and gripped the sides of her chair, trembling, physically holding herself back from the pain she wanted to inflict. He'd told her that he'd killed the entire pack that attacked him, but had he? Or were there more, haunting the woods like ghosts, waiting for Will to come back. But he wasn't coming back. He would never come back. He was lost to her. Forever.

She reached a shaky hand into her back pocket and pulled out her phone. She called Gabriel first, but there was no answer, so she dialed Hattie's number, a burner to be used only in case of an emergency.

"Michelle? What's wrong?" she answered.

"I'm not okay. I need help."

"Have you met with Gabriel?"

"Yeah, she took Sinclair. She's sending me blood bags, but I'm going through them too fast. I'm always hungry and *I'm so mad*. Jesus Christ, Hattie, I'm so mad all the time. I go from wanting to die to wanting to go on a murder binge."

"I'm so sorry, dear, but I told you this would happen. You should have stayed with me. I could have helped you."

"You wanted me to kill my baby."

"Yes, before the Queen did, when she was older and aware of her circumstances."

"Gabriel can protect her."

"Are you sure about that? I've seen the Queen do things that would curl your hair."

"My hair's already curly and if it's a smackdown between the vampire Queen and God's Messenger, I'm putting my money on the angel every time."

"Yes, fine. So, what do you need from me?"

"Can I come back to stay with you in Scotland? I know it's risky, but--"

"Risky's an understatement, but it doesn't matter. I was just packing my things to leave this place. I'm fairly certain Her Majesty's spies are closing in on me here. Text me your address and I'll come to you."

Allydia sat across from her descendant at the round dining table in the tiny apartment he was renting for the week. It smelled of stale cigarettes and shattered dreams. Whoever owned this place was a sad individual, indeed.

"My name is Allydia Cain," she began, noting how interested he seemed to be as she spoke, like he was starving for words. "I'm a vampire."

He laughed out loud. "A what?"

"Vampire. Queen of vampires, actually. I'm the first."

"You're joking."

"Something you should know about me," She opened her mouth and bared her fangs. He jumped back in his seat and she returned her teeth to their normal size. "I don't lie."

"What the," His voice trailed off as he stared.

"Before I was turned, I had three daughters. They went on to have children of their own who had children and so on for thousands of years. Lines died out over time and now *you* are the last of my descendants. Well, there is one other, an old Greek woman, but after the fright my father gave her, I may leave her be."

His face was blank, his mouth hanging open.

"My father is Cain, son of Adam. He doesn't age because he's been cursed by God. How familiar are you with religious literature?"

"Cain? As in, Cain and Abel?"

"Yes, that's right. He's everything you think he is and worse. As for me, I'm no danger to you. But, if the others find out who you are, you wouldn't be safe. That's why I told you to leave. Humans are little more than playthings and food to most of my people. They will not hesitate to use you in any way they can if they don't just kill you outright. That's why you must go. Do you understand?"

"But, Cain--"

"Has no clue you exist. As long as he doesn't see us together, you'll be fine."

He entwined his fingers as if in prayer and rested his chin on his hands, his eyes locked on hers. "Let me tell you a story, mm?"

"All right."

"Me mum grew up in Ahvaz. She had a good life. Family, friends. She grew up, got a good job. She was happy. When she was twenty, both her parents died in a plane crash. They were going on holiday for their anniversary. She was crushed. She decided to go on holiday herself. Took a trip to Italy where she had wine for the first time. She got wasted, completely sloshed, every night for a week. Her last night there, she did it up proper. Club hoppin', pub crawl, the whole thing. At one of them pubs, she met a man. He started chattin' her up, tellin' her she was tidy, she looked exotic. Said he fancied her, right? So, he followed her 'round the whole night like a dog on a leash and me mum got smitten. Took him back to her hotel and you can guess where that went, yeah? Next day, he's gone. No note, nothin'. She didn't even know his name. So, she went home, didn't think of it again. Then, the country's invaded. There's a war on. In the midst of that, she realized she hadn't gotten her monthly. So she fled. Took the last of her money and went to London where she had me. Life was hard, her bein' illegal, but we had a roof over our heads and food in our bellies, and on my life, I *never* heard that woman complain. She was amazin' and I loved her. Then, one day, I'm watchin' telly and there's a knock on the door. She looked out the spyhole and saw a bloke she didn't recognize. Thought he might be immigration enforcement, so she hid me in a hamper and told me to stay quiet. Through the openings in the wicker, I could see her let him in. I couldn't hear what was bein' said, but everything seemed fine for a while, til she got this look on her face. Same look she gave me when I fell off the back of the sofa and got a lump on my head. Terror mixed with fury. I saw her waving him toward the door, but he wouldn't leave. I watched him slap her across the face and I stayed hidden while he took an iron spike out of a briefcase and plunge it into her heart like it was his fuckin' job. Like he couldn't care less. He killed my mother. I can't leave without bringing him to justice."

"I understand," she told him. "He kidnapped three of my daughters and offered up the fourth to my stepmother as a sacrifice to make me what I am. He's a monster, maybe more so than I am. But, there is no justice for someone as cruel as my father. At least, not that can be administered by human hands."

"So, I should let it go, is what you're sayin'? How? And what about you?"

"What about me?"

"You're my ancestor, yeah? The only family I have left in the world besides that evil son of a bitch. You're tellin' me I can't get to know ya?

And I should also just ignore the fact that vampires are real creatures walkin' amongst us. How in the world am I supposed to do that?"

"You do it by going home, going to work, visiting with friends. You find someone to love and build a life with them. Have children. Create the family you've always wanted and that you deserve. You live your life and be grateful that you have it." She stood. "Go home, Navid. Be happy." She left, finally allowing the tears she'd been fighting to fall down her cheeks. She wept as she walked, wishing there was a way for her to have Navid in her life. But, there wasn't. Her existence put him in danger and as much as it pained her, he was better off without her.

Wyatt woke to the soft touch of Allydia's fingertips on his cheek. "You're back," he said, his voice scratchy as he lifted his head. "How was your trip? How are your, what, great-great, a hundred times great-grandkids?" He turned on the light and saw the tears streaming down her face. "What happened?" He scooted closer to her as she sat.

"My father hates me and I just had to tell my perfect, beautiful, amazing however-many-times grandson that he can never see me again because doing so could put his life in danger."

He wiped the tears from her cheeks and tucked her hair behind her ears. "I'm sorry. Is there anything I can do?"

"You can tell me what my father was doing here. Did he hurt you?"

"Hurt me? No."

"What, then?"

"It doesn't matter."

"Wyatt,"

"He's a dick. He gave me a bullshit speech, trying to defend himself. He thinks he did the right thing, taking your kids away. He thinks you're dangerous. He warned me that I should," He looked into her eyes, her heartbreak giving him pause. "It's not important."

"He warned you about what? Me?"

He took a sip of water from the bottle on the nightstand and put it back.

"He warned you about me. He said I would hurt you?"

"He said he thinks you'll kill me."

"That's absurd. You can't die."

"That's what I said."

She swallowed the lump in her throat as she held back more tears. "He told you to leave me."

"I told you, it doesn't matter."

She studied his face, looking for signs of deception. There weren't any.

"He's twisted. Resentful. Mad at God and everyone else, it seems like. He doesn't know what he's talking about. Besides, you think I'm gonna take relationship advice from someone that married *Lilith*?"

They both laughed.

"I *am* dangerous, though. I'd like to say, 'not to you' because I would never want to harm you, but when I found you in the bath and you yelled at me to leave and you hurt yourself..."

He touched her cheek, the guilt rising in his chest like stomach acid.

"The sight of your blood, the aroma of it, it did things to me. Things I'm not proud to admit."

"And you left. I know that you left so you wouldn't hurt me. I'm not worried about you attacking me. At all."

She nodded, a single tear falling from her eye.

"I'm here," he told her. "I'm right here and I'm not going anywhere."

More tears fell as she covered her mouth.

"What's wrong?"

"Navid," she whimpered. "That's his name. He said I have his mother's eyes. His mother, who my father killed in front of him when he was a child. He has no family but me. He's alone."

Wyatt pulled her into his chest and held her, kissing her head as she cried. "I'm sorry." He kissed her again. "I'm so sorry."

"I'd rather not discuss it further. Can we just sleep?"

"Yeah," he said, leaning back, positioning her in the crook of his arm. "Yeah, let's sleep."

Chapter 14

Malik bounced Sinclair in his arms as he rocked her, quietly singing "In My Life" as she howled, her tears soaking through his tee-shirt.

"I thought Gabriel said she liked Beatles songs!" he called to Valerie, who was in the nursery, busy putting a clean sheet on the crib mattress.

"She does!"

He sighed and went back to singing, but the baby continued to cry, kicking her legs and smacking her hand against his chest. After a few minutes, Malik gave up, carrying the hysterical child into her mother. "I've tried everything. She's been changed, fed, played with, and sang to. She's freaking out like she's scared of something."

"Give her to me," Valerie said, holding her hands out. She took a turn rocking her, rubbing her back, and humming the tune to "Let It Be". Sinclair continued to wail, pulling her mother's hair and beating her tiny fist against her shoulder. "Somebody's in a mood. What's your problem, Miss Perry? Do you have a tooth coming in?" She poked her finger in the child's mouth but felt no new protrusions.

"You think a bath would help? We could break out that lavender soap your sister brought over."

"I think she's just tired." She went back to humming, sitting in the rocking chair, and closing the blinds, dimming the room. After a few moments, the baby began to drift off, her cries now barely whimpers. Soon, she was quiet and relief washed over the exhausted parents.

Suddenly, a knock came on the front door. "You get it," Valerie ordered. "I am *not* moving. I don't care if it's a camera crew with a comically giant check, I'm not getting up *for shit*."

He laughed and backed out of the room, gently pulling the door closed behind him. The knocking turned to pounding as Malik walked back to the living room. Before he could answer, the door burst open, the man on the other side having kicked it in.

"The fuck?" Malik boomed.

Cain swung his briefcase, landing it squarely into Malik's jaw. He fell back, but quickly recovered, leaping to his feet and planting himself between the man and the hallway leading to the bedrooms. "You're messing with the wrong motherfucker."

"Am I? I believe you're exactly who I'm here for." He swiftly took the spike from the case and held it over his head, rushing toward the new father, causing him to change his position, dodging the weapon while wildly glancing around the room for one of his own.

Valerie emerged from the nursery, her brows furrowed in annoyance. "What in the holy fuck is going on--" She stopped, taking notice of the strange man in her apartment and the mess of what used to be her front door. "Who the fuck are you?"

"You must be Uriel," Cain huffed. "I thought you'd be at school. No matter. I'm almost done here. Just need to impale your human, then I'll be on my way."

In the distance, Sinclair again began to scream.

Cain's eyes lit up. "You have a child, angel? *Delicious.* I'll take them from you, as well." But as he took a step toward her, he was knocked to the ground by a cast iron pan to the back of the head. Malik stood over him, out of breath and sweating.

"Any ideas?"

Valerie shook her head and they both shrugged before heading back to the nursery and gathering up their crying daughter.

"Should we call the cops?" Malik packed the diaper bag while Valerie put Sinclair in her car seat.

"Nah, this is some 'other' shit. He knew who I was. Best take this mess straight to my sister.

Lucifer entered Mariana's apartment, yanking down the police tape that hung in front of the door. His heart pounded like a drum in his chest, the sound of his own blood pumping in his ears the only thing he could hear. He stepped slowly through the living room and down the hall, dreading what he'd find once he came to the bedroom, its door also taped off. He pulled it down and went inside, the sight of blood and the outline of a body on the carpet causing the veins in his neck to throb. All of the times he'd had to track down demons on Earth and in all the years he'd spent in Hell, nothing had ever made him as angry as he was in that moment. *Nothing.*

As he turned to leave, he noticed the writing on the mirror, letters written in blood that spelled out the word, *Akrotiri.*

"The fuck, bitch?" Valerie shouted as she let herself into the apartment.

Gabriel sighed, getting up from her spot at the island and putting her danish down on her plate. "It's Cain. I didn't think he'd go after *you,* Holy Fire, and everything. Something must've pissed him off *extra.*" She took Sinclair out of her seat and kissed her cheek. "Hey, pretty girl." The baby giggled and grabbed her finger. "Check the junk drawer for keys."

Valerie opened the kitchen drawer and rifled through unopened mail, bits of paper with what looked like shopping lists written on them, a stapler, three double-A batteries, and a dead glow stick before finding a pair of keys on a ring. "What are these to?"

"Your house. Well, my old house, but yours now. You're welcome!"

"Girl,"

"The house I grew up in. I just had it remodeled. Four bedrooms, three and a half baths, huge chef's kitchen. Take it. You'll be safe there."

"I'm not letting you buy me a house."

"I didn't buy it, I inherited it, and I have zero interest in moving back in. If you don't take it, I'll just sell it and it's not like I need the money."

Valerie folded her arms and bit her lip as she thought it over.

"Come on," Gabriel prodded. "Sinclair wants to go. Look how happy she is." The baby flashed a toothless grin and squawked in agreement.

"Fine," she reluctantly agreed, putting the child back in her seat. "Where is it?"

Gabriel picked up her phone and began typing. "Texting the address now."

Malik rubbed his temple. "You'll have to drive. I've got a migraine."

Valerie took the car keys and checked her phone, shooting Gabriel an irritated glare. "Bitch, what am I gonna do in *Connecticut*?"

She sat back down and took a bite of danish. Still chewing, she replied, "Keep your family alive."

Chapter 15

Wendy wandered around a busy shopping district in the town of Hamilton. There were people pushing strollers, riding bikes, talking on cell phones. There were buses and park benches, bars and restaurants. It all looked very normal. But as she got closer to the Waikato River, she began to sense it: the dark energy that filled the air like cigarette smoke in an otherwise sterile room. She dipped a hand into the water and was immediately bombarded by the dark magic. It was stronger than any she'd felt in the past and it was not human in origin. "What did you do?" she whispered to the long-dead witch that now threatened the island.

She spent hours searching, combing through the most remote places, hoping against hope that she was wrong, but she wasn't. She knew it in her bones. The witch hadn't been reincarnated as a human being. She'd come back as something else. Something dark. A vengeful spirit, her hate filling everything on the island. Every blade of grass, every grain of sand. It was all tainted. Soon, the people would become infected, turning on one another like rabid animals, *if* the island's structural integrity held out that long. It was pulling itself apart, she could tell by the fear she saw in the animals as they passed. From dogs tugging on leashes to birds screeching across the sky, they were all terrified. As she made her way back to town for supplies, the ground rumbled beneath her, throwing her to her knees and sending a flock of robins soaring from the trees and fluttering off into the distance. Time was running out. She had to act fast. Millions of lives depended on it.

"You were right," she said as she reentered the lodge, getting the attention of the coven who had been busy placing protection idols around the rooms, burning sage, and putting together protective hex bags for themselves and Wendy. She set her bags on the floor and put her hands on her hips. "I thought maybe there was nothing weird going on. I was dumb."

"So, you found her?" Charlotte asked, handing her a hex bag, hope filling her eyes.

"Oh, I found that crazy bitch, all right."

"Did you," another woman asked sheepishly. "You know, take care of it?"

"No. I can't handle this on my own. I mean, I probably could, with enough time, but there isn't any. She's tearing the island up. It'll be underwater in a few days if we don't stop her. This thing can't be reasoned with or bound."

"Well, dear," Alice chimed in. "We don't want you to *reason* with her. We want you to *kill* her."

"I'm afraid I can't do that, either. Not that I would. What kind of person do you think I am?"

"Excuse my language, dear, but why the hell not?"

"I'm not a murderer, Alice. Jesus. Savage much?"

"But, you know where she is?" Charlotte asked.

"Yeah. Bitch is everywhere. She's not human. She brought herself back as an angry Earth Spirit. Like I said, she can't be killed. I can't bind her magic, she's got no corporeal form, nothing I can make an effigy of. There's only one thing we can do and I'll need all of your help to get it done. We have to banish her."

"How do we do that?"

She picked up the shopping bags and grinned. "I bought supplies. I hope you're all well-hydrated."

Chapter 16

The women worked tirelessly, writing the ancient witch's name on three by three paper bags, wrapping them around walnuts, and tying them with black yarn. They then dropped their bundles in bottles filled with their own urine.

"Is the urine really necessary?" One of the women asked, holding her nose.

"Yeah," Wendy told her. "We could have used vinegar, but this is way more effective. I don't know about you ladies, but I don't want to take *any* chances."

"Is it okay if I'm scared?" one of the women asked.

"Sure. It's normal to be scared. We're going up against some powerful stuff. I'd be worried about you if you *weren't* scared."

"I just really wish you didn't need our help. We're not exactly...like you. Sorry, that was rude."

"It's fine. Listen, I wish I could've just handled this on my own, too. If she was a *person*, I'd take a picture of her, print it out, a five-minute binding spell," she rubbed her hands together. "All over. But this thing is everywhere. I need you guys. I know it's a lot, but I promise, you'll be fine."

"Are you entirely sure about that?" Charlotte asked, screwing the top on one of the bottles.

"Ninety percent." She winked.

"And the other ten?"

"My grandma always told me never to get cocky when it comes to magic. All done?"

The women nodded, placing the last of the bottles in the box. Wendy picked it up and shuffled out the door. "Load up! We've got a pissed off Earth Spirit to banish."

The women scattered across the island, each digging holes and burying their bottles at designated locations: the cities of Wellington, Napier, Gisborne, New Plymoth, Rotorua, Tauranga, Aukland, Wangarei, Paihia, Kaitaia, and beaches along the eastern shore, effectively encircling the entirety of the island. It was getting late when they met up on the shore of Lake Taupo, a caldera of the Taupo Volcano, the center of the island.

"You ladies ready?" Wendy asked, seeing in their faces that they weren't. They were terrified and with good reason. As they'd been working, the earthquakes had become more frequent, growing in intensity as the hours passed. Hine-nui-te-po knew what they were up to and she was displeased.

Charlotte fiddled with the hex bag that hung around her neck. "I think I can speak for everyone here when I say that we're nervous as shit, but we're ready to fight."

The women all nodded in agreement, some rubbing their arms for warmth, others checking to make sure their own hex bags were still in place. Wendy waved her hands toward herself, gathering them closer. "Everything will be fine. Half of magic is setting a clear intention. So, come on. Everyone hold hands in a circle, close your eyes, and picture a giant wave of bright, white light, pushing away the dark energy in the island." The women complied, joining hands, and forming a perfect circle. Wendy squeezed in, taking Charlotte's hand with her left and Alice's with her right. As she closed her eyes, the ground shook beneath them, threatening to knock them down. "Don't break the circle. Whatever you do, *do not let go.*"

Birds screeched across the sky above them as Wendy began to chant, "Whakakahoretia te kino", a Maori Karakia meaning simply, 'Get rid of evil'. The ladies joined in, repeating the phrase over and over as the sky went dark. The Earth shook violently, but the women continued, bending their knees as if they were riding a wave, all keeping their eyes shut tight for fear of what they might see. All, except for Wendy.

She stared sternly into the dense cloud of smoke that rose from the volcano as she chanted, doing her best to ignore the lava that had begun to flow down its sides. Slowly, what looked like a woman's face began to appear in the black plume. Its eyes were angry, nostrils flared, and its mouth was opened so wide, it looked like a caricature. From the billowing darkness came a piercing scream, filling the air and rustling the leaves of the trees behind them. Wendy felt Alice losing her grip, so she squeezed tighter, never taking her eyes off of the spirit.

After ninety or so seconds that felt like an eternity, the shrieking stopped. The ground went still and the smoke subsided, dissipating in the starry night sky. The women went quiet, ending their chanting, and opening their eyes.

"Is that it?" one of them wondered.

"Yep," Wendy told them, letting go of her new friends' hands and taking a deep breath, letting it out with an audible, "Ah."

"It's over?" Charlotte asked. "Just like that?"

"Just like that. She won't be back."

"But, how can you be sure?"

"This isn't my first rodeo."

After a moment of stunned silence, the women cheered, throwing up their arms and dancing in the sand.

"We have to celebrate!" Charlotte proclaimed. "Everyone, meet back at the hotel. I'll bring the booze. Party at Wendy's!"

Back at the lodge, the women drank beer and danced around the living room while listening to Split Enz on one of the ladies' phones. Wendy sat back on the sofa, smiling as she watched them. She took a sip of her drink and leaned her head back, barely able to keep her eyes open.

"Tired, dear?" Alice asked, sitting next to her.

"Yeah," she admitted. "It's good, though. My flight home leaves soon. I might just be able to sleep the whole way."

"Well, that's nice. Before I forget," she patted her knee and reached into her pocket. "Here's that pie recipe."

"Thank you, Alice."

"You're welcome, dear. I'm going to get another beer before Charlotte drinks them all. Such a lush."

Wendy laughed. "I didn't have you pegged for that big of a drinker."

"Oh, yes. I may need help getting up from the couch, but I can still drink these girls under the table. I'm old, not dead."

She laughed again, setting her drink on the end table and helping the older woman stand. As the women drunkenly attempted to sing along to "I See Red", all of them off-key and slurring their words, Wendy shook her head and muttered under her breath, "Not *just* a book club."

Chapter 17

Libby rocked back and forth in her porch swing, eyes closed, breathing in the balmy summer air. It would be her last summer, she knew, and she wanted to savor every bit of it.

"Quassatura," she heard as a sharp pain spread across her cheek. She held her hand to it, the blood appearing on her fingers causing her blood pressure to rise.

"What insolence is this?" the old woman hissed, grasping her cane as she stood. At the bottom of the porch steps, three women appeared, members of her own coven, their looks of determination fueling her anger.

"Sorry, Libby," Julia said. "I was just checking."

"Checking what?"

"If you had Grace's magic, you know, in you."

"What have you been smoking, child? If I had Grace's magic, I would have shared it with the rest of you. You know that."

The women climbed the steps, Julia in the lead. "I don't know anything except that without the Tituban magic, we're powerless against the other covens. I know you think I'm being paranoid, but--"

"Paranoid and treasonous!" Libby barked. "You *do not* attack one of your sisters, especially an elder. I should have you shunned."

"But, you can't because you're not our leader. We have no leader. And until Grace's magic is found, we're all but helpless. Now, if you don't mind, I'm just gonna come in and do a little search. See if you and our departed founder were in cahoots."

"Redipiscor!" Libby ordered, holding her hand out in front of her. The witches flew back, off the porch and onto the ground.

"I don't want to hurt you, old woman, but I will have that magic," Julia said through her teeth.

"Is that what this is about? You want Grace's power for yourself? *You* want to lead the coven?" Libby cackled. "*You*? You don't have the temperament, clearly, or the discipline. You're far too emotional, which is why half of your spells don't work the way you intend. If you took in *an ounce* of Grace's magic, it would burn you alive from the inside. Get off my property while I call the other elders so we can decide what to do about you." She went inside and picked up her phone, trying to remember how to do a group text. "Damn technology," she muttered. As she hit send, a cold chill went up her spine. She could feel the floor beneath her begin to rumble. Soon, the glass in the windows began to shake, pictures fell from walls, and lights flickered. The door flew open, the three witches storming in.

"I didn't want to do it this way," Julia said. "But if that magic's here, I *will* find it."

"Oh, sweetie, you have no idea who you're messing with. Ventus." The three were blown back in a gust of wind, pinned to the wall, the air moving so fast, they could hardly breathe. Libby ran from the room, dialing Poe's number as she hustled to her bedroom.

"Libby?" Poe answered.

"Yes, child, it's me. Listen, Julia, Sonya, and Hallie are here looking for Grace's magic. I know you don't have it, but I suspect you know where it is. I don't want you to tell me, I know Grace had her reasons for keeping it from us. Her magic, her decision. But, these girls are on a mission. Julia wants the power for herself and she'll do anything to get it. Under no circumstances can she be allowed to get her hands on it, do you hear me?"

"Yes, ma'am."

"I want you to run, child. Take only what you need and go, tonight. When she figures out none of us old broads has what she's after, she'll no doubt come after you."

"Okay. I'll take off. Thanks, Libby."

She ended the call and braced herself as the bedroom door flew open. "Where is it, Libby?" Julia snapped.

She locked her fingers around the cane. "I don't have it, and if I did, I certainly wouldn't give it to you."

"Obfoco!"

Libby held her hand to her throat as she began to choke. The three searched the room as she struggled to breathe, tossing the contents of her drawers onto the bed and pawing through her closet. Libby could feel herself growing weak, her peripheral vision filling with stars. With all of her energy, she lifted the cane and took a swing, landing a sharp blow to the back of Julia's knee. She buckled, her spell broken.

"Definitely treason." Libby whacked her again, this time in the shin, then the stomach. She turned her attention to the other two, swatting them both in the diaphragm, knocking the air out of them. She hit Julia once more, slamming the cane across her face before leaving the room in a mad dash for the front door. But as she rushed, she heard the fatal word being called out from behind.

"Ictum!"

She was stopped in her tracks by the unbelievable pain, like a bullet to the head. Her entire left side went numb as her cane fell to the floor. Her left eye closed, then the other. She collapsed, Sonya and Hallie looking on in shock as Julia stood over her. She bent down, able to feel the old woman's magic dissipate. She was dead.

"Check her phone," Julia ordered. "I want to know who she was talking to in there."

"This charm will protect you," Poe told the bunny as she placed the collar back around its neck. "Hold still. I won't hurt you." She picked up the scissors from the table and snipped a bit of fur from the rabbit's back, adding it to the mortar. She used the pestle to combine the hairs into the mixture and used a syringe to feed some to Raven before dipping her finger in and licking it. "Assuesco. Come on, let's pack." She ran through the house, throwing spellbooks and clothes in a backpack before picking the bunny up and placing her gently inside. She zipped it most of the way, leaving a pocket open so Raven could breathe, and headed for the door.

"Where are you off to?" she heard Julia ask. She turned, facing the three witches for the second time. "I know Libby called you. Warned you. She thinks you know where Grace's magic is. But you told me that's not true, right? And you wouldn't lie, would you, Poe?"

"I don't have it."

"I didn't ask if you had it. I know that you don't. I'm just wondering why you would keep it from us. We're sisters, aren't we?"

"You know, I thought so, but then you broke in my place and put a gash in my arm, so you'll have to forgive me if I'm not feeling the whole 'coven buddy' thing right now."

"Come on, Poe. Sweet, androgynous, summer child Poe. You can't fight us. Hand it over and we can all be friends again. I swear. No hard feelings."

"I don't--"

"Tell me where it is!"

She cocked her head and pursed her lips. "I wouldn't tell you where Grace hid her magic if my life depended on it."

"Are you sure? Because it literally does. Demeo."

Poe fell, dropping her pack.

"I won't ask again."

"Silentium!" She shot back, taking the witches' voices. Julia looked genuinely surprised that the younger witch had the power to pull off the spell as she tried to speak. Poe grabbed her backpack and leaped up, but Sonya threw her back to the ground. She and Hallie kicked her in the ribs and spine while Julia silently laughed.

With the pack lying on the floor, Raven slipped out, making a beeline for the witches. First, the bunny hopped up onto Sonya's shoulder and clamped down on the side of her neck, tearing out tissue as blood squirted from the wound. Hallie mouthed the words, "what the fuck" as the rabbit came for her next, running at her so fast, she couldn't see it anymore. *Where'd it go?* she thought, confused by the horrified stares on Julia and Poe's faces. She turned around and there it was, its fur soaked with so much blood, it dripped from its floppy ears. Julia had gone stark white, her mouth hanging open as she pointed. Finally, Hallie looked down and saw it, the gaping hole in her abdomen. The rabbit had run straight through her. She fell, dead before she hit the floor.

Poe gathered her senses and opened the pack. "Tersus," she said, the blood disappearing from Raven's fur. The bunny hopped into the bag and Poe zipped it most of the way. "Maneat!" She bolted from the house, Julia being rendered immobile for the moment and unable to follow her. The spell wouldn't last long, so she needed to hurry. There was only one place still safe, but for how long? It was only a matter of time before Julia found Wendy. She *had* to warn her.

Chapter 18

Lucifer was seething when he got to Gabriel's apartment. She set her soda can down on the kitchen counter as he approached her, the look in his eyes worrying her.

"Where is he?" he snarled.

"God, I'm so sorry. I didn't know--"

"Where?!"

She pleaded with her eyes. "He just attacked Malik. He's probably still there, but Lucifer--"

"I know the risks." He turned to go.

"Wait," she called after him, taking something from a small box on the counter and handing it to him. "Slip this in his pocket or something."

He looked at her, understanding mingling with the rage in his eyes. "Father's plan?"

Her voice cracked as she answered, "Yes."

He pursed his lips and nodded, slamming the door as he left. She slumped to the floor, pulling her legs into her chest and covering her mouth as tears slid down her cheeks, the sound of her own muffled sobs making her feel even worse. She put her head down on her knees, wishing she could wallow. But there was work to do. There was *always* work to do.

Valerie's neighbor stood outside the apartment, dialing nine-one-one as she peeked her head in to see the man lying on the floor. As he began to stir, the operator answered, "Nine-one-one, what's your emergency?"

"Hi, I think someone broke into my neighbor's--"

Lucifer snatched the phone from the woman's hand and crushed it in his, staring her down as her mouth fell open, her lip quivering in fear. *"Run away."* She made the sign of the cross and did as he commanded, running so quickly down the stairs that she almost fell.

Cain got to his feet, placing a hand on the back of his head and then checking it for blood. There was none. "You got my message." He laughed as he leaned on the bar.

"Wouldn't want to be interrupted." Lucifer hoisted the door up to cover the entrance. "Tell me, son of Adam. Did you forget who I am or are you just breathtakingly stupid?"

"I know exactly who you are. You and the other angels in your self-righteous show of force vaporized my last chance at--" He stopped, sitting on a stool and waving his hand. "It doesn't matter. It's over. I am forever alone. So scold me as you wish. Scream, throw things. It makes no difference. As long as you and I remain on Earth, I will continue to take everything you hold dear. I will kill everyone that means anything to you. Probably best to remain untangled. You wouldn't want to feel this grief again, would you?"

"You've gone mad." Lucifer stepped toward him. "Do you honestly think that's what I'm here for? A tantrum?"

Cain's expression turned from mockery to confused concern. "You wouldn't dare hurt me. You know the consequences."

He grasped him by the collar, lifted him from the stool, and slammed him to the floor, the terror in his eyes spurring him on. He held Cain's throat in his hand and leaned in, all but whispering, "Consequences be damned."

He punched him, first in the jaw, then in the eye. He broke his nose, cheek, and brow bones. When he got bored of that, he picked him up and heaved him across the room, sending him flailing into a window, cracking the glass.

"Stop this now!" Cain pleaded. "You know what will happen!"

"Save your breath." He kicked him in the groin and threw him over his shoulder. "The air is thin where we're going." He broke out the remaining glass and took off out the window rocketing to the clouds, Cain screaming as he clung to Lucifer's shirt.

"What are you doing?!"

Once above the clouds, they hovered in place, Lucifer tossing him forward and holding him up by the neck. "I want you to know, I'll have no regrets. I will enjoy this and the memory of it for all eternity." He plunged his fist into Cain's abdomen, ripping out organ after organ and discarding them, letting them fall haphazardly to the Earth. Cain seized, blood pouring from his mouth, his eyes starting to glaze over. Lucifer reached into his pocket, taking the device Gabriel had given him and shoving it into his adversary's mouth, forcing it closed until he swallowed. "My Father sends His regards." And with that, he let go, dropping Cain twenty-thousand feet to the pavement waiting below. When he could no longer hear his screams, he flew off, heading back toward his sister's apartment. Once there, he staggered to his bedroom, closed the door, and crashed onto the mattress.

Camael sat on what passed for a bed, leaning against the concrete wall of his cell, reading "Beyond Good and Evil" for the third time. The other inmates were loud but not louder than his sister's voice in his head. *Get the keys.*

What's up, G?

I know you have that guard's keys. It's time to use them. I'm parked across the street. Move your ass.

I told you--

I know why you're here. I've been filled in. You have a job to do. Now.

He closed his book and sat up, taking a deep breath, and preparing himself. He hadn't been sure that this day would ever come and now that it had, he wasn't sure he was ready for it.

Dude, be in your feelings after you're in the car.

Fine, I'm coming. He got up, retrieved the keys, and opened his cell. The other inmates went quiet as he crept past. He ignored their looks of shocked interest as he tried to sneak past the guards, but in quarters that tight, sneaking *anywhere* was impossible.

A guard turned and reached for his weapon. "What the--" But Cam knocked him unconscious before he could finish the sentence. He barrelled through guard after guard, punching some and simply pushing others to the ground. The alarm sounded, blaring as emergency lights flashed and the other men still locked in their own cells cheered.

Once out of his block, he tore steel doors from their hinges, making his way to the main entrance and out of the building. Bullets whizzed through the air, some lodging in his back and legs, but he barely noticed. He made it to the street and spotted Gabriel waving from her black sports car. She started it up as he hopped inside. She sped off, happy that it had occurred to her to cover her license plate before making the trip.

"So," he grinned. "Where to?"

Chapter 19

Hattie covered her fiery curls with a shawl and hurriedly took her bags from the trunk of the cab. Her eyes darted around the busy street, the lights from the airport across the way brightening the just-darkened sky above it so fully, it almost felt like day. The cab drove off and she stepped onto the road, anxious to get on a plane and out of her native land. It was no longer safe for her there and she knew it.

As she reached the sidewalk on the other side, a van with dark tinted windows screeched to a stop. Two men in black hoodies hopped out of the back and rushed her. She tried to run, but they were as fast as she was.

"Hey!" a man yelled. "Get away from her!"

"Stop!" another commanded.

"Someone call the police!" a woman begged.

The humans attempted to come to her aid but were swiftly knocked back by the goons. They tossed her into the van, got in themselves, and drove away, leaving the bystanders flummoxed, several of them already on their phones with the authorities.

The vampires chained her, wrapping her in iron links until she could no longer move her limbs. She struggled, but they were older and more powerful. It was inevitable. She was as good as dead.

Cain's eyes flew open, the sound of the splashing water to his left startling him awake. Had he landed a few inches over, he would have woken up at the bottom of the Hudson. He'd died hundreds of times over the centuries, and coming to underwater was his absolute least favorite way of realizing that he hadn't stayed dead. He got himself up, stepping out of the indention in the freshly cracked concrete. His clothes were torn and covered in blood, but he was no worse for the wear. He bent down to tie his shoe and began the long walk back to his hotel.

He unlocked the door and entered the room, his heart jumping and horror spreading across his face at the sight of the two people waiting for him inside.

"Wendy, Malik, *and* the bartender?" the woman asked. "Is there a stalker gene I don't know about?" He tried to back out of the room. "Uh, uh." She waved in its direction, causing it to slam shut behind him. She sat cross-legged on the desk while the man leered at him from a chair in the corner. He didn't know who *he* was, but he'd recognized Gabriel right away. After the beating he'd received from Lucifer, he was in no condition to grapple with God's Messenger.

"This is my brother, Cam. Camael. You might recognize him by his full name...The Wrath of God."

Cain's eyes grew wide as they fell on the man sitting silently, forearms on his thighs, hands folded, his expression cold and unchanged.

"How did you find me?"

"That thing Lucifer shoved down your gullet? Tracking device. Sends your location right to my phone. When you woke up from your tussle and started heading this way, it wasn't hard to figure out where you were going. This is the only hotel this far west."

"Tracking device? Hard to imagine angels needing the help of human technology to do God's will. Lucifer said God sent His regards. So, Messenger, does He want to tell me something? Is he angry with me? Or just disappointed?"

Gabriel continued, ignoring his questions. "I should have gotten him to you as soon as Dad told me to, but I put it off. I love my brother. I didn't want him to go. Had I known what you were up to, maybe I would've acted earlier. Maybe I wasn't supposed to act earlier. Who knows? Mysteries to be revealed at a later date, I guess."

"God's Wrath?"

"Totes. Only thing that can kill you permanently. See, God's salty that you basically wiped out your entire line. Seems you haven't learned your lesson and He's concerned that you'll find your last male heir and take him out before he procreates, which would be bad for some reason."

"My...there's another?"

"Oh, yeah. Allydia filled him in on your psychotic family history, put him on a plane back to where he came from. He'll be all right, eventually."

"And you've come to," He swallowed hard. "Kill me?"

"Don't get excited. You *will* die and you *will* go to Purgatory, but you'll never be reborn. You'll never set foot on this planet again."

"What do you mean? That's not possible. Elohim may be angry with me, but He *always* forgives."

"Yeah, but you're too much of a risk. Someday, when the human race goes extinct, God will welcome you home, you know," She pointed to the ceiling. "Up there. When He does, I hope you bring some knee pads, because you'll have some serious groveling to do. God will forgive you, but the souls of all the people you've killed, *your own relatives*, will need convincing."

"You're much more flippant than I remember."

"A lifetime of bullshit will do that to a girl."

"This is a lot of talking," Cam complained, sitting up straight. "Can I just kill this guy, already?"

"I'm just explaining to him why he's gotta die."

"You're stalling."

She rolled her eyes and crossed her arms.

"This is what I'm here for, G. I get it. It's all right."

Cain reached for the door, but it wouldn't budge. He scrambled to find a weapon, anything to defend himself with, but the drawer in the nightstand only contained a Bible. Adrenaline rushed through his veins and his blood pressure rose as he wished more than anything that he had returned to Uriel's apartment before coming back here to retrieve his--

"This?" Gabriel asked, taking his iron spike from the desk drawer.

He drew in a sharp breath. "Give that to me."

"Oh, sweetie. Now, you know that's not what's up." She tossed it to Cam who caught it, stood, and walked over, lumbering over Cain as he backed himself against the door.

"I want you to know," Cam told him, his voice steady. "I take no pleasure in this. I'm only doing it because I have to."

"*Angels*," Cain fumed. "Always so smug. You may be God's Wrath and you very well may be able to kill me once and for all but to be clear, I won't make it easy." In one fluid motion, he kneed Cam squarely in the testicles, bringing his foot down hard and stomping on his foot. He pushed his way past, retrieving the book from the nightstand, and swinging it around, slamming it into the side of Cam's face.

Cam grunted, wiping the blood from his lip. "Why are you tryin' to aggravate me?"

Cain leaped onto the bed and hopped down on the other side, putting himself directly in front of the other angel.

She flashed him a condescending smile. "I wouldn't."

"But, I must." He rushed behind her, wrapping his arm around her neck. He spotted a pen on the desk and grabbed it, biting the cap off, spitting it out, and holding the point to her throat. "I'll kill her. I'll jam this into her carotid. She'll bleed out so fast, she'll be dead before she has time to heal."

Camael's face contorted in hatred, his skin flushing, sweat beading on his brow.

Gabriel cleared her throat. "Oh, yeah, you done fucked up now."

Cam flew at them, yanking Cain's hand away from his sister's neck, and snapping his wrist. He flung him across the room into the wall as he screamed in pain. Cam's eyes were wild as he stepped closer, like a bull finally out of its cage.

Cain picked up a lamp and smashed it into his face, but the angel was unfazed. He went for the window, but Cam pulled him back, tossing him like a rag doll to the other side of the room. Again, he tried to open the door, and again, it wouldn't budge. He darted back to the nightstand, removing the drawer, and crashing it over Cam's head. Blood trickled down his temple, but he didn't pause for a second. He kept coming like the villain in a slasher film, unflinching as if he had no pain receptors. He was an automaton, built for one thing and one thing only.

He seized Cain's throat, slamming him hard against the door, his breathing that of wild boar, heavy and snarling. He twirled the plow, a low, guttural laugh escaping his lips as the second-generation human struggled to get free. This was it. They both knew it. This was the end.

With an exasperated groan, Camael drove the spike hard into Cain's chest, plunging it through the muscle and bone, and piercing his fast-beating heart. As he removed the weapon, Cain fell, his eyes rolling back, his body going limp.

Cam dropped the plow and backed away, turning to look at his sister, who was already beginning to cry. "Hey," he said, walking toward her as she got down from her spot on the desk. The sight of her in tears flipped his mood like a switch. All of the anger and violent impulses left him. He was himself again. "Don't be upset. You'll see me later."

"Not like this," she wept.

"Listen, I know it doesn't seem fair, everything done to Cain comes back on the perpetrator times seven, but I understand. You know I do. To be honest with you, it's just nice knowing I have a purpose."

She nodded, letting the tears stream down her flushed cheeks.

"You called in the bomb threat? Everyone else is out of here?"

Again, she nodded.

"Good." He patted her cheek and rubbed her arm. "You know what you gotta do, right?"

"I don't want to."

"But you'll do it, anyway?"

"Yeah."

He offered a sympathetic smile. "You know I love you."

"I know. I know that you do." She hugged him, wiping her tears on his sleeve. "I love you, too. I love you so *so* much."

As she pulled away, he laughed, looking down at the wet spot on his arm. "You'll be fine. The others will take care of you. You should open up to Barachiel more. Stop treating him like a child. I know he's got problems, but he'll be there for you. You know that."

"I will agree if you do me a favor."

"Anything."

"When you see Michael, tell him to take care of Lucifer when he gets there. He's been gone a long time and Heaven is, you know, *an adjustment.* And say 'hi' to Raph for me. Tell him I'm sorry I wasn't there to protect him."

"I will, but you know that wasn't your fault."

"Logically," she whimpered. "But most of the time, it feels like *everything* is my fault."

"Gabriel," He put his finger under her chin to lift her head, looking her in the eyes. "You're not God."

"No, I'm not. Can you imagine?"

They both laughed.

"So," he looked back at Cain's corpse. "How long before--" His hand flew to his chest, the sudden pain gripping him tight, like a hot poker searing through his internal organs. He dropped to his knees and toppled over onto his back, his face losing color and his mouth filling with blood.

Gabriel knelt next to him, hands shaking, her tears running down her cheeks, dripping from her face to her brother's chest. Blood spewed from his lips and trickled from his nose as he gasped for air. He trembled all over as Gabriel watched, unable to live with what was happening. "No," she squeaked. "I won't let you go." She placed her hands over his on his chest as light poured from them. She concentrated, shaking as she mustered everything in her to heal him, but nothing changed. He was still dying.

"It's no use," he gurgled. "I'm *supposed* to go. *It's okay.*" His gaze drifted from her to the ceiling, going distant, like he was looking at something she couldn't see. "G," he said, his voice barely above a whisper. "You didn't tell me it was so beautiful." His eyes closed, one last exhale escaping his lungs as his hand slid from his chest to the floor.

Gabriel covered her mouth, muffling her screams as she sobbed, squeezing her eyes shut as the grief swept her up like a hurricane. She couldn't handle this much pain. She was drowning.

After a few moments, she brushed the tears from her face, steadied her breath, and cracked her neck. She stood up, opened the window behind her, and sat on the sill. With a wave of her hand, both bodies erupted in plumes of smoke and Holy Fire. In a flash of light, Camael's true form burst from the flames, shooting up through the ceiling, and disappearing from her view. She blew a kiss in his direction, slung her leg over the window frame, and hopped out onto the sidewalk. She wiped her nose on her sleeve as she shuffled along the pavement. Her eyelids were heavy as she noticed the first hints of sunrise filling the sky with a purplish glow. Her chest felt heavy and her legs were numb. She lumbered her way to Wendy's, it being so much closer than home, barely aware of her surroundings, exhausted and desperate for bed.

Chapter 20

"Normally, we'd kill your progeny first." Hartley shackled Hattie to the post on the roof of the club, careful not to chip her recently manicured nails on the chains. "I don't know why the Queen wants it done this way, but it's not exactly my place to ask, so. Any last words?"

Hattie looked up at her in defiance, the concrete of the roof hot on her cheek and the holes, pouring blood from where her fangs used to be, aching in her gums. "I won't beg for my life."

"Good, I hate that shit."

She spat on her boots.

"Bitch, I just bought these!" She kicked her in the gut and stomped to the door, slamming it behind her, leaving Hattie alone to watch her first sunrise in decades.

She could hear her screams as she took her phone from her back pocket and dialed the Queen, peering through the tinted window in the door. She watched as Hattie cooked, her veins showing brightly through plumping skin. Her eyes popped, blood pouring from every orifice. After a few moments, her entire body exploded, sending bits of flesh, blood, and gore spewing in all directions. "Gross."

"Yes?" Allydia answered.

"It's done. Is there anything else you need before I go to bed?"

"No, Hartley, get some rest," the Queen told her. "You've done well. But when the sun sets again, find the girl."

Allydia set the phone back on the nightstand, plugging its cord in so it could charge while she slept. She looked fondly and then with concern at her lover asleep next to her. She knew he'd be displeased if he knew what she was up to, but what could she do? The last time a vampire sired without her consent and went unpunished, the consequences had been dire, to say the least. Hundreds had died when the fledgling lost control and gorged himself on an entire village before killing his maker. She couldn't let something like that happen again. It was her responsibility. They were *all* her responsibility, which is why from then on, she insisted on personally approving every turning. Right or wrong, the decision to make someone one of them would be hers, ensuring their loyalty and protecting them from one another. So, though she had been fond of Hattie, she had to reprimand her, if only as a warning to the others. Her behavior could *not* be tolerated.

As for the girl, though, she was torn. She was the product of an unsanctioned act and if she was anyone else, she wouldn't hesitate for a second in putting her down. But, the girl had meant something to Wyatt's son and if he found out that she'd killed her, he would never forgive her. She knew it. She knew it in her soul. He would leave her, his inner angel stronger than his feelings for her. If she was being honest with herself, the rebels weren't entirely wrong. Having him in her life *had* made her a little soft. Never before in her existence as a vampire had she concerned herself with the feelings or opinions of a man. She'd found them to be all but useless, unsatisfying, and obnoxious. But, not him. Wyatt was different. She was drawn to him like a moth to a flame, his light so bright, when she looked at him, nothing else could be seen. She put him above everything, dividing her loyalties and clouding her judgement. He made her question her decisions, her behavior, and her priorities. Being with him had changed her and she wasn't sure that she'd ever be her old self again. So, what to do? What should she do with the girl? She slipped off her clothes. She'd have to mull it over and make a decision after she had the girl in custody. For now, she'd focus on making herself, and her lover, happy.

She climbed on top of him and placed him inside her.

He drew in a sharp breath and opened his eyes, looking up at her and putting his hands on her hips. "Morning."

"Did you sleep well?"

"Not as well as I woke up."

She smiled and gripped the headboard as she moved, delighting in the pleasure washing over his face. Yes, having him in her life had made her soft. One could go as far as to say he made her weak. But, he also made her feel things she hadn't in centuries if she ever had at all. He made her feel cared for and appreciated. He made her feel like he wanted her and not just because of the pheromones. He made her feel needed.

As the sun climbed higher in the sky and her body grew tired, she let him take charge, rolling her onto her back and throwing her leg up around his. She bit her bottom lip, drawing a little blood and swallowing it, something she still had to do now and then when the pleasure was too great and she thought she might lose control. She didn't want to hurt him. She never wanted to hurt him.

Chapter 21

Wendy finished packing, picked up her suitcase, and made her way back to the living room where the coven waited to say 'goodbye'. She gave each woman a hug as they left through the patio door.

"If you're ever back our way, give me a call," Alice said. "You can come stay with me. No sense wasting money on a hotel."

"Thank you, Alice. I'll do that."

When the other ladies had gone, Charlotte gave her a quick hug, patting her back and smiling. "I just want to say, thank you so much. You really saved our bacon back there. I don't know what we would have done if you hadn't come."

"It was my pleasure," Wendy told her.

"I hope we didn't pull you away from anything too important."

"More important than this?"

She laughed. "Well, maybe some*one* important? There is someone special isn't there? Don't try to hide it. I have a sense about these things."

"Oh, do you?"

"Hey, you feel magic, I feel love. So?"

She bit her bottom lip. "*Maybe* there's *someone*."

"I knew it. And how do they feel about all this, taking over your grandmother's magical helpline, so to speak?"

"Oh, I haven't told her, yet."

Charlotte cast a judgemental glare her way.

"I said *yet*. She has a lot to deal with right now. Some guy her dad screwed over forever ago is still pissy about it, I guess, so she's got a situation to handle. Plus, I'm not really sure how to bring it up, you know? I've been doing this since I was a teenager. It's why I became a flight attendant, for the free travel to wherever I'm needed. My grandmother taught me, but it's been just me, on my own, for a long time, keeping this secret. I *will* tell her, though."

"All right, well, take my advice, do it sooner rather than later. Secrets are poison to a relationship. Just ask my ex-husband."

They both laughed as the older woman stepped out onto the patio. "And Wendy,"

"Yeah?"

"I only knew your grandmother by reputation, but I think she'd be really proud of you."

She smiled. "I hope so."

Chapter 22

Gabriel stumbled into Wendy's apartment, ignoring the fact that the door was unlocked when she got there. She plopped down on the couch and leaned her head back, annoyed that she'd have to wait a little longer to get some rest. "Sup, Poe?"

"How did you know I was here? How did you know my name?" She let the invisibility spell fall as she looked over the woman sitting next to her.

"I know most things."

"I'm looking for We--"

"She's in New Zealand. I *won't* be telling her you stopped by."

"Oh, are you her, I mean, are you guys like, a thing? Because *we* aren't. I'm Ace. I'm not into her, I swear."

"I'm not worried about that, kid. I haven't known Wendy that long, but I'm pretty sure she's not a pedophile. It's your witch war I don't want her getting dragged into." She stood up and shuffled to a window, opening it, and holding out her hand. "I appreciate you coming to warn her, but she can protect herself. Cute rabbit. Just the right amount of massacre-y." A checkbook flew into her hand from outside. She looked around the room for a pen, finding one on the coffee table next to a stack of mail.

"Is this real?" Poe wondered aloud.

She filled out the check for one million dollars and handed it to the girl. "Cash it. Hide out somewhere. Mostly, just try not to die. Wendy would be upset if something happened to you and if she cries, I'm gonna cry and I am way past my limit of depressing shit. Oh, fuck me. I probably broke a window at my place. Oh, well. Future problems."

"You're a witch, too?"

"No."

"But, how did you--"

"I'm something else. Listen, I'm not trying to be a dick, but I've had a real shitty night and it would be super awesome if you could go somewhere else now."

"Oh. Yeah, sure." She stood up and put her pack on, looking at the check in her hand for the first time. "Holy shit! A million dollars?"

"You're still here."

"I can't take this. You don't even know me."

She sighed, sitting back down. "Poe, real name Angela Hessen, born to a fourteen-year-old rape victim named Jessica Weber who died of an overdose when you were six days old. Adopted seven months later by the Hessens who kicked you out two years ago. After a short stint living on the streets, Grace found you and took you in. She recognized you as a direct descendant of Merga Bein, who, back in sixteen-o-three, used some powerful as shit magic to transfer her pregnancy to another witch before she was burned at the stake. You like tacos and the color purple. Spring is your favorite season and you wear black because you hope it'll make you seem scary or sad enough that people will leave you alone. Now, you're freaking out. You're thinking, 'How does this strange woman know all this?' 'Is she psychic?' 'I never knew my real mom's name before.' Girl, for real. I need to lay down. Please go away."

Poe stared, slack-jawed, and dumbfounded. "What the fuck are you?"

"I'm intuitive. I'm upset. I'm a little fucked up and I'm tired...of *everything*."

Chapter 23

Navid read his newspaper, patiently waiting at the gate of the airport until the sun had come up. Allydia had demanded he go back to London, but he never got on the plane. Instead, he waited, knowing that she and the rest of her kind would soon be fast asleep, allowing him to move freely among them as he investigated. He needed to know more, not only about his family and their past but about vampires. Knowing that they were real and not some comic book myth as he'd always thought was more than a shock; it was mind-blowing. He couldn't get his head around it. Vampires. It was insane. How could it be true? But, he'd seen it. He'd seen the fangs and the strange, dilated pupils with his own eyes. He'd heard the conversation between Allydia and the man that killed his mother. They hadn't known he was there. There was no reason for them to be lying. Moreover, Allydia had seemed sincere in her explanation of things. As a detective, he knew when someone was deceiving him. At least, he liked to think that he did.

Now that he knew her name, he was able to track down an address for his long-lost ancestor. Not many "Allydia Cain's" living in Manhattan, or anywhere else, for that matter. She was the only one, as far as he could tell. She owned property all over the world: apartments in Vancouver, Toronto, Tokyo, Paris, and Madrid. Hotels in Barcelona and Prague. Brothels in Amsterdam. Houses in Athens, Lisbon, and Milan. Medieval castles, now working museums, all over Europe. She owned nightclubs in Hamburg, Seville, Glasgow, Zurich, and Jerusalem. Game preserves in Nairobi and a shopping mall in Rabat. It was an impressive list, but what he was interested in right now were her holdings in the US. He scrolled through the list on his phone. There were nightclubs in Chicago, Los Angeles, New Orleans, and New York. He'd been to the Manhattan nightclub once before but it had been overrun with what he now knew to be vampires. He made a mental note to visit there again before moving on. Hotels in the French Quarter, on the Vegas Strip, and in Beverly Hills. Casinos in Reno and Atlantic City. And, finally, an apartment building on the Upper West Side. He jotted down the address, set the newspaper on his seat, and left the airport.

"West Eighty-Ninth and Amsterdam," he told the cabbie as he got in the back seat.

"Sure thing," he replied, turning the key and pulling out onto the road. "From out of town?"

"It's that obvious?"

"The accent gives it away."

"Right."

"Seein' any shows while you're here?"

"I've already seen one," he said, the memory of Allydia's teeth flashing in his mind. "Not sure I could handle another."

"Take my advice, kid. See as many as you can. Life is short. You might not get another chance."

Navid made quick work of picking the lock of the penthouse door, slipping inside undetected. He poked his head into every room, seeing that they were empty before moving on to the next. He peeked in drawers, went through closets and kitchen cabinets. He didn't know what he was looking for; he just needed to know more.

He opened the fridge and covered his mouth with the back of his hand. Inside were several bottles of wine, a bottle of rum, and blood bags. The bags hung from metal bars affixed to the ceiling of the appliance in four rows. Upon closer inspection, he could see that they were organized by blood type and expiration date. There was no food anywhere in the kitchen. This was it. This was what she lived on. He closed the fridge and wandered to the living room, noticing a door he hadn't seen in his initial walk-through. Behind it was a flight of stairs which he took to the roof, the scent of gardenias flooding his sinuses. They grew in large bushes in raised beds, the only plants in the rooftop garden. He picked one, brought it to his nose, and breathed in its sweet and refreshing fragrance.

He went downstairs, taking one last look around the apartment before deciding there was nothing of interest there. Now that he wasn't focused on his investigation, he could appreciate how beautiful the apartment was. There were antique chaises, ornate rugs, and gorgeous stenciling on the walls of the living room and bedrooms. The rich, hardwood floors flowed throughout and deep purple curtains covered every window. Allydia had excellent taste, if not a little over the top.

As he made his way to the front door to leave, he realized he was still carrying the flower he'd taken from the roof. Not wanting to leave any evidence of his presence, he shoved it in his pocket before exiting, making sure to lock up on his way out.

Navid broke into the nightclub with the same level of ease he had the apartment. It was dark, the main level having no windows, the dim lights just bright enough that he could make out the shapes of tables and booths around the walls. The room was mostly empty, serving as a dance floor most nights. Aside from the main entrance, there were two fire exits on either side of the room, their signs shining red above them. He swept the room, looking under tables and behind light fixtures, for what, he didn't know. This was his training, to go over everything, leaving no stone unturned. The place was spotless. Not a hint of the debauchery that must have gone on there at night between the creatures that haunted it.

He turned his eyes to the upper level and crept up the staircase. There, he found a VIP area, roped off, and a door. He ignored the booth, the door drawing him to it somehow. To his surprise, it was unlocked, so he went inside, his eyes widening at the sight of the room. There were beautiful paintings and tapestries hanging from the walls, settees, small tables, and a rug he recognized as being ancient Mesopotamian. He wasn't sure if it was Babylonian or Assyrian, but he knew it was old and probably priceless. He was still marveling at how perfectly preserved it seemed when his gaze lifted to the throne. Huge and ornately carved, the throne with its plush, mulberry seat loomed, as if it would come to life and swallow him whole at any moment.

He jumped, startled by what sounded like a doorknob turning. He turned to see a beautiful woman exiting what looked to be a bedroom.

"I'm sorry, my Queen," she blurted, rubbing the sleep from her eyes. "The sun was out and I didn't want to risk--" She stopped, confusion replacing panic in her expression. She rushed toward him, pinning him to the wall as she breathed in his scent. "I thought you were the Queen. You smell like the Queen. *What have you done with the Queen?*"

"Nothing," he stammered, remembering the flower in his pocket. He pulled it out and showed it to her. "It's just the gardenia. I took it from her garden. That's all."

"You steal from Her Majesty, break in here, and have the audacity to say, 'that's all'?"

"I'm sorry. I just wanted to learn more about her. I'd never lay a hand to hurt her, I swear it."

She smelled him again, almost touching her nose to his throat as he struggled to get free. "The gardenia, yes. But not just that. There's something else. Something in the blood. Who are you?"

He squirmed against her hand, but it was useless. She had him. "I don't think she'd want me telling you, miss."

She lowered her head and looked up at him, allowing her eyes to go black.

"All right, all right. I get it. You're creepy. But I could ask you the same question, mm? These are obviously her rooms. Who are you to be here when she's not?"

She stared, her face tight as she defended herself. "I am Hartley Morales, assistant to the Queen. I'm here because finishing work for Her Majesty left me stranded. Walking home in the daylight isn't exactly an option for me." She slid her hand up from his chest to his neck, applying a small amount of pressure without inhibiting his breathing. "Your turn."

His heart beat faster as he considered his options. Telling her who he was could be painting a giant target on his back. On the other hand, she was one snarky comment away from snapping his neck like a dry twig. He tried to think of a lie, but nothing he came up with would have made sense. As the adrenaline flooded his brain, he decided the best course of action was to spit it out and hope for the best.

"Fine. *Fine.* My name is Navid Parsi. I discovered Allydia stalking me back in London, so I followed her here. She told me I'm her descendant through my mother's line. I just wanted to find out more about her and where I come from. She told me it wouldn't be safe for me here. Told me to go home. Probably should've listened."

Hartley's face went pale, her eyes like saucers as she yanked her hand away. "Her trip," she realized. "A living relative. I can't believe it. Here I was thinking low-key Thor was her greatest weakness. At least *he* can take care of himself. You, you're helpless. If the rebels find out about *you*," She grabbed his collar. "You have to go."

She dragged him out of the room, past the VIP area, and down the stairs, texting as she went. "You shouldn't have come here," she lectured. "It's day, so it's probably all right, but I'm sending a human security guard to look out for you until you get on a plane, just in case."

"That's hardly necessary," he told her as she let him go at the bottom of the steps.

She smacked her lips. "Maybe, but I'm not risking the hellfire she'll reign down on me if something happens to you because I didn't take precautions. A *human*." She gave him a quick once over. "That's heavy." She took his arm and pulled him toward the exit.

"I'm a detective. I don't need a bodyguard."

"Um, yeah, you do. Don't worry about it. You won't even know he's there. Just get your ass home with a quickness." She opened the door and pushed him out, staying behind it to avoid the sun's rays.

Thrust out onto the sidewalk, he breathed a sigh of relief, the door slamming shut in front of him. "Well, that could have gone worse." He put his hand out to hail a cab as he thanked his lucky stars that nothing terrible had happened. Soon, one stopped and he got in. "JFK, please, mate."

The driver nodded and pulled away as Navid took one last look at the club, his hopes of getting to know more about his lineage dwindling as the building faded from view.

Chapter 24

"Stop right here, mate," Navid told the driver as he drove past the bakery, the light from its sign casting a glow on the dark street. The owner sat on the pavement outside, head in hands, openly weeping as police bustled around in the building.

"What's happened?" he asked, hurrying from the cab to his friend. He placed a hand on the man's shoulder and peeked inside. The place was trashed. Tables were flipped, chairs were broken, and smashed glass was everywhere. "Shit. They've come back?"

Babak nodded.

"I'm so sorry. I thought they'd gone for good 'round here. These ABM boys will never learn, will they? Don't you worry, though. I'll find the ones that done this. I swear, I'll--"

"It doesn't matter anymore, Navid. Nothing matters."

"What do you mean? They've got to pay for what they've done and I'll make sure they do, yeah? In the meantime, I'll help you clean up, get things settled."

"No. No, I won't be reopening. I'm done. I'm going home."

"Home? You mean to Tehran?"

"Yes."

"But, what about--"

"They killed her, Navid," he said, his voice booming in the night air. "They murdered my Shadi."

His mouth fell open as he dropped down to sit next to his friend.

"I was at the market. We were running low on eggs. I was only gone for fifteen minutes, maybe twenty. When I came back, I found her in the mess, blood all over. There was so much blood, I couldn't tell where it was coming from. Her whole body was soaked." He covered his mouth and sobbed.

Navid put his arm around him and fought back tears of his own. "I'm so sorry, my friend. I'm so, so sorry."

"I will take her home to be buried in Zahara's Paradise. I will demand the body washers be gentle. It is the least I can do. It is what she would want."

"Of course. Of course, take her home. Is there anything I can do for you? Anything at all?"

He shook his head.

"All right, how about I just sit with you then? I'll sit right here until you tell me you don't need me anymore, yeah?"

"Thank you. You're a good boy, Navid. One day, if you're lucky, you will find *your* Shadi. Someone to make you happy, feed you pastries until you get fat like me."

"I don't know about that. But, yeah, maybe if I'm really lucky." The two sat there in the dark, allowing the silence to wash over them as they mourned.

As soon as he opened the door to his flat, he wished he hadn't. Before he stepped foot inside, a hand flew out and jerked him in. It belonged to a large man, maybe six foot five, with long, unwashed, black hair. The door slammed behind him. He turned to see another man, shorter with blond hair and eyes so green, they looked like they'd been colored in with a marker. The big man tossed him onto the sofa and stood over him as the other sat down, draping his arm over the back of the couch and sucking on his teeth.

"Who might you be, then?" the blond man asked.

"I was about to ask that of you. Who are you? What do you want?"

"We ask the questions, bruv."

"This is my place, right? So, I'll be askin' whatever questions I like."

"Ah, is that right?"

'Yeah, mate. That's right."

"Do you hear that, Simon? He'll ask whatever he likes."

The big man snorted.

"Well, in that case, I'm Jack. This is my associate, Simon. We're here on King's business. See, he knows that that harpy that calls herself Queen was following you about, but what he can't figure is what for. He's stumped. But, I bet you know, don't ya?"

"King? What are you on about? What King?"

"Wrong answer, Nav." He socked him in the gut so hard, he thought he might throw up. The wind was knocked out of him and it took him a minute to catch his breath. "The King of our people is who I'm speakin' of, Nav. The true King. Now, sure, he's not the first of our kind or nothin', but he understands us. He's one of us, you get me? Unlike that bitch in her ivory tower, forcing us to fight for humans, takin' up with a lightning wizard, our King is for *us*. He's lookin' to unseat the harpy permanently, you understand? And he needs leverage. You, Navid Parsi, are that leverage. Only question is, how important are you to Her Majesty? What are you, eh? Boy toy? Blood bag? Inside man in law enforcement? What's so special about you that the old bag felt the need to creep around here like a virgin outside a whorehouse?"

"He's too pretty to be smart," Simon chimed in. "Probably not much of a detective. I'm guessing side piece."

"Is that it, Nav? Is the old bint letting you get your end away? Or has it not gotten that far? Rumor has it before she started shaggin' the American, she followed him 'round like a cat in heat, too. A desperate puppy, she was. Is that what's going on here? The Queen fancies ya?"

"That is absolutely not what's going on."

"What then? Come on, give us the dish."

He clenched his jaw.

"Oh, you won't tell me?"

"Sorry, boys. I'm not feeling particularly chatty."

"That's very disappointing, Nav. See, the King wants this information. Without it, he doesn't know if he should take you prisoner, or kill you offhand."

"I say we kill him," Simon grunted.

"Now, Simon, you know it's not our place to make those decisions."

"What is your place, Jack?" Navid sassed. "On your knees in front of some bloke calling himself your King?"

Jack slapped him, whipping his head to the side and causing his lip to bleed. "That was a warning, Nav. It'll be a lot easier on ya if you cooperate."

"Yeah," Simon smirked. "I'd hate to do you like your friend at the bakery."

He glared up at him, his cheeks burning. "What did you say?"

"The old lady. When you weren't here, we tried the bakery. No one there but her. We got a little frustrated, so we decided to have a laugh."

Navid's common sense left him as his heart pounded in his ears, fury burning through him like wildfire. He kicked his foot out hard, breaking Simon's shin before headbutting him in the chest, knocking him to the ground. He jumped up from his seat and turned to punch Jack squarely in the nose. While they were stunned, he made a beeline for the door. But, the vampires were fast, pulling him back and throwing him to the floor. Knowing there wasn't a minute to spare, he swept his leg, knocking Simon down. He landed with a thud as Navid got to his feet, dodging Jack's right hook. He avoided another hit and another, backing from the living room toward the kitchen. He feigned reaching for something on the bar with his left hand, distracting Jack just long enough to land a jab with his right.

"Oh, you'll pay for that, Nav," Jack warned, rubbing his jaw. In a blur, Jack was on him, pushing him to the floor and pounding his face and stomach with his pale, freckled fists.

"I wanna play," Simon said, hurrying over. He kicked him in the side over and over, crowing as he felt his ribs crack through his shoe.

"Hold on, hold on," Jack said, waving his hand at Simon. "Do you smell that?"

"Yeah," Simon gleaned. "Blood."

"No, somethin' else. Somethin' in it. You smell that?" They got down on the floor, sniffing Navid's wounds. "Could it be?" Jack licked the blood from a gash on Navid's cheek as he fought to keep conscious. "Well, I'll be goddamned."

"What is it?"

"It's her. It's the bloody Queen. This poor sod is one of hers. Blood of her blood."

"Aren't we all blood of her blood?"

"Yeah, technically, but this one's *human*. Don't ya get it?"

Simon stared blankly.

Jack rolled his eyes. "Come on, you can't be this dense. He's a human descendant of the Queen."

"He's a *what*?"

"Exactly! That's why she was so interested in seein' what he was up to. The old cow was pinin' for her real family."

"I didn't know she had any."

"Well, me, neither. I don't think anyone did. The King certainly hasn't the foggiest. You know what this means, don't ya?"

"What?"

"We bring him in, *alive*, we'll be heroes. The King will give us riches beyond our wildest dreams. Maybe Governorships, even."

"Alive?" His eyes went black. "I see what you're sayin' but that's a lot of blood going to waste."

"We'll pick up some skags once we've got him secure on the plane, right? He's our golden ticket, Simon. Best we don't fuck it up, yeah?"

"I guess."

"Good. Get the trunk ready. Let's see how flexible our boy here is." Simon went to the hall closet and dragged out a large steamer trunk. He opened it up, glancing inside to make sure there were enough air holes poked into the sides. Jack smiled down at Navid who lay half-unconscious and unable to move. "Come on, bruv. Don't want to keep His Majesty waiting."

Chapter 25

Lucifer's cold body lay draped on his bed, stale blood staining the sheets under his still-open mouth. It was empty, his true form having vacated hours before, on to another adventure.

His footsteps echoed in the suffocating silence of the sprawling nothing that was Purgatory. He trudged through the cold and dark, the hollowness of it more unsettling than the most depraved sewers of Hell. Above him, the souls hung, all of them unaware of the others just next to them, quiet and contemplative. It was a ghastly sight, even for Lucifer.

He trekked on, undeterred. Finally, he came upon the soul he'd been searching for. The figure of light hovered in front of him, still, content in its misery. He stood before it, watching with glee as the image of a face began to take form on what appeared to be its hanging head. Its glowing eyes looked up at him, warning him to leave it be. His eyes twinkled in the shimmer of the soul's incandescence and a sly smile crept across his face. "Hello, nephew."

ALUKAH

Too long a sacrifice can make a stone of a heart.

William Butler Yeats

Prologue

The man spilled thirty silver coins onto the sorcerer's table and tucked his long hair behind his ears. "Give me something to ease my guilt, shopkeeper. And, if no such thing exists, give me something to end my suffering for I am shamed and pained by wretched remorse."

The sorcerer could see the anguish in the man's eyes and took pity on him. "I have something," he said, reaching into a basket under the table. "It will not take away what you are feeling, but it will give you time to make amends. Is that what you want? To make things right?"

"I see no way of righting what I have done. My sin is far too great. But, if there *is* a way, I will have what you are selling."

"Very well." He held out an ornate bottle no larger than his index finger kept closed with a tiny piece of cork.

"A potion?" the man asked, taking the bottle and opening it, smelling the contents, and giving the sorcerer a suspicious glance. "Is this sheep's blood?"

"I assure you, it is not. Drink it and you will have your redemption."

Desperate, the man emptied the bottle into his throat, swallowing fast, hoping to avoid the salty iron taste of the deep red fluid. He placed the bottle on the table and cringed. He nodded to the sorcerer, left the bottle and the silver, and exited the shop, feeling no better than when he'd entered.

He sat under the tree, its deep pink flowers seeming to mock him with their beauty, demanding he be happy when he could not be. He wailed, letting the tears stream down his face uninterrupted as he sobbed. He labored to breathe as his stomach ached, his guilt and grief overwhelming. "Tell me what to do," he prayed, looking to the sky. "I will do anything you command. Give me a task and I shall complete it. What must I do to appease you?"

The clouds parted, opening up to the clear and starry night. The moon revealed itself and in its light, he could see a discarded rope lying on the ground a few feet away. He stood, walked over, and picked it up. "Is this what you demand of me, Lord?" His voice quivered as he worked the rope into a noose. "Shall this be my punishment?" He threw it over the sturdiest branch and tied it in place. "I can not be certain if you wish it, but I would rather feel the agony of death than live with the grievous sin I have committed. Please forgive me, Lord, and if you can not, know that I understand, for in this life and the next, I will never forgive myself." He climbed up the tree, sending the sparrows fleeing from their nests, placed the rope around his neck, and let go.

A group of men with torches came storming through the forest, calling for the man to show himself. Hungry for justice, they were stopped in their tracks when they saw the body hanging, limp, its eyes bulged and its tongue protruding.

"It's The Betrayer!" one of the men yelled upon closer inspection.

"Are you sure?" another asked.

"Yes! I'd recognize him anywhere, even in this state. The coward took his own life."

"How will we have justice *now*?"

"We will cut him down and bury his body in Akeldama."

"But, that's for foreigners."

"He was a stranger to us, was he not? Did we know what he was capable of? Did he share his plans with any of us? No. He did what he did in secret. He hid who he truly was from all of us. Akeldama is what he deserves."

The men took the body to the field, dug a hole, and dropped it in. They covered it and left it unmarked, spitting on it before turning to leave.

"Mmmff."

"Did you hear that?" one of the men asked.

"Hear what?" another responded.

"Mmmff."

"That."

"I did."

"As did I," another chimed in. The men turned, realizing that the sound was coming from the grave. They stared, horror covering their faces as their hearts began to race.

"Was he still alive?" the first man wondered.

"He couldn't have been," the second said. "Could he?"

The earth seemed to breathe, pulsating under the light of the full moon. The men watched in terror as one hand, then two appeared from underneath the soil.

"We buried him alive," one man uttered.

He clawed his way out, the others too stunned to move. He rose, the dirt falling away from his clothes as he climbed out and stood upright. "What has happened?"

The men stayed silent.

"What have you done to me?"

"You were dead," one of them told him. "We thought."

His mind went dark, his thoughts replaced by instinct alone. The sound of pounding in his ears was so incessant, he could hear nothing else. His eyes went black and his teeth seemed to grow, causing the others to scream and run. He chased them down, one by one, ripping out their throats with his newly formed fangs. The taste on his lips whipped him into a frenzy. He needed more of the salty liquid covering his mouth. His eyes shined in the moonlight as he bent over the dying men, clamped down on one neck after another, and drank. When the last man was dead, the pounding stopped. As he came to his senses, he realized that the noise he'd been hearing must have been their heartbeats. He stood in horror, looking down at the men he used to call friends. "What have I done?" he whispered, wiping the blood from his face. "What am I?"

He burst into the shop, filthy and covered in other men's blood. "Charlatan!" he shouted, startling the shopkeeper. "You offer no redemption. You've made me a demon!"

"Not a demon," the sorcerer corrected. "You are now as I am. Alukah."

His face went hot as he bounded toward the table. "You've made me a monster! An abomination!"

"I only gave you the option. Had you remained alive, no change would have befallen you."

"Take it away! Return me to my true self."

"This is who you are. There is no going back. Don't you understand? I've given you what you wanted."

"I did *not* ask for this."

"*Time.* So long as you stay out of the sun and keep your head and your heart, you will live forever. No matter how long it takes, you will one day find the redemption you seek. In the meantime, you'll possess strength beyond measure. Women will fall at your feet. Those things may seem fleeting, but they will be a source of happiness for you until you get the--"

The man gripped the sorcerer's throat, his rage once again taking over. He pulled out his trachea, the sound of his voice having become too irritating to take. He broke a chair over the shopkeeper's head, shattering it to pieces. He picked up one of the chair legs, leaped on top of him, and plunged it into the sorcerer's heart. When he'd gone still, the man got up and began to run.

He ran all night, faster than he'd ever run before. Faster than anyone should have been able to. He ran until he found himself in a country he didn't recognize in a tiny village on the other side of the Salt Sea. He felt weak, tired, and hungry. He sought refuge in an inn, but the keeper refused him, not recognizing his speech. Exhausted and overcome with what felt like starvation, he pounced, drinking the innkeeper dry before moving on, going from one room to the next, killing everyone in the building. Yet unsatisfied, he blew through the village, killing man, woman, and child, from house to house, feasting on an abundance of blood and misery. When he was finished, there was no one left. The village was dead.

He returned to the inn, the threat of sunrise upon him. He hid in the kitchen, the only room with no windows, found a bag of grain to put under his head, and went to sleep, his guilt rising in his chest as he drifted off. His slumber was restless, the screams of his victims emblazoned in his subconscious. He had nightmares of their cries, of their faces and he'd continue to have the same horrific dreams every day for the remainder of his life.

Chapter 1

Phindi walked the halls of the converted fortress, the vampires in her keep all quiet in their beds as the sun made its fiery rise above the thick, stone castle. Dated to 1477, she'd chosen the citadel in Alexandria as her command center for its strategic location. Centered between the two realms she now governed, Egypt was the perfect place to bridge her lands and monitor the happenings in both. There were rumors of someone calling himself 'King', but nothing substantiated, so she had her best spies out every night hunting for proof. In the meantime, she did her duty as Duchess by mediating disputes, paying the bills of those in her charge, overseeing the renovation of the building she occupied, and filling it with flame lilies. She couldn't stand most flowers. She found them frivolous and distracting, but she knew to be an effective leader she would have to be more than the Queen's general. She'd have to be seen not only as a warrior but as an ally, someone that cared about her people's problems and someone that they could relate to. Decorating her residence was one way of showing a softer side of herself, even if no such side existed, and flame lilies, while beautiful, are highly poisonous which Phindi saw as their one redeeming quality.

As she headed to her rooms, she heard a crash coming from the main hall followed by what sounded like a hundred men screaming. She looked down over the railing of the loft to the grand room below. The main entrance had been broken through and men poured in by the dozens, all cloaked in forest green and shouting, "For the King!" They wielded sleek, steel spikes, some burning their hands as they unsheathed them, the room now flooded with early morning daylight. They bounded up the stone staircase, determined, like hunters searching out their prey. Phindi took three seconds to get her bearings as she acclimated to her current predicament. Her home, her sanctuary, her fortress was being invaded.

"Rebels!" she boomed through the halls, pounding on the doors of the sleeping loyalists. She rushed to the armory at the end of the hallway, pulling swords and spears from their places on the walls and turning back to distribute them to her people, but by the time she'd returned, the fighting had already begun.

Half of the loyalists were slaughtered in their beds while the rest fought barehanded against the armed force, tearing heads from bodies and throwing their attackers over the railing. Phindi tossed weapons to her subordinates, leaving none for herself. She flew at the rebels, fangs bared, her arms outstretched. She drove her sharp nails into their abdomens, yanking out intestines before reaching up into their chests and clawing out their hearts.

As more men flooded the building, a voice came from behind. "Your Grace!" Phindi turned to see one of her fledglings holding her assegai. "Forgive me. I went into your rooms to retrieve it." The girl held it out to her and she took it, nodding in approval.

Above the entrance hung a massive banner, rolled up and largely ignored. Phindi leaped up onto the railing, took aim, and threw her spear at the gold cord holding it in place. The banner fell, its deep purple velvet blocking out the sun's rays, enabling the loyalists to descend, meeting the intruders in less confining quarters. They pounced, hacking off heads and running rebels through with their swords. Phindi leaped through the air, pulling her spear from the wall and landing confidently on her feet. She took her weapon in both hands, using it as a blunt instrument with which to knock her opponent to the ground before raising it above her head, her foot on the man's throat.

"Who sent you?" she demanded.

The man laughed, blood dribbling from the corner of his mouth. "My King."

"Who? Who is this self-proclaimed King that blasphemes against our Queen?"

"He is our redeemer. He saves us from your bitch Queen's tyranny."

Her eyes widened as her anger grew. "Your disrespect will not go unpunished. Know that on this day, you dishonor not the Queen, but yourself." She brought the spear down hard, sinking it in his chest and through his heart. His eyes went dim, the last bit of life leaving him. She pulled out the assegai and surveyed the room. A handful of her people remained, their shoulders slumped as they grieved the loss of their friends. Everyone else was dead. "Go to your rooms," she commanded. "It is day and you are exhausted."

"Will you inform the Queen of this treachery?" one of the girls asked.

"Yes, but not until I can offer her a solution to the problem. I will find out where this 'King' hides while he sends others to fight his battles. I will gather troops. I will form a plan and with Her Majesty's blessing, I will root out the traitor and scorch the earth to cleanse him from it."

The vampires bowed and scurried back up the steps to their rooms, locking themselves in for the day. Phindi looked over the bodies, spear in hand, resentment building like a wall in her chest, hard and strong. She would raise her army. She would find this King. She would have her revenge.

Chapter 2

"Can I come in?" Gabriel asked, her eyes bloodshot and her expression grim.

Wyatt stepped aside, closing the door behind her as she entered. "You knocked."

"Yeah."

"Have you ever knocked on a door in your life?"

"Once or twice. Can I talk to you?"

"Sure. I was about to have coffee. You want some?"

She cringed. He poured himself a cup, the morning sun lighting up the apartment in a flood of golden radiance.

"You sure? You look exhausted."

"I haven't slept."

"Soda?"

She nodded. He set his cup down and got the caffeinated beverage from the fridge. He slid it across to her as they sat at the island and she opened it, downing half the can before stopping to take a breath.

"So, what's going on? Another crisis? You need me to throw a ball of lightning at a Kraken or something?"

She shook her head, eyes fixed on the soda can.

"Lucifer giving you a hard time?"

She let out a grieved sigh. "No, Lucifer's probably dead."

He choked on his coffee. "Dead? Of what?"

"Oh, you know, not listening. I mean, I'm not *sure*, but I can't feel him anymore, so I'm assuming he's not on Earth, which means he's dead."

"Holy shit."

"That's not what I want to talk to you about, though."

"It's not? Because that's a pretty big deal."

"It's not. Listen, I don't normally talk to you about my problems because I don't want to burden you. You have enough to deal with. But, I can't go to Uriel with this without upsetting Sinclair, Wendy isn't back from New Zealand, and Lucifer's gone, so--"

"Hey," he said, reaching across the island and putting his hand over hers. "You can *always* talk to me."

She nodded, tears forming in her eyes. She looked up at him as they spilled down her cheeks. "I'm afraid you'll hate me."

"I won't," he promised, the pain on her face breaking his heart.

"I hope that's true." She brushed away her tears and took a deep breath before beginning. "When I was fifteen, my parents killed me...twice, after they killed my girlfriend and her family."

"Jesus Christ."

"Yeah. Pushed me down a flight of stairs, broke my neck. Then, shot me in the heart. My best friend saw it happen and he lost control. He killed them. He's been in prison for the last twenty years. He *was* in prison...until last night." She took a sip of soda, preparing herself to continue. "We met when we were ten. My parents took me to the city to see A Christmas Carol on Broadway. He was outside the theater panhandling, homeless, so I convinced James and Ester to bring him home. He stayed with us for a few days until my mom called social services and they took him away. He got put in foster care and I was scared I'd never see him again, so I ran away to find him. He was just a few streets over, so no one even realized I'd gone. We were inseparable for years after that. He took care of me when Ester would hit me or I'd get overwhelmed by all the thoughts in my head that weren't mine. He moved in after the Murphys' funeral so I wouldn't be alone. He waited until I found Uri and Raph. But, then he turned himself in. He was afraid he would hurt me or someone else. He was having a hard time reigning in who he was."

"Who he was?"

She sniffed as she fought to control her emotions. "He was one of us, B. Camael. The Wrath of God."

He raised his eyebrows. "Oh. So, he's out now?"

"He was." She wiped away more tears as she explained. "I visited him every week for the last twenty years. I told him everything that was going on with you and the others. I told him everything about everything. I grew up with him. He knew me, you know? And then, God came calling." Her tone turned resentful as she took another drink and slammed the can back on the counter.

"God? He spoke to you?"

"No, He just downloads information to my brain like a fucking laptop whenever He sees fit. It's pretty unpleasant. When I found out where Dia's descendants were, I also found out what Cam's purpose here was." She covered her mouth as she held back sobs. Unable to stifle her emotions, she continued through the tears, her voice going up an octave as she moved from the island to the sofa, sitting down and hugging her arms as if she were cold. "I had to tell him to break out of prison, drag him to a fight, and watch him die doing God's work. I had to burn his body so he could go home. I killed him, B. I killed my best friend."

He sat next to her on the couch and wrapped his arms around her shoulders, kissing the top of her head. "You didn't kill him."

"I did. *I did.* Because God commanded it. I always do what He wants me to. I *always* make it happen. Whatever it is that He wants done, I get that shit done. And I understand. The greater good and all that, but *fuck.*" She put her hand to her diaphragm as it got harder for her to breathe.

He held her closer, rubbing her arm, tears in his eyes now, as well. She made so much more sense to him now as a person. The weight of what God put on her, the responsibility, and the sacrifice. The abusive parents and traumatic childhood. He was amazed she hadn't fallen apart before now.

She cried into his chest for a few minutes, eventually calming down enough to have the hard part of the conversation. "There's more." She sat back, looking him in the eye, watching his expressions carefully, afraid of how he'd react. "The thing God wanted Cam to do," She paused, taking a shaky breath. "Was to kill Cain."

Wyatt's eyes grew wide, moving from his sister to the bedroom door where Allydia slept. "Cain killed him?"

"No, not exactly. Anything physically harmful that happens to Cain happens to whoever inflicted the damage times seven. God's Wrath is the only thing strong enough to kill him permanently, so when Cam killed Cain, he died, too."

"Oh, shit." He rubbed his chin. "I don't know how she's gonna feel about that."

"Relieved, I imagine. He was a shit father *before* he kidnapped her kids, called her a monster, and threatened to murder her. He's the reason she got all paranoid and hired a bunch of spies. She was scared he was coming after her."

"Then, why did you think I'd hate you? If you were doing what God forced you to and Allydia won't be hurt, why would I be angry?"

"Not about Cain. About the party."

He tilted his head. "What party?"

"In '97. Crystal something-or-other's birthday. East 48th street."

"Crystal Bowers. I remember that. Well, bits and pieces. I got pretty wasted that night."

"I'm so sorry." She sniffed again as more tears threatened to come.

"For what?"

"I was there. I saw you with that girl, standing by the speaker, beer in your hand. I watched you take her into a room and close the door. I knew who you were and I didn't say anything."

He went quiet, his expression somber, his eyes fixed on hers.

"I had a problem back then. I couldn't always handle the voices. Everyone's thoughts and feelings. It was a lot. And after my parents killed Ada, my girlfriend, my issue got out of control. I was, um," She wanted to look away, but she couldn't. She needed to see his reaction. "I was on heroin."

His features softened and he looked down at his hands in his lap.

"That night, I shot up more than a normal person would've been able to take. I was limp on the couch. I could barely make words. I couldn't hear your thoughts or feel your feelings, but I knew you were my brother. I didn't know your human name, but I was sure that you were Barachiel, Protector of Humanity, Leader of the Guardians, Angel of Blessings. *I knew it* and I just lay there, wallowing in my own bullshit. I'm so sorry, B. If I had known what would happen--"

"But, you didn't, did you?" He looked her in the eyes again. "You couldn't have. Not unless He wanted you to."

"I was stoned. I shouldn't have been. I should have been more responsible. I should have taken it more seriously."

"Taken what more seriously?"

"Who I am."

They were quiet for a moment while Wyatt gathered his thoughts. She'd expected him to be angry, but he wasn't. All she could feel him feeling for her was love and pity.

"I'm not mad at you, Gabriel. You were a kid with maybe the worst parents of all time plus *everyone* in your head. I can't imagine what that must be like."

She brushed away a final tear. "You don't hate me."

"No," he smiled. "Did I ever tell you how I met my wife?"

She knew the story, given that she knew everything about him as soon as she set eyes on him at his therapist's office a few years before, but she shook her head, knowing that he wanted to tell it.

"On nine-eleven, I was at my college's counselor's office not because I was upset about what had happened, but because I was seeing the ghosts of people that were killed. I thought I was having a meltdown. It was the worst 'hallucination' I'd ever had. So I was sitting there, waiting my turn, people crying all around me, and in walks Annie, calm as can be, carrying a twenty-four pack of water in her hands and a tote bag full of brownies she'd made over her shoulder. She gave everyone in the office a brownie and a bottle and asked if they were okay. She hugged people she'd never met and talked to them until they relaxed. She got to me last, gave me two brownies. Said I looked like I needed them more than anyone else there. She sat with me for *two hours* talking about everything and nothing. She made me laugh. She made me forget for a while that I was crazy. By the time it was my turn to see the counselor, the ghosts were gone and I felt fine. I think I fell in love with her right there." He tilted his head to make sure she was paying attention before he continued. "If you had told me who I was, *what* I was, I would have avoided two decades of mental illness and everything that went with it. But, I also would never have been in that counselor's office. I wouldn't have met Annie. I wouldn't have had Will."

She bit her bottom lip. "Do you think it would have been better that way? I know how much losing them hurt you."

"No," he insisted. "I would rather feel the pain of losing them every day than go through my entire life never having loved them. So, I don't blame you for ignoring me at that party. Whether it was God's will or just dumb luck, it doesn't matter. I'm grateful to have had them. No matter what happened, I know that they loved me."

She looked toward the bedroom door and back at him. "You know, Dia loves you, too. Hard."

"Does she?"

"*Hard*. Girl is all in. I haven't seen her like this ever. And, me and Uriel love you. And Sinclair. Not in the same gag-inducing way the vampire Queen does, but we do."

He laughed.

"So, don't go thinking there aren't people that care about you. And I don't give a fuck what happens from now until my feathery ass is back in Heaven, don't you even think about committing suicide again. My heart can't take it."

"I won't, I swear," he chuckled.

"Good. Is it okay if I take a nap on your couch? I'm stupid tired."

"Go ahead. I'll get you a pillow." He went to the hall closet, taking out a spare pillow and throw blanket. He set the pillow on one end of the couch and she immediately dropped her head onto it, curling up in the fetal position as he covered her with the blanket.

"Thanks, B. Love you."

"Love you, too." He went back to the island and finished his coffee, watching his sister sleep, having a new appreciation for her now that he knew what she'd been through. He'd always thought Annie was the strongest person he'd ever known, but he was wrong. Gabriel was.

Chapter 3

"Daddy," the small voice said, waking Malik from a dead sleep. "Daddy, wake up." He looked to his right and saw Valerie lying there, eyes closed, still asleep. "Daddy!" He jumped, finally seeing the girl at the side of the bed. She looked to be three or four years old, long, curly hair flowing down her back, wearing one of his wife's tee-shirts as a nightgown.

"What the..." He sat up, rubbing his eyes and turning on the light.

"Daddy, can you make eggs for breakfast?" the girl asked sweetly.

He stared, mouth agape. It took him several seconds to come to terms with who she was as it was just the night before that she'd taken her first steps. "Sinclair?"

She nodded. "Scrambled. And strawberries? Strawberries are my favorite."

"Um, sure, baby. Just let me get woken up. I'll be right there."

"Okay. Hurry, though." Her pupils dilated completely causing Malik's heart to jump to his throat. "I'm hungry." She skipped out of the room leaving him in a cold sweat. He looked back at a still sleeping Valerie, his heart thumping. She was oblivious and he was petrified.

"Mommy!" Sinclair cheered as Valerie entered the living room, Malik following closely behind.

"Holy shit," the mother muttered under her breath. The girl ran to her, putting her arms up to be held. Valerie complied, picking her up and carrying her on her hip to the dining table. "Looks like I'm gonna have to go shopping. You've outgrown all your clothes!"

Sinclair laughed.

"You'll need a big girl bed, too. Daddy said you want eggs for breakfast?"

"Yeah! And strawberries. And orange juice. And toast!"

"Oh! Okay, well, you heard her," she said to Malik who had already begun work in the kitchen. She turned her attention back to her daughter as she got her sat in a chair. "We'll have to get shoes and barrettes and headbands. Maybe after breakfast, we can braid your hair, how's that sound?"

"Yay!" the child beamed, clapping her hands and bouncing in her seat. "Can we also get some crayons? I really wanna draw."

"Of course! Crayons, finger paint, construction paper, all that stuff."

"Thank you, Mommy!"

Malik set plates in front of them and went back to the kitchen for the juice. As he poured, he glanced over at the table, watching anxiously as they ate. Maybe he'd been seeing things. It was early and he'd just woken up. But he knew what he saw. Her eyes had gone black. He was *sure*. According to his wife, that's something vampires did when they were about to bite someone. Had Sinclair been threatening him? Or was she just too young to control her instincts? Either way, between that and the hyper-fast aging, he was freaked out. *Get it together*, he thought, placing the cups in front of his wife and daughter. *This is your new normal. Learn to live with it.*

Chapter 4

"Well, that's good," Gabriel muttered as she peeked her head into Lucifer's room and found it empty. The sheets were stained with blood, but the bed was unoccupied, which meant that he'd recovered from the injuries he'd received during his bout with Cain. She shuffled to the kitchen, hoping there were some cookies left in the pantry, but as she passed the living room, she caught a glimpse of Lucifer on her balcony and he wasn't alone.

"What in the actual fuck?" she snapped as she went to meet him. On the floor between them lay what looked like a half-reanimated corpse, bloated, worms crawling out of its nose, moaning in anguish.

"Surprise!" Lucifer gleaned, clearly proud of himself. "It's our nephew. Well, it will be, once you heal his body. In retrospect, it may have been kinder to acquire him a fresh one, but in my excitement, I shoved his soul right back into the original. Must be unbearably painful."

"Jesus, Lucifer." She covered her mouth at the stench coming from the body. "He would have been reincarnated." She held her hand out, using her telekinesis to pull embalming fluid, muddy water, worms, and insects from the boy's stomach and lungs. He groaned, convulsing as the thread that had been keeping his eyes sewn shut broke, his milky eyes bulging.

"Yes, eventually, long after you all died and had gone back home. Losing Mariana has given me a new appreciation for human grief. Barachiel needs his son back *now*. Besides, don't you find it odd that the boy existed at all?"

"This is taking forever," she huffed as more and more sludge came seeping out of Will's nose and mouth.

"Don't you see? After my skirmish with Cain, I should have gone back to Hell, but I landed in Purgatory. *Purgatory*. I have no human soul. There was no reason for me to have ended up there. There's no explanation other than God made it so. He *must* want Will alive. Think about it, sister. There's no way our brother should have been able to procreate unless our Father wanted him to."

She sighed as the last of the fluid drained from Will's body. She placed her hands on his head and heart, his skin glowing from the inside at the touch. After a few moments, his appearance changed from a swollen, green, and gray zombie to the young man Gabriel had seen in Wyatt's memories. His eyes cleared, returning to their natural, grayish hue and color returned to his cheeks. He grasped her wrist, looking up at her in terror.

"You're all right," she assured him, helping him to sit up.

As he acclimated to his senses, he opened his mouth to speak. At first, only scratchy, broken syllables escaped his throat, but after a few seconds, words finally came. "Au-- Aunt Gabriel?"

She nodded, tears forming in her eyes.

"What-- How?"

"My doing," Lucifer chirped.

He turned his head to see his uncle standing behind him. On instinct, he heaved a bolt of lightning in his direction. Lucifer stepped aside to avoid getting hit.

"Feisty as ever, I see."

"Yo," Gabriel lectured, taking Will's hand and resting it by his side. "None of that."

He shifted his gaze back to her. "I was dead, wasn't I?"

"Yes," Lucifer told him. "It was unsightly. Very grim. I really should have taken a photograph."

Gabriel shot him a look before answering. "You were, but Lucifer brought you back."

"Is he stupid?"

"Kind of." She helped him up, his legs wobbling like a newborn deer as he stood.

"I resent that," Lucifer piped. "Just because you don't know why he was born, doesn't mean there isn't a reason."

"You have no idea what I know."

"I shouldn't be here," Will said, eyeing the railing. "After what I did, I don't deserve to--"

"What is with you people wanting to die?" Gabriel asked. "Seriously, is it something in your genes? Honestly. I have been through a lot of shit and I have never once wanted to fling myself from a building. *I'm a trash can* and I still love myself."

"Not the worst way to go," Lucifer interjected. "Certainly less painful than slicing open your wrists with a piece of broken glass. Then again, your father always has been a bit of a drama queen."

Will formed a ball of electricity in his hand as he stared his uncle down. "My father was a fucking saint. If I hear you disrespecting him again, I swear to God."

"He's alive," Gabriel told him.

The energy in his hand dissipated as his features softened. "What?"

"Yeah, Dia drinking so much of his blood when they first hooked up made him basically immortal. It's a whole thing."

"Is he," he stopped, choking back tears. "Is he okay?"

"Eh, better than he was."

"Where is he?"

"At his dad's place."

"I want to see him. I have to tell him I'm sorry. I have to--" He stumbled as he tried to take a step. Gabriel caught him and helped him walk inside.

"All right, kid. I'll take you to him. Shower first, though. You're covered in all manner of crap and you smell like a dumpster."

He nodded.

"You can borrow some of your uncle's clothes until we get you some new ones, *can't he*?"

"Of course," Lucifer agreed. "What's mine is yours. As long as I can be there when we surprise Barachiel."

"Yes, fine." She opened the door to the hall bathroom and took Will's face in her hands. "You know I love you, right?"

"Yeah. I love you, too."

"Good. So don't make me regret not letting you yeet yourself into traffic, okay?"

He nodded.

She brushed away a tear and hugged him. "I missed you."

He went into the bathroom and closed the door. When she heard the water running, Gabriel went back to join her brother in the living room. "You are dumb as shit."

"What?" he chuckled.

She pointed out onto the mess on the floor of the balcony. "You're cleaning that up."

Chapter 5

As night fell, Allydia emerged from Wyatt's bedroom already stunning in her leather pants and deep v-neck, cold-shoulder top. He wanted to scoop her up and take her right back to bed, but he couldn't let himself get distracted. He had to tell her about her father and he wasn't sure how she was going to take the news.

"Hey," he greeted as she sat next to him on the sofa. "You sleep okay?"

"As well as could be expected, I suppose."

"How are you feeling about Navid and everything?"

"All right. He's safe and that's what matters."

He rested his arm behind her on the back of the couch. "Gabriel was here today."

"I know. I can smell her on your furniture. Like chamomile and candy bars."

He fought the urge to laugh. "Something happened. Your father--"

"Are you hurt?" she fussed, looking him over.

"No, I wasn't there. But, baby, God's Wrath was."

"Wrath? You mean fire and brimstone, Sodom and Gomorrah, The Wrath of God? The angel Camael?"

"Yes."

She sat back and folded her arms. "I only met him once, in Hobah. Anger issues."

He placed a hand on her leg as he tried to find the words.

She tucked her hair behind her ears and held his hand. "Cain is dead, isn't he?"

"Yeah, baby, he is. I'm sorry."

She shook her head and put her fingers to his lips, a broken smile appearing on her otherwise solemn face. "I'm fine."

He kissed her hand. "Are you sure? I know what it's like to lose--"

"Our fathers were not the same. It's sweet of you to worry, but you don't have to. I spent centuries looking over my shoulder, afraid and hiding from him. The knowledge of his passing makes me feel," she thought for a moment. "Well, similar to how I feel when I'm with you."

He raised his eyebrows. "How's that?"

She touched his cheek and kissed him softly. "Safe." Her phone buzzed in her back pocket. She took it out to see a text from Hartley. "I have to go." She kissed him again and headed for the door. "I'll be back before you go to bed."

"See you then," he said as she closed the door behind her.

Yo, B, he heard in his head.

Gabriel, he replied. *You okay?*
Relatively. Is your girl with you?
She just left, why?
We're coming over.
Who's we?
You'll see.

"We're getting reports of rebel attacks all over Europe," Hartley said as she bowed her head and followed Allydia up to the throne room, walking through the path cleared by the crowd of vampires that danced on the main floor of the club. "Fires in the hotels in Barcelona and Prague. The nightclubs in Hamburg and Zurich. The brothel in Amsterdam is *gone*. Governors are reporting mass casualties. Numbers are still coming in, but--"

"How can this be?" she barked as they entered the room. Hartley closed the door and knelt before her. "There are plans for things like this. Contingencies. Every Governor is well-armed with stockpiles of weapons to distribute to their people. Every one of my children is well trained in self-defense. How are the rebels doing this?"

"They're attacking in the day, Your Majesty."

"They're *what*?"

"The day. They're cloaking themselves, risking death to butcher us in our sleep. No one is safe, my Queen. Not even under the sun."

"They're mad."

"They're organized. Someone is leading them. There are rumors of someone calling himself 'King'. I have people looking into it, but it seems that this person is ordering simultaneous attacks that are being carried out by those loyal to him. There are more traitors than we thought, Your Majesty. A lot more."

She paced the floor, arms crossed, her brow furrowed in thought and rage. "Call the Governors. All of them. Bring them here for an emergency conference. Offer assistance to whoever needs it and *find me this 'King'*."

"Yes, Your Majesty. I do have one piece of good news. We found the girl, Hattie's Sired. We have her downstairs."

"Show me."

They went back down the staircase to the main floor and opened the door to the lower level. They followed the steps down to a dimly lit room with damp, stone floors and cage-lined walls housing an army's-worth of various weapons. On the far side of the room sat a refrigerator with a stockpile of blood bags and opposite that was a cell. She could see the girl inside, huddled in a corner, and trembling.

Hartley handed Allydia a phone that was not her own, but that of the Queen's former assistant. "This is how we found her. My guys took this off Hattie in Scotland. The girl's was the only number that was ever called. Wasn't hard to trace."

"Thank you, Hartley. That will be all."

"Yes, Your Majesty." She bowed and hurried off to begin making calls.

"Your name is Michelle, yes?" she asked as she walked to the fridge, took a blood bag from it, and tossed it into the cell. The girl scrambled to get it open as fast as she could and guzzled the contents. Allydia tossed her another.

"Yes," the girl confirmed. "Michelle Iha."

"Do you know who I am?"

She nodded as she downed the contents of the second bag.

"I had your maker killed. It pained me, but it was necessary to maintain order. There's a faction of our kind that would see me removed. I can't allow any sign of weakness, do you understand?"

Again, she nodded, clearly frightened.

"There's an uprising I have to attend to, so for now, you'll remain here. When things have settled, I'll consider what to do with you more permanently." She spun on her heel and left the girl alone in the dungeon. Michelle leaned against the wall, crying into its cool stone. Hattie was gone and she was alone.

Chapter 6

Wyatt exited the bathroom to find Gabriel and Lucifer standing in his living room. "Oh, good," he said. "You're alive."

"I'm not the only one," Lucifer smirked, gesturing toward the kitchen. There, eating a piece of leftover pizza straight from the fridge, was Will. He turned to look at his father, dropped his food, and rushed toward him, throwing his arms around him in a tight embrace.

"I'm so sorry, Dad," the boy cried. "I'm so, so sorry."

Wyatt's eyes met Gabriel's, hope and confusion filling them as he all but begged her in his mind for this to be true. She nodded, giving him a reassuring smile. Tears streamed down his face as he hugged him, cradling the back of his head as he kissed his temple. He took his son's face in his hands and looked him over, shock giving way to curiosity. "How?"

"You're welcome," Lucifer chimed.

"You did this?"

"Of course. What are brothers for if not taking an excursion to the afterlife to rescue one's offspring from centuries of solitary torture? Now, if you'll excuse me, I haven't eaten since yesterday and I'm positively famished. Sister, will you be joining me?"

"Yeah, let's give these two some time to catch up." She waved her hand to get Wyatt's attention. *I know you want to tell him about Sinclair, but Michelle should. I'll call her.*

Okay, he agreed.

The two left, leaving father and son alone to talk. Wyatt still couldn't believe it. He didn't want to take his eyes off of Will for a second for fear that he would disappear. "Are you okay?" he asked, his voice shaking. "How do you feel?"

"Guilty," Will told him, tears spilling down his cheeks. "Sad. Disgusted with myself. I am so sorry, Dad. I don't know how to even *start* making things right. Is there a way? Because I'll do anything. Tell me how to fix it and I *will* because I don't--" he paused, stifling a sob. "I don't want you to hate me."

"Hey, I could never hate you, do you hear me?" He held his son's gaze, making sure he understood. "Grandpa was an accident. I know that. And, I can't die, so kill me again, kill me ten more times. I'll always come back and I'll always forgive you. *I'm* sorry. What Barachiel did to you," He sniffed and wiped away a tear. "I'm sorry."

"He was right, though. I'm a hazard. I threatened Lucifer with lightning twice in the first ten minutes I was back and he was the one that saved me."

"To be fair, I threaten Lucifer with lightning on a pretty regular basis. I wouldn't worry too much about it. He usually deserves it."

They both laughed.

"But, Michelle didn't," Will said, his features falling in despair. "I got mad that she told Gabriel I was losing it. I was upset that she was sent there to spy on me and I--" He covered his mouth as fresh tears poured down his cheeks. He took his hand away, trying to control his breathing as he spoke. "I just wanted her to leave me alone. I didn't mean to."

"Hey, hey, it's okay. Michelle's okay."

"What?" he whimpered. "I didn't kill her? I checked. She didn't have a pulse."

"Well, she did die, but she came right back...as a vampire."

Will's eyes were like saucers as he sat on a barstool at the island. "How is she?"

"I don't know. All right, I think."

"I need to see her. Where is she?"

"Relax, Gabriel's calling her now."

She set the phone back on the table as the waiter placed a plate in front of her. "Thank you," she said as he walked off. She took a bite of lasagna and tapped her fork against the plate, her eyes glued to the dark screen on her cellphone.

"What's got you in a mood now, Gabriel?" Lucifer asked, taking a sip of water.

"She's not answering."

"Who isn't?"

"Doesn't matter. Listen, I know I'm kind of dickish, but I'm really glad you're not dead."

"Well, thank you. I'm touched."

"For real, yesterday was a rolling dumpster fire and I'm really happy you survived it."

"What happened?"

"Camael killed Cain, like, for good."

"Wrath was here? I'm sorry I missed him. We had some good times in the old days. So, Camael's back in Heaven, then? I can't imagine him making it out of that alive."

"Yeah, he went back."

"And that displeases you?"

"Obvs."

"You were close?"

"Yeah."

"Well, then, I'm sorry. You will see him again, though. And, silver lining, the pebble in my shoe that was Cain, son of Adam, is finally no more. That's a good thing."

"I guess."

"And that was what I advised you to put off? Telling our fly-off-the-handle brother to do his duty?"

"Yep."

"Is it terrible that I'm glad you didn't listen to me?"

"Maybe a little, but I understand. Cain needed to be put down."

"Like a dog in the street." He raised his glass and took another sip.

"Like you would ever kill a dog."

"No, I wouldn't, but you know who I would kill, over and over again, no matter the consequences had our brother not stepped in?"

She rolled her eyes and sighed. "Cain."

"Cain. Cheers with me, sister." He picked up his glass again. "To Camael, always good for a laugh and the one and only Wrath of the Almighty."

She lifted her glass and clinked it to his, her enthusiasm lacking.

"Come, now. You know he's happy where he is."

"I know. I'm not worried about him, I just miss him." She took another bite as Lucifer cut into his eggplant Parmesan.

"It would seem, then, that we are both grieving the loss of someone we cared for. Perhaps we should form a support group. We could call it, 'Angels with Angst'. I'm sure we could recruit Barachiel to join. He's always distraught over one thing or another."

She snickered and took a sip of soda. "I am sorry about Mariana. She didn't deserve that."

"Yes, well, she too is in a better place. I know because I looked for her while I was in Purgatory and didn't find her."

"That's good, I guess."

"Yes. It's a dreadful place, that. I don't recommend taking an excursion there if you can avoid it."

"I'll keep that in mind."

"I've never felt something so empty. So completely devoid of--"

"Dude, I got it," she said, pointing to her temple.

"Ah, of course." He took a bite and studied her face. "What are you worried about then, if not Camael's well-being?"

She checked her phone. Still no text back. "Nothing."

He gave her a knowing squint and put his fork down.

"Fine. It's Will's girlfriend. She's not texting me back. She's a new vampire and I'm worried she's gone off and gotten herself killed."

"A vampire? Well, the apple doesn't fall far from the tree, does it?"

"She wasn't a vampire before he died."

"Well, that'll be a fun surprise, won't it?" he chuckled.

"Man, I hope Will's okay. I really don't want to have to send you to kill him again."

"You...you knew I was listening?"

"Of course I did."

He sat back and tilted his head. "So that Wyatt wouldn't blame you?"

She shrugged.

"How very manipulative of you. I'm impressed."

"I don't think B would see it that way, so shh."

"Your secret's safe with me."

"I told him about the party. He wasn't even mad. I forget sometimes how forgiving he is."

"Oh, *I* never do. You should have seen him after the Battle of Bravellir. He was sent to save King Herald, but the man all but begged to be allowed to die, thereby ensuring his legacy as a great warrior king, so I granted his wish. Barachiel was furious, but instead of giving me a lecture, he offered me a primitive form of jenever and sat with me while I complained. I was feeling particularly lonesome and--"

"I know all this."

"Then, how can you forget?"

"Because, man, I'm wrapped up in my own stupid shit a lot of the time. This human stuff is harder than it looks."

"Mm."

They finished their meals and Gabriel slid a credit card into the check presenter as the waiter scurried over to collect it. "Was everything to your liking?" the man asked.

"It was great," she told him.

"Yes, lovely, thank you," Lucifer said. The waiter nodded and walked off. "Tell me, sister. Do you think I'd be a good human?"

"No."

"You don't need to think about it a little?"

"Dude, do I have to remind you of the people in the church that time?"

"Do I have to remind *you* of the people in the theater that time?" he retorted.

"I didn't say *I* was good at being human. Shit, I might be more fucked up than *you*."

He raised an eyebrow and smirked.

She giggled. "Yeah, maybe not."

"Wendy!" Gabriel squealed, seeing her girlfriend sitting at the island as she and Lucifer entered the apartment. She darted over and kissed her repeatedly on the lips and cheeks. "I missed you so much. How was your trip?"

"Good. Hey, Lucifer. No bartender tonight?"

He glared at her.

"There's a lot to catch you up on."

"The bartender is no more, I'm afraid. Caught in Cain's revenge fantasy. Well, it's late. I'm off to bed." Lucifer headed down the hall. "See you in the morning."

"Night!" Gabriel sat next to her girlfriend, holding her hand and kissing it.

Wendy raised her eyebrows and pursed her lips. "What'd I miss?"

Chapter 7

Allydia used the key Wyatt had given her to enter his apartment and was horrified to find the Nephilim sitting casually on the sofa. She flew at him, baring her fangs and hissing. He jumped back in his seat as Wyatt stepped between them.

"It's okay," he told her, gently holding her back by the shoulders.

"It most certainly isn't. He's already killed you once. How is he even here? He should be rotting in the ground."

"Lucifer brought him back. I don't know the details and I don't care. What's important is that he's here."

She stared daggers at the boy, resisting the urge to lunge at him and tear his throat out with her teeth. "He's an abomination."

"What does that make you?" Will retorted.

"You have no idea what I am, the pain I will rain down on you if you so much as *breathe* on this man wrong."

"Relax," Wyatt said. "Nothing's gonna happen. We've been working on our meditation and--"

"*Meditation?*" she mocked. "Have you lost your mind? That boy is a menace. I give it a week, two at most before he's back to his monstrous ways."

"And, you'd know all about being a monster, wouldn't you?" Will snapped.

She glared at him. "I do what I do because I have to. I take no pleasure in hurting people. And, for the record, I haven't killed a human in years. Can you say the same?"

"Enough," Wyatt interrupted.

"She's got a point," Will conceded. "I don't know how long it'll be before I lose it again. Maybe I should stay with Aunt Gabriel for a while, just until we're sure I'm okay."

"That's hardly necessary."

"Let him go," Allydia begged.

"It's not that far and if I get out of control, Gabriel can stop me."

Wyatt folded his arms and furrowed his brow.

Will stood and patted his father's shoulder. "I don't want to hurt you, Dad."

Yo, B, he heard Gabriel say in his mind.

Yeah.

Michelle's not answering her phone. I called in a potential robbery to the house in Southport, but the cops said it's empty. Something's up.

"Allydia," he said, his tone accusatory as he met her gaze. "Do you know where Michelle is?"

"Michelle?" Will worried. "Dad, what's going on?"

Allydia frowned. "Don't ask me about this, Wyatt."

"Where?" he pressed.

"This is *my* business."

He closed the space between them, towering over her. She'd never seen him look so determined. *"Tell me."*

"Fine." She took a step back, feeling intimidated for the first time in centuries. "She's in the basement of the club, locked in a cell until I decide what to do with her."

"You put her in a cage?!" Will barked.

"She is not how you remember her."

"Let her go," Wyatt demanded.

"I can not. There are consequences to my actions. I have to consider--"

"Then, I'll get her myself." He pushed past her, Will following his father to the door.

"It is not your place," Allydia stated.

He turned back, looking furiously into her eyes, daring her with his words. "Stop me."

The men left, slamming the door behind them as the Queen composed herself, using her hand to fan her neck and chest. "Goddamn it, he's sexy."

Wyatt stormed through the club, his son at his heels. Vampires that recognized him from the battle in Iraq cleared a path, the fear in their expressions causing others to follow suit. At the back of the room, he spotted the door leading to the basement and quickened his pace, paying no attention to the hushed murmuring of the crowd around him.

"What are you doing here?" Hartley bleated, blocking his path.

"Get out of my way, Hartley," he commanded.

She arched an eyebrow. "Excuse me?"

"Step away from the lady," a half-drunk vampire said, coming up next to them.

Without altering his gaze, Wyatt shot a bolt of lightning into the man's chest, sending him reeling into a group of bystanders. "I don't want to hurt you, but you know I will." The Queen's assistant swallowed hard, pressing herself to the door behind her. Before she could decide whose punishment would be worse, his or her Queen's, she saw Allydia making her way toward them.

"Stop this now," she insisted.

He ignored his girlfriend's request, his eyes still fixed on Hartley's. *"Open the damn door."*

She looked to her Queen for instruction. She sighed and waved a hand, giving her the go-ahead, so she stepped aside. Will hurried past them, opening the door and bolting down the steps. Wyatt turned to address Allydia. "We need to talk." She gestured toward the steps leading upstairs, her annoyance clear in her expression. Before heading toward them, he stared daggers at Hartley as her hands trembled so hard, she nearly dropped her phone. "If anything happens to my son, I'll hold *you* responsible."

She slid back to her spot in front of the door, guarding it against further intruders as she watched the two go up to the second floor. She put her hand to her chest, glancing over to see the fallen vampire stand and take a glass of wine from a nearby table. "Well," she said under her breath. "That was dramatic."

Chapter 8

"Michelle?" Will called, his eyes adjusting to the darkness of the dungeon.

"Hello?" a weak voice called back. He dashed to it, finding the cell at the back of the room.

"Oh, God, Michelle," he breathed, stopping in front of the door. She was huddled in the corner, surrounded by empty blood bags, her hair disheveled, her dress torn, and her skin ashen.

She peered up at him, not believing her eyes. "Will?"

He gripped the bars and yanked the door off its hinges, flinging it aside and rushing in to kneel in front of her. He took her face in his hands, looking her over as she stared in wonder. "Are you okay? Are you hurt?"

She shook her head. "I'm fine. How are you here? Did I die again?"

Tears pooled in his eyes as he pushed the hair away from her face. "No. No, Lucifer brought me back. I don't know how or why, but...are you sure you're all right?"

She reached up and touched her fingertips to his chin. "You're real?"

"Yeah. Yeah, I'm real."

Her heart skipped in her chest as relief washed over. She kissed him hard, pulling herself up into his arms, almost knocking him over as she squeezed him. They embraced for several moments before Will stopped, tears of guilt tumbling down his cheeks.

"I'm so sorry," he whispered. "I never meant to hurt you."

"I know. I know you didn't." She ran her hand through his hair and down to his shoulder. "I can't tell you how much I've missed you. God, Will, I love you so much." She held him again, a swarm of butterflies fluttering in her stomach.

"I love you, too," he said, holding on to her like the last life preserver on the Titanic. "I feel like you're cutting me a lot of slack and I'm pretty sure I don't deserve it."

She laughed, kissing him again, softly at first, and then deeply, her body tingling as she pressed it against his. She pushed him down from his knees to a sitting position on the cool stone floor, positioning herself in his lap. She struggled to get his pants undone as she felt him stiffen beneath her, his hands running up her legs and under her dress. Just as she got the zipper unstuck, her fangs began to protrude, cutting his lip like a knife, the taste of his blood overwhelming her with lust and hunger. She leaped up, pushing him out of the way as she darted to the fridge across from the cell, threw the door open, and pulled out one blood bag after another, sucking down the contents, and dropping them to the floor.

He watched her, eyes wide as he gagged. "Oh, that's gross."

"You undermine me in front of my people," Allydia scolded as she and Wyatt entered her throne room, slamming the door behind them. "You attack them where they're meant to feel safe. *You disrespect me.*"

"You have a girl locked in a cage in an underground bunker. You don't get to be the one that's offended," he condescended, pacing around the room, hands on his hips, disgust in his eyes. "How could you do this?"

"I *had* to. There are *laws.*"

"That *you* created! Look around." He gestured to the lavish throne at the other end of the room. "No one tells you what to do."

"I do what I must to keep my people safe."

"Safe? From what? What could they possibly be afraid of?"

"Each other!" she shouted. "You think me cruel and brutal, but I do what I do for a reason. They are not *human*, Wyatt. They are predators with appetites and emotions you can not understand. Without a firm hand to lead them--"

"Stop." He crossed his arms, rubbing one of them as if for comfort. He bit his lip as he looked at her, the anger and despair mingling in his features catching her off guard. "I've stayed out of your business. I ignored your past against my better judgement. But this? And what about Hattie? What did you do to *her*?"

She closed her eyes for a moment as she folded her arms and sighed, clearing her throat in defiance as she returned his gaze.

He let out a deep, sorrowful breath. "Right. Okay, I need to end this."

"This?"

"Us. It's too crazy. I can't have you anywhere near my son."

Her bottom lip quivered as she spoke. "You would leave me so coldly?"

"I don't want to. Even after this, I don't want to be without you, but you've given me no choice."

"There is always a choice. You choose me or you choose to abandon me. *Again.*"

"I have to! I wish it could be different, believe me. You have no idea how much this is killing me. I love you, but I don't know what else to do."

She shifted her weight from one foot to the other as she struggled to maintain her composure. "That's the first time you've ever said that to me."

His features softened as he allowed his pain to show. He stepped forward, cupping her face in his hands and kissing her, a tear falling from his eye to her cheek. He slid his hands down to the sides of her neck as he rested his forehead on hers, breathing in the sweet scent of gardenia that hung in the air around her. "I'm sorry." He left the room, the Queen crumbling to the floor. She held her stomach as her mouth fell open in a silent scream.

"Your Majesty," Hartley yelped, hurrying in and dropping down next to her. She cradled her in her arms as she wailed, holding her head to her chest. She knew it wasn't her place to ask questions, so she didn't. Instead, she provided what comfort she could, being there for her Queen, as was her duty.

Chapter 9

Wyatt collapsed onto the couch, too broken to bother taking off his shoes. With Will and Michelle now safely at Gabriel's, he could finally deal with the emotions that had left him reeling, the events of the day swirling in his mind like a hurricane. He sat back, running a hand through his hair and breathing out slowly, tears welling in his eyes. "I did the right thing," he tried to convince himself. But, the quiet of the apartment weighed on him, his newfound loneliness crushing his chest like a discarded soda can. He wiped his face and turned his head sharply, thinking he'd seen something from the corner of his eye. He got up to investigate, checking all the rooms, but there was nothing. He went to the kitchen and got a bottle of water from the fridge, but as he turned the cap to open it, he was stopped in his tracks by a strange, familiar scent. He searched the place again, unable to locate a source, but he was sure of what he was smelling...lavender. "I'm losing it." He put the bottle down, took his phone from his pocket, found the number for his old therapist back in New Jersey, and hit 'call'.

"Yes," a sleepy voice answered. Wyatt looked at the clock on the oven and immediately felt guilty for not waiting until morning to make the call.

"Hi, Dr. Stratford. I'm sorry to be calling so late or...early. This is Wyatt Sinclair. I know it's been a while since my last session, but I was wondering if I could make an appointment for as soon as possible?"

"Mr. Sinclair? Yes, of course. Call Marjorie when the office opens at nine. I'll have her squeeze you into the first available. Is this an emergency? Are you having suicidal thoughts?"

"No. No, I just, um," He didn't know what to say. He wasn't even sure why he was calling. He couldn't exactly tell him the truth, that he just broke up with his vampire girlfriend because he was worried she'd kill his grown son who wasn't yet born three years ago when they'd last spoken, who died and was resurrected by Lucifer and that he was pretty sure he was now being haunted by his dead ex-wife. "It's been a weird day."

"Are you thinking of harming yourself or someone else?"

"No."

"Do you feel safe where you are?"

"Basically. Listen, I'm fine, I'm just upset and I'd like to talk."

"All right, Mr. Sinclair. Call the office in the morning and I'll see you soon."

He ended the call and put the phone on the counter, leaning against it and letting out a sigh of relief. He felt better just hearing the older man's voice, a sign to him that a visit to the psychiatrist was long overdue.

Gabriel finished hanging the blackout curtains in Wyatt's old bedroom while Michelle transferred blood bags from a medical cooler to a dorm fridge next to the nightstand. In the kitchen, Will organized the two hundred protein bars Gabriel had bought him by flavor in the pantry. She'd told him to wear cargo pants and always keep a few on him, just in case.

"William," Lucifer greeted as he entered the apartment. "Nice to see you. Gabriel tells me you'll be staying with us for a while lest you put your father in some sort of danger. What is my brother up to this evening? No doubt something scandalous with the vampire Queen."

Will shook his head. "He dumped her."

"You're kidding. I thought he'd moved past suicide attempts. Some things never change, I suppose."

"You said something like that earlier. What happened when I was gone?"

"Not my place to say."

"Like you care about decorum."

"Not generally, but contrary to what you may think of me, I do care about my brother and I'm quite certain he wouldn't want me burdening you with the events that took place in the days following your death."

Will formed a ball of electricity in his palm. "I can make you tell me."

Lucifer laughed. "I assure you, you can not."

"Fine." The lightning disappeared as he put his hands on the island, looking across to his uncle who sat on a stool, taking a peach from the bowl of fruit he'd insisted Gabriel buy. "Why'd you bring me back?"

"I have my reasons," Lucifer said, swallowing a mouthful of fruit.

"And those are?"

"Not your concern. I will say, though, that the look on your father's face when he realized you were back was worth all the effort." He stood and headed toward the hall. "Now, if you'll excuse me, it's late and I'm positively drained. I'll see you tomorrow. Oh, and William," He turned back, tossing the half-eaten peach into the trash. "Do keep in mind that should you again lose your way and bring any harm to my brother, I will tear out your heart and feed it to you before drowning you in the kitchen sink. Goodnight." He vanished into the room next to the one that would be Will's as Gabriel stepped into the hallway, rolling her eyes.

"Don't worry about him," she said, walking to the kitchen and taking a bag of chips from the pantry. She opened it and took one before tilting the bag toward her nephew. He grabbed a handful and sat.

"Why not? Would he not actually do it? Because that was really specific."

"Oh, he'd definitely do it. I just meant you shouldn't dwell on it. The chances of me letting you get that out of control again are pretty slim."

He almost choked as he swallowed his chips and reached for more. "You're threatening me, too? Not that I don't understand, but, *damn*."

"You know what you did, Will. I don't have to explain to you why we have concerns. *But*, I'm hoping that between me and Lucifer keeping an eye on you and your dad helping you with that meditation shit, this time will be different. And, if you start feeling rowdy, tell me this time, maybe, before you do something you can't take back. Okay?"

"Okay," he agreed.

"All right. I'm going to bed." She got up, leaving him the bag of chips, and walking toward her bedroom.

"Hey, do you think Allydia would hurt dad? Lucifer thinks--"

"Don't worry about it," she called back. "Your dad can take care of himself and if she tried anything, I'd fucking kill her."

"They asleep?" Michelle asked as Will came in, closing the door and setting a bottle of water on the nightstand.

"Yeah. A lot of death threats in this family. No wonder Dad took me to live somewhere else."

"I won't let anyone hurt you." She sat up on her knees on the bed, her tee-shirt, the only clothes she wore since her shower, just covering her backside.

"After what I did, I get it. They're right. I can't expect them to just be okay with me being here." His lip started to quiver as he spoke. "I don't know how you can still look at me without being scared or mad or *something*. How are you still looking at me like you love me?"

She held his face in her hands and looked deeply into his eyes, trying not to get lost in them. "I do love you. It broke me when Gabriel told me you were gone. *It broke me*. I know you wouldn't hurt me on purpose, even in that state. I know you, Will. You don't scare me. *You have me*." She kissed him sweetly. "You have me." She kissed him again, pulling him down on top of her as she lay back onto the blanket.

His thoughts faded as he glided his hands up her thighs, pushing up her shirt, and squeezing her hips. She slipped out of her shirt entirely, then pulled his off, as well. He kicked off his pants and boxer briefs and ran his hand up her body, his lips moving from hers to her neck. She placed her hand on the small of his back as he sank into her, his lips brushing her neck as he breathed her in, the perfume of her like birthday cake and magic. The familiar, warm ache replaced all other feelings as he buried his face in her hair, letting her wash away his guilt and regret as she moved beneath him.

She clung to him like hope as the sound of his heavy breathing in her ear sent shivers through her body. Her gums throbbed as her fangs descended. She turned her head, trying and failing to escape the sweet smell of his skin and the blood just beneath it. She raised her fist to her mouth and bit down on it, sucking the blood from her own hand as a wave of euphoria flooded through her. Relief washed over her as she realized she could keep herself from harming him. She would never forgive herself if she bit him. He was back. Her only love was back and he was everything.

Chapter 10

Malik lay breathless in the dark, unable to sleep, his heart thumping in his chest. He couldn't get the image of his daughter's eyes flashing black and the threatening tone of her voice when she'd said she was hungry out of his head. He wanted to talk to his wife about his anxiety but was afraid she'd get angry. Sinclair was family and he knew how important that was to her. He knew that she loved him, but when it came down to it, her child would always be more important. Sinclair was her blood. He was an option. Still, he couldn't shake the feeling that something was off. He had to say something. He just had to be careful about how he went about it.

"Val," he whispered. "Valerie."

"Mmm."

"Val, wake up. I need to talk to you."

She opened one eye and glared at the clock. "Boy, it is five in the morning. I am not in the mood."

"No, Val. I really need to talk to you. Before Sinclair gets up."

She smacked her lips. "What is it?"

"I think something's off."

"What do you mean, 'off'?"

"When she came in here asking for eggs, her eyes turned *black*. Not like there was a shadow or something. Her pupils got *giant*."

"Okay."

"Okay? That's all you got to say?"

"Well, she's part vampire. It's bound to happen."

"What the-- how are you so calm about this?"

"Why are you in a tizzy right now? I told you what she was."

"Yeah, but--"

"She's a tiny child. What do you think is gonna happen?"

He gave her a knowing look.

"Boy, you're crazy. She is all right. Besides, you think Gabriel would leave her here if she thought she was dangerous?"

"Daddy?" a soft voice came from the doorway.

He cleared his throat and sat up. "Yeah, baby. Did you have a bad dream?"

"No." She came in and sat next to him on the edge of the bed, looking up at him with pleading eyes. "I just wanted to tell you you don't have to be afraid."

He swallowed the lump in his throat. "Afraid of what?"

"Me. I would never hurt you, Daddy. I promise."

"He knows that, baby," Valerie told her. "Go back to bed. Sun's not even up yet."

"Okay, Mommy." She hopped down and pattered back to her room.

"See?" Valerie smiled. "She's fine. Now, go to sleep. I'm tired."

He lay back, clutching the comforter to his chest, his heart beating faster now than it had before he'd woken his wife.

Malik never slept. Instead, he got out of bed at six, made a big breakfast, and woke Valerie and Sinclair up with an idea he thought might help make things at least *seem* more normal.

"What do you say, after breakfast, we all go to the park?"

"YAY!" Sinclair exclaimed, jumping up from her seat and throwing her arms around his neck.

"I think that's a great idea," Valerie agreed.

"All right, eat up! There's a park a couple blocks away. We can walk there as soon as we're done."

"Thank you, Daddy!" Sinclair gleaned, shoveling bite after bite of pancake and hash brown into her mouth. Valerie flashed him an approving smile and the family finished eating, excited for the day ahead.

Sinclair held tightly to Malik's hand as they stepped onto the soft grass. The sounds of the other children playing happily made her smile from ear to ear. She couldn't wait to join them.

"Okay, I need you to stay where we can see you, right there on the playground. Don't go off into the woods over there. You could get lost."

"Okay, Daddy."

"Remember to be nice to the other kids and if you get scared or hurt, just yell. We'll be right here."

"Most importantly," Valerie said. "Have fun."

"I will! Bye, Mommy! Bye, Daddy!" She let go of her father's hand and skipped off, climbing up to the top of a slide and giggling all the way down. She had a blast, playing on the jungle gym and swings, hanging from the monkey bars, and sliding down the fireman's pole. She laughed to herself as she thought about her grandfather doing that countless times for work and wondered if it had been as fun for him as it was for her.

As her feet hit the bouncy pieces of recycled tires underneath the pole, she noticed a six-year-old boy sitting alone under a tree close to the edge of the forest. She walked over and sat on the ground in front of him. "Hi. I'm Sinclair. You wanna play?" He nodded shyly. She picked up a stick and drew a tic-tac-toe board in the dirt between them. They took turns holding the stick, drawing x's and o's until one of them won the game, scribbling them out, and starting over.

They played for about twenty minutes before the boy's father called from a bench, "Logan! Five more minutes, then it's time to go!"

"Look at that," Valerie said, gesturing to the kids. "She made a friend."

"I see," Malik said. "Maybe you were right."

"I was what? I'm sorry, can you say that again? I don't think I heard you."

He laughed and put his arm around her. "*You were right.* She's perfectly fine. I overreacted. You happy?"

"More than happy. I'm content." They shared a kiss and kept talking, taking their eyes off the kids just long enough for Sinclair to leave her new friend and have a quick chat with his father.

"Logan's daddy?" she asked the man who didn't look up from his phone.

"Mm-hmm."

"I saw the bruises on his arms. I know what you did. I'm asking you to stop it."

The man looked up from his screen and scanned the park to see if anyone had heard. Luckily, it looked like no one had. "Go away, little girl, before something bad happens to you."

Her expression turned stern as she stepped closer. "I asked nicely."

"Stay out of my business, kid."

Her hands became fists as she stared him down. She looked so serious and determined, unlike any four-year-old he'd ever seen. He almost laughed at her. Almost.

His hand flew to his chest as he felt a jolt followed by searing pain spread from his heart down his left arm. He panicked, unable to catch his breath.

"Don't put your hands on that boy again," she said through gritted teeth. "If you do, I'll know and you will *not* live to regret it, do you understand?"

His face went ghost white as he trembled, the pain in his chest unlike anything he'd ever felt. "What the fuck?" he choked as he slumped in his seat.

"You get it," she decided, skipping off and hugging her new friend goodbye. Just like that, the pain was gone. He gasped for air as sweat trickled down his temples, the color returning to his face.

"Aw," Valerie said as they turned back to see the children hugging. "How sweet is that?"

"Adorable," Malik agreed.

Behind the trees, the old woman watched, her long, spindly legs peeking out from her black, shapeless dress. Her wild, gray hair was largely unkempt, half piled up in a loose bun, unwashed, and attracting flies. She sniffed the air in the girl's direction, making sure to stay out of sight. She smelled the air again as the child rushed off to be with her parents. A crooked smile crept across the woman's face as she scratchily whispered, "Delicious."

Chapter 11

"Chocolate or fruity?" Gabriel asked, opening the pantry door.

"Fruity," Wendy said, sitting at the island. Gabriel took the red box from its spot on the shelf and opened it, pouring tiny, brightly colored flakes into two bowls before getting milk from the fridge. She poured the milk and got two spoons from a drawer, handing one to her girlfriend before sitting herself and taking a bite.

"That's hardly breakfast," Lucifer commented as he entered the kitchen.

"Hey," Gabriel picked up the box and pointed to the nutrition label. "It has eleven vitamins and minerals."

"Yes, well, clay contains iron, zinc, and calcium. I don't suggest eating that, either." He took a banana from the fruit bowl and went to the living room where he turned on the television and settled on the sofa to watch the last few minutes of the morning news.

Gabriel rolled her eyes as she took another bite. Wendy looked back to make sure Lucifer couldn't hear her before asking, "Is it weird that I find Satan endearing?"

She snickered. "Don't let him hear you call him 'Satan'. He hates that."

"Noted. Is it okay if I use your shower? I have a flight I'm already running late for."

"Again?" Gabriel complained. "I'm beginning to really resent your job."

"Just a day trip. I'll be back by dinner."

"Yeah, go ahead. What's mine is yours. And everyone else's, apparently."

"So, Will and his girlfriend got settled in okay?"

Gabriel shuddered, almost throwing up her cereal. "I don't want to think about it."

"Okay," Wendy chuckled. "Listen, before I go, there's something I've been meaning to tell you."

She put her spoon down and arched an eyebrow. "You got a side piece? Am *I* the side piece?"

She laughed. "No. Sometimes, when I go to work, I'm not just doing flight attendant stuff. Sometimes, I'm doing witch stuff."

"Witch stuff?"

"Like in New Zealand. No one called in sick. I went because there was a coven that needed help banishing an evil Earth Spirit. They were weak sauce. If I hadn't shown up--"

"You lied?"

"Yeah. Yeah, I didn't want to bother you while you were busy with that whole Cain thing. I figured you'd just worry and get distracted. I'm sorry. Are you mad?"

She chewed on her bottom lip. "I don't know. I've never felt like this before."

"Like what?"

Gabriel crossed her arms and thought for a moment before finding the right word. "Deceived."

"No one's ever lied to you before?"

"Of course, but I always *knew* they were lying and I always knew why. It didn't bother me. This is like, painful."

"I'm so sorry. I'll never lie again, I swear. I've just never told anyone about this. It was something my grandma always told me to keep to myself just in case."

"In case what?"

"Tituban magic is strong. In the wrong hands, it can be used to do all kinds of damage *if* it doesn't kill the witch trying to wield it first. If certain people knew who I was, really bad things could happen. I have to be careful. Please don't take this personally."

"Okay."

Wendy gobbled up the last of her cereal and kissed her cheek before rushing off to the bathroom.

Gabriel jumped up and threw her boots on. "Yo,"

"Hmm?" Lucifer acknowledged.

"Stay with the kids. I'm going out for a while."

He waved her off, never looking away from the TV. "Fine, fine."

She wasn't sure what to do with the strange emotions she was feeling. She was confused and in need of answers, so she decided to consult an expert.

"I need relationship advice." She burst in, swinging the door closed and planting herself at the kitchen island.

"So, you came *here*?" Wyatt asked.

"You were with the same chick forever. You kept a marriage going for *years* even though you were out of your mind most of the time, so, yes. I came here. Also, you're three blocks away and Uriel's in fucking Connecticut."

He shrugged and sat opposite her. "All right. What's up?"

"Wendy's been keeping stuff from me. Some side hustle where she goes off to who knows where to help other witches with their problems. How worried should I be about this? She *lied*."

"Well," he folded his hands. "Why'd she lie?"

"To protect herself from evil witches and to keep me from worrying, supposedly."

"You believe her?"

"I guess."

"I'd cut her some slack. You haven't been together long. She's probably not used to letting somebody in on her secrets. You might be the first person she's dated that knows she's a witch at all."

"Mm-hmm. Mm-hmm. *But, she lied.* She lied right to my face and I had no idea. Could say anything and I'd never know if it was true or not. How do I know she won't lie to me again?"

"You don't. You can't. It's the risk we all take to be with someone. I know you've never had to before, but if you want a relationship with her, you have to trust her."

"Trust," she pondered. "Interesting. Like faith."

"Exactly."

"Hmm."

"Crisis averted?"

"We'll see."

He leaned forward. "Can I ask *you* something?"

"Always."

He swallowed hard, not sure if he wanted to know the answer, but he had to ask. "You know everything about me."

"Yeah."

"Things I don't know about myself."

"Totes."

He took a deep breath. "Why do I love her?"

She tilted her head as her eyes softened. "You know why."

He shook his head.

"Because you're dumb."

He cast her an annoyed glare.

"Okay, serious now?"

"Please."

She cleared her throat. "It's a lot of things. You love her because she loves you. She puts you on a pedestal so high, you can't see the ground. You love her because you see her the way she was before. You see who she is underneath who she has to be. And, you love her because you need to."

He stared at her, his heart leaping to his throat. "I felt that in my bone marrow."

"You asked."

"You should be a therapist."

"Pfftt, like I have patience for that shit."

"I broke up with her," he lamented. "How do you think she's taking it?"

She gave him a knowing look. "Badly."

Chapter 12

"Thank you so much for coming," the girl said as she let Wendy into her dorm room. Her eye was black and swollen, her cheek bruised, and her lip split. "I didn't know who else to call. My mom said you helped people like us, even if we aren't practicing, so I--"

"First things first." She waved her hand over the twenty-year-old's face. "Pulchra."

"What was that?" She touched her eyelid and looked in the mirror above her desk, shocked at the transformation.

"No reason you should be reminded of what happened every time you look at yourself. It wasn't your fault, you know that, right? Some men are just trash." The girl nodded. "The glamour will hold until you've healed all the way. You have a picture?"

"Yeah." She took a photo from the desk drawer and handed it to her. "From Spring Break."

She tore it in half, discarding the girl's image so that only her abusive ex's face remained. She pressed it between her hands and closed her eyes while repeating the phrase, "Discede procul aeternum." After a few minutes, she opened her eyes. "You got a lighter?"

The girl hurried, rummaging through her drawers, finally finding a blue disposable lighter she'd used to light a joint the weekend before. She handed it over and Wendy lit the picture on fire, tossing it in the empty waste bin.

"Let that burn to ash. It'll put itself out when the spell's complete. Need anything else?"

She raised her eyebrows in shock. "No. Is that it?"

"Yeah, he won't bother you again. Remember, let that thing burn." She headed out the door.

"Thank you!" the girl called.

She waved. "Any time."

Back on the plane, Wendy couldn't help but feel guilty about keeping Gabriel in the dark about her extracurricular activities. After all, she'd trusted *her* with who *she* was. Angels, demons, vampires, all of it. Cain had spooked her, though. She could tell when she told her about him breaking into her place. She needed to focus and Wendy didn't want to be a distraction. Still, it had upset her to learn that she'd lied to her and she didn't want to be a source of pain for her new lover ever again. She'd make it up to her somehow.

Her phone buzzed in her pocket and she took it out, looking down at the screen and smiling. It was a text from the college girl thanking her again. She saw on her ex's social media accounts that he was packing up and moving to Japan. He didn't know why, he just felt like he needed to.

She laughed as she put the phone away and gazed out the window, the sky on fire with the sunset. She regretted not telling Gabriel about her work sooner, but she never once regretted the work itself. All her years of hiding who she was and all the time she'd spent practicing with her grandmother had been worth it. Helping witches who couldn't help themselves was her calling and she loved doing it. As much as being God's Messenger was a part of Gabriel, this was who Wendy was and who she'd always be.

Chapter 13

Allydia woke up on the floor, her assistant big-spooning her as the sun left the sky. She got up, waking Hartley as she smoothed her hair. She stood, glided to her throne, and sat, slinging one leg over the arm as the assistant scrambled to kneel before her.

"Good evening, Your Majesty," Hartley said, clearing her throat and adjusting her top.

"Good evening. I apologize for my outburst last night. You should never have seen me in that condition. Thank you for comforting me."

"Of course."

They were silent for a while as Allydia thought things over. Hartley kept her head bowed, her fingers laced behind her back, her gaze averted.

"I don't remember what freedom feels like," Allydia blurted, cutting the air with her words. "I'm not sure I've ever known it."

"Your Majesty?"

"I've spent thousands of years creating a kingdom, taking power for myself because I'd felt so helpless in my human life. I was little more than a servant to my father. He beat me, ridiculed me, showed me no mercy. Still, I stayed with him, even after I was married, so he wouldn't have to roam this world alone. He needed me. And, when my family was gone, I replaced them with all of you. Tell me, do you need me? Do any of you?"

"We love you, my Queen," she choked out.

"That's not what I asked."

Her bottom lip quivered as she dared to make eye contact. "We would, all of us, be dead if not for you. You saved us, not only from death but from our lives. You saved me from prejudice and judgement, bigotry, and hate. My own family cast me out. I died for being just a little of who I was and you gave me," She started to cry. "You gave me everything."

Allydia slid off her seat and onto her knees, wiping the tears from her assistant's cheeks, and searched her face. "Are you happy?"

"My Queen, I am a thousand times happier today than at any other time in my life and that is thanks to you."

She showed a whisper of a smile. "It was all worth it, then." She hugged her, putting her hand to the back of her head. She'd never shown Hartley physical affection like this before and the feeling of her Queen's arms around her was overwhelming. She slowly hugged her back, unable to swallow the lump in her throat. She sobbed into Allydia's shoulder, decades of repressed emotion pouring out in a waterfall of tears. "You're invaluable to me, Hartley. I'm so grateful for your presence in my life. Your family may have abandoned you, but I never will. No matter what happens, I want you to know that."

She pulled away and used her sleeve to clean the smudged mascara from her face. "I know that, Your Majesty." She caught a breath in her throat as she remembered what she'd been too afraid to ask about the night before.

"What is it?"

"I just thought I should ask, with the rebels wreaking havoc," She turned her head to listen for anyone near the door, not wanting the others to hear. There was no one. "Did Navid get home safely?"

Her eyes flashed. "How do you know that name?" She bolted up, Hartley too, standing on instinct.

"He was here, prowling. I sent him home. I didn't realize you had living rel--"

"Did you have him followed?"

"Of course, Your Majesty. Security was with him until he was safely on his flight."

She scowled, taking her phone from her pocket and calling his number. No answer. She stormed toward the door. "When the governors start to arrive, inform them that they are to stay here until I return."

"Where are you going, my Queen?"

"London."

She stood in Navid's apartment. Broken furniture and glass littered the floor while the stench of blood hung in the air like smog, thick and inescapable. Fury burned in her chest as she looked for clues as to who may have taken him, but there were none. The bakery she'd followed him to had been boarded up and abandoned. He was gone, no doubt a pawn in this 'King's' twisted game. But, if this unnamed vampire wanted to play, she would show him exactly who he was toying with.

Back at the club, the Governors began trickling in. Hartley got them up to speed and assigned them apartments on the third floor while she waited for further instructions.

"Hart?" a voice called. She turned in its direction and spotted a man she hadn't seen in decades. "It is you! You look unbelievable!"

"It's 'Hartley' now."

"I see that." He looked her up and down, a wide smile curling up his lips. "Seriously, you look *amazing*."

"You think so?" She couldn't help but flirt. Oliver had been an old flame, someone she'd dated back in the nineties. He'd attracted her right away with his Australian accent and chiseled features, but things fizzled, as they always did between her and other vampires. As much fun as she'd had with him, something never felt quite right. Her, probably.

"I do. You look...well, you look like you were always meant to."

She gave a proud smile, noticing how handsome he still was. "So, it's been a while. How have you been?"

"Busy. I opened a casino in Atlantic City."

"Finally! Congratulations. I know it was your dream."

"Yeah, it was. Still is. It's better than I could have hoped. People love throwing money away to forget their problems."

"That they do."

"So, I hear there's a pack of ruffians causing trouble."

"Something like that."

"Well, I'm sure the Queen has it under control. She's nothing if not capable."

Her phone rang and she held up her hand to excuse herself as she answered it. "Yes?"

"It's Phindi. I need to speak to Her Majesty at once."

"She isn't here. Can I help you with something?"

"You are loyal to the Queen, yes?"

"Of course."

"You can be trusted?"

"Yes, Genera-- I mean, *Duchess*. Your Grace. I am assistant to the Queen and I--"

"Yes, fine. I have information on the so-called 'King'. He's in Jordan. I've found his precise location and I need the Queen's permission to launch a full-scale attack. I have an army ready and waiting just out of his sight. And, there's something else. He's holding a man. A human. He's taken him prisoner and is keeping him hostage. I don't understand his reasoning for this, but the man has been given water and food. If he'd not been so badly beaten, I would think he was being kept as a pet."

Allydia appeared in a blur, snatching the phone from Hartley's hand. "Duchess Phindi, this is your Queen. Bring me the human alive. As for the 'King' and his sycophants, do what you must. Anything you have to. By sword, scythe, or sun, *kill them all*." She handed the phone back to her assistant. "Text me his exact location." Hartley nodded, the fire in the Queen's eyes sending a chill up her spine.

Allydia went to the center of the floor, her presence filling the room. "Attention." The music stopped. The lights went up. All eyes were on her. "As you may know, there are those among you that would see me overthrown. They call me 'distracted', 'weak', and 'unfit to lead'. If anyone here feels this way, I demand that you now come forward and state plainly that you oppose me." The crowd was silent, each vampire steady in their obedience to her. All, but five. She snuffed them out by the way their hands shook ever so slightly when she spoke and the grimaces they tried to hide. She moved faster than even they could see, plucking each one from the crowd, tearing their heads from their bodies with her bare hands, pulling hearts from chests and eyes from sockets, and piling up the parts at her feet for the others to see. "Anyone else?" she growled, licking blood from her palm. "Now is the time. With me or against, make your choice known."

The vampires bowed their heads, each taking a knee.

"Good." She turned her attention to Hartley. "Lock it down. If anyone threatens the faithful,"

"I will eviscerate them, my Queen."

She lowered her head. "Call everyone. Tell them to be ready for rebel attacks, even in the day. I'll handle the 'King' myself." She kicked a heart out of the way as she moved toward the door. "And get someone to clean this shit up."

Allydia cried as she washed the blood of the children that had forsaken her from her hands. Their betrayal was enough to cause her heartache, but what hurt more was the realization that this was the first shower she'd taken in her own apartment in weeks. She'd become accustomed to waking up and going to sleep at Wyatt's, his scent filling every room, his energy soothing. Now, just minutes before sunrise, she'd have to go to bed alone. Her stomach churned as she wept, covering her face with her hands under the scalding water. She knew that she was breaking, but she couldn't allow it. She had to rescue Navid and save her people. Only when that was done could she mourn. Only then could she decide how to proceed.

Chapter 14

Navid struggled with the shackles that dug into his wrists as he fought the dizziness that threatened to overtake him...again. He'd been in and out of consciousness since he'd been thrown in the cell, mostly due to the way he was being held there: by chains, upside down, hanging from the ceiling.

When he'd first arrived, vampires had swarmed him, stripping off his shirt and scratching his chest and back, licking his wounds as he tried to break free, all wanting a taste, every one of them gobsmacked by the familiarity they sensed in his blood. Some showed signs of trepidation while others laughed maniacally, savoring his flavor on their lips like a fine wine. Only when their leader, the one they called 'King', shooed them away did they leave him be. He'd brought him falafel, dates, and water, all of which he'd refused for fear of being poisoned. The food sat, untouched on the dusty floor and had begun to attract flies. He was drenched in sweat, dehydrated, and starving. His jaw ached from the gag in his mouth holding it open while muffling his angry screams. He growled in frustration as he tried to climb up the chain, hoping to release it from the hook on the ceiling, but his arms were too weak. Just when he thought he might pass out again, the cell door swung open.

"That's an unsettling shade of purple," the 'King' said, studying his face. "Toasted plum, I'd call it." With one hand, he unhooked the chain, dropping Navid hard on the floor. He winced as searing pain spread through his back and shoulders. He rolled to his side, facing his captor, wishing he had the fluid to waste by spitting on him, if only he weren't gagged. "You should eat, Navid." He knelt down and slid a new plate of food toward him which he batted away like a defiant cat. "Have it your way." He tucked his shoulder-length hair behind his ears as he looked down at his hostage, almost feeling sorry for him. "I'm not going to kill you. If I'd wanted to, I would have already and I wouldn't taint your food. I would just eat you. Do you know why you're here?"

He shook his head, though he had a pretty good idea. He'd heard bits and pieces of vampire chatter since he'd arrived, not to mention the blathering by Jack and Simon. This 'King' was staging a coup against Allydia and was using him as leverage. Didn't take a genius to figure it out. But, if he could keep him talking long enough, maybe the wooziness would subside and he could use his chains to strangle him and make a run for it. Not a solid plan, considering the place was overrun with vamps, but what choice did he have?

"You're here because it will infuriate the Queen. Nothing more, nothing less. When this is over, I *will* let you go."

He scrunched his eyebrows in confusion.

The King sighed. "You see, the Queen has always been feared. Respected. Beloved. That changed, however, when she all but disappeared for three years. She abandoned her people. Left them to their own devices. When she finally emerged from her sabbatical, she had the nerve to require their service in a war that was not their own. They fought and died in a battle for what? Do you know? Because none of us do. She rejects her own kind and instead takes a human lover and now we discover she has a living descendant. It seems that the Queen's priorities have shifted. Her people are simply learning to adapt to their new reality. They need someone new to lead them. They see me as their savior." He burst out laughing, causing Navid to jump in his skin. "*Me*. It's absurd. Do you not see the irony?" The bound man's expression told him that he didn't. "Oh, of course, you don't. Allow me to introduce myself properly. Some call me The Betrayer, a name earned yet still hurtful. My given name is Judas Iscariot."

Navid's eyes grew to saucers as his labored breathing quickened. His heart thudded against his chest and his mind raced. The gravity of what he was saying hit him like a ton of bricks. Could this be true? And, if it was, what did that mean? The implications were mind-blowing.

Judas turned his head to listen for eavesdroppers before addressing him again, his tone hushed. "The Queen's army marches as we speak. Most of my followers are here, awaiting battle. A few are scattered, awaiting orders. You'll be safe as long as you remain chained. The Queen has no intention of surrendering her crown. She is too proud. It is what I'm counting on. I have no interest in ruling over these foul creatures. My goal is the complete destruction of their kind."

Navid tilted his head, more confused than ever.

"Their gullibility and old-world misogyny make it easy to sew seeds of unrest. I control them like puppets on a string." He leaned in, twisted determination coloring his face, his voice dropping an octave. "I've barely lifted a finger in this fight. They were itching for war, so I've given them one. A civil war that will end this putrid empire once and for all."

Michelle crawled into bed, wrapping her arm around Will's waist and resting her head on his chest. He'd been asleep for hours, but as the sun began to make its ascension, she was just getting tired. His body was warm against her skin and the sound of his heartbeat was soothing, like a lullaby encouraging her to drift off. She listened to the air fill and escape his lungs, so grateful for the sound of it, she almost cried. As she began to fall asleep, she drew in a sharp breath, startled by the realization that she'd completely forgotten to tell him. She'd been so thrilled to have him back, it hadn't occurred to her that he should know. She had to tell him...now.

"Will," she whispered, sitting up and gently nudging him. "Will, wake up."

"Hmm?" He rubbed his eyes and sat up. "What time is it?"

"Six-thirty. I need to tell you something. Something important."

"Are you okay?"

"I'm fine, I'm just...a vampire."

"Are you hungry? You can drink if you want. It was kind of gross at first, but it doesn't bother me anymore. You have some bags left, right?"

"No, I'm not hungry, it's something else. I'm not sure how to say this, so I'm just gonna start at the beginning."

"All right." He took her hand, seeing how serious she was giving him a twinge of anxiety.

"After I turned, I went with the vampire that made me to her place in Scotland. We had to hide because if the Queen found out she'd sired someone without permission, she would have killed us both. I was hungry all the time. Like, more than normal. Hattie kept me in blood, but it was never enough. After a few weeks, it was clear why." She cleared her throat, stalling for time. "I started...showing."

He did a double-take. "You started *what*?"

"I was pregnant, Will."

His muscles tensed and his chin dropped. "You...how?"

"The morning after pill must not have worked. Maybe it was expired or something, I don't know. But, I was pregnant before I turned, so--"

He looked her over, putting his hand to her belly, the vacancy evident by the flatness of her abs. "But," His eyes shined with tears as he assumed the worst. "The baby died?"

"No," she told him, grabbing his hands and holding them to her heart. "No. Because of my weird vampire physiology or something and your Nephilim hyper-speed aging thing, she grew *fast*. Like, so fast, my ribs broke from the muscles underneath stretching out so quick. She didn't die, Will. She's fine. She's perfect."

"She?" Tears sprung from his eyes like water from a fountain.

"Her name's Sinclair, for you." She, too, began to cry. "I tried, but I couldn't keep her. I wanted to, you have no idea. When she looked up at me with your eyes," She stopped, choking back sobs as she tried to rein in her emotions. "But, I was afraid."

"Of what?"

"Of me. I was scared to death that I would," She covered her mouth, squeezing her eyes shut as the pain of missing her baby proved too great to contain.

"Okay," He held her close to him and settled back against the pillows. "It's okay. I understand." He kissed the top of her head and rubbed her arm. "It's early. You should sleep. We can talk about it tonight."

She sniffed, her eyelids feeling heavy. "Gabriel says she's okay, but I wish I could see for myself. But, I can't. I can't risk it. I would die if something happened to her because of me."

He lifted his head. "Gabriel?"

"Yeah, I gave her to your aunt. She's the only person I could trust."

"Mm. Okay, get some sleep." But she was out before he finished the sentence.

Chapter 15

"Where's my daughter?" Will exploded, causing Gabriel to choke on her banana.

"Boy, you are lucky Lucifer's still asleep. He can't know about her, yet. And, don't tell him I was eating fruit. I don't want to give him the satisfaction."

He threw a ball of lightning past her and into the kitchen wall. "Where?!"

"Yo!"

"Tell me or I'll--"

"You'll what?" She stood from her seat at the island and stepped toward him, arms crossed and eyebrows furrowed. "You're upset, confused, clearly pissed. But, don't forget who I am. God knows *I* never can."

"What'd you do with her?"

"I didn't hurt her. What kind of monster do you think I am?"

"The kind that would send a girl who should have been in college to spy on her nephew and kill him if she had to."

"She was never supposed to *kill* you. She was supposed to tell me if *I* needed to."

"I swear to Christ."

"She's with Uriel, your Aunt Valerie. She's fine, I swear. She made a friend at the park yesterday. Did him a favor. She's doing well. You don't have to be so grouchy. Eat something and settle the fuck down."

She went to the pantry, grabbed a box of granola bars, and tossed it to him. He tore it open, stripping a bar of its wrapper and gobbling it up in two big bites. He took another from the box and sat, his body finally beginning to relax.

She got a glass and filled it with milk, setting it in front of him and returning the jug to the fridge. "I would never hurt Sinclair," she promised, sitting across from him and taking a granola bar for herself. "She's different than you. She's in full control of her powers and her emotions and thoughts are always in check. I don't have to worry about her like I do you."

"Can I tell you something?"

"Any time."

He looked her in the eyes, hands trembling as he fumbled with another wrapper. "I'm worried about me, too."

Her eyes softened and she patted his hand. "You'll be okay."

"You don't know that. Look what I just did."

"Will,"

"The headaches are back. Not bad, but it's starting, just like before. When I'm with Michelle, I'm fine. I feel like me. But, any other time, it's like a bomb waiting to go off and the seconds are ticking down and I don't know how much time I have before--"

"Shut your mouth. Nothing's gonna happen, you hear me? I won't lose you again. Especially after what it did to," She stopped herself, taking a bite of her breakfast and looking down at the counter.

"What it did to who? To Dad?"

She looked back up and chewed, not wanting to answer.

"Lucifer wouldn't tell me, either, but it doesn't take a genius to figure it out. He tried to kill himself again, didn't he?"

She swallowed hard, knowing her brother had no intention of ever telling his son about what happened after he died. "I shouldn't tell you."

"But, he did, right? He tried? What'd he do? Slit his wrists? Pills like in college?"

"No. No, not pills."

"What, then?"

"Why are you asking about this? He's okay now."

"Because I'm back. But, if you have to--"

"No."

"But, if you do, I don't want him to fall apart."

"He didn't get better because you came back. He got better because," She dropped her granola bar at the sudden realization. "Because of her."

"Her? The vampire Queen?"

She nodded.

"She helped him? She actually cared about him?"

"Yeah, dude, she loves him. I've never felt love like that and I know everything everyone around me ever feels. Except you. And Wendy, which is nervous-making, I'm not gonna lie."

"I didn't know it was that serious. I mean, I thought I saw something in her eyes when she looked at him, but..." He swallowed another bite. "So, now she's gone, and if I have to die,"

"He'll feel alone again. *Shit*. Well, that's it. You can't die. Ever. You have to suck it the fuck up and figure out a way to control your shit because I will *not* lose my brother, do you understand?"

"Yes, ma'am," he muttered.

She folded her arms and bit her lip as she slowed her breathing, trying to get her heart to stop booming in her ears.

"I should go to Dad's."

"He's on his way to New Jersey. He'll be back in a few hours."

"What's he doing in New Jersey?"

"It's been some time, Mr. Sinclair. Tell me, what's spurred this sudden return to therapy?" Dr. Stratford sat with hands folded in his lap, his notebook and prescription pad at the ready on the table next to him.

"I broke up with my girlfriend and I'm not sure how I feel about it," he confessed, noticing how the small office seemed like a time capsule, not having changed a bit in the last few years. Even the doctor looked the same, the only difference being the frames of his glasses were black now instead of silver. "Her job is, um, demanding. There are things she does there that I don't, I don't know, approve of? I can't get past it."

"Hmm. I think I understand. Being the partner of someone that does sex work can invoke feelings of jealousy, inadequacy,"

"What? No, she's not a sex worker. She's...in charge of things. Policy-making and law enforcement. Sort of."

"Ah, so she works in government. I'm sorry. When you said 'approve', I just assumed. My own moral bias. I apologize. Continue."

"The point is, there are things about her that I hate. Things she's done. Things she continues to do. *I hate them.* But, I love her. Despite everything, I am completely in love with her. I'm in so deep, I can't see daylight. Literally, sometimes. It's like my heart and my head are on different pages. Different chapters. Different goddamn books altogether. My brain keeps telling me to stay away from her, but it *hurts.* I have physical pain in my *gut.* I crave her like food. I *need* her like a drug. It's not normal."

"That's an interesting word." He picked up the pen and jotted it down. "What do you think 'normal' is?"

"I don't know." He thought for a second, recalling the last time he'd ended a relationship. "When Annie left, I was sad. I felt lost. Discarded. Unimportant. This is something else. I'm not moping around and crying all day. I'm having a hard time breathing."

The therapist tapped his pen to his lips. "Perhaps, you're reacting to this breakup differently because you feel differently about this woman than you did your wife."

"You think I love her more than I did Annie?"

"I didn't say 'more'. I said 'differently'. Every relationship, romantic or otherwise, is different. Different dynamics, different personalities. For instance, last we spoke, Annie had suggested you get in-patient treatment for your hallucinations. How does this new woman feel about that?"

"I haven't had any since before I met her," he blurted, realizing immediately what a mistake that was.

"You haven't? How is that possible?"

He gulped, saying the only thing that came to mind. "My sister's a billionaire."

"Ah," he said, taking his glasses off and setting them on the table. "A sister? I don't believe you ever mentioned her before."

"I didn't know she existed until recently."

"Well, I see much has changed."

"Yeah."

"Listen, we could do a deep dive of why you feel the way you do and how you may or may not be able to reconcile your feelings for this woman with what you know to be true in your mind, but that could take weeks and I don't know when you'll get around to coming back, so I'll say this plainly. Take my advice: Always make decisions based on what your head tells you is right. Your heart is dumb as shit."

Wyatt erupted in laughter. "You cursed? I don't think I've ever heard you say 'shit' in my *life*." He held his stomach as he bellowed.

"Well, you're not the only one whose life has changed over the years. Do you remember that woman that interrupted our session a few years ago?"

He thought back to when he'd first met Gabriel right here in this office. "Yes."

"After some soul searching, I decided she was right. I *have* wasted my talents. In a few months, I'll be retiring to work on playing full time. I may never play Lincoln Center, but the piano is my passion. So, while it may be unprofessional, from now until I lock up the office for the last time, I'll use the words that drive the point home most effectively."

"Well, they sure did," he chuckled.

On the drive home, Wyatt thought about what the doctor had said, giving it careful consideration. He was probably right. His common sense was telling him to stay away. More than that, his instinct to protect his son demanded it. Still, he couldn't shake this feeling. It sat on his diaphragm like a boulder, radiating through him, begging him to change his mind and plead with her to come back to him.

I sent Will to your place, he heard his sister's voice in his head.

Is he okay?

He's fine. A little shaky. Michelle told him about Sinclair.

On my way.

Chapter 16

"Did you know?" Will asked as his father returned home.

He closed the door and dropped his keys on the island, sitting across from his son, three protein bar wrappers and a half-empty two-liter between them. "Yeah. I wanted to tell you, but it wasn't my place."

"For God's sake, what is it with you people thinking things are or aren't your place? If you know something that affects someone else, you should tell them."

"Michelle's her mother. She had the right to tell you herself."

He rolled his eyes.

"How do you feel about this? Three's kind of young to have a kid. Must be weird."

"Shut up," Will snickered, picking up a wrapper and throwing it at him.

He laughed.

"Gabriel said she's at Valerie's. She said she's happy there. Do you think that's true?"

"I think Gabriel would know if she wasn't."

"Yeah." He pursed his lips and rested his elbows on the counter, touching his linked fingers to his chin. "I'm really sorry, Dad."

"About what?"

"I don't know, man, pick something. Murder, property damage, making you a grandfather in your thirties, upsetting you so bad you tried to kill yourself."

"Who told you that? Lucifer?"

"Nobody had to tell me. It doesn't take a genius to figure out that the guy who attempted suicide a bunch of times because his dad was an ice cube would do it again when his inner angel killed his own son, although, I am one."

He arched an eyebrow and sighed. "Yes, you're a genius and I have some issues, but I'm all right. You don't have to worry about me."

"But, what if--"

"Let's go." He stood, picking up his keys and walking toward the door.

"Where?"

"To see my granddaughter."

"So, this is Will," Valerie said, ushering them inside.

"Yes, ma'am," Will replied.

"Did you just call me 'ma'am'? Sweetie, I know you think that's polite, but don't do that again."

Wyatt laughed.

"And you," she turned her attention to her brother, casting him a judgemental glare. "You need to visit more often. I know it's a trip, but I miss you."

"Grandpa!" Sinclair squealed from the top of the stairs.

Valerie grinned. "Speaking of people who miss you."

The child stepped carefully down the staircase and hurried to where they stood, holding her arms in the air for Wyatt to pick her up, which he did.

"Hey," he gleaned. "You got big."

"I know! You should have seen my dad's face. I thought he was gonna have an accident."

He laughed again, setting her feet on the floor. "Is he here?"

"No, he's at work," Valerie told him.

"Daddy!" Sinclair beamed as if noticing Will for the first time. She rushed over and hugged his leg. He froze, her warm reaction to him hitting him like water to the face. He hadn't expected her to know who he was. He thought there'd be an awkward introduction giving him time to get comfortable. But, she'd recognized him somehow and there was no stalling.

"Come see my room! My mom painted a whole wall with chalkboard paint." She took his hand and led him up the steps. He looked back to Wyatt who waved him on with a reassuring smile.

"See?" She pointed to the wall as they entered the room. It was covered in an elaborate scene: a sun in the top right corner, grass and flowers of various shades of pink and purple, and a rainbow stretching across a blue sky. "I can draw anything I want and when I want to draw something else, I can just erase it and start over. I made you something." She stood in front of a small table set low to the ground and took a piece of paper from the pile to her left. He knelt down as she handed it to him. "That's me, you, and Mommy," she pointed out. He looked down at the picture, impressed with how accurately she'd sketched them out with colored pencils, matching their skin tones and the color of their eyes perfectly.

"Good job, sweetie."

"Thanks. Can you give it to Mommy? I know she's afraid to come."

He tilted his head, surprised at how her words tugged at his heartstrings. "Yeah, I'll give it to her."

"Thanks, Daddy. It's okay, I understand. I know why she gave me away. She did the right thing. Can you tell her I miss her and I love her and I'm not mad?"

His eyes were pools as he nodded.

"Don't cry. I'm not sad. My mom and dad are really nice and now that you're back, you can come visit all the time."

"I will. All the time."

"Yay! You should go now, though. My dad's almost home and he'll feel threatened if he sees you here. It'll be awkward. He'll get better about it, though."

"Okay," he said, wiping away a stray tear. "I'll see you really soon."

She threw her arms around his neck and squeezed tight before whispering in his ear, "I know you're scared, but you don't have to be. Everything's gonna be okay, I promise. I love you, Daddy." She kissed his cheek and let him go.

"I love you, too, sweetie."

"I know."

Chapter 17

"Cake!" Gabriel cheered as Wendy opened the bakery box and presented it to her. Chocolate ribbons adorned the perimeter of the round layer cake while 'I'm sorry' was spelled out in vanilla cursive on the top. "You didn't have to do that."

"Yes, I did. I shouldn't have lied. Even if I could justify not saying anything about that part of my life before, lying about why I was going to New Zealand was really sucky of me. Oh, I almost forgot." She pulled a plastic container from her shoulder bag. "While I was there, I had these incredible meat pies. You have to try one." She removed the lid and handed her a pie before taking one for herself.

"You baked?"

"I'm multifaceted."

"Holy crap!" she said, mouth full.

"Right?"

"Lucifer, come taste this!"

He reluctantly got up from his spot on the sofa and joined them in the kitchen.

"It's real food like you like." Gabriel handed him a pie and took another bite of hers.

He gave it a sniff and took a bite, raising his eyebrows in approval and taking it with him back to the living room.

"Don't get crumbs on my couch!"

"I really am sorry about lying," Wendy said. "I've never been able to trust anyone with this before."

"Yeah, well, I've never had to trust anyone ever, which is something I need to work on, according to my brother."

Lucifer scoffed from the sofa. "You went to Barachiel for relationship advice? Are you mad?"

"Like *you* would have been a better choice." Gabriel retorted.

He shrugged. "Fair point."

"For the record," Wendy said, tucking Gabriel's hair behind her ear. "You've been a great girlfriend."

"Really?"

"Outstanding."

"Well, you are an excellent baker."

"Thank you. Maybe later, I'll show you some of my *other* talents."

"I'm pretty sure I've seen those."

"I still have some tricks up my sleeve."

Gabriel laughed.

"For the love of," Lucifer huffed, exasperated. "Can you two please take your incessant flirtations to a less common room? Some of us are trying to read in peace."

"Gladly." Gabriel flashed a devious smile as she walked toward her bedroom, beckoning Wendy to follow. "Bring the cake."

The old witch took the chicken bones from the pocket of her apron and arranged them in a circle in her palm. She turned them, one by one, as she uttered the incantation, "Otevřít dveře." In the apparent emptiness of the forest, a shimmering translucence appeared before her. She stepped through it, entering the unseen cottage, hidden to all but her. She replaced the bones and shuffled to the kitchen where a stew pot set simmering on the stove. She took the herbs she'd just picked from her apron and tossed them in, inhaling the aroma with her crooked nose. She picked up the large wooden spoon from the butcher block counter and gave the broth a stir, scraping up the bits that had stuck to the bottom while she was outside. An eyeball and two tiny fingers floated to the top as she tasted the hot liquid. She smacked her lips a few times and added a dash of salt, stirring it again before putting a lid on it and hobbling to the rocking chair just a few feet away in the living room. She sat, saving her energy. She'd need all she could muster when she finally went for the girl. She was almost out of food and the child from the park with the smokey eyes and the deadly abilities was powerful enough to fuel her existence for months if not years. From what she'd observed, she was sure once she got a taste of the girl's flesh, she'd be stronger than ever. She just had to get close.

As the sun set, Will waited anxiously for Michelle to wake up. He sat on the edge of the bed, holding the drawing their daughter had made for them, tearing up as he thought about what he'd say and how she'd react.

"Will," She opened her eyes and sat up. "Why are you sitting there like that? Is something wrong?"

"I just need to talk to you."

"Are you okay?"

"I'm fine. I went to see Sinclair today."

"What?" She stared at him, hope and worry in her eyes. "Is she all right?"

His lip quivered as he handed her the drawing. "She's perfect. She wanted me to give this to you. It's us."

Tears spilled down her cheeks as she studied the drawing. "How old is she now? She was just a baby."

"She's about four or five. She's aging a little faster than I did, but--"

"And she's okay? She's happy? Safe?"

"Yeah, she said Valerie and Malik are really nice. She said," he caught a breath in his throat. "She said she loves you and misses you and she understands why you gave her away. She said we can visit whenever we want."

She covered her mouth, stifling the cries that begged to escape her throat.

He took his phone from his pocket and showed her the picture he'd taken of her standing in front of the rainbow she'd created on her chalkboard wall. She looked down at the screen, sobbing into her hand. She closed her eyes, shoving the phone away, shaking as she wiped the tears from her face.

"I can never visit her."

"Of course you can," he told her. "She said--"

"It doesn't matter what she said, she's a kid. She doesn't understand what I am, what I could do to her. Besides, if another vampire sees me with her and figures out she's mine, they'll kill her. Not to mention, Lucifer. If you and your dad are hanging out, he won't care about where you're going. But, if I tag along? He might follow us just to make sure I don't try to eat you both."

"My dad wouldn't have to go with us."

"Yes, he would. I can't trust myself and I know in my soul that if I went feral, you wouldn't have the heart to stop me before I did something horrible. But, he would. Your dad would protect you and Sinclair with his life because that's what he does." She dropped her head, fighting back more tears. "I hate what I am. I hate everything about it. If you weren't back, I don't know how much longer I would've been able to hang on, Queen's dungeon or not."

"Hey," he lifted her chin. "You can do anything. You're amazing."

She smiled through fresh tears and kissed him softly before getting up and pulling on a pair of jeans. "I need to be alone for a while."

"Are you sure?"

"Yeah," She kissed him again and headed for the door. "I'm going for a walk. I'll be back soon."

He watched her go, wishing there was something he could do to make her feel better. As the pain in his head grew in intensity, he rubbed his temples and tried to focus on something else. He looked at Sinclair's picture on his phone, calming himself, taking a deep breath, grateful that she was safe where she was, away from Allydia and away from Lucifer.

Michelle wandered the streets for hours, ignoring the hunger growing within her, pushing it down, too overcome with emotion to worry about things as trivial as feeding. She swallowed her tears and concentrated on her steps, the sound her ballet flats made against the pavement, and the feeling of the night air turning crisper with the approaching Fall.

In the distance, she heard a woman scream. "Not your business," she told herself. But, as the stranger cried for help again, Michelle's instinct to help overpowered the one to self-preserve. She bolted toward the noise, deep into a wooded area of the park. There, she came upon a woman in leggings and a sports bra being dragged by the ponytail by a man twice her size. The two women locked eyes, the jogger's pleading for help as she fought to break free from the tall man's grasp. Without hesitation, Michelle threw herself at him, knocking him to the ground, forcing his hands away from his would-be victim.

"Run," Michelle warned the woman, who had already begun dialing nine-one-one. She hurried off just as the man sprung up and slapped Michelle across the face. She licked the blood from her lip, fangs descending, her pupils dilating. "That was dumb." She leaped up, striking him down with a back-handed smack. She flung herself on top of him, holding him down by the shoulders. Before she knew what she was doing, she clamped onto his carotid artery, draining him as he struggled beneath her, a fight no human could win.

When she'd had her fill, her mind cleared. She'd killed him. The guilt came immediately, hanging on her heart like a beehive on a thin branch, too heavy to withstand. She cried again, this time not because she missed her daughter, but because she missed herself.

Chapter 18

Phindi looked over her troops, more than two thousand strong, faces smeared in red paint to honor their Queen and flame lily petals covering their armor. They carried swords, machetes, and daggers, their bodies tense in anticipation of battle and their hearts set on revenge. They waited, somewhat impatiently, for the order from the general-turned-Duchess as she assessed the opposition that approached from less than fifteen thousand yards away. Most marched forward while others stood guard at the entrance to a narrow canyon. Beyond that, she knew, was where the so-called King was hiding.

She pounded her assegai on the desert floor as her soldiers stomped in unison, whooping and snarling, anxious to get to the fight. She lifted her spear and the crowd went quiet. She turned to face the oncoming enemy and shouted in her native tongue, "Iwa!"

They shot themselves as if from a cannon at the other side, piercing hearts and slicing off heads with relative ease. The enemy army wore no armor, instead donning the same green, hooded cloaks as the men that stormed her sanctuary. Though not a match for Phindi's trained soldiers, they outnumbered them three to one. It would take time, skill, and luck for her side to prevail. The King's men refused to back down, even as their numbers dwindled, death coming to them bloody and swift. Some seemed to carry no weapons and hurled themselves at the soldiers like cannon fodder, their skin burning as it touched the petals soaked in the sap of the flame lilies that Phindi had concentrated.

She plowed through the hooded men, butchering one after another as they came for her. It seemed too easy as the armies now became evenly numbered, Phindi losing five hundred or so soldiers to their forty-five-hundred dead. As she got closer to the entrance, she felt a sharp sting in her shoulder followed by a heat spreading through her arm. She turned her head to see herself bleeding from what looked like a bullet wound emitting a bright, white light. "UV bullets," she hissed, digging the projectile out of her flesh and crushing it in her fist. Shots rang out as the traitors opened fire, the Queen's army dropping like flies to the blood-stained sand. "Get the guns!" she ordered, flying through the crowd, chopping off hands and collecting the weapons more modern than her own and using them against their previous possessors. Her soldiers obeyed, attacking their enemies even in the face of death. Most were mowed down, but others were successful in their efforts, retrieving guns for themselves and slaughtering the hooded men that stood between them and the King.

In the end, every traitor was killed along with more than nineteen-hundred of Phildi's soldiers. Only eighty-six faithful remained, bloodied and bruised, but not broken. They made their way to the entrance, hell-bent on taking down the would-be King once and for all. But, as Phindi began to step through, a light flashed, filling the canyon and searing the exposed skin of her hand and arm. She yelped, jumping back, her face twisted in rage. "Take the cloaks!" she commanded, rushing to the corpse of a fallen traitor and stripping the body of its hood. She winced, recognizing the man as one of her own soldiers. He'd gone missing the day of the battle in Iraq. She'd assumed he'd been killed there. She never would have suspected him of being a turncoat. Her disappointment only fueled her anger as she covered herself and marched back to the canyon. A few of her soldiers beat her to it, though, eager to avenge their brothers and sisters, but even through the fabric of the cloaks, their blood boiled, their skin swelling and turning purple as they cooked from the inside out. Their screams echoed in the night as they perished faster than if they'd been standing in direct sunlight. Whatever was lighting up the canyon was far more powerful than anything Phindi had ever seen.

"What do we do now, Your Grace?" a soldier asked.

She thought for a moment, tapping her assegai on the ground, livid and disappointed in herself. "The only thing we can do. I will contact the Queen for further instructions."

Wyatt sat staring at the bottle of whiskey on his coffee table, alone, his chest heavy and his stomach in knots. No matter how hard he tried to convince himself that leaving Allydia had been the right thing to do, he couldn't get her out of his mind. The look on her face when he ended things, the quivering of her lip as he kissed her goodbye, and the smell of gardenia that lingered in the air crushed him and no amount of advice or therapy helped. He was lost for her and fighting the urge to run back to her and beg forgiveness was even more painful than missing her.

He rocked the bottle back and forth, his lips pursed, and his eyes slits as he fought to maintain control. A single tear slid down his cheek and he wiped it away, a low growl in his throat as he covered his mouth, his leg shaking.

Outside, Allydia watched, sorrow meeting concern as she cursed the glass between them, wishing with everything in her that she could be inside where she belonged. She belonged with him and she *would* find a way.

"Yes," she said, answering her phone. As she listened to Phindi's account of the battle in Jordan, fire replaced the emptiness in her gut. "I'm on my way."

"With respect, Your Majesty," Phindi said. "It is not safe. Even you won't survive this light weapon. How will you protect yourself?"

"I'm not coming alone." She ended the call and leaped down to the street, on her way to call in a favor.

Inside, Wyatt breathed a heavy sigh, standing from his seat and taking the bottle to the kitchen. He opened it and poured the contents into the sink, watching with a twinge of regret as it disappeared down the drain. He tossed the bottle in the trash and was suddenly smacked in the face by the overpowering scent of lavender. He slowly made his way back to the living room where there, sitting on the couch as if she owned it, was his dead wife's ghost. His heart skipped a beat as he caught his breath. She was beautiful, as stunning as the day they were married. His eyes pooled as she turned to look at him, a kind smile on her soft pink lips.

"Come sit with me," she said, her voice like a song in his ears. He did as he was told, unable to take his eyes off of her, her skin glowing, her hair like gold. "How are you, really?"

"I-I don't know. Sad, I guess. Stressed. Worried."

"About what?"

Tears fell as his face remained still. "Will. He doesn't think I see it, but I know he's feeling shaky. I'm afraid of what he'll do and I'm scared that I'll," he swallowed a lump in his throat as more tears trailed down his cheeks.

"You don't have to worry about Will," she told him. "He'll be just fine, I promise."

"How can you know that?"

"Where I am, there's no such thing as not knowing."

"Then why'd you ask how I was?"

"Because you needed to say it out loud. Now, tell me about the vampire."

"Are you sure? That seems kind of inappropriate."

She laughed. "Maybe, but you need to work out your feelings before something bad happens. I don't want to see you up here for a long long time. So, spill. What's the dilemma?"

"She's a murderer that threatened our son's life. She had his girlfriend in a cage in a dungeon."

"True, but she loves you."

He wiped more tears from his face. "That doesn't matter."

"Of course it does. She can make her threats all day, but she would never lay a hand on Will. She knows you'd never forgive her if she did. She is head over heels. She loves you as much as I do and trust me, that's a lot. She will never hurt Will or you. As far as her being a murderer, that's horrible and it might take some effort for you to look past it, but for your sanity, you should really consider it."

"You're serious?"

"I know you, Wyatt. You need her. She keeps you from falling apart."

"You're not wrong about that," he conceded. "I'm sorry. I'm so sorry, baby. I had no idea--"

"I know. It's okay. Dying wasn't the best time I've ever had, but holding Will and looking down into that sweet baby's face was well worth it. I have no regrets. Now, I have to go, but I want you to promise me that you'll take care of yourself."

He took a shaky breath. "I promise."

"And, Wyatt, I want you to know this, I mean *really* know it. What happened to me wasn't your fault."

He nodded.

"You're a good dad, Wyatt. I'm sorry I ran away without telling you you were gonna be one. I should have trusted you. *You* should trust yourself now. Do what's in your heart." She blew him a kiss and faded, disappearing, the scent of lavender scrubbed from the air.

He fell back in his seat, wiping away the remaining tears, his head spinning. "Do what's in my heart." He sat up, resting his elbows on his knees, covering his face, and screaming into his hands.

Chapter 19

It had been hours and Michelle was still not back from her walk. Will paced the floor of the living room as the others slept, his head pounding and his blood pressure climbing. His mind raced with worry as his heart drummed in his ears. He looked again at the picture of his daughter on his phone, hoping the image would calm him. Instead, it triggered a borage of intrusive thoughts and paranoid delusions. His brain filled with images of her being hurt, beaten, and drowned all at the hands of his devilish uncle. He tried to shake them, telling himself they weren't real, that Lucifer had no idea she existed. But, the visions kept coming, flashing in his mind in bits and pieces, eventually replacing all logic with a rabid sense of urgency. His breathing quickened and his steps became deliberate, taking him swiftly to his uncle's bedroom.

He threw the door open and pounced, leaping onto the bed and wrapping his hands around Lucifer's throat.

"What mischief is this?" he choked, but as he grabbed his nephew's arms to pull them away, white-hot electricity flowed through them causing him to seize, the skin of his neck crackling like bacon.

"I won't let you hurt her!" Will screamed, his eyes wild, his cheeks red. "I'll kill you before I let you anywhere near her!"

Foam dribbled from Lucifer's mouth as he shook. Finally, he was able to push the boy off, but he came right back, punching him in the jaw with electrified fists.

"Damn it, Will!" Gabriel yelled, using her telekinesis to toss him to the floor. He stood, moving like a predator back to the bed. She waved her hand, pushing him back against the wall and holding him there. "The fuck's your problem?"

"He's rambling on about me doing harm to his girlfriend as if I have any interest in that." Lucifer healed, getting out of bed and cracking his neck. "While I do find vampires generally to be vile and ridiculous creatures, she seems perfectly--"

Will broke free of Gabriel's hold and jumped onto the bed, balls of lightning at the ready as he fixed his gaze on his stunned uncle.

"Somnus," they heard from the hall. Will collapsed, unconscious, his head hitting the pillow as if it belonged there. They turned to see Wendy, arms folded, shaking her head. "The violence in this family, I swear. You should really work on just loving each other. You okay?"

"No worse for the wear. If you'll excuse me, I'm feeling a bit peckish." He moved past them and went to the kitchen.

"And, you?"

Gabriel bit her lip, placed her hands on her hips, and took a deep breath. "Not really."

"What was that all about?"

"He's losing it…again. I don't know what to do."

"Yes, you do," Will said, sitting up, light-headed and groggy.

Wendy's mouth fell open. "How are you awake?"

Gabriel sighed. "He's special."

"Lucifer should have left me where I was." He sat on the edge of the bed and rubbed his temple.

"Shut your hole."

"You know I'm right." His shoulders slumped, the rage gone from his now somber face.

"Boy,"

"You know what I'll do. It'll be Lucifer, then you, then whoever walks through that door next. Dad. Michelle. You see what I am. You have to kill me."

"What the hell?" Wendy snapped.

"I'll get in the tub myself. All you have to do is hold me under if I try to fight it." He got up, looking his aunt in the eye, tears starting to form in his. "I can't control what's going on in my head. You have to stop me before I do something that can't be undone."

Gabriel took a shaky breath, fighting back tears of her own as she wrapped her arms around him, hugging him tight and smoothing the back of his hair.

"Tell them I'm sorry."

She nodded.

"Look out for Dad."

"Of course."

"Damn," Wendy blurted. "It is not that deep."

They turned to look at her, still lurking in the doorway. Gabriel wiped the tears from her cheeks. "You don't understand."

"No, I get it. Can't control his powers, they're making him crazy. He's dangerous, blah, blah. It's nothing a little self-control spell can't fix."

Their mouths hung open. He stepped closer to her, studying her face for signs of deception. "Are you serious?"

"Yeah. Give me like, forty-five minutes to gather up the ingredients. Try not to kill anyone in the meantime." She hurried to the front door and left the apartment leaving the two awestruck and staring at each other in disbelief.

"Can she really do that?" Will wondered. "Can she fix me?"

"I don't know. I guess we'll find out."

"All right." She sat on the floor of Gabriel's living room and took the supplies from her bag. She spread out a six-by-six green cloth and spilled a handful of garden soil in the center. Next, she placed a lace agate in the dirt followed by a nugget of frankincense. Then, she sprinkled a pinch of motherwort and took a sip of water, not wanting her throat to go dry as she recited the incantation.

"Are you sure this'll work?" Gabriel asked.

"Leave her alone," Lucifer lectured from the sofa. "Tituban witches have been pulling off miracles for centuries. No reason to doubt this one now."

"Don't worry," Wendy smiled. "I got this." She rubbed her hands together and began the spell. "Earth within and Earth below, teach him what he needs to know. Not so quick to flare or flow, but like stone both strong and slow." She bundled up the cloth around the other ingredients and tied it with a black thread before tossing it to Will who sat mesmerized across from her. "Go put that under your bed and never move it. When you wake up tomorrow, you'll be all better."

"That's it?"

"Yep."

He got up and went to his room, shoving the parcel under his bed against the wall directly underneath the middle of the headboard.

"That's really all it takes?" Gabriel asked.

"Yeah."

"Well, damn, no wonder you're the witch community's on-call fixer."

She giggled, getting up and heading to the kitchen to wash her hands.

"Did you see that shit?"

"Mm-hmm," Lucifer acknowledged, not looking up from his book.

"You think it'll work?"

"I assume so."

"Why aren't you more excited?"

"I'm ecstatic. Thrilled beyond words. Jumping out of my skin."

"Dude,"

He rolled his eyes and put his book down. "I'm very happy that our previously savage nephew will soon be in complete control of his faculties. I'm just also tired and still slightly aggravated by his latest outburst."

She gasped, clutching her hand to her stomach.

"What is it?"

"Barachiel," she whispered, not wanting Will to hear. "He's in trouble."

Chapter 20

Wyatt was awoken by the sound of his front door being kicked open. He flew out of bed, already gathering energy as he went to the living room to see who'd broken in. Before him stood a dozen male vampires, fangs exposed in twisted grins as they eyed him like steak, licking their lips, nearly panting at the sight of him. One stepped forward, drool leaking to his chin. "You do look tasty. I guess that's what she sees in you."

"What do you want?"

"Dinner."

He looked over the group, taking note of their positions in the room.

"You're the one the bitch Queen chose over us. We were forsaken for *you, a human.*"

"Not just human," he corrected, forming a ball of electricity and eyeing the lumbering brute. "I was *going* to give you a chance to change your mind, but then you had to go and be disrespectful. *No one* calls my girl a bitch." He threw a bolt of lightning into the vampire's chest, sending him flying into the wall on the other side of the room.

"You do not scare us with your parlor tricks, Lightning Bearer," one of them hissed. "You may be strong, but we are many." They attacked, surrounding him in a sea of fangs and maniacal laughter. He fought them off, using all the energy he could handle to throw bolts and balls of lightning in all directions. The air sizzled and snapped, every hair on his body standing on end.

Yo, B, what's wrong? He heard Gabriel ask.

Angry vampire hoard.

I got you. Hold up your hand like you want to answer a question in class.

He did, using his free hand to punch a vampire in the nose, breaking the bone and knocking him out cold. He turned to the sound of a window breaking and was puzzled by the sight of a wooden mallet flying toward him. He caught it and on instinct whipped it back, driving a hole through the forehead of a vampire trying to sneak up behind him. He spun around, facing the raging beasts as they came for him. He lunged at them, one after another, bashing heads in, cloaked in a field of electricity. Every vampire that got close was sent reeling, falling to the floor in a seizing heap. He crushed their skulls with the hammer, taking out his pent-up aggression on his attackers, leaving none standing.

His chest heaved as he caught his breath, the bodies strewn in a bloody mess on the hardwood.

Do you need us to come help? Gabriel asked.

No, I'm fine. It's over.

From the corner of the room, he heard a low gurgling, the grumblings of a dying man.

"You're not dead?" he asked, approaching the one who'd insulted Allydia. He was slumped against the wall, bleeding from the head, his stomach burned and smoking.

He coughed, his arms too weak to cover his mouth. "It will not be that easy to kill me, human."

He crouched in front of him. "So, you're telling me this rebellion Allydia was talking about is because of *me*?"

He spat blood on the floor. "You don't know? She left us *for years* to pine for you. She is derelict in her duty. She had an obligation to *us*. But you charmed her away so we must follow another."

"Another?"

He laughed before coughing again. "We do as our King commands and soon, he will tear your whore Queen into pieces. He will slaughter that cun--"

Wyatt drove the handle of the mallet into the vampire's heart, unwilling to listen to anymore. Blood spurted from the creature's mouth as the light faded from his eyes. His head fell forward, his life extinguished. Wyatt stood, letting out a sigh of relief as he walked through the bodies to the sofa. He dropped onto it, suddenly aware of how tired he was not just physically, but emotionally. He was exhausted, sick and tired of denying himself what he needed. Annie was right. He needed Allydia, but how could he rationalize being with her? He'd have to give it some serious thought, just as soon as he cleaned up this mess.

"What kind of trouble?" Lucifer asked for the third time.

"He's fine now," Gabriel told him, walking toward the door to let Allydia in. She opened it, startling the vampire who hadn't yet knocked. She quickly composed herself, clearing her throat and coming inside.

"We had an agreement."

"I know."

"The price for my aid in your Father's war was the deliverance of my descendants."

Gabriel crossed her arms. "And, I delivered them to you."

"Navid is in danger, held captive, no doubt afraid for his life. You *will* do as I ask."

"I shouldn't get involved."

"Hey, Allydia," Wendy said as she exited the bathroom.

"Hello."

"You okay?"

"No."

"This isn't my business," Gabriel told her.

"Be that as it may," Allydia seethed. "I require your assistance."

"Dia,"

"Messenger."

"It isn't my place."

"As if any of you care to stay out of the affairs of others."

"Girl, you had that child in a cage. What did you think he would--"

"Don't change the subject. We are talking about Navid. He's been kidnapped by a deluded psychopath and I need your help in freeing him. I do not ask for help easily, but I do it now because it is necessary."

"Who's Navid?" Wendy asked.

Allydia tapped her fingers on the counter. "My grandson."

Gabriel rolled her eyes. "One hundred and eighty-second great-grandson. You're barely related at all."

"You have a living relative?" Lucifer asked. "Does he share your penchant for mild stalking?"

Allydia glared at him. "Yes, actually."

"Don't chime in," Gabriel told him.

"You're really not gonna help her?" Wendy shamed.

"It's vampire business and it's all the way in Jordan."

"It's her kid, kind of. If you can help, you should."

She sighed. "Well, if you're gonna guilt me into it. Fine, but only because he had his goons attack Barachiel earlier."

Panic flashed in Allydia's eyes.

"He's fine." She shifted her gaze to Lucifer. "Just in case more show up, though,"

"On my way." He rushed out the door just as Michelle was coming in.

"Will!" the girl yelled, terrified of what the Queen would do to her. He stumbled out of the bedroom, half-asleep and rubbing his eyes.

"You're back," he said, giving her a peck on the lips. She pointed towards Allydia who cast them an annoyed glance before addressing Gabriel again.

"Let's go. It reeks of immaturity in here."

Gabriel snickered and kissed Wendy on the cheek. "Can you stay with the kids?"

"Of course."

"We're not children," Will said. "We don't need a babysitter."

Gabriel smacked her lips. "She's a baby vampire and you're three."

Allydia did her best to hide her amusement as she and Gabriel walked past them to leave. Gabriel stopped in front of her nephew and grabbed his face with one hand.

"How do you feel?"

"Well, my cheeks hurt a little, but fine, otherwise."

She laughed, letting go. "How's your head?"

"Great. I think it worked."

"You're welcome," Wendy called.

"Thank you," he chuckled.

"Okay, be good," Gabriel instructed. "I'll be back by this time tomorrow. Get some sleep. Love you."

"Love you, too." As Gabriel left, Will and Michelle retreated to their bedroom.

"What are you thanking the witch for?" Michelle asked.

He sat on the bed and took a protein bar from the nightstand. "She did a spell to help me stay calm. I should be in full control of myself now."

"You were slipping again?"

"Oh, yeah. Big time. I almost killed Lucifer. I got it in my head that he was gonna kill Sinclair. I could see him doing it like it was happening right in front of me like it was real. Oh, there's a pouch of rocks and dirt under the bed. Wendy said to leave it there for the spell. How was your walk?"

She wanted to shelter him from the events of the evening, to allow him the happiness she could see all over his face as he'd told her about his night. After a few seconds, she simply said, "Dark."

Chapter 21

"Well, this is a fine mess," Lucifer commented as he entered his brother's apartment, taking note of the blood-soaked paper towels that littered the floor.

"Yeah," Wyatt said, sweeping glass into a dustbin. "I never would have thought shoving corpses in an incinerator would be an average Wednesday night for me, but here we are. Gabriel send you to check on me?"

"Just a precaution."

"Mm-hmm."

"So, you'll be pleased to know that your progeny has been cured of his affliction."

He stopped what he was doing. "What?"

"Our sister's witch worked a spell calming his mind and giving him control over his powers and temper."

"You're telling me he's...normal?"

"Aside from the ability to put on a rather impressive light show and an immeasurable capacity to retain knowledge, yes. Good thing, too. I overheard him practically begging Gabriel to put him out of his misery."

He dropped the broom. "Why would he do that?"

"He gave himself a fright trying to kill me."

"He tried to kill you?"

"Like father like son."

"What did you do?"

"Nothing, I was fast asleep. The boy convinced himself I was plotting to murder his girlfriend. Before you ask, I wasn't."

"Is that why you're here instead of Gabriel? She didn't trust you two alone together?"

"No, she's off to Jordan with the vampire Queen to rescue her much-removed grandson from something or other, I wasn't really listening. You'll be interested to know that when Gabriel mentioned you being attacked, your beloved showed signs of concern."

He raised an eyebrow.

"I thought so."

"I think I made a mistake."

"Of course you did. I'm surprised she didn't order the attack herself."

"She's angry?"

"No," Lucifer considered. "She seemed to be in mourning. I'd venture to guess that if you wanted her back, you could have her. If she doesn't get herself killed in the meantime."

He picked up the broom and leaned it against the wall. "Did I thank you for bringing Will back?"

"You didn't need to."

"Thank you. Seriously."

"It was nothing."

"It wasn't nothing. It was huge. I almost regret kicking your ass when I thought it was you that killed him."

"Almost?"

He laughed and brought him in for a hug, patting his back a few times before letting him go.

"All right, that's enough affection. You're clearly exhausted. Go to bed. I'll finish cleaning this up."

"Really?" Wyatt asked.

"Yes, yes. You've earned it, what with avoiding being quartered by creatures of the night and all."

He laughed again. "Okay, thanks. Goodnight."

"Goodnight."

Wyatt disappeared into his bedroom while Lucifer swept more glass into the bin. He smiled to himself, his brother's gratitude like a warm hand over his heart. He would never admit it, but Barachiel's approval meant a lot to him, in human form or otherwise.

As the sun began to rise, the last of the guests finally went to bed. Governors and diplomats had apartments on the third floor while everyone else slept on cots in the cellar. It wasn't ideal, but if the traitors infiltrated the club during the day, it would look empty to them at first glance. Since no one usually spent the day there, it would be reasonable for the rebels to assume the building was empty and go, leaving the slumbering vampires alive and oblivious to the fact that they were ever there at all.

Hartley made one last lap around the building ensuring all locks were locked, her UV gun strapped to her hip just in case. She planned to sleep with it on the nightstand in the Queen's personal quarters, wanting to be close enough to hear if there were any intruders. When she was sure the building was secure, she headed up to the throne room where she found Oliver waiting for her, shirtless with a bottle of rum.

"What are you doing?" she giggled.

"I remembered rum is your favorite as is my chest."

She laughed out loud. "This is the Queen's throne room. We can't do this here."

"What about in there?" He tilted his head toward the bedroom.

"We shouldn't. It would be highly inappropriate."

"Come on, she doesn't have to know."

"Oliver,"

"When I saw you downstairs, I thought you looked like a snack. When I realized who you were, I had to have you. Tell me you don't want me and I'll go. Do you want me to go?"

"No, I don't," she gleaned. "And, I'm not a *snack*. I'm a fucking buffet because I'm a lot and you're never really sure where to start." She turned her head and ran a painted fingernail down the side of her neck. "I suggest right here."

"As you wish," he said, tossing the bottle into the throne and nibbling at her neck, wrapping his huge arms around her slender frame. She laughed again as he lifted her up and carried her to the bed. He kissed her hard as he removed the rest of his clothing before flipping her over and sliding her pants off. He kissed the back of her neck while he got a bit of lotion from the bedside table and smoothed it over himself. She gasped as he slowly entered her, lifting her hips and reaching around to caress her. She covered her mouth, muffling her cries of pleasure, feeling it necessary to be as quiet as possible as to not wake the others. She gripped the headboard, steadying herself on her knees as all thoughts of the danger they were in left her mind.

When they were done, they fell asleep there in the Queen's bed, tangled up in each other's arms, too spent to bother covering themselves.

Chapter 22

"Sorry about that whole trying-to-murder-you-in-your-sleep thing," Will said, refilling his uncle's cup with coffee.

"That's all right, William. We all have days where we feel particularly homicidal. Besides, the feast you've made has more than made up for it. I've been living on take-out for months. Your aunt keeps nothing of substance in her kitchen aside from a carton of orange juice that I'm fairly certain expired last year."

"You could go shopping, cook for yourself."

He squinted and shook his head. "That sounds rather dull."

"Morning," Wyatt said, emerging from his bedroom.

"Hey, Dad. I made breakfast. Sit down, I'll get you a plate." Will took a plate from the cabinet and piled it high with two pancakes, scrambled eggs, bacon, and mixed berries. He set it in front of his father before pouring him a cup of coffee.

"Your son's quite the chef, Barachiel," Lucifer complimented, taking a sip of coffee and placing his cup back on the counter. "I don't think I've eaten so much since The Field of the Cloth of Gold."

Will thought for a second. "June, fifteen-twenty."

"Yes. You know your history."

"I know a lot of things."

He stood, taking one more sip from his cup before putting it down for the final time. "Very good. Well, I'm off. I called someone about fixing your window. They should be here momentarily."

"You didn't have to do that," Wyatt said.

Lucifer patted his back. "I don't *have* to do anything. But, it needs to be attended to. Wouldn't want a bird to fly in, would we?" He headed toward the door.

"Bye," Wyatt called.

He waved without looking back and left the apartment.

"He's not as bad as I thought he'd be," Will said.

"He has his moments."

"He told me about the vampires. You okay?"

"I'm fine. Speaking of vampires,"

"Michelle wouldn't hurt a fly."

"I'm not talking about her, although, I feel like I should tell you to be careful."

"Allydia, then?"

He nodded, taking a bite of his pancakes. "God, I missed these."

"You want to get back with her?"

"I don't think 'want' is a strong enough word."

"You know what I'm gonna say, right?"

"That she's a monster and a murderer and I should run away screaming?"

Will laughed. "I think you figured that out on your own. No, I was gonna say you should do whatever you want. You don't have to ask my permission."

"I wasn't."

"No, you were just gauging how I'd feel about it before making a decision that would inevitably be whatever you thought I'd be most comfortable with. You're still doing it."

"Doing what?"

"Putting everyone else first. Listen, Dad, you don't have to worry about me. I almost killed *Lucifer* last night. Gabriel couldn't even stop me. Wendy had to knock me out with some magic word."

"She's done that to me, too. Best sleep of my life."

"For me, too, for thirty seconds. She told me it should've kept me under for eight hours. I'm stronger than all of you. And, now that I'm able to control myself, there's no reason for you to be concerned. Your girlfriend can't hurt me. More importantly, you deserve to be happy. If the Queen of all vampires is what you need to live your best life, go get her."

"My best life?" he chuckled.

"Dad,"

"Okay, you're right. I was putting your feelings first. I probably always will and not just because that's who I am as a person. You're my kid. I have to consider--"

"I'm not a kid. I *have* a kid."

"You're three."

"I wish you'd all stop saying that. You know I'm like, twenty-seven."

"Yeah, well, I was changing your diapers three years ago."

"That's really gross."

"You have no idea."

"So, are you gonna call her?"

"Lucifer said she's in Jordan. I'll find her when she gets back. I probably have some serious groveling to do. This is the second time I've bailed. Should talk to her in person."

"Mm."

"There's something I should tell you."

Will took a bite of bacon from his third plate of the morning and looked up with raised eyebrows.

"Your mom stopped by."

He choked. After a few coughs, he took a gulp of milk and put his glass down. "What?"

"She said she loves us and she has no regrets. Seeing you in the hospital is her favorite memory. She's happy she had you."

Will's eyes were huge. "But, she's...I don't understand."

"She was a ghost."

"Oh."

"She went back to Heaven."

"Okay."

They sat in awkward silence as they finished their breakfast. As Wyatt took his last sip of coffee, a pigeon burst in through the broken window, panic-flying around the living room, knocking over a lamp. He put his cup down and sighed. "Damn it."

Chapter 23

"That's a lot of exploded vampires," Gabriel said, turning her nose up at the thousands of corpses that littered the desert floor. Even in the dark of night, it was a disgusting scene.

"We buried our dead before the sun rose," Phindi explained. "But the traitors did not deserve that kindness."

"All right, but someone is bound to see this."

"You will burn the bodies when we leave," Allydia told Gabriel, her impatience clear in her tone causing Phindi's stomach to flip.

"Apologies, Your Majesty. I should have disposed of the rebels' bodies. I let my emotions get the best of me. It will not happen again."

"It's fine, Duchess."

"Again, I apologize, my Queen. I have failed. I could not deliver the man who calls himself King to you. I can not get through the tunnel of ultraviolet light."

Gabriel stepped forward, rolling her eyes as she walked toward the canyon. "I can." She got to the entrance, pulled her sunglasses down over her eyes, and stepped inside. Along the eighty-mile-high cliffs were hundreds of spotlights filling the narrow passage with so much UV light, Gabriel's skin was beginning to darken. "Death by tanning bed." She went back to the group. "Hope you guys don't mind walking over broken glass." She held her hands in front of her and closed her eyes. After a few seconds, the lights shattered, raining down glass so loudly, the vampires had to cover their ears. Finally, it was dark.

Phindi held back a smile as she looked to her Queen for approval.

"If you find the hostage before I do, bring him to me *alive*."

"Yes, Your Majesty."

Allydia nodded, stepping aside to make way for what was left of her army to begin their assault. Gabriel stood behind her, in no mood to get trampled.

"For the Queen!" Phindi shouted, raising her assegai.

"For the Queen!" the rest cheered. They flew through the canyon, all but ignoring the cuts they got on their legs as they moved through the two feet of glass.

Gabriel stood next to Allydia and folded her arms. "I feel like they could have just thrown rocks at them and accomplished the same thing without dragging me all the way here."

The Queen arched an eyebrow.

"Your boy's in a cell. Take the stairs on the right when you first get inside."

She looked at her with a puzzled expression.

"I can hear his thoughts. He's scared. And dehydrated. You should hurry."

She spun on her heel and bolted into the canyon. Gabriel tilted her head as she heard something familiar. "Is that? *No way.*" She chuckled as she, too, slowly made her way into the canyon.

On the other end of the passageway was a large courtyard now flooded with battling vampires. The faithful sliced, shot and hacked their way through a force triple their size, slaughtering the lot of them while taking massive casualties of their own. Allydia barreled through, ripping out the throats of any hood-wearer in her path. She reached the massive door flanked by two Roman columns built into the side of the mountain. Without hesitation, she stormed inside, locating the staircase Gabriel had described and making a beeline for it. Not far behind, Gabriel entered the building, having snuck past the fighting vampires who seemed to have no interest in what she was doing there.

Downstairs, Navid clung to life by his fingernails, lying on the floor, his lips chapped, and his breathing shallow. Judas had removed his gag to attempt to feed him, but he wouldn't accept food. He didn't want to risk being poisoned or fed vampire blood. As he felt himself slip away, he began to regret that decision.

"Navid!" Allydia gasped, rushing to open the cell door.

"A-All," He couldn't form the words. His throat was too dry.

"It's all right," she told him, breaking the shackles from his wrists and ankles. "You'll be all right." But, as she was about to help him to his feet to leave, six rebel vampires slammed the cell door shut with Allydia and Navid still inside. They cackled as they gloated in their apparent victory.

"Not so big and bad are you now, *Your Majesty,*" one mocked.

"When your friends outside are dealt with, we'll be back," another threatened. "Maybe show you what you're missing, being with that human lightning rod of yours instead of your own kind."

"I think you've forgotten to whom you're speaking," she said.

"We know exactly who you are, bitch, and we'll be back for you." He grabbed his genitals and stuck his tongue out while the others laughed.

She knelt down and whispered in her grandson's ear, "Close your eyes. I don't want you to see me this way."

He nodded and squeezed his eyes shut as she stood, sauntering to the door, never taking her eyes off the vulgar traitor. With one powerful kick, she knocked the door off its hinges and into the men standing behind it. In a blur, she plunged her hand into their chests, pulling their hearts from their bodies as they fell, the dumb looks of shock on their faces with them now for eternity. She used one of their cloaks to wipe the blood from her skin before turning back to the cell. Seeing it up close, she noticed the small palm leaves embroidered on the deep green fabric. It would have been beautiful had it not been worn by such a treasonous sycophant.

She helped Navid up, putting his arm around her shoulder as he stood. He opened his eyes to see the mutilated corpses on the ground and was so grateful to be free, it didn't occur to him to be frightened of the long-lost relative that had saved him.

In the makeshift throne room at the center of the building, Gabriel couldn't help but laugh. "Judas? Oh, my Christmas. It's been *forever.*"

"And, who might you be?" he asked sitting in the stone seat perched on a small platform a few steps above the rest of the floor.

"It's me, Gabriel. It's okay that you don't recognize me, new body and everything."

"Messenger?" He stood from his seat and stepped down to meet her. "It *has* been some time. What are you doing here?"

"Not sure, to be honest with you. I try to stay out of politics. It's not my place to interfere in this kind of stuff, you know? Besides, Dia could've handled this on her own. All I did was turn off a light, which I maintain could have been done without me. But, you pissed me off, so, here I am."

"You misunderstand my motives, Angel. I don't seek power for myself. I want to destroy the vampiric race once and for all. It's what I was meant to do, to live long enough to make amends for what I did."

"No, I get it. Still dumb as shit."

"How have I offended thee? I have no quarrel with you."

"No, you *want* no quarrel with me, but you fell ass-backward into one. I would have stayed out of it, but you put my brother in danger. That was unwise."

"Your brother?" He stepped back, stroking his beard as he came to the realization. "The Lightning Wielder? He's an angel?"

"Obvs. What did you think he was?"

He shrugged. "Wizard. Warlock. Street magician. So, the Queen's taken up with an angel. Amazing. If I may ask, which angel is he?"

"The best one," Allydia said, entering the room, nearly carrying an exhausted Navid with her.

Gabriel hurried to them, helping Navid sit on the floor before taking a bottle of water from her bag and opening it, holding it to his lips. She placed her other hand on his back, healing the cuts that covered his torso. After a few sips of water, he took the bottle from her and looked her over, eyes wide with wonder. She took her hand away as he looked down at himself and back at her.

"Gabriel," she introduced herself. "Messenger of God, archangel, yappaby shmappaby. We should get you on the plane into some air conditioning. I have snacks. Chips, cupcakes, cookies." They stood and she began leading him away. "We'll get you some real food when we land. Some steak, maybe?" He looked back at Allydia with concern. "She's coming. This'll just take her like, a second."

When they were gone, Allydia rushed Judas, gripping his throat and throwing him down into his throne. He didn't fight back. Instead, he laughed.

"It's too late, Your Majesty. By now, they're dead, all of them. I have won."

She fumed, her whole body trembling with rage. "I should have forced your maker to kill you when you slaughtered that village."

He scoffed. "I killed my maker *before* I butchered that village. I was tricked into becoming one of you. I wanted him to pay for what he did to me."

"I took pity on you. When I found you alone in that inn, I showed you mercy."

"You shouldn't have."

She screamed, pounding her fist into his chest, breaking his ribs. She tore open his shirt and clawed at his flesh, peeling back the skin and muscle and prying open his chest. She reached into the cavity and plucked out his heart, holding it before him.

He smiled and in a voice barely audible even to her, he gurgled, "I am redeemed."

Outside, Gabriel cleared a path, waving her hand at the mess of glass in the canyon and leading Navid through. Phindi and a handful of faithful were all that remained of the vampires, the rest broken and battered in lifeless heaps on the blood-soaked sand.

"Messenger," Allydia called as she exited the building. Gabriel turned, stopping as the Queen approached her, her soldiers at her heels. Stern and stoic, Allydia gave her command. "Burn it all." Gabriel nodded and the group exited the canyon, stepping around the bodies that peppered the landscape. When they were clear, Gabriel flicked her wrist, igniting the corpses within and without. Navid's eyes grew wide as he watched the flames over his shoulder, the stench of the smoke wafting through the night air turning his stomach.

The battle was over, but at what cost? Allydia was heartbroken, her entire life feeling like a waste.

Phindi and her soldiers headed back to Egypt in disgrace, unable to make eye contact with their disappointed Queen.

Chapter 24

Hartley woke to the smell of smoke. She tried to turn the bedside lamp on, but it didn't light. The power had been shut off. In the distance, screams echoed through the club, snapping her to attention. She jumped up, throwing her clothes on and smacking Oliver on the back. "Wake up!"

"What?" He sat up, rubbing his eyes. "Is it still day?"

"I don't know, but there's a fire. Get your sexy ass up. We have to go."

He quickly complied, getting into his clothes and following her out of the room, through the throne room, and into the VIP area. The smoke was thick, but even through the dark haze, Hartley could make out several hooded figures holding closed the door to the basement. "Hey!" she shouted down to them before opening fire, hitting each one in the head with UV bullets, their treasonous bodies falling with thuds to the floor. She leaped down over the railing while Oliver hurried down the steps. She rushed to the door, kicking the rebels out of her way and opening it up, getting punched in the face by the heat of billowing smoke. She fell back as Oliver met her, both horrified as a man on fire tumbled from the cellar door and fell, no more than a giant lump of smoldering charcoal.

"The diplomats," Oliver breathed, bolting back to the staircase and following it up to the third floor, Hartley close behind. But, as they reached the landing, they were stopped in their tracks by an all-consuming wall of fire.

"Do you hear that?" Hartley shuddered.

"What? I don't hear anything."

"Exactly. The screaming stopped." They exchanged terrified, knowing glances before turning to race down the steps. Halfway to the bottom, the staircase gave out, dropping them down in a pile of rubble. They clawed their way out and headed to the door, opening it just enough to see if sunlight would meet them should they exit. Light poured in and they slammed the door back. Hartley made a beeline for the dead rebels and tore two of their cloaks away. She raced back to the door and handed one to Oliver. They covered themselves and stumbled out onto the sidewalk, a firetruck already pulling up in front of them. They retreated to an alley and hid there, neither of them sure how to answer questions about how the fire started or who had shot the men whose bodies had not yet burned.

"Are you all right?" Oliver asked, looking her over.

"Yeah. You?"

"Could be worse, I reckon."

She took her phone from her pocket and began dialing.

"Who are you calling?"

She held the phone to her ear and cleared her throat. "Everyone."

Navid slept across the aisle, an empty bag of cheese puffs still in his hand, while Allydia sulked.

"I'm sorry about your people," Gabriel said, sitting in front of her.

"Are you?"

"Well, I'm sorry you're sad."

"That's something, I suppose."

"I know this is a bad time, and I know you're not thinking about it, but I'm also familiar with you, so it needs to be said."

She cast her a look of derision. "What?"

"I don't want to be a dick, but you know what I'll do to you if you hurt my brother, right?"

She leaned back and rolled her eyes. "It is your brother that inflicts pain."

She gave her a confused stare. "Did you forget who he is? Protector of Humanity. He might not care much about *himself* most of the time, but his kid? You mess with Will's shit and all that Barachiel instinct comes flooding to the surface like a fucking dam broke."

"The boy is a menace."

"Wendy fixed him. He's fine now."

She raised an eyebrow. "Really?"

"Mm-hmm. I didn't think it was possible, but that bitch has *skills*." She looked over at Navid and back at her. "I mean, come on. Look what you just did for Navid. A hundred and eighty-two generations removed *and* you just met. Imagine if it had been Fatima, Naima, Sada, or Thaddea."

"You invoke the names of my daughters?"

"And imagine if, on top of all that maternal instinct, your sole purpose for existing was to protect people. To save them. It was who you were on your deepest level. If the tables were turned, how would you have reacted? What wouldn't you sacrifice for your children?"

She glanced over at her sleeping grandson and back at Gabriel. "He sacrificed nothing. He's disgusted by me. Afraid."

"Bitch, he is *broken in half.* He came to *me* looking for answers. *Me.* Do you know how fucked up a person has to be to--"

"I saw him struggling. I didn't dare hope that his melancholy was for me."

"Girl, with the stalking. For real."

"So, the Nephilim is under control?"

"Looks like. He did almost kill Lucifer first, though. It was hilarious. I mean, horrible and upsetting, but the look on Lucifer's face when I couldn't hold Will back," She laughed. "Ah, I wish I'd gotten a picture."

"You're sure he poses no threat to Wyatt?"

She nodded.

"Interesting."

Navid woke up coughing and Allydia went to sit next to him, handing him a water bottle and rubbing his back. He took a drink and looked up, his eyes fixed to Gabriel.

"Uh, oh," she said.

"What?" Allydia asked.

"He's star-struck."

"You're Gabriel?" he asked. "As in, Muhammed's first revelation?"

"Sort of."

"You met him?"

"Yeah."

His jaw dropped.

"Dude, get it together."

"I'm sorry, it's just...you're the most beautiful thing I've ever seen."

"She has a girlfriend," Allydia discouraged.

"I don't mean like that. I mean, that too, but, well, you're a bloody angel! A creature of divinity. Love and light and all that."

Gabriel crossed her arms and shook her head. "You need a nap."

He drew in a sharp breath as he suddenly felt ashamed of his lack of respect. "I'm so sorry." He slid off his seat and onto his knees, putting his head down in reverence.

"Oh, dude, no. No, don't do that."

"I'm sorry, I don't know what the appropriate thing to do is."

"*Not that*. Makes me wildly uncomfortable. I'm not *God*. Plus, I'm pretty much human right now, so." She waved her hand dismissively and he got back in his seat.

"You can understand his reaction, Messenger," Allydia warned. "You will treat him with kindness."

Navid looked shocked. "Are you threatening an angel?"

"She's also sleeping with one," Gabriel chimed.

Allydia scowled.

"What?"

"You're what?!" he gasped.

"It's not your concern," she said, handing him a bag of chips. "You should eat something else."

"He was gonna find out," Gabriel defended.

He opened the bag. "That's allowed?"

"It's not *not* allowed."

"My head is spinnin'."

"Eat," Allydia instructed, "Then go back to sleep. We'll be home in a few hours. You'll stay with me until I'm sure no one's left to harm you." She went back to her seat across from Gabriel as Navid ate, staring at the two women in front of him in amazement. "So," she said, turning her attention back to the angel. "Tell me about Lucifer's face when he thought his life was in danger."

Navid choked. "Lucifer?!"

Chapter 25

The old witch hid in the trees, watching for the girl with the power of death. Days had passed and she was beginning to lose hope. Finally, as if by answered prayer, the child returned, her parents helping her across the monkey bars. She looked older somehow as if she'd aged a year. She'd have to act fast. If the girl aged into double digits, she'd be of no use to her. Her patience wearing thin and her stomach grumbling, she followed the family to their house, creeping behind the fence as they entered the backyard.

Malik prepped the grill for the last barbecue of the season while Sinclair played in her sandbox and Valerie went inside to get the meat. Suddenly, the gate flew open, and the croan burst through.

"Baba Yaga!" Sinclair cried, pointing to the old woman.

"Baba what?" Malik asked as he stepped in front of her. "The hell do you want?"

"The child," she hissed. "I *need* the child."

"Lady, you best--"

She whacked him in the face with her cane made from an old broom handle, splitting his lip. She thumped him again, in the head and then in the stomach.

"Mommy!" Sinclair screeched.

Valerie looked out the kitchen window and saw the old lady beating her husband with a stick. "The fuck?" she muttered.

With Malik on the ground, the wind knocked out of him, Valerie hurried to get her sword from the top of the hall closet, running out to the yard as the witch approached Sinclair.

"Bitch, you best get the fuck off my property!"

"The mother," the woman bemoaned. She ran at her, bringing the cane down hard against Valerie's blade. They sparred, exchanging blows, neither wavering for a second. Sinclair sprang up, trying to make a break for it.

"Uh, uh, pretty," the witch crooned, bringing her hand up, causing the sand to rise and swirl around her in a tornado of filth.

"Oh, it's like *that*? Okay, I see you." Valerie cracked her neck, the sword erupting in flame. The witch stepped back, her shock quickly dissolving as her desperation forced her to continue. She slammed her cane into the sword again, but after a few strikes, the wood charred and ignited. She dropped it and curled her fingers toward the ground, lifting a large chunk of earth up, breaking it free from the rest. But, before she could raise it high enough to threaten the angel, Malik leaped up, snatched the sword from his wife's hands, and drove it deep into the old croan's chest. Her clothes caught flame and she screamed, her whole body going up in a plume of embers and ash. The ground returned and the sand fell, freeing Sinclair.

"Daddy!" she yelped, running into her father's arms as he knelt down, hugging her tight.

"Are you okay?" he fretted.

She nodded, a wide smile spreading across her face.

"I love you so much," he told her, fighting back tears. "I love you so so much."

She giggled. "I know."

Allydia stood in the rubble of what used to be her club. Oliver sat on the sidewalk, head in hands, as Hartley updated the Queen.

"The delegation from Norway was en route when the attacks occurred, so they're safe. They landed just after sunset. Governors from the Philippines and Nepal are also secure. I sent them to a hotel on Madison and 50th. Phindi and her group are in Alexandria and the Governor of Paris has barricaded himself in his chalet and refuses to leave. Everyone else is," She took a beat, placing her hand over her heart.

"And the rebels?" Allydia asked.

"Dead."

"You're sure?"

"Yes, Your Majesty. The ones that didn't die in the attacks were dealt with by my humans. I left none alive, I assure you."

"How many of us are left?"

She choked back her tears. "Twenty-nine, including us."

"Total?"

She nodded. "Their attacks were coordinated, Your Majesty. Small groups of traitors infiltrated every one of our homes and businesses simultaneously. They all but wiped us out." She brushed away the tears she could no longer fight.

Allydia appeared cold, even as her heart sank. "Transfer ten million dollars from my personal accounts to each survivor, including yourself. Contact the insurance company. Rebuild the club as you see fit. Make it a sanctuary for our people. Keep them safe."

She looked puzzled. "Forgive me, my Queen, but this sounds like goodbye."

"What did I promise you after you stayed with me the night that Wyatt broke my heart?"

"You said you'd never abandon me," she said, her lip quivering.

"And I never will. So, this is not goodbye. Do you trust me?"

"Of course, my Queen."

"Good. I will see you again, have no doubt." She cupped her face in her hands. "Until that time, stay strong, have faith in your capabilities, and be happy."

She nodded, stifling more tears.

"Good to see you alive, Oliver."

He stood and bowed his head. "And you, Your Majesty."

"I trust your casino is insured."

"Yes, Your Majesty."

"Perhaps I'll visit it once you've made any necessary repairs."

"I would be honored, Your Majesty."

"I have some business to attend to," she said, turning to go. "Take care of each other."

Chapter 26

Navid sat at Allydia's dining table, still drowsy and starving. Gabriel opened the takeout containers of steak, mashed potatoes, haricot verts, and yeast rolls, and handed him a plastic knife and fork. She took a bite of bread and picked up her own fork, casting him an annoyed glare. "You're staring."

"Sorry, I just can't believe I'm on a date with an angel."

"Not a date."

"No, I know, but, you know what I mean."

"I'm just here until Dia gets back to make sure you don't get kidnapped or eaten."

"Yeah, I know, but I'm freakin' out, right? How am I supposed to behave around you?"

"Dude, just eat."

"Should I call you 'Messenger' like Allydia does? Or would you prefer the full 'Messenger of God'?"

"My name's Gabriel."

"Right, but--"

"Bro, it would be way less annoying for me if you'd just treat me like a normal person."

"All right, but I don't know if I can."

"Give it a shot."

"I'll do my best." He took a bite of potatoes and glanced around the room. "Why does she even have a table?"

"Appearances."

"Right."

"Your dad's in Edinburgh, by the way."

He coughed up a bit of bread. "What?"

"He's a curator at the national museum there. After college, he took a trip to Scotland and fell in love with it. He's been there ever since."

"How..."

"I know things."

"Ah."

"I'm telling you this because you have a deep-seated desire for family. I'm not saying you shouldn't spend time with Dia. She loves you like a son. I'm just saying, she's not the only game in town."

"You're sayin' I've got a dad in the UK, not eight hours from where I live?"

She took a sip of soda. "Mm-hmm."

"And, you know this because of your angel powers or whatever?"

"Yep."

"Well, I'll be damned."

"Nah, you're good."

"What's he like?"

"Uh, tall, swarthy, fifty. Smart. Still kind of a man-whore, never settled down. Plays the violin. Still drinks a lot of wine."

"I don't know what to say."

She shrugged, taking a bite of potatoes.

He cut into his steak, unable to take his eyes off her.

"Dude, stop staring."

"Right, sorry." He lowered his head and took a bite, his gaze still fixed on her.

"Dude!"

Navid is safe now. Meet me at your apartment, Allydia texted to Gabriel as she stood outside the door. She knocked, ready to swallow her pride.

"Allydia Cain, as I live and breathe," Lucifer greeted, stepping aside to let her in.

"Where's the boy?"

"Asleep, I'm afraid. Is there something I can help you with?"

"No." She sat at the island. "I was hoping to make amends."

He sat across from her. "Oh, I wouldn't worry about that. Young William isn't the type to hold grudges, unlike your father. Did you know he murdered the woman I was seeing recently because of what happened between us in Akrotiri?"

"No, I didn't. My condolences."

"And, mine to you on the loss of your father."

"Unnecessary, but thank you."

"I did have a bit of fun torturing him before Wrath did him in. I would apologize, but you know better than anyone how badly he deserved it."

"I do. I almost hurt him myself after he told Wyatt to leave me. How is he?"

"Pensive."

"Hmm."

"So, you found your descendant all right, I assume?"

"Yes. Judas was the one behind the rebellion and his kidnapping."

He laughed. "Judas Iscariot?"

She nodded.

"Oh, that's hilarious."

"Speaking of things being hilarious, Gabriel told me about your run-in with the Nephilim."

"I was sleeping. He caught me off guard."

"Uh-huh."

"What's going on?" Will said, shuffling to the kitchen.

"Will, good of you to join us," Lucifer said.

"I'm just getting a snack." He pulled a box of cereal from the pantry and took a mixing bowl from the cabinet.

"Sit for a moment. Your girlfriend's Queen would like a word. If you'll both excuse me, I'm off to bed." He headed down the hall, leaving the two alone. Will sat, pouring the contents of the box into the bowl.

"What's up?"

She crossed her legs and cleared her throat. "I wanted to apologize for my behavior. I shouldn't have frightened you and locking Michelle in a cage was perhaps a little rash."

"You don't have to apologize. I know you're just doing it because you want to get back with my dad. It's okay. I'm not mad."

"You're not?"

He folded his hands and looked her in the eyes. "My dad never makes himself a priority. He gave up everything to make sure I grew up safe, including you. He worked a job that bored him in a place far away from everyone he cared about. He was lonely and miserable, but he didn't care because *I* was okay. He has more than earned the right to be with someone that makes him happy. I don't know if you're the best person for him, but I see how you look at him. Even when you were pissed off, it was clear how much you love him. I would be a crap son if I stood in the way of his happiness."

Her eyes softened. It was like she was looking at him for the first time. "You're a good son, Will. Your father obviously raised you well."

"Yes, he did. Oh, milk! Duh." He got up and went to the fridge just as Gabriel walked in.

"Dia," she said.

"I need to speak with you."

"Go ahead," Will said, pouring the milk and putting it back. "I'm gonna take this to my room. I'll probably pass back out as soon as I finish it."

"Night," Gabriel called after him as he left.

"Goodnight!" he called back as he closed the bedroom door behind him.

"Well?" Allydia asked.

"You're crazy."

"And?"

"And, it's a big ask."

"Can she do it?"

"I don't know. It's never been done."

"Messenger,"

"I understand. But, Jesus, Dia, are you sure?"

"I've fulfilled my commitment to your Father, yes?"

"Yes."

"Then, what do you care?"

"I care," Gabriel defended. "I consider us friends. Plus, my brother would never forgive me if--"

"Everything I do is for your brother. You can see into my past. You know my heart. Have I ever cared about anyone more than him?"

She softened her expression. "No."

"So, you will call your witch. Ask her to free me of this burden. Undo what has been done."

"All right. If that's what you want."

"You know that it is."

"Fine." She took her phone from her pocket and dialed Wendy's number.

"Can you do it?" Gabriel asked.

Wendy went to the desk and opened the drawer, waving her hand over the cat's eye necklace, removing its warding so she could access it. "Yeah, I can do it. I'll be right over." She ended the call and shoved the phone in her pocket before picking up a letter opener and jamming it into the tip of her finger, squeezing a few drops of blood onto the amulet. She took a deep breath and blew it out her mouth, not looking forward to the pain that would come with what she was about to do. The truth was, she'd put it off for too long already. Gabriel's friend needing help was the push she needed to get it over with. She braced herself against the wall. "Here goes nothin'." She took another breath and squeezed the necklace tight in her fist. "Solvo."

The cat's eye cracked open, spilling brilliant blue light from its center, filling the room with shimmering radiance. She tried to cover her eyes, but her arms were yanked down by the force of the magic. It spun around her, lifting her from the floor and turning her around as it blew through, forcing its way in. She cried out as her temperature rose, her skin flushing and her eyes glowing like bioluminescent algae. Her heartbeat was like a drum roll in her ears as she was pulled away from the wall and bent backward as much as her spine would allow as the last of the sparkling incandescence worked its way in through her open mouth as she screamed.

She dropped to the floor, the room going dark and the blue of her eyes returning to their normal shade. As her temperature went down and her heart rate settled, she caught her breath, never being so happy for something to be over in her life.

Chapter 27

Wendy lit the black candle with a red interior and placed it on the floor above Allydia's head as she lay in Gabriel's living room.

"Last chance to change your mind," Gabriel said from the ottoman.

"You sure?" Wendy asked.

Allydia nodded, folding her hands over her diaphragm and closing her eyes. "Proceed."

"All right then." She rubbed her hands together and held them over the vampire's chest, taking deep breaths as she prepared.

Yo, B, you should get over here, Gabriel thought to her brother.

Everything okay? he replied.

Dia's having Wendy do a spell on her. It's risky. She could die.

What? Stop her!

Can't. She begged to have it done.

I'm coming.

"Revorsio esse verus hominem," Wendy said. "Revorsio esse verus hominem." She repeated the phrase for several minutes as Allydia's body started to tremble.

"Is she okay?" Gabriel asked.

Wendy ignored her, continuing to chant. Allydia shook, her eyes rolling to the back of her head.

"Wendy, is she okay?!"

Wyatt burst in the door, racing to kneel next to the vampire opposite Wendy. "What are you doing to her?!" She kept chanting, her eyes twinkling like stars in shades of electric blue. Wyatt held Allydia's hand and touched her forehead. "She's burning up!" From underneath her skirt, a slow-moving puddle of blood emerged. "What the hell is happening?!"

"It's how she died," Gabriel told him, dropping to her knees next to him. "Uterine atony after childbirth." She placed a hand over her abdomen to heal it, but Wendy smacked it away. "Did she just--"

"REVORSIO ESSE VERUS HOMINEM!" Wendy fell back as the candle blew itself out and Allydia stopped moving. The witch caught her breath as she moved out of the way. "It's done."

Gabriel rushed around to take Wendy's spot across from her brother, put one hand over Allydia's abdomen, and the other on her head. Her skin glowed as her veins became visible. The angel looked pained as her hands began to shake. "This is taking too long." Her eyes met Wyatt's and he could see the worry in them as his heart beat out of his chest.

He squeezed Allydia's hand and brought it to his lips as a tear slid down his cheek. "Come back. Please, come back." Finally, a shallow breath escaped Allydia's throat, then another and another, each one deeper than the last. Gabriel backed away, lowering her head in relief as her friend's skin began to brighten, color returning to her face with more vibrancy than before. Wyatt breathed a sigh of relief and kissed her hand again.

"It worked?" Gabriel asked.

"Yep," Wendy said, standing up. "I need some water." She went to the kitchen and got a bottle from the fridge.

"What did she do?" Wyatt asked.

"She removed Lilith's spell. Put her back the way she was."

"You're kidding. You mean she's..."

"Human. A hundred percent regular-ass person. Hella dangerous. For a while there, I didn't think I'd be able to fix her." She got up and stomped to the kitchen. "You and I need to have a discussion about boundaries."

"You can't interrupt me mid-spell," Wendy defended.

"I wasn't interrupting, I was just trying to--"

"She had to be all the way back exactly as she was right before the original spell was done or it wouldn't have worked. You have to trust me on these things."

She sat on a stool and crossed her legs. "I'm working on it."

"Mm," Allydia moaned as she opened her eyes. "Wyatt," She reached up and touched his chin. "You're here."

He smiled through his tears, awash in emotion. "Yeah, I'm here. Why did you do this? You could have died."

"A risk worth taking."

"Why?"

"Forever without you would have been a pain worse than death. Besides, you need me."

"You didn't have to do this."

"Yes, I did."

He wiped his face and tucked her hair behind her ear. "I love you."

"And, I love you," She ran her fingertips over his lips. "More than anyone is ever going to."

He bent down and kissed her, cradling her face in his hands.

"Aw, that's sweet," Wendy commented.

Gabriel sighed. "Yeah, they're pretty cute when they're not dying or making me nauseous with their sex memories."

She laughed.

"Hey, were your eyes glowing earlier?"

"Probably."

"Freaky."

"Yeah."

"Is that common for you?"

"New development."

"Pretty impressive stuff you did tonight."

"I learned another trick while you were gone," Wendy teased.

"Really? Did you get a new spellbook?"

"No, I watched porn."

Gabriel laughed. "Well, we shouldn't let that education go to waste." They scampered off to Gabriel's bedroom, leaving Wyatt and Allydia alone to bask in the warmth of their reunion.

Chapter 28

Poe shot up in bed, her fluffy familiar sleeping soundly on the pillow next to her. Even from her Bourbon Street hotel room thirteen hundred miles away, she could feel Grace's magic being set free. There was no way the others didn't feel it, too.

She hopped out of bed and threw on a pair of jeans. She tossed the rest of her belongings in her backpack, not bothering to change her shirt from the one she'd been sleeping in, and looked up flights on her phone. She booked the soonest one and slipped her boots on, tying them as fast as she could. *What am I doing?* she thought. Grace's magic being released meant one of three things: Wendy needed it for a powerful spell and took it into herself, which was best-case scenario, Wendy activated it to protect herself from someone or something she couldn't handle on her own, *or* Julia somehow got her hands on it, killed Wendy, and used her blood to take the magic for herself. If Wendy was in trouble, there wasn't much she could do to help. She wasn't nearly as strong as a born-Tituban witch and she'd barely made it out of town alive last time she stood against Julia and her minions. Still, she had an obligation to try. Wendy only had Grace's magic because she brought it to her. It had been her mentor's dying wish, to see her family's magic passed to someone with Tituban blood. After she'd crossed over and her power was securely in the amulet, it acted as a compass, leading Poe directly to Wendy. She could have hidden it, sealed it away, and dropped it in the ocean. It's what she thought she *should* do. But, Grace was like a mother to her, and not honoring her wishes wasn't an option. Still, her stomach twisted with guilt as she smoothed the covers, leaving the room looking as nice as when she'd arrived.

"Come on, Raven," she said, patting the bed and holding open the pack. The bunny woke up and hopped over, climbing into the bag. "We're going home."

Julia looked up at the Tribeca apartment building, a shiver running down her spine as the remnants of magic emanating from four stories above lingered, dancing on the air like fireflies in the dark of the early morning. She couldn't tell who had activated Grace's magic, but whether it be Poe, an elder witch, or a stranger, there was one thing she was sure of: they wouldn't have it for long.

In the near distance, she heard the incessant cawing of a crow. She held out her arm as the bird swooped down and perched itself there, its weight a familiar comfort. "We've found it, Griffin," she told the animal. "Soon, Grace's magic will belong to us, as it was always meant to."

COVEN

Happiness is not found in things you possess, but in what you have the courage to release.

William Butler Yeats

Prologue

Tituba placed her infant daughter inside the circle of white candles, the moonlight peeking through the trees cascading its approving glow on the baby's smiling face. She sat on her knees, confident in the protection the forest provided, far away from the prying eyes of the townspeople that would hang her if they knew what she was. She placed her hand on Violet's head and said the words, quietly, but with conviction. "Ne agnosceretur sicut pythonissam." The child giggled as Tituba smiled down at her, relieved that it was done. She bent down and whispered into her daughter's ear, "You will remember this spell. Teach it to your children and your children's children so your generations will always be protected."

She blew out the candles and placed them back in the hollowed-out tree stump she used for hiding spellbooks and ingredients, covering it with rocks before gathering her newborn in her arms.

"Tituba," a voice whispered in the dark.

"Who's there?" She froze, every muscle in her body tense as she clutched the baby to her chest. She scanned the trees and saw the figure of a girl fast approaching.

"It's me, Sarah."

"Oh!" She let out a sigh of relief. "You gave me quite the fright. What are you doing out here at this hour, child? If your father catches you, he'll string you up and me along with you."

"I need to ask you something and I didn't want anyone else to hear."

"All right, well, spit it out, girl. It's late and we need to get you home."

She looked back to make sure she wasn't followed before speaking again. "I need your help. You know, *magic help.*"

"Now I *know* you're trying to get me hanged."

"I'm serious, Tituba, please. My mother practiced the craft and she said if I ever needed something, that you were the only person I could go to."

She gently bounced the baby as she closed her eyes, remembering her friend, the girl's mother, who'd recently passed from the pox. "What is it that you want, child?"

"I want you to bring her back. Her and my sister. Bring them back before my father dies of a broken heart."

Tituba's expression turned dark as she stared into the teenager's eyes. "You know I can not."

"Why not?" Sarah whined. "I heard Goody Sawyer talking to her cousin last week and she said--"

"You listen to me, girl," she snapped. "Goody Sawyer is not the same as me. What she does is dark and dangerous and will not result in a happy family reunion. Life and death are not interchangeable. Once a soul has reached its next destination, there is no retrieving it. Not for *us*, anyway. To try is an invitation for wickedness, do you understand?"

She crossed her arms, her lips pouted.

"You stay far away from Goody Sawyer, do you hear me?"

"You can't tell me what to do. You're just a slave."

She scowled. "Little girl, I may be a slave, but I am not *your* slave. You will speak to me respectfully unless you want me to tell your father I found you out at this hour."

"You wouldn't. You'd have to explain why *you* were out."

She laughed. "I have a new baby. Babies cry. Sometimes, a walk in the fresh night air is the only thing that settles them. No one would question why *I* was out of bed at this hour."

"Fine. I'll stay away from Goody Sawyer."

"Good. Just get this out of your head, now. I know you've been put through the mill, but you have to accept life for what it is."

Sarah dropped her arms. "What's that?"

The witch kissed the top of her baby's head, her gaze still fixed on the girl. "Tragic with blinding flashes of beautiful happiness."

"If Tituba won't help me, I will help myself," Sarah whispered as she snuck into Goody Sawyer's bedroom through an open window. She quickly searched the room, making sure to put things back the way she'd found them before moving on to another drawer or cabinet. It was no use. There was nothing there that could help her. Crushed, she walked back to the window, resigned to her defeat. But, as she lifted a leg to climb back out, a floorboard creaked. She backed up and knelt down, lifting the board. Her eyes lit up at the discovery of a leather-bound book with a strange symbol on the front: a square with a vertical line cutting through the center of an X. She opened it to find page after page of chants, lists of ingredients, and odd symbols. "A spellbook," she muttered. She shoved the small book into her reticule, replaced the floorboard, and hopped out the window, hastily making her way to the woods to begin her studies.

The other girls laughed while Sarah used a stick to carve an inverted pentagram in the soft soil of the forest floor. All, except one.

"I think this is a bad idea," Elizabeth blurted as Sarah placed candles at each of the points. She began to light them, dismissing her friend's concerns.

"It's harmless, Lizzie. The book says I can summon him here and make him do my bidding. As long as we don't break the circle, he can't harm us."

Temperance took one last bite of her apple before tossing it to the ground. "I bet nothing happens at all."

"I hope you're right," Elizabeth said, nervously twirling her hair.

"It makes no difference what you think, as long as you recite the words exactly. The book says, 'Five voices speaking as one'. Do you all remember it?" The girls nodded, taking each other's hands around the symbol. "All right. Let's begin. Emergo nunc survus. Emergo nunc servus." The others joined in the chant, repeating the phrase over and over. After several minutes of nothing happening, Elizabeth let go.

"This is pointless."

"I agree," Temperance said, folding her arms. "The sun will set soon. We should get back."

"Please," Sarah begged. "Just a few more minutes." But, the girls were bored, letting go of each other's hands and casting pitiful glances her way.

"I'm sorry, Sarah," Caroline said, already walking away.

Ruth followed her. "Me, too, Sarah. I almost thought it might work."

Temperance patted Sarah's shoulder before joining the others.

"I'm sorry for your loss," Elizabeth told her. "But, it's probably for the best he didn't come. Any gifts given by the Devil would surely come at a price." She, too, left the clearing, leaving Sarah alone to hide what they'd been doing. She blew out the candles and hid them in the hollowed-out tree trunk before smoothing over the dirt, wiping out any trace of the symbol she'd drawn there just a few minutes before. She sat on the ground, head in hands as she wiped away a stray tear. Suddenly, she heard a twig snap. She popped her head up, hoping her friends had returned to try the spell again.

"Are you back?" But, no one answered. She stood, peeking through the trees in the direction of the sound of rustling leaves. "Hello?" When no response came, she turned to retrieve her bag but was stopped in her tracks by a vision of pure evil. It was a figure of a man, except it had no face, no clothes, and no color. It was as if a shadow had come to life. It stood before her, ominous and solid as the trees that surrounded her. Her hand flew to her chest as she struggled to get her breath, her heart beating so fast, she thought it would explode. As she looked over the strange figure, she whispered to herself, "It worked."

"I heard your call," the shadow hissed, its voice little more than a low growl.

"Can you bring my mother and sister back?" she blurted.

The figure tilted its head as dozens of snakes seemed to appear from nowhere, slithering over her shoes and around her ankles. She didn't scream, determined to remain in control of the situation. She ignored the creatures, steadying her breathing as the shadow drew closer. "That is your request?"

"Yes." She swallowed hard as the figure towered over her, the smell of rotted eggs emanating from it as it seemed to grow in size.

"I will do as you ask," it snarled. "But, what you want requires a sacrifice. The blood of a child. Bring me a child, and you will have what you desire." And, with that, it was gone. The snakes disappeared and Sarah was left with a decision to make.

Meanwhile, in the woods, the girls hurried to get home before dark. Caroline and Ruth skipped arm-in-arm while Temperance and Elizabeth followed. Elizabeth kept her head down as she walked, guilt creeping into her thoughts.

"Is it terrible that I'm glad nothing happened?"

"Terrible?" Temperance asked. "I don't think so. The Devil is *not* someone to toy with. Truth be told, though, I think it's all nonsense and superstition. Tituba is a slave deluding herself into thinking she has some control over her circumstances. Goody Sawyer is just bored."

"I hope that's true." They continued to walk as the sun got lower in the sky, carefree, having no reason to think they were in any danger. But, seeping up out of the earth appeared four dark figures. The stench of sulfur surrounded them as they slithered along the forest floor, each attaching itself to one of the girls. They screamed, the demons' touch like fire against their skin. The shadowy figures climbed up the girls' bodies as they tried to run, but the weight of the entities pulled them down to the ground as they covered them entirely. The shadows sank in, absorbing through their new hosts' skin, filling every organ, every cell with their wretched, foul essence.

They rose, wicked grins spreading across the faces of those who used to be Sarah's friends. They ran their hands over their new bodies, delighting in the flesh and the feeling of air moving through their noses and lungs. It had been ages since any of them had been on Earth and they were ready to have some fun.

Once in town, the demons went wild, pulling people's hair, tipping over wagons, and killing a horse with their bare hands. The townspeople fled, hiding in their homes and storm cellars, sure the girls had been possessed by the Devil. The four danced in the street, lifting their dresses over their heads and cackling.

"Such a spectacle," a voice came from the shadows. "You really should learn a bit of discretion. I had no trouble finding you at all."

"Jailer!" the one occupying Temperance howled. "You will not take us back!"

"But, I will," Lucifer said, stepping into the last light of the day. "I always do."

They ran, the one occupying Elizabeth racing back into the woods while the rest bolted toward the church. Lucifer followed the three into the building, shaking his head in derision. "It never ceases to amaze me how unimaginably stupid you demons are. You were out in the open. You could have scattered, maybe saved yourselves. But, you *chose* to be trapped. What was the logic in that decision? Baffling."

They backed away, their eyes wide with fear. "Leave us be, Lucifer!" the one in Ruth screeched. "We won't go with you!"

"Well," he smirked. "Not willingly, I imagine." He rushed them, placing a hand on one of their heads. But, before he could expel the demon, the others began fighting back, hitting him with Bibles and biting at his arms and chest. He rolled his eyes. "Fine. We'll do this the quick way, then." He slammed one demon onto the floor and tore its intestines out, blood spurting from its mouth and nose. He snapped another's neck and grabbed the last one by the hair, pulling it back and looking into its eyes. "As I said, I'll *always* take you back." He plunged his hand into the demon's chest and yanked out its heart, tossing it aside as the body fell. When all three demons had slipped out of their hosts and slithered their way back to their cages, Lucifer turned, sighing with regret to see a handful of parishioners hiding between the pews. He thought about addressing them, explaining what had happened, but there was still a demon out there and he had no time for coddling a few frightened humans. He left the church, on his way to finish the task at hand.

Back in the woods, the demon residing in Elizabeth became hysterical. It clawed at the ground, desperate to dig a hole big enough to hide in until Lucifer moved on, tricked into thinking it had kept running.

"Elizabeth?" Tituba called, coming upon her as she gathered evening primrose. "What are you doing out here in the dark?"

"Never you mind," the demon seethed, not looking up from its work.

The faint scent of sulfur hit Tituba's nose as she stopped, dropping her flower basket and gasping.

"Move along, witch," the demon hissed, still digging.

"I won't," she said, instead running up on the demon, grasping it by the head and yelling, "Apage ire in domum suam!"

Its eyes flew open wide as the inky shadow slowly tore away, sliding down to the ground and disappearing into the grass.

"Well, it looks as though you've done my job for me," Lucifer said. "I'm impressed. And, what might your name be, love?"

"Tituba Indian. And, you are?"

"Irrelevant, it would seem. Gratitude. Your assistance is much appreciated."

"Tituba?" the girl breathed, sitting up and rubbing her head. "What happened?"

"You just fainted, girl. Go on home now."

She nodded, getting up and walking away, casting Lucifer a suspicious glance as she passed.

In the distance, they could hear a baby crying. "Violet." Tituba ran toward the sound, Lucifer following out of sheer curiosity. They came to the clearing and there they found Sarah with the infant, stolen from her crib. "What are you doing, girl?"

"I'm sorry," Sarah said through tears. "He said he'd bring them back. I just had to give him..." She looked down at the crying child's face. "I have to."

"Subsisto," Tituba ordered, causing the girl to freeze where she stood. She took her baby back, rocking her as her crying quieted. "Who told you to do this?"

The girl was immobile but for her eyes and mouth. Fresh tears came as she said the words, "The Devil."

Lucifer guffawed.

Tituba gawked at him. "Why is that funny?"

He composed himself, unable to keep from smiling. "I can assure you, the Devil told her no such thing. He does not take children as payment for favors. The idea of it is absurd."

"It's true," Sarah insisted. "He--" She stopped, the egg smell returning. Snakes rose from the grass, slithering over their feet, wrapping themselves around their ankles as even the fireflies seemed to flee in panic.

The dark figure began to take form in front of them as Lucifer's expression turned cold. "Moloch."

"Take her," Tituba said, handing the baby to Lucifer.

"Take her? Are you so trusting? I am a stranger to you."

She looked into his eyes, seeing in a way others could not. "I have nothing to fear from you, Bringer of Light. Others may fear you, but I see your heart." She scurried to the hollowed-out tree trunk and rifled through books, candles, and potions. Finally, she got to a small, bronze statue of a man with the head of a cow, its seven chambers wide open.

"I should be fighting this beast, not babysitting. You have no idea what you're up against."

She gave him a condescending smile before setting her gaze on the figure. "Capti sunt vobis." The beast bellowed pained screams into the night as it was blown apart, reduced to ash, and sucked wailing into the statue. "Cinccino." The chambers locked, trapping the monster inside. She placed the statue back in the trunk, this time waving a hand over it, reciting the words, "Operimentum lutum," as dirt sprung from the ground, covering the trunk in two feet of earth.

Lucifer stared in awe, fascinated by the power this witch possessed. "Your mother's a force of nature," he whispered to the baby in his arms. "Perhaps, you'll grow up one day to be just as skilled. For the sake of humanity, I hope that you do." The child giggled and he smiled, finding a moment of peace in the infant's blissful ignorance.

"As for you," Tituba scolded, turning her attention back to Sarah. "What you did tonight was unforgivable. You can no longer be trusted with the power of speech. I am sorry, but I can not risk you doing something this feeble again. I must take your words, if for no other reason than to protect my daughter from your rampant stupidity."

"No!" Sarah yelped. "Tituba, please! I'm sorry!"

"Nec ultra addas loqui."

The girl mouthed the word 'please', but no sound came from her throat. She stared in horror at Tituba's stoic face, pleading with her eyes to give her voice back.

"Iam moveri," Tituba said, releasing the girl from her frozen position. She put her hand to her throat, silently screaming as tears streamed down her freckled cheeks. She ran away, leaving Tituba to take her daughter from Lucifer, bouncing her as she sighed. "I did not enjoy doing that."

"Yes, well, it needed doing," he told her. "That girl is a fool and would no doubt dabble in more things of which she has no business. I'd venture to say you did her a favor."

She looked him over, squinting as she made her assessment. "You and I are cut from the same cloth, I think."

He laughed. "My dear woman, you have no idea how wrong you are about that." But, as he walked her home, he couldn't help but feel a strange connection; a spark of hopeful peace between them. He could have been wrong, but if he wasn't mistaken, what he was feeling was the beginnings of friendship.

Chapter 1

Her scent was like oxygen as Will breathed her in, the sweet vanilla on her skin enveloping his senses as he kissed her neck and shoulder. Michelle moved beneath him, her hands on his back as their legs intertwined. Her breathing quickened as she climaxed, the feeling of air moving so quickly through her lungs frightening her as she hadn't experienced the sensation in months. When they were finished, he rolled to his side of the bed and her hand flew to her chest as she felt her heart beating much more rapidly than before.

"Something's wrong with me," she panted, sitting up.

He sprung up next to her and put a hand on her back. "What?"

"I don't know. I feel," her hand slid down to her lower abdomen. "I have to go to the bathroom. I have to go to the *bathroom*?" She got up and went to the restroom. A minute later, she came back, hands still wet from washing. Her eyes were like saucers as she held her stomach, her heart beating out of her chest. "I went to the bathroom."

"Uh, congratulations?"

She rolled her eyes. "*Vampires don't pee, Will.*" She went to the window and tentatively slipped her hand between it and the blackout curtains. The sun had come up just a few minutes before and its light should have cooked her skin like meat under a broiler, but it didn't. She pulled it back and looked at it, the shock on her face causing Will to stand. She looked at him, eyes wild, before pulling the curtain back and standing directly in front of the glass. Again, nothing happened. She was fine. "What the fuck?"

"Kinda giving the neighbors a show."

"Look at me!" She spun around, a cautious smile curling her lips.

"Oh, I'm looking," he said, putting his hand to his chin.

"Look outside, Will. It's *day*!"

As the post-coital fog lifted from his brain, he finally understood. "Are you..."

"GABRIEL!" she shouted, throwing a tee-shirt on and racing from their room to the angel's.

"What fresh hell?" Gabriel complained, rubbing her eyes and sitting up in bed.

"What am I?"

She gagged. "Oh, my Christ. You smell like semen. Please get out of here with that shit. You're gonna give me nightmares."

"That's my bad," Will said, buttoning his jeans as he joined them.

"I know it's your bad. That's my problem. You two really need your own place. This is not okay. Move into Tae's. It's just sitting there."

"Gabriel," Michelle bubbled, sitting in front of her on the bed.

She huffed, "I'm gonna have to burn this blanket."

"*What am I?*"

She folded her arms. "What do you me--" She stopped, tilting her head as it became clear. "Holy shit." She leaped out of bed, the strap of her satin nightgown falling off her shoulder. She replaced it and banged on the bathroom door where her girlfriend was taking a shower. "WENDY!"

Allydia basked in the early-morning sun, allowing herself to feel the warmth of it for the first time in thousands of years. The cool, early-fall air blew in through the open window, waking Wyatt from a dreamless sleep. She inhaled deeper than she had in millennia, not out of habit or emotional reaction, but because she needed to. She closed her eyes, her mind calm, and her soul at peace.

"What are you doing?" he asked, getting out of bed and standing behind her.

She smiled as he wrapped his arms around her. "Breathing."

"You have goosebumps."

She laughed, inspecting her arm. "I do! I don't know that that's ever happened before."

He kissed the side of her head and gazed out the window overlooking the courtyard as he rested his chin on her shoulder. "How do you feel?"

She rubbed his arm and stared up into the bright, cloudless sky. "Like myself. I feel more like myself than I have since the night I died. I am worried, though."

"About what?"

She closed the window and turned to face him, biting her lip and looking up at him with fear in her eyes. "I'm human now. Nothing special. The pheromones are gone. What if you come to discover that without them, you don't want me anymore?"

He tucked her hair behind her ear and touched her cheek. "First, human doesn't mean not special. You don't need superpowers to hold my interest and I definitely don't have to be drugged to want you." He took her face in his hands. "I love you...full stop. No more separations. No more doubts. It's me and you...the end, okay?"

She nodded and he kissed her, sliding his hands down her neck and shoulders. She pulled away and gasped, her hand flying to her stomach.

"What?" he asked.

"I'm hungry," she giggled. Her smile broadened. "Wyatt, I'm hungry! I can eat *food!*" She ran past him, making a beeline for the kitchen as he chuckled and followed. She stood in front of the open fridge pulling random things from it, having no idea what any of it tasted like or what ingredients went together. She gathered kiwi's, an orange, a block of cheddar, and two steaks. "What can I make with this?"

He laughed, taking the items and putting them back where they'd come from. "Nothing good if you mixed them all together." He gestured to the island. "Sit down, I'll make you something. What did you like to eat before?"

She sat. "Lentil soup, a lot of fruit. My favorite thing was flatbread I made with barley flour and water. I may still remember how to do it. Do you think I could find a millstone in working condition?"

"A *millstone*? I doubt it." He poured her a glass of orange juice and placed a kiwi in a bowl, cutting it in half and handing her a spoon. "Why don't you snack on that while I make some eggs and toast?"

She took a sip of juice, her eyes lighting up as she set the glass down and smacked her lips.

"What do you think?"

"Tart."

He snickered, placing bread in the toaster and cracking eggs into a pan. She dug her spoon into the flesh of the kiwi and took a bite. She put the spoon down and covered her mouth as she swallowed. He looked over at her as he whisked. "You okay?"

She reached for her juice. "I like the sweet part in the center." She took another sip and put it down, puckering her lips and squeezing her eyes shut. "Is all of your fruit so sour?"

He smiled, taking a banana from the bunch and handing it to her. She looked it over, her eyebrows scrunched. He laughed, taking it and peeling it for her before handing it back. She took a bite, raising her eyebrows in approval.

"Better?"

She nodded emphatically, swallowing, and taking another mouthful. He took two plates from the cabinet and spooned the scrambled eggs onto them before buttering the freshly popped-up toast. He slid a plate in front of her and handed her a fork before sitting and beginning to eat. She watched him and mimicked his movements, taking a bite of toast, then a forkful of eggs. "This is very good," she told him, pointing to the toast. "It's the butter. It used to take me half an hour to churn butter for the day. Now, you can just buy it. So convenient." They continued eating as he watched her, smiling to himself as he reveled in her happiness. In the entire time he'd known her, he'd never seen her so relaxed, so comfortable in her own skin. *This* was who she truly was and who she was always meant to be.

"Holy crap balls," Wendy said, Michelle's chin in her hand. "I guess I didn't know my own strength."

"What does that mean?" Gabriel asked, joining the others in the kitchen after throwing on a tee-shirt and pair of jeans.

"To do the spell to cure Allydia, I needed more power, so I absorbed my dead great-aunt's. She left it to me, it was purely consensual. Apparently, I didn't just take away Allydia's vampirism, I took away vampirism all together." She cringed, hoping no one would be too upset with her. "I feel really bad. I didn't mean to like, commit genocide."

"Did I hear 'genocide'?" Lucifer asked, emerging from his room, looking like a men's magazine cover model somehow first thing in the morning.

Gabriel threw him an orange.

"Thank you."

"She accidentally made all the vampires human."

"She did? Well done, Wendy, though I don't think that counts as proper genocide. Mutilation, maybe. We should celebrate. Perhaps young William can make us all a decent breakfast?"

Michelle's ears perked up. "Oh, my God, I've missed bacon so hard."

Will laughed. "On it."

Yo, B, Gabriel thought.

Yeah? He responded.

There's something Dia needs to know.

Chapter 2

The crow perched itself on the fire escape as Julia searched inside, rifling through drawers and looking over stacks of mail. She looked over the envelopes, the corner of her lip turning up in a satisfied smirk. "Wendy." Her locator spell had led her to this apartment, but the resident was nowhere to be found. She did, however, find the broken Catseye lying haphazardly on the floor, clearly discarded after its contents were purged. There was still a bit of blood smeared on its edge, a handy ingredient, so she pocketed the necklace and continued to look for anything else that might prove useful. As she opened the hall closet, she felt her sisters enter the building. She rushed to find anything else that might be of use, hoping to find something that would give her a clue about where the mystery witch might be, who her friends were, or where she worked. But, all she found in the closet were towels, blankets, and, sitting on the floor, a large trunk with a heavy-duty padlock. She knelt and held her hand over the metal lock. "Patefacio sursum." The lock broke and fell to the floor just as the other witches opened the door and came into the apartment. They were all there, the six remaining witches of her coven, not including Poe, who she was still livid about letting slip through her fingers. She stood to greet them, knowing full well the punishment she was about to receive. If Libby's message hadn't made it to them, Poe surely had. She would be marked a traitor, banned from coven gatherings of any kind for at least a month but up to a year while she proved her loyalty, doing menial spells and any other grunt work the coven deemed necessary. Her hope was that she could find this Wendy on her own and deliver her to the elders, thereby ensuring her place as not only a member of the coven but as its new leader.

"Julia," Donna said, stepping out in front of the others, all with their arms crossed, cold stares on each of their faces. "What have you found?"

"Nothing, yet," she lied. "Just this trunk. I just got the lock off."

"It's time for you to go, not just from this place, but from the coven."

"What? What do you mean?"

"We know what you did to Libby. We know that you corrupted two of our sisters. Your actions got *them* killed, as well. There is no redemption for what you've done."

"You don't understand. I was just trying to find Grace's magic. It belongs to us! I was just--"

"Enough," Donna boomed, her voice rattling the windows and causing a gust of wind to blow Julia's long red hair off her shoulders. "You have betrayed your coven, a crime from which there is no coming back."

"But--"

"Julia, you are shunned." They turned their backs to her, keeping their eyes on the wall as they waited for her to leave. Her stomach dropped, their abandonment like a death. She held a shaky hand to her diaphragm as she tried to steady her breathing, the loss like a kick to the chest. Tears puddled in her eyes as she made her way to the door. From the hall, she looked back at them, their eyes still averted. Donna began to close the door, leaving enough of an opening that Julia could still hear her. "If your thoughts turn to revenge, remember that we still have your measure."

The door slammed, leaving Julia truly alone for the first time in her life. She wiped her tears and took the Catseye from her pocket, rage replacing hurt as she put it back, more determined than ever to make Grace's magic her own.

Inside, Donna went to the trunk, opening it to find Wendy's supplies: Goofer dust, grave dirt, candles, a variety of crystals and herbs, and at the bottom, wrapped in a linen cloth, was a spellbook. She opened the leather-bound book, its weight heavy and size lumbering. She gasped, her eyes widening, her mouth hanging open.

"A grimoire?" Nicole asked.

"No," Donna said, her voice quivering as she ran her hand over the first page. "A book of shadows."

"Whose?"

She carefully re-wrapped it, gently putting it back where she'd found it. She stood and closed the closet door, her heart racing as she told the others, "Tituba's."

Her words were met with gasps, Nicole dropping the letter she'd picked up to learn the name of the person living there. "Are you serious?"

She steadied herself against the wall and nodded. "Grace said she'd had a sister, but that she died years ago. She never mentioned Eva having children."

"Wendy," Nicole said, picking up the envelope and showing it to her.

"A blood relative. A born-Tituban witch. Someone that can carry the power of her magic without being destroyed by it. Grace didn't *hide* her magic. She chose her heir. She gifted us with a new leader, as powerful as she was, if not more so. This Wendy has Tituba's original spells. All of her knowledge. The things she could teach us! Grace didn't betray us. *She saved us.*"

Julia stood outside the building, cloaked and waiting. After a while of pacing, she spotted Poe hurrying to the entrance. She bolted toward her, but Griffon got to her first, the bird knocking her down and clawing at her face. The girl screamed, trying to shoo it away, but it was relentless, scratching at the skin of her cheeks and forehead, drawing blood as it cawed. It finally flew off as Julia approached, giving Poe the chance to stand up. As she was brushing the street-dust off her pants, Julia grabbed her from behind, wrapping her arms around the girl so tightly, she could barely breathe. Julia snickered. "You're not the only one with a familiar willing to do their bidding. Come on. You and I need to have a chat. Domum." The crow flew over the now empty sidewalk, its talons dripping with blood. It squawked again as it took off in the direction of the place Julia had teleported to, leaving the witches still inside the building none the wiser.

Chapter 3

"Giovanni La Rosa," Navid muttered. After nearly an hour of sifting through hundreds of social media accounts under the name, he finally found the one associated with his father. His profile listed him as being fifty years old, originally from Catania, Sicily, now living and working in Edinburgh. "There you are, Dad." The picture in the profile was unnerving. Navid covered his mouth as he noticed the similarities in their faces. Their cheekbones, smiles, and noses all matched. He felt like he was looking into his own future, one with a black jumper, a glass of red wine, and salt-and-pepper hair. Looking closer, he realized he recognized the restaurant the photo had been taken in. The blue, high-back chairs were a dead giveaway. He'd been there a few years before. He'd had the Cullen skink and a Blood, Smoke, and Sand. Had they crossed paths and never known it?

As he scrolled down the page, he noticed something strange. Every picture on his dad's timeline was of him with a different woman, all beautiful, and all at least twenty years younger than him. The captions read, *With Samantha at the park* and, *Beach day with Ingrid.* In one, he'd written, *Scuba diving with Holly and Sabine,* except they were very obviously in someone's flat and through the window in the background he could see that it was snowing. "Oh, that's just not right." He clicked on the "friends" list and noticed immediately that every person he was following was a gorgeous woman. "At least they're all adults." He closed the laptop and sat back in his chair, staring at the top of the computer like it had offended him somehow. He tapped his fingers on it, mulling over if he should reach out or not. Just as he was about to reopen the computer to run a background check, a knock came on the door. He went to the kitchen and grabbed a butcher knife before opening it. "Oh, hello." He stepped aside, letting a frantic Hartley in and closing the door behind her. "Apologies for the knife," he said, putting it back where he'd gotten it. "Can never be too careful, some of your lot wanting me dead and all."

"Where's the queen?" she asked, stomping through the apartment, poking her head in every room.

"Not here. Said she had somethin' to do last night. Hey, how are you out in the daylight?"

"That was *my* question." She paced the floor, her hands trembling as she checked her phone. "It's dying. Perfect."

"There's a charging station on the kitchen counter. You're free to use it."

"I know where it is." She marched to the kitchen and slammed her phone on the charging pad, trying desperately to control her anxiety. But, her heart felt like it was going a mile a minute and for the first time since the Civil Rights Era, she was sweating. "Look at me," she snapped, opening the fridge, ignoring the blood bags still hanging inside and taking a bunch of grapes. "Look at this crazy shit." She shoved several in her mouth and ate them, dropping the rest onto the counter.

"I'm sorry, miss, but you're gonna have to give me more to go on."

"I'm *human*."

"Ah. I did notice you look a little different. Wasn't gonna say nothin' as not to offend. A little more color in the cheeks. Still very pretty, just a wee less menacing."

"Are you hitting on me?"

"No, oh, God, sorry! I didn't mean to make you uncomfortable."

"You didn't, I just don't think you know..." She folded her arms and squinted as she found the words. "I'm pretty sure you're straight and I'm carrying a little more baggage than the girls you're used to." She looked down at herself and back up at him.

He arched an eyebrow as the front door flew open.

"Hartley, are you all right?" Allydia said, coming in and giving her assistant a once-over. "I tracked your phone. How do you feel?"

"How did this happen?" She looked at her queen, realizing she, too, was no longer a vampire.

"A witch did a spell, removing the original one that turned me. I didn't think it would affect anyone else."

"Well, it did. It affected *everyone else*. Oliver, the diplomats, Phindi, and the rest. We're *all* human."

Navid nodded to his grandmother and went to the living room, giving the women some privacy.

Allydia brushed her assistant's cheek. "You look flushed. Are you hurt?"

"No, I'm just freaking out! I don't know how to be," she waved a hand over the length of her body. "*This*."

"It's an adjustment."

"I'm weak. Look how thin I am! Someone could snap me like a dry twig. How will I survive?"

"Strength isn't in size, Hartley. It's in discipline. If you're concerned about your safety, take a self-defense class. Krav Maga or Jiu-Jitsu."

"I mastered both of those decades ago, at your instruction."

"Oh, that's right. Well, you see then, you have nothing to fear."

"I'm a trans woman in America. I'd be insane *not* to be afraid."

"Then, do as the humans do. Carry mace, don't go out alone after dark, and if someone attacks you, yell 'fire' instead of 'rape' or 'help' because people will be more likely to assist you."

"That's incredibly depressing."

"Yes. We may have been predators in our time, but humans can be the most evil creatures on Earth. You'll have to be careful now, but you will be fine."

She took a deep breath and nodded, taking her phone from the charger and slipping it into her back pocket. "I'll let everyone know."

"Thank you. But, Hartley, I'm no longer your queen. You are free. Do whatever you wish. Live your life the way you see fit. Go to the beach, watch a sunrise. Have fun and be happy."

"I'll try, Your," she stopped herself. "*Allydia*. That'll take some getting used to." She left, feeling only slightly calmer than she had when she'd arrived.

"How are you feeling?" Allydia asked, entering the living room where Navid sat at the computer.

"Better. So, vampires have gone extinct?"

"It would appear so."

"I hate to bring this up, but isn't that exactly what Judas wanted?"

She shot him a look and folded her arms.

"Sorry."

"Have you eaten?"

"Yeah, your angel friend had a boatload of groceries sent over. The freezer in there is full of ice cream in flavors I've never heard of. One has a picture of a late-night chat show host on the package with bits of waffle cone already mixed in. It's incredible. Remind me to thank her properly if I ever see her again."

She gave him a knowing look.

"What?"

"Even if she wasn't taken, she would never be good enough for you."

"What are you on about? I wasn't..."

She raised her eyebrows.

"And what do you mean, 'not good enough'? She's a bloody angel. There's literally nothing better than that."

"Gabriel isn't a *bad* person, she's just...preoccupied. Her loyalty is to her Father. Her siblings come second and while I can tell she holds a deep affection for the woman she's seeing, she will always be last on her list of priorities. God's Messenger will always put her duty first. As it should be, of course, but you deserve to be someone's whole world."

"That's sweet of you to say, Gran, but--"

"Did you just call me 'Gran'?"

"Uh, yeah, sorry. It just seems disrespectful to call you by your given name, seein' as how you're my ancestor and all. Is it too weird?"

"It's a little weird."

"Right, yeah, sorry."

"I like it, though. It makes me feel important. After giving up my kingdom, it's nice to feel connected to someone, like I matter."

"Of course you matter," he said standing up and looking her in the eye. "Aside from a sleazy womanizing father across the pond, you're the only family I've got. Don't think for a second that you don't matter, especially to me."

She smiled. "Thank you, Navid." She looked behind her in the direction of the kitchen and back at him. "Now, tell me more about this ice cream."

Chapter 4

Poe fought to break free of her mullein prison, but the more she struggled against the thick stalks woven around her, the tighter they became, eventually squeezing so hard around her abdomen that she could hardly breathe.

"Arctius," Julia said, summoning more flowers to bind her arms to her sides. The watchful eyes of the coven would have made interrogating the girl impossible in the city. Now, though, in the seclusion of Grace's cottage in Tarrytown, Julia was free to do what was necessary to get the information she needed, no matter how unpleasant the method may be. "Who's Wendy?"

"Like I'd tell *you*," Poe shot back.

She sighed and folded her arms, tapping her foot on the soft grass. "Bestiola." Scurrying from all directions, thousands of ants, beetles, and spiders made their way to Poe who stood helpless, tangled in a web of yellow and green. They crawled up her legs and over the rest of her body, so many in number that she could hear them as they moved. But, even as her heart pounded in her chest, she remained defiant.

"Bugs?" she mocked. "They're harmless. Your torturing skills are severely lacking, bitch."

Julia furrowed her brow. "Mures inclusi essent."

"Oh, shit," Poe whispered as hundreds of rats burrowed out from underground and sped toward her. They climbed up her legs, the weight of them so heavy that she fell onto her back. They swarmed her, nipping at her nose and earlobes. She tried again to get out of her entanglement, but it was no use. Julia's magic was stronger than hers. "I'll never tell you!" she shouted through the deafening squeaks of the earth-covered rats. "You'll never find her!"

Julia's patience had worn thin. She watched as the vermin ate away at the girl's skin, tapping her fingers on her arm as she pondered her next move. "Nice of you to join," she said as the crow landed on the fence to her left. It squawked as if in response and fluttered its wings. "If she won't talk, should I just kill her?" It squawked again. "That's what I think, too. Arctius." This time, a six-foot stalk curled around Poe's neck, choking the life from her in a slow and steady fashion. "Tell me again how my torturing skills are lacking."

The young witch's heart beat out of control as her face began to turn blue. Her eyes rolled back in her head and the morning sunlight grew dim as consciousness faded. The sound of the rats and insects disappeared. Even her heartbeat, which was like thunder in her ears a moment before was gone, replaced by the sound of an unfamiliar woman's voice, her heavy German accent making her words almost unintelligible to the girl on the brink of death.

"Wake up, Enkelin," the voice demanded. "This witch can not best you. She is *weak* where *you* are *strong*."

Who are you? she thought. *Am I hallucinating?*

"I am the source of your power, Enkelin. Take all of it, everything I have, and rise up. Become the witch you were meant to be."

Color came back to her face as she gasped for air, the rats and insects fleeing from her as if she were a sinking ship. The flowers, too, loosened and recoiled, freeing her from her floral coffin.

"What the..." Julia muttered.

Poe steadied her breathing as her eyes glowed emerald green, realizing who the mystery voice had belonged to, the words slipping from her no longer scratchy throat. "Merga Bein." In one quick motion, she was on her feet, her combat boots sinking into the soil farther than they should have for a girl as slight as she.

Julia looked on in horror as Poe stepped toward her, her calm, deliberate movements making her stomach flip. "That's why Grace was so obsessed with you," she panted. "You're a descendant of one of the most powerful witches of all time. She brought you in to strengthen the coven, so she could leave her magic to this Wendy person. Who is she? How is she related to Grace? Where is she?!"

Poe stared, her shimmering eyes causing a lump to form in Julia's throat. She swallowed it, doing her best to appear unafraid...and failing. The young witch raised her arms at her sides and held them there for a moment before clapping her hands together, sending a shock wave in her kidnapper's direction, knocking her back all the way from the garden through the back door of the house. She broke through the screen door and fell onto her back, the window above the sink shattering from the force of the sonic boom. She sat up, giving a puzzled glance to the rabbit sitting on the table looking unbothered as it continued to eat from a food dish. She hurried to her feet and rushed to the living room and out the front door where she found Poe waiting, eyes still sparkling. Julia nearly fell over at the sight of the girl.

"Supernatet," Poe said, her voice like a razor through the air. Julia gasped as she was lifted from the ground, made to hover as Poe moved closer.

The teenager raised her hand, but before she could complete the spell, Julia yelped, "Alio!" and disappeared, teleporting off to who knows where leaving Poe alone with her new-found strength.

Phindi sat uncomfortably in the seat of the plane, the cursed sun mocking her through the small window as she stared ahead, unwilling to give it even a second of her attention. After getting Hartley's call and learning of the queen's abandonment, her remaining soldiers fled from the citadel, excited to begin their new lives as humans. Gifted with the queen's riches, they ventured out on their own, relishing their sudden freedom and bathing in the light of the nearest star that would have broiled them alive not twenty-four hours earlier. They disgusted her, their willingness to let this injustice stand confounding and aggravating her. The fiercest warriors on Earth, now relegated to mediocrity. She was livid, but more than that, she felt betrayed. Hartley had explained that the queen only meant to shackle *herself* to mortality, that the rest of them being dragged into the muck along with her was an accident of an over-zealous witch. But, that made her treachery even worse. She meant to leave them, cast them aside in favor of an ill-conceived human life. *Human.* It was absurd. The longer she sat there, the angrier she became, the mingling smells of the other passengers' meals making her stomach turn. She had no plan for what she'd do when she landed on the queen's doorstep. She hadn't thought it through and was still having trouble forming a cohesive sentence, let alone a plan of action. She only knew she wanted to cause her former queen pain. She wanted to hurt her, directly and with her bare hands. She wanted to make her suffer.

Chapter 5

Wendy opened the door to her apartment to find a group of women waiting for her inside. She could feel their power before she'd entered the building and immediately recognized them as some of the witches that attended her great-aunt's funeral. "Grace's coven," she said, closing the door behind her and dropping her keys on the coffee table.

"How did you know that?" one of them asked. "What am I saying? *Of course,* you knew."

Another stood from her spot on the sofa, trembling as she slowly approached. She was older than the rest as evidenced by her crow's feet and the wisps of gray that framed her face. Wendy was made uncomfortable by the intensity with which the woman stared at her, the hope in her eyes perplexing. "You look just like her."

Wendy took a step back. "Is that why you're staring so hard? Because it's creepy."

"I'm sorry," the woman said, blinking a few times. "You just look so much like Grace. It's uncanny. I'm Donna. This is Nicole, Linda, Ashley, Melissa, and Stephanie."

She looked over the group, all sitting politely with hands folded in their laps, their expressions ranging from shocked to anticipatory. The one called Stephanie, a woman in her early twenties, was visibly shaking while Melissa looked to be on the verge of tears. "Why are you here?"

"We felt Grace's magic and tracked it. We thought we'd find it here, but only the residue remained. Why can't I feel it on you? You're Wendy, Grace's niece, right?"

"Grand-niece. I won't give you her power. It would kill you. I'm sorry, I can feel that you're all powerful witches, but this would definitely leave you a drooling mess."

"Oh, of course, no, we don't want to take it." She looked back at her sisters who gave her an approving nod. She took a shaky breath before addressing her again. "We're asking you to join our coven. Not only join, but lead us as our Priestess."

She scoffed. "You're joking."

Donna looked puzzled. "We found Tituba's book of shadows in your closet. We know how powerful you are."

"You what now?" She stomped to the closet and dug through her belongings until she found the book, flipping through the pages until she was sure it was intact.

"We didn't steal anything," Donna promised.

"We wouldn't dare," She heard Nicole murmur.

She replaced the book and closed the closet door, furrowing her brow as she turned back to look at the women. "You broke in here, went through my stuff, and now you want me to join your coven? What if I hadn't taken Grace's magic into me? If it was still in the Catseye, what would you have done? Steal it? Try to activate it yourselves?"

The ladies shifted in their seats as Donna wrung her hands. "W-w-we'd have done the same thing," she stammered. "Find out who you were and then wait. We are a peaceful coven. We only wanted to know why Grace hid her magic from us. Now, we understand. She left it to a blood relative. It makes perfect sense. She chose you to lead us."

"Lady, I'm not sure she even knew I existed. She probably just wanted to keep you all from getting yourselves killed."

Donna looked hurt by the assertion but held her composure. "Either way, you are the last born-Tituban witch. This coven is yours...if you'll have it."

Wendy sighed. "Listen, guys, you seem like a lovely group of chicks. Maybe a touch Stepford, but aside from the whole breaking-and-entering thing, probably perfectly nice. But, I've never been part of a real coven, let alone been one's Priestess. I can see how important this is to you, but, I'm sorry. I'm not your girl."

Donna's posture straightened and her face went hard. "Very well. Let's go, ladies." She turned and led the others single-file out the door. Tears now flowed down Melissa's cheeks as she took one last look at Wendy before closing the door behind her.

Wendy folded her arms, chewing on her bottom lip as she weighed her options, knowing there really were none. "Son of a bitch." She went into her bedroom and grabbed a suitcase, opening it up and throwing clothes inside. She knew she'd never be safe there now that her identity had been discovered. If Grace's coven didn't attack her, another would. Tituban magic was too tempting. She'd have to abandon the apartment, maybe change her name. She'd have to stay with Gabriel for a few days until she got settled. She'd been spending most nights at her place, anyway. "Shouldn't be a problem."

She whipped her head around at the sudden banging on the front door. She zipped the suitcase and sleuthed to the living room, feeling the immense power coming from the witch waiting in the hall. She looked out the peephole and saw Poe nervously looking behind her. She opened the door and pulled her in, slamming it closed and locking it before heading back to the bedroom where she took another suitcase from the closet and began filling it.

"Hey, Poe. Your coven was just here, rifling through my shit. Looks like I'm going on the lam."

"The coven? Was Julia with them?"

"Who? No, no one named Julia. Donna, Nicole,"

"Are you sure? Julia wasn't here?"

"You okay, Poe? You look flushed. Also, did you get like, nine-thousand times more powerful since the last time I saw you?"

"Probably over nine-thousand. We have to go. *Now.*"

"That's why I'm packing."

"No. *Right now.* Julia just tortured me in my own backyard trying to get information about you. If the coven was here without her, that means she's probably been shunned. They must know about her killing Libby and--"

"Wait, wait, wait. That was a lot of what-the-fuck keywords just then. Torture? Killing? Who's Julia?"

"She's been trying to find Grace's magic. She wanted to take over the coven, but if they kicked her out,"

"She'll want it for herself."

"Exactly." Poe looked out the window to the street, making sure she hadn't been followed. "I tried to warn you about her, but your friend sent me away."

"What friend?"

"The psychic one. Brown hair, fancy boots, knew where I get my magic from. She was here when I came by before. Gave me *a million dollars* so I could get out of town. Probably saved my ass."

Wendy's cheeks went hot. "Would it be okay if I stay with you for a few days?"

"Sure. Are you allergic to rabbits?"

"No."

"Cool. Let's go."

She took Tituba's book of shadows from the closet and shoved it in a suitcase before zipping it. "I just have a stop to make first."

Gabriel laughed out loud. "Over nine-thousand. That's *hysterical.*"

Wendy stormed into her girlfriend's apartment, Poe trailing behind, carrying both suitcases.

"Wendy," Lucifer greeted from the couch, putting his newspaper down. "Who's your friend?"

Wendy leaned against the island and crossed her arms. "Poe, Lucifer. Lucifer, Poe."

Poe dropped the luggage. "Not like *Lucifer,* Lucifer, right?"

"The one and only," he smirked.

"Holy shit."

"You're mad," Gabriel said, pushing Wendy's hair behind her ear. She smacked her hand away.

"Yeah, I'm mad. You should have told me about Julia when you found out. She tortured Poe. You should have--"

"My brother died that night!" Gabriel shot back, her eyes widening in anger and confusion. "I couldn't handle it if something happened to you. I was trying to protect you."

"I don't need protection. I've been taking care of myself for a long time. You shouldn't have hidden it from me."

"Like you hid New Zealand? Or your side hustle as a one-stop-shop problem solver for witches? You lied to protect yourself. How can you be mad when *I* was trying to protect you, *too*?"

"That was *my* secret to keep. This is different. People have died. Poe almost died. More people could *die*."

"Yeah, people like *you*! After what happened to Cam, I couldn't risk it."

"I'm sorry about your brother, you know I am. But, you can't hide things from me, especially witch stuff. I know it's not saving-the-world shit like you're used to, but it *is* life and death. So, I'm gonna go figure out how to deal with this Julia thing, and then...I don't know."

"You don't know about what?"

She pursed her lips. "Us. I need some time to think." She spun on her heel and left the apartment, Poe picking up the bags and scurrying behind.

"That was a bit melodramatic," Lucifer said, getting up and walking to the door, closing it as he looked back at his sister who'd gone pale, her lip quivering as she stared into nothing. "Sister," He hesitantly moved closer as he noticed the blender and toaster beginning to shake on the counter. Her breathing quickened as things around the room began to float. The remote, his paper, even the ottoman lifted from its spot on the floor. "Gabriel, I believe you're losing control of your powers. Let's take some deep breaths, shall we?"

He was right. She had lost all control. She squeezed her eyes shut as the sound of his thoughts pounded in her head like a TV at full volume. The downstairs neighbors' thinking about where they should go for lunch filled her brain with images of burgers, sandwiches, and fries. She was bombarded by emotions from all directions. It was impossible to tell which were hers and which were other people's. It was like she was a teenager again, the sensory overload too much for her mind to take. She shook as an argument from a couple on the street several stories below boomed in her head. She started to hyperventilate as she fell to her knees. She could feel the heat rising in her chest as her skin began to glow. Tears sprung from her eyes as she opened them, seeing the worried look on her brother's face. He was too close. As her tears evaporated from the heat, she was able to scream out a single word of warning. "RUN!" Bar stools, the sofa, and the refrigerator all floated up from the floor. Kitchen drawers flew open, sending silverware flying. A butter knife implanted itself in Lucifer's leg. He pulled it out, dropping it to the ground as the bedroom doors burst open, blankets and pillows being thrown into the hall where picture frames fell, smashing onto the hardwood. Lucifer's eyes grew wide as he saw Gabriel's hair float up. She screamed, throwing her head back as appliances and furniture crashed to the floor and her body was engulfed in flames. He flew back, shielding himself behind the island, avoiding the initial blast. She continued to scream through the plumes of smoke and fire as Lucifer peeked over the counter. When he was sure it was safe, he rushed to open the kitchen window, pulling in a gust of wind strong enough to put out the flames. It knocked her into the hall where he followed, covering her charred skin in a comforter as she healed.

"I'm sorry," she panted.

He knelt next to her, picking up a shard of glass and tossing it aside. "I've never seen you so upset. I'm by no means an expert on heartbreak, but does it really justify suicide by Holy Fire?"

"It was an accident," she grunted, standing up and going to her room where she threw on some non-burned-to-ashes clothes. She put her hand to her temple as she winced, the thoughts and feelings of others still ringing in her overworked mind. She emerged from her room, hopping on one foot as she put her boots on. She passed her brother and found her phone on the kitchen floor. The screen was only a little cracked, so she put it in her pocket and headed for the door.

"Gabriel," Lucifer called after her. She stopped to look at him. "She will come to her senses."

She nodded, having no idea if he was right, but appreciating the sincerity in his tone all the same. "I'm going out." She left, closing the door behind her harder than she intended to.

He leaned on the island and shook his head. "Well, nothing good can come from that."

Chapter 6

Michelle breathed in the late-morning air as the sun warmed her skin. The early-autumn breeze blew through her curls as she watched Will come back to the park bench, two ice cream cones in hand. He offered her one and sat, looking out at the sea of people going about their day in the park, walking dogs, playing Frisbee, and having picnics. By the time Michelle had taken two bites, he was nearly finished. She held hers out to him, still full from the massive breakfast he'd prepared for her earlier.

"Are you sure?" he asked.

"I'm not hungry."

He took it, happily eating as she smiled at him.

"I never asked, how do you like the city?"

He swallowed his last bite and put his arm around her. "Jury's still out. It's definitely different than Southport. Louder. And, there's a smell."

"Garbage mixed with cooking street food," she told him. "You get used to it."

"Hmm."

"I feel like I should tell you something."

His heart jumped as he turned to face her.

"When I was a," she glanced around before whispering, "Vampire," She cleared her throat. "I did some things."

He took a deep breath, fearing the worst. "Things? Like, with dudes?"

She scrunched her eyebrows and tilted her head. "Dudes?"

"I mean, I'll understand. I was dead, so,"

"What? No, I didn't," She looked around again. "I didn't *sleep* with anyone. I meant like, violent things. Last night, when I was on my walk, a guy was trying to kill some girl, so I," She covered her mouth, fearful of what he'd think of her once he knew the truth.

He put his hand on her knee. "You protected her?"

"Yeah," she said, covering his hand with hers. "Yeah, but,"

"But, nothing. You saw someone that needed help and you helped them. I can't fault you for that."

"There was another time, in Southport, when I was hiding from Allydia. That guy from the bowling alley tried to kidnap me off the street and I," Tears welled in her eyes. "What I did to him was--"

"I don't care."

She looked confused. "You don't care?"

"No. That guy was a monster. If you hadn't stopped me, I would have killed him myself that night. Besides, you weren't yourself. I know you'd never hurt anyone on purpose as a human."

"How can you be sure?"

He wiped away her tears. "Because you're crying just thinking about it."

She laughed and held his hand, kissing the back of it before taking a serious tone. "You know I don't blame you for the things you did before, either, right?"

"I know," His eyes darkened as he thought about the donut shop burning, the smell of his father's smoldering flesh, and the look on his grandfather's face as he died. "But, I do."

"You weren't right, Will."

"No, I wasn't. But, I thought I was. I thought I was doing the right thing, burning down the town, killing my dad. I really believed I was saving them...from me. Gabriel's girlfriend swears she fixed me, but there will always be this part of me that won't believe it. I'll never be able to trust my own judgement. Not fully."

She touched his cheek and gave him a reassuring smile. "I'll just have to keep an eye on you, then." He smiled back and kissed her, relaxing his shoulders as her lips soothed him, still hardly able to believe that he was lucky enough to be loved by someone as amazing as her.

"Allydia's not here," Navid said, stepping aside to let Gabriel in. His heart skipped a beat when he saw her, so he averted his glance, hoping not to make an ass of himself. "She's off at her bloke's."

"Don't care." She hurried past him, opening kitchen drawers and cabinets, rummaging through them before moving on to the hall closet.

"Hey, I wanted to say thanks for all the food. It was very kind of you. What are you lookin' for?" he asked as she slammed it shut.

"Where'd she put it?"

"What?"

She went to the living room, looking under couch cushions and putting her hands on her hips when it seemed her search had been fruitless. "The drugs. She used to keep all kinds, not that she ever did them. Just in case she had a guest that wanted to partake, you understand. She must have gotten rid of them before she invited you to stay because, you know," she gestured to him. "Cop."

"Detective, but fair enough."

She shut her eyes, the sound of other people's thoughts like a punch to the head.

"Are you all right?"

She squinted, the sensory overload making it hard to focus. "No."

"Do you need to go to hospital?"

She laughed. "They wouldn't know what to do with me."

"Would you like some tea? I have Chamomile, Earl Grey, Assam,"

She took a closer look at him, his feelings beginning to drown out the noise from the street and surrounding apartments. "You're worried about me."

"Well, yeah. You come in here, turnin' the place upside down hunting for drugs, obviously in some kinda pain. Anyone right in the head would be."

"You'd be surprised." She gawked at him, his genuine concern for her well-being helping to settle her mind even as it confused her.

"Now, you're the one starin'."

"Sorry, I'm just not used to people, you know, giving a shit."

"I find that hard to believe."

"I'm sorry I freaked you out, storming in here like that. My girlfriend dumped me and I kind of lost it. Maybe dumped? Not sure."

His mouth fell open. "Is she daft?"

She couldn't help but take offense. "No."

"I mean, pardon my sayin', but you're stunnin', not to mention the powerful angel bit. I don't care if she *is* a mega-powerful witch, she's lucky to have your attention. Bird must be off her trolley."

"Dude, don't flirt with me right now. I will climb you like Everest."

He was taken aback, swallowing hard as he tried not to appear nervous. "I thought you were gay."

"Pan."

"Oh." He raised his eyebrows, holding his hands in front of himself as he tried to will away his growing erection. "And, you know everything about me? How I'm feelin'?"

"Yeah."

"Well, *that's* not embarrassin'."

She eyed him like a wild animal, unsure of where his emotions ended and hers began. His desire became her own as she was overwhelmed, not by the thoughts of others, but by her sudden attraction to him. She looked down at his hands and back up at him. "You've got *nothing* to be embarrassed about."

His heart beat faster as he took a step back, his legs bumping into the sofa. "I'm trying very hard not to kiss you."

She closed the space between them, the smell of his cologne enveloping her senses. Her forehead brushed his cheek as he bit his lip. She closed her eyes. "I shouldn't let you."

"It's inappropriate, yeah?"

"Very." She looked up at him again, putting her fingertips to his chin before standing on her tiptoes and kissing him. He closed his eyes, letting his hands wander to her waist. As their kissing grew in intensity, he wrapped his arms around her, pulling her close. She tore his shirt off and pushed him down onto the couch before climbing on top of him and throwing her own shirt to the floor. "Bro, I am gonna worship that D like it's a fucking deity." She kissed him again, removing her bra and dropping it to the floor. She slid her hands over his chest, up to his neck, and back down again while he ran his over her thighs as they straddled him. "Mm," she grunted as her mind began to clear. She grabbed his face and pushed away, sighing as she debated. "Probably a bad idea, right?"

"The worst," he agreed, going in for another kiss. She held back.

"See, normally when I'm upset, I jump on the nearest dick and ride it until I calm down. But, you're not looking for a casual hook-up. You're a decent dude. I'd just be using you for your body, and you deserve better."

"I'm all right with it. Use me. Use me all day."

She laughed and stood. "Sorry, but there might still be a chance I can fix things with Wendy but there definitely won't be if I do, you know, you." She felt bad for him, sitting there all worked up with nowhere to go. She sighed. "Give me your phone."

"What for?" He took it from his pocket and handed it over.

She took a picture of herself from the neck down and tossed it back to him. "Here. For the spank bank." She put her clothes back on and left, making sure the door was locked to give him some privacy.

Navid sat alone, his heart still beating out of control, beads of sweat on his temples. "Well, that was...somethin'." He looked down at his phone and shrugged, setting it on the arm of the sofa and unzipping his pants.

Outside, Gabriel was again bombarded by noise. The thoughts of pedestrians, cab drivers, and bike messengers all flooded her brain. She needed a quiet place. She needed her brother.

While Allydia took a nap in his bedroom, Wyatt made a list of things he thought might make her more comfortable as she got re-acclimated to human life. Sunglasses, sweaters, and the ice cream she'd told him she recently discovered. He planned to surprise her with the gifts, but as he was about to leave, Gabriel burst through the door, flying into his arms and sobbing into his chest. He held her close and rubbed her back. "What happened?"

"Shh," she ordered, letting the sound of his heartbeat, strong and steady, drown out the other noises in her head. She was shaking, so he smoothed the back of her hair and kissed the top of her head.

"Okay," he whispered, resting his cheek on her head. "You're okay."

Chapter 7

The crow perched itself on top of the dilapidated cabin as Julia stepped off of Moll Dyer Road and trekked the rest of the way through the woods to meet him. Outside, the cabin looked as if it had been left to rot since 1697. The wood was grayed and crumbling. Even the grass surrounding the building had been dead so long, only a few brown and yellow blades sprung from the dry soil. She knew, though, that this was the preferred meeting place of the Dyer coven, one of the oldest and most powerful covens in the country. Leonardtown was steeped in their history and Julia hoped to enlist the sisters in her effort to take Grace's magic by force. She would offer to join them, bringing that power with her, strengthening their coven even more, making them a force to be reckoned with beyond their wildest imaginations. She went over the pitch in her head as she prepared to knock on the door, Griffin's impatient squawking distracting her from her thoughts. "Pipe down," she hissed, closing her eyes and taking a deep breath. The bird went quiet and she cracked her neck, taking one final shaky breath before rapping on the door.

An African-American woman answered, the scowl on her face making Julia's heart leap to her throat. She was tall in stature with broad shoulders and striking features. Her lumbering presence accompanied by the massive amount of power flowing from her was intimidating, to say the least. Julia felt like a child before her at five-three and a hundred and twenty pounds. She could feel her freckled cheeks blush as she nervously tried to remember her speech.

"Well, come on in, then," the woman huffed, stepping aside as she walked through and closing the door behind her. Inside was a different universe, a small palace of marble-covered floors and gold-lined walls. Eleven more women filled the room lit brightly with crystal chandeliers that seemed to glow of their own accord. *A full coven*, she thought. They wouldn't need another member. Still, she was sure they'd want her once they heard what she was offering.

"A witch," the first woman informed the others. They looked her over, some with interest, others with derision.

"Mediocre at best," a blonde in the corner assessed.

"Teleportation powers," another said. "Seems handy."

"She reeks of desperation," a middle-aged brunette dismissed.

"You've been shunned," an older woman determined, approaching her with a skeptical glare. "I can smell it all over you. Who were you with? Too weak to be a Gowdie. Too white to be a Laveau. You a Kyteler heir? I thought they stopped practicing in what, the eighteen hundreds?"

"Yes, I am and they did," she answered, painfully aware of all the eyes on her. "I was with the Tituban coven in New York."

"Grace's coven?" the older woman asked, her eyebrows raised.

She's impressed, Julia thought. *I'm in.* She nodded.

"I heard about your Priestess. My condolences."

"Thank you. That's why I'm here."

"Is it? Because from where I'm standing, it looks like you're here to find a new coven to take you in."

"Well, yes, ma'am, but I don't come empty-handed. Grace hid her magic from the rest of us. I tracked it to an apartment in Tribeca where it had been claimed by an outsider."

"That's not possible," the woman argued. "The only way someone from outside the coven would have access to a fallen Priestesses' magic would be if..." She stepped back. "*A blood relative?*"

Julia nodded. "I'm offering to join our covens, once I take Grace's over. I have a bit of the witch's blood. I can use it to track her and siphon the magic from--"

"Are you out of your mind?!" she laughed, the other women in the room looking shocked as they, too, held back nervous laughter. "If there's a blood-born Tiutuban witch carrying Grace's magic on top of her own, you should run and hide, not plot war with your coven."

She clenched her jaw, speaking as calmly as she could through gritted teeth. "Grace's magic belongs to the coven. If they won't take me back, her power will be *mine*. I need allies."

"Girl, what you need is a psych evaluation. I knew Grace. We tussled back in the day. The amount of power she wielded would crush you under its weight. *If* you *somehow* shook it free of the Ttuban witch, it would *boil you alive.* I would advise you to forget about this, but you seem set, so I'll ask you to take your leave...and don't come back."

She held her hand out as if to say 'stop', sending Julia sliding back to the reopened door and out onto the porch. The door slammed in front of her, dashing her hopes as she heard the clacking of three locks latching. From the roof, the crow squawked and flapped its wings.

She turned and stomped back toward the road. "Shut up, Griffin."

Every witch in North America worth her salt knew the story of Isobel Gowdie. After a torture-forced confession in Auldearn, she'd tricked her executioners into hanging and burning the long-dead body of a local child in her place. The boy had died of fever, his corpse buried on the outskirts of Nairn for fear of contamination. It had been easy to dig him up and apply the glamour. Once everyone was convinced she was dead, Isobel fled to The New World where she used maleficium to coerce the founder of Providence to grant her asylum. By the next summer, she'd formed a new coven, using blood magic to spread her power evenly to all members. With her DNA now part of them, they had children who would carry the magic, as well. Now, more than three hundred and fifty years later, the Gowdie coven was made up strictly of the descendants of Isobel's original coven. Outsiders were forbidden from setting foot on their property, a towering three-story, seven-bedroom Italianate in College Hill with a four-car garage and guest house. Witches from all over the world knew to stay away from the Cushing Street mansion for fear of being executed on sight. The Gowdies were solitary, ruthless, and played by their own set of rules. They were the only one of the original covens that allowed male members. The rest had outlawed them when a group of male witches formed a secret society in 1854 whose sole purpose was to annex several territories as slave states and rule over all non-witches in those places, using the forced labor of the "ungifted" to amass fortunes for their members. Men were deemed too power-hungry and self-serving to handle magic, so from then on, when a male witch was born, his powers were stripped. The Gowdies deemed the practice unnecessary and cruel and refused to partake in what they saw as a criminal act. Their male witches were as much a part of their coven as the women, with the same rights and responsibilities as the rest. They'd even had male leaders over the years, the last Priest having died by suicide in October of 1987 when he'd lost his personal fortune in the stock market crash. Now, his daughter, Blair was High Priestess. In her late forties and as beautiful as ever, Blair ran the coven like a machine. Half the members were related to her in one way or another and the other half were either in love with her or terrified of her. She slinked around the mansion imposing her will on the others with minimal effort, none of them daring to oppose her under any circumstances. They weren't victims, however, each of them as sinister as she, taking joy in the pain they inflicted on their victims. They used any sort of dark magic necessary to accomplish their goals, which were generally money-based and indulgent. They compelled bank tellers to rob their employers' vaults and leave the sacks of cash at their doorstep. They glamoured themselves to appear as the spouses of politicians, only revealing their true faces once in the act of adultery, having secret cameras taking incriminating pictures for the purpose of blackmailing them later. When one of them would get sick, whether it be a cold or cancer, they'd transfer their ailment to someone in town that had annoyed them in some way. As far as witches went, the Gowdies were as devious and heartless as they came.

Now, standing just a few feet from their door, Julia was wondering if she'd made a mistake in coming to them. Even Griffin refused to land on anything closer than a tree across the street. She stood under its branches and thought it over. If they agreed to help her siphon Grace's magic, they'd no doubt want a piece of it for themselves. On the other hand, without them, she was alone and she was in no way strong enough to go against this Wendy on her own. She *could* try the Leveaus in New Orleans, but they were sure to send her away, the kind of magic they practiced requiring a delicate balance of light and dark. They'd see what she was trying to do as selfish and may even bind her powers as a precaution against upsetting the natural order of things. If she pissed off the Gowdies, though, she could end up dead.

Before she'd made a decision, she found herself inside the giant house, surrounded by well-dressed witches of varying ages. There were several redheads and blondes with similar features; siblings, she assumed. The rest were of varying ethnicities, all sharing the same bothered expression as they sized her up. She immediately recognized Blair. Her beauty was notorious. Her full lips and bright eyes were the envy of insecure witches all over the East, though rumors spread that it was all a show, a glamour to cover her true face. That could have been jealousy, of course, but no one would ever know with how secretive the Gowdie coven was.

The Priestess folded her slender arms and tapped her glossy red nails on her porcelain skin as she looked her over. "Tituban," she mused. "How is your coven still functioning without Grace? She was the only one of you with any real power."

"You're telling me," she croaked, unnerved by the way they'd blinked her into the house.

"The Dyers called, said you were hell-bent on doing something foolish. You've come seeking assistance?"

She nodded. The group looked amused.

"She's cute," one of the blonde men said. "Can I keep her?"

"Do you mind sharing, cousin?" another man asked.

"Not at all."

"Just let me play with her a little first," an Asian woman sneered.

"I'll get the video camera."

"She won't be staying," Blair told them, ignoring the disappointed looks on their faces. She waved at them to stand behind her, ensuring she couldn't flee. They followed orders as she shifted her weight from one foot to another and bit the inside of her cheek. "You want us to what, distract the witch while you take her power for yourself?"

She swallowed hard. "Basically."

"And in return for our help, you'll join us, enriching our coven?"

"Well,"

"And, we should agree? We should bend to your will? You, a shunned witch lacking in discipline or decorum, holding less magic in her entire body than I do in my big toe?" The others snickered. "Honestly, I can't decide if I should admire your conviction or pity you for your obvious lack of intellect."

She fumed, her cheeks burning hot as she clenched her fists at her sides.

Blair tossed her strawberry blonde locks off her shoulder and shook her head. "What you offer is insufficient. We don't work for others and we don't take in a lesser coven's rejects. Pure Tituban magic, though, *that's* of interest. So I have a counter. You give me what I need to find this Tituban witch and I won't carve out your entrails and use them in my next divination."

She stared daggers at the Priestess, her anger boiling over.

"You won't talk? That's fine. I don't need you to." She grabbed the sides of Julia's head, her eyes boring into hers, her face turning red. "Zeige mir."

Julia began to convulse as Blair searched her mind, the images of memories flashing in her minds-eye like movie clips. She saw the name 'Wendy' on the letter in the New York apartment. She saw the girl, Poe, tangled up and tortured. She saw the name of the town where Grace's coven resided and she saw the address of the house Julia thought would be the most likely place Wendy would be hiding. Blair let go, leaving Julia to fall in a heap on the dark hardwood. "Tarrytown," she smirked, looking back at the others. "Packs some snacks. We're going on a road trip."

Suddenly, Julia was back out on the sidewalk across the street, fetal on the ground under the tree where the crow still perched. She held a hand to her head as she got to her feet. Dizzy and unwanting of any further attention from the Gowdies, she teleported herself back to her house in Tarrytown.

A block away from the mansion, a man slumped in the driver's seat of a rusted-out pickup, cell phone in hand, its camera pointed at the bird that now took flight. He looked back to the house as he sent the video to his boss and pulled up his number. He hit 'call' and put the phone to his ear. "Something's up," he told the person on the other end, picking up his binoculars and looking through them into the front window of the coven's sanctuary. He could see them in what looked like an important conversation, their leader grinning from ear to ear. "I'll keep you posted."

She sat at her kitchen table, head in hands, tears of frustration pooling in her eyes. She had to get to Wendy before the Gowdies. If they got hold of Grace's magic, that was it. She'd be without a coven and without any real power forever. She couldn't let it happen. She went to a drawer and pulled out the book she'd swiped from Grace's house the last time she was there. There had to be something useful in it. *Something* to help her take back what was rightfully hers.

After a few minutes of flipping through pages of family anecdotes and herbal remedies, she came upon a page written in a different ink. It was faded, clearly older than the other pages, and had a peculiar energy about it as if the paper itself served as a warning. Written in Latin, it described the events of a spell gone wrong in old Salem. A young girl had inadvertently summoned a creature of some kind, a strange man referring to it as 'Moloch'. The girl had promised it something in return for the power to bring the dead back to life. The creature had agreed, but Tituba put an end to it, capturing the monster in a statue with seven locks and burying it in one of her hiding places.

She slammed the book shut and sat back in her chair, arms crossed and brow furrowed. She knew Tituba's woods well. Grace had taken the coven there several times over the years for special occasions: the birth of a new witch, May Eve, Litha, and even a few weddings were performed there, the witches eager to have their unions blessed by Tituba's spirit. Julia was sure she would have no problem finding the statue if that's what she decided to do. Unlocking it may be trickier, but she could figure it out. It was risky, though. She knew by the vibes coming from the page that this creature was mischievous if not altogether dark. What would it want in return for its help? Would it even do as she asked? She'd have to consider it carefully, given that the ramifications were unknown. She'd have to hurry, though. The Gowdies were on their way.

Chapter 8

Hartley stood on the doorstep of the brick railroad-style apartment on 73rd Street in Queens, the sound of a dog barking a few doors down startling her as she took in her surroundings. It had been more than fifty years since she'd been here but it looked exactly the same. Same geometric pattern in the front window, same peaked porch roof above the door. Even the patch of dirt that acted as her front yard that she'd spend hours a day playing in as a child remained identical, not a speck of green in sight. She wasn't entirely sure what she was doing there, except that she felt she needed to come. Allydia had told her to live her life as she saw fit, that she was free. She didn't feel that way, though. For decades, she avoided this place, the memories too upsetting to relive. It haunted her like the screams of the Wailing Woman from the ghost story her mother had told her all those years ago. Now, standing in front of her childhood home, Hartley felt more afraid than she had when she'd first heard the tale as a five-year-old. She took a breath and tightened her ponytail, jumping from one foot to the other, and closing her eyes. "Let's go, bitch," she muttered to herself. She knocked on the door and stood still, opening her eyes as a woman in pink scrubs answered. She looked to be in her early fifties, heavy set with high cheekbones and dull eyes. Definitely *not* her mother.

"Can I help you?" the nurse asked politely.

She was flustered but quickly regained her composure. "I'm sorry, I was looking for Gloria Morales."

The woman's face lit up. "Oh, of course, come in!" She let her in and closed the door, locking the deadbolt as Hartley glanced around the room. It was exactly the same, from the herringbone pattern on the floor to the plastic on the sofa. A portrait of white Jesus still hung on the living room wall and crosses adorned the tops of every door frame. Growing up here had felt so oppressive and foreboding. Now, though, as she took in the familiar scent of lemon furniture polish, it seemed smaller somehow. It was just a building. It had no power over her.

"Gloria doesn't get many visitors these days, aside from Father Daniel, of course," the woman said. "He comes a few times a week. How do you know her?"

As she looked around, it occurred to her that her mother still hadn't made an appearance. Who was this woman and why was she there? "I'm her...granddaughter."

"Oh! I'm sorry, I'm just surprised. She's never mentioned you. I'm sure you're anxious to see her. She's right through there." She pointed to the door of her parents' bedroom. "I'll leave you two alone, let you catch up. It's my lunch break, anyway. She shouldn't need anything. She's been relatively comfortable the last few days. I'll be back in about an hour." The woman left, locking the door back from the outside.

Hartley felt her heart begin to race as she approached the bedroom door. Her mother was ninety-one and from what she'd discerned, not in the best of health. Her stomach twisted at the thought of what she might find on the other side of the door as she turned the knob. What would she say? Why was she even there?

"Wanda?" the old woman asked, her voice soft. She tried to lift her head to get a look at the woman entering her room but was too weak, tired from the heavy doses of medication she was on. She was lying in a hospital bed, the top half raised slightly. She looked frail, not like the tough-as-nails mother she'd been raised by.

"No, Gloria," she said, stepping closer. "My name's Hartley. Your son, Hart, was my father."

"Hart?" She squinted with cloudy eyes to see her face.

Hartley sat in the chair next to the bed. "Yes, ma'am. I'm your granddaughter."

Gloria's expression went from confused to joyful. "Hart! My baby! I'm so happy to see you!" She took her face in her hands and kissed both cheeks.

"No, ma'am," she lied. "I'm *Hartley*, your--"

She laughed. "Las tonterias. My vision may be going along with the rest of me, but I would recognize my sweet boy anywhere. How could I not know who you are? You are my soul. My heart. Where did you think your name came from, mm? How are you, Papi?"

She didn't know what to say. Being called by her deadname didn't bother her as much as the fact that her mother seemed to have forgotten how horribly she'd let her father treat her back in the day. The beatings when he'd find her wearing her mother's makeup. The lectures about morality. The slurs. The "therapy". She had no idea how with it her mother was, what medicine she was taking, or even what disease she had. She didn't know if she knew what she was saying or if she was too doped up to know right from left, but this was her shot. This was her chance to get it all off her chest. The abuse, the torture, the pain. She'd hear it all. She'd be made to remember it the way Hartley had for all those years. She'd tell her how cruel they'd been. How ignorant and self-righteous. She'd tell her how miserable she'd been growing up in that household of zealots and how happy she'd been since coming out as trans. She'd spill her truth on her like candy from a pinata and leave before she had the chance to respond. It was time. This was her opportunity. But, as she sat there, looking into her mother's milky eyes, knowing this may be the last time she'd ever see her alive, she couldn't do it. No matter what she'd done, no matter what she'd let her father do, she was still her mother and she couldn't bear to break her heart.

Tears slid down her rouged cheeks and she lowered her head as she held her mother's hand. "I'm fine, Mami."

"Why are you crying, my angel? Are you worried about your father? Because he can't hurt you anymore."

She lifted her eyes to look at her again. "What do you mean?"

"It took a few weeks," Gloria said, her voice getting fainter. "Just a pinch every night. Not enough that he could taste it. Every dinner for three weeks."

Her eyes grew to saucers, remembering her father's obituary in the paper twenty or so years before. All it had said about how he'd died was that it had been 'natural causes'. He was in his late sixties by then, so she hadn't questioned it. The truth was, she hadn't much cared. The man was horrible and deserved whatever heart attack or stroke that had taken him. But, this? "What are you saying, Mami?"

"He was a proud man, your father. Would never admit when he was wrong. But, I could tell, he knew. He knew what he did to you was a sin. Kicking you out, disowning you like that. I begged him to bring you home. For thirty years, I begged him. But, he was stubborn. After that final dinner, his favorite, Sopa De Lima, my begging came to an end." Her eyes fluttered closed and her breathing slowed.

Hartley covered her mouth, shocked by what she was hearing.

"I was so happy that...the last thing I saw in his eyes...was regret." She began to quietly snore as Hartley wiped the tears from her face with trembling hands.

"Holy shit," she whispered. All this time, she thought she'd been so willing to commit acts of torture and kill people with no real remorse because she'd been a vampire. Turns out, it was genetic.

Back at her apartment, Hartley cuddled with her cat on the couch, taking refuge from the day and its unrelenting sunshine. Marilyn seemed unfazed by the change in her owner, purring happily on her lap as she always did. Vampire or human, it made no difference to her. "As long as I keep you in food and catnip, you're a content kitty, huh?" Hartley said, petting her back as she drifted off for a nap. A knock came on the door, startling the cat who jumped up and found a new place to sleep in the corner of the sofa. Hartley got up and answered it, surprised to see Oliver standing on the other side. "I thought you went back to Atlantic City," she said, letting him in and closing the door behind him.

"I was going to but," He put his hands on his hips, his pained expression causing her to tilt her head like a confused dog. He grunted and took her hands in his. "Come with me."

"What?"

"Live with me."

"You're crazy."

"I'm serious. Aside from the genocide, nearly getting burned alive, and the sudden change in species, being with you again has been incredible."

She laughed. "I think you need to eat something."

"I need *you*, Hartley. Come on. What else have you got to do today? Just try it. Give it a week. If you hate it, you can always leave me...shattered in a million pieces and contemplating celibacy as a lifestyle choice."

She laughed again and folded her arms, his charming accent giving her butterflies. "I'd have to bring Marilyn."

"A threesome? I didn't think you liked to share but if that's what you want--"

"My cat," she tittered, glancing over to the couch and back at him.

He looked at the ball of fur curled up in the corner and laughed. "Oh! Yeah, sure. Bring the cat. Get a dog. We can have an entire menagerie if you like. What do ya say?"

She chewed on her bottom lip and squinted at him, shaking her head and giving him a sly smile. "All right, we can *try it* but only because you look extra cute in that shirt. Green was always your color."

"Yes!" He scooped her up and swung her around as she giggled, forgetting for a moment about her mother's confession and how pitiful she looked lying in the hospital bed. Now, she just felt happy and she wanted to stay in that bliss for as long as she could.

Chapter 9

"So, your girlfriend's an angel? Lucifer's real?" Poe asked as they entered the house in Tarrytown.

"Yeah," Wendy told her.

"I think my head's gonna explode."

"Don't tell anyone. I'm pretty sure it would be like, Apocalyptically bad if word got out. And, I'm not sure she's my girlfriend anymore."

She scoffed as she put Wendy's bags on the bed in Grace's old room. "You'll forgive her. She was just looking out for you."

"I guess. Who's this?" She bent down and smiled, petting the rabbit that hopped into the room to greet them.

"That's Raven."

"Your familiar?"

She nodded, passing by and walking to the kitchen where she got a fresh bowl of greens together for the bunny's lunch.

Wendy followed, sitting at the table as Poe dropped into a chair, resting her chin on her fist. "Thanks for letting me crash here."

"No problem. So, you don't have a familiar?"

"No," Wendy said. "What I do can get pretty dangerous and I always thought it'd be better to go it alone. Didn't want anyone else to get hurt if I messed something up."

"Oh," she said, raising a knowing eyebrow.

"What?"

"You're not used to anyone caring about you."

"So?"

"So, when your girl tried to protect you, it freaked you out."

"It didn't *freak me out*. It pissed me off."

"Did it *really*, or was it just a good excuse to end things before she could get hurt by some witchy bullshit?"

She folded her hands. "I'm pretty sure God's Messenger can't be taken down by a rogue witch with a hard-on for my magic."

"I'm not talking about Julia, specifically. And, maybe she can't be hurt by her, or *anything*. But, your subconscious doesn't know that."

She pursed her lips and let out an exasperated sigh. "You're making some good points, Poe. Gotta say...it's kind of obnoxious."

A crash came from the living room, jolting them from their seats. "Julia," Poe whispered.

"Doubt it," Wendy said, feeling the immense power coming from the front door. "Feels like..." They went to the living room where a group of twelve witches stood, all wearing the same smug grin. "Gowdies."

"Which one of you is the Tituban witch?" a woman in a flowing red dress asked, stepping toward them.

"Blair, right?" Wendy said, giving her a once-over. "The rumors are true, then. You're smokin'."

"Flattery," Blair chirped. "Unexpected, but it won't distract me. I've come for Grace's magic. Hand it over willingly and I won't butcher the child."

"I'm not a child," Poe snapped.

"Shh." Wendy held her arm out to keep her a few steps behind her, keeping her eyes on the Priestess. "How did you find me?"

Blair rolled her eyes. "Ugh, that imbecile from Grace's coven tried to acquire my services in taking your power for herself. She apparently didn't know what she was walking into."

"I won't give you my power. If it didn't kill you, it would make you even more power-hungry and megalomaniacal than you already are."

She laughed. "Dear girl, how naive do you think I am? Grace's magic is powerful beyond measure. I wouldn't dare take it all into myself. I'm not suicidal."

Wendy wrinkled her brow.

"No, no. I will share the power with my family. That magic would incinerate just one of us, but divide it by twelve..." She held her hands out and flicked her fingers causing the room to shake. After a few seconds, the whole house was rattling.

"Sturm!" a redhead shouted. Thunder clapped above them so loud, it sounded like it was coming from inside the house. A man opened his mouth, sucking in a deep breath and blowing it out, filling the room with a gust of wind so strong, it knocked Poe to the floor.

"It's real cute," Wendy called over the noise. "But, it won't affect me."

Blair scrunched her nose. "Ubertragen!"

"Is that German?"

She held her hand out in front of her as if asking for money. "UBERTRAGEN!"

"I'm gonna have to look that up, hold on!" Wendy took her phone from her pocket and typed the word into a translator app. "Oh! 'Transfer'! That won't work on me!"

The house quaked more, flinging pictures from the walls as Blair's face turned a deep shade of red.

"Hey, you match your dress!"

"Gib es vorbei!"

"It won't work!" she yelled again, hardly able to hear her own voice over the interior thunderstorm. "I can't...I can't be...UGH! Quiescis!" The room went still. "Much better," she said, grateful for the quiet. "Like I was trying to tell you, I can't be spelled."

"Of course you can!" Blair defied. "Ubertragen!"

She sighed. "No, really, I can't. Ancient magic. I'm warded from any supernatural harm. You guys aren't, though. Supernatet."

All twelve Gowdie witches lifted from the ground, hovering in midair, the horror on their faces causing Poe to giggle.

Wendy clasped her hands in front of her as she walked around the room, stepping between the floating witches and shaking her head. "You Gowdies, man. You're all terrorism and greed. Did you not get enough hugs as kids, or what?"

"Lass mich gehen!" the mouth-breather griped.

"Is that another spell, or are you just bitching?"

"Fine!" Blair relented, annoyance and dread in her voice. "We'll go. We won't come for you again."

"See, I wish I could believe you."

"What are you gonna do with them?" Poe asked.

"What someone should've done a long time ago." She went to the bedroom and opened one of the suitcases. "I knew this would come in handy one of these days." She held up an instant camera and took a photo of the group.

Blair's face fell, going stark white as her eyes widened. "What are you doing?"

Wendy shook the picture as it developed and walked back to stand next to Poe. "Got any ribbon?"

"Sure," she said, scurrying to the kitchen and fetching a spool of black ribbon from a drawer. She handed it to Wendy.

"Don't!" Blair begged.

Wendy ignored her, wrapping the photo with the ribbon until the entire image was covered. "Scissors?"

"Oh, right." Poe rushed back to retrieve a pair of orange-handled sewing scissors and brought them back. Wendy snipped the ribbon and handed the spool and scissors to Poe, tucking the end in so nothing was left loose.

"You wouldn't dare!" Blair shouted. The others squirmed, unable to break free from Wendy's floating prison.

"You brought this on yourself," she told her, taking the picture in both hands. She cleared her throat. "Sunt vinctum ex usura magicae aeternum."

The group screamed, sweat dripping from their foreheads as they realized what had been done to them.

"NO!" Blair bellowed.

"It had to be done," Wendy said. "You people have given magic a bad name for centuries. I don't know why no one bound your powers before now."

"No one's been strong enough," Poe explained. "Grace wanted to. She told me she tried a few times years ago, but it never worked. Damn, you're like, Super Witch."

She snickered. "Maybe I'll get tee-shirts made."

"You'll pay for this!" Blair warned. "We'll get our powers back and we'll--"

She rolled her eyes. "Relinquo." They disappeared, sent back to their house in Providence with a single word. "Well, that was exciting. Let's go bury this and get some lunch. I'm starving."

Poe nodded, following her through the kitchen and out the back door, Raven hopping along behind them.

The early afternoon sun all but disappeared behind the leaves of the massive oak trees as Julia headed deep into the forest. Sparse rays peppered the landscape, providing just enough light to lead her to the clearing where Tituba used to perform her most sacred rituals. "Ostendeo," she demanded. The ground opened before her, centuries of earth and rock making way for the perfectly preserved tree stump to rise up, its secrets no longer hidden. She reached inside, pulling out candles and bundles of dried herbs. Finally, she found what she'd been looking for, the small bronze statue that held the key to all of her ambitions. It was hideous, its face that of a cow's twisted in anguish. Its body resembled a naked man's, the hands stretched out as if in offering. "Seven locks," she muttered, looking it over, the seams of the chambers barely visible. She cracked her neck and began. "Laxo." One chamber burst open from the statue's right leg. "Revelabit." Four more sprung open from its back. "Recludo." A tiny chamber emerged from the top of the figure's head. She blew out an uneasy breath as she prepared to give the last command. She closed her eyes and gripped the figure tight, as if it would slip away before she could finish the spell, ruining her plans. She leaned against a tree and opened her eyes. "Dabit fructum." She heard a sharp click inside the figure as sulfuric smoke seeped from its openings. She coughed, waving the black fog away, still holding tight to the idol. The dark cloud wafted a few feet away, slowly forming an opaque shadow in the shape of a faceless man. She swallowed the bile that came up in her throat as the smell grew stronger and the shadow moved closer.

"Why have you freed me, witch?" the creature hissed, its voice low and snarling.

She trembled against the tree, squeezing her fingers so tightly around one of the open chambers of the figure that she drew blood. "I seek assistance."

It lurched its neck and slithered to only a few inches from her face. "You are stronger than the last girl that summoned me to this place. She had no real power. But, *you*," It was so close, it was almost touching her. "You could be of use."

"I need more power," she told it. "There's a witch that took--"

"I care nothing for your reasons. If power is what you desire, power is what I shall provide. But, nothing comes without a price."

"W-What do you want?"

"A child. One young, preferably still suckling. Bring one to me, and I will give you what you want."

"I can't do that," she said, her heart sinking as it backed away and turned its back to her. She walked toward it, her stomach aching with disappointment. "Please. I can't kidnap a baby. It's too terrible. There must be something else. Blood? I'll open a vein right now. You want to be worshiped? Here." She dropped to her knees. "I'll praise you, sing songs of your awesome power. Anything. Just tell me what to do."

It turned, putting a hand to its chin. It circled her, the leaves on the ground not making a sound as he stepped on them. "Get to your feet."

She did as she was told.

"There is something else I will have." It stood before her, hands on hips.

"Name it."

It dipped its head. "Take off your clothes."

She drew in a sharp breath. "Take off..."

"Remove your clothing and lay yourself down. Give yourself to me of your own free will and I will grant your request."

Her mind raced as she tried to quickly make a decision, but she couldn't think straight. Between the nausea from the stench and the panic over her last chance of getting what she wanted slipping through her fingers, it felt to her like there was only one option. She kicked off her shoes and pulled her top off over her head. She shimmied out of her jeans and unhooked her bra, slipping it off and dropping it to the ground. Finally, she slid off her panties and got down on her knees before lying back on the soft grass. She kept her eyes fixed on the creature as it came down on top of her, seeming to have no weight, though she could feel it on her skin, its touch slimy as if it was covered in a layer of mucus. It spread her legs wide, a strange growl emanating from its throat. It held her hands above her head as she felt it enter her, filling her completely with its slippery phallus. She closed her eyes, biting her lip as it thrust into her over and over again. As sick as she felt and as terrified as she was, her body couldn't help but react, her back arching and her hips rocking beneath the shadow's greasy touch. She groaned in pleasure, indifferent to the crow in the tree above, screeching, and flapping its wings so hard that feathers loosened and fell in a halo around her head. It flew off, the stench of sulfur making it, too feel sick.

Chapter 10

"You ready?" Will asked. Michelle squeezed his hand, her face beaming as they waited on the porch of Malik and Valerie's Connecticut home.

"I think so," she said, pressing the doorbell, hopping a little in anticipation.

"Will!" Valerie said, opening the door and giving her nephew a hug. "Come in, Sinclair's waiting for you." She let them in and closed the door. "You must be Michelle. I hear you're human again. Good for you. Vampires always gave me the heebies."

"Yes, ma'am. Me, too."

"Did you just," Valerie rolled her eyes. "What is with you two and this 'ma'am' shit?"

"Oh, I'm sorry, um,"

"Valerie."

"Right. Valerie. I was just trying to be polite."

"I know, I know," she sighed as she led them to the living room.

"Mommy!" Sinclair squealed, racing to meet them, wrapping her arms around Michelle's waist. "I'm so glad you came!"

"I'll give you all some privacy," Valerie said, patting Will on the shoulder before retreating to another room.

"Did you like my picture?" the child asked, pulling away.

"Yeah, baby," Michelle told her, fighting back tears. "It was really good."

"Hey, sweetie," Will said.

"Hi, Daddy. My other dad's waiting for you in the kitchen. He wants to make sure you're not dangerous anymore. I told him you were fine now, but he doesn't think I know what I'm talking about. Spoiler alert, I do."

He laughed. "Okay, I'll go talk to him. Be right back." He went to the kitchen, leaving mother and daughter alone for the first time in what seemed like forever.

Michelle knelt down to get a better look at Sinclair's face, seeing so much of herself there. She was the perfect combination of her and Will. She had her nose, mouth, and chin, and Will's cheeks and eyes. She had long, flowing curls held back with colorful barrettes and dimples that made Michelle's heart melt. She couldn't believe how fast she'd grown. She looked to be six or seven and spoke like a twelve-year-old. Michelle rubbed the girl's arms and smiled. "I missed you."

"I missed you, too. I'm really glad you're back. I have so much to show you! Come on!" She took her hand and led her back to the entry and up the staircase. "Did Daddy tell you about my chalkboard wall?"

In the kitchen, the men stared awkwardly at one another on opposite sides of the island. Will scratched his head then folded his hands in front of him while Malik remained still, arms folded, a skeptical scowl on his face. The silence lasted too long. Will decided he needed to break the ice. "So, Sinclair said you think I'm still psycho."

He pursed his lips, widening his eyes in surprise.

"I'm okay now. A witch did a spell. It's all under control."

"Val told me."

"But, you aren't sure."

"I'm not sure of much these days. Demons, vampires, witches. All seem like things to avoid. Magic spells. Too good to be true, if you ask me."

"That's valid. I do feel a lot better, though. And, I swear, I would never do anything to hurt Sinclair. You have to know that."

"Oh, I believe you. How long's that gonna last is the question."

Will cleared his throat, fiddling with his fingers as the room grew quiet again. "So, Malik, what do you do?"

"I'm a chef."

"Really? I got a degree in Culinary Arts. Online, but still. Where do you cook?"

"I'm a private chef and I teach classes here and there."

"Do you like it?"

"Love it."

"Can I ask you a question?"

He shrugged.

"Why don't you cook in a restaurant? You're an hour away from the food capital of the world. I'd think you'd want to be more a part of it."

"I like what I do. I don't have anyone telling me what to do. I'm my own boss. That's what's important to me."

"So, why not open your own restaurant?"

Malik chuckled. "Well, that's a nice thought, kid, but it's kind of a pipe dream. Sixty percent of new restaurants close in the first year, eighty by year five. You need a prime location to have a chance at all, and those are tens of thousands a month in rent alone. A food truck, maybe, one day. That's the smarter play."

Will leaned in, his expression quizzical. "You teaching my daughter to think that small?"

"Hey," Michelle said, entering the room and placing a hand on her boyfriend's shoulder. "Time to go. Sinclair said she needs a nap."

Malik looked at the clock on the stove. "Yep, it's about that time. I'll show you out." He got up and ushered the young couple to the front door. "See you again soon." He closed the door abruptly as Michelle cast Will a confused side-eye.

"What was that about?"

He shrugged.

They walked back to the car, stopping to give the house a final look. She sighed.

He opened the door for her. "What's wrong?"

"I didn't want to go," she admitted. "She's so awesome, Will. I love her so much."

"I know. Me, too."

She stared up at her daughter's bedroom window, tears forming in her eyes as she made the determination. "I want her back."

"Thanks for letting me hang out," Gabriel said, watching as Wyatt got her another soda from the fridge. He set it on the island in front of her and sat down, opening a can for himself and taking a sip.

"You're always welcome here, you know that."

"Yeah. I thought I'd be intruding on your time with Dia. I didn't know she'd be asleep for hours."

"She's not exactly used to her new sleep schedule."

She giggled. "No, I guess not."

"So, you ready to talk about what happened? Maybe start with why you smell like charcoal?"

"Your damn firefighter instincts," she said, taking a drink before putting the can down. "I set myself on fire a little earlier. Not a little. A lot. Lucifer had to gale-force wind me onto my ass to put me out."

He raised an eyebrow.

"It was an accident. You're not the only one that can lose control of their powers in an emotional fit. Pretty sure I broke my oven, too, not that it matters."

"Why were you upset?"

"Fight with Wendy."

"Ah."

"We might have broken up. She was super pissed."

"What'd you do?"

"I didn't tell her one of her witch friends was in trouble and now some other witch chick is salty about Wendy having her dead aunt's magic instead of her. I don't know, it seemed pretty petty to me."

"Why didn't you tell her?"

"The same reason you wouldn't have told her if you were me. I was protecting her. Those crazy bitches are out there killing each other trying to steal *her* magic. I don't know if she's a match for them. From what I saw in her friend's head, they're all pretty badass. I just watched Cam die like, twenty minutes before that girl showed up. I couldn't risk losing Wendy, too. Now, I may have, anyway."

"I'm sorry."

She shrugged, taking another sip of soda.

He stood and picked his keys up from the counter. "All right, well, I have to go." He scribbled a note telling Allydia he'd be back in a few hours. "Stay as long as you want, just lock up when you leave. Talk more later?"

"Actually, can I come with you?"

"To therapy?"

"Yeah. You don't have anything important to talk about and I could use some advice."

He laughed. "Okay, sure. It's not like it'll be the first time you've taken over one of my sessions."

Chapter 11

Allydia found the note on the counter and clicked her nails on the cool stone. She noticed two soda cans on the island, one of them marked by a smear of pale pink lipgloss. She felt a twinge of jealousy rise in her chest until she realized she'd seen that shade before. "Gabriel." She relaxed her shoulders and took a sip from the can she assumed belonged to Wyatt. The bubbles tickled her tongue and burned her throat as she swallowed the intensely sweet liquid. She set the can back in its spot and cleared her throat. "They drink this on purpose?"

A thunderous banging came from the door. Allydia's spine straightened as she was keenly aware of how much weaker she was than she used to be. Who would be pounding so hard on Wyatt's door and what would she do if they were dangerous? She thought back to what she'd told Hartley about self-defense. She'd also been trained by various senseis over thousands of years. She may not have superior strength and speed anymore, but she was far from helpless.

She went to the door and opened it, taking a step back in surprise when she saw who was standing on the other side. "Phindi, what are you--" But she was cut off before she could finish the question, taking a hard jab to the chin. "Ow!" she yelped.

"How could you do this to me?" the woman barked. "To all of us?" She went to hit her again, but Allydia blocked her punches, one after another as the former general pushed her way inside. "You betrayed us! The traitor was right. It was *you* who lost your way."

"It wasn't meant to affect the rest of you," she told her, jumping back to avoid a kick to the abdomen. "I only wanted a chance at freedom. I thought you would carry on as you were without me."

"Carry on without you?" she exploded. "*There is no us without you!* You were the dam that held back the raging sea. You were the mother of our kind. I served you faithfully for generations. I loved you!" She picked up a barstool and smashed it against the counter, shattering it against the stone. She took a broken leg and spun it in her hand as she edged closer, Allydia backing away.

"I'm sorry, Phindi. You were an excellent soldier. I care for you, truly. But, the burden of what I'd become was too great. I'd nearly forgotten who I was. And, when it cost me the man I love, I--"

"You chose *him*!" she shouted. "You chose *him* over your people! A *human*!" She charged, her makeshift stake raised. "Perhaps, after I kill you I'll wait for him to return and slaughter him, as well!"

"Hey!"

Phindi turned to the male voice calling from behind and was immediately thrown to the ground by a ball of electricity. She was stunned, but not badly hurt, the lightning of a fairly low voltage. She tried to get up, but the man stepped into the apartment, hand out, ready to fire again if she made a move. She clenched her jaw. "Another lightning wielder?"

"Thank you, Will," Allydia said as Michelle closed the door behind them. She stood between the couple and her attacker, kneeling and brushing Phindi's cheek. "I'm sorry, Duchess. Hurting you was not my intention."

Tears streamed down her face, her chest heaving as she fell apart. "What do I do now? I have nothing. *What am I* if not a warrior for the queen?"

Will chimed in, "You could go into private security."

The former vampires gave him condescending glares.

"What? It's not a ridiculous idea. I hear Cardinal Rain's looking for new management."

Dr. Stratford shifted in his seat, made visibly uncomfortable by Gabriel's presence. He turned his glance to Wyatt who sat next to her, his elbow resting on the arm of the couch, his legs crossed, ankle over knee. "Your sister?" the doctor verified.

He nodded. "Yeah. We have the same dad."

Gabriel erupted in laughter while Wyatt stifled a snicker.

"That's amusing to you?" the doctor wondered.

"It's funny because it's true."

"All right," He took off his glasses and set them on the table next to him. "So, Mr. Sinclair, why have you brought your sister to your session? Are you having trouble navigating your new-found family dynamics? Are there unresolved feelings surrounding her discovering you? Any resentments? Jealousy?"

"No."

"I'm kind of hijacking his session," she told him. "He was just gonna talk about how his girlfriend made a huge sacrifice to get him back and he feels guilty about that, blah, blah, blah. I told him on the way here she'd been thinking about it for a while. His dumping her was just the straw that broke the camel's back. He's got no reason to feel bad. Guilt-ridden is kind of his default setting, though, so."

He shot her an annoyed glance.

"What? That is accurate."

"I'm sorry, young lady," the doctor said. "But, I'm retiring soon and no longer taking new patients. Unless this is a joint session to discuss--"

She took a wad of hundred dollar bills from her back pocket and threw it on the coffee table. The doctor looked at it and back to her before putting his glasses back on and picking up a notebook and pen. "What do you want to talk about?"

"I need better coping mechanisms," she told him. "Back in the day, it was drugs. Then, it was dick. Now, I'm just sort of flailing around with no distractions and it's like," She grimaced. "Not awesome."

"Well, there are several healthy ways to deal with stress. Meditation, exercise, healthy eating..."

"That all sounds really terrible."

He arched an eyebrow. "All right, in that case, what you need to do is get to the root of what's causing you to feel upset."

"Well, right now I'm freaking out because I had a big fight with my girlfriend. I've never been in a real relationship before. Intimacy issues, fear of abandonment, and a general lack of interest have made them seem like a giant pain in the ass. But, this girl's amazing and I think I fucked it up by lying to her and I'm afraid I won't be able to fix it."

"Was the lie to conceal infidelity?"

"No, I didn't tell her about someone stopping by her place one night. They were involved in something that I thought might be dangerous for her, so I sent them away. She found out, now she's mad."

He lowered his glasses and put his pen down. "That's it?"

"Yeah."

"You tried to protect her from a shady character and that upset her?"

Wyatt sat forward. "Did you just say 'shady'?"

Gabriel nodded.

The doctor placed his glasses and notebook on the table and leaned back in his seat. "Give it a few days. She'll get over it. If she doesn't, she's too immature for an adult relationship and you're better off without her."

Wyatt burst out laughing. "I am *loving* this new you."

She twirled her hair and crossed her legs. "Should I buy her something big, like a house or a car or something? Some kind of grand gesture to smooth it over?"

The doctor shook his head. "That's not necessary. What she probably needs is a sincere apology. Money doesn't solve every problem and you can't just buy people."

She cocked her head, glancing at the money on the table.

He cleared his throat. "Touche."

Chapter 12

Eight-year-old Wendy let out a blood-curdling scream as her parents were gunned down in front of her, the man with the rifle having smashed through the front door like a SWAT team member on crystal meth. Her mother was dead before she hit the floor and her father writhed in a pool of blood on the cream-colored carpet.

"Why?" he gurgled as the gunman stood over him.

He sneered, his thick mustache glistening in the bright sunlight that poured in through the hole where the door used to be. "Thou shalt not suffer a witch to live."

"I'm not a witch," he defended. "My powers were stripped when I was a baby."

"Not you." He altered his gaze to the girl who now hyperventilated in the corner.

"No!" her father begged. "She's just a little girl!"

He raised the rifle, pointing it at the girl. "Witches are never children. They're born evil. If you could go back and kill Stalin in his crib, wouldn't you?"

"Wendy, run!"

The man turned his gun back on her father and shot him between the eyes. Wendy screamed again, buckets of tears falling from her sorrowful eyes. The shooter pointed his weapon at her again but before he could pull the trigger, Wendy shouted, "Calidi!" The metal of the weapon instantly burned hot, searing the skin of his hand. He dropped the gun, crying out in pain. She took a few quick breaths and reminded herself, "I'm a witch. I'm a witch. I can do *anything. I'm a witch.*"

"I'm gonna kill you, you little bitch!"

She wiped away her tears and pointed to the man's left eye. "Dissilio!" It burst in his head, exploding like an over-filled water balloon. He howled, his charred hand flying up to cover the mess dribbling from his eye socket. While he was distracted, she made a break for it, speeding by him and out the door.

She raced through the field across the street and into the woods. She kept running to the other side of the forest to her grandmother's cottage, her tears again streaming down her now flushed cheeks.

"What's happened?" the old woman fretted, meeting Wendy on the front porch and cupping her small face in her wrinkled hands.

"The man," she panted. "Had a gun. He broke in. He killed them!" She began to sob, throwing her arms around her grandmother's waist.

She caught a breath in her throat. "My Daniel?"

"He said we're evil. Are we bad, Grandma?"

"No, sweetheart," the woman told her, brushing her own tears from her eyes and patting her on the back. "Just different. Some men fear what they can't control and that fear drives them to villainy." She knelt down to look her in the eyes. "You're a good girl, Wendy. But, no matter what you do or where you go, there will always be men who want to extinguish your power and witches that want to take it for themselves. You'll have to be guarded and careful, always. Promise me."

She gulped back a sob and nodded. "I promise, Grandma. What do I do now? I'm all alone."

She took her in her arms and squeezed her tight. "You're not alone. I'll always be with you, my sweet girl. I'll always be right here."

Shots rang out, dozens of bullets crashing through every window of the cabin as the witches inside shrieked, some ducking for cover while others perished instantly from bullets to the head or heart. The barrage continued as four men armed to the teeth busted through the door, their assault weapons smoking as they sprayed the women with round after round. When the screaming stopped, their leader held a fist in the air, signaling the others to hold their fire. He ran his fingers over his graying mustache before adjusting his eyepatch and taking stock of the carnage. He could make out eleven bodies strewn across the floor, the sight delighting him, but leaving him yet unsatisfied.

"We're missing one," he barked. "Fan out. Bitch has got to be here somewhere."

The men tore through the cabin, tossing furniture around as they stepped over the corpses of the fallen witches.

"You hear that?" one of the men asked. The group went quiet as they listened.

They heard what sounded like whispering, the same three words repeated over and over. "Caedis haec homines."

"Where's it coming from?" he asked.

"Stay frosty, boys," the leader said, raising his rifle. They looked everywhere, but couldn't find the source of the chanting. It got louder, echoing through the room as if it was being piped through a speaker system. The one-eyed man held his breath as he listened, cocking his head, a vicious smirk crossing his lips. He hoisted his gun straight up, squeezing the trigger, a single bullet releasing from the chamber. Above them, the woman yelped, blood dripping from her stomach wound onto the leader's shoulder. The men took aim, but the older man again made a fist. The witch had pinned herself to the ceiling using a flight spell, but as she bled out, she grew too weak to maintain it. She fell, landing with a thud on the floor in front of them. The leader laughed, holding his rifle in one hand

and dragging the witch by her hair with the other. He threw her up against the wall in a sitting position, her skin already having lost most of its color. He knew he only had a couple of minutes to get the information from her before she was dead, so he wasted no time in questioning her. "Hey," he shouted, smacking her across the face to perk her up. "Dyer bitch. Don't conk out on me, yet. What's going on in your community of vipers, hmm?"

"What?" she breathed, barely able to keep her eyes open.

"Must be something big. Word has it the Gowdies left their compound and headed to New York. Now, why would they do something like that? I've had eyes on them for years and they never leave their little corner of the world, so what's so important that the entire coven would up and take a trip like that?"

"Caedis haec homines." Her head slumped as she began to fade.

"Oh, no you don't." He smacked her again, holding her head up, his fist gripping her hair. "What are they after? What's got you bitches all in a tizzy?"

"Wendy," she laughed.

"What? Did you say, 'Wendy'?"

"The Tituban." Blood slipped from her lips as her eyes rolled back. "She's the last. She contains all of her ancestors' power." She flashed a blood-stained smile as she coughed. "You may kill me, but you are all dead. She will discover what you've done and she will make you suffer. She'll skin you alive and hang you by your--"

"Wendy? Why does that name sound familiar?" He scratched underneath his eyepatch and laughed as the memory surfaced. "The kid?! Oh, I'm looking forward to this."

"Caedis haec homines."

"Are you doing a spell?" he cackled. "Yeah, those don't affect us anymore. A couple years back, we paid one of your kind to ward us from magic...right before we slit her throat."

Her eyes widened as they glossed over, a final, gurgling breath escaping her lips as her body went limp.

"Well done, boys," he said, standing upright and patting one of his men on the shoulder. "This coven is officially destroyed."

The men cheered, shooting their guns in the air and giving each other high-fives.

"No time to celebrate," the one-eyed man told them, heading for the door. "We've got a witch to hunt."

Chapter 13

Hartley leaned back, closing her eyes as she breathed in the salty ocean air, grateful for the shade the boardwalk above provided from the late-day sun. She sat comfortably on the blanket, digging her toes in the cool sand as she reflected on the events of the day. In the last twelve hours, she'd gone from vampire to human, single to having a live-in boyfriend, and from hating her mother to feeling sorry for and disturbed by her. "What a day."

"Fries for the lady," Oliver said, joining her on the blanket and opening a take-out container. She took one, dipping it in cheese sauce and taking a bite.

"Holy shit."

"Aren't they great? I've discovered any food tastes delicious if it's been deep-fried and covered in cheese." He took one as well, looking out onto the waves.

"Can I ask you something?"

"Anything, darling."

"Did your parents know you were...you know..."

"What? Pan?"

She nodded, taking another bite.

"I think they suspected."

"You never told them?"

"They never asked."

She raised an eyebrow.

He turned to face her. "I never told them because it seemed like they would have rather not known. Talking about things like sexuality just wasn't done then."

"Oh."

"What's the matter? Is someone giving you shit? Just give me a name."

She shook her head. "I went to visit my mom today."

He looked surprised. "You did? She's still alive?"

"Not for long from the looks of her. I don't know, I just..."

He held her hand. "What?"

"My parents did everything they could think of to change me. They made me feel worthless and ugly and...unloved. They hurt me. I don't know if I can forgive her."

He kissed her hand and held it to his chest. "Maybe you don't have to. Maybe it's not about her."

"What do you mean?"

"I mean, it's been decades since you've seen her, right?"

She nodded.

"And, if you never saw her again, how would that affect you, really?"

She shrugged.

"So, maybe forgiving what she did isn't necessary. Maybe all you need is closure."

"How do I get that?"

"Beats me," he said taking another fry and popping it in his mouth. He chewed and swallowed before speaking again. "But, whatever it is you need to do, you do it. No second-guessing, no stifling yourself for somebody else's comfort. You do whatever it takes to bring yourself peace because no matter what some old woman or anyone else might think of you, you deserve to be happy exactly the way you are."

She looked at him fondly as he kissed her hand again. "You know what?"

"What?"

"You might be the best decision I've made in years. Well, second best."

"All I felt was a huge spike in Julia's power," Poe said, crunching leaves under her biker boots as they trekked through the dense woods.

"I felt it, too, but that wasn't just Julia's magic getting stronger," Wendy told her. "There was something dark attached to it. Something old. If I'm right, we are in a pig farm's amount of shit." They came to the clearing, the faint smell of sulfur still lingering in the air.

"What the hell happened?" Poe asked, seeing the uprooted tree stump surrounded by centuries of silt and sandy loam.

Wendy furrowed her brow as she spotted the brass figure in a pile of leaves, split apart, a crack running through its center from the top down. All seven chambers had been unlocked. "Mother--"

"What is that thing?"

"Grace never told you the Moloch story?" She knelt down to gather up the candles and the rest of Tituba's belongings.

"No."

She stood and glanced around to make sure she hadn't left anything. "Back in the day, some girl summoned some kind of monster to get it to bring her dead relatives back to life. It demanded a human sacrifice, so the girl offered up Tituba's daughter. Tituba stopped her and trapped the monster in this idol. Some guy called it 'Moloch'."

"What guy?"

"I don't know. Tituba just referred to him as 'The Bringer of Light'." Her eyes widened and her mouth fell open. "You've got to be kidding me."

"Bringer of Light? Like--"

"Lucifer, yeah, probably. Oh, my God! I can't believe I never put that together before."

"What do we do now?" Poe asked. "The idol's broken. It's useless."

"It doesn't matter. That thing's been locked up so long, it can't function on its own. It needs a witch to act as a conduit. Without Julia's magic to cling to, it's nothing. All we have to do is take her power."

"Like with the Gowdies?"

"No, not bind it. Remove it completely. The stripping spell done on male witches when they're babies, *that's* what we need."

"We'd need her measure."

"I know." She began the long walk out of the woods, Poe following closely behind. "We'll need the coven."

Chapter 14

Allydia sat across from Phindi in the quiet 116th Street restaurant, watching her eat as she took a sip of Bissap. "How is your Fataya?"

"Fine," she mumbled. "How are your Nems?"

"Lovely. I had forgotten how much I used to love food. You know, for as long as I'd gone without it, I don't think it ever occurred to me to miss it."

She slammed her fist down on the table, startling the people at the next table. "This man, are you certain he is worth all of this? That he is worthy of you?"

She set her glass down and folded her hands. "I didn't do this only for him. I spent thousands of years trying to fix what was broken in me, creating a family to replace the one my father had taken. No matter how many of you I turned, there was always something missing."

She lowered her head. "We were not enough."

"No, because the thing that was missing was *me*. I had forgotten who I was. I lost myself somewhere between responsibility and repetition. I was *tired*, Phindi. But, to answer your question, yes, he is worth it. He is worth all the stars in heaven. More precious than any diamond. I would give my life to remain in his favor and I would burn this world to the ground to bring justice to anyone who might dare try to take him from me, do you understand?"

She nearly choked on her last bite of food as she nodded. "Yes, my Queen."

"Good." Her eyes softened. "I know it's hard, adjusting to this human life. I will help you in any way you need."

"What I *need* is purpose."

Allydia picked up her glass. "We will think of something."

"So, since Allydia's human now, are we just gonna forgive her for that whole locking-me-in-a-cage thing?" Michelle asked, sitting next to Will on the couch in his father's apartment.

"That's entirely up to you," he told her. "I'll hate her if you want me to."

She sank back into the cushions and crossed her legs. "Your dad really loves her, doesn't he?"

"Yeah, I think he really does."

She sighed, resting her head on his shoulder as he put his arm around her. "I guess I can let it go, but only because I think I could take her now."

He laughed. "That's very big of you."

"I know, right? I'm a goddamn saint." She giggled, wrapping an arm around his waist. "Will,"

He kissed her head. "Hmm?"

"I miss her."

He rested his cheek on top of her head, knowing they were no longer talking about the ex-vampire queen. "Me, too."

"I was serious earlier. I want her back."

He rubbed her shoulder. "I know."

"She was so happy. Safe. She loves it there, I could tell." She brushed away a stray tear as Will held her close. "I can't just uproot her, it would break her heart. And Valerie and Malik seem like good parents, right? I mean, they have to be. She loves them. She's got drawings she's done of them all over her room. Her whole life has been with them. It's just not fair." She wiped away more tears as they came, her voice going up an octave as she spoke through the sobs. "She's growing up so fast. *So fast* and we're missing it. We should be with her. We should be..." She covered her mouth, her crying now out of control. He kissed her head again then pulled away, taking his phone from his back pocket and calling his aunt.

"Hello?" Valerie answered.

"Hey, Aunt Valerie, it's Will. I want to apologize. I think I may have insulted Malik earlier. I kind of implied he wasn't ambitious enough."

She laughed. "Yeah, he said something about you making a comment."

"Is he mad?"

"No, sweetie. He laughed it off, said you're too young to know what you're talking about."

"Oh," he said, blowing by the insult. "Well, good...I guess. Listen, I know you don't know me that well and I don't exactly have the best track record when it comes to being, you know, *sane*, but I was wondering if I could ask a favor."

"Boy, you're family. That's all I need to know about you. Besides, if sanity was a prerequisite for speaking, everyone in this family would have to cut their tongues out. What do you need?"

"It's big."

"That's all right."

"Really big."

"Boy, I love you, but my patience is wearing thin."

"I was wondering if it might be okay if me and Michelle," He looked at her as she sat forward, head tilted as she listened.

"If you and Michelle what?"

"If we moved in with you?"

Michelle gasped, covering her mouth with one hand and holding her stomach with the other.

"We just miss Sinclair already," he continued. "And, I don't mean we want to take over or anything. You and Malik are her parents, we just," He placed a hand on his girlfriend's knee. "We just want to be part of it."

"Daddy!" he could hear Sinclair squeal in the background. "Tell him yes, Mommy! Tell Daddy it's okay! Please?!"

Valerie laughed. "Well, I don't have a choice, now, do I?"

"Are you sure?" Will asked, not wanting to get his hopes up for nothing. "I know it's weird."

"Oh, sweetie, weird is so normal for this family, we should put it on a crest. Pack your stuff. I'll have a room ready for you."

"Thank you, Valerie. You have no idea how much this means to us."

"I'll see you soon."

"Yes, you will. Thank you. Bye." He hit 'end call' and put the phone on the coffee table. Michelle sat, jaw agape, eyes fixed on this man, this love of her life. She stared, eyes wide as he noticed her gawking. "Oh, God, did I overstep?" he wondered. "I did. I made a decision for both of us without asking you first. I'm sorry. Is that not what you wanted? I can call her back. I can--"

"Will," she breathed.

"What?"

"Will you marry me?"

"Yes."

"Really? You don't need a second to think about it?"

"Wait, do you mean tonight or ever? Yes to either."

She laughed. "How about this weekend?"

"Yes." He took her face in his hands and kissed her before resting his forehead on hers. "The answer will always be yes. Anything you want, for the rest of my life, you'll have it. I'm gonna give you everything."

Chapter 15

Hey, Gabriel thought to Lucifer. *You busy?*

He scanned the bar for potential playmates. The room was full of beautiful women, but two, in particular, caught his fancy. Both had long, dark hair, their full lips and easy smiles reminding him of Mariana. They sat huddled together in a booth, laughing over the rims of their martini glasses. *Yes.*

Will wants us at B's place. Says he has an announcement. Meet us there?

He smirked as he headed for the table. *Can't. I'm on the prowl.* "Hello, ladies. Mind if I join you?"

They giggled, the one on the left patting the seat next to her.

"Is he coming?" Wyatt asked as he opened the door to his apartment and waited for her to enter before going in himself.

"No," she grumbled. "Says he's busy."

"Doing what?"

"Ho-ing."

"Hey!" Will cheered, pouring them flutes of sparkling cider. "Where have you been? We're celebrating!"

They took the glasses, Gabriel laughing under her breath as she took a sip of the fizzy beverage. Michelle rushed over, Will wrapping his arm around her as she stood next to him.

"Celebrating what?" Wyatt asked.

Michelle beamed, holding up her left hand, showing off the two-carat, white gold halo engagement ring. "We're getting married!"

"Sunday," Will chimed.

"And, we're moving in with Valerie to be close to Sinclair."

"Come eat! I made a ton of food." The couple scampered to the kitchen, Wyatt remaining motionless in the entry.

"You're freaking out," Gabriel said.

"Little bit."

She laughed. "They'll be fine. I can't see in *his* head, but she's all about him. Honestly, who are we to judge? It's a healthier relationship than either of ours."

"You got me there." They clinked glasses. "Where'd he get the money for that ring?"

"I gave him a credit card."

"Of course you did."

"What?"

He shook his head.

"Don't give me shit. I've had a very hard day."

He laughed. "All right. So, you gonna apologize to Wendy?"

"Probably. I should give her a little space first, though, right? She was pretty pissed."

"Yeah, let her cool off a little."

"Yeah."

"Guys!" Will called. "Get in here! I made steak and lava cake."

"He said lava cake," Gabriel bubbled, rushing toward the kitchen.

Wyatt laughed as he followed, taking another sip of cider and joining the others around the island.

Gabriel raised her glass. "To Will and Michelle." They all clinked glasses and began to eat. "So, how offended will you be if I don't eat the asparagus? Like, you'll still give me the cake, right?"

Will chuckled. "Yeah, Aunt Gabriel. You can still have cake. And, I made you two."

She pinched his cheek. "That's why I love you, kid."

Lucifer gazed out the hotel room window, the newly-darkened sky reflecting his feelings of emptiness as he succumbed to his melancholy. Even with two women on top of him, one gyrating on his genitals, the other behind her, kissing her neck and fondling her breasts, he couldn't help but feel bored. Perhaps he'd cared more for Mariana than he'd let himself admit. He let out a mournful sigh and put his hands behind his head. "It's not the same."

Allydia and Phindi stood outside of the four-story building on Wooster and Broome, its black steps leading to the glass storefront glistening under the light of the pale moon.

"What do you think?" the former queen asked. "Gym on the first floor, offices on the third. You could live on the fourth and teach self-defense on the second."

"I don't know," Phindi said, hugging her arms against the cool evening breeze. "Running a business? I wouldn't know where to begin."

"Then you'll hire a manager, someone with experience to run day-to-day operations while you focus on instructing."

"And, you are sure there is a need?"

"I am. Hartley reminded me today of the brutality of men. As long as humanity persists, there will be a need for those who are seen as weak to learn to protect themselves from the strong. You've been my fiercest warrior, but now, the fighting is done. Put your skills to a worthy purpose. You protected my kingdom. Now, teach others to protect themselves."

Phindi looked up to the fourth-floor windows and back down to the storefront, a single potted plant sitting outside of its black-trimmed windows; life against the brick and mortar. She dipped her head then turned to face her former queen. "Then, I accept this challenge. I will make you proud."

"I know that, Phindi. You always do."

Chapter 16

Emergency. Meet at the covenstead NOW.

Donna read the group text from Poe and put her phone in her back pocket before walking down the steps to her basement. The open, mostly empty room had served as the coven's meeting place since Grace's death and while it was conveniently located in her own house, it also meant that she was now in possession of and responsible for all of the coven's most sacred belongings. It was an honor but a burden, knowing that if anything should happen to her home, whether it be fire or flood, the coven's most important items would also be lost. Still, she'd been humbled by her sisters' confidence in her and did her best to ensure the safety of their grimoires, potions, and measures, the last being arguably the most important things a coven retained. The knotted cords functioned as talismans for each witch in the coven, giving the group the ability to control or even kill its members. They were symbols of loyalty, binding each witch to the rest in perfect love and perfect trust. She kept them in a fireproof safe built into the wall opposite the door along with the other sacred objects just as her fallen Priestess had when they resided in *her* home.

"Donna,"

She jumped, startled as she turned to see Julia standing in the corner. "You aren't welcome here anymore."

"I'm giving you a chance to reconsider."

"Reconsider what? Shunning you? I won't." She studied her as she became aware of her increase in power. It was significant and something about it was off. It felt malevolent and as she stepped closer, the odd scent of sulfur filled her nose, making her queasy. "What did you do?"

A sly grin crept across her face. "What I had to." She closed the space between them and as she drew closer, Donna became lightheaded, needing to steady herself against the wall. "You feel it, don't you?" Julia gleaned. "The power?"

She went ghost white, sweat forming on her temples. "What have you done?" She swallowed the bile coming up in her throat and she fought to regulate her breathing. "What I feel coming from you isn't human. What have you attached yourself to?"

"It doesn't matter. I can take it back for us. I have everything we need to take Grace's magic by force. Make me Priestess. I'll lead this coven in a new, glorious age. We'll put the Dyers to shame. The Gowdies will be *nothing* compared to us. Give me control and there will be nothing we can't do."

"I don't know what dark entity you've gotten mixed up with, but even with its help, you are no match for a Tituban witch. It's time for you to go." She opened her mouth wide, releasing a low vibration that pulsed through the room.

Julia squeezed her eyes shut as the wave went through her, causing her diaphragm to seize and her lungs to empty themselves of air with no way of taking in more. A gust of wind began to push Julia backward, her heels dragging across the wooden planks as she fought to hold her ground. After a few seconds of getting her bearings, she planted her feet, cracking her neck and opening her eyes to reveal the now glistening obsidian spheres, like black lacquer pools where her eyes used to be. She flittered her fingers toward the ground as she grinned, conjuring up dozens of snakes. They slithered their way to Donna, wrapping themselves around her ankles and up her legs.

"Evanescet," Donna commanded, but the snakes remained.

"You're the most powerful in our circle and your magic is useless against me." Julia stepped toward her. "You should have accepted me."

The older witch clenched her jaw and turned, stumbling toward the safe.

"What are you gonna do?" Julia scoffed. "Hit me with a lust potion?" But, as she opened the safe, a knot of dread formed in her stomach. As Donna reached inside, Julia whispered, "My measure." She screamed, lifting off her feet and flying toward her. She knocked her to the ground, climbing on top of her and wrestling the cord away. She pinned her down while serpents of varying species slid over her body. Donna's blood pressure dropped and her heart-rate sped out of control as the stench of sulfur overwhelmed her. Julia licked her lips, seeming to get a twisted pleasure from her former sister's panic as an eight-foot black Mussurana glided up Donna's body to her throat, wrapping itself around her neck and beginning the constriction. Her face went blue and her eyes bulged as the blood vessels in the sclera burst, turning red what was once white. Julia exhaled, getting to her feet as the snakes disappeared underneath the floorboards, their job done. Donna was dead, leaving the coven even weaker than before.

Julia threaded her measure through her fingers as she hovered over the fresh corpse, her eyes returning to their original shade. The coven would never accept her now. That was fine. She didn't need them. She'd take Grace's power for herself and if anyone got in her way, they'd just have to die, too.

Wendy and Poe found the coven waiting for them in Donna's basement. They sat in a crescent, Donna's body under a sheet on the floor in front of them. Most were still in tears, but Nicole was stone-faced and ready for revenge. She got up to meet them, putting herself between them and the body.

Poe gasped. "Donna?"

Nicole nodded. "Linda did some candle scrying. Julia took her measure and killed her. It was Julia but also something...*else*. You can still feel it. It's dark."

"I know what it is," Wendy told her. "I know it feels like it's super powerful, but it's been locked up for centuries. It's barely functioning. It needs a witch to latch onto or else it's basically just a creepy shadow."

"Julia wants Grace's magic," Linda said from her seat, her hands trembling. "I saw her intentions in the flame. She wants to take us over," She looked Wendy in the eyes. "And kill you."

She smacked her lips. "Things have been trying to kill me my whole life, but your girl's still here. I'm sorry about your friend." She returned her gaze to Nicole. "No one else is dying today."

"You didn't see what I saw," Linda choked, sniffing and wiping her cheek with the back of her sleeve.

Wendy's expression turned hard. "Get in a circle." She knelt down and opened her bag, taking out Tituba's white candles. The women looked at each other and shrugged before standing and forming a circle. She placed the candles around them and began lighting them.

Poe knelt next to her. "What are you doing?"

"Get in the circle, Poe," she ordered.

Her tone made the girl's heart jump. She got up, standing with her sisters as they watched. The women grew nervous as Wendy stepped over Donna's body to pick up a chair and move it to the center of the circle. She stood on it and took a deep breath. They looked up at her, joining hands and exchanging worried glances.

"What's the plan?" Poe asked.

Wendy rolled her neck then cracked her knuckles. "Bait and fucking switch."

Chapter 17

Lucifer downed his third beer of the hour and tapped his napkin signaling for more. The bartender reluctantly poured him another. "Last one, man."

Lucifer took a sip and put the glass down. "I assure you, I can handle it."

"If you say so. You wanna talk about it?"

"About what?"

"Whatever's got you drinkin'?"

He put his elbows on the bar and thought for a moment. "I think I've been here too long."

"Aight. Let me call you a cab."

"Not here at the bar. On Earth. I've allowed myself attachments. I've acquired disappointment. What's worse is that I find myself without purpose. No enemy to battle. No demon to put back in his place. No evil to vanquish. No part to play in a Divine plan. I'm simply *here*. How do you people do it?"

He cocked his head and raised an eyebrow. "Us people?"

"Yes, humans. You go bumbling through life with no direction, no instruction, aside from the educations provided to you by other humans which is mediocre at best and offensive in its ignorance. And, when you do manage to formulate a plan, more often than not it gets torn to shreds by forces out of your control. How do you go on every day as if it's all fine?" He took another drink. "I'm beginning to have a new appreciation for my brother's repeated attempts at ending his misery once and for all." He took another swig as the bartender sighed.

"I did not need this today," he muttered to himself. "Listen, man, I don't know what you're going through, but taking yourself out isn't a thing to do. If you can't give a shit about yourself, think about the people you'd be leaving behind."

He fiddled with his glass, watching the amber fluid as it swirled. "My sister *would* be quite upset with me. Well, one of them. The other would be indifferent, I imagine. You know, I have no idea how my brother would react. For all the times he's tried to murder me, I think he's starting to come around." He looked up at him. "Honestly, how do you live these lives of constant failures, mistakes, and tragedies?"

"Listen, man, life can fuck you over. A lot. No doubt. But, you keep pushin', keep chippin' away at whatever that goal is. What choice you got? Lay down and die? I don't know about you, but my momma didn't raise a little bitch. So, I'm gonna get my ass up every mornin' and get to work, and if I never get what I want outta life, at least when I get to the pearly gates I can say I gave it everything I had. I kept my nose clean, I treated people decent, and I did everything I could. At the end of the day, it don't matter how many times you get knocked down. What matters is how many times you get back up."

Lucifer tapped his fingers to his lips. "That's very wise." He stood and shook the man's hand. He was preparing to go when a patron shuffled up behind him, blocking his path.

"Hey, boy," the man gruffed. "Get me another whiskey."

Lucifer turned his head to see the drunk, then looked back at the bartender whose jaw had become tight. He leaned in, speaking as quietly as could be heard in the noisy bar. "'Boy' is still a slur, is it not? I've heard my sister call my nephew that, but he's as white as they come. It's a bit confusing. You look perturbed, so I'm assuming it's still offensive, yes?"

The bartender nodded as he wrung his hands, his whole body visibly tense.

"Well, then," Lucifer shot back his elbow, slamming it into the racist's face, shattering his nose and knocking him out cold. He finished his beer and set the glass down, grinning as the bartender lifted his eyes and put his fist to his mouth. Lucifer paid his tab and leaned on the bar. "Would you like me to kill him for you?"

Allydia got back to Wyatt's as Will and Michelle sat down to watch the eleven o'clock news. "Children," she greeted.

"Hey," Will said. "I saved you a plate. It's in the oven. You might want to start with the cake, though. Gabriel's on a sugar bender."

"Isn't she always? Thank you, Will. And, thank you for your assistance with Phindi earlier."

"Everything okay there?"

"Yes, fine. She was just feeling a little lost, needed some direction."

"Hey," Wyatt said as he came into the room, giving Allydia a quick kiss. "Did they tell you?"

"Tell me what?"

Michelle sat forward and held out her hand to show her the engagement ring.

Allydia looked to Wyatt to gauge his reaction before making a judgement. He shoved his hands in his pockets and lifted his eyebrows as he simpered. She shifted her gaze back to the couple and smiled. "Well, congratulations."

"Thank you," Michelle beamed, patting Will on the knee to get his attention. "Let's go shopping for Sinclair's flower girl dress tomorrow. I don't want to put it off to the last minute."

"Who's Sinclair?" The room went quiet, all three of them looking bug-eyed at her, Michelle covering her mouth in regret at what she'd let slip.

"It's fine," Gabriel called from the island as she finished her second piece of cake. "B, maybe take her in the other room to tell her, though. She might react badly. But, I mean, she's human now. What's she gonna do, complain?"

"Come on," Wyatt said, taking her hand and leading her into his bedroom. He closed the door and stood in front of it as she cleared her throat.

"Wyatt," she hesitated, folding her arms and doing her best to keep from looking agitated.

"It's all right."

"It doesn't feel all right."

"I'm sorry," he told her. "I couldn't tell you. Gabriel said you would have killed her."

"Did you..." She dug her nails into her arms as she tried to hold it together. "When Will was a child and we were apart..."

"Oh, no! No, I didn't...she's not *mine*."

She let out a sigh of relief and relaxed her shoulders.

"She's Will's."

She stared at him blankly. "What?"

"His and Michelle's. Michelle was a vampire when she had her, so Gabriel thought you'd--"

"Get out of my way."

"Calm down."

"How old is she, in appearance?"

"About seven. Why?"

"She hasn't come into her full power, yet. There's still time."

"We're not *killing her*, Allydia."

"You've never dealt with something like this," she warned. "Human/vampire hybrids aren't like other vampires. Vampires kill for food or in passion. Their emotions were nearly impossible to keep in check. Hybrids are calculating, premeditated."

"Sounds like someone else I know."

She bit her lip. "I did what I had to to keep my people in line. These things--"

"She's not a *thing*. She's my granddaughter. She's a sweet little girl that likes to draw and go to the park. She's a kid."

"So was Hitler, once. Had I known what he'd become when I met him, I would have killed him, too."

He did a double-take. "You met Hitler?"

"Briefly. He was in a waiting room at a hospital in Linz when I was there for...dinner. He was a teenager, I think. I didn't pay much attention. He was no one at the time. Listen to me, Wyatt. Hybrids are the most powerful creatures on Earth. They can survive almost anything once they mature. If we wait too long, there will be nothing we can do."

"Allydia,"

"They get hyper-focused. Fixated. They set a goal and nothing will keep them from achieving it."

"You sure we're not talking about you?"

She cast him a condescending glare. "Hybrids alone are methodical and cunning serial killers with no capacity for remorse or empathy. Pair that with what you know a Nephilim to be and tell me you're not at all concerned."

He sighed and crossed his arms. "Gabriel says she's okay."

"Well, you'll have to excuse my unwillingness to put too much faith in your sister's judgement after she let your son live."

He stared daggers at her.

"I'm sorry. I'm happy that it all worked out. I am. I've come to appreciate Will and he obviously loves you very much, but you know what he was. Imagine that at ten times the power and with foresight." Hot tears formed in the corners of her eyes as she stepped closer. "When she gets to full power, I will be useless in a fight. I'm human. I won't be able to protect you."

His eyes softened and he cupped her face in his hands. "I don't need you to protect me. I've got a family of archangels for that."

She laughed, wiping a tear from her cheek.

He smiled. "Nothing's gonna happen to me, okay? Sinclair's not dangerous. If she was, Gabriel probably would have killed her without ever telling me she existed, right?"

"Maybe."

He kissed her. "Everything will be fine, I promise."

She nodded, unconvinced.

From the kitchen, Gabriel side-eyed the bedroom door as she took a sip of soda.

"Everything okay?" Will asked from the couch.

She snapped to attention. "Yeah. Everything's fine." She peered at the door again, taking another long sip and placing the can back on the counter. "Everything's gonna be just fine."

Chapter 18

Wendy trekked through the dense foliage of the forest floor, the cool night air still like an undisturbed lake. Poe had described a small clearing at the center of the woods behind Grace's house where her great-aunt had performed her sacred rituals and most difficult spells. Wendy headed to the spot, hoping to tap into any residual energy that might have been left there.

The pale light of the quarter moon was barely visible through the just-turning leaves of the towering oak trees. In the distance, she could hear the caw of a crow as the branches above her began to tremor. She stopped, peering up into the darkness. After a few seconds, the figure of a woman crouching in the tree became clear and from above her Wendy could hear the quiet command. "Transuerso."

She giggled. "Hey, you *are* strong. That almost tickled."

Julia hopped to a lower branch, her face now visible. "Tranuerso!"

"Won't work," Wendy told her. "You wanna come down here? I'm starting to get a crick in my neck."

"TRANSUERSO!"

She sighed. "What's it gonna be? Big fight or save us some time and just toss me the measure now?"

Incensed, Julia leaped from the tree, flinging herself onto Wendy and knocking her to the ground. She smacked her, first with her right hand, then her left.

"Subsisto!"

Julia's hands became immobile at Wendy's command. "I will have your power," she seethed as the forest floor began to move, every inch as far as her eyes could see now lousy with snakes.

Wendy shuddered at the sight of them. "Well, that's not what you want. Sursum." She rose up, sending Julia staggering backward.

"Da mihi!" Julia demanded.

"You know what? I don't think I will."

Her eyes shined black, reflecting the moonlight like onyx glass. She lifted off the ground, hovering above her as she spread her arms open wide. Thunder clapped as thirty-mile-an-hour winds pelted the landscape with hail. "Deditionem tuus potentia!"

"Nope."

Her face twisted in rage, her chest heaving. "Morietur!"

"*Die*? Really? That's rude." Wendy unfurled the measure she'd swiped from Julia's pocket.

"How did you get that?!"

"Nicked it when you were taking your frustrations out on my face. Did you really think I'd let you hit me for no reason? You girls ready?"

"Ready." Poe emerged from the trees, taking the cord and rushing it back to Nicole's awaiting hands just a few feet away in Grace's clearing. Linda lit the candles as Nicole began fraying the edges of the measure.

Julia gasped. "Where did they come from? Why couldn't I feel their magic?"

"I worked one of Tituba's spells. My grandma used it on me when I was a kid to protect me from, well, people like you. From now on, no one outside of the coven will recognize them as witches."

Linda lit the last candle and began to chant, "Praesidio in loco isto."

"No!" Julia flew toward them but was repelled by an invisible wall. She watched in horror as Nicole pulled a single strand from the cord and drop it into the silver ritual bowl. She turned back to Wendy, jaw clenched, and face flushed. "You'll pay."

Wendy scrunched her nose. "Will I, though?"

"MORIETUR!"

"Have you still not figured this out? I'm warded. I can't be spelled."

A sinister smirk appeared on her lips as she pulled the Catseye from her pocket.

"What is that?" Wendy asked, squinting to see.

"You should have checked both pockets."

She stepped closer, still unable to make out the small object in the dark.

"You can't ward yourself from your own blood. Coquito."

Wendy felt a rush of heat flow through her, starting at her heart and making its way through her entire circulatory system. She fell to her knees as Julia cackled. "Cook," she choked, her hand resting on her chest as she began to panic, the realization of what was happening causing her mind to race. She was dying and there was nothing she could do to stop it. Her blood was boiling in her veins.

She dropped onto her back, snakes slithering up her legs and over her abdomen. Her skin turned beet-red as she began to sweat. *I should have forgiven Gabriel*, she thought. *I shouldn't have pushed her away.*

"AUFERETUR!" Poe yelled, running between the women, her eyes sparkling like emeralds. Julia was thrown into the trees, Poe rocketing up to meet her. The two clashed, clawing at each other like jackals as they slammed into branches, careening through the air like out-of-control space junk. They plummeted to the ground like meteors, cratering the forest floor, spewing dirt and snake pieces in all directions.

Julia got the upper hand, pinning the sixteen-year-old in the depression with her mind as she herself floated out, a satisfied sneer on her pale lips. "Your power may be increased, but you are *nothing* compared to me. You're a child out of her depth. You should have stayed in hiding. Operculum!"

The ground beneath her began to rumble as she struggled to break free of Julia's spell. The walls of soil around her crumbled, filling the pit, and entombing the young witch.

Julia laughed, turning her attention back to the coven as she stepped over Wendy lying screaming in agony on the grass. She held her hands out, using everything she had to penetrate the protection spell. Just as she was beginning to make progress, the sound of an explosion rang out from behind. She spun around and was confronted by a dirt-covered Poe, her eyes shining even more brightly than before.

"I may be a kid, but I can still whoop your ass." The girl waved a hand in her enemy's direction and bellowed, "Quercus!" Julia was hurled into a massive oak, her head bloodied on the bark as she collapsed unconscious to the forest floor.

Poe hurried to kneel next to Wendy who lay barely alive, wheezing and crying blood tears. "Amoveatur," she ordered, her eyes returning to normal.

Wendy coughed, gulping in air as the redness in her skin disappeared. She sat up, still too lightheaded to stand as her temperature went down. She patted her friend's arm and steadied her breathing. "Thanks, Poe."

Julia stood, her face twisted in rage as she touched the back of her head and looked at the blood on her hand when she pulled it away.

Wendy tried to stand, but her legs were like jelly. "I'm not really up to snuff. You got this?"

Poe hopped up and stretched her arms over her chest. "Yeah, I'm good."

Wendy crawled to join the others in the circle as Julia bounded forward.

"Adflicto!" Poe shouted, causing her adversary's spine to snap.

She fell but soon recovered, the monster inside her healing the break almost immediately. "Sursus deorsum!"

Poe was flung upside down in the air, hovering as if she were being held by her ankles.

"We have to hurry," Wendy asserted. Nicole dropped a match in the bowl, sending a green flame to jump then dissipate. She looked at the group, each one nodding to convey their readiness. In unison, the witches spoke the sacred words, "Nunc marcus finis eius magicae."

"NO!" Julia cried as her eyes lost their sheen. Tears poured down her cheeks as the air stilled, the clouds moved out, and the snakes slithered back to where they'd come from.

Poe crashed to the ground, released from the former witch's spell. Julia fell to her knees, powerless and devastated. She sobbed, covering her face with shaky hands as Nicole approached, her face like stone.

She looked down at her, hands clenched behind her back. "We banish you, Julia of the Kyteler line. You will leave the State of New York, never to return for any reason. And, let me make this crystal clear for you.

If I ever see you again, I will kill you." She went back to her sisters, leaving Julia to cry alone. There was no coming back from this, no revenge to be had. She was nothing.

Chapter 19

Hartley listened to the waves crashing outside the Atlantic City apartment. She lay in bed, unnerved by how tired she already was as Oliver slept quietly next to her. Up until now, midnight had been her noon, her "day" barely started. Now, she could hardly keep her eyes open as the cool ocean breeze coming in through the open window filled the air with a clean saltiness, lulling her to sleep. These new hours would take some getting used to.

As she drifted off, her phone rang. She answered it quickly as not to disturb her new-ish boyfriend. "Yes?"

"Is this Hartley?" the woman on the other end asked.

"It is."

"Hello, doll. This is Wanda, your grandmother's nurse. I just wanted to let you know that Gloria passed peacefully in her sleep about an hour ago."

She sat up, her heart leaping to her throat.

"She was very happy to see you and your father today. I've never seen her smile that much."

"My father?"

"Yes. She said seeing her son again was the best gift she could've asked for. I must have missed him. Can you give him the news? I don't have a number for him. Thank God you left yours. Nothing's more tragic than learning about the death of a loved one in the obituaries."

"Um, of course. Yes, I'll tell him."

"Thank you, dear. Now, Father Daniel has been by to perform the last rites and has scheduled her service for three this Saturday at St. Anthony's. Will I see you there?"

"Um,"

A dog barked in the background. "Oh, shoot. Forgot to let the dog out. I have to go. I'm so sorry for your loss."

"Thank you." She ended the call and set the phone on the nightstand, lying back and pulling the sheets up to her chin. She stared up at the ceiling, unsure of how to feel. Her mind was swirling with the revelations of the day, her eyelids heavy. In his sleep, Oliver rolled over and threw an arm over her waist. She hugged it, grateful to have someone there with her. She fell asleep, unaware of the single tear that slid down her cheek.

The coven gathered in Grace's living room to discuss what to do now that Donna was gone. Wendy sat at the kitchen table, cuddling Raven as Poe made tea for the group. As she waited for the kettle, Poe took a seat next to her friend and folded her hands, pleading with her eyes.

"What?" Wendy asked, already knowing the answer.

"Well? Are you gonna join us, or what?"

"Or what."

She stuck out her lip.

"Don't give me that face," she giggled.

"We need you."

"You don't."

"Wendy,"

"Look, Poe, I understand how important covens can be. Aside from the occasional need for the power of multiple witches, the sisterhood, the bonds that you all have...it's awesome. I had that with my grandma back in the day. But, the coven is just...not where I belong."

She put her elbow on the table. "Where is, then? The city?"

"Probably."

"With Gabriel?"

She sighed and put the bunny on the table, petting its ears. "Feels that way."

"Well, you know we're always around if you need us."

"Same."

"Thank you, Wendy," Nicole said, entering the room and sitting across the table. "We appreciate everything you did for us today. If there's anything we can do to repay you in the future, don't hesitate to call."

She nodded.

"Poe, the girls have been talking. It may be unorthodox, but we would like *you* to be our new Priestess."

"What?" she coughed.

Wendy patted her back.

"Tonight, you proved yourself to be the most powerful among us. You showed bravery and compassion. And, Grace loved you like a daughter. It's only fitting that you should take her place."

She cleared her throat. "I don't know what to say."

"Say you'll do it," Wendy winked.

"I-I accept."

"Wonderful. I'll tell the others." She got up and went back to the living room as the kettle began to whistle. Wendy stood and poured the water into the teapot while Poe remained motionless, jaw agape.

Wendy sat back down, letting the tea steep. "You okay?"

"Not really."

She laughed. "You'll be fine. I have a feeling this is what Grace was grooming you for. I didn't know her, but if she was anything like her sister, she knew what she was doing."

"I'm only sixteen."

"All right, so, maybe that's not *ideal*." She laughed. "But, you have five sisters in there that love you and trust you. And, you have family in me."

"I do?"

She smacked her lips. "Girl, we're practically cousins."

She smiled and hugged her. "Thanks, Wendy."

"No problem. Hey, I think your rabbit's jealous."

They looked at the bunny now up on its hind legs, its front paws covering its face. They laughed as Poe picked it up, snuggling it under her chin. "You think you'll ever get a familiar?"

She considered it, conceding that Raven was super cute. "Maybe. One day."

Wendy knocked on Gabriel's door, but there was no answer. She tried opening it, but it was locked. She glanced around the hall. It was empty. "Recludo." The bolt unlocked and she let herself in. She went to the bedroom where she expected Gabriel to be sleeping, but it was empty. No one was home. She sat on the ottoman, tapping her fingers on the soft fabric, and waited.

Chapter 20

Will and Michelle lay unconscious in front of the TV, having fallen asleep during the monologue of a late-night talk show. Allydia, too, had gone to bed while Wyatt and Gabriel stayed up talking.

"You're not tired?" he asked.

"I am," she replied, spinning her empty soda can on the island.

"But, you don't want to go home."

"Not especially."

He sat next to her, arm on the counter as he faced her. "You're miserable. Maybe you should call her."

"It's not just that," she admitted. "It's all the things. God's work, secrets I have to keep. It's getting to be too much and I don't know how I'm gonna keep doing it."

"You'll do it, whatever it is because you have to. You always do. My friend Tim would say you have broad shoulders. Anything that gets put on them, you'll carry."

She looked away as she nodded in resentful agreement.

"But, it *is* okay to take a break once in a while."

She scoffed. "That hasn't been my experience."

He laughed. "All right, but you set yourself *on fire* today. You'd be dead if Lucifer hadn't saved you. Think about that sentence and tell me you don't need a break."

She laughed out loud. "Satan as a savior is pretty funny. Although, he *is* a good dude, just kind of fucked up."

"Yeah."

"He's growing on you."

He rolled his eyes.

"You care about him."

"Stop," he smirked.

She giggled. "He's your new best friend. You're gonna start having sleepovers and braiding each other's hair."

"Okay."

"It's nice. You *should* get along. He's a lot, but he loves you."

He looked amused. "He loves me?"

"Don't tell him I told you, but he's desperate for your approval. He sees you as a kind of moral authority. He respects you."

"Really?"

"He brought Will back because he couldn't stand to see you so upset. I know you remember how Barachiel feels about him."

He crossed his arms and sighed.

"You've been great friends basically since you were created. You just don't remember it."

"He's all right."

"Besties."

He shook his head.

"I'm gonna have necklaces made."

"Geez."

"No! Friendship bracelets."

"You need a nap."

Lucifer stumbled down the street, his buzz not quite inebriation. He took a swig from his nearly empty whiskey bottle, still in the bag it came in as not to alert police. He'd hoped to feel the effects of the alcohol more fully, but it would seem he hadn't had enough. He couldn't help but be disappointed in the bartender's refusal to take him up on his offer of bigot-homicide as he thought about the last time he'd taken his frustrations out on men who had offended a barkeep he'd come to admire. He finished the bottle and dropped it in a trashcan as he passed, wondering what kind of trouble he could get into before the night was through.

The streets were unusually quiet. Or was it just later than he thought? Only a few people walked by and street traffic moved freely, not a single traffic jam his entire walk. He took his phone from his pocket and checked the time. 2:07 AM. "Ah," he said to himself. He leaned against a lamppost and scrolled through his old messages, reading back conversations he'd had with Mariana that he hadn't been able to delete.

Ready for round two?

Of course!

Be there shortly.

Not the most romantic words ever written, but they plucked at his heartstrings all the same.

He replaced the phone and took in his surroundings. The lights, the vibrancy, the pollution. "I don't belong here." He shoved his hands in his pockets and began walking, aimless in the dark.

Chapter 21

The one-eyed man held a finger to his lips as he waved his men closer to the apartment door. "Remember, we're taking our time with this one. No shootin'. We're gonna do this old school."

The three men nodded, evil grins plastered on their faces as they rubbed their hands together in anticipation.

"Don't kill her, now. That's *my* right. Hurt her real bad, but *I* put the nail in the coffin."

Again, they nodded.

"Let's get to it, then." He kicked the door in, leaving a scuff mark where his boot hit.

Wendy shot up from her seat on the ottoman. Assuming they were burglars, she waved a hand at them. "Auferetur!" But, the men just laughed. "What the hell?"

"Wendy, right?" the leader asked, stepping forward.

"Foris!"

"That won't work on us. We took precautions."

"What do you want?"

He drew closer. "I know it's been some years, but, I was wondering, do you remember me?"

She studied the man's face as her heart pounded in her ears. She caught a breath in her throat as her bottom lip began to quiver.

"That's right."

"You killed my parents," she breathed.

"You took my eye. Some might call that square. I say, we have unfinished business."

Seeing that there was no way out, adrenaline coursing through her veins, she punched him in the mouth, causing drops of blood to spill from his lip to the floor.

He rubbed his face. "Oh, you're spunky, I'll give you that." He backhanded her, knocking her to the ground and kicking her in the abdomen. "Come on, boys. Time to teach this witch bitch a lesson."

They snickered and whooped as they bounded over, taking turns kicking her in the back and head. They pounded on her with their fists, one of them pinning her to the floor with his knee on her diaphragm. She couldn't breathe as blood poured from her mouth and broken nose. Her eyes swelled shut from repeated punches and her shattered ribs had punctured one of her lungs. She'd gone numb, probably from shock. She couldn't move, limp on the hardwood as the men continued their assault.

The one-eyed man shooed the others away as he straddled her waist and hit her again. "I'm gonna enjoy watching you die."

As he wrapped his thick fingers around her throat, she heard a familiar voice in the distance. "Well, well, well. I had planned on going straight to bed, but butchering a handful of intruders is probably just the thing I need to ensure a good night's rest."

"Mind your business, buddy," one of the men barked, pointing his rifle at him. Lucifer smirked and snatched it away, breaking it over his knee and discarding the pieces before headbutting the stunned witch hunter, rendering him unconscious.

"Who's next?"

The two foot-soldiers raised their weapons, spraying the room with bullets, Lucifer's body riddled with quick-healing wounds. He lunged at them, yanking the guns from their hands and tossing them to the ground. He picked one of the men up and threw him into a wall before smashing the other's head on the kitchen counter, crushing it like a rotted piece of fruit. The first man got to his feet and staggered toward him, Lucifer laughing at the determined look on his face.

He grabbed him by the collar and tossed him to the floor. "It was unwise of you to come to this place." He lifted his boot and slammed it down on the intruder's head, cracking his skull and killing him instantly. "And, then there's you." He stomped toward the man with the eyepatch, his cheeks crimson with rage at the sight of Wendy's condition.

"Who the hell are you?" the man shouted, standing up and pulling his pistol.

He rolled his head back. "So many titles. "Shining One. Light-Bearer. Watch-Keeper of the Damned. God's Strongest and, of course, Favorite of the Almighty."

His hand began to shake. "S-Sa--"

He gripped him by the throat with one hand while disarming him with the other. "*I am not Satan.*"

The man grabbed his wrist, struggling to get free as he choked.

He pulled him close, teeth clenched as he spoke in a soft, deep tone. "My name is *Lucifer.*" He spun him around and snapped his neck, dropping his body to the floor and brushing his hands together as he looked over the rest, making sure no man was left breathing. "I'd almost forgotten how much I enjoyed a good slaughter." His eyes fell to the broken witch. "Wendy," he whispered, falling to his knees next to her, holding her face in his hands as he inspected her head wounds. *Gabriel,*

Sup?

Wendy's hurt. Come home now. I fear she doesn't have much time.

Coming.

He tapped her cheek to try to coax her awake, but she was too far gone. He listened for a heartbeat. It was slow, her breathing rattled and shallow.

"Just sit tight," he pleaded. "Gabriel's on her way." But, there was no time. Her chest fell and didn't rise again. "Come on, love," He felt for a pulse but couldn't find one. "Must you be so impatient? I haven't healed anyone in sixty-five years and it never was my strong suit. Can you not hang on until Gabriel arrives?" He sighed, placing one hand on her forehead and one over her heart. "Fine. I will make the attempt." He pursed his lips and growled as he concentrated, sweat beading at his temples. His whole body trembled as he sought to make things right. His bloodshot eyes began to tear as he feared he'd be unable to heal her. "You mustn't leave."

Finally, his hands began to glow, lighting up her skin with the power of a thousand stars. Her swelling went down, her nose righted itself. Her broken bones came back together and her lungs filled with air.

She sprung up, her eyes flying open as she gasped and clutched her chest. Lucifer fell back, exhausted, lying in a pool of sweat.

She slid next to him, still too weak to stand. "You okay?"

"Fine," he panted.

"Wendy?!" Gabriel called as she rushed into the apartment.

"I'm all right," she said as Gabriel dropped to the floor in front of her.

She ran her hands over her, checking for wounds before kissing her and running her hands through her hair. "I'm sorry. I should've told you about--"

"I'm sorry, too. I overreacted. The truth is, I'm pretty sure I'm in love with you."

She wiped away a tear and kissed her again.

"Well, I'm off to bed," Lucifer said, sitting himself up. "Do clean up this mess before the corpses give off a smell."

Gabriel threw her arms around her brother's neck, almost knocking him back down. "Thank you."

"It was nothing." He patted her back and pulled away so he could stand.

"Really. I owe you. Huge."

"I'll keep it in mind. Goodnight." He shuffled off to his room, leaving the two alone among the bodies.

"What the hell happened?"

"Witch hunters," Wendy huffed.

"Ah."

"Did you know Lucifer knew Tituba?"

"Yeah. You didn't?"

She shook her head.

"Oh, yeah. They hung out a few times in the 1690s. He even made a special trip topside when he found out she'd been arrested. Had to *buy* her to get her released. He still feels weird about that. Slavery really pissed him off."

Everything all right? She heard Wyatt in her head.

Fine. Lucifer saved her. I told you he's a good dude. She glanced around at the dead bodies. *Maybe a little messy.*

Chapter 22

Hartley peeked her head into the chapel. The priest had already begun speaking, so she tiptoed in and found a seat at the back of the church where she hoped to go unnoticed. In the pews ahead of her she saw her mother's nurse, a woman she vaguely recognized as being one of her mother's friends that babysat her when she was young, and about thirty people she'd never seen before. The smell of incense made her queasy as she listened to the eulogy, the priest's words hitting harder than she'd expected.

"Gloria was a pillar of her community. From her work at the women's shelter and the soup kitchen to her charitable donations to cancer research, crisis relief, and back-to-school preparedness programs, she was a shining example of what a servant of God should be. Helping others was what gave her joy. When it came to the church, she was one of the most devoted members I've ever seen, leading Bible study, singing in the choir, and hosting fundraisers twice a year to raise money for repairs and maintenance for our beloved church home. No one here will ever forget the fire that gutted this very sanctuary twelve years ago. The city almost had the building condemned. But, Gloria went out, going door-to-door, raising funds to bring us back from the brink. All told, she raised over one point six million dollars. We're only here today because of her love for God and our church family. No one will ever be able to replace Gloria Morales. She will be missed for generations to come." He made the sign of the cross, as did the crowd. Hartley noticed several people crying, including the nurse. The priest himself looked to be getting misty. "At this time, I'd like to invite friends and family to come to the pulpit and say a few words."

Wanda stood, going to the head of the room and smoothing a piece of paper out in front of her. "First, I'd like to thank you all for welcoming me. I didn't know Gloria for very long and when we met, she was already pretty far along in her illness. Still, she'd have moments of clarity. They could last a few days or just a few minutes. In one of those moments, she wrote this letter to all of you. She asked me to read it at her funeral." She cleared her throat and looked down at the page. "To my friends and church family, I love you. You've made my time on this earth easier and less painful. You picked me up when I was down. You gave me strength when I was weak. You helped me see what was broken in me and gave me the courage to right the wrongs that had shattered me. You lifted me up and I have no words for how grateful I am for that. To Father Daniel, your visits have meant the world to me. Most people couldn't stand to see me in this state, but you have been here for me. I am truly blessed to have your prayers, guidance, and friendship. Thank you. And, to my son,"

Hartley's ears perked up, her stomach flipping as she bit her bottom lip.

"My sweet, beautiful baby boy, you may never hear this and that's my fault. I wasn't there for you the way I should have been. I didn't know how to parent a child like you. I was a bad mother. I know that and I'm sorry. I hope that the actions I took in the past were enough to give you some peace of mind. That knowing you're safe, at least from one person who didn't understand you, is of some comfort to you. Even though I didn't get to watch you become the person you were meant to be, or see you fall in love, or even smile without pain in your eyes, I can feel you in my heart every day. I love you more than you'll ever know and I hope that life gives you everything you ask of it.

And, to everyone listening, don't cry for me. Don't grieve what's lost. Instead, love what's in front of you. Be kind, do good works, and love yourselves the way you wish to be loved. I'll see you all again one day. Goodbye."

Hartley covered her mouth as tears rolled down her cheeks.

"Hartley, dear, is that you?" Wanda asked. The crowd turned to look at her.

She wiped her face and sat up straight. "Y-yes."

"Would you like to say something? Everyone, this is Hartley, Gloria's granddaughter."

She was a deer in headlights as they stared. Slowly, she stood, smoothing her charcoal-black Etsuko dress and making her way to the pulpit. She glanced down at the closed casket, breathing a sigh of relief that she didn't actually have to see her mother's dead body. Wanda gave her arm a quick pat before handing her the letter and taking her seat.

"I'm not really sure what to say," Hartley admitted. "I hadn't spoken to Gloria in years. I thought coming here would be easier. I didn't expect to be so emotional." She paused, swallowing hard as she gathered her nerve. "I didn't know her the way all of you did. I grew up being worried about what she thought of me. I was downright afraid if I'm being honest." She blew out a mournful breath. "I don't think I can ever forget how she made me feel as a scared, lonely, queer kid just looking for *one person* to stick up for me and not having that. I don't know that I can ever forgive her for not being what I needed her to be. But, I do think I can come to terms with it now." She wiped the last tear from her face. "I'm ready to move on."

Lucifer sauntered into Gabriel's apartment the morning of the wedding carrying a large envelope. "Sister, I'm glad I caught you."

Gabriel swallowed a bite of pumpkin pie-flavored toaster pastry and crossed her legs, resting her elbows on the island. "You're leaving?"

"I'm having a bit of an existential crisis. Thought I might do some traveling. Would you mind giving this to William and extending my apologies to the happy couple for missing the blessed event?"

She opened the envelope and pulled out the deed, leaving the keys inside. "You bought them a building in Brooklyn?"

"Just a six-story on Dekalb. Nothing overtly pretentious."

"Sixteen million dollars?"

"Fifteen point eight and that money was going to waste just sitting in your account."

"What do you expect them to do with twenty-eight apartments and three commercial spaces?"

"Whatever they like. Michelle's inheritance will run out eventually. Raphael was a surgeon, not a titan of industry. This gives them security. Options. I'm surprised *you* didn't think of it. What did you get them?"

"I'm paying for the wedding."

"And?"

"Nothing."

"Come now, Gabriel."

She bit her bottom lip and averted her glance. "*And*, a trip to the Moon."

"A *what*?"

"A private company's doing them now."

"How much is that?"

She shifted in her seat. "Eighty-one million."

He raised his eyebrows.

"Each."

He laughed.

"Hey, it is a once-in-a-lifetime experience."

"It would have to be."

She put the page back in the envelope and resealed it. "I'll give them your present."

"Thank you." He turned to go. "I'll be back."

"Lucifer," She got up and walked over to him, giving him a hug and patting his back. "Take care of yourself."

"I always do."

Hartley sat on the edge of the bed staring at the three pills in her palm. *This is it*, she thought. *No going back*. She popped them in her mouth, estrogen, progesterone, and anti-androgen. She took a sip of water and swallowed them down. Now that she was human, her body could change. In a few years, her outside would finally match her inside.

She walked to the window as she tied her hair up in a messy bun, closing it against the cool ocean breeze that gave her chills. She watched the sunlight glisten on the waves as they crashed against the beach and admired the wispy clouds that floated in the havelock sky.

She left Oliver in bed while she went to the kitchen to make breakfast. She had never been a good cook, but she'd recently discovered she could make anything that came in a tube. So, she set the oven to three hundred and fifty degrees, banged a package of cinnamon rolls on the counter, and opened it, placing the icing cup on the stove and separating the rolls of dough onto the sheet pan. She washed her hands, put the pan in the oven, and set the timer. She sat at the bar, taking her phone from the charger and smiling. Her life was blissfully normal and for the first time maybe ever, she didn't feel afraid.

She went into her texts and found Allydia's number. Her cat leaped into her lap and then to the counter, her tail smacking Hartley in the face. She giggled and typed the words, *Thank you*. She hit 'send' and put the phone down before getting the cat's food in her bowl and again sitting, resting her cheek on her hand as she allowed herself to feel something she'd never dreamed was in her reach...happiness.

Allydia texted back, *You're most welcome* and put her phone down on the charger in her kitchen as Navid came in to meet her.

"That's a nice dress," he commented. "What are you all gussied up for?"

"A wedding." She glared at the suitcase in his hand. "What's this?"

"Just packin' up the few things I bought while I was here."

"You're leaving?"

"Yeah, it's about time I get back to work. We can't all be independently wealthy."

She leaned on the counter. "I've funded your savings and current accounts to eighty-five thousand pounds and deposited twenty million dollars into a Swiss account under your name."

He blinked and shook his head. "You what?"

"I must have forgotten to mention it. I would have put more in your UK accounts, but they're only insured up to--"

"You didn't have to do that."

She squinted for a second. "Of course I did. What's the point of having money if not to take care of people?"

"Thank you, but recent events aside, I can actually take care of myself."

"I'm sure you can. It's not an insult." She walked past him and made her way to her bedroom where she opened a drawer full of various types of jewelry. He followed her, standing in the doorway as she retrieved a diamond tennis bracelet and carefully put it on her wrist.

"I can't take your money. It makes me feel a bit like a child."

"You *are* my child," she asserted as she placed diamond studs in her ears. "In a way. If you never touch the money, it won't hurt my feelings. It's there in case you need it and that gives me peace of mind. When are you going?"

"In the morning. Flight leaves at ten."

"You should come to the wedding, then. Do you have a suit? Let's buy you a suit."

"Whose wedding is it?"

"Wyatt's son's. And his niece's, sort of."

"Oh, that's, um..."

"They're not related by blood. Wyatt and the bride's uncle are both angels."

"Whew, I was worried I'd stumbled onto something I'd be better off not knowin'. You know, I don't think you ever told me which angel your man is."

"Oh, he's Barachiel, Protector of Humanity."

"Really?"

"Yes. Why do you say 'really' like that?"

"Just strikes me as odd, guardian angel takin' up with the queen of vampires. How'd you manage it?"

She clicked her tongue and tossed her hair over her shoulder. "Persistence."

"Will there be other angels there?"

"Yes. Uriel who goes by Valerie, and Gabriel, of course." She noticed him cross his arms at the sound of her name. "She'll be there with her girlfriend, the witch that turned me back. Will that make you uncomfortable?"

"No," he said, feigning a casual tone.

She didn't quite believe him but moved on. "Good. Michelle, the bride, is human as is Uriel's husband, Malik. Uriel and Malik have adopted Will and Michelle's daughter, Sinclair, who's part Nephilim and part vampire. Because she was born and not bitten, she retains her vampire nature. I am uneasy about it, but I've spoken to Gabriel and she claims the girl is a danger to no one. Something about the way she said it, though."

He stared, wide-eyed, his concern obvious.

"No harm will come to you, I promise."

"You sure about that?"

She used her finger to make a cross over her heart.

He snickered.

"Now, let's go get you a suit. We'll have to hurry. We have a plane to catch."

"A plane? Where is this wedding?"

Chapter 23

"It feels like it's been a lifetime since I've been here," Will said as Wyatt fixed his tie. Standing in his childhood bedroom in Southport, he tried to push the memories of the last time he was there from his mind, but they haunted his thoughts like malevolent spirits, ready to send him into a meltdown at any moment. Beating the pizza guy half to death, what he'd done to his father...the wolves. He was feeling unsteady, but he kept himself together. It was important to Michelle that they get married in the place where they'd first said 'I love you', so he pushed through his demons. *Anything* to make her happy.

"It kind of was," Wyatt teased, seeing how uneasy his son was and attempting to lighten his mood. "I mean, you did die."

He snorted.

"You sure you're ready for this?"

"Honestly? She's the *only* thing I'm sure about. Like, in life."

He gave a quiet smile as he finished adjusting the tie and straightened his own.

"What?"

"Nothing, just," He finished with his tie and picked up his jacket. "That's exactly how I felt when I married your mother."

"You still miss her?"

"I think part of me always will." He felt himself getting emotional, so he took a deep breath as he put on the jacket, not wanting to ruin his son's day. "She'd be really proud of you."

"You think so?"

"Are you kidding? Michelle's way out of your league. If your mom was here, she'd run up to the altar and high-five you as soon as you said, 'I do'."

Will burst out laughing. "Just because you're right, doesn't mean you have to be rude."

He laughed.

"So, do you have any advice?"

"Marriage advice?" He cringed and crossed his arms as he thought. "Well, I guess I'd say, don't panic when you argue, because you *will* argue. A lot. It's normal. What you have to do is stay on topic, never insult her, and remember that at the end of the day, what you're really fighting for is the health of your relationship. Put that first and everything else will fall into place. Easier said than done, but do your best to keep it in mind."

"That's solid advice."

"I'm wise beyond my years," Wyatt joked.

"Aren't you really, like, two-hundred-thousand years old?"

He laughed again. "Probably. I'd have to ask Gabriel for an exact number."

"It's not that hard to figure out. You were created to protect people and people, as we know them, didn't exist until--"

He shook his head. "All right, smart-ass." He handed Will his jacket and patted him on the shoulder. "Let's get you married."

Locked away in Wyatt's old bedroom, out of sight from her fiance's prying eyes, Michelle let Gabriel help her with her makeup. There was no way she was letting Will see her before she walked down the aisle. Yes, it was superstitious, but with her luck, she wasn't taking any chances.

As the angel applied a small amount of highlighter to her cheekbones, Michelle wondered something. "Does it feel ridiculous that you had to get online-ordained to perform the ceremony, given who you are?"

"A little," she admitted.

"My uncle called you 'the highest authority on Earth'. Seems silly you need a piece of paper to prove you can do something."

"A piece of paper like a marriage license?" she teased.

She grinned. "Haha."

She put the brush down and picked up the mascara. "Look up."

She did as she was told and Gabriel applied a final coat to her long lashes.

"Just so you know, I'm not an authority on anything. I'm an errand boy. I relay messages. That's really it." She put the tube down and stood, waving her hand for Michelle to do the same, which she did. She held the Cinderella-like dress open for her to step into and pulled it up around her.

"You're more than that. You're like a second mother to me."

"Well, that's terrifying. You know I'm not a role model, right?"

"I hate to break it to you, but you don't get to decide how I perceive you."

She bit her tongue. "Fair enough." She zipped her up and stood her in front of the mirror.

"Holy crap." She lit up as she admired the dress, its lace bodice with cap sleeves and plunging neckline accentuated her body perfectly and the full skirt made entirely from fairy-tale 3D lace made to look like leaves was hyper-dramatic, just as she'd requested. She'd never seen herself as beautiful but now, staring at her reflection as Gabriel added a few more bobby pins to her sparkling crystal tiara to keep it firmly in place, she was floored by how stunning she was.

"So weird when hot girls don't know they're hot," Gabriel commented.

"Hey," She turned to look at her. "I know you don't need to hear it, but thank you. None of this would be happening if not for you. I don't just mean the wedding. I mean any of it. If you hadn't sent me here..." She stopped, choking back tears, and fanning her face.

"Okay, okay. Don't ruin your makeup getting all up in your feelings already. I'm not doing that shit again." She got a tissue from the makeup bag and dabbed it under her friend's eyes.

She took the tissue and blew out a calming breath.

"Better?"

She nodded. "I mean it, though. You gave me a whole family when I'd lost mine. I'll always be grateful for that. I love you." She hugged her, careful not to let her freshly made-up face touch Gabriel's rose-red dress.

"I love you, too, girl." She hugged her back, chewing on her lip as she stifled her own worried tears. "I really do."

Gabriel knelt in front of Sinclair to hand her the white wicker basket of rose petals and smoothed back a hair that had strayed out from underneath her crystal headband. She adjusted the girl's shoe that had somehow slipped off in the back and when she was finished, she brushed the curls from her shoulders, flashing a half-hearted smile. "Beautiful as always."

"Gabriel,"

"Hmm?"

"Grandpa was right. You should take a break. You deserve it."

"That's kind of you to say, but--"

"Gabriel," she touched her cheek. "You're doing a good job."

Her eyes swelled with tears as Sinclair kissed her cheek and threw her arms around her neck. She held her for a few seconds as she got her emotions in check.

"Are you ready, baby?" Michelle asked as she met them at the edge of the forest.

"Ready, Mommy!" she beamed, handing Gabriel a tissue she pulled from her left shoe.

Gabriel blotted her damp cheeks and held back a chuckle as she stood.

The bride bent down and pointed to the white linen runner that stretched from where they stood to the clearing in front of the creek. "Just follow that cloth all the way to the end. When you get to Daddy, sit down with Malik and Valerie, okay?"

"I got it, Mommy." She skipped down the path lit by twinkly lights that covered every tree on either side.

"Are you sure she'll be all right? The sun's going down and it's a long way to the wedding."

Gabriel scoffed. "Strongest creature on Earth, remember? Nothing's gonna fuck with her out here."

"Okay." She took a deep breath and blew it out slowly as she steadied her nerves.

"Didn't you take public speaking in school?"

"Yeah."

"There are only seven people down there."

"That's not what I'm nervous about and you know it."

Gabriel shot her a condescending glare.

"I wish you could tell me, you know, for sure."

"Hey," Gabriel smiled. "I don't need superpowers to be able to tell that that boy loves you."

"What if--"

"No 'what if's'."

"But--"

"A couple of years ago, he was about five and I brought him as a present his own laptop. B hadn't let him on the internet yet because he'd read like, *all* the parenting books and thought it was too soon." She rolled her eyes. "So, I talked him into letting me give it to him, which took some arm twisting, but I mean, come on. The kid's a genius. It would have been cruel to stifle him, right? So, he opens the box and I get it all plugged in and set up and I'm telling you, his face lit up like a goddamn Christmas tree. He did everything on that computer from that day on. School, shopping, the occasional trolling of politicians on social media. It was his link to the outside world. It meant everything to him."

"That's cute, but what does it have to do with anything?"

"Because, dummy, he looks at you the same way he looked at that laptop for the first time, with hope and excitement. When you talk, he hangs on every word like he might fall off a cliff. When you leave the room, for a split second, I can see a little twinge of sadness on his face. Will loves you. The only thing you have to worry about is making sure you always remember that. Golden rule that shit."

"What?"

"Marriage. Just like anything else, it works like magic. Do unto him as you'd have him do unto you."

"Ah," she laughed.

"I didn't mean it that way, filthy." She waved her hands in front of herself to try to get the image out of her head.

"It works that way, too, though."

She gagged. "You're grossing me out now."

The music started, "Once Upon A Time...Storybook Love", wafting through the trees on the PA system Gabriel had installed, run by the DJ who'd set up just out of sight of the actual ceremony.

"I guess it's time," Michelle said, grinning from ear to ear.

"All right, girl. Go get your man."

Chapter 24

The setting sun cast a rosy hue through the trees as Will stood at the altar, his skin glowing under the lights that twinkled all around him, in the trees and cascading down from the Spanish Dress and white rose-covered arbor. In front of him, the aisle ran deep into the woods. On one side sat Malik, Valerie, and Wendy. On the other, his father, Allydia, and Navid, who he'd never met, but seemed like a nice enough guy. Behind him, the sound of the rushing creek filled the air. He squeezed his hands together in front of him, the anticipation driving him crazy. As beautiful as this all was, he just wanted to be married. He couldn't wait to make Michelle his wife. He only hoped he would always do right by her.

Allydia could see the torment Wyatt was trying to hide in his eyes. She held his hand and rubbed his arm. She remembered the last time they were in this place, Wyatt cradling Will's limp body in the grass as he cried and feeling helpless as she had no way of easing his pain. "Is it hard to be back here?"

"A little." He kissed her hand, trying to ignore the memories that flashed in his mind. "A little."

"He looks happy."

Wyatt smiled. "He does, doesn't he?"

"It really is beautiful out here."

"It can be."

Overhead, they heard one song fade out and another begin, Haley Reinhart's version of "Can't Help Falling In Love". The small crowd turned to see Sinclair skipping down the aisle, tossing red and white rose petals from a basket, her face lit up with a smile that could melt the coldest of hearts. She bounced up to Will. "Happy wedding, Daddy!"

"Thank you, sweetie," he giggled. She took her seat on Valerie's lap as Gabriel made her way to the altar, standing behind Will and facing the crowd. Finally, emerging from the trees like a fairy princess, Michelle made her entrance. Will's knees went weak as his heart raced, the sight of her giving him life. He caught himself, having to take a step back so he wouldn't fall as he whispered to himself, "I am *not* good enough for her."

She stepped to the altar, taking Will's hand as the couple faced their officiant.

Gabriel took the bride's bouquet and cleared her throat as the music stopped. "We are gathered here today to celebrate the joining of William Ross Sinclair and Michelle Narissa Iha in Holy Matrimony. Who gives this woman to be married to this man?"

Sinclair raised her hand. "I do!"

They all laughed as Gabriel gave her a wink and continued. "I won't ask if anyone objects because I already know that no one does. So, at this time, the couple will make their vows. Michelle."

She nodded, holding tightly to Will's hands. "There was a time when I didn't think I'd ever love anyone. I was cynical. Love was a pipe dream, and risky, and I wasn't even sure if I wanted it. But, you wrecking-balled my walls down with a *look*. I fell so hard, I thought I might break something. I am so stupid in love with you, the thought of being without you makes me want to die. So, I will spend every day making sure you never doubt it. I love you, Will, and you will *always* have me."

He kissed her hands and choked back tears as he drew in a breath, looking down at her and trying to maintain his balance. "Michelle, I could go on and on forever about how perfect and amazing you are and how unbelievably lucky I am because, *my God*, I am lucky. I could tell you all the things I'll do to make you happy because you deserve everything. I could make promises I have no idea if I'll be able to keep. I could recite poetry or sing a song, although, I don't think anyone wants to hear that."

A burst of laughter came from the crowd.

"But, what it all boils down to is that I love you. *I love you* and for the rest of my life and every life after, that will always be true."

Gabriel fanned her eyes. "You kids. All right, Will, repeat after me. With this ring, I thee wed."

He took the diamond infinity band from his pocket and placed it on her finger. "With this ring, I thee wed."

Gabriel handed Michelle Will's ring. "Michelle, repeat after me. With this ring, I thee wed."

She put the white gold band on his finger. "With this ring, I thee wed."

"Awesome. By the power vested in me by I'mOrdained.com, the state of Indiana, and God Him-freakin'-self, I now pronounce you husband and wife. Go ahead and kiss."

"Crash Into Me" played over the speakers as Will took his new wife's face in his hands and kissed her, so lost in the moment he didn't hear the guests' applause.

A proud smile fell on Wyatt's face as he brushed away a single tear. Allydia put her hand on his knee and as he held it, she rested her head on his shoulder. "They're very sweet. I'm glad I didn't kill them."

He laughed, patting the back of her hand.

"Daddy!" Sinclair called from her seat, breaking the trance. Will pulled away as he and Michelle turned to look at their beaming daughter, Gabriel handing back Michelle's bouquet.

"Yeah, sweetie?"

"Is it over? I'm starving."

He laughed, "Yeah, sweetie, it's over."

"Great!" She hopped down and darted back into the woods on her way to the reception Gabriel had set up in Wyatt's old backyard. The bride and groom followed, holding hands and giggling as they disappeared beyond the trees.

Wendy got up to meet Gabriel at the altar, plucking a rose from the arbor and handing it to her. "They're cute together, huh?"

"Yeah. I just wish I didn't have to hear every carnal thought she had about him."

She covered her mouth and snickered.

"You laugh, but it legit makes me nauseous. There are things an aunt isn't supposed to know about her nephew. It's not right."

She took her hand away and held it to her stomach as she cracked up.

"I'm glad my suffering amuses you."

"It really does. I'm sorry," She calmed herself. "I'm sorry, it must be terrible." She leaned in to whisper in her ear. "Do you think we could sneak away for a while? I'm not wearing anything under this dress. Maybe we could replace those dirty thoughts with--"

"Yep." She took her hand and led her into the woods.

Navid watched them leave, the last of the guests still at the clearing. He bowed his head as he followed the aisle into the forest, bitter acceptance settling in his gut as he reminded himself that she was an angel of God and he was just a man, undeserving but blessed to have been in her presence at all.

Sinclair sat quietly, devouring her second piece of cake while the adults gathered on the dance floor, chit-chatting while they waited for the music to start. With no warning, Michelle hurried to the edge of the smooth wood platform and flung her bouquet into the crowd. It hit Allydia in the chest, causing her to grasp it on instinct. The other guests clapped as she examined her prize.

"These are lovely. I'll just go inside and put them in some water." She gave Wyatt a quick peck on the cheek before heading toward the house. They exchanged smiles and waves as she went in through the back door.

"So," Navid said, taking his ancestor's place next to Wyatt and folding his arms. "You're an angel, yeah?"

"Apparently."

"And, what does that mean, exactly?"

He gave him a puzzled glare. "What do you mean?"

"Well, you have angel business, right? Savin' the world and whatnot."

"Occasionally."

"And, that takes priority, yeah? I mean, God's will be done and all that."

"I guess."

"So, what's that mean for her?"

"Allydia?"

"Yeah, mate. She's human now. She can't be gettin' mixed up in whatever antics you and your angel buddies got goin' on at any given time. So, tell me, *Barachiel*, what exactly are your intentions with my gran?"

Wyatt was silent for a moment before erupting in laughter.

Navid squinted, scrunching his brow, his face stern.

Wyatt could see the seriousness on the man's face and went quiet. He tried, but after a few seconds, he couldn't hold back any longer. He put his hand to his chest and bowled over in a fit of laughter, wiping away tears as he patted Navid on the back.

Finally, the Death Cab For Cutie version of "Earth Angel" began to play, the crowd dispersing as Will and Michelle took the floor for their first dance as husband and wife.

Navid sat down and took a sip of champagne as Gabriel walked over to stand next to Wyatt. She looked up at him, a wide smile covering her face.

"What?" he asked.

"You feel that, right?"

"Feel what?"

She coyly averted her glance. "Well, I don't want to scare you."

He chuckled. "What?"

She leaned in, speaking in hushed tones as if she were telling him a secret. "Don't freak out, but," She looked around as he leaned in closer. "You're happy."

He laughed and let out a sigh. "I think you're right."

"Um, duh."

"What about you? That whole Wendy thing get resolved?"

"Oh, yeah. We made up...a bunch of times. We just made up again in the woods about half an hour ago."

He squeezed his eyes shut and shook his head. "Unnecessary."

She giggled.

"So, you're good? Everything's right with the world?"

She glanced over to see Wendy holding out a leaf in front of Sinclair who watched in awe as the witch waved her hand over it, changing its red autumn coloring back to green. She shifted her gaze back to her brother and smiled. "For the most part."

"Anything you need help with?"

She took his arm and watched the couple dance, putting her head on his shoulder as she calmed her nerves. "I'll keep you posted."

Chapter 25

The house was dark, the only light coming in through the draped windows. The living room was cold, the heat having never been turned on with the changing of the season. Bills and advertisements piled at the threshold under the mail slot as the phone on the charger rang to no answer. The call went to voicemail and the room again was silent. In the corner, the Gothic iron birdcage hung from the ceiling, left undisturbed for weeks. The crow inside lay still on the newspaper-lined bottom, dead from dehydration.

Lying stiff on the loop pile carpet, Julia's body rested where she'd fallen, overcome with pain and exhaustion. The life had left her long before, but something in her remained, growing...evolving.

The corpse's belly had swollen to twice its normal size and now, as night fell over the dead witch's home, the stretched skin began to move as if something were underneath, fighting its way out. After a few moments, the skin and muscle tore open, dozens of snakes bursting forth from the cavity. A tar-like substance followed, oozing out onto the floor as the overpowering stench of sulfur escaped the body, filling the room with its noxious odor.

The body's glassy stare seemed purposefully fixed on the ceiling above, as if she'd known. Even the dead were terrified of what was to come.

SINCLAIR

Either thou or I, or both, must go with him.

Romeo and Juliet, Act 3, Scene 1

Prologue

Twenty-two-year-old Wyatt slumped in his seat on the sofa in Clear View's rec room, the combination of Risperidone and Lithium making him lethargic. As tired as he felt, he couldn't sleep. His hallucinations had always been bad but since arriving at the upstate mental hospital, they had grown in frequency and intensity. What used to be sporadic was now constant with not one figment of his imagination but several, and all the time. Even now, heavily medicated and half-conscious, he saw a man staring out the caged window, his robe slightly opened, a bit of drool dribbling from his dry, parted lips. The man didn't seem to be aware of his surroundings, but why would he be? He wasn't real, just like the woman twirling in front of the television and the teenager that paced the floor mumbling obscenities.

"Come on, asshole," Wyatt whispered to himself. "Get it together. They're not real."

"Excuse me?" an orderly asked, leaving his post at the door and walking toward him.

"Nothing, I'm just talking to myself." Wyatt hung his head and muttered, "What else is new?"

"Really? Because it sounded like you called me an asshole. Did you just call me an asshole?"

"What? No. I was--"

"Because I don't think it would be in your best interest to insult me, do you?"

Wyatt lifted his head, his steely eyes boring into the would-be bully. Through gritted teeth, he tried to defuse the situation, knowing the consequences of having an outburst in a place like this. "I wasn't speaking to you."

"Are you giving me attitude?" He bent down, his face now only inches from Wyatt's. "Because it sounds like you're giving me an attitude."

He trembled with rage as he tried to control his emotions and remain seated. Every part of him wanted to rip the man to shreds. It took everything in him to stay still as he gripped the edge of the couch cushion and clenched his jaw. "I'm not."

"That sounds like backtalk to me." The orderly stood and cracked his neck. "Maybe you need a lesson in manners. What is it you're here for? Hallucinations? What do you think, bitch? Am I real or something your fucked up brain invented?"

Wyatt seethed as the orderly laughed.

"See, I think you have no idea what's real and what's in your head. You don't even know if *you're* real, do you?"

Wyatt bit his lip so hard he drew blood as the fatigue he'd been feeling was replaced with a surge of adrenaline. His heart pounded in his chest as his breathing quickened. His knuckles went white as his fingers dug holes in the sofa's pleather seat.

"Is Wyatt even your name? Maybe you're not even here. Maybe--"

But, before he could finish, Wyatt was on his feet, hurling himself into the man and knocking him to the ground. He sat on his chest and punched him, first in the eye and then breaking his nose. Blood splattered as he continued his assault, the other patients screaming and cowering in corners. Two more orderlies came to their coworker's rescue, prying Wyatt off of him and dragging him away. He fought them, pushing and punching. One got him in a choke-hold, but Wyatt grabbed his arm and raised it to his mouth, biting down on the man's flesh causing him to scream in pain.

A nurse rushed over, tapping the glass of a syringe as she got close.

Wyatt grunted as the first orderly got to his feet, aiding the others in restraining him. "No," he demanded. "No more drugs." But, her compassionless eyes never even looked at his face. She rubbed a spot on his arm with alcohol and administered the injection. Almost immediately, he felt weak, his legs giving out underneath him. He did his best to struggle as the men dragged him to his room, but it was no use. He was fading fast and as they strapped him to the bed, he didn't even feel it as the first man punched him in the stomach and diaphragm.

The others left the room while the first orderly spat on him, landing one more blow to his abdomen before turning the light off and closing the door as he left. Just when he thought things couldn't get much worse, the woman's voice was back. It had been a few days since he'd heard it, but now it was clear as day, ringing in his head as loud as ever.

Tell me where you are. She sounded upset, almost like she was crying. *I can't help you if you don't tell me. Answer me, please.*

His eyes rolled back as the medicine worked its magic. *At least I'll finally get some sleep,* he thought, his eyes closing, the world and the woman's voice fading into oblivion.

Chapter 1

Sinclair dragged the toes of her shoes through the bits of tire that cushioned the ground under the swing as she sat, head resting on the chain as she watched the children with their parents playing happily on the other side of the park. She didn't avert her glance when Gabriel approached and sat next to her or when she pulled a candy bar from her bag and handed it to her.

"Thanks," the girl said, eyes still on the family of strangers as she peeled open the wrapper and took a bite.

"Your mother's worried sick," Gabriel said, taking a bite of her own candy bar and following her niece's stare.

"Which one?"

"Uriel. Michelle's so busy trying to make your first birthday party perfect, she doesn't even know you're gone."

"I'm thirteen."

"Not according to the calendar."

"You know what I mean."

"Yeah, I do."

She took another bite and swallowed before speaking again, glancing over to her aunt who finished her candy and put the wrapper in her bag. "She's going to a lot of trouble?"

"She's making a cake from scratch. Her skills in the kitchen are almost as bad as mine. I don't have high hopes of it being edible. Girl's lucky she met your dad. Without him feeding her decent meals, she'd eat...well, like I do."

"So, effort, is what you're saying."

She met her niece's gaze, the pain in her expression breaking her heart. "She wants it to be special for you. She starts school soon and she's having some anxiety about being away from you for that many hours a day. And she feels guilty."

"She doesn't need to."

"I told her, but what do *I* know?"

She laughed, taking one last bite of candy and giving the wrapper to her aunt who put it in her purse. She again looked to the family across the park and held on to the swing's chains, resting her head on the warm metal. "I'm getting too old for this, aren't I?"

Gabriel's heart was heavy as she patted the girl's back.

"Okay. You can take me home now."

Gabriel gripped the chains of her own swing. "We can stay a little longer." She kicked her feet out and swung back and forth, a tiny smile forming on Sinclair's lips as she, too began to swing.

Michelle peeked through the window in the oven to see the cake had finally risen. She breathed a sigh of relief as she checked the timer and scurried back to the dining room to begin filling purple and white balloons with helium. Clusters of twinkle lights hung from every inch of the ceiling and streamers papered the walls so completely, not a speck of paint showed through. The party was taking shape and she couldn't wait to see her daughter's reaction to the room's transformation.

As she fiddled with the rented helium tank, she heard the front door slam. She went to investigate, seeing Sinclair bolting up the stairs and heading to her room.

"Thanks for bringing her home," Valerie told Gabriel as they stood in the entry. "I about had a heart attack."

"Where was she?" Michelle asked, worry covering her face as she approached.

"Just at the park again," Gabriel said.

Valerie crossed her arms and shook her head. "This is the third time this month that girl has run off."

Michelle leaned on the banister and rolled her eyes. "She's just going down the street to the park. She's thirteen, not three."

Valerie smacked her lips. "You weren't here when that Baba whatever-the-hell attacked her. I still have nightmares about it. I don't want her going out alone. Who knows what other monsters might be waiting to--"

"She's fine," Gabriel interrupted. "She's not five anymore. If something tried fucking with her *now*, God help them."

Valerie bit her bottom lip, casting an annoyed glare at her sister. "Why you always gotta undermine me?"

"I just don't want you to worry for no reason."

"I have *every* reason."

Gabriel saw the memories flashing in Valerie's mind, the beatings doled out by various abusive foster parents, the bullies at school, and the time spent alone, neglected for days on end, sometimes with no food. Her features softened as she placed a hand on her sister's shoulder. "Sinclair isn't you and *you* are *not* the people that raised you. You're a good mother. Believe me, I would tell you if you weren't."

She laughed.

"She just needs a little time alone. Okay, I have to go. Wendy's moving in today and I promised I'd help her unpack."

Valerie raised her eyebrows. "Moving in? That's a big step for you, seein' as how up until you met her, you were handing your ass out like Halloween candy."

"Hey," She held a finger up in protest, then dropped it. "All right, that's valid."

Valerie walked Gabriel to her car leaving Michelle to look up to the second floor, too impatient to give her daughter the space Gabriel said she needed. She hurried up the steps and knocked on Sinclair's door before opening it.

"Can I come in?"

The girl shrugged.

She slipped into the room, closing the door behind her. Sinclair was at the chalkboard, furiously drawing something Michelle couldn't make out. It was a sea of orange, red, and gray with no real shape to it. She sat on the bed and watched, the cold determination on the girl's face unnerving. "Are you okay?"

"As okay as ever," she answered, her eyes fixed on her work.

"You freaked Valerie out leaving like that."

"I didn't mean to."

"I know. She's just being overprotective. Maybe let one of us know before you head out next time."

She stopped what she was doing, glanced over to her mother, and nodded.

"You sure you're okay?"

Sinclair relaxed her shoulders and looked around the room. "This used to be Gabriel's room when she was a kid. I feel sad for her. Some really bad things happened to her in this house."

"Like what?"

"Just parent stuff."

"Oh. Well, you don't have to worry about Gabriel. She turned out fine. No matter what life throws at her, she catches it and makes it her bitch." She covered her mouth. "I'm so sorry. Don't repeat that word in front of Valerie. She'll give me a lecture and I don't need her telling me how to parent one more time today."

She smiled. "You know I've heard her say way worse, right?"

"Yeah. I suspect she beats *herself* up over it, too. So, is that what's been bothering you? Gabriel told you some horror story from her childhood and it's put you in a mood?"

She sighed heavily, looking up as if in deep thought as she put the chalk down. She brushed the residue from her hands and sat next to her mother. "Do you think she's happy?"

"Well, she's moving in with her girlfriend, so probably."

"Yeah. Mom,"

"What, baby?"

"Are you happy?"

She smiled and put her hand on her knee. "Yeah, baby, I'm happy. Why wouldn't I be?"

"Gabriel said you feel guilty about school."

She clicked her tongue. "Your aunt should really mind her business sometimes."

"I don't want you to feel bad about--"

"I'm all right. Mom guilt is a totally normal thing. I know logically that you're growing up and you don't need me as much. I've put off school long enough. It's time to get my crap together. But, I feel bad about being gone a lot, just like any mom with a job does. It's nothing for you to worry about, okay?"

She nodded.

"Okay," She kissed her head and stood. "Now, stay out of the dining room for a while. It's not ready, yet."

"Okay, Mom."

She left the room, Sinclair's cold gaze returning to the chalkboard. She went back to it, picking up the orange chalk, and beginning again.

Chapter 2

"What do you think?" Will asked as he and Malik stood in the center of the empty room that looked more like a warehouse than an office building.

Malik glanced around at the exposed beams and ductwork, the studs, and the huge window at the front of the building. "It's big. What are you gonna do with it?"

"I'm converting it to a restaurant."

"Oh, congrats. You've certainly got the space for it here."

"Yeah," Will crossed his arms. "It's just," He paused.

"Just what?"

"I mean, don't get me wrong, cooking's great. But, if I'm being honest, it's just a hobby for me. I don't love it the way you do."

"Most people don't," he winked.

"Do you want it?"

"Want what?"

"The restaurant."

Malik stepped back. "Boy, you trippin'. I'm not about to work for *you*."

He laughed. "I don't want you to work for me. This would be *your* place. I'd just be an investor."

"I appreciate you thinking of me, kid, but I don't need any favors."

"Who's doing you a favor? I've been eating your food for months. I know how good you are. You could make us both a *ton* of money."

"I don't know, man. Getting into business with family? What if it fails?"

Will shrugged. "Then, I just rent the space to someone else. No harm done."

He chuckled. "That's cold."

"All the apartments are rented. I have an on-site handyman and an office next door where I basically sit and count my money all day. I'm bored. I need a project but I don't want to run a restaurant. *You* do."

He looked around again and rubbed his chin.

"And, who knows? If this place does well, maybe I open more restaurants around town."

"Well, look at you, four years old and already a mogul."

He gave him an exasperated glare. "That joke's getting really old."

"Maybe, but you're not."

"Are you in, or what?"

Malik sighed. "Why not?"

"Awesome." They shook hands, both men smiling. "Let's get to work."

"All right, Pearl," Wendy said, placing the terrarium on top of the dresser and turning on the red UVA light. "We're not just staying the night this time. We live here now. I know it'll be an adjustment for you, but you'll get used to it. You like Gabriel, right?"

"You're talking to the lizard?" Gabriel asked, sauntering into the room and sitting on the bed.

"She's a snow leopard gecko, thank you, and yes, I'm talking to her. This is a big move for her. She needs reassuring."

"*She* does, or *you* do?"

Wendy turned, a playful smirk curling her lips. "I'm fine. I've never lived with anyone, so it's a little weird, but a good weird." She sat, brushing the long, dark hair off her girlfriend's shoulder. "First day of summer vacation weird. Pearl, though, will have to get used to being in a new environment. Hopefully, feeling how calm I am settles her nerves."

"If you say so." Gabriel ran a hand over Wendy's thigh. "Far be it from me to question the communication between a witch and her familiar."

She touched her cheek and went in for a kiss, but before their lips could meet, her phone buzzed in her pocket. She pulled it out and read the text. "It's Lucifer. He's in Tristan da Cunha. Pretty." She turned the screen so Gabriel could see the picture he'd sent of the remote island from above.

"That's super interesting. So, you were saying?" She leaned in but the phone buzzed again.

"He says he's running out of quiet places to think."

She rolled her eyes. "How sad for him."

"He says he's even starting to miss you."

"For Christ's sake." She stood and took her own phone from her back pocket, texting to her brother, *I miss you, too, but I need you to stop texting my girl now. It's moving day and I'm tryna christen this new mattress.*

"What did you say?"

"I said I miss him, too."

Her phone buzzed again and as she read the text, she couldn't help but laugh. "He says, 'Apparently, I've interrupted something tawdry. I'll speak to you later'."

"Okay, phones up." She took both cells and dropped them in the nightstand's drawer before crawling across the bed to Wendy on the other side. She kissed her delicately before pulling her top off. "I hope Pearl's not shy because there's about to be a show."

As the two kissed again, removing each other's clothes, the gecko scurried in her habitat, drinking from her bowl, and hiding in her ceramic cave. The phone buzzed again, but this time, the women were too preoccupied to notice.

Lucifer laughed as he put his phone away, taking in the ocean view, the water so blue, it almost made him forget how unhappy he was. He was still, after all his time, unable to settle his conscience. Racked with guilt and shame, feeling that every day he remained on Earth was another day he failed as a son, he wandered, searching for meaning in his now directionless existence. He wished that he could enjoy his time on Earth, knowing that in just over two hundred years, his Father would wake and send him back to the depths, either as Watch Keeper or as a new inmate. But, there was no joy to be had. He'd disobeyed, putting human lives before his duty. He'd defied God's command and he knew better than anyone that there was no coming back from that.

Wyatt looked over his notes as the instructor drew a cross-section of a heart on the whiteboard. The man put the marker down and addressed the class of would-be paramedics. "So we've talked about STEMI, ST elevation, ST depression, and T rate inversion. Tomorrow, we'll be discussing cardiac axis and axis deviation. Think of the cardiac axis as the mean vector in which the electrical activity of the heart flows. So, you've got your SA node here," He picked the marker back up and wrote the letters 'SA' in the top left corner of the heart. "And you've got your intra--" He caught a glimpse of the clock on the back wall and stopped. "Hey, sorry, guys. I've kept you over again. We'll get back to this tomorrow. Have a great day."

Wyatt and the other students gathered their belongings and left the classroom. As he exited the community college, he found Allydia waiting for him, coffee and danish in hand.

"My hero," he said, taking the cup and gulping down the warm contents.

She took his books so he could eat as they walked. "You left without eating. It isn't healthy."

"I was running late."

"Learning to take care of others shouldn't interfere with taking care of yourself."

He swallowed a bite of danish. "It's sweet of you to worry about me, but I'm all right."

"All right isn't good enough for you. You deserve amazing."

"Aw, look at you caring about me," he teased.

"Are you sure this is what you want to be doing?"

"School? Yeah, why?"

"You've been tired."

"I'm just not used to getting up this early. It'll be fine once I get my schedule fixed."

They walked in silence for a while as he finished his breakfast. He tossed his trash in a bin as they approached the subway.

Allydia stopped at the entrance, touching his arm as she looked up at him. "I don't want you to think I disapprove."

"I don't."

"I think it's noble what you're doing. I'm very proud of you."

"Thank you, but I don't know if I'd call it 'noble'."

"It's training to save lives. What would *you* call it?"

"I don't know, it just feels like," He took the books and looked them over before returning her gaze. "What I'm supposed to do."

"There is no 'supposed to' in this life, Wyatt. There is only what you decide. You choose what you do and you have chosen kindness, service to others. There is nothing more noble than that."

He tucked her hair behind her ear. "I'm not sure if that's incredibly insightful or if you just love me."

She flashed a mischievous grin. "I'm fairly certain it's both."

He laughed and gave her a quick kiss before leading her to the subway. "Sometimes, I forget you've been collecting wisdom for thousands of years."

Chapter 3

Navid paced in the alley, hugging his arms as his patience wore thin. He'd been waiting for over an hour and he was beginning to think his informant wasn't going to show. Finally, a man scurried into the alley, hands trembling as he lit a cigarette. "You him?" he asked, blowing out a puff of menthol-laced smoke.

Navid nodded.

The man looked behind him, eyes wild.

"Were you followed?"

"I don't think so." He took another drag and set his eyes on Navid. "You can never be too careful with them Mare Boys, though, yeah?"

"That's facts. So, what've you got for me?"

"They just pulled a job in Hackney. Not sure what they nicked, but they filled a whole van with boxes. Must be important to 'em because even Duncan was there."

His ears perked up. "Duncan Laurence?"

"Who else, mate? Yeah, the big guy himself. He watched 'em load up the boxes, never gettin' *his* hands dirty, then they drove off. I followed them, just like you said. They're hole up in a warehouse near Olympic Park."

"Of course, they are."

"These bloke's ain't messin' round, yeah? You go in, you best be packin' because they will be."

"Don't worry about me, mate." He lifted his shirt to show off the Glock 17 in its belt holster. "I'm Flyin' Squad. I haven't been unarmed for six months."

The man took a step back. "That gun's real serious."

"Yeah, well," Navid put his shirt back down. "So am I."

Navid sleuthed in through a broken window of the long-abandoned warehouse, scanning the room as he positioned himself behind a tower of pallets. There were five men, all in jeans and tee-shirts unloading crate after crate from a windowless van. A sixth man wearing dark slacks and a brightly-colored flower-print button-down took stock of a crate's contents as it was placed before him, writing on a legal pad and nodding for another to be opened when he was finished.

"Duncan," Navid muttered as he took out his phone and quickly snapped several pictures of the van's license plate, the men's faces, and the crates which, with the help of his phone's zoom, he could see were full of watches, each worth at least twenty-four thousand pounds retail. With his zoom he could also see that the men all carried pistols, the jeans-wearers' shoved down the back of their pants, and the flower-shirted man sporting a shoulder holster.

In the distance, he could hear water dripping. Not surprising given the condition of the building. There were probably leaks everywhere. But, it hadn't rained in days. As he took one last picture of the side of the van, he noticed a small puddle seeping out from underneath it. It was leaking oil at a rapid rate. If they gave chase, that would make it easier to follow or track them. "Good to know," the detective whispered to himself.

"Is someone there?" Duncan called. The others pulled their guns and pointed them in the direction their leader was looking.

Navid held his breath for a second. He'd spent the last several months gathering information on this gang and Duncan Laurence in particular. He knew his address, his daily routine, even the name of his favorite actress. He knew his associates, his relatives, and his barber. He knew he hated olives, liked bacon more than anyone he'd ever met, and had a soft spot for beagles. He knew he'd had a vasectomy in his twenties and had come to regret it when, just last week, his wife filed for divorce on the grounds of fraud. Apparently, he'd never disclosed that bit of information. Navid had been surveilling the head of the Mare Boys for months but he'd never been able to catch him in any wrongdoing. This was the break he needed. He couldn't let it slip through his fingers.

"Oi!" Duncan called again. "Who's there?" He set his paper and pen on the crate in front of him and walked around it, stomping toward what he could now see was a man sitting on the dirty cement leaned up against a stack of pallets. He waved his hand, signaling the others to put their guns down. The man was passed out, phone in hand, mouth hanging open. Duncan kicked his leg, waking the man and laughing. "He's sloshed!"

The others chuckled as they threw tarps over their ill-gotten gains, hiding them from the drunk stranger.

Navid squinted up at him, slurring his words. "You're not Penelope."

"No, mate. You're in the wrong spot. Do you know who I am?"

Navid shook his head.

"Good. That's real good. Do you know any of my friends?"

He glanced around the corner of the pallets and back up at him, shaking his head again.

"Brilliant. And, do you know what we're doin' here?"

Navid feigned sleepiness as he stood, catching himself on the pallets as he pretended to be dizzy. "Looks like," He pointed to a rusted-out forklift. "Workin'?"

"You could say that, yeah. And, what exactly are *you* doin' here?" He snatched the phone and opened the picture file. His eyebrows raised and his lips curled into a sickening grin. "Well, well, well. I see why you were disappointed that I wasn't Penelope." He turned the screen to show the others the picture Gabriel had taken of herself all those months before. They whistled and whooped in approval as he turned the screen back, giving it another once-over. "She's *fit*. What are you doin' here? If I was you, the only way I'd get outta *her* bed is in a body bag."

Navid grabbed the phone and shoved it in his pocket. "That's a bit disrespectful, innit?"

"Probably, yeah. But, you know what else is disrespectful? Stumblin' into *my* place, sozzled, knackered, and uninvited."

"Good thing I'm stone-cold sober, then," he said, his tone changed and his words clear. "Bright-eyed and bushy-tailed. And, I've got a warrant, so, no invitation needed." He winked before punching him in the nose and swiping the gun from the gang leader's holster. He spun him around, Duncan holding his nose and wincing in pain. He held him to his chest while pointing the gun at the others. "All right, then. Down they go, nice and easy." The men traded ornery looks, snickering as they set their eyes on the detective and opened fire.

Duncan was shot in the leg, falling to the ground as Navid dropped him, diving behind the pallets of wood. They charged toward him, shooting haphazardly in his direction. He returned fire, hitting the two closest in the abdomens.

"Let's just go, man!" one of them shouted. The three still standing made a break for the van, two hopping in the back and shutting the doors while the last climbed in the driver's seat.

Navid pulled the trigger again, but the gun was out of bullets. He threw it to the floor and pulled out his own gun. As the van sped toward the exit, Navid pursed his lips, cracked his neck, and took one final shot. The bullet hit the leaking oil tank, exploding the van in a ball of fire and sending metal and glass flying. The detective ducked down, covering his head as the back of the pallet wall got singed.

Duncan dragged himself across the concrete, determined to make his escape.

"Not today, mate." Navid grabbed him by his injured leg and yanked him back, pinning his arms to his back and cuffing him.

"What the fuck, Navid?!" A woman's voice echoed from behind.

"Hey, Pen," he greeted. "Nice of you to join."

The female detective and a handful of bobbies stormed in. The officers checked the van for survivors, finding the driver with a head wound but still breathing.

"We don't just blow shit up, Navid. This isn't America."

He laughed, pulling Duncan up with him as he stood. An officer rushed over and dragged him off. "Have fun in prison, blank-shooter!"

"And, taunting a suspect?" she lectured. "I know you've been after this guy for a while, but--"

"I'm just havin' a bit of fun. I deserve it, yeah?"

She furrowed her brow and watched through the open doors as officers loaded the suspects into the Transit. "You do get results, I'll give you that."

He checked the time on his phone. "All right. I'll meet you at the station to get this paperwork squared away."

She tilted her head. "It's late. You should get some sleep. Paperwork can wait until morning."

"You know what they say. Why put off until tomorrow what can be done today?"

"See, this. This right here."

"What?"

She shook her head. "This is why we didn't last. You never stop workin'. You get four hours of sleep a night, if that, and when you're not doin' the job, you're wishin' you were."

"Lot's of criminals on the streets, Pen. And, if I'm rememberin' right, the reason we didn't work was because you was out shaggin' your ex while I was in hospital with a gunshot wound."

"It was a flesh wound and I didn't know you were hurt until after. Besides, I was only seein' him because I was unhappy with how things were between us. Your head was never out of the job, yeah? Doesn't matter. Point is, you're workin' too hard. Go home. Get some rest. Paperwork can wait."

"Yes, ma'am," he scoffed.

"I mean it. And, see about takin' some vacation time. It's not like you're not due. I say this with love, right? You need a break. Take a trip. Visit some family. Take care of yourself." She patted his arm and walked over to join the officers in examining the contents of the crates.

He sighed, not wanting to admit it to himself, but knowing she was right. "Family," he snorted. He looked down at his phone, pulling up his father's profile. He'd updated his cover photo with an image of him with yet another woman, laughing and holding glasses of red wine. "He does always seem to have a good time," he muttered to himself. Maybe visiting his long-lost dad wasn't the worst idea after all.

Chapter 4

"Excellent work, ladies," Phindi said as she wrapped up the class. "Before you go, what is rule number one?"

Twenty women responded in unison, "Anything to get away."

"Very good. I will see you all next week." She walked from her spot at the head of the room to the back where she had a display of items for sale. She stood behind the counter in case any of her self-defense students needed anything. As they filtered out, she eyed a woman who'd kept her sunglasses on the entire class. "Courtney," she called.

The woman jumped as she picked up her duffel bag. "Yes?"

"Come here, please."

She reluctantly made her way to the counter, adjusting her glasses to fit closer to her face. "Yes?"

She gestured toward her eyes. "Your sunglasses. Remove them, please."

"I-I'd rather not."

"I insist." Her tone was stern, her voice unwavering.

She slowly pulled the glasses down and off revealing a swollen and black left eye.

"As I suspected." She glanced around the room to make sure they were alone and pulled something out from underneath the counter.

Courtney examined the small metal object in her teacher's hand. "A barrette?"

"Not just a barrette. See here?" She pointed to its side. "A serrated edge. Wear it like this." She clipped it in the woman's hair just above her temple. "On the side of your dominant hand so it's easily accessible. When you are threatened and he is close, you simply pull it out and slash across the face, like this," She motioned over her own face to demonstrate. "Under one eye and across the bridge of the nose to the other side. Then, you run."

She swallowed hard, her eyes wide. "It works? It's so small."

"Just like you. Small but effective. I've watched you in class. You are capable of wielding much power. Strength does not come from size but from intention."

"How much?"

"There is no charge today. All I ask is that you make a promise, not to me but to yourself. If he does something like that to you again," She pointed to her eye as she slid her glasses back on. "You will leave and never return. You must remember, *pain* is not love."

She nodded. "Thank you."

The woman hurried out leaving Phindi to reflect on the conversation, one she'd had with at least a dozen women since she'd opened the gym to self-defense training. Sometimes, they came back the next week in better spirits, freed from their abusers. Other times, they didn't come back at all. She hoped to see Courtney again as she wondered what had happened to the ones that never returned.

Navid stood outside the museum, shifting his weight from one foot to the other as he tried to will his palms to stay dry. "What am I doing here?" he muttered to himself. "I must be one brick short." He shoved his hands into his pockets. "This was a mistake." He blew out a deep breath as he looked over the pale-blond sandstone and colonnaded pillars of the Neoclassical building. Everything in him was telling him to leave. His anxiety was through the roof. Gang members, murderers, bullets buzzing by his head, those he could handle without breaking a sweat. But, this, a meeting with his biological father was sending his heart racing.

Just as he was turning to go, he heard a voice from behind. "Navid?" He looked back. "It is you!" The older man with the light Italian accent rushed toward him, arms outstretched. He grabbed his shoulders and kissed both cheeks before taking his face in his hands as he looked him over. "Your photographs didn't do you justice! You're my spitting image! You have your mother's lips, though. You must get all the ladies, yes?"

"Not *all* of them," he said, a bit taken aback by his dad's warm reception. He'd only just sent him a message via social media that morning explaining who he was and asking if he had any interest in getting acquainted. He'd invited him for a visit immediately saying that he'd always wondered what had happened to his mother after their brief "romance". Navid had told him about his early years and that his mother had been killed so he was then adopted. His father had offered condolences and asked for pictures, which Navid sent.

Giovanni took a step back to get a better look at him. "I'm so glad you've come! You will stay with me, I insist. I'm having a party later tonight. Just a few friends. You must come."

"All right," Navid agreed.

He put his arm around his son and ushered him away from the building. "Have you been to Edinburgh before?"

"I have, actually."

"Wonderful, isn't it? Such interesting people. We should go to dinner. Have you tried Cullen skink? I know a fantastic place."

Navid smiled as they walked. Maybe he and his father had some things in common, after all.

They entered the Ramsay Garden flat, the geometric pattern of the coffered ceiling catching Navid's eye as he noticed the distinct tap his father's Italian leather loafers made on the old Scots Pine floors. Crystal chandeliers hung in the center of every room including an office nook off the living room with curved walls that couldn't have been more than a couple of feet wide. Tasteful burgundy Kashan rugs decorated the floors while shuttered windows and built-in cabinetry lined the walls.

"Nice place."

"Oh, thank you," Giovanni said, looking around the living room as if seeing it for the first time. "I kept it as true to its history as I could, with a few modern conveniences, of course."

He looked down the hall, the number of doors seeming excessive for a man living alone. "How many bedrooms?"

"Three. Mine is at the end of the hall, you can take the one on the left. It has its own en suite."

"Why so many, if you don't mind me askin'?"

"Well, one never knows when one might have guests." He winked as a knock came on the door. He answered it, letting in nine women, all beautiful and all salaciously dressed. "Welcome, ladies. This is my son, Navid. He's on vacation." A few seconds after he'd closed the door, another knock came, this one louder, more insistent. "Excuse me."

"Navid," one of the women said, standing inappropriately close to him. "That's a pretty name. Where are you from?"

"London," he replied, taking a step back, the pungency of her perfume tickling his throat.

"No, I mean where are you *really* from?"

He furrowed his brow. "I'm *really* from London. I was born there, right? So, that's where I'm from."

"Don't be racist, Isla," another woman said, giving her a gentle nudge. "Don't you hear the Cockney accent? He's as British as they come, he is." She tossed her auburn curls over her shoulder and smiled up at him. "So, you're on vacation? What do you do?"

"I'm a detective." He shifted his gaze to the front door where his father shook the hands of five men as they entered. He couldn't be sure from the distance, but it looked to him like they were slipping money into his hand.

The woman's eyes grew wide and her face fell. "A detective?"

"That's right." He returned her stare, confused by the change in her expression.

"Does your father know that?"

"Yeah, I mentioned it. Why?"

"No reason." She hurried off, joining the others as they mingled with the new party guests.

"Well, that's not suspicious at all." He approached his father who greeted him with a broad smile.

"Navid, my boy. Are you having a good time? The ladies to your liking?"

"Everythin's on the up and up here, yeah?"

"What do you mean?"

He watched as the woman called Isla guided a man by the tie to one of the guest rooms. "I'm pretty sure you know exactly what I mean."

"Fine," he laughed, lowering his voice. "They're prostitutes. Who cares? They've all been tested if that's what you're concerned with."

"It's not."

"Don't get all poliziotto on me. It's perfectly legal here as long as no pimps are involved and I assure you, they are all here of their own accord. Why do you think I moved to this country? For the food?" He scoffed. "What I wouldn't give for proper arancini. But, it's worth it, no?"

He cast him a judgemental glare. "I saw you take money from those men. Comes off real pimpy to me."

"Just a door fee," he smirked. "For the party. Recouping my wine cost, that's all."

"Right." He rolled his eyes.

"Don't be so stuffy, Navid. Have some fun. You're on vacation, after all." He patted his shoulder and walked off to chat up one of the women.

"I knew this was a bloody mistake," he sighed. As he turned to leave, a man in an expensive suit and gold cufflinks breezed by. He was tall with pale skin and jet-black hair, the left side of the front of his jacket puffed out like he carried something hefty in an inside pocket. He couldn't put his finger on it, but there was something off about him that made Navid's cop sense tingle. Navid went to his father, the women dispersing at the sight of him. He got Giovanni's attention and gestured to the strange man. "Who is that, then?"

"I don't know," he admitted. "I don't remember seeing him before."

"So, you don't know anything about him?"

He shook his head.

"But, you let him in your place?"

"He must have come with one of the others. My parties are exclusive. One must be invited."

"But, not by you personally?"

He let out an exasperated sigh. "Lighten up, Navid! It's a party! With your looks, you could have your pick of ladies. My treat. Enjoy yourself." He rejoined the party guests while Navid watched the stranger take two women into the room that was meant to be his. His eyes became slits as the door closed. Something wasn't right about the man in the fancy suit and he was determined to find out what.

Inside the bedroom, the two women giggled as they sat on their knees on the four-poster bed. The man looked them over as he took the scourge from his jacket pocket. "Take off your clothes," he ordered, dropping the whip to his side as it snapped with electricity. The women did as they were told, lying back on the pillows as he made his way toward them, a crooked grin spreading across his dry lips.

Chapter 5

"Make a wish," Michelle said as Sinclair drew in a deep breath.

"Make it a good one," Valerie added.

Sinclair blew out the single candle as her family applauded and sang 'Happy Birthday'. Michelle cut the cake and placed the pieces on purple paper plates, handing each one to Valerie who then set them in front of the guests.

Will scooped ice cream and set a bowl in front of his daughter, kissing her cheek. "Did you get everything you wanted?"

She offered a half-hearted smile. "I always do."

He laughed and passed out bowls while Gabriel, Wendy, Allydia, and Malik ate. Wyatt sat at the other end of the table watching his granddaughter's face. She was pensive, trying to appear fine in front of the others, but she didn't fool him. He recognized that look. It was the same face Will had made when he first learned what he was. She was worried and as she snuck away, the party guests chatting happily, seemingly unaware of the concern in her features, Wyatt sighed, following her to where she sat on the staircase.

"You wanna talk about it?" He sat next to her, tying the loose string of his work boot.

She looked down at her hands in her lap. "Not really."

"Okay." He sat quietly, pretending to check his phone for text messages. After a while, she lifted her head and laced her fingers.

"Grandpa?"

He put his phone back in his pocket. "Yeah, sweetie?"

"I'm really sorry."

"For what?"

Tears pooled in her eyes as she fought to maintain her composure.

"Hey," He put his arm around her. "What's wrong?"

She sniffed. "I'm afraid."

"Of what?"

Her face was sullen as she struggled to find the words. "Growing up."

"You're worried about your powers?"

She averted her eyes and wiped away a tear. "I don't want any of you to get hurt."

He kissed the side of her head. "We won't."

"How can you be sure?"

He lifted her chin, looking her in the eyes and wiping away the fresh tears that spilled down her cheeks, a reassuring smile spreading across his lips. "We're pretty scrappy."

She laughed.

"There you are," Michelle said as she walked through the living room and into the foyer. "Your ice cream's starting to melt."

"I'm coming." Sinclair went with her mother back to the dining room and as the two disappeared from sight, Wyatt's expression changed. His smile faded and worry filled his eyes.

He crept up the steps and snuck into the girl's bedroom. Sinclair had always expressed herself through her art. He thought he might find some clues as to why she was so distraught in one of her sketchbooks but as he opened the door, the picture on the chalkboard wall made his heart jump. It was vivid, fire and smoke leaping from the black, gray figures lining the bottom in what looked like a river of blood. Through the haze, he could see a neon billboard. He recognized it almost immediately.

"Wyatt?" Allydia called from the hall behind him. "I've been looking everywhere for you. What are you--" She stopped, standing just behind him in the doorway. "Well, that's ominous. What is it?"

He swallowed hard, unable to take his eyes off the grim scene. "Times Square."

While Malik showered, Valerie climbed into bed, exhausted and ready to get some much-needed rest. But, before her head hit the pillow, she was gripped by a strangely familiar vision.

The street was empty save a few abandoned cars as several inches of rain slowly drained away, the rushing of the water in the sewer underneath so loud, it nearly drowned out the car alarm blaring in the distance. The air was thick with the stench of sulfur as she began to hear them, a few at first then hundreds. "Holy shit," she whispered, recognizing the raptor-like screech from a vision she'd had years before. It grew in intensity as it drew closer...the sound of screaming demons.

The voices were thousands now, shaking the ground and rattling windows. She put her hands to her ears, frantically looking around to see where they were coming from, but she couldn't pinpoint a location. They were all around her, everywhere and nowhere, the twisted laughs of the damned booming through the night like jets hitting Mach ten. Water turned to blood running over Valerie's feet as fires erupted on the street.

Her sight was obstructed by thick smoke as the noise grew so intense, it made her teeth chatter. She began to choke as she squeezed her eyes closed, coughing as tears ran down her cheeks.

She gasped, sitting up in bed, her hand flying to her chest as she fought to catch her breath. "It's over," she whispered to herself. "You're okay."

From the hall, Sinclair watched, arms folded, chewing the inside of her cheek in the dark. She backed away and headed to her room, Valerie never knowing she'd been there at all.

Hey! Valerie thought to her sister.

Gabriel responded, *What up, fam?*

Lucifer closed the gate to Hell, right?

He did.

Where is he now?

An island in the south Atlantic.

Still on his bullshit?

Yeah, trying to find himself or some kind of purpose or whatever. Like, I get it, but this has gone on for too long, I feel.

So, he can't open the gate back up, right?

No.

Valerie bit her lip. *You sure?*

Totes. Are you okay? It's late and I was just drifting off.

I'm fine. Just curious. Night.

Night.

Had she just passed out and had a weird dream, or was this a true vision? If it was the latter, she needed to tell her sister asap, but with the gate closed, it was impossible. It must have been a dream. "You're just tired," she told herself. But, after decades of premonitions, she knew in her bones her vision was real. She closed her eyes, hugging her pillow as she fell asleep, too tired to fight it. *Tomorrow,* she thought. *I'll think about it tomorrow.*

Chapter 6

Navid waited in his father's flat until morning when the strange man left. He followed him to an antique shop in Grassmarket where he stayed hidden but within earshot, listening to the conversation between the raven-haired man and the shop girl.

"Excuse me, miss?" he asked, his voice low and raspy.

"Yes, sir, can I help you?" she replied, too-red lipstick covering her thin lips.

"I'm looking for the owner of this store. Last I heard, he was going by 'Cain Adamson'. Is he here?"

Her face fell. "Are you friends?"

"I wouldn't say *that*."

Her shoulders relaxed. "Oh, good. I mean, not *good*, but...Mr. Adamson went missing about a year ago." She went behind the counter and took a business card from the drawer. She held it out to him. "This is his lawyer. He's been handling the estate and the like."

He took the card and nodded before spinning on his heel and exiting the shop. When he was sure he was gone, Navid approached the counter, pulling up a photo he'd taken of his ancestor when he'd been spying on him the night he'd met Allydia. He flashed his badge, taking the girl by surprise.

"Have I done something wrong?"

"No," he said, showing her the screen. "I just have a question. Is this the man you call Cain Adamson?"

Her eyes widened with hope. "Yes, that's him. Have you found him?"

"Sorry, love," He put his phone back in his pocket. "Your boss is dead."

She went pale. "What?"

He took a brochure from the counter and wrote his number on it, sliding it across to her and gesturing toward the entrance. "If you see that man again, give me a call, yeah?"

She nodded, taking the paper and placing it in the drawer. "He didn't kill him, right? He was looking for him."

"No, he didn't. He's a person of interest in a different case. Could be dangerous. Can I get one of those cards you gave him?"

She nodded, taking one from the drawer and handing it to him. "He did seem like a sleekit bastard. If he'd shaken my hand, I'd have to count my fingers after. Felt a little like I might boak when he was close. Do you know who *did* kill Mr. Adamson?"

"Yeah, he's been taken care of, as well. You don't have to worry about him comin' round."

She put her hand to her heart and breathed a sigh of relief.

"I've got to get back to work. Have a nice day." He turned to go.

"You, too!" she called after him, checking out his backside as he walked. As he left, she took the pamphlet from the drawer and twirled her hair as she looked at what he'd written. "Navid." She glanced up to the door, seeing him hurry off after his suspect. He hadn't flirted with her, but he'd been working. Maybe she'd call him later, whether the pale man came back or not.

Navid caught up to the man at the lawyer's office where he stood outside the window, using a hearing aid to listen in on the conversation inside.

The man flashed a sleazy grin as the lawyer asked how he knew Mr. Adamson. "Oh, we go way back. We did business together once in the old country."

The lawyer looked the man over, a suspicious eyebrow raised. "And, what country is that?"

"It hardly matters now, does it? The venture ended when he discovered I needed payment that he couldn't provide. Well, not *couldn't*. It was well within his ability. He just refused on moral grounds. *Him*." He laughed. "As if his ethical standards are so high."

"Yes, well, unfortunately, he's been missing for a little over a year. With no next of kin that we know of, his accounts have been frozen. The estate pays out what's needed to maintain his business and property but otherwise--"

"No next of kin, are you sure?"

"None that we can verify. There *is* a girl in the US he granted access to. She's the last living person with a claim to his considerable assets. But," He stopped, realizing he shouldn't be giving the stranger this much information. Why was he?

He leaned in, hands folded on the desk between them. "But, what?"

"She, she," He couldn't stop himself from talking. "She's in a coma."

"Where?"

He began to sweat. "A hospital in New York."

"And, what is her name?"

His eyes bulged as he loosened his tie. "I, I shouldn't,"

His eyes became slits. "*Her name*."

"Ta, Tamsen Flagler."

He smiled, standing and adjusting his suit jacket. "And, what do I need to do to get access to Cain's accounts?"

The lawyer's hands shook violently as he reached behind to open a file cabinet, taking out a document and filling in the names and dates. "She would have to sign this." He held out the paper.

"That's it?" He snatched it away and looked it over.

The lawyer nodded as he began to feel queasy.

"Thank you. That will be all." He left the office, Navid keeping behind a bush as he dropped the hearing aid back in his pocket and pulled out his phone. He hadn't yet found it necessary to tap into the money Allydia had given him but chartering a flight to the States to beat this man to where he was going seemed like reason enough. Once that was done, he called his grandmother. When no answer came, he left a message.

"Hey, Gran. I'm on my way to New York. Somethin's fishy. It involves your dad. I'll call you when I know more."

He picked up his things from his father's flat, Giovanni still passed out from the shenanigans of the night before. He left a note saying he had urgent business involving a case and they'd speak again shortly. He wasn't sure if he would actually ever see his father again. He wasn't his favorite person by any means. He was morally corrupt and engaged in thinly veiled illegal activity. On the other hand, he *was* his dad and if there was a way to have even a casual holidays-and-birthdays-only relationship with him, he'd regret it if he didn't try.

He left the building and got in the black taxi. As he headed to the airport, he tried calling Allydia again before realizing it was only five AM in New York. "Idiot," he whispered to himself.

"What's that?" the driver barked.

"Not you. I was talkin' to myself. Forgot about the time change."

"Ah."

He sat back in his seat and gazed out the window at the beautiful old buildings as they passed. He thought about the dinner he'd had with his father before the illicit party, how they'd talked and laughed.

"So," the driver asked. "You're leaving us, then? Going back to where you came from?"

"No. Somewhere else."

"Ah, well. You think you'll be back?"

He sighed. "Maybe...one day."

Chapter 7

"You're finally up," Valerie said as Sinclair lumbered into the kitchen wearing jeans and a tee-shirt that was clearly too big for her. "Are those Michelle's clothes?"

The girl rolled her eyes as she opened the door to the walk-in pantry. "She won't mind." She went inside and began eating, shoveling snack bars, pretzels, and cookies in her mouth, barely chewing before swallowing the massive amount of food.

Valerie followed her into the pantry and handed her a bottle of water. "Were you up late?"

"No, I just needed to rest. Big day." She inhaled a granola bar and took the water.

Valerie laughed. "You got plans?"

She chugged half the bottle and replaced the cap. "You should eat something."

"I had breakfast with everyone else while you were still asleep."

"Something else. You need your protein."

"Girl, what is with you lately? One minute you're condescending and jumping rope with my last nerve and the next you're worried about my eating habits. Everyone else is gone for the day. It's just you and me. Tell me what's going on with you."

She put the bottle on a shelf and bit her lip. "You know I love you, right? Even when I'm awful. It's not your fault. I'm just...feeling overwhelmed."

"I love you, too, baby." She hugged her. "Why are you feeling like that?"

She pulled away, holding back tears. "I don't want to upset you."

She smirked. "I've been through a lot worse than teen angst. I can handle it, I promise."

A tear ran down Sinclair's cheek. "I'm sorry."

"For what, baby?"

As she reached for her water, her hand grazed a jar of jam, knocking it off the shelf and sending it crashing to the floor. "Sorry."

"It's all right, I'll get it." Valerie knelt down to clean up the mess. She winced as a broken shard sliced through her thumb. "Son of a--" She looked up to see Sinclair staring down at her hand. Her eyes went black and as her breathing quickened, her teeth began to extend. Valerie's heart leaped to her throat as she jumped back.

The girl covered her mouth, her eyes returning to normal as Valerie's skin healed itself. She dropped her hand to her stomach as fresh tears formed. "I'm so sorry." She fled the pantry and made a beeline for the front door.

"It's okay, I understand!" Valerie called after her. She raced to catch up.

"I'll make it up to you. Everything."

"What are you talking about?"

"Tonight." And with that, she was gone, moving so fast, Valerie couldn't even see which direction she'd gone.

"Shit."

Valerie searched everywhere for her daughter. The park first and the woods beyond it, the beach, and both of her favorite museums. She was nowhere to be found. Valerie returned home and called Wyatt, leaving a message asking if he could come to help look for her. She didn't want to involve her sister if she didn't have to. She had overstepped one too many times when it came to Sinclair. Just because she knew what she was thinking didn't mean she knew what was best for her. Gabriel wasn't her mother, *she* was. So, even though she hated invading her daughter's privacy and she'd never snooped before, she *needed* to find her. Maybe there was something in her room that would give her a clue about where she would go. She opened the door and what she saw on the chalkboard made her stomach drop. The smoke, the fire...the bodies. It was so similar to her vision, there was no way it was a coincidence.

Begrudgingly, she contacted her sister. *Hey.*

Gabriel responded, *What's the haps?*

She sat on the bed, eyes still fixed on the picture. *I think we need to talk.*

Chapter 8

The man strolled into the hospital room, not noticing Navid standing a few feet away in the hall. He took the chart from the end of the bed and flipped through it before tossing it over his shoulder. Navid peered in and watched as the pale man removed the girl's feeding tube and whispered something in her ear.

Her eyes flew open as she gasped for air, beads of sweat forming at her temples. The monitor beeped rapidly as her heart rate spiked.

"Hello, Tamsen," the man cooed. "Don't be afraid. Everything's fine. *Remain calm.*"

Her breathing slowed to normal and the monitor's noise quieted to an even, rhythmic pace.

"Good. That's very good, Tamsen." He handed her the document and a pen. "Sign this now."

She did as she was told, unable to take her eyes off of his pupils which seemed to change shape as he stared back at her.

"Lovely. Thank you." He took the items and hurried off, leaving her confused and blowing past Navid who pretended to be checking his phone for messages.

Navid waited until the man got on the elevator and the doors closed before entering the room himself. "Are you all right, miss?" he asked as she sat up. She looked around the room, taking in her surroundings, and putting together what must have happened.

"I'm not sure. How long have I been here?"

"I don't know, miss. I'm not a doctor. Would you like me to fetch one?"

"Who are you?"

"I'm a detective." He flashed his badge. "I followed that man here from Edinburgh. Have you seen him before?"

She shook her head.

"How did you know Cain Adamson?"

"What do you mean, 'did'?"

"He's dead. Were you friends or--"

"That's not possible."

"I assure you, it is."

She tilted her head as she looked him over. "Who did you say you were?"

"I'm a detective from London. I've been following the man that--"

"How did Cain die?"

"He was murdered."

"Well, he'd have to be, wouldn't he? By who?"

"The killer's also dead, ma'am. You don't have to worry."

"Okay, but, is Cain *dead* dead or just dead for now?"

He furrowed his brow. "Miss, how did you know Cain?"

"I didn't. She did."

"Who?"

"It doesn't matter. She's gone now. They got rid of her."

"Who's gone?"

"You remind me of someone. Have we met?"

"No. Are you all right, love? Should I call for a doctor?"

She reached a hand out to touch his cheek. "So familiar."

He gently brushed her hand away. "Who knew Cain? Why did he give you access to all of his money?"

"She had ways of making him do what she wanted. He wouldn't have sex with her because he said I was too young, so she convinced him it was necessary. The money would pay for the army."

"You're not makin' any sense, love. Let me get you a doctor." He turned to go but she grasped his arm, the realization causing her to jump. He turned to face her, confusion and shock mingling with annoyance on his face.

"Sorry, it's just," She let go of his arm, her eyes wide as she stared up at him. "Do you know Allydia Cain?"

Phindi unlocked the door to open the gym for the day and did one final inspection of the equipment before taking her place behind the counter. She smoothed the front of her red tank top and sprayed the counter with disinfectant, wiping it down with a cloth. As she placed the cleaning supplies under the counter, a man with what looked like a newly-formed scab running across the bridge of his nose marched through the door. She stood upright, taking a defensive stance as she was all too familiar with men that carried themselves this way, chest puffed out, fists clenched, and jaw tight.

"You the owner?" the man in the baseball cap snarled.

She nodded, taking a pen from the cup on the glass counter, knowing it could be used to puncture his carotid, poke through his eye, or stab him in the hand should he grab her.

He lifted his shirt, revealing a small handgun tucked into the front of his faded jeans. "You should've minded your business, bitch." He reached for the gun as Phindi stepped back, keenly aware of her mortality, recent as it may be.

He pulled the gun and aimed it at her.

"What do have there, mate?" Navid asked as he strode in.

The man turned as the detective grabbed his wrist, squeezing so hard he dropped the weapon while Navid punched him in the solar plexus. He went down, the breath being forced out of him. Navid punched him in the nose, knocking him out cold.

"You all right, love?"

Phindi nodded, her mouth agape.

"Can I get one of them jump-ropes?" He gestured to the wall behind her where items for sale hung.

She tossed him a rope.

"Thanks." He rolled the man over onto his stomach and bound his hands, then his feet, hogtying the would-be assassin on the smooth gray floor. He called the local police and put his phone back in his pocket.

Phindi composed herself and smoothed her short hair. "I don't remember you being this attractive."

He raised his eyebrows. "Well, in my defense, the last time you saw me, I was starvin', dehydrated, and covered in my own blood. Have you seen my Gran? She's not answerin' calls or texts and her apartment's empty aside from the furniture."

"She moved in with Wyatt last month, though she's spent most of her time with him since becoming human. She's probably at their apartment. I will write the address down for you." She tore off a piece of blank receipt paper and scribbled the address on it before reaching across the counter to hand it to him.

He took it. "Thank you."

"Are you betrothed?"

"Betrothed?" he chuckled. "No, I'm not betrothed."

"Is there anyone you are courting for the purpose of eventual betrothal?"

"No, I'm not *courting* anyone at the moment."

"I am impressed with your skills in close combat and the efficiency with which you disarmed that man."

"Just job trainin'."

"The Queen mentioned. Detective, yes?"

"Yeah."

"You have a nice face and your body looks strong."

"Um, thanks?"

"Do you find me attractive?"

He raised his eyebrows again, feeling his shoulders tense. "Excuse me?"

"My face, is it to your liking?"

"Uh, yes, you're quite lovely."

"And, my body?"

"What?"

She stepped back and held her arms out to give him a better view. "Do you have a desire for it?"

He cleared his throat. "It would be ungentlemanly of me to comment."

"You are polite. That is a rare quality in a man. And, your accent is very charming."

"Phindi, is this your way of flirtin' with me?"

"Is it working?"

He pressed his tongue to the inside of his cheek. "Yeah."

"Would you like to have dinner with me?"

"I absolutely would."

"Excellent. I will seek your grandmother's permission and if she agrees, you will plan a date and text me the details. Is this acceptable?"

"Sure, but I'm fairly certain you don't need anyone's permission to date me but mine."

"I haven't dated a man without the Queen's consent since 1897."

"Oh."

"NYPD," an officer said as he and two others came through the door.

Navid showed him his badge and explained what happened while a female officer spoke to Phindi. She, too, explained the details of the incident.

"Navid was very brave and carried himself with dignity and strength." She looked past the officer and made eyes at her new suitor. He smiled back as the two male police officers laughed, mocking the suspect and nudging him awake. They dragged him out to the cruiser and threw him in the back while Phindi's interviewer placed the gun in an evidence bag.

"If you have any more problems, don't hesitate to call," she said as she left.

"Thank you," Phindi replied, but her eyes were fixed on Navid.

"I should go," he told her. "I really need to speak to my Gran."

"As do I."

"Right. I'll see you later."

"Yes, you will."

He left the gym, a smile plastered on his face. Phindi took her phone from under the counter and made the call.

Chapter 9

Allydia searched the bedroom for her phone. Her alarm hadn't woken her and Wyatt left her to sleep before heading to class which, even though she knew he meant it as a gesture of kindness, had aggravated her. What if something happened to him while he was gone? Or to her? She wouldn't have had a chance to say goodbye. It wasn't something that he thought about, but since becoming human again she was all too aware of how fleeting life could be. She wanted to make sure he always knew how much he meant to her...just in case.

The bedroom turned up nothing so she moved her efforts to the living room where she heard a faint buzzing come from the sofa. She slid her hand between the cushions and found the cell phone vibrating with an incoming call.

"Yes, Phindi," she answered.

"My Queen, I am calling to seek permission to pursue a romantic relationship with your relation, Navid. He has shown interest and has agreed to a social engagement of his choosing pending your approval."

"I see."

"Do you approve?"

She considered it, sitting on the couch and crossing her legs as she thought. "I have no objection. His private life is his own and you no longer answer to me. Date who you wish but I would caution you against bringing heartache to my grandson. I'm no longer your Queen but I am still fiercely protective of those I love, do you understand?"

"Of course your ma-- *Allydia*. Navid was here looking for you. It seemed urgent."

"All right, I'll call him now. Thank you." She ended the call and pulled up her grandson's number. "Phindi and Navid," she muttered to herself while the phone rang. "Eh, he could do worse."

"Gran?" he answered.

"Hello, Navid. Phindi said you were looking for me."

"Yeah, can you meet me at your old place?"

She stood, his tone causing her throat to go dry with anxiety. "Of course. Is everything all right?"

"I'm not sure. Just hurry, yeah?"

"On my way." She ended the call and rushed out the door, locking it behind her. *Meeting Navid at the old apartment,* she texted Wyatt, knowing he wouldn't see it until after school. *See you soon. Love you.*

Standing on the steps in front of Times Tower, Sinclair began to hyperventilate. Dozens of people passed by, some bumping into her as they walked. They were everywhere, milling about all with seemingly important places to be. Even the small children holding tightly to their parent's hands looked busy and the lights flashing all around were giving her a headache. It was loud, overcrowded, and chaotic. It was not a place she wanted to be.

She gripped the railing as she made her way down the steps, her mother's shoes, being a size too big, almost causing her to trip. She blew out a relieved breath when she got to the ground but the calm was swiftly replaced by an overwhelming sense of dread. Being part Nephilim, the sun didn't affect her the way it did a full vampire, but it still made her a little weak, her powers, as well as their side-effects, becoming stronger the older she got. As the dizziness grew, so did her inability to control her emotions. The heat from the late-morning sun felt hot on her skin. She tried to cover her neck with her hair, but it did no good, the radiation penetrating through her thick curls with ease.

She clutched her chest, her heart beating out of control and her stomach in knots. Hot tears spilled down her cheeks as she felt her knees starting to buckle. Her head felt like it would explode and the world around her went dim. She felt the hair on the back of her neck stand up as her hands began to tingle. She tried to stop it but she couldn't. The air around her snapped with the sound of electricity as her whole body sparked. As she battled herself, she heard her aunt's voice calling to her from a few feet away.

"Sinclair!" Gabriel raced to her, her presence instantly calming the trembling girl. The electricity dissipated as the angel took her niece's face in her hands. "Hey, you're okay. Look at me."

Sinclair locked eyes with her as her pupils fluctuated, growing to double their original size, contracting to normal and back to oversized in a matter of seconds.

"Okay, okay," Gabriel pulled her to her chest and wrapped her arms tightly around her. She kissed the top of her head and smoothed the back of her hair. "I'm right here. You're all right. You're all right."

Sinclair breathed in her aunt's scent, the chamomile and chocolate soothing her nerves as her heart rate slowly returned to normal.

Gabriel fought tears of her own as she continued to hold the girl. *Yo.*

Hello, sister, Lucifer replied. *You sound concerned. Is everything all right?*

A tear fell to her cheek. *Finish up your sightseeing. It's time to come home.*

Chapter 10

Blair fussed with the stippling brush, her full-coverage foundation doing little to cover the wrinkles around her eyes and mouth. No amount of makeup could hide how tired her eyes looked or how sunken her cheeks were. She did her best to make herself presentable, but she was embarrassed to show her real face, even to her own siblings. Yes, it was vain, and in the grand scheme of things, it mattered very little. Still, she obsessed, painting her face with more blush than was necessary in a sad attempt at looking younger. "I may be powerless," she muttered to herself. "But, I will *not* be ugly."

In the months since her coven's magic had been bound, all the spells they'd worked in the past had been undone. Her glamour was removed. Her brother was in the hospital, dying of a cancer she'd previously transferred to someone else. Unable to compel the townspeople to steal for them, the coven was running out of money fast. When the bank began threatening to foreclose on their house, three members left, getting jobs and sharing an apartment on Chestnut Street downtown. She'd felt betrayed but with her magic gone, she had no means of revenge. The remaining members mostly stayed in their rooms, finding it hard to look her in the eye, their impatience palpable.

Attempts had been made to undo the Tituban's binding spell, but no coven would dare help them and without magic, the Gowdies were as weak and pathetic as any other human. Blair wasn't just angry and mournful of the loss of her abilities, she was disgusted by what she'd become...normal.

As she finished applying a layer of lipgloss to her thinning lips, a knock came on the front door. She went downstairs to answer it, but before she'd made it to ground level, the door flew open as if by its own power and a man sauntered through, glancing around, his features twisted in disapproval.

"Who the hell are you?" she barked, preparing to turn and race back up the steps.

The pale man ran a finger along the banister before rubbing the dust from his skin. "You've really let the place go, haven't you?"

"The maid quit months ago. Who are you?"

He adjusted his jacket and looked her in the eye. "I'm a friend of Julia's. She came to you for assistance once. Do you remember?"

She scoffed, stepping down to stand directly in front of him, deciding that showing signs of fear was more dangerous than confronting a potential threat head-on. "The rejected Tituban? Yes, I remember." She felt lightheaded being this close to him. There was something odd about him, his presence alone causing her skin to crawl.

"Yes. You refused to help her. Now, she's dead. Had you provided her with what she asked for, she would have had the strength to withstand what I did to her. Sadly, with her magic stripped, she was left unprotected."

"What *you* did to her?"

"A necessary evil, as they say."

She took a step back. "What are you?"

A sickening smirk crossed his lips. "Old."

"What do you want?"

"I want you to give me what you deprived dear Julia of: assistance. It's the least you can do, given the fate she endured because of your selfishness."

She laughed. "There was no helping her. She was weak. I would have had to do her job *for* her. She was completely useless."

He snatched her up by the throat, lifting her from the ground with one hand as she struggled to breathe. His eyes flashed as his jaw tightened. "Julia was the vessel by which I entered this world. She freed me from captivity and by her blood, I was made flesh. Her sacrifice will not be forgotten and you will not insult her again."

Her feet dangled as the stench of sulfur filled her nose causing her eyes to water. The room grew dim as she choked, her painted nails clawing at his wrists. He dropped her, her knees hitting the floor as he crossed his arms.

"Clearly, you've lost your magic. The rest of your coven is as worthless as you are, I assume?"

She rubbed her neck and cleared her throat, casting him a defiant glare.

"Hmm." He stroked his chin as he thought. "Julia considered you to be the most powerful coven on this continent. She feared you."

"Everyone did," she coughed, getting to her feet. "But, as you said, we're worthless now. No magic, impoverished. My own brother's dying and I'm powerless to stop it. You want assistance? I have nothing to give."

He tilted his head, his features softening. "Would you like it back?"

"What?"

"All of it. The fear in a man's eyes when he realizes what he's up against. The control over others, including those in your coven. The magic. The *respect*."

She swallowed hard, his stare intense. "Of course, but--"

"I could restore you." He lifted her chin and turned her face to the mirror on the wall next to her. She gasped. Her wrinkles were gone. The bags under her eyes, gone. Her skin was bright and dewy, her lips full and smooth.

She put a hand to her cheek, unable to believe what she was seeing.

"I could give it all back, everything you've lost. I could make you whole. I could heal your brother and provide you with more money than you'd be able to spend in ten lifetimes. But, it would come at a cost."

She blinked a few times and turned again to face him. "A cost?"

He nodded.

"What is it that you'd want?"

He grinned. "Obedience."

Chapter 11

He could hear Annie screaming from the hall as he hyperventilated in the bathroom, pounding the back of his head against the door. He felt as though his mind was tearing itself apart, his reason floating away like a feather on the wind. He tried to pull himself together but his heart pounded so hard in his chest, he thought he might die. For a moment, he'd forgotten his name.

"Wyatt!" his wife called. "Wyatt, let me in!"

But, he wouldn't. He couldn't risk hurting her and no matter how many times she'd seen him like this, he still felt guilty for putting her through it. He knew she was afraid of him and the look on her face when he had these episodes broke his heart. Tears poured down his cheeks as he screamed, banging his fist on the side of his head.

Where are you? he heard in his mind.

He grimaced as if the sound hurt him. "Not now."

Tell me.

He screamed again, back fisting a hole in the closet door.

"WYATT!"

He covered his ears in a feeble attempt to block out the noise.

Annie beat on the door, the concern in her voice now mingling with impatience. "I'm coming in!"

He got to his feet, stumbling to the sink where he splashed cold water on his face now flushed from the adrenaline coursing through his veins. As he patted his skin dry with the towel hanging on the ring above the light switch, he looked at the reflection staring back at him in the brushed nickel framed mirror. He jumped back, not recognizing the face of the man in the mirror. He had shoulder-length, blond hair, a square jaw covered by golden stubble, and eyes so blue they nearly glowed.

Wyatt squeezed his eyes shut. "It's not real." He took several breaths as he tried to settle himself. "It's another hallucination. *It's not real.*" But, when he opened his eyes, the strange face remained, peering at him from the other side of the glass.

Tell me where you are.

"Leave me alone!" he shouted. His chest heaved as he fought to catch his breath, the sound of his heart thumping so loud that he didn't hear his wife using a bobby pin to pick the lock. As she burst into the room, he yelled, "You're not real!", slamming his fist into the mirror, sending bloody shards crashing to the vanity below.

Wyatt was jolted awake by the automated announcement cutting through the white noise of the subway as it headed north. He rubbed the sleep from his eyes, pushing the memory from his mind and focusing his attention on the composition book in his lap, going over his notes from that morning's class. He hadn't thought about that day in years, the incident that finally chased Annie away. It felt like a lifetime ago but if he was being honest with himself, it was still too painful for him to think about. He had other priorities: Will, Allydia, and Sinclair. They, along with his siblings, were what mattered now. They were the ones that needed him. *No reason to dwell on the past*, he thought, his hands trembling as he turned the page and continued to read.

Gabriel had just dropped Sinclair off at home when she felt her brother's panic. She hurried back to the city, blowing through every stop sign and red light she came across. She flew into his apartment only a few seconds after he'd walked in, himself.

Relief washed over her as she took in his thoughts. "Oh, good. Just memories. I thought something bad happened."

"I'm fine." He closed the door behind her and took a seat at the island. "It's just been a while since I've had any dreams. You're jumpy, though."

She sat next to him. "Hazard of the job."

"Mm." He rested his elbow on the counter, his expression pensive. She rubbed his back while she waited for him to get out the words she knew he wanted to say. He gave himself a second before beginning. "You know, sometimes, for a second I'll think, 'What if this is all in my head? What if I'm really in a psych ward somewhere, drugged and strapped to a bed, hallucinating this whole life?' Because it's crazy, right? Demons and vampires, monsters, and angels. They're not supposed to exist. Maybe Annie didn't leave me, she just had me committed. But, then I look at Will or Allydia or you, and I don't care. What you've given me, *family* is everything. As twisted as it might be, I wouldn't trade it...even if it's imaginary."

Gabriel sniffed back the tears that threatened to come, the look in her brother's eyes crushing her like a tin can. She raised her hand and smacked him across the face, leaving a red mark on his cheek.

"Ow!" he laughed. "What was that for?"

"You felt that, right?"

He massaged his stinging face. "Kind of hard to miss."

"That's because *I'm real*. Dumbass."

Chapter 12

With their magic restored, the Gowdies skipped through town, emboldened, and out for blood. Blair gleaned as she watched her brother, now healed, blow up fire hydrants with the snap of his fingers. They cackled as water shot up and flooded the street, a rainbow forming in the air above.

They turned onto Chestnut, spotting the cars of their former members in front of the plain brick building, its black door leading to the apartment they now shared. A twisted grin spread over Blair's ruby lips as she held out her left hand, palm up.

"What are you thinking?" her brother asked as the others ran ahead into the building.

She smirked, raising her right hand and slapping it down onto her left causing the roofs of the cars to cave in, smashing the windows, their alarms ringing out into the otherwise quiet morning.

He laughed.

She brushed her hands together. "No escape now."

They joined the rest of the coven, racing up the steps to the third floor, the witches too impatient to wait for the elevator. In the hall, they waited for Blair to give the order. She led them to the apartment, raising a hand as if in greeting.

She turned to face them. "Show no mercy." She flicked her fingers, the door flying off its hinges into the living room where the three traitors sat drinking coffee.

"What the hell?" Kevin barked, nearly choking on his latte. Denise and Fiona just stared, the color draining from their faces as their hearts leaped to their throats.

The nine filed in, squawking and hissing as they blew out can lights and tore furniture apart with their bare hands.

"You betrayed my sister," Bennett explained. "Remind me, what's the punishment for abandoning one's coven?"

Kevin barreled toward him, balling his fists but Bennett threw him back with the flick of a wrist. He flew into the television, crashing into the screen and convulsing as electric current flowed through him. He fell face-first onto the floor, a puddle of foam escaping his lips as his eyes glossed over and the shaking stopped.

Fiona screamed, ducking behind Denise, the two now cowering in the corner. "Unsichtbar!" Denise yelped, but the women could still be seen.

Blair snorted. "Oh, *you* didn't get your powers back. Only loyal members of the coven were given back what was taken by the Tituban. *You* are traitors."

"Hey," Cyrus interrupted. "I don't mean to be a downer but is this necessary?"

"Excuse me?" Blair snapped.

"No disrespect but I mean, we're killing our own now?"

She glared at him, her nostrils flaring as she held herself back from slaughtering him, too. "They are *not* our own. *They abandoned us.* They left us when we needed them."

"Yeah, but--"

"But fucking nothing! They die. Those are the rules."

"The coven's rules or yours?"

"I *am* the coven! Now, get on board or you'll die, too." She faced the women again. "They'll get what they deserve."

Denise and Fiona screamed as the others pounced, clawing at their skin and gouging out their eyes. Blood and flesh fell to the ground in bits as the witches shrieked. Cyrus covered his mouth, horrified by what he was seeing. While everyone else was distracted, he slipped out and headed for the stairs. "Indespectus," he whispered, cloaking himself in an invisibility spell. He sprinted from the building, heading to the only place he thought might be safe.

"The Tituban," Cyrus said, clearing his throat as Poe opened the door. "Where is she?"

"Why would I tell you?" she asked, sensing his power. "And, how did you get your magic back?"

He looked behind him, feeling Blair's eyes on him even though she was nowhere to be seen. "Some guy Blair's taken up with. He's...off. Can I come in, please?"

She could tell that he was scared, which was odd for a Gowdie. She felt his magic, weaker than hers but only by a little. She was confident she could take him in a fight but it'd be close. "I guess." She let him in and locked the door behind him. "Why are you here?"

He coughed. "The coven's gone rabid. Blair's always been kind of fucked up but she's on another level, killing our friends." He cleared his throat again. "Everyone else is going along like it's normal. They're so happy to have their magic, they'll do anything she says."

"Didn't they always?"

He coughed into his elbow. "Yeah, but that was," He looked down at his sleeve, specks of blood now glistening on his skin. "They're coming." He flew through the house to the back door, rushing out into the garden.

"What are you doing?" she called, hurrying after him.

"I thought I saw some larkspur out here." His eyes darted around at the various plants and flowers. "There." He ran toward the blue and violet flowers but before he could reach them, he fell to his knees, hacking up blood and tissue as his lungs seemed to disintegrate.

"Subsisto cantamen!" Poe shouted over her guest's wheezing. He continued to cough, her spell having no effect.

He looked up at her with pleading eyes as she repeated the spell. Still, it did nothing. He grabbed her ankle. "Kill...her."

"Blair?"

He nodded. "And," he struggled to get out the words as he continued to choke. He pulled his phone from his pocket and showed her the screen. "That...guy." He bowled over, cups of blood followed by what looked like hundreds of dermestids pouring out of his mouth, the insects spreading over his face and devouring his flesh. Poe tried to bat them away but more came, leaving nothing left of his head but his skull.

She wretched, backing away as the bugs vanished before her eyes. "Goddamn Gowdies, man."

Chapter 13

Pearl chirped as she crawled over Wendy's open palm. The witch gently stroked the gecko's head and back, laughing to herself at how Gabriel would roll her eyes at the sight of the tiny creature playing on the kitchen island. "We eat here," she'd say. She didn't understand the witch/familiar bond and that was okay. Wendy didn't understand most of Gabriel's angel stuff, so they were even. She did feel like she was hiding something from her, though. Something was bothering her that she obviously didn't want to talk about. Wendy would let it go, for now. No sense starting an argument over something that was probably none of her business, anyway.

She jumped up, feeling the magic emanating from the hallway. She opened the door to see Poe, fist raised.

"Not even gonna let me knock?" Poe quipped.

"Sorry." Wendy closed the door and waited a few seconds before Poe tapped on the wood. She opened it again, a sly grin on her face.

"You're ridiculous."

"You're whiny," she giggled, letting the girl in and closing the door behind her.

"You finally got a familiar?" She sat at the island, touching a finger to the gecko's tail.

"Yeah, some dude was selling her on the street and she was so freakin' precious, I couldn't resist. What's up?"

"One of the Gowdies showed up at my house today."

She arched an eyebrow, sitting across from her. "Why?"

"They have their magic back."

"How? I bound them."

"Some guy." She slid the phone she'd taken off Cyrus' body across the counter, showing her the picture of the man. "He said there was something off about him. He asked me to kill him *and* Blair."

"His priestess? That's--"

"Treason, yeah. Something's going on, I'm telling you. He was scared and you know Gowdies. They're not afraid of anything."

"Where's your informant now?"

"Dead. Spelled. I tried, but I couldn't stop it. Whoever this guy is that's giving them power, he's *strong*."

Wendy examined the photo. "I don't recognize him. He does put off mad creeper vibes, though." She went to a drawer and got some ribbon and a pair of scissors. She wrapped the phone and did the incantation. When she was finished, she pursed her lips. "Hmm."

"What?"

"It didn't work. Here, help me out." She took Poe's hands and wrapped them around the phone, placing her own over them. She did the spell again and again and was still disappointed. "It's not working."

"How is that possible?"

She put her hands on her hips and bit her lip. "He's too powerful."

"How, though?" Poe wondered. "Not to be arrogant or anything, but aren't we like, the strongest witches ever?"

"Maybe not," she shrugged.

"We are, though. *You* are, at least."

She folded her arms and chewed on her lip as she thought. "Send the pic to the other covens. See if anyone's seen him before."

"Okay, but Wendy,"

"Hmm?"

"What the hell is this guy?"

Moloch winced at the sting of Wendy's spell. "Tituba," he seethed.

"What?" Blair asked.

He pushed her head back down. "I didn't tell you to stop."

She went back to servicing him while he rested his elbow on the arm of the solid gold throne he'd installed in the Gowdies' formal living room, its snake embellishments winding around the legs and back. He watched the members of the coven indulging in the pleasures of the flesh on the floor, sofa, chairs, and chaise, mind-controlled townspeople doing as they were commanded. As amusing as the sexual escapades of humans were to watch, he grew perturbed. The Tituban that had bested Julia was now coming for him. This new threat along with the one he'd sensed upon his arrival in the States had him concerned. He needed more power.

He glanced over to the gold statues flanking the fireplace, their nude bodies and faces twisted in terror more arousing to him than the orgy he was witnessing or the woman's mouth around his genitals.

"What did you call them, again?" he asked.

Blair popped her head up, looking in the direction he was gesturing toward. "Oh, Denise and Fiona." She went back to her work as he smiled.

"That's right. Denise and Fiona. Just lovely." He closed his eyes and enjoyed the moment knowing that soon, he'd leave this place to acquire new allies, these more vengeful and depraved than even himself.

Chapter 14

Allydia stepped into her old apartment, barely getting the door closed before Navid rushed to meet her.

"What's wrong? Are you hurt?" she fretted, looking him over for signs of injury.

"No, I'm fine. Someone says she's got an important message for you and would only tell you in person. Made me bust her out of hospital."

"Hospital?"

He ushered her into the living room where Tamsen waited. She stepped forward, locking eyes with the former vampire. Allydia grunted, lunging at the girl who jumped back, falling onto the couch.

Navid stepped between them. "What are you doin'?!"

"She thinks I'm her," Tamsen said, standing and gesturing for him to step aside, her eyes still fixed on Allydia's. "Lilith's gone. I'm just Tamsen."

She wasn't convinced. "If she's gone, how are you standing?"

"Someone woke me up from my coma. It doesn't matter. I have to warn you."

She tilted her head. "Warn me?"

She nodded. "When Lilith was hurt and she thought the angels might find her here, she did a divination using the intestines from that guy."

"Tobin," she remembered, sorrow coloring her face as she crossed her arms.

"Yeah. She did the spell and found out that--"

"How do you know this?"

She shifted her weight from one foot to another, rubbing her arm as if she were cold. "I remember...everything. Everything Lilith knew, I know. Her plans, her spells, her," she grimaced as she swallowed. "Eating habits. Hell."

"And, you're still functioning? I'm impressed."

"The man at the hospital, I think he did something to me. I don't feel much of anything besides...calm."

"You owe him a favor, then. The last person I saw Lilith vacate was such a mess, she gouged her own eyes out in the hopes of ridding herself of the images left in her mind."

"That's...horrifying. Anyway, she wanted to see if her plan to destroy the Gate would work, but instead, she saw something else."

"Something else?"

"Something that scared her so bad, she almost went back to Hell willingly."

Allydia rolled her eyes. "The only thing that ever scared Lilith was her brother."

"Her brother?" Navid asked.

"Lucifer."

"Oh, well, sure."

"Navid, can you please give us a minute?"

Allydia cast her an annoyed glare. "You can speak freely."

"It's all right," he said, kissing his grandmother on the cheek. "I've got a date to prepare for, anyway. See that she gets back to hospital when you're done talkin', yeah? I don't want to get thrown in American prison for kidnappin'." He left the room and the apartment, locking the door behind him.

"So," Allydia said. "What had my stepmother so anxious that you felt it necessary to bring to my attention? Crows feet? A man growing tired of her?"

Tamsen squinted. "This is why she called you 'flippant'."

She sighed. "Did she fear the wrath of my father? If so, you have nothing to worry about. He's no longer a threat to *anyone*."

She shook her head. "You should sit down."

Lucifer took one last peaceful stroll around the island, breathing in the fresh ocean air and feeling the sun on his face. He'd miss it here, the quiet and the nature. But, his sister had sounded worried when she'd all but ordered him back. Whatever was bothering her must have been something she couldn't, or just didn't want to, handle on her own.

He went into the jungle, far enough away from any of the locals that no one would see him take off. He glanced around to make sure he was alone and bolted up, hovering over the trees and reveling in the island's beauty for a final time. He flew off, away from this paradise and on his way home.

When Gabriel left, Wyatt made himself some lunch. As he ate his sandwich, he realized he'd never turned his phone back on after class. He took it from his jeans pocket and took a sip of soda while it powered on. He munched on chips while he went through his texts, one from Allydia saying she was meeting Navid and another from Valerie.

Malik and Will are in a meeting with a contractor and not answering their phones. Sinclair ran away again and I can't find her. Can you--

He stopped reading and bolted from his seat at the island to the front door. He was in such a hurry, he almost forgot to lock up. He knew something was going on with his granddaughter, but running away? He had to find her before she got hurt or worse, hurt someone else.

Chapter 15

"Why the hell are we in *Yonkers*?" Blair complained, the rest of her coven silent, they too wondering why they'd been dragged to this decrepit building, the long-abandoned power station giving them all chills.

"I need more allies," Moloch explained. "Ones with no regard for their physical well-being, willing to use brute force to carry out my wishes, no matter the cost."

"And, you'll find them here?" she scoffed. "In a graffiti-covered relic?"

"Not *in* it," he sneered. "Under it."

She scrunched her eyebrows. "Raising the dead is a risky game. I don't recommend it."

He snickered. "Not the dead. The *damned*. Now, be good little witches and fetch me some humans. Keep them docile until I return."

"How many?"

"As many as you can. Thousands. More."

A breath stuck in her throat. "I don't have the power to control that many people at the same time."

His eyes flashed as he grabbed her by the throat. Her skin became ashen as her eyes went black. He pulled her close and through gritted teeth, he whispered, "Yes, you do." He let her go, smiling as she walked off to do his bidding. The others were hesitant, but with a flick of her wrist, they followed.

Once alone, Moloch entered the building, the shuffling of his brown and gray jackboots on the damp floor echoing through the room. After a few moments of searching, he finally felt it. "There you are." He closed his eyes and focused his power through his hands. At first, the gate to Hell was only made visible, the closed portal looking like little more than a void in the fabric of space. But, as he concentrated, sweat dripping from his pores, it slowly started to unravel, shattering like glass under the weight of his command. With one final push, the gate to Hell blew apart, revealing a crater of unknowable depth. He laughed as he caught his breath, relaxing his arms. He took a few seconds to prepare himself, restoring his energy and mustering his courage. Even for him, this wouldn't be easy.

"I hope this is all right," Navid said, pulling out a chair for Phindi. She sat, looking up at him in approval.

"It's very nice," she told him. "I especially like the charming portrait of the dog." She pointed up to the black-and-white painting hanging on the wall next to the table. He chuckled as he sat across from her.

"I haven't spent much time in New York, so I didn't know where a good place to eat was. I just did an internet search of romantic lunch spots in Brooklyn and this was the first place that popped up." He glanced around at the white-painted brick, wooden columns, and exposed pipes. "It's a lot more industrial than I thought it'd be."

"It's what they call 'trendy'. I don't know that I'd consider it romantic, but I do like the atmosphere. I have very high hopes for this place and for this date."

He shifted in his seat. "No pressure, right?"

"There is no reason to be nervous," she said. "My attraction to you grows by the minute."

He cleared his throat. "Thank you."

"Do you like my dress?"

"Yes, it's very nice."

"It is lilac, a bright color to catch your attention."

"I see," he said, taking a sip of water.

"And, it is low-cut to draw your eye to my exposed cleavage."

He choked, almost having to spit his water back into the glass.

She looked over the menu. "Do you know what you want?"

He skimmed the menu and nodded. "Yeah."

She rested her chin on her fist and flashed a sly smile. "So do I."

His eyes widened as he chugged the rest of his water.

"What can I get you?" a waiter asked, too overwhelmed by the lunch rush to notice the sparks flying at the table.

"I'll have a Caesar salad with grilled chicken," Phindi answered, her gaze still fixed on her date.

"The same," Navid said. "And, can we get an order of truffle parm fries?"

"Sure thing," the waiter said, hurrying off.

Their food arrived within minutes, each taking fries from the shared plate in between bites of salad and sips of soda. They talked about work and current events, laughing at each other's jokes and enjoying one another's company.

"So, you exploded the van?" she asked, clearly impressed.

He shrugged.

They both laughed. When it was time for dessert, they exchanged longing glances over molten chocolate cake, spooning bites into their mouths as they stared at each other.

"There is only one test left," Phindi said, breaking the silence between them.

"Test?"

"Of compatibility."

"Ah."

"So, you agree?"

"Agree to what?"

"We must engage in sexual congress."

He dropped his spoon and looked around the busy restaurant to see if anyone had heard.

"Am I making you uncomfortable?"

"No, no," He cleared his throat again. "I just--"

"We should do it now while I am fully aroused and freshly shaven."

He swallowed hard before waving to the waiter. "Check, please!"

They burst through the door of Phindi's loft, kissing passionately and tearing at each other's clothes. By the time the door was shut, they were naked aside from their undergarments, which quickly fell away as well. They collapsed onto the murphy bed, not bothering to get under the covers. He rested himself between her legs as they made out, his lips moving from hers to her neck. She ran her fingers through his soft hair, anticipating the moment of his entry when her body suddenly stiffened. She yanked his head back to look him in the eye.

"Do you have a condom?"

His face fell. "Oh, bollocks. I don't, I'm sorry. I didn't want to presume." He pushed himself off of her and sat up.

"It's all right, I have some in the medicine cabinet." She got up and went to the bathroom to fetch them. She tossed him the box. "I was warned that disease is rampant now, so I bought those, just in case."

"That's smart thinkin'," he said, ripping open the package and putting on the condom. "I'm clean, but--"

"I haven't been with a man since becoming human," she blurted.

"Uh, all right."

"I tell you this because I am not sure of my strength."

"Your--"

"I fear I may hurt you in my exuberance."

"Oh," he pulled her back down onto the bed and covered her body with his. "I wouldn't worry about that, love. I'm nothin' if not durable."

Chapter 16

The stench of sulfur filled obsidian halls as Moloch investigated the pit humans called Hell. Iron cages lined the walls, the coal floor leaving his boots filthy. A chill ran through him as he buttoned his suit jacket, surprised that he could see his breath. "The rumors aren't true, then," he said to no one in particular as he peered through the bars of various cells. "It's not hot at all down here."

"Who are you?" A voice came from behind.

He turned to face what he assumed to be a demon, his shape that of a man with a mutilated face and leathered skin the color of a rotting apple. His nose appeared flat against his face as though it had been crushed and his eyes shined like a cat's in an unnatural shade of gold.

"Are you in charge here?" Moloch asked.

"For now. How did you get in here?"

"Destructive ingenuity. I'm Moloch."

"Belphegor. Aren't you one of the false gods of the Canaanites?"

"*False*?" He adjusted his jacket and cracked his neck. "That's insulting. Just because your father *technically*--"

Belphegor's patience ran thin. "*Why are you here*?"

He sighed. "I've come to make you an offer." He held his arms out toward the cages. "All of you."

Voices from inside the cells began to chatter.

"An offer? From a defunct pagan deity?" He scoffed, the demons surrounding them cackling as they banged on their cell doors. "You have nothing."

"On the contrary," Moloch snapped his fingers, popping open every cage in Perdition. Demons flooded the halls, their ill-formed bodies packed in the space like taupe and onyx raisins. "I have everything I need...almost."

"Get back in your cells!" Belphegor boomed, but the demons resisted.

"We want to hear what he's got to say!" one of them shouted. Cheers erupted from the crowd in varying levels of shrill.

Moloch flashed a sleazy grin as he addressed the horde. "How long has it been since you've breathed clean air? Seen the light of the Sun? Felt the touch of a woman?"

The crowd grumbled.

"Would you like to once again?"

His question was met with raucous agreement.

"I can give you the world! Your jailer thinks I have nothing to offer but I can free you, break your shackles and lead you to a future where we make the rules. We decide who is and isn't worthy of the thing so brutally taken from you: *life. Life* is what I have to offer."

"How?" a demon called from the masses.

"By joining me. You will be my army as I rule over the Earth as its King. Elohim cast you out but stand with me and the world will be yours!"

The crowd again cheered, thousands of voices merging as one deafening screech.

"Wait, wait, wait!" Belphegor said. "How did you open the gate? Once it's been locked, only God can unseal it."

"God or *a* god. And, I didn't *unseal* it. I dismantled it entirely. The gate has been obliterated."

His gleaming eyes widened. "Everyone back in your cages! *Now!*"

Moloch rolled his eyes, making a fist as Belphegor's head caved in on itself. Soon, his whole body was pulverized, reduced to a compressed heap on the soot-covered floor. For a few seconds, all of Hell was silent. Then, more cheers along with applause rose from the mob. They celebrated, freedom finally within reach.

Still in her cage, Lilith trembled, holding it shut even as others tried to let her out. Her bright eyes shown through the tar-like substance that coated her as she watched the demons rally. She squeezed them shut, memories of what she'd seen when last she was on Earth playing in her mind like a movie reel. She shivered, gripping the bars as the others made their way to the newly-destroyed gate. As Hell grew quiet, she crumpled to the floor, balling herself up and hugging her legs. If the body she'd conjured for herself were real and functioned as such, she would have cried.

Phindi and Navid lay panting next to each other on sweat-soaked sheets, the blanket bunched up at their feet. Pillows, once at the head of the bed had been tossed to the floor, discarded as a hindrance to movement. They stared blankly up at the ceiling, limp, both too spent to care about the buzzing of a phone coming from the pile of clothes a few feet away.

"My legs are numb," Phindi said between heavy breaths. "That was amazing."

Navid nodded in agreement, still unable to form words.

"Did you enjoy it?"

He blinked a few times and let out a slow breath. "Immensely."

"That is a relief."

"A relief?"

"Yes, because I will want to do it again very soon."

"You and me both, I'd say."

"Excellent. I just need a twenty-minute nap first. I haven't been this fatigued in the day since I was a vampire."

He angled his head to look at her. "Do you miss it, bein' a vampire?"

She returned his gaze, rolling onto her side to face him. "I used to. When my queen stripped me of my power, my immortality, I was angry. I felt betrayed. But, I quickly came to appreciate the gift she'd given me...*freedom*. Freedom to be whomever I choose, to do as I see fit. I had been fighting one battle or another since my father trained me as a warrior. I was born for war. I was bred for it. I had never known another way. Now, I do as I please." She traced his bicep with her finger. "The first time your grandmother saved me, pulled my dying body from the battlefield, she gave me a new life in service to her. The second time, by restoring my humanity, setting me free, she saved my soul."

He rolled over and brushed her cheek, his fondness for her evident to her by the look in his eyes. "I'm glad you're happy."

She touched his hand and held it to her face while she spoke. "We are compatible, yes?"

"I think we are."

She smiled sweetly before kissing him, climbing on top of him, and reaching for the last condom on the nightstand.

"I thought you needed a nap?"

"Sleep can wait," she said, tearing open the wrapper and sliding the condom over him. "You should not have to."

Chapter 17

"Okay, Pearl, time for a snack." Wendy put the gecko in her terrarium before taking six mealworms from the plastic container and dropping them in the food dish. The lizard chirped and scurried toward the dish to feed. From the other side of the apartment, Wendy heard the front door open and close.

"Babe, are you home?" Gabriel called, setting her keys and phone on the kitchen island.

"Yeah," she called back, going to meet her.

Gabriel looked relieved as she grabbed her girlfriend's face and kissed her hard, pulling away abruptly and sitting on a stool. "I have to talk to you."

"You okay?" She sat next to her, covering her hand with hers.

"Not really." She squeezed her hand before patting the back of it and letting it go. There's something I haven't told you."

"I figured. You've been acting a little sus lately."

"I'm sorry."

"Angel stuff?"

She nodded. "I wanted to tell you. I *needed* to talk about it but," She put her fingers to her temple, closing her eyes and gritting her teeth at the sudden searing pain. "Fuck me."

"Headache? Do you need some--"

She grunted, shaking her head. "There's nothing you can do." Her eyes flew open and fixed on the door. "Oh, shit."

"What?"

The door flew open, Allydia storming in, a look of terror covering her ashen face. Tamsen came in behind her, hovering in the foyer.

"What's wrong?" Wendy asked the former vampire. "You look like you've seen ten ghosts."

"Tamsen," Gabriel said. "This is Wendy. She's a witch."

Wendy did a double-take. "We're just announcing that shit to strangers now?"

She ignored her question, doling out instructions. "Give her all of Lilith's spells. She's gonna need them. Wendy, when she's done put her in a cab to her parents' place upstate. Dia, get Michelle and Navid. Take them to the Southport house. The city's not safe." She stumbled to a kitchen drawer and took out a notebook and pen, handing them to the silent girl. Tamsen sat at the island and began to write.

"Will Wyatt survive this?" Allydia croaked.

She looked her in the eye, her expression hard. "I don't know, yet."

Allydia bit her lip, a single tear dropping from her eye as she hurried out of the apartment, slamming the door and racing to the elevator.

"Okay, what the fudge?" Wendy asked.

"It's too late," Gabriel said, wincing in pain as she grabbed the sides of her head. "I can't explain." She fell to the floor, squeezing her eyes shut as blood dribbled from her nose. She clutched her stomach as she curled herself into a ball, taking shallow, labored breaths.

Tamsen took a quick glance at the angel on the floor, barely registering the scene as she continued to write.

"Gabriel!" Wendy knelt next to her. "Percuro!" she demanded. "PERCURO!"

The spell was useless. Gabriel continued to writhe in unimaginable pain, going pale and coughing up blood.

"It's okay," Wendy cried, retrieving the phone from the counter. "I know what to do."

Lucifer coasted at a leisurely pace over the Atlantic, enjoying the view of the ocean beneath him. In the distance, he could just make out the iconic New York City skyline, the Empire State Building like a beacon calling him home.

He felt his phone buzz in his pocket and took it out, seeing it was Gabriel that was calling. "Sister," he answered. "Don't be impatient. I can almost see your apartment from here."

"Lucifer, it's Wendy," the voice on the other end quivered.

He stopped where he was, floating over the water at an altitude too high for ships to see him. "What's wrong, love? You sound distraught."

"Something's wrong with Gabriel. She had a headache and then she grabbed her stomach and she's coughing up blood and, oh, God!"

"What? What is it?!"

"I think she's having a seizure!"

He looked toward the city and shoved his phone back in his pocket, taking off so fast, he created a sonic boom.

Chapter 18

Tamsen had retreated to the guestroom to finish her work by the time Lucifer arrived, flinging open the balcony door and rushing to crouch next to Gabriel on the floor.

"How long has she been like this?" he asked, placing a hand on her forehead.

"Ten minutes, maybe," Wendy told him, her voice shaking as tears streamed down her face.

"She's burning up."

"What's wrong with her?"

He pursed his lips.

"Why aren't you doing anything? Help her!"

"I can't."

"Why the hell not?! You fixed me when I was hurt. Doesn't your angel healing shit work on illnesses?"

"This isn't a sickness, pet. She's receiving the wo--"

Gabriel stopped moving, stopped breathing, her body limp on the hardwood.

"Hey," Wendy whimpered, lightly slapping her girlfriend's cheek. "Wake up."

"It's all right, love," Lucifer assured, his voice barely above a whisper.

"Get up," she sobbed. "Get--"

Gabriel's eyes flew open as she sucked in a deep breath. Lucifer sighed in relief, standing as Wendy threw her arms around her neck. "I thought you were dead."

"Just for a second," she said, pulling away, her eyes wide as she stared up at her brother. "Lucifer," She stood, taking his hand and placing it on her head. "Listen."

He closed his eyes as he took in her thoughts, his pulse quickening and his hands going clammy. His mouth fell open as he stumbled back, catching himself on the island.

She wiped the blood from her mouth and went to the fridge, getting a bottle of water. She took a long swig and replaced the cap while the others stared after her.

"Are you okay?" Wendy asked, still shaking with nerves.

"Ish." She walked back to kiss her on the cheek before turning her attention to her brother who was barely holding himself upright. She tilted her head, giving him a knowing look. "I need a ride."

"Did you find her?" Wyatt asked as Valerie met him at the front door, letting him in and closing it behind him.

"Yeah," she told him. "Gabriel brought her home hours ago but she went right to her room and won't come out. I'm worried about her. I thought it was just normal teenager bullshit but for a second today, she had fangs. That's never happened before. And, she's drawing some really fucked up shit."

"I saw. What does Gabriel say?"

She rolled her eyes, leaning on the banister, and smacking her lips. "She just said, 'hang tight' and hee hee'd into the wind. I swear, that bitch has been on my every last for months, acting like she knows better than *me* how to raise *my* child."

"Yeah," He said, hugging his arms, remembering when she'd given Will a computer when he was five and the many lectures she'd given him about stifling his development. "She did the same thing with Will. The thing was, though, as much as it aggravates me to say,"

"She wasn't wrong." She sighed. "I know. She never is. That's what makes it so annoying."

Wyatt nodded. "You mind if I talk to her?"

She shrugged. "Give it a shot. She just yells at me to leave her alone. Maybe she'll respond better to you."

He'd taken the first step up the staircase when he felt a tremor. "Does Connecticut get earthquakes?"

"Not any we should be able to feel." She gripped the banister as the shaking went from barely detectable to strong enough that the chandelier rattled. "What the--"

From her room, they heard Sinclair scream. They started up the steps but were nearly knocked over as Gabriel rushed in and bolted past them.

"Get them out of here!" she called to Lucifer hurrying in behind. Without hesitation, he gripped the two by their arms and dragged them from the house at hyper-speed. Standing in the yard, he blocked them as they attempted to get back inside.

"Move!" Valerie shouted as he held her back.

"I can't," he said, holding her by the shoulders and staring into her eyes, the tone of his voice giving her pause. "I'm sorry."

The ground quaked again, setting off Wyatt's car alarm. He took his keys from his pocket and turned it off. "The hell's going on, Lucifer?"

"We need to stay here," he said, shifting his gaze to Wyatt while keeping a firm hand on his sister's shoulder. "Trust me, brother."

He pursed his lips, rubbing the stubble on his face and folding his arms. "I might be crazy, but I think I do."

Valerie again tried to push past him. "If you don't get out my way, I swear to fuck, I will Holy Fire your ass into motherfuckin' oblivion."

"You must trust me, Uriel," Lucifer said, the look of compassion in his eyes confusing her more. "I won't let anything happen to you."

Inside, Gabriel burst into the bedroom to find Sinclair convulsing on the floor, blood spewing from her mouth and nose. "Hey," she said, inching into the room. "Hey, I'm here. I'm right here."

"Gabriel," the girl choked as she fought to stop the trembling.

"Yeah." She knelt next to her, holding her hand and kissing her on the forehead. "I'm right here with you."

"I'm afraid," she said, her voice barely above a whisper as tears spilled down her cheeks.

"I know." Tears gathered in Gabriel's eyes, too as she did her best to appear strong. "It'll be over in a minute."

Sinclair's face twisted in pain and she screamed again, bolts of white-hot lightning shooting out from her body in all directions. Gabriel was thrown back into the chalkboard wall, her head splitting the drawing of a neon billboard in two. She fell to the floor, holding a hand up in front of her to deflect the barrage of electrical discharges being flung from Sinclair's changing body.

The sound of snapping bones cut through the girl's cries with an eerie resonance while skin and muscles stretched. Fangs grew and receded as her eyes flashed black. Lightning struck the bed and curtains, starting fires that grew too fast for Gabriel to put out while she deflected bolt after bolt, her telekinesis the only thing preventing her from being struck again.

What's going on? Wyatt sounded in her head. *I see smoke.*

It's all right, she replied. *We'll be out in a second.*

A flood of electricity poured from Sinclair's solar plexus, Gabriel barely able to keep it from engulfing her in a plume of pure energy. She closed her eyes as the intense light crept up and around her. The house shook, pictures and light fixtures falling from their places, smashing on the hardwood below.

Opening her eyes just enough that she could see, Gabriel took one last look around the room she grew up in, taking a mental photo as she said to herself, "Can't say I'll miss it." Bits of plaster broke free from the ceiling as Sinclair's howls intensified. As the lightning subsided and the girl went quiet, a beam came crashing down, filling the air with a cloud of drywall dust.

Outside, the three siblings waited, the brothers watching the house from the grass as Valerie paced on the sidewalk behind them. Wyatt held his arms, biting his lip as Lucifer attempted to comfort him.

"Gabriel will be fine," he said, patting his shoulder.

"And my granddaughter? Will she be all right?"

He tipped his head and raised an eyebrow. "I suppose that depends."

"On what?"

"Your definition of 'all right'."

From the house, they heard what sounded like an explosion. Windows blew out as the roof caved in on itself, waves of lightning ripping through the air above them. Valerie covered her face and dropped to her knees while Wyatt took a step forward. "I'm going in."

Lucifer grasped his arm. "You mustn't."

"Let go."

"Do you remember what happened last time you were hit with a jolt like that?"

"I survived."

"Do I have to remind you that your vampire sweetheart is no longer a vampire? Should she die, a burning similar to the one you received from your son will send Barachiel straight back to Heaven and Wyatt will cease to be."

"The odds of that happening are--"

"It doesn't matter how slight the chances, I will not risk it. Come Hell or high water, you will live to see the end of this day."

Another boom shook the house, this one too strong for the foundation to withstand. The building crumbled before them, reduced to a pile of rubble as Lucifer moved to shield the others from the fallout.

"Sinclair!" Valerie yelped as her brother held her back.

Smoke and dust filled the air, the sudden silence the loudest thing Wyatt had ever heard. *Gabriel,* he called in his mind. No answer. *Gabriel!* His chest tightened, his eyes darting around, unable to see through to where the building used to stand. Finally, behind the cloud of ash came the sound of his sister coughing.

I'm fine, she answered. *Just clawing my way of out my damn childhood.*

As the dust settled, two figures appeared. In front, a grown Sinclair, her mother's clothes, oversized just a few minutes before, now fitting perfectly. Gabriel followed, brushing dust from her pants.

"Damn it," she complained. "These pants are ruined. You know how hard it is to find pants this comfortable?"

"Not really," Sinclair giggled.

"They are *yoga* pants that look like *dress* pants. *Boot-cut.* I'm gonna have to scour the internet--"

"Baby?" Valerie said, rushing to her daughter, holding her face in her hands as she looked her over. "Are you okay?"

She smiled and nodded.

Valerie let out a sigh of relief as she hugged her. "So, this is it?" She pulled away and gave her another once-over. "You're done growing?"

"Yeah, I'm done."

"How do you feel?" Wyatt asked, remembering how scared Will had been when he'd grown to adulthood overnight.

"Honestly?" She put her hands on her hips. "Hungry."

"Well, let's get you something to eat, then." Valerie turned to walk to her car but was stopped by a change in Wyatt's expression. He looked confused. "What?" She followed his glance and saw Lucifer, a tear sliding down his cheek as he stared, transfixed by the woman in front of him.

"I'm sorry," he said, his voice quiet, averting his eyes.

"Just breathe," Gabriel told him, her compassionate tone causing Valerie and Wyatt to exchange baffled looks.

Another tear fell from Lucifer's eye as he put a shaky hand to his chest, breathing out slowly as he dropped to his knees. He sniffed back more tears as he bowed his head. "Forgive my staring. I was overwhelmed. I didn't think I'd ever see you again...Father."

Valerie grabbed Wyatt's arm to steady herself, both taken aback at what they were hearing.

Sinclair lifted Lucifer's chin, looking him in the eye.

He trembled as more tears fell. "I've failed you."

"You've done no such thing." She took his hand and pulled him up, wiping the tears from his face. "You're exactly where you're meant to be."

Wyatt's legs went numb, his mouth going dry, and his heart racing. "Sinclair?"

She turned her head, smiled at him, and winked.

Chapter 19

Wyatt drove back to the city, Gabriel next to him and Sinclair in the backseat, dreamily looking out the window like she didn't have a care in the world. His knuckles were white around the steering wheel, his jaw clenched. He stared ahead, ignoring the awkwardness of the silence in the car.

Gabriel tapped her fingers on her knee, biting her tongue and rolling her head on the back of her seat. When she couldn't take her brother's frustration anymore, she let out an exasperated sigh. "I'm sorry I didn't tell you."

He kept his eyes on the road, his head tilting slightly as he decided to stop ignoring her. "Why didn't you?"

"I don't make the rules."

His steely glare moved to Sinclair's reflection in the rear-view mirror then back to the road. "How long have you known?"

"Are you kidding me?" Gabriel removed a chunk of debris from her hair. "I'm gonna be pulling this shit out of my hair for weeks."

"How long?"

She bit her bottom lip and cleared her throat. "Since Michelle brought her to me."

"A year?" He shook his head. "Her whole life."

"I'm sorry!"

"Would you have loved me the same if you'd known?" Sinclair chimed in.

He looked in the mirror at her again.

"Would you be in school, working toward a goal, starting a new career? Would you be happy and content as you are now, or would you have spent the last year worried about why I was here, crippled by dread and letting life pass you by like cars on the highway?"

Gabriel plucked more drywall from her chestnut locks. "She's got you there."

He cast her an annoyed side-eye.

"Besides," Sinclair clarified. "I'm not really *here*, here. I'm still asleep. My subconscious is just kind of borrowing Sinclair's body. It's like I'm in a lucid dream."

"I just saw Lucifer grovel at your feet like a dog," he dismissed. "You're definitely here."

She chuckled. "He's a good boy."

Gabriel snickered.

"Because you said 'dog' and Lucifer's my boy, like, my son. You get it."

He flashed his sister an unamused glance.

"Dad jokes, remember?"

He rolled his eyes. "I thought with the Gate closed, nothing but human souls could get in or out."

"'Nothing' doesn't really pertain to me. However, had it been destroyed, I wouldn't have been able to repair it until I woke up, which means I wouldn't be able to be here now."

"Why *are* you here?"

She went back to looking out the window. "When we get back. For now, I'd like to enjoy the ride."

Lucifer sat in Valerie's passenger seat as she followed the others to Gabriel's apartment. He'd started to calm down, though his hands still had a slight tremble.

"She's God?!" Valerie blurted, cutting the quiet like a chainsaw.

"Settle yourself, sister. Wouldn't want to cause an accident."

"God?!"

"Just a bit of Him."

"Which bit?"

He chuckled.

"And, if Sinclair's God, is she even Sinclair? Is she a real person at all? What the fu--"

"I'm sure He'll explain."

She glanced over at him, her features softening. "How are you?"

"Me?"

"Yeah. This must be another level of fucked up for *you*. Are you okay?"

He thought for a moment. "Do you know what? For the first time in a very long time, I think I am."

Chapter 20

"Navid!" Allydia pounded on the door of Phindi's loft. "Navid, I tracked your phone! Let me in!" When no answer came, she used the key she'd been given for emergencies and opened the door herself. She found the two scrambling to put their clothes back on and turned her back, an exasperated sigh escaping her lips.

"Boundaries, Gran!" Navid shouted as he zipped his trousers.

"I apologize but you weren't answering your phone."

"Kind of busy." He threw on his shirt while Phindi adjusted her dress.

"Is everything all right?" Phindi asked.

"No," she said, peeking over her shoulder to make sure they were decent before turning to face them. "Elohim has returned."

Navid's jaw dropped. "Isn't that--"

"Yes."

Phindi put her hand to her heart. "The Creator?"

"Yes. We have to go."

"Go?" Phindi asked. "Where could we go to hide from God?"

"We're not hiding from God, I don't think. His Messenger told me to get you somewhere safe, so that's what I'm doing. We just have to pick up Wyatt's daughter-in-law first. Get your shoes on."

Navid fumbled as he tied his laces. "Gabriel told you? Is she all right?"

"She's fine," Allydia said, casting him a suspicious glare.

He rolled his eyes.

"What are these looks?" Phindi asked, gesturing between them.

Allydia tapped her fingers on her arm.

"It's nothing," Navid insisted.

Phindi raised an eyebrow.

"Really. I had a *mild* crush. *Had*, past tense."

Allydia tossed her hair over her shoulder. "I never approved."

"You were involved with the angel?"

"No. It was just a crush."

Allydia scoffed.

"*Fine*, we made out, briefly, *once*. Pants were on the entire time."

The women were silent.

"I've had two girlfriends since then, not including you." He touched Phindi's arm. "I do not still have a thing for Gabriel. I swear."

"I warned Phindi not to hurt you," Allydia told him, turning to lead them out of the apartment. "But, if you treat her badly, I'll slap *you* around a little, as well."

After new-student orientation, Michelle wandered the campus grounds, admiring its buildings, some of which were over three hundred years old, and breathing in its rich history. She spent hours in the natural history museum, prying herself away only when she'd realized she'd skipped lunch and was starving. She leaned against the massive stone a sculpture of a triceratops stood on as she took one last look around, smiling to herself. "Tae would be proud," she said under her breath, the quiet breeze feeling like peace against her skin. "This is where I belong."

"Michelle!" she heard in the distance, breaking her contemplation.

She stepped away from the stone and onto the sidewalk indented with dinosaur-shaped paw prints and saw Allydia, her grandson who she hadn't seen since her wedding, and the ex-vampire Will had shocked months earlier. "Allydia? What are you doing here?"

"Ivy League," the former vampire approved. "Wise choice."

"Thank you. It's the closest school to Sinclair that I got into."

"I don't think that need be a consideration anymore."

"What?"

"We must go now. Come."

"Why? What's going on?"

"Just come. I don't know how much time we have and you're making a scene."

"Old woman, I will *show you* making a scene if you don't tell me what's happening *right now.*"

Allydia tilted her head and arched an eyebrow. "Rude," she scolded. "But, fine." She glanced around to make sure no one was in earshot. "Elohim has returned in the form of your daughter. I don't know the details as to why but Gabriel instructed me to fetch you and get you to safety and I learned long ago that her Father isn't one to be trifled with, so *let's go.*"

Her jaw dropped, the color draining from her face as she remained motionless on the pavement.

Allydia huffed. "Phindi, be a dear?"

She nodded, rushing forward and throwing the girl over her shoulder. They hurried back to the car, piling in and speeding away, on their way to the airport and to safety.

On the plane, Michelle made several frantic attempts to get in touch with Will. Every call was sent straight to voicemail, every text left unseen. "Fucking contractors," she muttered.

Allydia and Phindi chatted while Navid sat opposite them, mesmerized by his new girlfriend's graceful movements. She smoothed her baby hair and dragged her fingers down the side of her face, over her chest, and to her lap where she folded her hands, never taking her eyes off her former queen. She listened intently to every word spoken before responding, her words always honest, clear, and direct. There were no games with her. She meant every word she said and spoke with abandon, unafraid to ask for what she wanted or to be exactly who she was. She was spectacular. *Don't be an idiot*, he thought. *You've spent one day with the girl. It's way too early to be catching feelings*. But, as he watched her, he couldn't help but feel like this relationship would be different because *she* was different. Unlike the women he was used to dating, she was unabashed, genuine, and forthright. She was real. No matter how much he tried to dismiss his emotions as ridiculous, a strange knowledge had come over him, a sixth sense of sorts. He knew it in his bones. She was the one.

For a moment, their eyes met causing his heart to flutter. They exchanged smiles before she went back to her conversation and he looked down at his phone. He scrolled through his pictures, found the one Gabriel had taken of herself, and deleted it.

Chapter 21

Sinclair finished her fifth pudding cup and took a bite of her peanut butter and strawberry jam sandwich. "I've been craving one of these all day." She took the sandwich with her, eating as she rifled through Gabriel's pantry for more snacks. The others sat at the island, lined up on the side opposite the kitchen, watching in awkward silence. "Score," she said, grabbing a box of cinnamon cereal and shoving the last bit of sandwich in her mouth as she got a bowl from a cupboard.

"Would you like me to order you a proper meal?" Lucifer offered.

"Unnecessary." She dumped the cereal in the bowl, poured milk over it, got a spoon, and dug in.

Lucifer gave Gabriel a disapproving scowl. "This is your fault."

She shrugged. "Be grateful it's not blood."

"Don't bicker," Sinclair scolded.

"Yes, Father," Lucifer agreed.

"Sorry," Gabriel said.

Wyatt and Valerie exchanged surprised looks.

"So, are you gonna tell us what you're doing here or should we just guess?" Wyatt asked, evoking a stunned look from Lucifer.

She finished her cereal and placed her dishes in the sink before making her way back to the pantry. "Oh, you know, stopping a big bad, saving the world, same old, same old. Gabriel, do you have any," She grabbed a box of toaster pastries. "Never mind. Found them." She opened a pouch and put the pastries in the toaster.

Valerie took a deep breath as she gathered the nerve to ask, "So, are you still Sinclair, or are you strictly--"

"Hey, Dad," Will said, entering the apartment and closing the door. "I got your message to meet you here. That meeting took *forever*. What's u--" He stopped, seeing the woman in the kitchen that bore an uncanny resemblance to his daughter. "Sinclair?"

"Hey, Dad," she said as the pastries popped up. She took them out of the toaster and handed him one. "Hungry?"

He took it. "Starving." He took a bite. "Growth spurt, huh?"

"You could say that."

"Are you older than me?"

"Uh...yeah."

Gabriel giggled.

"Thirteen to thirty," Lucifer informed him. "He thinks He's funny."

"I'm hilarious," she defended. "I made a marine mammal that surfs in boats' wakes. They do it on porpoise."

Gabriel covered her mouth and laughed.

Will gobbled the last of his snack and got a bottle of water from the fridge. "Okay, I'm confused."

Wyatt stood, but before he had a chance to speak, Lucifer blurted, "She's God."

Wyatt smacked him upside the head.

Lucifer rubbed the back of his head. "What?!"

Sinclair flashed a stern look. "Barachiel, don't hurt your brother."

Will choked on his water. "She's what, now?"

"God," Sinclair told him, handing him a protein bar from the pantry.

There was a moment of silence while he processed. He took another sip of water and put the bottle down. "For how long?"

"Forever. Sinclair's human soul was in charge while she grew up, having her own experiences, living her life. I was in the background, mostly, poking my head out on a rare occasion."

He furrowed his brow. "Was she aware of you?"

"Of course. And, she's still in here, just," She pointed to her temple and clicked her tongue. "Taking a break. She's got to take a back seat while I get some work done. Speaking of work, Lucifer,"

"Yes, Father," he said, standing.

"I need the city evacuated. Now."

"As you wish." He hurried from the apartment, eager to please his Father.

"Uriel, take your sword to the roof and get comfortable with it again. You're a tad rusty."

She raised an eyebrow, not getting up from her seat. "It's kind of buried under a house right now."

Sinclair went to the fridge and pulled out a block of cheddar, tossing it to Valerie. "I guess you could fight with this."

She caught it, giving her a puzzled look.

Gabriel laughed.

Sinclair flashed an amused smile. "It's extra sharp."

Wyatt groaned as he slapped his palm to his forehead. Valerie sighed as she put the cheese back in the fridge and sat back down.

Sinclair picked a piece of lint off of Gabriel's shoulder and gave her an imploring look.

Gabriel sighed, waving her hand in the direction of the balcony doors, opening them with her mind. "I really wish you would've said something earlier." Sinclair smirked as Gabriel raised her hand. "People are gonna think they're seeing a damn UFO."

Through the open doors, the sword came whizzing in, spiraling through the air at breakneck speed. Will covered his head, ducking as Wyatt and Valerie leaned out of the way. Gabriel caught it by the hilt and held it out to Valerie who took it, shaking her head.

"I guess I better hop to, then," Valerie said, getting up from her seat. "Wouldn't want to piss off the Almighty."

Sinclair winked at her as she left and turned her attention back to Gabriel. "Take Wendy to Tarrytown. Have her gather the witches and teach them Lilith's spells. Oh, and Tituba's exorcising spell. Can't forget that."

Gabriel nodded in agreement. "Which witches?"

She finished her pastry, her eyes darkening as her tone became more serious. "All of them."

Gabriel stood and called over her shoulder, "You down?"

On the couch in the living room sat a petrified Wendy, clutching the notebook Tamsen had filled with Lilith's spells before going home to her parents. Her mouth hung open as she trembled, shakily getting to her feet and following her girlfriend out the door.

Sinclair waved goodbye and as the door closed, she met Will's stare. "I know you're upset but just in case I don't get a chance to tell you later, you've been a really good dad."

He scrunched his eyebrows, staring at her for a few seconds before dropping his water bottle in the trash can. "I need a walk."

"Will," Wyatt called after him, but Sinclair placed a hand on his shoulder, forcing him down onto a stool.

"He needs a minute."

Will slammed the door behind him, leaving his father alone with his daughter-turned-God. Wyatt glared at Sinclair who sat on the other side of the island, taking a sip of her water. He chewed the inside of his cheek as his mind raced, his shoulders tightening as he thought about what to say.

"We have some time," Sinclair said, replacing the bottle's cap. "Go ahead and ask."

He averted his glance. "It's probably not my place."

She laughed. "You're an archangel of the Lord. Your usual *place* is in the Throne Room of Heaven. You can ask me questions. You may not always like my answers but you are always free to ask."

He folded his hands in his lap and returned her gaze.

"You're wondering why I let bad things happen, why I don't just snap my fingers and fix the world's problems. You want to know why I let people suffer."

He let out a tentative breath, not wanting to offend God by daring to question Him but too curious to dismiss it. "Kind of."

She moved around the island to sit next to him, facing him as she spoke. "Have you liked every decision Will's made?"

"What?"

"When he wanted to marry Michelle so fast?"

"Well,"

"When he burned half a town to the ground? When he killed your father? When he killed *you?*"

His jaw tightened. "Did I *like--*"

"No, of course, you didn't. But, you loved him, anyway. You forgave him. And, if he did something equally as horrible at some point in the future, you'd forgive him again. You would love him through anything."

"Of course."

"And, when he was little and learning to ride a bike, did you hold onto his shoulders and keep him steady forever or did you let him fall?"

"I let go," he said, beginning to understand. "He had to fall a few times to learn to balance."

She brushed a stray hair away from his eyes. "He did. And, as he's your child, you are all mine. I love people as you love him. They're not pets to be trained. Human souls need freedom to learn and grow, just as you have."

"Me?"

She nodded. "You don't remember it but before you were Wyatt, you had become discontented. As Barachiel, you did as I asked but you were just going through the motions, saving people because I'd told you to and for no other reason. Your empathy had dwindled. For that reason and many others, I put you in Wyatt Sinclair, knowing what life would be like for you. I gave you the opportunity to not only see the best and worst of human existence but to *feel* it. To *know* it so that next time I command you to keep someone from jumping off a bridge, you'll sympathize with the pain they're going through. When I ask you to bless someone with a baby, you'll understand the joy it will bring to those parents, and when I tell you to save a child who would die if not for your protection, you'll do it wholeheartedly because you know the devastation of losing a child yourself."

His hands trembled as his heart beat out of his chest, his eyes wide with anger and shock. "You put me through hell for *job training*?"

"Yes, but I also put you in Allydia's path, so...you're welcome."

"*What?*"

"What Lilith did to her was atrocious, making her a killer, giving her the bloodlust. She never would have agreed to be saved like that if she'd been given the choice. Her kids got taken, her father abandoned her, and I had to let it happen. I needed her army to defend the Gate so I could slip through when Sinclair was born. I've always felt guilty about that so I had Gabriel introduce you."

"You had her...you orchestrated my relationship?"

"Don't get offended. I didn't manipulate your feelings. I just knew that if she met you, the part of her that was still *her* would fall hopelessly in love with you and that you would eventually love her, too. She would protect you and the others when you needed her to and your influence would give her the final push she needed to cure herself and unwittingly eliminate vampirism which would be one less thing for me to worry about and *then*, Allydia would have the life she always deserved. You would find joy and feel from her the unconditional love you hadn't known before as

Wyatt. You would know what it meant to be someone's top priority and you would build a life with her that, over time, would eradicate the torment you sometimes still feel from your past. That love will heal you and sustain you for the rest of your time on this planet."

He blinked. "I don't know what to say."

She shrugged. "Say, 'Thanks, Dad'."

He laughed. "Thanks, I guess."

"Not the most sincere but I'll take it."

"I have another question."

"Sure."

"You basically just told me you planned for me to have Will but Gabriel said we can't--"

"Angels normally can't, which is another reason I needed you here. Only Barachiel could use the loophole."

"Loophole?"

"Annie prayed for a baby. As worried as she was about your presumed mental illness being passed on, she still wanted to be a mother more than anything. I knew that Wyatt would do anything to keep from losing her and Barachiel would be affected by that and he would answer her prayer. She got cold feet when she thought she'd have to choose between you and her son. Luckily for me, Nephilim grow fast."

"Wait, you're saying--"

"I'm only as strong as the body I'm in when I'm on Earth normally, let alone when I'm unconscious. It has to be that way. The last time I showed my true face, a guy climbed down a mountain thirty years older than when he'd climbed up. So, I needed to be half-Nephilim and half-vampire. It's the strongest combination of--"

"You puppet-mastered my son and his wife, too?!"

"*Again*, not their feelings, just their circumstances. I didn't make them fall in love, I just knew they would. I didn't make them have sex, I just made sure the pharmacist Michelle went to for the morning after pill would give her a box that expired almost ten years ago. I set that in motion before I went to bed."

His jaw dropped.

"What?" Outside, thunder clapped as the sky darkened. She looked to the window and smiled. "My baby."

Chapter 22

Thunder clapped so loud it rattled the windows of the cafe Will now sat in, sipping coffee and staring out the window onto the Hudson. He'd wandered from Gabriel's apartment down West 70th Street and stopped here when the rain started, hoping to wait out the storm that only seemed to grow in intensity.

His phone buzzed on the table, Michelle's image lighting up the screen. He picked it up, eager to speak to her. "Hey, I need to talk to you about something."

"Allydia told me," she said. "Sinclair's God?!"

"For now. Apparently, He came with her when she was born and she's known the whole time. I don't," He pinched the bridge of his nose and squeezed his eyes shut. "I don't understand why she never said anything."

"Maybe He wouldn't let her? Divine plan or some bullshit?"

"I don't know. He said she's still in there, still alive, still aware. I just hope when He's done doing whatever He needs to do, He gets the hell out of her and takes His all-knowing ass back to Heaven. I can't--" He stopped, noticing a couple listening in on his conversation with puzzled looks on their faces. "Anyway, how are you? Are you okay?"

"Not really but how could I be, right? Gabriel had Allydia drag me off campus and now I'm on a plane to Indiana while my family's in who knows what kind of danger. I'm with the chick that locked me in a cage, another ex-vampire, and a guy with a gun."

His ears perked up. "What guy? Why does he have a gun?"

"Allydia's great-great-whatever grandson. He's a detective."

"Oh," he said, his shoulders relaxing. "You mean Navid. I talked to him a little at the wedding. He seems okay."

"Yeah, I guess him and that Phindi girl are a thing now."

"Really? Huh. Well, that's--" Another clap of thunder shook the building so hard, a picture fell from the wall. Patrons jumped and choked on their drinks. Will peered out the window through sheets of rain. In the distance, standing in the middle of the river, he could see a figure, arms outstretched, palms facing the sky. "Hey, I need to call you back."

"Is everything okay?"

"I doubt it. Love you."

"Love you, too."

He ended the call and placed some money on the table. As he got up to leave, the room went dark. He turned back to the window and saw a wall of water come barreling toward it. "Look out!" he shouted, throwing himself at the waiter that had come to clear his table and shielding him as the glass shattered and a wave of river-water came rushing in. People screamed, running to the other side of the room as the building flooded.

"This way!" the manager called, opening the door to the kitchen and ushering customers through to the service entrance.

"Thanks, cutie," the waiter said, giving Will a wink before hurrying to the back.

When the room was cleared, Will headed to the front door, angrily mumbling to himself, "Lucifer."

"Hey!" Will shouted through the downpour. He stood on the edge of the river, his slacks and button-down soaked through. Behind him, cars drifted on the now flooded street. Streetlights were down, windows were broken. As he cupped his hands around his mouth to yell again, a stop sign flew by, carried by one hundred and fifty mile an hour winds, nearly taking his head off. He dodged it and bellowed, "Lucifer!"

The figure on the river turned and made its way to the shore, walking on top of the water as if it were pavement.

"It is you," Will said. "Of course, it is. What the hell are you doing?"

"What my Father commanded," Lucifer said. "You shouldn't be out here."

Will's phone buzzed in his pocket. He took it out, glanced at it, and put it back. "The Mayor's ordered a city-wide evacuation."

"Ah, well done, me, then." He smacked his nephew's back and pushed him toward the street. "Let's get you out of all this water before you drown and my brother has my head."

They trudged across to a building, Lucifer prying open the gate and breaking a window, shoving his hand inside and unlocking the door. They hurried in, their shoes half-submerged in the shallow water filling the room.

Will slammed the door shut, the wind outside no match for his inhuman strength. "I'm gonna need some information."

"My Father didn't tell you?"

He crossed his arms. "I didn't exactly give Him a chance. Why's He here? What the hell is going on?"

He leaned against the wall, taking a much-needed break. "It would seem a misguided witch released something she shouldn't have and now that the beast has been made flesh, he'll destroy this world and swallow the lot of you whole should my Father fail in His attempt to rescue you. I wouldn't worry too much if I were you, though. God isn't really one for failure."

"Right," he said, unconvinced. "Who's this monster?"

"His name is Moloch. He seeks power. He craves worship, feeds on it. The more souls that follow him, the stronger he becomes. Anyone unwilling to submit will be tortured and eliminated. Even his own minions are fair game for his whims. I once watched him flog a woman he called 'wife' for giving him a toothy--"

"Moloch, like child sacrifice and hellfire Moloch?"

"I see your education included religious studies. Very good. Yes, one and the same. In his true form, he's barely a threat but once corporeal he can gain worshipers and worshipers give him strength. Only my Father can defeat him and he will. He's done it before."

"How'd He do it before?"

He snickered. "He gave humanity a set of rules, most of which you all continue to ignore, the first being--"

"No gods before Him," he said, shaking his head. "So, He made people stop worshiping him."

"Yes. After some years, Moloch was rendered little more than a ghost. However, God has been wary of interfering in humanity's belief structures in the last few thousand years. I'm not sure what His plan is now."

"But, you're doing what He tells you, anyway?"

He tilted his head. "Of course. Have you forgotten who I am?" He stepped away from the wall, closing the space between them. "I will do as my Father commands. I need no context, no explanation. As long as He allows it, I will serve Him to the best of my ability. My advice to you is if you are asked to help in His efforts, you work as though the world depends on it because it probably does. Otherwise, stay out of His way."

Valerie ducked in the doorway, the rain coming down in sheets onto the roof of her sister's building. "Time for a break," she said, pulling her phone from her pocket and calling her husband.

"Hey, baby," he answered. "After a few meetings, I'm pretty sure we found our contractor. What have you been up to?"

"Angel shit," she told him. "Listen, I need you to go to your parents' in New Jersey."

"What for?"

"You see this storm, right?"

"Yeah, there's an evacuation order but--"

"But, nothing. Get out of town. I'll call you when it's safe to come back."

"You're not coming with me?"

She rested the tip of her sword on the floor of the stairwell. "This storm isn't Mother Nature, it's Lucifer."

"Lucifer? Why?"

"It is a long and fucked up story which I will tell you when I'm done with what I gotta do."

"What do you have to do?"

"I'm not sure yet. Fight someone or some thing. It's big." She looked out onto the pounding rain, her eyes falling as the nerves set in. "You know I love you, right?"

"Val, you're starting to scare me. Should I be worried? Because I am."

"I'm fine. I'll see you soon." She ended the call and shoved the phone back in her pocket. "I hope."

Chapter 23

Once safely at the house in Southport, Allydia retreated to the kitchen where she sat alone at the table desperately trying to get her anxiety under control. Navid and Phindi chatted on the sofa while Michelle paced the backyard, the early evening air like silk on her skin. The warm breeze did little to soothe her as she ended her call with Will. She went inside and sat at the table across from Allydia who took the opportunity to get out of her own head.

"Are you all right?"

"Nope," Michelle said, crossing her legs.

"How is your husband?"

"Freaked."

"And, his father?"

She dropped her phone onto the table. "You haven't talked to him?"

"I'm sure he's busy."

She leaned back in her chair, just noticing how concerned Allydia looked. "He loves you."

She nodded, her gaze distant.

"Are you...*insecure*?"

She tossed her hair over her shoulder and cleared her throat.

"You *are*."

She folded her arms and dropped her head.

"As much as seeing you squirm gives me joy, and it does, like, *a lot*, I have to tell you, I've seen how Will's dad looks at you. It's the same way Will looks at me. You're being crazy. That man loves you."

She lifted her chin, her eyes pooling with tears. "He's an angel and God has come calling. I am insignificant at best and at worst," She wiped away a tear that dripped to her cheek. "I was a *monster*. You don't know a quarter of the things I've done, the atrocities I've committed. I am irredeemable. God could demand he leave me or worse, restore his memories, make him Barachiel once more in which case he would flee from me of his own volition."

Her features softened as she leaned forward. "Listen, I don't know what God would do but my daughter would never ask anyone to give up someone they love, especially not her grandfather. She adores him. If there's even a smidge of her left in there, she won't ask him to."

"Elohim doesn't *ask*," Allydia retorted. "He forces your hand. He manipulates. If He wants us apart, He will make it happen."

Michelle pursed her lips and covered Allydia's hand with hers.

She looked at her with shock then gratitude, patting the back of her hand. "So, you forgive me, then, for kidnapping you?"

"Which time?" Michelle scoffed.

Allydia smiled. "Either?"

"I mean, I guess but only because you're sad."

In the living room, Navid went on and on about how amazing he thought it was that God was on Earth. "I wonder if I'll get to meet Him," he said, so excited by the idea that he didn't register Phindi's hand on his thigh.

"Do you not see how frightened the others are?" she asked. "He is the Creator, the one they call 'God Almighty'. Are you not afraid?"

"Not of *Him*. Maybe a little of whatever He's here fightin'. On the other hand, why should I be scared of that, either? If He's here, no chance that's posin' a problem for us, right?"

She looked him over, staring deep into his eyes which seemed to dance as they looked back at her.

He held her hand. "What?"

"You are strong, brave, and foolishly optimistic. If we survive the night, I will give you many children."

As the sun set over the city, residents scrambled to flee the flooded streets. Traffic backed up on bridges as car horns blared, the unrelenting rain making seeing to drive difficult.

A man slammed his fist into his steering wheel as he gritted his teeth, his wiper blades all but useless against the downpour. He rolled his window down and poked his head out, hoping to see the car in front of him inching forward. It didn't move. He honked again, waving to the other cars as he shouted, "Come on!"

He readjusted himself in his seat and had begun to put the window back up when he heard something strange in the distance. Over the pounding rain and car horns, another sound emerged. It was high-pitched, almost shrill but also guttural, like a wild animal dying alone in the woods. He looked through the windshield and in the mirrors but saw nothing but a gray wall of water. The noise got louder, its source drawing closer. Curious, he unbuckled his seat-belt and got out of the car.

The sky darkened as the shrieking persisted, so loud now that the bridge began to shake. The man put a hand over his eyes like a visor, desperate to see what could be making the horrific howl. After a few seconds, what looked like a shadow appeared above him. He squinted, unable to make it out.

Before he could think, the shadow rushed him, its mutilated face so terrifying, he couldn't even scream.

Chapter 24

Gabriel sat cross-legged on a log in the woods behind Poe's house as Wendy addressed Grace's coven, the angel's patience razor-thin as they had little time to get their ducks in a row.

The witches stood in a circle, holding hands and surrounding Wendy who concentrated on the faces of the women she saw in her mind's eye, hoping that she'd translated Lilith's teleportation spell properly. Tamsen had written it in Arabic and there was no way the others would be able to learn the spells in the time allotted if they were in a language most of them were unfamiliar with. Latin would have to do.

"Ad hunc locum," Wendy said, repeating the phrase once for every witch she meant to summon. One by one, they materialized inside the circle, the Priestesses of all the remaining major covens on Earth: From the United States, the Bassets, Bishops, and Leveaus. The Clarkes and Rigbeys from England and the Balfours from Scotland. From Italy, the Cantinis. The Nassars from Saudi Arabia and the Esus from Nigeria. From Ireland, the Meaths. From Australia, the Pauers. The Liangs from China, the Chantraines from France, and from New Zealand, Charlotte.

"Welcome," Wendy greeted as Grace's coven released their hands, allowing the women to spread out. "I apologize for bringing you here with no notice but we're pressed for time, so--"

"Why have you summoned us to this place?" the Leaveau Priestess snapped, pulling a curved blade from her belt and holding it in front of her.

Wendy sighed. "As I was saying, there's not a lot of time, so I'll get right to it. An old god called Moloch has come back to Earth. He's power-hungry, strong, and straight-up evil. Manhattan is under siege. If he's successful there, it's just a matter of time before he takes over the rest of the country and he won't stop with the US. The world is at risk. We need your help."

"Moloch?" the Nassar witch gasped. "But, how?"

"A shunned witch released him from Tituba's trap," Poe explained. "Now that he's corporeal--"

"A shunned witch?" the Leveau asked. "From *your* coven?"

"Yes."

She guffawed. "So, this is *your* responsibility. Why should we put ourselves at risk, *our sisters* at risk to clean up your mess?"

"That's valid," Wendy said. "But, and I hate to be that guy, who helped you when your dumbass sister let a fucking zombie loose in the French Quarter?"

The Leveau cleared her throat. "I appreciate that, Wendy. I do. But--"

"But, what?" Charlotte piped in. "You just don't believe in repaying debts?" She looked over the crowd, making sure to make eye contact with every witch there. "The island where I live would be underwater right now if not for this woman. I don't know what she's done for the rest of you but I'd venture to guess it's not nothing considering she's been our community's lifeline for the last what, fifteen years?" She moved to stand next to Wendy. "Millions of people would've died, including me, had she not saved our kiwi asses, so me and my girls will be there," She turned to face her. "Whatever you need."

"Wendy banished my daughter's abusive boyfriend," the Basset witch chimed. "She protected her. Count us in."

"Us, too," said the Bishop witch.

The Leveau Priestess put her hands on her hips after sliding the knife back between her belt and her dress. "I don't discount the Tituban's worthiness but this is *Moloch*. Have you all not heard the stories? The sacrifices of children? The torture? *He burned his enemies alive.*"

"Oh, for fuck's sake," Gabriel huffed, checking her phone and putting it back in her pocket as she stood. "We don't have time for this. Somebody kill me."

Wendy took a step back. "Huh?"

"I mean it, kill me. Now."

"Are you high?"

"Not since the 90s. I'm serious, let's go. Fucking kill me."

"No one's gonna *kill* you. What's wrong with you?"

"Fine, I'll do it myself." She waved a hand at the Leveau witch, freeing the knife from her belt and hurling it toward herself. It plunged into her chest, piercing her heart. She pulled it out and dropped it to the grass as blood spurted from her mouth.

Wendy screamed as a collective gasp sounded from the crowd. Blood poured from Gabriel's wound as her lifeless body fell, hitting the ground with a thud. Wendy covered her mouth, Poe catching her as her legs went weak.

A split-second later, the angel Gabriel exploded out of the body in a fiery glow. The energy-being had six wings and stood taller than the trees, its face indistinguishable from the rest of its incandescent body, a swirling inferno in the shape of a human. The angel lifted from the ground, hovering over the witches who huddled together, some curious, some terrified.

"I am Gabriel, Messenger of the Lord your God," a deep voice boomed from above. "A threat to all of humanity is eminent. Without your help, civilization as you know it will end. You have been summoned by the Almighty to do His work. The consequences of refusal will be swift and dire. Make your choice but be warned, if His efforts should fail, the blood of the innocent will be on your hands."

The figure of light shrunk down, disappearing into the corpse's chest. Wendy watched with tearful anticipation as the stunned crowd remained silent. Finally, Gabriel's eyes flew open as her hand jumped to her chest. She coughed as she took her first few breaths, Wendy kneeling beside her.

"Fuck me." She sat up. "Nope." She lay back down again, Wendy holding her hand. "That sucked *all* the balls."

"Are you okay?" Wendy asked, brushing the hair off her forehead.

"On a scale from meh to roadkill, I'm a solid shit factory."

"That's what you really look like?"

She took a few more deep breaths. "I don't really look like *anything*. That's just what people expect."

"We'll be there," the Meath Priestess called.

"Us, too," piped the Chantraine.

"And us," said the Esu.

The Liang witch nodded in agreement. "We are in, as well."

All the women nodded, all except the Leveau. She remained stiff, her expression stern as she retrieved her knife, wiping the blood from it on the grass.

Gabriel sat up and Wendy stood, taking a pile of papers from her bag and handing them out to the others. "Teach the spells to your covens and meet us at the designated time and place. Instructions are on the first page." She handed the Leveau Priestess a bundle of pages. "I appreciate all of your help. It won't be forgotten."

She gathered everyone inside the circle and made the command, "Reditu." The Priestesses disappeared, sent back to where they'd come from.

Grace's coven headed through the forest back to Poe's to practice the new spells while Gabriel leaned against the log, trying to get her bearings.

Poe joined Wendy a few feet away, eyes fixed on the exhausted angel. "You're girl, though!"

Wendy beamed. "*Right?*"

Chapter 25

Lucifer's face twisted in rage as he looked out the window.

"What?" Will asked.

He growled, flinging the door open and stepping out, waving his hand toward the sky, the rain instantly stopping, the clouds clearing.

Will followed him, the two standing knee-deep in water as Lucifer watched the skies.

"What are you looking at?" But as he followed his uncle's line of sight, he saw them, too, the thin, black wraith's streaking across the sky. There were thousands of them, descending into buildings and across the river.

"They're everywhere," Lucifer lamented.

"What the hell are those things?"

"Demons, let loose by Moloch, no doubt." He looked him up and down. "You nearly murdered me once."

"You want me to apologize again?"

"You're strong. Come with me."

"Where?"

He pulled him close, wrapping his arms around him and gripping him tightly as he struggled. "Hell."

"What?!"

They lifted off, springing from the flooded street and shooting into the night, Will kicking as they flew.

They touched down outside the abandoned power station, Will shoving away as soon as his feet hit the ground. "What the hell's wrong with you? You don't just fly people places without their consent."

"My apologies, William. I forgot my manners, time being scarce, you understand." He trudged into the building, Will following behind.

He coughed. "What is that?" He covered his nose with his shirt.

"Sulfur," Lucifer said as they moved through the building, the concrete floor becoming more and more cracked the closer they got to their destination. Finally, they came upon the crater, a gaping hole so deep, they couldn't see the bottom.

"Is that--"

"They've gone," Lucifer seethed, staring into the abyss.

"Who?"

"All of them. It's empty but for one. Only my sister remains. I can feel her, cowering, afraid to face our Father after everything she's done." He turned his back to the opening and began to leave. "Stay here. If Lilith steps foot out of this hole, use everything you've got."

"Everything I've got to what?"

He stormed out, angry determination coloring his voice as he answered, "Kill her."

"So, what should I call you?" Wyatt asked. "God? Elohim? Dad?"

"Sinclair's fine."

He arched an eyebrow.

"I'm still her, just also me. I know it's confusing."

"Truer words."

She pursed her lips, gazing out the window with furrowed brow.

"What's wrong?"

"The demons know I'm here. Moloch's mobilized them." She looked him in the eyes. "I know I've put you through it and you're not entirely happy with me right now."

He blinked, flashing her a contemptuous glare.

"I understand. But, I need you now, Barachiel. Are you with me?"

He leaned back and sighed. "Yeah, I'm with you."

"You're sure?"

"I haven't slept through an Apocalypse, yet. No reason to start with this one."

"Well, that's very good to hear because the demons have been set free and the people they're possessing need help. They can still be saved if we work quickly."

"What do you need me to do?"

"The witches will have to put their hands on them for the exorcisms. Once the demons have been removed, I need you to get those people to safety. Shock whoever you need to, but don't kill anyone. Those are innocent people, do you understand?"

He nodded, looking down at his hands folded on the counter.

"We won't be able to save them *all* but," She stopped, tilting her head, her features softening. "Hey,"

He met her gaze.

"You know how much I love you, right?"

"Are you speaking as Sinclair or God?"

"Yes."

He bit the inside of his cheek as tears threatened to form.

"One of the reasons I chose you to be here was because I needed to feel loved, too. Not devotion or fear. Not worship or admiration. Just real love from someone that didn't think I could do anything for them, that didn't expect me to be perfect or even helpful. Expectationless. Because of you, I've had that. Will, Michelle, Uriel, even Malik all love me more because I come from you. The traits I inherited from you through Will have endeared me to them. Your bravery and kindness, your unflinching honesty...your eyes. It wasn't Barachiel that gave me a family, it was Wyatt. *Wyatt* gave me true, unconditional love and I will always be grateful for that."

Tears spilled down his cheeks as she came around the island to hug him, rubbing his back and kissing the side of his head.

"I should tell you something else because I know you're curious." She wiped away his tears and brushed his hair away from his eyes. "Your parents aren't in Purgatory. They're together. They're happy."

He broke down, hugging her again and sobbing into her shoulder.

She placed a hand on the back of his head. "It's okay," she whispered. "I love you, Grandpa."

Chapter 26

Lucifer stormed down 7th Avenue, the floodwater clearing the pavement in front of him as he walked. He drove the river back to its rightful place, his face twisted in rage as his eyes fixed on the standoff happening in front of Times Tower. There they were, the demons that had escaped, every monster in Hell now occupying some poor human's body, lined up on the street, ready to do battle.

In front of them were seven witches whose power he could feel from fifty feet away. They'd clearly been advanced by the monster that stood front and center. Even in human form, Lucifer could see the wretched creature hiding beneath the surface, this thing that called himself a god.

Opposite the horde of evil stood his Father as the woman, Sinclair. The determination in her face gave Lucifer chills having seen the look more times than he could count. There was a time when he and God had battled side by side every century or so before The Almighty had decided to stop coddling humanity. Now, they'd fight together once more, the thought of it sending a shiver of excitement down his spine.

Wyatt stood on Sinclair's left with Valerie next to him as Lucifer took his place to her right. Behind them, Gabriel, Wendy, Poe, and her coven lined up, awaiting orders.

"Elohim," Moloch sneered.

"Tituba's bitch," she mocked in response.

Wyatt lifted his eyebrows, surprised by her language.

Moloch rolled his neck, ignoring the insult. "This world is mine, old man. You should start fresh somewhere else. I hear your precious humans are making great advancements in the colonization of Mars. Perhaps you could follow them there."

"Or, alternatively, you could make like a tree."

He tilted his head like a confused collie.

"*Leave.*"

He snorted. "Ah, I'd almost forgotten about your jokes. Funny, but you won't be laughing when I slaughter your children and the women foolhardy enough to follow you here. Seriously, you've come to stop me with *this*, a few angels and a handful of witches? All of Hell is at my back."

She leaned her head back. "Gabriel, what time is it?"

She checked her phone. "Nine on the dot." As she slid her phone back in her pocket, the other covens began to appear, teleporting in one by one. Thirteen covens materialized, one hundred and fifty-six women, all armed to the teeth with magic including Tituba's exorcism spell.

Poe furrowed her brow as she looked over the crowd. "The Leveau's aren't here."

"I see that," Wendy sighed. "Here's hoping we don't need them."

Across the divide, Blair placed a hand on Moloch's arm. "See the blonde with the better-than-everyone attitude?" She pointed in Wendy's direction.

He nodded.

"I want her to myself."

"So, have her." He took off his jacket and threw it to the ground, yanking off his tie as his body began to swell. Muscle tore through his clothes as he grew to twelve feet tall, his head doubling in size while massive horns sprouted from his elongated face. His skin glistened a muted shade of bronze in the moonlight, his head now that of a bull. His feet were replaced with hooves while his fingers formed razor-sharp claws. Steam wafted from his snout as gasps erupted from both camps.

Blair put her hand to her chest and licked her lips. "How are you sexier this way?"

He grunted down at her before turning his attention back to Sinclair, the low rumble of his voice booming in the still night air. "We were friends once, were we not, Elohim?"

She held her palms up at her sides, gathering energy. "No," she corrected. "You've always been a dick." She snapped her wrists forward, directing white-hot bolts of lightning into the beast's chest.

He stumbled back but corrected himself quickly as the energy dissipated. He lowered his head and let out a snarl before giving the order, "Attack!"

The demons charged, some wielding shards of obsidian and granite as swords, others without weapons relying on their superior strength to win the day.

Gabriel crouched in front of Sinclair, her hands held out as if to say 'stop', her telekinesis holding the horde at a distance while Sinclair shot bolt after bolt of lightning into Moloch's sizable torso.

Lucifer cracked his neck and winked at his brother. "Time to get to work." He bounded into the crowd, exorcising demons with one hand while fighting off more with the other. As the bodies of the unoccupied fell, Wyatt rushed to them, carrying them two at a time to the shelter of an abandoned fast-food restaurant several yards away.

The witches hurried to join the fight, shouting, "Ne transgrediaris!", immobilizing demons before reciting the exorcism spell. Wyatt scurried to help the freed humans to safety, throwing low-voltage balls of lightning at any demon that got in his way.

"What's happening?" a woman asked as he helped her sit in an empty booth. The others looked to him for answers.

"I don't know how to answer that," he told them. "Not without sounding like a lunatic."

"We were possessed, weren't we?" a young man asked, his hands shaking as he struggled to zip his hoodie.

Wyatt let out a sympathetic sigh.

"That's what happened to us, right?" the man asked. "That thing out there with the horns, that's the Devil, right? And, we were possessed by his demons?"

"Not exactly."

"What do you mean, 'not exactly'?" the woman snapped.

"We'll explain everything when this is all over. For now, stay here." He moved to leave but a man blocked his path.

"Who's 'we'?" he asked.

"I really don't have time for this."

"Make time."

Wyatt looked over the man's shoulder to see the battle unfolding in the street. Witches lay on the ground covered in blood while others were being beaten. "Get out of my way."

"Not until you tell us what--"

"People are getting killed!" he barked in the man's face. "I know you're scared but I don't have time to make you feel better right now. Move or I will move you."

The man's lip quivered as he stepped aside, the others in the building huddling together as Wyatt stormed out.

Back outside, he threw one bolt of lightning after another, clearing a path for the recently freed to race to safety. He came to the body of an older woman wearing a flower-print dress, a gaping head-wound pouring blood onto the wet pavement.

"Alice?" a woman yelped, crawling over and checking the body's neck for a pulse. "Oh, God, Alice!"

"Alice?" Wendy pointed the way for the man she'd just exorcised and came to kneel next to the corpse. She covered her mouth, tears forming in her eyes.

"Those monsters killed her," the grieving woman sobbed.

"I'm so sorry, Charlotte," Wendy said. "I shouldn't have let you come." She stood to address Wyatt. "Can you get them out of here, please?"

He nodded, patting her on the shoulder before picking up Alice's limp body. He escorted Charlotte and her coven to the restaurant, laying the dead witch in a booth, her sisters crying around her. The unpossessed looked on, tears of their own beginning to fall as panic turned to guilt for taking up their rescuer's time. Wyatt ignored their shameful glances and rushed back to where he was needed.

Wendy took her aggression out on the Gowdies, who now formed a barrier between Moloch and Sinclair's lightning. They deflected it, waving it away into buildings and billboards, rendering her ineffectual.

"Iikhmad," she growled, using Lilith's suppression spell to tamp down the witches' power as she stood before them.

"Absterben!" one of them shouted.

"Stirb jetzt!" another chimed in.

Wendy's jaw clenched as she stared them down, unable to control her anger. "Not tonight, bitches. Khudh alqua."

The Gowdies faces fell in horror as clouds of green light emanated from them and floated away, circling around Wendy before entering through her ears, nose, and mouth.

"What are you doing?" Gabriel asked as she fought to keep Moloch and the demons at bay.

"I took their power," she told her, stepping forward to face Blair who had been unaffected by Lilith's spells. "And, now I'll take yours."

The Gowdies ran, powerless and afraid as Blair's eyes went black. "You're no match for me anymore, Tituban."

She smirked. "Well, let's find out. Praefoco!"

She remained still.

"Subsisto!"

Nothing.

"Ignis!"

Blair rolled her onyx eyes and laughed. "As I said, no match. Herzbruch."

Wendy's hand flew to her chest as pain radiated from her heart down her left arm. She gasped for air as Blair laughed.

"Wendy!" Gabriel cried.

"Leave it alone," Sinclair instructed as she continued her assault on Moloch.

"She's dying!"

"I almost have him," she said through gritted teeth.

Moloch convulsed, barely keeping himself upright as electricity pumped through him.

Wendy fell to her knees, the color draining from her face as Gabriel pleaded.

"I have to help her."

Sinclair trembled as she increased the voltage. "Just...one...minute."

"She doesn't have a minute!"

Wendy collapsed onto the pavement, rolling her head to look into Gabriel's eyes. She whispered, "I'm sorry," before grabbing her hand. "Impartio."

Slowly, Wendy began to heal as Gabriel's abilities were shared with her. Gabriel watched, fascinated as Wendy waved her free hand in Blair's direction, engulfing her in a mushroom cloud of holy fire. The blast knocked the two sides apart, flinging Sinclair, Gabriel, and Wendy into the glowing, red staircase.

With Gabriel unconscious, Moloch and the remaining demons were free to move as they pleased. They marched toward the women while witches shouted out every spell they could think of to slow them down. Most were stopped in their tracks while Wyatt heaved lightning at the demons still moving. Valerie planted herself between the women and the horde, her sword igniting as she stood guard.

The women got to their feet as Moloch seethed. As his followers grew fewer in number, he became weaker. "No more games," he grunted, opening his mouth wide, releasing a black cloud of toxic gas.

Sulfur filled the air, choking the angels and witches. They coughed, their eyes watering. Wyatt pushed through, getting as many people to safety as he could. Soon, though, there were no freed humans left. The witches were suffocating, lying helpless on the ground as they struggled to breathe. Moloch approached the steps, the glint of victory in his eye.

"I've had just about enough of you," Lucifer said, getting between him and his sister. He flew into him, knocking the beast on his ass. He pried up the statue of Francis Duffy, breaking it free from its concrete pedestal.

Moloch stood, laughing, his hooves clonking as he stepped forward. "What are you planning on doing with that trinket?"

"What I always do...my damnedest." He swung the eight-foot-tall statue like a baseball bat, slamming it into the monster's face, the crack so loud, the crowd stood still. The beast's head turned, a few giant teeth falling from his smiling mouth. He laughed again.

Lucifer erupted with rage, hitting him over and over in the stomach and chest but his punches had no effect. Moloch remained unmoved, his maniacal laugh angering his opponent even more.

"Angels," Moloch mocked, wrapping his enormous hand around Lucifer's throat and lifting him off the ground. "Hardly worth the time it takes to snuff them out."

Lucifer kicked and punched but he couldn't break free from the beast's grip. Sinclair raced toward them but before she could reach them, Blair stepped in her path.

A sinister grin crept across the witch's lips, her ash-covered skin seeming to glow. "Geh weg." With that, Sinclair went flying into a billboard, smashing its orange lights, causing them to spark and blink out. She fell sixty-eight stories to the ground, her skull crushed on the sidewalk like overripe fruit.

Lucifer growled as he fought harder but it was no use. The beast had him.

Lucifer, he heard in his head. *Look at me.*

He couldn't move his head but he altered his glance to set eyes on his sister who held her throat, coughing as she sat up, keeping demons back with her mind. Tears sprung from her eyes as he listened to what she had to say. His eyes became saucers and he went ghost-white. She nodded and gave him a smile as he was consumed by Moloch's bright-white hellfire, dead so fast, he didn't have time to scream. The monster dropped his arm, nothing left of the angel he'd been holding but a cracked, charred cellphone that clinked on the pavement as Moloch brushed the dust from his hands.

He'd been so amused with himself, he hadn't heard the angel's brother screaming his name or the sound of his heavy footsteps as he bounded toward him.

Wyatt leaped on his back, grabbing the sides of his massive head and releasing every bit of energy he could muster. He took it from the air, the clouds, and the billboards. Electricity poured into the beast, causing his eyes to roll back and foam to sputter from his mouth.

Barachiel, stop! Gabriel begged.

I've got him.

You don't. Run!

But, it was too late. Moloch reached back with one clawed-hand and pulled Wyatt off, flinging him into the side of a building. He crashed through the wall and into an office space, his spine shattered on impact.

Gabriel looked to her sister standing next to her. *Don't do it.*

Valerie wiped the tears from her eyes. *Bitch, what the fuck do I have to lose?* She raced toward Moloch, sword raised. She plunged it in his gut, the wound combusting. But, as she pulled her weapon out of the monster's flesh, he bellowed a hearty laugh, the holy fire absorbing into his skin as if it were a welcome guest. He lifted his hand and swatted her away like a fly.

Poe crawled to Wendy on the steps. "We're getting slaughtered." She covered her nose and mouth with her shirt as she tried to breathe, coughing with every inhale. "There aren't many of us left."

The demons drew closer, Gabriel growing weaker by the second as the sulfur overtook her. She wouldn't be able to hold them off much longer.

Blair stood next to Moloch, both of them grinning as they waited for the angel to fall, leaving the door open for them to kill the rest of their enemies, including God.

"I don't know what to do," Wendy choked. "It's hopeless."

Gabriel's apartment sat empty, boxes of Wendy's clothes, books, and dishes left unopened in various rooms. It was dark, the only light still on being the UVA lamp over the lizard's terrarium. In her habitat, Pearl shuffled from one side to the other, her tiny heart beating a mile a minute. She rammed herself against the glass, Wendy's distress calling her like a beacon. She threw her pocket-sized body at the front of the terrarium, again and again, her tail thwapping against the glass with every strike. The noise echoed through the otherwise silent apartment. Had anyone been home, they would have been able to hear it all the way in the kitchen where the only other noise was the sound of the refrigerator's low hum.

After a few minutes, the noise from the habitat in the bedroom stopped. No more thwapping, no more shuffling. The apartment was quiet.

Moments later, another noise echoed from the bedroom, cutting through the air with sharp clarity. It was the sound of glass cracking.

Chapter 27

Wyatt came to in the dimly lit office, the sounds of the continuing battle several stories below coming in through the gaping hole in the wall. He tried to stand but barely got himself rolled to his back before the pain searing down his spine became overwhelming. He winced as his jaw tightened and his arms fell to his sides. He could feel his vertebra repairing themselves, the shards fusing together like jagged puzzle pieces. His legs were numb and his back was on fire. As desperate as he was to get back to the fight, he wasn't going anywhere until his spine healed. He looked up at the fluorescent lights, most of which were turned off for the day, and tried to come to terms with the fact that this might be his last night on Earth. He'd wanted to die so many times but not now. Now, he had things to live for, people that depended on him, people that loved him and that he loved. He couldn't let it end this way, not with that thing out there terrorizing the city. He had to survive this and if he couldn't, he at least had to take that monster down with him.

He grunted in agony as he took his phone from his pocket. The screen was cracked but it still worked. He found Will in the contacts and hit 'call'.

"Dad?" Will answered.

"Hey," he said, his voice scratchy. "Where are you? Are you okay?"

"I'm fine except Lucifer dragged me to the mouth of Hell to kill his sister if she tries to escape. Just another typical Tuesday night in this family."

Wyatt chuckled.

"Are *you* okay? You sound like you're in pain."

"Oh, I'll be fine in a few minutes but listen, if you don't hear from me again by morning--"

"Why wouldn't I hear from you?"

"*If* you don't hear from me, I want you to go to the house in Southport. It'll be safe there for a little while, at least."

"You're freaking me out, Dad. Are you saying there's a chance tha--"

"Promise you'll go."

"All right, I promise but how could Moloch win? Lucifer said--"

"Lucifer's dead."

"*What?*"

"Moloch incinerated him."

"Holy shit."

"I don't know what's gonna happen when I get back down there. I won't lie to you, it's not looking good. But, me and your aunts are gonna do everything we can. We always do."

"What about Sinclair?"

A tear rolled down the side of his face and into his ear as he remembered seeing his granddaughter's body fall and crash onto the pavement.

"Dad, where's Sinclair?!"

"I love you, Will."

"Dad!"

"Be good." He ended the call and wiped the tears from his face before calling Allydia.

"Wyatt, are you all right?" she answered, her voice frantic.

"For now." The pain in his back was starting to lessen and the feeling in his legs went from nonexistent to pins and needles. "You're safe?"

"Yes, we're fine."

"Good. So, I was wondering, if I'm still alive tomorrow, do you want to get married?"

She was silent for a moment.

"Allydia?"

"No."

"No?"

"No, tomorrow is much too soon. I'll need time to prepare, plan. Next spring?"

A relieved laugh tumbled from his lips as he smiled. "Whatever you want." He sat up, his spine fully mended. "I should get back."

"Of course. Wyatt,"

"Hmm?"

"Be careful."

He smiled again. "Love you, too." He ended the call and stood, his legs still shaky. He took a few wobbly steps to the opening in the wall and looked down at the battle below. He couldn't make out what was happening, he just knew it wasn't over, and as long as it wasn't over, there was still hope.

Wyatt limped from the building and through the sulfuric smog to find unoccupied humans scrambling to get away from the fighting. He guided them through the crowd, throwing balls of lightning at the demons that tried to stop him. He ushered the humans to the restaurant and turned back. There were a handful of witches still performing exorcisms but most had either been killed or were lying on the ground choking on toxic air. In the distance, he could see Wendy and a few more witches lying on the steps while Valerie swung her fiery sword, clanking it against the spears of rock some of the demons carried. She was fighting three at a time and even from afar, he could see she was exhausted.

Gabriel was on her knees, covering her nose and mouth with her shirt, still holding Moloch and the demons back. Wyatt let out a sigh of relief as he saw Sinclair walk up behind her.

"I can't keep doing this," Gabriel told her. "I can't breathe."

Poe was on the verge of passing out but as she lay there, coughing and eyes watering, her defeated expression altered. She beamed, smiling from ear to ear as she tapped Wendy's arm.

Wendy scrunched her brow and followed her friend's gaze. There, at the top of the staircase stood the Leveau coven.

Wendy rested her head back on the steps. "About fucking time."

The New Orleans witches took only a moment to assess the situation before their Priestess called out the first spell. "Evacuandam!"

"Evacuandam!" the coven repeated, their voices carrying over the crowd as though amplified by invisible loudspeakers. On their word, the cloud of sulfur dissipated, thinning out until it had completely disappeared.

Wendy, Poe, and the witches in the crowd caught their breath. Poe's coven remained intact while the rest had endured mass casualties. Their numbers had dwindled but they stayed on mission, exorcising as many demons as they could.

"It doesn't matter," Blair taunted. "The Leveaus are street performers compared to me. Poison air or not, you can't win."

Wendy offered her hand to the Leveau Priestess. "Take what you need." She took it, keeping her eyes fixed on the black-eyed witch as the rest of her coven joined her at the bottom of the steps. Poe held out her hand, too, the Priestess taking it in hers and gesturing to the coven to join hands, as well. They lined up, hand in hand as they awaited orders.

"Street performers?" the Priestess snapped. "We are not here for your entertainment, bitch." She glanced over to where Gabriel fought to hold Moloch off, noticing the woman standing behind her. There was a power radiating from her that she couldn't explain. It was breathtaking. She turned her attention back to Blair and said, "We're here to save the world. Conteram seorsum."

"Conteram seorsum!" the witches repeated.

Blair laughed. "You can't break me. You're weak. I'm," She looked down at her arms, dark lines spreading over their skin. "What the," The cuts grew deeper, blood seeping from them as she watched in terrified amazement. "What did you do?!"

"Conteram seorsum!" they shouted again, their voices echoing in the night.

Sweat beaded at Blair's temples as she started to hyperventilate, the cracks moving up her shoulders to her neck and face. She screamed as pieces of her fell to the ground, her body shattering like glass and crumbling to the pavement in a pile of wet flesh.

"Decrusto," the Priestess spat.

"Decrusto," the others repeated, the mounds of flesh and shards of bone disintegrating into blood and dust.

"Exteriores spatium."

"Exteriores spatium!" The muddy mixture lifted from the ground and floated up like a balloon, into the sky and out of the atmosphere.

The witches let go of one another. "You're late," Wendy said.

"Wasn't sure I was coming," the Priestess admitted.

"I'm glad you did."

She looked out over the crowd. "That's a lot of demons."

"Yep."

"Looks like we've got our work cut out for us. Come on, ladies."

They exchanged respectful nods as the Priestess led her coven into the battle.

Wendy's heart sank as she looked over to see Gabriel on her knees, hunched over with one hand up in front of her. Moloch was getting closer and she could see the exhaustion on her girlfriend's face. She wouldn't be able to hold him off much longer. She rushed to her, ducking to avoid the lightning Sinclair continued to pump into Moloch's chest.

"What do you need?" she asked. "How can I help?"

"I don't think you can," Gabriel told her, her voice strained.

"There's got to be something we can do," Poe said as she approached.

Gabriel thought for a second. "Help my brother. Get as many people out of there as you can...*fast*. There's only one way this ends."

The two nodded and bolted into the crowd, finding Wyatt and helping him take survivors to the makeshift shelter.

"There are too many," Gabriel told Sinclair. "I know you know I'm right."

"Just a few more minutes," she growled.

"I don't have any more minutes in me. I'm falling apart. I know you want to save these people but I can't keep them back any longer and if Moloch doesn't lose followers like, right the fuck now, he's gonna kill us all."

Sinclair remained determined, ignoring Gabriel and continuing her assault.

Gabriel's elbow hit the ground as she struggled to keep going, Moloch inching forward as she weakened. *I don't think I'm gonna make it*, she thought to Wyatt. *Moloch's closing in and he'll definitely squash me like a bug to get to Sinclair. Do me a favor.*

Of course, he thought back.

Gather the witches and people you've saved. Tell Wendy to use Lilith's teleportation spell to take you all somewhere else. Somewhere far.

You want us to leave? But, there are still thousands of--

There's no saving them. I have to use my last bit of energy to light their demon asses up.

She doesn't want those people to die.

I know. She's being stubborn, like always. God's way or the highway. But, we're out of time.

You're talking about defying God. Isn't that--

Yeah, He'll be uber pissed and I'll probably end up in a cage. I might even mope around all depressed and shit like Lucifer's been doing but I have no choice. It's kill a few thousand people or hand the planet over to this monster and a bunch of demons. We've tried it His way. It's time to use some common, human sense. Get those people out of there.

Gabriel,

Just fucking do it. She scanned the crowd to see Wyatt, Wendy, and Poe ushering a large group of people into the restaurant. *Is that all of them?*

Yeah, but--

Good. She set herself up and held out her free hand.

Gabriel, are you sure?

But, before she had time to answer, a strange noise blared in the distance, a shriek so shrill, it silenced the horde of demons trying to push through Gabriel's barrier.

What the hell was that? Wyatt asked.

I have no idea. Gabriel dropped her arm and looked around. "What is that?"

Sinclair stopped what she was doing and listened. "It can't be."

Another cry echoed in the dark, this time followed by the thunderous sound of massive, flapping wings.

Everyone looked up, including Wyatt who stood in the doorway of the restaurant, stunned by what he was seeing.

Another screech came from the animal as it drew closer and in the neon light of the billboards, everyone could finally see what it was: a black and white striped, thirty-foot dragon.

"Are you fucking kidding me?" Wyatt muttered as Wendy came out from inside to stand next to him. Their eyes were wide as their mouths hung open.

She knew as soon as she saw it but the word still came out as a question. "Pearl?"

Back on the steps, Gabriel glared at Sinclair who couldn't take her eyes off the creature. "Dragons are real?!"

Without altering her gaze, she answered by holding out her hand and tilting it from one side to the other.

The dragon shot down over the crowd of demons, opening its mouth to reveal rows of razor-sharp teeth. The demons tried to run but it was too late. From the back of Pearl's throat and out her open mouth, a wave of lava-hot fire erupted, burning demons to ash by the hundreds within seconds.

"Holy shit," Wyatt and Wendy whispered in unison as the dragon made a u-turn in the air and took another pass, incinerating hundreds more.

"You have a dragon?!" Poe asked, squeezing between them to get a better look.

"I have a *gecko*," Wendy said.

"You sure about that?"

Pearl flew over the crowd once more, setting hundreds more ablaze in one fell swoop. The remaining demons fled, abandoning the abomination they had once called 'savior'.

Gabriel's eyes rolled to the back of her head as she collapsed, fatigue overtaking her. Now unconscious, there was no longer anything keeping Sinclair and Moloch separated. With no followers left, however, Moloch was at a disadvantage. He was weaker but still self-assured. He rushed forward, his hooves splitting the concrete apart as they slammed down with every step.

"Fuck it," Wyatt said, racing toward the beast.

"What do you think you're doing?" Valerie asked, stepping in front of him.

He looked past her to see Sinclair's eyes go black, fangs descending as her arms stretched out to gather electricity from the air around her. He shrugged. "Helping?"

Valerie looked back, seeing the monster headed straight for her daughter. "Yeah, all right." Her sword again lit as the siblings ran toward them.

Sinclair pulled every bit of electricity from the surrounding billboards and buildings as she could, the air around her sizzling and snapping as lightbulbs and screens exploded, spraying glass and darkening the street. She let out a bellowing scream as she emptied the electricity into the monster's torso. He stepped back, grunting as he righted himself.

Wyatt, too, threw a steady stream of lightning at the beast, aiming at his head while Valerie crept up from behind. Moloch fell to his knees but kept coming, crawling on all fours, his shining eyes fixed on his enemy.

Gabriel awoke just in time to see Valerie raise her sword, its fire shining in beautiful, sunset hues against the blue and white bolts of lightning flooding into the monster's body.

Sinclair and Wyatt halted their electrocutions as Valerie plunged her blade into the beast's back, piercing his heart, and erupting out his chest. "Teach you to mess with *my* family, ugly ass cattle lookin' motherfucker." She pulled her weapon from his body, blood sputtering from his mouth, his eyes raised in surprise as he held a hand to the cauterized wound.

Gabriel sat herself up, waving a hand in Moloch's direction, this time her Holy Fire taking hold, engulfing him in flames. He screamed, his cries muffled by the fire. After a few moments, they stopped. He fell forward, his body turning to ash. As the flames died, so did he.

Valerie dropped her sword, its flame going out as it clinked on the cement.

"Everybody all right?" Wyatt asked.

Valerie nodded.

Gabriel struggled to stand. "More or less."

Sinclair wiped a tear from her eye, touching each of them on the arm before stepping over the smoldering pile of ash and walking onto the scorched battlefield.

"She'll get over it," Gabriel told them. "People dying just...isn't God's *favorite* thing."

Pearl flew over the street toward the restaurant, shrinking down to her original size and resting in Wendy's open palms. "You okay, pretty girl?" Wendy cooed as the gecko seemed to hiccup, a tiny puff of smoke escaping her smiling lizard lips.

Poe studied the animal, her eyes filled with wonder. "I knew familiars were as powerful as their witches but *my God*."

"What?" Sinclair called from a few yards away.

Poe froze. "Nothing, Ma'am. Sir. Ma'am. Your Holiness." She leaned in to whisper to Wendy. "She's God, right?"

Wendy nodded.

"Super weird."

"You're telling me. I babysat her once."

Gabriel joined Sinclair among the ashes of the dead. "Barachiel's gonna marry Dia. He's gonna be okay, I think."

Sinclair smiled. "I believe he will be."

"Not sure about Uri, to be honest."

She smiled again. "Don't worry about your sister. I've got her covered. As for you," She brushed a few stray hairs out of Gabriel's eyes. "You've done well. I'm very proud of you."

She nodded, tears welling in her eyes.

"Gabriel," She took her face in her hands. "You can rest now. Take a break. Live your life. Be Taran Murphy for a while. I won't call on you again. Well, not for a couple of hundred years, anyway."

Tears spilled down her cheeks and Sinclair wiped them away.

"You'll make them understand?"

She nodded as she sniffed back more tears.

"Thank you, Gabriel." She kissed her cheek and walked off, leaving the angel alone to cry in the dark.

Chapter 28

Shrieks of the damned pierced the night as their shadowy figures swirled around Will before diving into the chasm they'd clawed their way out of just hours before. Their wailing was so loud and the sight of them so ominous, Will had to cover his ears and flee his post, leaving the demolished gate to Hell unmonitored. He stumbled out of the building, ducking to avoid getting hit by one of the dark figures as it sped past. Thousands of the wraiths rushed in as Will hurried to escape them, tripping in the gravel and falling on his rear. He sat there, ears covered, watching as they filtered in. After a few moments, they were gone, their shrill cries replaced by welcome silence. He dropped his hands, letting out a sigh of relief as he saw Sinclair approaching from his left.

"Is it over?" he asked.

"Almost," she said, offering a hand to help him up.

He took it and stood. "My dad?"

"He's fine. Your aunts and Wendy, too."

His shoulders relaxed as he let out a breath.

"I have to go now."

He nodded. "Will Sinclair remember being...you?"

Her eyes softened and she tilted her head, touching his cheek before hugging her arms. "No, she won't. Listen, Hell's gate isn't open, it's broken, decimated. In this body, I can't just blink it fixed. It requires a spell...and a sacrifice."

His jaw tightened. "What kind of sacrifice?"

"Blood, for starters, of someone from our line. Your father's line. Sinclair blood. Did you read The Da Vinci Code?"

He shook his head. "How much?"

She bit the inside of her cheek. "Just...all of it."

"No."

"Mine, not yours."

"Out of the question."

"Well, if that's upsetting you, I don't even want to tell you the second part."

"Second part?"

"To seal the gate completely, the spell requires another ingredient." She put her hand to her chest. "The heart of the divine."

He took a step back as the color drained from his face.

"Please stop freaking out. It's okay."

"*Okay*?!"

"If the gate isn't sealed now, the demons that just got sucked back into Hell will climb right back out, not to mention the thousands that are still out there."

"No. You might be God but you're in my daughter. I forbid it."

"You what?"

"I forbid it. You're not killing my daughter. Figure something else out."

"Sinclair has known who she was since the moment she was born. She always knew it would end this way. She understands why it's necessary. You should, too."

"I said *'no'*." He formed a ball of lightning in his hand and threw it at her, hitting her in the stomach and knocking her to the ground.

She looked up at him in annoyed confusion. "Really?"

He shocked her again, this time with more voltage.

"Are you serious?" She got to her feet. "I'm God."

He threw a bolt of lightning hard into her chest, its force sending her reeling back and into the gravel. He stood over her, another orb of energy forming in his palm. "Fuck God."

She scurried out of the way just as he threw the ball down, narrowly avoiding a shock to the face. She raced around to the other side of the building and back in a blur, now carrying a heavy, rusted chain. "I won't fight you but you won't stop me." She used her hyper-speed to rush him, wrapping him in the chain from neck to ankle.

He struggled against the iron as she closed the space between them.

"When you and Michelle are ready, Sinclair's human soul will be back. Maybe she'll be a boy next time. Do you have a preference?"

He shook his head, tears pooling in his eyes. "Please, don't do this."

"What kind of God would I be if I let my Creation be destroyed? There are thousands of demons out there and thousands more beneath our feet. How many people do you think they'll kill? What kind of pain they'll cause? What unimaginable torture will they inflict? I have to do this. Hey," She lifted his chin as tears slid down his cheeks. "You'll be okay. You all will be. I made sure." She wiped away his tears and kissed his cheek before pushing him to the ground. He winced as his chained back slammed into the gravel and concrete. "Stay here. When you make your way out of that, go home. Stay out of this building. You shouldn't see any part of this."

"Stop!" he cried as she entered the decrepit building. "Wait, please! Stop!"

She ignored him, taking one determined step after another toward the dark fissure. Once upon it, she sat down, legs dangling over the edge into the void. She let her fangs grow, holding her left wrist to her quivering lips. With her pointed teeth, she tore open the artery, cringing as she held her arm out over the chasm, letting the blood drain.

She took a deep breath and began the spell. "Ghalq hadha bawwaba." Inside, the walls started to close in, rock and earth fusing to fill in the deepest parts of the breach. She pulled her legs up and sat on her knees, whispering to herself, "This is gonna suck." She took another breath before starting again. "'Aydaan," She put her fingertips to her chest and sank them in, penetrating the muscle and breaking through bone. "Aihtafaz," she grunted as she wrapped her fingers around her fast-beating heart. "Mugfal." Her whole body shook as she ripped the heart from her chest, dropping it into the chasm. As her eyes rolled back, her face falling and her muscles going limp, the shards of Hell's gate came together, the mass of vacancy fully repaired.

Outside, the ground vibrated with the sound of thousands of demons fast approaching. They howled as they were pulled out of the bodies they'd been occupying, through the air, over Will, and into the building.

"No!" he shouted, fighting harder to get free of his chains. "Sinclair!" It took less than a minute for all the remaining demons to be hauled back to their rightful place, the gate's lock now secure. In the quiet of his solitude, Will sobbed, his arms aching against the iron that bound him. Finally, one link broke, snapping apart and clinking on the rocky ground. Another link cracked, then another. Soon, enough of the chain had been broken that he could move his arms and wiggle himself free.

He raced inside, dismissing Sinclair's instructions to go straight home. He tore through the building back to where Lucifer had left him. There, he found her, her hands and arms covered in blood, a gaping wound where her heart used to be. "No," he whimpered, kneeling next to her and gathering her in his arms, holding her the way his father had once held him, tears pouring down his face as he brushed the hair away from his daughter's empty eyes. He rocked her, kissing her head and weeping, his heart completely broken.

Chapter 29

"They'll be all right?" Wyatt asked as the spared humans filed out of the restaurant, their dead stares having him question the witches' decision to spell them.

"They'll be fine," Wendy told him. "They'll go home, go to bed, and wake up tomorrow like nothing happened. They won't remember a thing."

"Are you all right? I know you lost a lot of friends tonight."

She let out a breath, holding back tears as she pet Pearl's head. "I did." She looked up at him with a sympathetic smile. "But, you lost a brother."

He dropped his head and chewed on his lip.

"Go be with your family. I'll finish up here, give you a few minutes before I come over and do the supportive girlfriend thing." She turned her gaze to Gabriel who still stood on the battlefield. "Maybe I'll make her a cake. Or brownies. Or cookies? There's an oatmeal butterscotch recipe I've been wanting to try."

"I'd go with all three."

They both laughed. "Okay. All three it is. And, I'll bring some by your place, too."

"Thank you."

She nodded as he touched her arm and walked away.

Valerie sat on the steps, their red light flickering as she rested. Her phone buzzed in her pocket and she answered it, happy to see Malik's number lighting up the screen.

"Hey, I was just about to call you."

"So, it's over?" he asked, hope in his voice.

"Yeah. It's definitely over."

"And, you're okay?"

"As okay as I can be, I guess. Gabriel says we're done with our angel shit. No more visions, no more monsters."

"Are you serious?"

"That's what the girl said."

"I am real glad to hear that because I just got a call from the adoption agency."

"Now? It's the middle of the night."

"Someone chose us."

She sprang up. "What?"

"She's in labor right now in Albany. I'm already in the car on my way."

Her stomach flipped as tears of joy welled in her eyes. "Text me the hospital's address. I'll meet you there." She ended the call and darted off, blowing by Wyatt as he walked over to meet Gabriel.

God's Messenger crouched down to pick up what was left of Lucifer's cellphone, now little more than a lump of charcoal. She held it to her chest as her brother knelt next to her.

"You okay?" he asked.

"Not really." She fiddled with the phone, pieces of it breaking off in her hands. "It's been a day."

He nodded in agreement.

"It's gonna be weird not having him around, making snide comments, criticizing my eating habits."

"Well, if you want, I can pick up the slack in that department. You do eat way too much sugar."

She laughed. "Almost. Next time, try it with a little more flair."

He chuckled. "I'll work on it. Maybe I'll fake a British accent."

"I'd appreciate that," she giggled, fresh tears falling from her puffy, red eyes.

Wyatt ran a finger over the phone, tears of his own threatening to spill. "I'm gonna miss him."

"You'll see him again."

He blinked, raising his eyebrows. "I'm going to Hell?"

She wiped away her tears and looked up at him, a soft laugh escaping her upturned lips. "No."

Lucifer floated through Heaven's great halls, nostalgia washing over him as he was enveloped in the warmth of pure light. Wandering past the levels in which human souls resided, he made his way to the angelic realm. Once there, he quickly bypassed the Cherubim, finding himself where his existence had begun, in the Choir of the Seraphim.

"Lucifer," he heard a voice call.

"Yes," he responded, recognizing it immediately.

Before him materialized the figure of a man with bright blue eyes and five-o'clock shadow. This must have been the appearance of the human he'd been born into nearly forty years prior.

"Camael. It's good to see you. I was sorry to have missed you on Earth."

"That's all right. That version of me would have found you obnoxious."

He laughed. "You're probably right."

"It's good to see you, too. Gabriel told me to look out for you when you got here. Said you'd need time to adjust."

"She did, did she? Why am I not surprised? Always feeling the need to control things, that one."

"She just loves you. We all do. You're going to have to get used to feeling that again."

"You're here!" another voice called. Forming in the ether was the image of the man that had called himself Tae.

"I am. It's nice to see you again, Raphael."

"How is my niece? Did she get into the university she wanted?"

Lucifer held back a snicker. "We'll talk later."

"Brother!" Michael cheered, manifesting before him in a glittery haze. He appeared as a tall man with dark, shoulder-length curls and golden-brown eyes. "It's been too long."

"Agreed."

Michael hugged his brother and patted him on the back. "I've missed you."

"Likewise."

"Tell me, what is Hell like?"

"Perhaps a story for another time."

"Of course. I'll admit, when Father told us you'd be back, I was almost afflicted with emotion."

He chuckled. "I'd recommend avoiding it. Wouldn't want to hurt yourself."

"He's still asleep but He said He'll see you as soon as He wakes."

Lucifer looked to the gleaming set of doors a few feet away, the low vibration of his Father's energy emanating from just beyond them. He moved to stand in front of them, placing a hand on the smooth surface. "I'll just wait here, then."

"For two hundred years?" Michael asked.

"Getting even the smallest of glimpses of Him on Earth was enough to remind me of how much I needed Him. I've endured the ache of Separation for thousands of years. Two hundred will go by like minutes."

He stood next to him and put his arm around his shoulders. "If that's what you want, I'll wait with you."

Lucifer smiled, staring eagerly at the doors, the happiest he'd ever been.

The End